*The Sing-song Girls of Shanghai*

Weatherhead Books on Asia

# The *Sing-song*

# Han Bangqing

# *Girls of Shanghai*

First translated by Eileen Chang

*Revised and edited by Eva Hung*

COLUMBIA UNIVERSITY PRESS :: NEW YORK

COLUMBIA UNIVERSITY PRESS

*Publishers Since 1893*

New York    Chichester, West Sussex

Copyright © 2005 University of Southern California

All rights reserved

The illustrations appearing on the title page and page 1
are reprinted from *Renditions*, nos. 17 and 18, with
permission from the Research Centre for Translation, Chinese University of Hong Kong.

*This publication has been supported by the Richard W. Weatherhead
Publication Fund of the East Asian Institute, Columbia University.*

: :

*The University of Southern California would like to thank
Mr. Stephen C. Soong and Mrs. Mae Soong for their generous donation of the manuscript of Eileen Chang's draft translation
of this novel. Columbia University Press and the University of
Southern California Library would like to thank Lillian Pu Yang,
whose initial efforts to reconstruct the manuscript and bring this work
to the attention of scholars led to the publishing contract between
USC and Columbia University Presss.*

Library of Congress Cataloging-in-Publication Data

Han, Bangqing, 1856–1894.
[Hai shang hua lie zhuan. English]
The sing-song girls of Shanghai / Han Bangqing ;
first translated by Eileen chang ; revised and edited
by Eva Hung.
p. cm. — (Weatherhead books on Asia)
Includes bibliographical references.
ISBN 0–231–12268–3 (cloth : alk. paper)
1. Han, Bangqing, 1856–1894—Translations into
English.   I. Title.   II. Series.
PL2710.A58H313   2005
895.1'348—dc22                        2005043234

*Columbia University Press books are printed on permanent and
durable acid-free paper.*
*Printed in the United States of America*
c 10 9 8 7 6 5 4 3 2 1

CONTENTS ::

*Sing-song Girls of Shanghai* (*Haishanghua liezhuan*, 1894, hereafter referred to as *Sing-song Girls*) is the greatest late Qing courtesan novel, and next to *Flowers in the Mirror* (*Jinghuayuan*, 1830), it may well be the greatest work of nineteenth-century Chinese fiction. The novel provides a panoramic portrait of life in the Shanghai pleasure quarters during the last decades of the nineteenth century. In sixty-four chapters, it describes more than two dozen courtesans and their patrons, seen in the twin sports of desiring and being desired, and it inquires into the moral and psychological consequences of their romantic adventures.

The author of *Sing-song girls* is Han Bangqing (1856–1894). A native of Lou County in Songjiang Prefecture, Han spent his youth in Beijing with his father, a low-ranking governmental official. Despite his reputation as a child prodigy, Han repeatedly failed the civil service examinations. He eventually gave up hope of an official career and settled in Shanghai, becoming a regular contributor to the newspaper *Shenbao* with a column about the demimonde. *Sing-song Girls* was allegedly based on Han Bangqing's personal experience. He is said to have been a regular patron of Shanghai brothels and made the boudoirs of some of his favorite courtesans into scenes of intimate investigation.

Han Bangqing's decadent lifestyle may sound much like that led by many other drifting scholars from the late Qing period. In Han's case, however, two things merit attention. In 1892 Han Bangqing founded a magazine entitled *Haishang qishu* (A book of Shanghai wonders), a biweekly that featured his collection of Gothic short stories, *Taixian mangao* (Sketches of Taixian), and his novel, *Sing-song Girls*, in serialization. Although it lasted for only eight months, *Haishang qishu* appears to be "the first literary magazine in Chinese history."[1] By writing fiction and running a literary magazine for commercial purposes, Han Bangqing has also been regarded as the "first professional literary writer" of modern China.[2]

Second, *Sing-song Girls* is a novel that highlights Shanghai as the geographical locale that gives meaning to the story narrated. As the first "modern" city in China, Shanghai was not merely a rising metropolis that served as the new center of foreign and domestic trades. It conveyed an urban aura different from that of traditional cities, thanks to the creation of new social groups, economic relationships, and habits of consumption.[3] Shanghai thrived on account of the competition and interaction between and among foreign and indigenous forces, practices, and institutions; and the upper-class courtesan houses, located mostly in the foreign concessions, stood out as some of the most visible sites—almost a "public sphere—in which such competition and interaction were carried out. It is against this transactional and transient background that the sing-song girls gathered and parted like flowers drifting on the surface of an unfathomable sea, as the reverse of the name of Shanghai, *haishang*, suggests.

Ironically enough, *Sing-song Girls* has never been popular among general readers. People usually attribute this unpopularity to the fact that it is written in the Wu dialect and therefore is unreadable to readers from other regions of China. Actually, the novel should not be all that unintelligible to Chinese readers, as the Wu dialect is used mostly by courtesan characters to reflect the refined linguistic taste of their profession. Moreover, the language problem was overcome thanks to the acclaimed novelist Eileen Chang, who translated the dialectal part of the book into Mandarin Chinese in 1983.[4] Chang is also to be credited for having produced the original English version of the novel.

The real reason for the novel's unpopularity might lie in the fact that it does not read like the courtesan novel we generally know. Compared with conventional courtesan novels of the late Qing period, *Sing-song Girls* falls short of the sentimental narcissism that characterizes *A Precious Mirror of Flowers* (*Pinhua baojian*, 1849) and *Traces of Flowers and Moon* (*Huayuehen*, 1872), and it never emulates *Nine-Tailed Turtle* (*Jiuweigui*, 1911) in sensationalizing the sordid dealings of the prostitutes and their clients. Han Bangqing narrates everything in a matter-of-fact style, to the point where even the most glamorous banquets and the most sensuous rendezvous sound like familiar and familial routines. As it is, his novel seduces us by rendering a special linguistic sensation one would not have expected after having read traditional courtesan novels. It initiates a way of describing desire and passion in the courtesan house from a perspective that would only later be likened to the fiction of psychological realism.

The courtesans and their customers in *Sing-song Girls* appear as a group of amazingly ordinary women and men. They meet, fall in love, quarrel, break up, and are reunited just like ordinary couples, but, on the other hand, they know they are only playing roles commensurable with those of husband and wife. While they could not care less about composing love letters and poems to each other, as clichéd formulae would have it, they are equally not at all obsessed with what goes on in bed. Eileen Chang is right in pointing out that "there is no sensuous quality [in the novel], though the novel's topic is the pleasure quarters of Shanghai eighty years ago."[5] The demarcation lines between love and lust, vanity and disillusionment, which are so handily drawn in most courtesan novels, here cannot be identified with ease. Thus critics have concluded that *Sing-song Girls* excels most Chinese fiction since *The Dream of the Red Chamber* (*Honglou meng*, 1791).[6]

The realism of the novel brings into question not only the lifestyle of courtesans as received or imagined by society but also the cultural, aesthetic motivations of reading and writing the courtesan romance as such. One should also see the novel's lifelike atmosphere as an "effect of the real," an effect that arises as the novel pits itself against the narrative conventions of the courtesan novel. At his best, Han Bangqing plays in his novel with a fascinating contradiction of goals: he writes to upset the unlikely romantic myth of courtesan life, yet his realistic endeavor works also to ensure the continued existence of that myth, which, however questionable, has become part of the cultural capital circulated among the characters and contemporary readers alike.

::

*Sing-song Girls* features numerous episodes about the romantic games in the courtesan house, but the most compelling are those dealing with the theatrics of desire and virtue. Han Bangqing understands that being a courtesan is a profession, or an art, of faking virtues and indulging desires. His novel thus excels in featuring a gallery of courtesans who are not paragons of virtue but first-rate players upon desire in the name of virtue: love, fidelity, generosity, and even chastity. Making love is literally the artificial staging of erotic desire in accordance with a set of gestures of virtue and the much-awaited sex scene often comes only as an afterthought.

Nevertheless, engaging drama often happens, with the girls spoiling the delicate balance between desire and virtue, fantasy and necessity, by consuming one at the expense of the other. When our sirens are enchanted by their own devastating songs, they become parodies of their bitter profession. Paradoxically, when they fail to carry out their professional arts, these sing-song girls show, either in personality or in action, a magnanimity that would have been endorsed by the virtuous romances they are employed to simulate.

There is yet another twist in Han Bangqing's taxonomy of desire. When a girl is determined to carry out "genuine" virtue above all else, she may do so in such a fervent way as to cultivate a new kind of desire. An excess of virtue often verges on a transgression of virtue; a fanatic passion to be virtuous tends to place itself ambiguously in the courtyard of desire. Contrasted to most late Qing courtesan novels, which mouth crude moral pretensions as an excuse for debauchery, *Sing-song Girls* ventures to mix virtues with temptations in a truly dialogical way.

Three examples will point up the various facets of the sing-song girls' adventures. The affair between the courtesan Water Blossom (Li Shufang) and the scholar Jade Tao (Tao Yufu) can be picked out as one of the most romantic in the novel. Water Blossom and Jade fall in love at first sight. As their affair matures, Jade proposes to marry Water Blossom as his wife, not concubine, a proposal naturally causing his family's vehement opposition. In the meantime, Water Blossom has contracted tuberculosis. As there is no hope of a solution to the dilemma of the marriage, Water Blossom slowly withers away and dies a pitiful death.

While the love affair may first look like a Chinese version of *La dame aux camélias*, which had yet to be translated into Chinese in 1892,[7] it tells more about morality as conceived in courtesan circles. Water Blossom knows her position from the outset, but she is not immune to the temptation of becoming a wife in a scholarly family: a happy ending as promised by any conventional courtesan romance. Ironically, after the marriage plan is denied by Jade Tao's family, Water Blossom turns out to be a person much tougher than expected: if she cannot be a wife worthy of a scholar's family, she can be a courtesan proud of her profession.

It is now Water Blossom's turn to take the initiative. Thus even when she is dying, she turns down time and again Jade Tao's suggestion to move out of her boudoir to rest in a quieter place; she does not want to die as the kept woman of her lover. One may well imagine that, if Jade had not proposed the fatal formal marriage, the lovers would have ended up living together happily as husband and concubine. But the aborted proposal brings out the self-esteem hidden in Water Blossom's mind, driving her to achieve a kind of virtue people often take for self-abandon. However quixotic it may appear, her death in the midst of the hustle and bustle of Shanghai prostitution houses becomes a sign of moral triumph, not only over the hypocrisy of so-called decent society but also over the humble role she originally might have taken in compliance with social expectation.

In sharp contrast to this love story is the triangle of Lotuson Wang (Wang Liansheng), Little Rouge (Shen Xiaohong), and Constance Zhang (Zhang Huizhen). As their story starts, Wang, a midranking official temporarily staying in Shanghai, has been going steady with his favorite courtesan, Little Rouge. Their relationship is in danger when Wang discovers Little Rouge is secretly developing a liaison with an opera singer, behavior despised by both customers and other courtesans, because of social bias and the notoriety of opera singers' lifestyles. Out of revenge, Wang starts a closer relation with Constance Zhang.

In a world where love and treachery masquerade hand in hand, neither Little Rouge's nor Wang's new affair should have led to trouble. But in this case, Little Rouge is simply outraged by her old patron's betrayal. Little Rouge storms into her rival's place, ruining all the furniture, and fights with Constance on the floor. Throughout the whole scene and afterward, Wang might feel embarrassed, but he never really loses his temper. He eventually goes back to Little Rouge to ask her pardon. The story thus partakes of a domestic quality rarely seen in courtesan novels. Whereas Little Rouge seems to play the contradictory roles of both an adulterous mistress and a jealous wife, Wang, in his turn, unwittingly allows himself to assume the double roles of cuckold and unfaithful husband.

The character of Little Rouge merits particular attention. She appreciates her relation with Wang (of course partially for financial reasons), but she feels just as strongly about her new lover. The passion that drives her to destroy Constance's chamber, thus declaring in public her possessive love for Wang, simultaneously motivates her to run her own intrigue, at the expense of Wang's love (and money) for her. The environment where she lives and thrives teaches her no domestic scruples; her professional promiscuity nevertheless sends her to undergo the trial of passion in a doubly severe way. She sticks to her unreliable new lover toward the end of the novel, at the cost of losing most of her customers. And one of the greatest prices she pays is to let Constance marry Wang in her place as concubine, an ideal domestic role most courtesans were supposed to take after ending their careers.

Little Rouge's story does not end here. There is no doubt that she is greatly humiliated by Lotuson Wang's marrying Constance Zhang as his concubine. But a similar humiliation falls on Wang only too soon, when the newly wed Constance is caught committing adultery with her husband's cousin.

Problems involved here are not just infidelity or moral retribution, or just different ethical assumptions held by (ex-)courtesans and their customers, but the endless self-delusion and desire to seize what is unavailable or forbidden, sparing no one. If even a marital relation cannot check the overflow of desire, why be serious about an affair of betrayal outside the bonds of marriage? Or, the other way around, shouldn't one cherish more a romance with a courtesan like Little Rouge, because it demonstrates the intensity of emotional bondage, however short-lived, under impossible conditions?

Thus, possibly with these thoughts in mind, Wang visits Little Rouge again after learning that business has sunk to the very bottom. Instead of Little Rouge, he is greeted by her servants. He takes up an opium pipe when "without good reasons, two tears dropped from his eyes."[8] It is at this moment that Wang seems to come to an awareness that he and Little Rouge are after all in the same boat, endlessly drifting in the stream of desire, while his residual passion for her helps him ascend to the plane of compassionate understanding.

My third example is the case of Second Treasure (Zhao Erbao), which serves as the underlying plotline for the entire novel. One can hardly miss the naturalist aspect of Second Treasure's story. She comes from the countryside and yearns for the glamour of Shanghai. She is lured into the courtesan trade, and in a short time she has made herself a popular success.

Precisely because this success comes so easily, Second Treasure is twice as susceptible as her fellow sisters to the spell of the fantastic scholar-courtesan romance. She falls in love with a wealthy young man, Nature Shi (Shi Tianran), and, at the latter's suggestion, she willingly gives up everything for a future as a decent wife. What follows is not difficult to guess. Shi never comes back, and Second Treasure finds herself deep in debt for the dowry she has prepared.

Second Treasure is described as too vain and naive to see the misfortunes awaiting her. But this does not mean that Han Bangqing intends only to criticize his heroine. He seems to indicate that these courtesans are all too human when they are deluded by the impossible dreams and virtues they of all people should see through and that the sad clichés of fiction do happen and are made to happen repeatedly simply because they are part of the real human condition.

For this reason, it is extremely suggestive that the novel ends with Second Treasure's awakening from a dream. In the dream, she is first harassed by an old patron and then followed surprisingly by the messengers sent by Nature Shi for the overdue wedding. Overjoyed as she is, Second Treasure is shrewd enough to keep her mother from telling anyone the longings and pains they have been through. But then Second Treasure is reminded that Nature Shi is actually long dead, and with this warning, the messengers suddenly turn into monsters, threatening to grab her and take her away.

It is at this moment that Second Treasure wakes up, and the novel comes to a sudden end. This device of "waking from a dream" (*jing-meng*) reads like a parody of the famous dreaming and awakening scenes in Tang Xianzu's (1550–1616) *Peony Pavilion* (*Mudanting*, 1599) and in fact bears imprints of the climax of Jin Shengtan's (1608–1661) seventy-chapter edition of *The Water Margin* (*Shuihuzhuan*, ca. fifteenth century) where Lu Junyi awakes from an ominous dream foretelling his and his sworn brothers' future. An interesting dialectic can be discerned here. In the dream, Second Treasure has shown us her capacity to love, suffer, and forgive—virtues celebrated by all great courtesan romances. But in the novel's realistic context, these are virtues more dreamed of than upheld by courtesans and their patrons. Here, Han Bangqing lays bare his scheme of realism on two levels: first by letting his girls indulge their dreams and then by making them take reality as a dream. Awakening from the dream, would Second Treasure come to an understanding that dreams vanish as fast as nightmares and that she might have been deceived not only by her desires but also by those self-imposed virtues, virtues that might be vanity for her?

Both Eileen Chang and Hu Shi highly praise Second Treasure's generosity and selfless love.[9] In so doing, they have ignored the dreamlike quality of Second Treasure's virtues and therefore exposed themselves as wishful consumers rather than critics of romantic idealization in courtesan literature. Whereas Second Treasure has awakened from her dream, Chang and Hu still think that the dream should come true and that a courtesan is desirable because she acts out virtues that would jeopardize her profession. The last paradox of *Sing-song Girls* thus is its secret, anticipatory retort to even its most sympathetic defenders, showing how easily the grounds of realism and fantasy can be confused at every level of the courtesan romance.

::

I have discussed *Sing-song Girls* as a masterpiece that helped modernize late imperial Chinese fiction at least in three aspects, representing a new typology of desire, an arguably modern rhetoric of realism, and a unique instance of the urban novel. As Eileen Chang observes, in a cultural and ethical environment where the individual pursuit of romantic love could still be overruled by the norm of prearranged marriage, Han Bangqing made the brothel a substitute Eden, a garden in which the forbidden fruit of free love was made available to Chinese intruders.[10] The tragicomedies enacted by the characters of *Sing-song Girls* appear surprisingly moving, in the sense that these men and women are shown as lonely souls, seeking consolation in the most unlikely circumstances, and that they find bliss, however tentatively, in their fall.

The desire so equivocally defined by *Sing-song Girls* lends light to the realistic project embedded in the novel's narrative scheme, one that surpasses in many ways the foreign models to be introduced and sanctioned by writers of the next generation in the name of the modern. Whereas nineteenth-century European novels such as *Madame Bovary* and *Anna Karenina* base their dialectic of desire and realism on the tension between adultery and fidelity and between the crime of romantic yearning and realistic punishment, *Sing-song Girls* denies such a (melo-)dramatic dilemma by making its heroines professionals of romance. Emma Bovary's romantic fiasco has been treated as a climactic moment in European realist discourse. In Emma's futile effort to bridge the gap between words and the world, between what she wishes to become and what she can be, (nineteenth-century) realism manifests itself as a discourse that articulates desire by narrating the inaccessibility of the desired object. By contrast, the courtesans in *Sing-song Girls* take an even more treacherous path in desiring love, since they are trained from the outset to *embody* the fickleness and unreliability of love. Thus when they plunge themselves into the sport of romance, these girls appear to be twice as vulnerable as their European counterparts.

The city of Shanghai plays a crucial role in etching this drama of desire and the discourse of realism. This is a city that sees hundreds of girls descend into a world of no return; indeed, with its ever-changing facets, Shanghai may well appear as a vamp, mysterious, seductive, and dangerous. Not unlike most characters under his pen, Han Bangqing, too, was an immigrant to Shanghai and stayed in the city till his death. A connoisseur of courtesan culture, Han Bangqing could not actualize his own drama of love and lust without invoking the city's magic name. Shanghai as the embodiment of the city is a touchstone through which the novel's intelligibility can be verified, and yet this effect of the real is found nowhere better than in the observed circulation of values and desires. A paradox: to write a realistic Shanghai means to celebrate the city's capacity continually to demand investment of desire, in power, money, land, and bodies and to refuse final judgments as contrary to the fluid nature of the urban economy.

Mixing both the cosmopolitan and local color unique to Shanghai, *Sing-song Girls* renders an urban regionalism that anticipates the literary style and attitude later called the Shanghai style, or *haipai*. The *haipai* school comprises writers who assume postures ranging from the newly imported flaneur to the old-style literatus and features a hybrid of trends as far apart as Mandarin Ducks and Butterflies fiction and neoimpressionist sketches. Arising from and nourished by a commercial culture, the Shanghai style is flamboyant and changeable, with dilettantism and frivolity as its twin trademarks. But beneath their flamboyant style lies the writers' inflamed desire to catch up with time; tear down the ostentatious and frivolous facade of the text, and one finds a desolate city threatened with the menacing power of modernization. At a time when realism was sanctioned as the canon of modern Chinese literature, the Shanghai-style writers played with the canon in such a way as to reveal the impotence of its promises.

The neoimpressionist texts by writers such as Shi Zhecun, Liu Na'ou, and Mu Shiying have won increasing attention in recent years, thanks to their patent modernist sensibilities.[11] Forty years before the neoimpressionist writers shocked their readers with recourse to exotic styles and nonchalant mannerisms, Han Bangqing's *Sing-song Girls* had quietly broken the same rules by inserting an indigenous modernity into the traditional discourse of courtesan fiction. As argued above, the novel in many ways anticipates or even surpasses the May Fourth practice of romanticism and realism; its achievement has long been underestimated. It was Eileen Chang, the precocious woman writer of wartime Shanghai, who came to appreciate the modernity of the aesthetics of *Sing-song Girls* and put this aesthetics into practice during the Japanese occupation period, while her weakness for Western middle-brow romantic literature further enriched her personal vision of Shanghai. As she puts it, the courtesan house as highlighted by *Sing-song Girls* no longer serves as the major topos of twentieth-century Chinese romantic imagination,[12] but the taxonomy of desire the novel evokes has survived to become the emotional index of life in Shanghai. Suffice it to say that Chang would become the finest interpreter of the fin-de-siècle cult of the Shanghai-style fiction of the forties, under the shadow of Japanese aggression and Communist revolution.

::

Eileen Chang came to the United States in 1955, and she spent the rest of her life in increasing reclusion. Perhaps contrary to her wishes, however, she has been fervently embraced by Chinese readers in Taiwan, Hong Kong, and overseas since the sixties, thanks to the praise of C. T. Hsia, then a professor at Columbia University, and other critics. C. T. Hsia's full-length study of Eileen Chang was published in *Wenxue zazhi* (Literary magazine), a leading literary journal in Taiwan, edited by T. A. Hsia, as early as 1957. This marked the beginning of Chang studies. Chang became an important phenomenon for all Chinese communities in the eighties and nineties.

If one asks why Chang's works now appear more compelling than ever, the answer may be that her inquiries into human frailties and trivialities, stylized portraits of Chinese mannerisms, and celebrations of historical contingencies make her a perfect contrast to the discourse of orthodoxy represented by such writers as Lu Xun, Mao Dun, and Ding Ling. Above all, we may say that as early as half a century ago, Chang was practicing a premature fin-de-siècle poetics.

Chang was never a productive writer, and she wrote only a handful of works in the last thirty years of her career. But *Sing-song Girls* remained one of the few projects she continued to take interest in. As mentioned above, a slightly truncated Mandarin Chinese translation of the novel came out in 1983; meanwhile, Chang kept working on the novel's English version. But except for the first two chapters, which were published in the translation journal *Renditions* in Hong Kong in 1982, little information about her progress was made public. As time moved on, Chang even left her friends with the impression that the manuscript was never completed and that it had been lost in the course of her numerous moves.

*Sing-song Girls* was made into a movie in 1998 by the famous Taiwan director Hou Hsiao-hien, and the script writer was Chu T'ien-wen, author of *The Notes of A Desolate Man* (New York: Columbia, 1999) and longtime admirer of Eileen Chang. Hou's movie was well received worldwide, and Chang's rendition of the novel again became a focus of public interest.

After her death, Chang's estate was entrusted to her friends in Hong Kong, Stephen C. Soong, founding editor of *Renditions*, and Mae Soong. In 1997 Professor Dominic Cheung of the University of Southern California sought from the Soongs the favor of donating select manuscripts by Chang for a memorial exhibition at the USC. Among the materials Cheung subsequently obtained was a box of manuscripts typed in English. Ms. Lillian Yang of the East Asian Library took an interest in several piles of unidentified manuscripts. Their content appeared obscure to everyone; Yang did research on them, consulting C. T. Hsia's writings and other sources. This led to a discovery most exhilarating to worldwide Chang fans: the manuscript was none other than the purportedly lost translation of *Sing-song Girls*.

Among Chang's papers was a full rendition of the original in sixty-four chapters, along with two additional revised but incomplete versions of the first. After reviewing all three versions, Yang selected the better revised chapters and merged them into one. As such, the reconstructed manuscript Yang sent to Columbia University Press reflects Chang's own revisions to her original draft.

Still, as it stood, this composite manuscript remained unpolished; to make it publishable, more work had to be done. Thanks to Professors C. T. Hsia's and Joseph Lau's recommendation, Columbia University Press and the Weatherhead East Asian Institute, Columbia University, were able to enlist Dr. Eva Hung, director of the Translation Center at the Chinese University of Hong Kong, to undertake the editing and revision of Chang's manuscript. Dr. Hung is an internationally renowned translation historian and a first-rate translator and fiction writer in her own right. As she points out in her afterword, the time and energy she invested in revising and editing Chang's manuscript almost amounted to retranslating the original from scratch. She was willing to take up the laborious task, over a period of almost three years, because of her respect for Chang's achievements as well as her own commitment to literary scholarship: such collaborative work had long been a practice in the history of Chinese translation.

Dean Jerry Campbell and East Asian Library director Kenneth Klein of the University of Southern California lent their generous support as Lillian Yang was preparing Chang's manuscript. Ms. Jennifer Crewe, editorial director of Columbia University, played the key role in coordinating the editorial work. Her confidence in Chang's work and her willingness to promote Chinese literature over the years are most commendable.

In 1981, at the recommendation of C. T. Hsia, Eileen Chang expressed a strong interest in seeing *Sing-song Girls* published by Columbia University Press; she even welcomed Hsia's proposal to write a preface to her translation.[13] Chang changed her mind the following year, perhaps for financial or other reasons, and her manuscript fell out of sight. Now, twenty-five years later, thanks to the aforementioned efforts, Chang's wish to introduce *Sing-song Girls* to the English-speaking world has finally been fulfilled, and by the publisher she first considered, Columbia University Press.

*Notes*

1. The literary supplement of *Shenbao*, *Yinghuan suoji* (Sketches of the world), first published in 1872, has been generally regarded as the first literary periodical in late imperial China; however, featuring a wide range of subjects, the supplement appears more like a publication of miscellaneous interests. Hang Bangqing's *Haishang qishu* specialized in fiction and can be called the first literary magazine in a

more professional sense. See Chen Bohai and Yuan Jin, *Shanghai jindai wenxueshi* (A history of literature from Shanghai in late imperial China) (Shanghai: Shanghai renmin chubanshe, 1993), p. 241.

2. Chen and Yuan, *Shanghai jindai wenxueshi*, p. 241.

3. See Yu Xingmin and Tang Jiwu's informative account of the rise of Shanghai in *Shanghai: Jindaihua de zaochaner* (Shanghai: The premature baby of Chinese modernization) (Taipei: Jiuda wenhua chuban gongsi, 1992).

4. Eileen Chang's annotated translation of *Haishanghua* was published by Huangguan chubanshe (Taipei) in 1983.

5. Eileen Chang, *Zhangkan*, (Taipei: Huangguan chubanshe, 1994), p. 177.

6. Hu Shi, preface to *Haishanghua liezhuan*, in *Hu Shi zuopin ji* (Works by Hu Shi) (Taipei: Yuanliu, 1986), 13:8; Zhang Ailing (Eileen Chang), *Hongloumeng yan* (The nightmare of *The Story of the Stone*) (Taipei: Huangguan chubanshe, 1994), p. 9; and idem, afterword to the Mandarin version of *Haishanghua*, pp. 591–608.

7. Lin Shu's translation of the novel was not published till 1899.

8. Han Bangqing, *Haishanghua*, Mandarin translation by Eileen Chang, p. 432.

9. See Hu Shi's introduction to *Haishanghua*, p. 135, and Eileen Chang's afterword to the Mandarin version of *Haishanghua*, p. 599.

10. Chang, afterword, p. 596.

11. Leo Ou-fan Lee should be regarded as one of the most important promoters behind the reappraisal of the neoimpressionist school. See the introduction to his *Xinganjue pai xiaoshuo xuan* (A collection of neoimpressionist fiction) (Taipei: Yunchen wenhua, 1987), pp. 1–8. Also see Yan Jiayan, "Lun xinganjui pai" (On neoimpressionism), in idem, *Shiji de zuyin* (Footsteps of the century) (Hong Kong: Tiandi tushu gongsi, 1995), pp. 100–137; and Wu Fuhui, "Shiji zhibing" (The malaise of the century, in *Wenxueshi* [Studies in literary history] 1 (1993): 157–173.

12. Eileen Chang, afterword to *Haishanghua*, pp. 596, 608.

13. C. T. Hsia, "Zhang Ailing geiwo de xinjian" (Eileen Chang's correspondence with me, 11), *Lianhe wenxue* (Unitas) 14, no. 11 (1998): 79–80.

*Eileen Chang*


Chapter 1 begins with a short foreword followed by a prologue. The foreword describes the novel as an exposé of the wiles of the prostitutes of the trading port Shanghai and stresses that it is in no way pornographic. In the prologue, the author, under his pen name Hua Yeh Lien Nung,[1] or "Flowers Feel For Me Too," dreams that he is walking on a sea completely covered with flowers, a simple conceit, as Shanghai means "On the Sea," and a flower is a common euphemism for a prostitute. In his dream, he sees chrysanthemums, plum blossoms, lotus flowers, and orchids tossed by the waves and plagued by pests. These flowers, which weather autumn chill or winter snows, rise above mud or withstand loneliness in empty hills, fare worse than the less highly regarded varieties and soon sink and drown; which so distresses our author that he totters and falls into the sea himself—dropping from a great height onto the Lu Stone Bridge that separates the Chinese district and foreign settlements in Shanghai. He wakes up to find himself on the bridge, an indication that he is still dreaming—a dreamer living in dreamland—and bumps into a young man rushing up the bridge, the prologue thus merging into the story proper.

The sentiment in the prologue shows where the author's sympathies lie and is clearly at variance with the moralistic introduction, which is just the routine disclaimer of all traditional Chinese novels that touch on the subject of sex. Closely modeled on *Dream of the Red Chamber*'s preface-cum-prologue, but without its charm and originality, this section of the book, so uncharacteristic, would bore foreign readers and put them off before they had even begun and would only serve to mislead the student of Chinese literature looking for underlying myths and philosophies. Not a best-seller when first published in 1892, this little-known masterpiece went out of print a second time in the 1930s after its discovery by Hu Shih and others in the May Fourth Movement.[2] Perhaps understandably concerned about its reception abroad, I finally took the liberty of cutting the opening pages.

The epilogue is omitted for similar reasons. Weakest in scenic description, where he was generally formalistic and used conventional literary expressions, the author here pictures at great length the joys of mountain climbing without gaining the top and its panoramic view, thus explaining why most of his subplots are left dangling, but with deducible and inevitable endings.

As Hu Shih pointed out, a poem and an erudite pornographic tale have been worked into the book just to show off the author's prowess in other realms of belles-entendres such as "Blood flowed, floating pestles away," a quotation from the classics about the amount of blood shed in a battle. Unfortunately, the other quotations with double meanings are not as translatable. Neither are the scholarly drinking games that often give quotations a clever twist. The poem would be unwieldy and labored in translation and would create an effect quite different from that intended. These are the only excisions I have made and patched over, I hope unnoticeably, to maintain continuity and pace.

I had long been familiar with the book but, until I translated it, had never realized that on their first night together Green Phoenix came to Prosperity Lo from another man's bed, which should be no surprise in a whorehouse but was still a shock because of the domestic atmosphere of these sing-song houses, and especially after all her posturings. In this and a few other instances of extreme subtlety, my footnotes are more like commentary, at the risk of being intrusive.

*Eileen Chang*


*Notes*

1. [In pinyin romanization, Huayeliannong. *E.H.*]
2. [In pinyin romanization, Hu Shi. *E.H.*]

*The Zhao Family*

Simplicity Zhao, a first-time visitor to Shanghai who falls for high-class courtesans and cheap prostitutes alike.

Second Treasure, sister of Simplicity who comes to Shanghai in search of him and ends up as a courtesan.

Madam Hong, mother of Simplicity and Second Treasure, sister of Benevolence Hong.

Clever, originally a servant girl at the Wei house in Generosity Alley, she later joins the Zhaos' establishment and strikes up a relationship with Simplicity.

Flora Zhang, a friend of Second Treasure who accompanies her to Shanghai and, like her, becomes a courtesan.

Nature Shi, the scion of a well-known family and Second Treasure's regular client whom she hopes to marry.

*Hall of Beauties on West Chessboard Street*

Woodsy, a courtesan in this second-class house.

Jewel, a virgin courtesan and sister of Woodsy.

Mama Yeung, the maid of the house.

Lichee Zhuang, owner of a lottery store and a regular client of Woodsy.

Fortune Shi, a regular client of Jewel and Third Treasure of Tranquillity Alley. He entices Second Treasure and Flora Zhang into prostitution.

Lai the Turtle, the son of a high-ranking government official, is an uncouth man disliked and feared by all the courtesans he visits.

## The Zhou House in Sunshine Alley

Orchid Zhou, Twin Pearl's real mother and head of this first-class establishment.

Twin Pearl, leading courtesan of the house.

Twin Jade, a new girl purchased by Orchid Zhou.

Twin Jewel, a courtesan who feels displaced by Twin Jade.

Mama Yang, a maid in the Zhou house.

Golden, the maid with a reputation for being an unfaithful wife.

Worth, Golden's husband and a manservant of the house.

Eldest, the son of Worth and Golden.

Clever Baby, a servant girl of the house.

Benevolence Hong, uncle of Simplicity Zhao and regular client of Twin Pearl. He owns a ginseng store in South End and often runs errands for Lotuson Wang.

Modesty Zhu, younger brother of Amity Zhu and regular client of Twin Jade.

## The Huang House in Generosity Alley

Second Sister Huang, owner of this first-class house and quite well known when she was young.

Green Phoenix, leading courtesan of the house who purchases her own freedom.

Gold Phoenix, a virgin courtesan of the house.

Pearl Phoenix, a courtesan of the house considered lazy by everyone.

Mama Zhao, the maid of the house.

Little Treasure, a servant girl of the house.

Prosperity Luo, a regular client of Lute Jiang and later of Green Phoenix. He is an official with the rank of alternate magistrate.

Promotion, the steward of Prosperity Luo.

Vigor Qian, the favorite client of Green Phoenix. He lives on Avenue Road.

Mrs. Qian, wife of Vigor Qian, an easygoing woman.

Gold Flower, a girl bought by Third Sister Chu and placed temporarily in the Huang house.

## The Lin House in Generosity Alley

White Fragrance, leading courtesan of the house.

Green Fragrance, a virgin courtesan and younger sister of White Fragrance.

Amity Zhu, older brother of Modesty Zhu and a regular client of White Fragrance.

Whistler Tang, Amity Zhu's business partner and an occasional client of Green Fragrance.

Devotion Yin, a young man of some literary fame and a regular client of Green Fragrance.

### The Wei House in Generosity Alley

Sister Wei, owner of this top-class establishment.

Sunset, a top-class courtesan.[1]

Mallow Yao, a regular client of Sunset and a henpecked husband.

Mrs. Yao, wife of Mallow Yao, a woman prone to jealousy.

Dragon Ma, a regular client of Sunset and private secretary to the official Harmony Qi.

### The Li House in East Prosperity Alley

Fair Sister Li, real mother of Water Blossom and owner of this first-class house.

Water Blossom, leading courtesan of the house who wants to marry Jade Tao. The frustration of her wish leads to ill health and an early death.

River Blossom, a childish virgin courtesan.

Big Goldie, the maid of the house.

Beckon, a servant girl in the house.

Jade Tao, Water Blossom's lover who wants to marry her. His family objects to his taking a prostitute as wife.

### Big Feet Yao's House in East Co-prosperity Alley

Snow Scent, a courtesan working for herself.

Little Sister, Snow Scent's maid and Clever's aunt.

Elan Ge, a Chinese banker and regular client of Snow Scent.

Wenjun Yao, a tomboyish courtesan who finds favor with Second Bai Gao.

Second Bai Gao, a young man of some literary fame who finds the normal run of courtesans unattractive.

### Generosity Alley

Grace Yang, a courtesan suspected of involvement in a gambling scam.

Thrive, Grace Yang's maid.

Crane Li, a regular client of Grace Yang and nephew of Pragmatic Li. He is a gambler who is cheated by everyone.

Second Kuang, Crane Li's steward and a client of the low-class prostitute Third Pan.

Laurel Zhao, a courtesan in her midtwenties who is an opium addict. She rents rooms in the same house as Grace Yang.

Belle Tan, a first-class courtesan.

Cloud Tao, a regular client of Belle and elder brother of Jade Tao. He lives in the Old City.

### East Civic Peace Alley

Lute Jiang, a first-class courtesan and Prosperity Luo's regular girl until he took up with Green Phoenix.

Tigress, a servant girl at Lute Jiang's, probably so named because she was born in the year of the tiger.

Script Li, a regular client of Lute Jiang and Bright Pearl of Tripod Alley. He is a high-ranking official and a man of great wealth.

### Co-security Alley

Clever Gem, a first-class courtesan.

Ocean, Clever Gem's maid.

Big Silver, Clever Gem's servant girl.

Cloudlet Chen, owner of a lottery shop and a regular client of Clever Gem.

Constant Blessing, Cloudlet Chen's steward and a client of the low-class prostitute Second Wang.

### Hall of Spring

Love Gem, sister of Clever Gem and a courtesan in this second-class house.

### Great Prosperity Alley

Third Sister Chu, mother of Perfection and formerly a well-known figure in the brothel world.

Perfection Chu, a young married woman who has just become a streetwalker.

Pragmatic Li, a regular client of Perfection and an old client of Bright Pearl. A miser, he prefers the cheaper girls.

### Nobility Alley

White Orchid, a second-class courtesan.

Sister Gold, White Orchid's maid.

Pine Wu, a regular client of White Orchid. He comes from the same hometown as Simplicity Zhao and works in a foreign firm.

Clement Zhou, the owner of a gambling den who teams up with Pine Wu in a scam.

Iron Hua, a regular client of White Orchid.

## Tripod Alley

Bright Pearl, a wealthy semiretired courtesan who is getting on in years.

## Lucky Spring Alley

Constance Zhang, Lotuson Wang's new flame. He helps her set up her business.

Lotuson Wang, a regular client of both Constance and Little Rouge of Floral Alley. He is an official who deals with affairs related to foreigners.

Talisman, the steward of Lotuson Wang.

## Floral Alley

Little Rouge, a first-class courtesan and Lotuson Wang's regular girl until he met Constance.

Pearlie, Little Rouge's maid.

Goldie, Little Rouge's servant girl.

Little Willow, an opera actor and Little Rouge's lover.

Thatch Fang, an older man with literary pretensions. He later marries Laurel Zhao.

Jade Wenjun, a courtesan with literary pretensions.

## Tranquillity Alley

Third Treasure, a virgin courtesan.

Bamboo Hu, bookkeeper at Cloudlet Chen's lottery shop and a regular client of Third Treasure.

## Auspicious Cloud Alley

Cassia Ma, a second-class courtesan who wins Mrs. Yao's trust.

## Security Alley

Third Pan, a low-class prostitute.

Verdure Xu, a regular client of Third Pan and a rather rough character.

Longevity Zhang, the steward of Amity Zhu and a client of Third Pan. He is the lover of the maid Golden.

*Beaten Dog Bridge*

Second Wang, a low-class prostitute.

Rustic Zhang, a regular client of Second Wang and cousin of Flora Zhang. He comes to Shanghai with Simplicity Zhao and manages to find a job.

*Rustic Retreat*

Harmony Qi, a wealthy elderly Chinese official who prides himself on being a champion of young lovers.

Aroma Su, a courtesan who comes back into the business when she fails to get along with the wife of the man she married. Her sister, Essence, is one of Qi's concubines.

Pendant, a teenage member of Qi's private theater troupe whose sexual favor he enjoys.

Hairpin, a teenage member of Qi's private theater troupe whose sexual favor he enjoys.

*Note*

1. [For an explanation of the distinction between top-class and first-class courtesans, see "The World of the Shanghai Courtesans." *E.H.*]

*The Sing-song Girls of Shanghai*

CHAPTER 1 :: *Simplicity Zhao visits his uncle on Salt Melon Street, and Benevolence Hong makes a match at the Hall of Beauties*

A young man was seen rushing over Lu Stone Bridge, which linked Shanghai's Chinese district to the foreign settlements. He was dressed in a golden brown box jacket of glossy Nanjing silk, under which was an off-white cotton archery gown.[1] Surprised by the busy scene, he bumped into a ricksha and fell smack on the ground, splashing mud all over himself. Scrambling quickly to his feet, he seized the ricksha puller, shouting and cursing wildly at him, deaf to remonstrances. A Chinese policeman in a dark blue cotton uniform came over to question him. "My name is Simplicity Zhao, and I'm bound for Salt Melon Street," said the young man. "But out of the blue came this blockhead who ran me over with a ricksha! Look at the mud on my jacket. He'll have to pay for it."

"You could have been more careful yourself. I shouldn't press the matter," the policeman said.

Simplicity Zhao grumbled on for a bit but finally had to loosen his grip on the ricksha man and watch him pad away. A crowd of spectators had gathered at the crossroads, talking and laughing. Simplicity Zhao tried to brush the dirt off his clothes, complaining in despair, "How can I go and see my uncle like this?"

Even the policeman couldn't help laughing. "Why don't you go over to the teahouse and get a towel to wipe yourself down?"

Following his advice, Simplicity went to the Waterway Teahouse

: :

1. A knee-length gown of Manchu origin worn for freedom of movement. By the nineteenth century, it no longer had anything to do with archery.

by the bridge, where he took a seat near the street and removed his jacket. A waiter brought him a basin of hot water and a towel. He wrung the towel dry and wiped his jacket carefully, until not a trace of mud was left. Then he put it back on, took a sip of tea, paid the bill, and headed straight for the central market on Salt Melon Street. Here he saw the signboard of the Flourishing Ginseng Store and ambled into its small walled courtyard, asking loudly for Mr. Benevolence Hong. A young salesclerk answered, invited him in, took his name, and hurried in to announce him.

Soon Benevolence Hong bustled out. Though Simplicity had not seen his uncle for a long time, he still remembered well the hollow cheeks and protuberant eyes. He quickly walked up to the man and greeted him on one knee. Benevolence Hong hastened to return the salutation and asked him to take the seat of honor, inquiring meanwhile, "How is your esteemed mother? Did she come with you? Where are you staying?"

"My humble quarters are at the Welcome Inn on Treasured Merit Street. Mother did not come but told me to pay you her respects, sir," Simplicity replied.

While they talked, the young clerk served tobacco and tea. Benevolence Hong asked his nephew what had brought him to Shanghai.

"Nothing in particular," Simplicity said. "I'm hoping to find some employment."

"Just now, though, there aren't any good opportunities in Shanghai," said Benevolence.

"Mother says I'm not getting any younger, and there's nothing for me to do at home, so it's better for me to go out into the world and learn to do business."

"There's certainly something in that. How old are you?"

"Seventeen."

"You have an esteemed sister, too. I haven't seen her either for several years. How old is she? Is she betrothed yet?"

"Not yet. She's fifteen."

"Who else is there in your family?"

"Just the three of us and a maidservant."

"With so few people, your expenses are probably low."

"Even so, we also have to pinch and skimp much more than before."

There was a clock on a table carved from tree roots. As they talked, it struck twelve, whereupon Benevolence asked Simplicity to stay for a casual meal and summoned the clerk to give him the instructions. A little later, four plates of cold cuts, two main courses, and a jug of wine were brought in. Uncle and nephew sat facing each other, drinking and chatting about recent developments and how things were in the countryside.

"Are you staying alone at the inn? Isn't there anyone to look after you?" asked Benevolence.

"A friend of mine from a rice merchant's has also come to Shanghai to look for work. His name is Rustic Zhang, and he's staying with me."

"That's all right then."

After lunch, they wiped their face with a towel and rinsed their mouths. Benevolence handed Simplicity a water pipe. "Do stay for a while. I'll go and finish a few small chores and then see you back to the inn."

Simplicity agreed politely, whereupon Benevolence hurriedly left the room.

Simplicity sat smoking the water pipe until he got good and tired of it. The clock had struck two by the time Benevolence came out. He summoned the clerk again to leave some instructions and then went with Simplicity to his room at the Welcome Inn.[2] There was already a man in the room, lying there smoking opium. After a brief greeting, Benevolence asked, "Mr. Rustic Zhang, I presume?"

"At your service," said Rustic. "And you, Uncle, must be Mr. Benevolence Hong."

"You do me too great an honor to call me Uncle."

"I apologize for not having called on you to pay my respects."

After this exchange of civilities, they sat down. Simplicity produced a water pipe and offered it to Benevolence.

"This is my nephew's first visit to Shanghai. He is absolutely dependent on your great kindness," said Benevolence.

Rustic said, "Alas, I am all too aware of my own inadequacy. But since we came to town together, it's only natural that we should look out for each other."

After more courtesies, Benevolence passed him the water pipe. Taking it in one hand, Rustic gestured with his other hand toward the couch, inviting Benevolence to share a pipe of opium with him.[3]

"No, thanks," Benevolence declined, and they sat down again.

Sitting to one side, Simplicity listened to their conversation, which drifted gradually to the topic of courtesans. He was just about to slip in a question or two when Rustic passed him the water pipe, so he took the opportunity to whisper into the latter's ear.

: :

2. Inns catering to officials and the very rich provided full board with accommodation. Those for ordinary travelers only provided the hard furnishing; guests had to bring their own bedding, and meals were not provided. Welcome Inn falls into the latter category.

3. [Opium smoking was prevalent and quite legal in China of the late Qing dynasty (late nineteenth to early twentieth century). Among the well-off, it was a regular part of entertaining guests. E.H.]

"Ha!" Rustic turned to Benevolence. "My brother Simplicity says he'd like to take a look at the sing-song houses. Is that all right?"

"Where shall we go?" said Benevolence.

"Let's take a stroll along Chessboard Street," said Rustic.

"I remember there's a courtesan called Jewel at the Hall of Beauties on West Chessboard Street. She's not bad," said Benevolence.

"Then let's go," Simplicity broke in.

Rustic grinned. Even Benevolence could not help smiling.

Simplicity told Rustic to put away his opium tray and then waited while he changed into a new outfit—a melon-ribbed cap, Beijing-style trimmed slippers, and a padded gown of shiny gray Hangzhou silk topped by a glossy box jacket of sapphire-blue Nanjing silk. Rustic then proceeded to fold up one by one all the clothes he had changed out of before he was finally ready to go. At the door, he and Benevolence each pressed the other to take the lead.

Impatiently, Simplicity pulled the door to, locked it, and followed them out. After turning a couple of street corners, they were on West Chessboard Street. Outside one of the doors, there was an iron stand with an octagonal glass lantern inscribed in vermilion with the words "The Hall of Beauties." Benevolence led the way in. The menservants knew him and shouted at once, "Mama Yeung, a friend of Young Mr. Zhuang."[4] Somebody answered upstairs and came stumping to the head of the stairs to greet them.

The maid Mama Yeung watched as the three men came up and said, "Oh, it's Young Mr. Hong. Please come in and take a seat." A servant girl of thirteen or fourteen had propped up the bamboo curtain with a stick to let them through. There was already a man in the room. He was lying on the couch, his arms round a courtesan, cuddling with her. Only when Benevolence walked in did he get up to greet the newcomers, cupping his hands palm over fist to salute Rustic and Simplicity and asking for their family names. Benevolence answered for them and turned toward Rustic, saying, "This is Mr. Lichee Zhuang."

"Honored," Rustic murmured.

The courtesan hid behind Lichee Zhuang, waiting till everyone had taken their seats before she came up to offer them watermelon seeds. The servant girl also brought water pipes and filled them for the clients.

"I was just going to look for you," Lichee Zhuang said to Benevo-

: :

4. Women in second-class houses addressed all patrons as Young Mr. So-and-so. By the early twentieth century, the custom had spread to the best houses, as everyone liked to be called young.

lence Hong. "I've got a lot of stuff here. See if anyone can help dispose of them." He fished a folder out of his pocket and handed it to Benevolence. Benevolence saw that on the list were items of jewelry, curios, paintings, calligraphy, and clothes, all numbered and with prices written next to them.

"This sort of thing . . . " Benevolence said, frowning. "Well, they're hard to sell. I heard Script Li of Hangzhou is here. D'you want to try him?"

"I've told Cloudlet Chen to take this to Li. There's been no news yet."

"Where's all the stuff?"

"Right here, over at Longevity Bookstore. Would you care to go and take a look?"

"What's the point? I don't know the first thing about this kind of stuff."

Simplicity, impatient with their conversation, turned to give the courtesan a good looking-over. She had a very fair round face and regular and exquisite features. Loveliest of all were her smiling lips— so small they formed a vermilion dot—and her mercurial eyes oozed tenderness. Since she was at home, she was dressed casually and for ornament wore only a silver filigree butterfly in her hair. Her cotton blouse was the color of dawn's first light, set off by a sleeveless jacket of black crinkled crepe with satin pipings and pink crinkled crepe trousers trimmed with off-white satin and three bands of embroidered lace.

She felt Simplicity's gaze and, smiling, walked to the big foreign mirror against the wall and studied herself from all angles, smoothing her sidelocks. Entranced, he followed her with his eyes. Suddenly he heard Benevolence Hong call out, "Miss Woodsy, shall I make a match for your little sister Jewel?" Only then did he realize that this courtesan was Woodsy Lu, not Jewel.

He saw her turn around and answer, "Why not? You'd be doing my sister a good turn." She shouted for Mama Yeung, who happened to come in at that very moment to offer them towels and more tea. She told her to summon Jewel and add more teacups.[5]

"Which is the gentleman?" Mama Yeung asked.

"Young Mr. Zhao." Benevolence Hong pointed to Simplicity.

Mama Yeung eyed him sideways. "Oh, so this is Young Mr. Zhao? I'll get Jewel." She took the towels and ran out, thump, thump, thump.

Not long afterward came the sound of bound feet, creakety creak

: :

5. [Etiquette of the sing-song houses is explained in the essay "The World of the Shanghai Courtesans." *E.H.*]

all the way.[6] That must be Jewel coming. Simplicity Zhao had his eyes on the door curtain and saw her walk in, pick up the plate of watermelon seeds, and pass it around, first to "Young Mr. Zhuang" and then to "Young Mr. Hong." When she got to Rustic and Simplicity, she asked for their names and gave Simplicity a little smile. He saw that she, too, had a small round face, exactly like Woodsy's. She was younger and not as tall, but if they were not seen together it would be quite impossible to tell them apart.

Jewel put down the plate and seated herself shoulder to shoulder with Simplicity, which embarrassed him a little. He didn't know whether to remain seated or walk away. Fortunately, Mama Yeung came hurrying in again. "Young Mr. Zhao, please come this way."

"Everybody, please come over together," said Jewel.

At this, they all stood up, inviting each other to take the lead.

"I'll lead the way," Lichee Zhuang said. He was about to walk ahead when Woodsy grabbed him by the sleeve. "You stay here. Let them go."

Benevolence Hong looked over his shoulder with a smile and, together with Rustic and Simplicity, followed Mama Yeung into Jewel's room. It was right next door to Woodsy's and was similarly furnished, with a dressing mirror, a clock, golden hanging scrolls, and colorfully painted silk lanterns. They sat around casually as Mama Yeung bustled about adding teacups and summoned the servant girl to fill the water pipes. Then a manservant brought in a plate of nuts and sweetmeats, which Jewel offered to everyone before sitting down next to Simplicity again.

"Where is Young Mr. Zhao's residence?" asked Mama Yeung, who was standing next to Benevolence.

"He is staying at the Welcome Inn with Young Mr. Zhang."

"Has Young Mr. Zhang got a girl?" Mama Yeung turned to Rustic, who smiled and shook his head. "He hasn't? Then we must fix him up with one, too," she said.

"Fix me up with a girl? How about you?" said Rustic, at which everybody roared with laughter.

Mama Yeung laughed and continued, "Wouldn't it be more fun if you got yourself fixed up and came and visited together with Young Mr. Zhao?"

With a sardonic laugh, Rustic went and lay down on the couch to smoke.

"Come, Young Mr. Zhao, you be the matchmaker," Mama Yeung turned to Simplicity.

Simplicity, busy fooling around with Jewel, pretended not to hear.

: :

6. "Creakety creak" represents the noise made by the wooden soles of bound-feet shoes.

Jewel snatched her hand away from his. "Hey, you're to be the matchmaker. Say something!"

He still did not speak.

"Go on, say something," she urged.

Hard pressed, he glanced at Rustic and made to address him, but Rustic ignored him and went on smoking.

Simplicity was saved from his embarrassment by Lichee Zhuang, who had just come in through the door curtain. He took the opportunity to stand up and invite Zhuang to take a seat. Mama Yeung, seeing that there was nothing doing, went out with the servant girl.

Lichee Zhuang sat down opposite Benevolence and talked about things in the business world. Rustic was still lying on the couch, smoking. Jewel held Simplicity's hands tightly in her own and forbade him to move. She would only chat with him, one minute saying she wanted to go to the theater, the next that she wanted a drinking party. Simplicity just grinned. She went so far as to draw up her feet and roll into his arms. But when he stuck a hand up her sleeve, she held her bosom tight and cried out desperately, "Stop it!"

Rustic had just finished smoking a couple of pellets of opium. "You should pass up the dumplings and go for the buns!" he said smiling.

Simplicity did not understand. "What did you say?"

Jewel set her feet down quickly and tugged at him. "Don't listen to him. He's making fun of you." She glared at Rustic and pulled the corners of her mouth down. "You won't get yourself a girl, but when it comes to wagging your tongue, you're tops, right?"

This dampened Rustic's spirits. He got up sheepishly to look at the clock.

Sensing that Rustic wanted to go, Benevolence Hong also stood up. "Let's go and have dinner."

On hearing this, Simplicity hastily fished out a silver dollar and tossed it into the candy dish. Jewel said, "Do stay a little longer," and then called out to Woodsy, "Elder Sister, they're leaving."

Woodsy hurried over and said something to Lichee Zhuang in a low voice. Then she and Jewel saw the men out to the staircase landing, both saying, "Come together again soon." The four men made affirmative noises as they walked down the stairs.

CHAPTER 2 :: *A callow youth trying a pipe is just good for a laugh, and a virgin courtesan attending a party is unscathed by a gibe*

The four men left the Hall of Beauties and walked up West Chessboard Street into the House of Satisfaction diagonally across the way, where they took a small private room behind the main parlor. Having served them tobacco and tea, the waiter took their order. Benevolence Hong ordered a basic menu with the addition of a soup and another main course.[1] The waiter laid the tablecloth, set out two large plates of nuts and sweetmeats, and turned up the gaslight. Looking at the clock, they saw it was already past six. Benevolence Hong called for warmed wine and invited Rustic Zhang to take the seat of honor. Rustic adamantly refused and instead urged Lichee Zhuang to take the seat. He himself sat in the second place, Simplicity Zhao in the third, and Benevolence Hong in the host's.

The waiter brought the first two courses in small bowls, and Lichee Zhuang started to talk business again with Benevolence Hong. Rustic managed to put in a word now and then, but Simplicity, who did not understand any of it, soon lost interest. He could hear the lively sound of music and singing coming from the "study" next to the parlor and, unable to sit still any longer, slipped out on the pretext of going to the toilet. He peeped through the windowpane next door and saw six diners seated at a round table, surrounded by courtesans and their maids and servant girls. The women filled the room. The fat man sitting facing the window had a purplish dark complexion and three strands of black whiskers. He had called two girls to keep him company. The one on his right was singing a Beijing opera aria, "Plucking Mulberry Leaves." As her face was hidden by her lute, Simplicity could not tell what she looked like. The girl on the left was older but quite pretty. Seeing that the fat man had lost at the drinking game "guess fingers," she offered to take the penalty cup of wine for him. The fat man refused, shoved her hand away, and bent down to pick up the cup himself. But just before he reached it, the courtesan on his right halted her playing, quietly took the cup, and gave it to her maid to drink. The fat man did not see what she had done and ended up drinking from an empty cup. Everybody laughed uproariously.

Simplicity Zhao watched, full of envy. Then a killjoy of a waiter came and asked him to rejoin the feast, so he had to return to the table. While they partook of the first six courses served in small bowls, Lichee Zhuang gesticulated and talked endlessly. The waiter, seeing that they were not drinking much, served up the main dishes and the rice. Benevolence Hong again offered a cup of wine all round, and then they each had some congee, wiped their faces with hot towels, and sat around the room chatting. The waiter brought the bill. Benevolence glanced cursorily at it and told him to put it

: :

1. Ordering a basic menu involved just setting the number of dishes for each category of food and leaving it to the chef to make up the menu.

on the account of Flourishing Ginseng Store. The waiter answered "Yes, sir," again and again.

The four of them walked out, deferring again to one another at the door. Just as they got to the main parlor, the fat man from the study walked in after having gone to the outhouse, his face flushed with drink. The minute he saw Benevolence, he invited him to join his party, saying, "Well met, Mr. Hong, well met indeed! Please come and join us." Brooking no protest, he grabbed Benevolence and also cornered the other three, urging them to join his party, "Come on in and have a chat."

Lichee Zhuang excused himself and left. Rustic Zhang signaled Simplicity with his eyes, so the two also excused themselves. They bade farewell to Benevolence Hong and walked out of the House of Satisfaction.

"Why did you want to leave? I know we just happened along, but we could have gone in and made the most of it!" Simplicity Zhao grumbled as he walked along.

Rustic Zhang clucked his tongue and told him off. "They've got high-class courtesans in there. Imagine how humiliating it'd be if you'd gone and called some second-class ones."

Simplicity saw his point. After a moment of reflection, he said, "Lichee Zhuang is probably at Woodsy's. Let's go to Jewel's, too, for a cup of tea, what d'you say?"

Rustic sneered again. "He went on his own, so why go bothering him? You'd only be a nuisance!"

"Then where shall we go?"

Rustic sneered and then said with deliberation, "You're not to blame. Being a first-timer in Shanghai, naturally you don't know the rules of the game. If you ask me, you'd be well advised to stay away from the second-class houses, let alone the top ones. They're all used to people making a splash. You can spend thirty or forty dollars on a girl, and it means nothing to her. Besides, Jewel is still a virgin. Can you afford several hundred dollars for her deflowering? It'll definitely cost you more than a hundred. That's just not worth it. If you want to have some fun, you'd better stick to the straightforward places."

"And where are these places?"

"If you're interested, I'll take you there. They may be smaller than the best houses, but the girls are not much different."

"Then let's go."

Rustic stopped to get his bearings and found that they were right in front of the Galaxy Jewelry Store. "If you really want to go, it's this way." They walked southward across the Beaten Dog Bridge to the very end of New Street in the French concession, where the last house had a sooty glass lamp hanging over its door. Just beyond the threshold was a staircase. Simplicity walked up with Rustic and found there was only half a room upstairs. It was very narrow, with one end completely taken up by a large Cantonese lacquered bed. Facing the staircase was a makeshift opium divan, just some boards set up on a couple of benches. A pine dressing table stood by the window, with a high-back chair on each side. These simple furnishings were enough to give an air of exquisite clutter, it being so crowded.

Seeing no one in the room, Simplicity whispered to Rustic, "Is this a second-class house?"

"Not second-class, just Second," Rustic said smiling.

"Is Second cheaper than second-class?"

Rustic smiled and made no reply. Suddenly, they heard someone shouting loudly downstairs, "Come over here, Second Miss." The voice called out twice. Then they heard someone answer in the distance and come laughing and chattering in their direction.

Simplicity still persisted with his questions, so Rustic told him hastily, "This is a flowered smoking den."

"Then why did you say Second?"

"The girl's name is Second Wang. Sit down, and hold your tongue."

Rustic's voice had hardly died away when Second Wang came upstairs, so Simplicity kept quiet. The minute Second Wang saw Rustic, she leaped at him, crying, "You're a fine one—you liar! You told me you were only going home for two or three months, but you've been away all this time! Two or three months, my foot! More like two or three years! I sent the maid to look for you several times at the inn. They said you hadn't come back, but I didn't believe it. Old Mrs. Filial Guo next door went searching for you, too, and was told you wouldn't be coming back again. Fart mouth! D'you ever stick to your word? Mind you, *I* don't forget it. If you hadn't come, I'd have ferreted you out myself and dealt with you in my own way. See how you'd have liked that!"

Rustic put on a smiling face and pleaded with her. "Don't be angry. Let me tell you something." He whispered into her ear.

He had only said one or two things when she jumped up and pulled a long face. "Smart, aren't you! You want to pass your wet shirt on to someone else and be well rid of it, is that it?"

"No!" Rustic cried out anxiously. "Just hear me out."

So Second Wang again crawled into his arms to listen to whatever it was he was murmuring. He signaled with a jerk of his mouth, and she turned round to glance sideways at Simplicity. Rustic said something more.

"And what about you?" she said.

"Why, nothing changes as far as I'm concerned."

Only then did she relent. She got up to trim the lamp wick and asked Simplicity's last name, scrutinizing him from head to toe. Simplicity turned around, pretending to look at the scroll on the wall.

A middle-aged maid came shuffling upstairs with a kettle of water in one hand and two boxes of opium paste in the other. Seeing Rustic, she also exclaimed, "Aiyo, it's Mr. Zhang! We thought you were gone forever. It seems you *do* have a conscience after all!"

"Tut-tut, if *he* has a conscience, dogs don't eat shit," said Second Wang.

"I'm here now, and still I'm told I have no conscience," Rustic said smiling. "Starting from tomorrow, I'll never set foot in this house again!"

"You wouldn't dare!" Second Wang said smiling.

While they were talking, the middle-aged maid had put the boxes of opium on the tray, lit the opium lamp, poured tea, and taken the kettle downstairs. Second Wang started to toast the opium, leaning against Rustic. Seeing Simplicity sitting by himself, she beckoned him over, "Come and make yourself comfortable on the couch."

He accepted the invitation with alacrity and lay down on the humbler side of the divan.[2] He watched as she toasted and rolled a pellet of opium, fixed it on the pipe, and handed it to Rustic, who sucked it all in in one long soughing breath. She made another, and he finished that, too. At the third pipe, he said, "No more," and she turned the pipe around and offered it to Simplicity. As Simplicity was not used to smoking, the opening on the pipe bowl got clogged before he was halfway through. She took the pipe and poked a needle through. He tried but got stuck again. She giggled. This fed the fire already kindled in him and made his heart itch more than ever. She cleared the hole in the pipe bowl, and as she held it for him over the flame, he took the opportunity to squeeze her wrist. She snatched her hand away and pinched him on the thigh with all her strength, so hard it ached and stung and tingled all at once. After Simplicity finished smoking, he stole a glance at Rustic. His eyes were closed, and he seemed to be dozing.

"Rustic," he whispered twice. Rustic's only response was to lift a hand and wave it from side to side, indicating he was not to be disturbed.

"He's stoned. Let him be," Second said.

Now she came over to Simplicity's side, holding a long pick for toasting opium, and leaned against him. His heart was as hot as

: :

2. [The right-hand side was considered the honored side and the left the humble side. *E.H.*]

burning charcoal, but with Rustic in the way, he dared not make a move. He just stared at her snow-white face, pitch-black eyebrows, crystalline eyes, and blood-red lips. The more he looked, the more infatuated he became, and the greater his infatuation, the harder he stared.

Seeing him like that, she asked with a smile, "What are you staring at?"

He was about to reply and could not find the words, so he just grinned.

She knew he was a boy who had not yet tasted meat, but that bashful air of his still exasperated her. Having filled the pipe, she pushed the mouthpiece to his lips, saying, "Here, be my guest." She then stood up, took a cup of tea from the table, and sipped at it. When she turned around and saw that he was not smoking, she handed him her cup. "Would you like some tea?" she asked.

Flustered, he sat up in a hurry and reached out for the cup with both hands. In so doing, he bumped right against her, splashing tea all over himself and nearly breaking the cup. She burst out laughing so loudly that even Rustic woke up, rubbing his eyes and asking, "What are you two laughing at?"

Rustic's dazed look made Second double up with more laughter, and she clapped her hands in mirth. Simplicity started laughing, too.

Rustic sat up and yawned, and then said to Simplicity, "Let's go."

Simplicity knew Rustic was in a hurry to get back because this opium wasn't doing anything for him, so he had to comply. Second Wang did some more whispering with Rustic, and then he went straight downstairs. Simplicity was about to follow when she clutched his sleeve, whispering, "Come on your own tomorrow."

He nodded and made haste to catch up with Rustic. They returned to the inn, went into their room, and lit the lamp. Rustic still needed another smoke. Simplicity went to bed first and lay there thinking there was much truth in what Rustic had said earlier. "Besides," his thoughts continued, "Second seems to fancy me. This must be fate." But he could not put Jewel out of his mind. When all was said and done, she was prettier than Second. He certainly wouldn't have enough money for both of them. Thinking now of this girl, now of that one, he tossed and turned and was unable to sleep.

Presently, Rustic had smoked his fill, cleaned out the ashes, washed his hands, and was ready for bed. Simplicity, however, draped some clothes over his shoulders and sat up again. He took a few puffs on the water pipe and then lay down once more, and before he knew it he was fast asleep.

At six the next morning, he was already up and called the hotel attendant for hot water to wash his face. He decided to go out for breakfast and take the opportunity to amuse himself a little. Rustic was still snoring away, so he closed the door and walked alone down Treasured Merit Street. He had a bowl of stewed pork noodles for twenty-eight copper coins at the Fountainhead Restaurant on the corner of Pebble Road. From there, he turned onto Fourth Avenue, peering around him before setting off again with a long leisurely stride. He happened to come across the garbage carts making their way along the street. Several workers were shoveling up garbage and tossing it into the carts, with some of it spraying in all directions. Afraid his clothes would get soiled, he was about to turn back, when he saw that Generosity Alley was just up ahead. He had heard this was where the sing-song houses of the two highest categories were located, so he went in to look around. He saw that every house in the alley had a slip of red paper pasted on the door, with the courtesan's name written on it. One of the houses had a carved stone gateway and a black lacquered signboard. The gilt characters read "Residence of Sunset Wei, minstrel."[3]

Simplicity stood at the door and looked in. He saw maids with uncombed hair washing and starching clothes in the courtyard and menservants sitting cross-legged in the parlor cleaning all kinds of foreign glass lamps. A servant girl of fourteen or fifteen rushed out of the front door muttering and ran straight into his arms. Before Simplicity could tell her off, the girl started cursing him, "You'd bump into your mother and kill her, wouldn't you? Haven't you got eyes in your head?" The minute he heard the piping voice, his anger melted away. Then he saw her handsome looks and dainty figure, and he grinned instead. The girl brushed him aside, turned around, and ran down the street. Just then an old woman came running out the door, shouting the name Clever and beckoning, "Come back." At this, the servant girl retraced her steps slowly, pouting and muttering to herself.

The old woman was about to go in when she saw Simplicity. A little taken aback, she stood there, trying to make him out. Embarrassed, he sheepishly retreated out of the alley. The garbage carts had moved on, so he went to the Splendid Assembly Teahouse and

: :

3. [Storytelling in a musical rhythm, which was a type of minstrelsy, originally had male and female performers, but only the latter caught on in Shanghai. When these women turned into prostitutes, they kept the proud title of "minstrel" and ranked above the first-class courtesans. For more information, see "The World of the Shanghai Courtesans," p. 540. *E.H.*]

ordered some tea upstairs. He sat there drinking seven or eight refills and did not return to the inn till it was almost noon.

By then, Rustic was up. The hotel attendant brought lunch, and
after they had finished eating, they washed their faces. Simplicity
wanted to go to the Hall of Beauties for a cup of tea.

"At this hour, the courtesans are still in bed. What d'you want to
go there for?" Rustic asked smiling.

There was nothing Simplicity could do. Rustic set out his opium
tray and lay down to smoke. Simplicity lay down, too. He stared
blankly at the top of his bed curtains, his thoughts working up and
down like creaking pulleys. He pushed his right hand against his
front teeth and bit his nails. A while later, he got up and started
pacing up and down the room, goodness knows how many hundred
times. Rustic had only had one pellet of opium, so he could not very
well hurry him just then. He sighed and lay down again. Chuckling
to himself, Rustic ignored him.

Simplicity could not help urging Rustic to hurry four or five times
before Rustic had finally smoked his fill. Rather unwillingly, Rustic
went out with Simplicity, heading straight for the Hall of Beauties.
They found two menservants playing mah-jongg with the maids in
the parlor. One of them quickly left his tiles to shout up the stairs,
"Guests coming up."

Simplicity, taking several steps in one stride, had already got to
the top of the stairs. Rustic followed him into Jewel's room and saw
her seated at the table by the window in front of a mirror box of
purple cedar, getting her hair done. Mama Yeung, who was standing
behind her, was attending to it with a fine-toothed comb while the
servant girl cleared away the fallen hairs. Rustic and Simplicity sat
down on the high-back chairs on either side of the table.

"Have you had lunch?" Jewel asked smiling.

"Yes, a while ago," said Rustic.

"So early?" she said.

"They're always like that at the inns," Mama Yeung broke in.
"They like to serve lunch at midday. Not like us here in the sing-
song houses, no telling how late we'd be!"

As they talked, the servant girl lit the opium lamp, gave Simplicity
the water pipe, and filled it for him. Jewel invited Rustic to smoke
on the divan, and he lay down with the opium pipe. A manservant
brought a kettle to make tea, and Mama Yeung prepared some hot
towels. Simplicity watched as Jewel finished her coiffure, took off
her blue cotton shawl, and replaced it with a black crinkled crepe
sleeveless jacket. She then walked over to the foreign mirror on the
wall to look herself over. Suddenly, they heard someone calling for

Mama Yeung next door. It was Woodsy's voice. Mama Yeung quickly folded up the mirror and went over to Woodsy's room.

"Is Young Mr. Zhuang here?" Rustic asked.

Jewel nodded in the affirmative, and Simplicity immediately expressed a wish to go and greet him, but Rustic emphatically forbade him to do so. Jewel also pulled him back by the sleeve, saying, "Sit still." He took the opportunity to sit down on the rattan chair in front of the bed. Jewel sat on his knees and whispered something in his ear. He looked bewildered. She whispered again, but he still could not make out what she was saying.

Exasperated, she said between clenched teeth, "You!" After a moment's reflection, she pulled him up to his feet and said, "Come over here, and I'll tell you."

The two of them lay down on the bed with their backs to Rustic, and only then was communication gradually established between them. After a while, Jewel suddenly giggled, "Aiyo! Stop it!" In another moment came a cry of distress, "Aiyo! Come quick, Mama Yeung!" followed by continuous cries of "Aiyoyo." Mama Yeung ran over from the next room, laughing and scolding, "Stop it, Young Mr. Zhao." Simplicity had to let go, and Jewel got up to smooth her sidelocks. Mama Yeung picked up a silver filigree butterfly by the pillow and put it in Jewel's hair, saying, "How Young Mr. Zhao can horse around! But our Miss Jewel is a virgin courtesan!"

Simplicity just grinned and went and lay down opposite Rustic on the humbler side of the divan. He whispered, "Jewel asked me to give a drinking party for her."

"So?" Rustic said.

"I promised."

Rustic sneered and, after a long pause, said, "Don't you realize that Jewel is a virgin courtesan?"

Jewel broke in, "What about it? Aren't virgin courtesans allowed to have drinking parties?"

Rustic laughed. "So, they can have drinking parties but no horsing around. What viragoes!"

"Young Mr. Zhang," said Jewel. "Don't take any notice of what Mama Yeung says. You're Young Mr. Zhao's friend, and we hope you'll be our friend, too. You don't want to make Young Mr. Zhao pick on us, do you? That's surely beneath a young gentleman like you."

"I didn't say anything wrong when I asked Young Mr. Zhao to stop horsing around," said Mama Yeung. "And if I did say something that offended Young Mr. Zhao, the young sir has the gift of the gab. He doesn't need anyone to prompt him."

"Lucky for us that our Young Mr. Zhao is understanding," said Jewel. "A fine state of affairs it would be if he listened to his friends."

She had scarcely finished speaking when a shout came from downstairs: "Mama Yeung, Young Mr. Hong coming up."

Jewel quieted down, and Mama Yeung hurried out to welcome the new guest. Simplicity also got to his feet. But the footsteps that came up the stairs went into Lichee Zhuang's room next door.

CHAPTER 3 :: *A professional name links the new girl to the belles of the family, and etiquette places a young man in the seat of honor*

Soon afterward, both Benevolence Hong and Lichee Zhuang came over to Jewel's room. Rustic Zhang and Simplicity Zhao hastened to greet them and invited them to sit down. Simplicity asked Rustic to broach the subject of his dinner party. Rustic sneered a little, but before he could raise the matter, Jewel saw what Simplicity was after and broke in, "What's so embarrassing about a dinner party? Young Mr. Zhao would like to ask you two gentlemen to dinner. Now, isn't that simple enough?"

Simplicity had no choice but to reiterate the invitation.

"I'm of course at your disposal," Lichee Zhuang said pleasantly.

Benevolence Hong pondered. "Will it be just the four of us?"

"We're too few," Simplicity said and turned to Rustic Zhang. "D'you know where to find Pine Wu?"

"He's at the Fidelity Company, but I don't think he'd come if you just send him an invitation. You and I will have to deliver the invitation in person," Rustic replied.

"Then may I trouble you to go there on my behalf?"

Rustic gave his assent. Simplicity then begged Benevolence Hong to invite a couple of other guests for him.

"Let's ask Cloudlet Chen," suggested Lichee Zhuang.

Benevolence Hong replied, "I'll come back later with whoever I run into," and so saying stood up. "I'll be back at six. Now I need to take care of a few things first."

Simplicity again repeated his earnest request for Benevolence's assistance. Jewel saw him out of the room, but Lichee Zhuang ran after him and said, "If you do see Cloudlet Chen, please say I'd like to know whether he has taken my things over to Script Li's yet."

Benevolence Hong promised to do so and then walked down the stairs and headed out of West Chessboard Street. A ricksha happened to pass by. He took it and rode to West Floral Alley on Fourth Avenue. Having paid the ricksha man, he went into the residence of Little Rouge at the mouth of the alley.

"Pearlie," he called out in the small courtyard.

A maid looked out from an upstairs window. "Mr. Hong, do come up."

"Is Mr. Wang here?"

"No, sir," said Pearlie. "He hasn't been for three or four days now. D'you know where he is?"

"I haven't seen him for a few days, either. Where's the maestro?"

"She's gone for a drive in a carriage. Come up and rest for a while, sir."

Benevolence Hong had already turned to go, saying casually, "Never mind."

"If you see Mr. Wang, do bring him along," Pearlie called out.

Benevolence Hong gave an affirmative grunt as he departed. Crossing to Third Avenue through Co-security Alley, he arrived at Twin Pearl's house in Sunshine Alley and walked straight through the parlor. It was all quiet. A lone manservant called out, "Mr. Hong's here." No answer came from upstairs. Benevolence went up, but the stillness was undisturbed. He lifted the door curtain himself, walked in, and, finding no one about, sat down on the divan. Only now did Twin Pearl come over from the room opposite, walking in slow graceful steps and holding her water pipe.

Seeing Benevolence, she asked with a smile, "Where did you go last night after you left the restaurant?"

"I went home."

"I thought you'd gone with friends to a party, so I told the maids to wait up for you for quite a while. Turns out you went home!"

"Sorry about that," he said smiling.

Twin Pearl also smiled. She sat down on the stool in front of the divan and filled the water pipe for him. As he reached for it, she said, "I'll hold it for you," and put the pipe to his lips. He inhaled it in one breath. Suddenly, the sound of shouting and cursing came through the front door and surged into the parlor, followed by the noise of people coming to blows.

"What is it?" Benevolence asked, startled.

"It's Golden and her family again," said Twin Pearl. "No end of quarreling night and day. It's partly Worth's fault, too."

Benevolence went to the window to peer down. He saw the maid Golden pulling at the pigtail of her husband, Worth, but he didn't move an inch. Now he laid his hand on her topknot, and, with one hefty push, she went straight down. Lying face down on the floor and unable to struggle to her feet, Golden nevertheless kept yelling,

"Beat me if you dare!" Worth, without a word, pinned her down with one foot and started hitting her with his fist. His blows rained down all over her body, from shoulders to buttocks, and she started screaming like a pig being butchered.

Twin Pearl could stand it no longer. She shouted out of the window, "What d'you think you're doing? Have you no shame?"

Everybody downstairs also shouted in unison for them to stop. Only then did Worth let go. Twin Pearl took Benevolence by the arm and turned around. "Just ignore them," she said with a smile and passed him the water pipe.

A moment later, Golden came upstairs, her mouth in a pout, and her face covered in tears.

"You *will* quarrel night and day, whether there are guests here or not, is that it?" said Twin Pearl.

"He pawned my fur-lined jacket, and then he dared beat me!" Golden complained and started to cry again.

Twin Pearl said, "What more can we say? If you were a bit smarter, you wouldn't get the dirty end of the stick every time."

That took the wind out of Golden. She took the teacups and tea leaves, went into the parlor, and sat there weeping.

Then Worth came into the room with a kettle of hot water.

"What were you beating her for?" Twin Pearl asked.

"You know only too well, Third Maestro," Worth said with a smile.

"She said you pawned her fur-lined jacket, is that true?"

Worth sneered. "Third Maestro, why don't you ask her what happened to the savings club money that was collected the day before yesterday? I said we should send our eldest to learn a trade, and that'd cost five or six dollars, but when I asked her for the club money, she couldn't come up with it. That's why I pawned the fur-lined jacket, which only fetched four-fifty. Just thinking about it makes me burst with rage!"

"The money from the savings club was what she put aside from her own earnings. Are you saying she's not allowed to spend it?"

"You know the situation only too well, Third Maestro," he said smiling. "If she did really spend it, I'm easy, but what expenses d'you suppose she's got? If you throw money into the Whampoo River, you'd at least hear a bit of sound; with her, you don't even get that."

Twin Pearl smiled and said nothing. Worth made tea, prepared a hot towel, and then went downstairs. Benevolence moved close to Twin Pearl and asked in a whisper, "How many lovers does Golden have?"

She quickly held up a hand to silence him. "Don't speak out of turn. You may be saying this for fun, but if Worth should hear you, there'd be no end to their rows."

"I don't see why you should bother keeping her secrets. Even I have heard something about it."

"Nonsense!" she said sharply. "Sit down, I have something to tell you."

Benevolence returned to his seat.

"Did my mother say anything to you?" she asked.

He bowed his head and thought for a moment. "Was it about buying a new girl?"

She nodded. "It's all settled, but it costs five hundred dollars."

"Well, is she pretty?"

"She'll get here any time now. I haven't seen her yet. I expect she's prettier than Twin Jewel anyway."

"Which room will she get?"

"The one across from mine. Twin Jewel will move downstairs."

He sighed. "I'm sure in her heart Twin Jewel wants to do well, too. The trouble with her is she's not smart enough for this business."

"My mother has spent quite a lot of money on Twin Jewel, too."

"You go on being nice to her, and see if you can persuade your mother to be more philosophical about it. Just think of it as charity."

As they were talking, they heard the steps of unbound feet running into the parlor, and a voice saying repeatedly, "She's coming! She's coming!" He hurried over to the window again and saw that it was the servant girl Clever Baby, still panting from her great rush.

Knowing the new girl had arrived, he leaned over the windowsill with Twin Pearl, waiting. They saw Twin Pearl's mother, Orchid Zhou, coming through the door, leading a virgin courtesan by the elbow. Clever Baby walked ahead of them, and they all came upstairs. Orchid Zhou led the girl straight up to Benevolence. "Mr. Hong, take a look. What d'you think of our little maestro?"

He stepped closer to look the girl straight in the face. Clever Baby told her to greet Mr. Hong. She murmured something indistinctly, so embarrassed that she turned away, flushed scarlet to the ears.

He saw that she had the kind of charm that would arouse both love and sympathy. "Excellent!" he said in earnest. "My hearty congratulations! This girl will bring you a fortune."

"Thank you, sir. Coming from you, it'll no doubt come true. I only hope she'll make a real effort. If she could be like her three sisters, it'd be good enough for me." Orchid Zhou pointed to Twin Pearl as she said this.

He turned to smile at Twin Pearl.

"My elder sisters are all right now, both of them married. I'm left all by myself because nobody wants me, and you'll have to keep me until I'm old and dead. What's so good about that?" Twin Pearl said to her mother.

Orchid Zhou guffawed. "You have Mr. Hong here. When you marry Mr. Hong, you'll be twice as well off as Twin Joy. Isn't that so, Mr. Hong?"

He just smiled.

"Think of a name for us first, Mr. Hong," said Orchid Zhou. "When she proves that she knows the business, we'll give you Twin Pearl."

"What about calling her Twin Jade?" he suggested.

"Isn't there anything that sounds better? Everybody's Twin this and Twin that, what a bore!" said Twin Pearl.

"Twin Jade is fine," said Orchid Zhou. "In our business, the important thing is to be well-known. Call her Twin Jade, and everyone in Shanghai can tell she's a sister of Twin Pearl and the other Zhou girls. That's a lot better than using a new unknown name."

Clever Baby, who was standing to one side, laughed. "That sounds rather like the eldest maestro's name, doesn't it? Twin Joy and Twin Jade, don't they sound about the same?"

"What d'you know? About the same!" Twin Pearl told her off with a smile. "Go and get me the handkerchief hanging out on the veranda."

With Clever Baby gone, Orchid Zhou took Twin Jade to the room opposite. Seeing that it was getting dark, Benevolence Hong also got ready to leave.

"What's the hurry?" said Twin Pearl.

"I have to go and see a friend."

She stood up as though she would walk him to the door but then remained standing there and just said to him, "If you're going home later, drop by for a minute first; don't forget."

He said all right and walked out of her room. By then the maid Golden was no longer in the parlor, so she must have gone elsewhere. As he approached the staircase landing, he heard the faint sound of someone weeping in the little mezzanine room. He peeped through the curtain. Instead of Golden, he found Twin Jewel, the other girl Orchid Zhou owned. She sat there with her face to the wall crying and brushing away her tears. To comfort her, he stepped into the room and tried to make conversation. He asked, "What are you doing here all alone?"

Seeing that it was Benevolence, Twin Jewel quickly got up, gave him a smile, and greeted him by name. Then she bowed her head and remained silent.

"Are you moving downstairs?"

She just nodded.

"The downstairs room is actually more convenient than upstairs."

She played with the hem of her jacket and remained silent. Unable to go further into the subject, he just said, "When you have time, go upstairs and visit with your elder sister. It'd be nice just to chat with her."

Only then did Twin Jewel murmur assent. Whereupon Benevolence Hong withdrew and went downstairs, with Twin Jewel seeing him off as far as the staircase.

Benevolence left Sunshine Alley and turned east, heading for the Auspicious Luzon Lottery Store in South Brocade Alley. He saw the bookkeeper Bamboo Hu standing at the door looking around. As Benevolence went up to greet him, Hu hastened to invite him in.

Without bothering to sit down, Benevolence asked, "Is Cloudlet here?"

"Amity Zhu came a while back and went out with him. It looked like a dinner party," said Hu.

So Benevolence decided to invite Hu instead. "Then let's go to a dinner party, too."

Bamboo Hu declined repeatedly, but Benevolence would brook no excuses. He just dragged Hu along to West Chessboard Street. Arriving at Jewel's room at the Hall of Beauties, they saw that Simplicity Zhao and Rustic Zhang were there with another guest. Benevolence thought that would be Pine Wu and upon inquiring was proved right. As Bamboo Hu did not know anyone there, they all introduced themselves and then sat down to chat casually.

By the time lamps were lit, only Lichee Zhuang was missing. When they asked Woodsy, she said he had gone shopping at Bowling Alley.[1] The menservants set up the round tabletop, lined up the high-back chairs, and lit all the lanterns, which were paneled with silk framed with spotted bamboo. Simplicity, whose patience was sorely taxed by the waiting, started to pace the room, but the servant girl seized him and made him sit down again. Rustic Zhang and Pine Wu lay head to head on the divan, not smoking opium but talking about some con-

: :

1. [A bowling club was set up by the British soon after their concession was founded, and Bowling Alley was created in 1857. The site was subsequently sold, and the building torn down, but locals continued to refer to that junction of First Avenue (now Nanjing Road, see the map on p. 536) as Bowling Alley. One of the exhibits we can see today in the Shanghai History Museum is a tram dating from the Republican era showing "Bowling Alley" as its destination. E.H.]

fidential business in low voices. The Lu sisters Woodsy and Jewel sat side by side on the bed pointing to those present, talking and joking about them behind their backs. Bamboo Hu, who had little to say, looked at the calligraphy and paintings hanging scrolls on the wall.

Benevolence Hong told Mama Yeung to fetch an inkstone and a writing brush so he could write out the chits for summoning girls to the party. First he wrote two names: Woodsy and Twin Pearl. Bamboo Hu was for summoning Third Treasure of Tranquility Alley, and he wrote that down. Then he asked Pine Wu and Rustic Zhang whom they wanted. Pine named White Orchid of Nobility Alley, and Rustic named Cassia of Auspicious Cloud Alley.

Simplicity looked on as the writing was done. He suddenly got an idea and turned to Rustic Zhang, saying, "Let's summon Second Wang, too; that'd be fun." This brought a harsh look from Rustic. Simplicity was contrite.

Thinking Simplicity also wanted to summon a girl, Pine Wu spoke against it, saying, "You're the host here, so you shouldn't call any other girls."

Simplicity was going to say it was not exactly a courtesan he had in mind but could not find the right words. Luckily, the menservants shouted downstairs just then, announcing, "Young Mr. Zhuang coming up." Woodsy rushed out upon hearing this, and Simplicity took the opportunity to walk off and welcome Lichee Zhuang. After Lichee had come in and greeted everybody, he went next door with Woodsy.

Benevolence Hong called for hot towels. Mama Yeung answered and took the call chits downstairs with her. By the time the menservants had prepared the hot towels, Lichee Zhuang had also come over. They all wiped their faces. Lifting the wine kettle high, Simplicity Zhao respectfully indicated that Bamboo Hu should take the seat of honor. Greatly surprised, Bamboo adamantly declined even though Benevolence also joined in to persuade him. And so Simplicity had to settle for placing Pine Wu in the seat of honor and letting Bamboo take the second seat. The others all took their places after brief attempts at offering precedence to each other.

Jewel came forward to pour a round of wine. Simplicity held up his cup to salute his guests, and everybody thanked him and drank. The first course, as was the rule, was shark's fin. Simplicity was just about to help serve everyone when they stopped him, saying, "Don't stand on ceremony; best to be casual." Without much ado, he obeyed and just said "Help yourselves" once. After shark's fin came the things served in small bowls. Woodsy had changed into party clothes and had just come over.

"The maestros," Mama Yeung announced.

As Woodsy and Jewel could not sing, two musicians just sat outside the curtain and played some tunes with their wind and stringed instruments. When they had finished playing, the girls summoned to the party arrived one after another. Like the Lu girls, Rustic Zhang's girl, Cassia, was no singer, either. The minute White Orchid appeared, she asked Third Treasure, "Did you sing?"

Third Treasure's maid understood what she meant. "After you," the maid answered.

White Orchid tuned her *pipa* and sang a Suzhou prelude, followed by an air from Beijing opera. Lichee Zhuang was the first to get into the mood and called for big cups for the wine games. Mama Yeung went next door to get three large chicken-pattern wine cups and set them in front of him.

"I'll hold ten cups in the bank," Lichee said.

On hearing this, Pine Wu immediately rolled up his sleeves, bared his arms, and started the finger game with Lichee. After White Orchid had finished singing, she drank the penalty wine for Pine Wu. Having taken two cups, she drank two more as reserve credit and then apologized, "Sorry, I have to move on to another party now."

Twin Pearl arrived late, after White Orchid had gone. Benevolence Hong noticed that Golden's eyes were swollen to the size of walnuts, so he took the water pipe from her and prepared it himself. Golden turned around and stood with her back to the party. Twin Pearl opened her nutmeg box, took out an invitation card, and handed it to Benevolence Hong. He took it and saw it was from Amity Zhu, asking him to attend a dinner party at White Fragrance's house in Generosity Alley. On the back of the card, there was another line of minute writing, which read: "P.S. There's an important matter that I need to consult you about in person. Pray come quickly upon receipt of this message." This last line was marked with thick circles for emphasis.

Benevolence had no idea what all this was about, so he asked Twin Pearl, "When did the invitation come?"

"It's been quite a while now. Are you going?"

"I have no idea what it is that's so urgent."

"Shall we send a man there to find out?"

He nodded in agreement.

She called Golden over and gave her the instructions. "Get someone to go over to White Fragrance's house in Generosity Alley and see if the party's over. Ask Mr. Zhu if there is anything urgent. If not, just say Mr. Hong sends his apologies."

Golden went downstairs to tell the sedan-chair bearers. Lichee Zhuang reached out for the invitation, asking, "Is it written by Amity?"

"That's what puzzles me. The invitation is in Prosperity Luo's handwriting. I wonder who's the one with the urgent business?" Benevolence replied.

"What does Prosperity Luo do?" asked Lichee.

"He's a native of Shandong and has an official position as alternate magistrate in Jiangsu province. He's here in Shanghai on business. Did you see a fat man last night at the House of Satisfaction? That's him."

Simplicity Zhao did not know until then that the fat man was called Prosperity Luo. He committed it to memory. The next thing Lichee said to Benevolence was, "If you're going, you've got to play me for a few cups first."

Benevolence stuck out his fist and played for five cups. The sedan-chair bearers were back by then and reported, "Dinner was about over, but they said to ask Mr. Hong to come with his girl. They're waiting."

So Benevolence excused himself and made ready to leave. Simplicity, not daring to detain him, saw him out. The menservants hastened to bring a hot towel. Benevolence gave his face a quick wipe and then went out and walked leisurely to Treasured Merit Street, heading straight for Generosity Alley. By the time he got to White Fragrance's door, Twin Pearl's sedan chair was already there waiting for him. They went upstairs together.

All he saw was a table littered with cups and game chips, and men and women sitting around it in some disarray. The party was drawing to a close, and the lamps were burning low. There were only four men at the table. Besides Prosperity Luo and Cloudlet Chen, there was Whistler Tang, a trusted friend of Amity Zhu's. He saw all three of them quite frequently. Only one man at the table was unknown to him: a tall young man with clean-cut features. When they got talking, Benevolence learned that his name was Ge, Elan to his friends. He was from Suzhou, a well-known heir to a fortune.

Benevolence Hong offered his respects again, bringing his hands together, palm over fist. "My desire to meet you was like a thirst. I'm lucky to have the opportunity today."

On hearing this fulsome praise, Prosperity Luo pushed a large wine tumbler toward Benevolence, saying, "For you to moisten your throat, so you won't die of your thirst."

Benevolence smiled, a little embarrassed. He took the cup and put it on the table and then sat down casually in a vacant chair. Twin Pearl sat behind him. White Fragrance's maid got him another cup and chopsticks, and White Fragrance poured him a cup of wine herself. But Prosperity Luo insisted that he drain the huge cup of wine.

"You people have finished your feast," Benevolence said with a smile. "It's a bit late for me to drink. If you're serious about inviting me, set another table!"

At this, Prosperity Luo jumped to his feet and said, "Then leave your drink. Let's go!"

CHAPTER 4 :: *Benevolence acts as comprador to help a friend, and Pearlie signals to her girl to curb her jealousy*

Whistler Tang made Prosperity Luo sit down, saying, "What's the hurry? I suggest that Maestro Lute send a maid home first to make arrangements for a dinner party. Since Benevolence has just got here, we should now let him have his turn as banker. When Amity comes back, we'll all go over to Lute's place, and they should be ready by then, right? If you go now, you'd just be waiting around— no point in that, is there?"

"You're right, you're perfectly right," Prosperity Luo said. Of the two girls he had called, one was his steady girl, Lute. She told her maid to go home and see to the preparations. "Come back when the table is set."

Benevolence looked around and found that Amity Zhu was indeed absent. In his stead, White Fragrance and Whistler Tang were playing host. White Fragrance's younger sister Green Fragrance, as the "girl at home" summoned by Whistler Tang, also helped out.

Benevolence asked in surprise, "It's Amity's party, where's he gone off to?"

"Script Li sent word for him to go over there. He'll be back in no time," replied Whistler Tang.

"Now that you mention Script Li, I'm reminded of something." Benevolence Hong turned to Cloudlet Chen. "Lichee wants to know if you have taken his list to Script Li."

"I asked Amity to take it along just now. Seems to me the prices are set a bit too high," said Cloudlet Chen.

"D'you know where the things came from?" Benevolence Hong said.

"It's said to be a Cantonese family. I don't know the details, either."

"Now it's my turn to question you: have you become a detective?" Prosperity Luo asked Benevolence Hong. "Our Maestro Twin Pearl here has a Cantonese guest; she doesn't know enough about him. Have you found out for her?"

Everybody laughed, Benevolence along with them.

"Where would I get a Cantonese guest?" said Twin Pearl. "Now you'll have to find me one."

Prosperity Luo was about to retort, but Benevolence intervened. "Don't talk nonsense. I'll put up ten cups for the bank, now you try to break it."

Prosperity Luo rolled up his sleeves to play the finger game and lost the very first round.

"I'll finish the game first and then drink all the penalty cups in one go," he said.

He went five rounds and lost them all. Lute drank a penalty cup for him. The other courtesan whom he had just started to see, Green Phoenix, also reached out for the wine.

"No wonder you want to play the finger game," said Benevolence Hong. "You've got all these people to drink for you."

"All substitutes keep off! I'll do the drinking myself," said Prosperity Luo.

Benevolence Hong applauded, laughing.

"Better stick with your substitutes," said Cloudlet Chen.

Whistler Tang helped pour some wine and passed a cup to Green Phoenix. Knowing that Prosperity Luo was taking the party to Lute's place, she said, "I have to go now. Shall I drink a couple more penalty cups as a reserve?"

Prosperity Luo shook his head. "Never mind." So Green Phoenix left.

Whistler Tang persuaded Prosperity Luo to take a break and told Cloudlet Chen to take on Benevolence Hong for five rounds, too. Whistler Tang himself was the next to play. That left only Elan Ge.

Ge had twisted around in his seat to talk to his girl, Snow Scent. They had been whispering into each other's ears, and he'd never even noticed that Benevolence Hong had been banker all this time. He turned around only when Whistler Tang asked him to play.

"What is it?" he asked.

"I know you're passionate lovers," said Prosperity Luo, "but do keep it down at this table. You don't want to act it out for us to see, do you?"

Snow Scent flung her handkerchief in Prosperity Luo's face. "As for you, you never have a single decent thing to say."

Benevolence Hong saluted Elan Ge. "I await your instructions."

Elan Ge had no choice but to play a couple of rounds and drink up. Then he went back to talking to Snow Scent.

Impatient by now, Prosperity Luo stuck out his fist to challenge Benevolence Hong again, and this time he won. Benevolence lost nine out of his ten cups. Prosperity Luo thought it was his chance to break the bank, but unfortunately he lost again. Just then, they heard the menservants shout out downstairs, "Mr. Zhu coming up."

Cloudlet Chen hastened to stop Prosperity Luo. "Let Amity play a round, and we'll wind up the game."

It sounded reasonable, so Prosperity Luo played no more. Amity Zhu hurriedly sat down, saying repeatedly, "Forgive my absence." Then he asked, "Who is banker?"

Instead of continuing the game Benevolence Hong asked, "What's that important matter you want to consult me on?"

Amity Zhu was bewildered. "Eh? I haven't got any important matter, not me."

Prosperity Luo could not help saying with a smile, "Isn't a dinner party in a sing-song house important enough?"

Benevolence Hong also smiled. "I knew you were the one who made a fuss about nothing."

"All right, my fault. Quick, play the game before you go."

"Since there's only one round left, let's just forget it. I'll give everyone a toast instead," said Amity.

They replied in unison, "Whatever you say."

Amity Zhu collected six of the large wine cups and filled them. Everyone drank up and left the table to sit casually around the room while the menservants busied themselves preparing hot towels. Lute's maid, who had reported back a while earlier, now came up again to hasten the guests. Elan Ge, Prosperity Luo, and Amity Zhu had their own sedan chairs, and Cloudlet Chen his private ricksha. All the courtesans were to follow their guests to Lute's place. Only Whistler Tang and Benevolence Hong were going on foot, so the two of them started out ahead of the party.

They left White Fragrance's house, and just as they came to the mouth of Generosity Alley, another man was about to turn into it. On seeing them, he quickly moved to one side and stood at attention to greet Benevolence respectfully.

Benevolence Hong saw that it was Talisman, Lotuson Wang's steward. He asked, "Where's your master?"

"My master is in Lucky Spring Alley. He hopes you will drop by for a chat, sir."

"Whose house is he visiting?"

"Name's Constance, sir. My master has only just started seeing her in the last couple of days."

On hearing this, Benevolence Hong turned to Whistler Tang and said, "I'll go over there for a minute; be right with you. Please tell them to start without me at Lute's." Whistler Tang told him to hurry back and went on by himself.

Benevolence Hong followed Talisman to Lucky Spring Alley. It was dark in the narrow lane, and they had to feel their way past two or three houses. Then they pushed open a big double door and went in.

"Mr. Hong's here," Talisman called aloud.

Somebody answered upstairs, but things remained quiet.

"What about bringing a foreign lamp down here?" Talisman called again.

"Coming, coming!" the voice upstairs answered.

After another long wait, an old serving woman came down the stairs holding a tin plate reflector lamp, saying, "Do please come up, Mr. Hong."

Benevolence saw rosewood tables and chairs piled up in the parlor; it looked like they were moving house. Upstairs, a paraffin lamp hung in the middle of the room, lighting up all four corners. It was as bright as the full moon, but the place was empty except for a large bed and a dressing table. Even the window curtains, bed curtains, lamps, and mirrors had been packed and cleared away. Lotuson Wang was seated at the dressing table, with four small dishes set before him, having a simple supper. The courtesan eating with him would be Constance.

Benevolence walked into the room and said pleasantly, "So, you're enjoying yourself alone."

Lotuson rose to greet him. Seeing the tipsy look on Benevolence's face, he asked, "Have you been drinking?"

"At two parties," said Benevolence. "They sent you several invitations. Now Prosperity Luo has taken the party to Lute's. D'you feel like going?"

Lotuson smiled and shook his head.

As Benevolence perched himself on the bed, Constance brought him a water pipe. Taking it, Benevolence hastened to say, "Don't stand on ceremony. Please get on with your meal."

"I've finished," she said with a smile.

Benevolence saw that she had amiability written all over her face. She was kind and approachable, and he guessed that she was probably a second-class courtesan who only entertained at home. "I see that you're moving, right?" he asked.

She nodded and said yes.

"Where to?"

"Big Feet Yao's house in East Co-prosperity Alley. My room will be right across from Snow Scent's."

"Are you just renting the room, or are you working for them?"

"I'm renting. It costs thirty dollars a month, though!"

"That's nothing. Mr. Wang alone will be spending five to six hundred a season. There's no danger of your not making ends meet."

As they talked, Lotuson had finished eating, wiped his face, and rinsed his mouth. The old serving woman came in with an opium tray. She asked Constance, "Where should I put it?"

"On the bed, of course. Would it be on the floor?" said Constance.

The old woman guffawed and took the tray to the bed. "Oh dear, Mr. Hong will surely kill himself with laughter over this!"

"Go downstairs after you've tidied up, and stop chattering," said Constance.

Only then did the old woman gather up the dishes, cups, and chopsticks and go downstairs.

After that, Constance invited Lotuson to have his smoke. He went over to the bed, lay down opposite Benevolence, and said to him, "I asked you here because I need to buy two things: a marble rosewood couch and a set of lantern panels with pictures of birds framed in spotted bamboo. Best if you could get them for me tomorrow."

"Where should I send them?" asked Benevolence.

"To Big Feet Yao's house. The west room on the first floor."

Benevolence looked at Constance and grinned. "Get somebody else to buy them for you. I'm not doing it. If Little Rouge hears of it, she's going to slap my face."

Lotuson smiled and said nothing.

"Mr. Hong, why is it that you, too, are afraid of Little Rouge?" asked Constance.

"Why wouldn't I be? You ask Mr. Wang. She's a spitfire!"

"Mr. Hong, I'd be grateful if you would look out for me, for Mr. Wang's sake," she said.

"And how will you show your gratitude?"

"I'll invite you to a dinner party, all right?"

"Who wants dinner parties from you? It's not as if I've never been to any. Are they such a rarity?"

"Then what should I do?"

"Instead of a party, just treat me to your buns. That's easy for you and won't cost you anything, right?"

She giggled. "You're all the same; there's not one good one among you!"

Benevolence laughed and stood up. "If there's anything else, tell me now. I have to be going."

"No, that's it." said Lotuson. "I'd like you to come to a dinner party the day after tomorrow. When you see Prosperity and the others, tell them for me. I'll send you the proper invitations tomorrow."

Benevolence promised to do so and went on his way to the dinner party at Lute's place in East Civic Peace Alley.

When Benevolence had gone, Constance came over to the bed and leaned against Lotuson to prepare the opium for him. Lotuson smoked some seven or eight pellets in succession and after that gradually closed his eyes.

"Shall we retire for the night, Mr. Wang?" she whispered.

He nodded his consent, so she removed the opium tray, and they went to bed.

The next day, they did not get up until one in the afternoon. After they had washed, the old serving woman brought congee, and they each ate some. Constance remained at the dressing table to do her hair. The old woman again set the opium tray on the bed, where Lotuson smoked by himself, thinking that it'd be necessary to go to Little Rouge's now and tell her a lie. He'd break the news to her gradually. Having made up his mind, he put on his jacket and made ready to go.

"Where're you going?" Constance was quick to ask.

"I'll drop in at Little Rouge's."

"Won't you have lunch before you go?" said Constance.

"No, I'm all right."

"Will you be coming back later?"

He thought for a moment. "What time are you moving over to East Co-prosperity Alley tomorrow?"

"Early in the morning."

"Then I'll be there at one in the afternoon."

"Do drop in later today if you have time."

He said all right as he ambled downstairs. Talisman followed him out of Lucky Spring Alley, and they headed eastward. As they approached West Floral Alley, Lotuson told Talisman to go home and fetch his sedan chair. He then turned into the alley. The maid, Pearlie, had already caught sight of him.

"Aiyo!" she shouted, "Mr. Wang is here!" She hurried out into the courtyard, grabbed him by the sleeve, and called out again, "Maestro, Mr. Wang is here!" She only let go of him when they got to the staircase.

Lotuson went upstairs at a leisurely pace. Little Rouge came out of her room to greet him with just the semblance of a smile. "I say, Mr. Wang, you've got a nerve . . ." she choked in midsentence.

The sadness on her face made him feel guilty. He put on a grin, went into her room, and sat down. Little Rouge came in after him and leaned against him, holding his hand.

"Tell me, where have you been these three days?"

"I was in the Old City. A friend of mine was celebrating his birthday, and the feast went on for three days."

She sneered. "D'you think I was born yesterday?"

Pearlie brought him a towel to wipe his face.

"When you were in the Old City, did you go home at night?" Little Rouge asked again.

"No, I just stayed at my friend's place."

"So your friend is a brothel keeper," said Little Rouge.

He could not help laughing.

Little Rouge also laughed. "Pearlie, just listen to him! The day before yesterday I sent Goldie to look for you at your house. They said your sedan chair was there, but you weren't home. You've got good legs, I must say, going all the way to the Old City on foot. Or did you take a carriage and jump over the city wall in it?"

Pearlie guffawed. "Mr. Wang is getting up to a bit of trickery now. Where did he get such a good idea, to say he was in the Old City?"

"He kept his secret well, though. Even his friends couldn't find him, and not for lack of trying," said Little Rouge.

"Mr. Wang, you're a patron of long standing," said Pearlie. "Even if you want to see somebody else, it doesn't matter. It's not as though our maestro won't let you!"

"Whoever you choose to see is none of my business. And yet you *had* to keep it from me and make it look as though I'm jealous and wouldn't let you go. Now *that's* infuriating!" said Little Rouge.

In the face of this perfect duet, Lotuson could only remain silent. He made an awkward attempt at a smile. Finally, when Pearlie had finished her chores and gone downstairs, he said to Little Rouge, "You mustn't listen to idle gossip. We've been together for three or four years; don't you know me by now? Even if I want to see somebody else, I'll tell you all about it first. Why would I keep it from you?"

"I wouldn't know why," said Little Rouge. "Ask yourself. All along you've been calling other girls to occasional parties, one from this house and another from that. Have I ever said anything? Yet now you want to keep it from me; what for?"

"But there's nothing going on. I'm not keeping anything from you."

"I think I know the reason, though. You're not so much keeping it from me as planning to jilt me for someone else, right? I'd like to see you do that!"

When Lotuson heard this, he changed color and looked away. He said with a sneer, "I didn't come for three days, and you call it jilting you. Have you forgotten all the things I said to you before?"

"That's the whole point. If you haven't forgotten, then tell me: Where have you been these three days? Who's the girl? If you'd only tell me, I wouldn't be quarreling with you."

"What would you have me tell you? I said I was in the Old City, and you won't believe me."

"You're still trying to pull the wool over my eyes! I'll ask you again when I've found out."

"Very well then. Since you're too angry to talk about this right now, we'll wait a couple of days. When you're in a better mood, I'll tell you all about it."

She snorted and was silent for a long while.

"Let's have a smoke," he coaxed her.

So she went to the divan with him, hand in hand. He took off his jacket and lay down to smoke. But she just sat passively at the other end. He wanted to make some light conversation but could find nothing to say.

Suddenly they heard footsteps coming up the stairs. It was the servant girl, Goldie. As soon as she saw Lotuson, she said, "Mr. Wang, I've just been to your residence to invite you here, but you're here already!" Then she said, "Why didn't you come the last few days, Mr. Wang? Were you angry with us?"

He made no reply.

Little Rouge said testily, "Why would he be angry? I'll slap your face for that! Angry, indeed!"

Goldie said, "Mr. Wang, when you don't come, our maestro gets so upset we have to go again and again to invite you. Don't be like that again, please?" So saying, she moved a cup of tea over to the opium tray, hung up his jacket, and was about to go.

Seeing the blank look on Little Rouge's face, Lotuson said, "Let's get a bite to eat, all right?"

"Just tell her what you want," Little Rouge replied.

"You'll have some, too, won't you? Let's eat together. If you don't want any, we won't bother."

"Then tell her what you'd like."

He knew she liked fried noodles with shrimp, so he ordered that. Little Rouge told Goldie just to call down for the servants below to order it from the Garden of Plenty. Shortly afterward, the noodles were delivered, and Lotuson asked Little Rouge to join him.

She frowned. "I don't know why, but there's a sour taste in my mouth.[1] I've got no appetite."

"Have a little anyway."

Reluctantly, she put a tiny amount on a small plate and ate it. Lotuson, too, did not eat more than a few mouthfuls before he called to have the dish taken away.

Pearlie brought a hot towel and reported, "Your steward is here with your sedan chair."

"Did he say what it's about?" Lotuson asked.

Pearlie called toward the window, "Master Talisman!" Hearing

: :

1. This is a pun on the common Chinese metaphor for jealousy, drinking vinegar. E.H.]

this, Talisman came upstairs at once and handed Lotuson an invitation. He opened it, saw that it was from Elan Ge for a dinner party that night at Snow Scent's, and set it aside. Talisman withdrew. Lotuson returned to the divan to smoke. Then he suddenly thought of something and told Pearlie to bring his jacket.

Pearlie took the jacket down from the clothes rack, but Little Rouge stopped her with a bark. "What's the hurry? Where d'you want to go?"

Pearlie signaled Little Rouge with a glance, saying, "Let him go to the party." That put a stop to Little Rouge.

Lotuson happened to look up and see it. He wondered what Pearlie was up to. Could they have found out about Constance?

As he was wondering, Pearlie helped him put on his jacket, saying, "When you get to the party, send us a call chit right away. Don't go and get anybody else, now."

"What are you saying this for?" said Little Rouge. "Let him call whoever he wants."

After putting on his jacket, Lotuson held Little Rouge by the hand and asked with a smile, "Aren't you going to see me out?"

She wrenched her hand free and sat down in a chair instead. He pressed close to her and whispered many little endearments. She just looked down and started to clean and groom her fingernails, completely ignoring him. After a long while, she finally said, "I don't know what's the matter with your heart, it's changed so."

"Why d'you say I've changed?"

"Ask yourself."

He still pressed for an answer. She pushed him off with both hands. "Go! Just go! Even the sight of you makes me mad!"

He pretended to smile and left.


CHAPTER 5 :: *An empty slot is speedily filled by a new love, and a new arrangement is kept from an old flame*

It was evening. The lamps had just been lit when Lotuson Wang got in the sedan chair that took him to Snow Scent's house in East Co-prosperity Alley. Talisman announced him, and a maid propped up the bamboo curtain and welcomed him into the room. He saw that only Amity Zhu and Elan Ge had arrived; they were chatting. Lotuson went in, and they saluted each other and sat down. Then Lotuson called Talisman over to tell him, "Go to Yao's across the way to see if the things for the upstairs room have all arrived."

After Talisman was gone, Elan Ge asked, "I saw your note today and thought, but there isn't any Constance in this alley! Then the menservants said there's a Constance moving in across the way to-morrow—is that so?"

"I've never come across the name Constance, either," said Amity Zhu. "Where did you find her?"

"I'll thank you all not to mention it later when Little Rouge is here, all right?" Lotuson said smiling. The other two laughed up-roariously.

A moment later, Talisman came back to report. "Everything is ready in the room. They said the four lamps and the bed were de-livered only a little while ago. The bed is set out already, and the lamps are hung up."

"Now go to Lucky Spring Alley and tell them," Lotuson ordered.

Talisman said "yes, sir" and withdrew. Before he left, he told the two sedan-chair bearers, "Don't go away, you two, not till I'm back."

When he approached the end of the alley, a shadowy figure loomed up in the dark and took his arm. He saw that it was Amity Zhu's stew-ard named Longevity Zhang.

"What is it?" he said, annoyed. "You gave me a start!"

"Where're you going?" asked Longevity.

"Let's go and have some fun."

The two of them walked with arms around each other's shoul-ders to Constance's in Lucky Spring Alley. They told the old serving woman to send word upstairs.

"Is Mr. Wang coming?" Constance opened the window to ask Tal-isman.

"Master is at a dinner party. He's probably not coming," he said.

"Who did he call to the party?" said Constance.

"I don't know."

"Is it Little Rouge?"

"I've no idea."

"I see you have your master's interest at heart!" she said with a smile. "Who else can it be if it's not Little Rouge?"

Talisman made no answer. As he walked out of the alley with Lon-gevity, they discussed where to go for a little sport.

"Well, there's only Orchid Alley."

"It's too far away."

"Or we could go to Third Pan's and see if Verdure Xu is there."

"Let's do that."

The two of them turned toward Security Alley and groped in the darkness to Third Pan's door. They first peeped in through the gap in the door. When they tried to push it open, they found it was latched. Longevity knocked twice, but there was no answer. He kept knocking, and finally a maid asked from within, "Who is it?"

"It's me," Talisman answered.

"Our Miss has gone out. Sorry," said the maid.

"Open the door anyway," said Talisman.

They waited for a long time, but it was still dead quiet inside; the door remained shut. Longevity lost his temper. He turned sideways and started kicking hard at the door, making a racket and cursing at the same time.

"Coming! Coming!" Alarmed, the maid opened the door. On seeing them, she said, "Why, it's Master Zhang and Master Talisman! I was wondering who it was."

"Is Master Xu here?" Talisman asked.

"No, sir."

Longevity saw there was a light in the side chamber, so he barged into the room with Talisman at his heels. They saw a man come out from behind the bed curtains clapping his hands and stamping his feet in great mirth. It was none other than Verdure Xu.

"So we're intruding!" the two said in unison. "Sorry to disturb you."

The maid who came in behind them laughed, saying, "Why, I thought Master Xu was gone, but here he is—in bed!"

Verdure Xu lit up the opium lamp on the couch and invited Longevity Zhang to smoke. Longevity, telling Talisman to go ahead, pulled open the bed curtains and crawled straight in. There came the noise of tangled limbs tussling in bed, and then a woman shouted, "What d'you think you're doing? Don't you ever get enough?"

The maid hurried forth to make peace, "Please don't, Master Zhang!" But Longevity refused to let go. Verdure Xu grabbed him and pulled him up in one quick movement, saying, "All you do is horse around! There's a time for everything. Don't you have any sense at all?"

Longevity brushed his own cheek with a finger—a gesture indicating "shame on you." "Giving your girl a hand, eh? But is she your girl? Shameless!"

The streetwalker Third Pan draped her padded jacket over her shoulders and got off the bed. Longevity kept staring and making grimaces at her. She pulled a face and gave him the evil eye.

He pretended to duck his head between his shoulders in fright. "Oh, dear! Oh, dear! I'm so scared!"

Stumped for a better reply, she could only come up with, "Watch it, or I'll lose my temper!"

"Lose your temper? Even if you're to lose your trousers, I . . ." Then he stopped and went up to whisper a few words into her ear.

Third Pan cried out in exasperation, "Listen to him, Master Xu! Listen to what this good friend of yours is saying!"

Verdure Xu pleaded with Longevity, "It's all my fault; I'd be much obliged if you'd overlook it, my good brother."

Longevity said, "That's all right, since you're begging to be let off. Otherwise I'd want to ask her: we're all friends here, is Master Xu longer than Master Zhang by three inches?"

"You have your sweetheart, Master Zhang," she answered. "I can't please you, so there's only Master Xu to help me out a bit."

"Listen to the way she says Master Xu," Longevity said to Talisman. "Now, that makes him happy, doesn't it? He's so happy, his soul will be called away!"

Talisman said, "No, I don't want to listen. Nobody ever calls *my* name!"

"You're a good friend, Master Talisman," she said smiling. "Why don't you put in a good word for me?"

"Speaking of friends . . ." said Longevity.

Verdure Xu roared out, cutting him short, "I'll give you a clout in the face if you dare say any more."

"Fine, fine. Let's just say I'm scared of you, all right?" said Longevity.

"So! The joke's on me now!" Verdure Xu rolled up his sleeves and rushed over to beat Longevity, who escaped hurriedly into the courtyard with Verdure in hot pursuit. Longevity pulled out the door bolt and rushed into the alley, heading east. Just then someone came out of the dark and bumped into him.

"What's going on?" the man exclaimed. The voice sounded familiar.

Verdure Xu walked up to him and asked, "Is it Constant Blessing?"

The man answered to the name. So Verdure Xu took him by his arm and returned to the house, calling to Longevity, "Come in, I'll let you off this time." Longevity crept in after them, bolted the door, and peeped at the man through the bamboo curtain. It was Cloudlet Chen's steward, Constant Blessing. Longevity hurried in to ask him:

"Is the party over?"

"How would it be over so soon? The girls' call chits have just been sent downstairs."

Longevity Zhang thought for a moment. "Talisman, I have to go."

"I'm coming with you," said Verdure Xu. So saying, they left in a flurry. Third Pan did not even have time to see them out.

The four of them walked out of the alley together and headed east until they got to Pebble Road. Longevity continued ahead innocently. Verdure Xu grabbed him to tell him to go south.

"I'm not going," Longevity said to Talisman.

Verdure Xu pushed him from behind. "Not going, eh? Try being stubborn!"

Longevity nearly fell down. He had no choice but to cross Zheng's Wooden Bridge with them. When they got to New Street, a serving woman standing by the roadside rushed over and called out, "Master Constant!" She pulled him along by the sleeve and kept talking as she walked on, leading them to a house. She pushed the door open and walked in. In the house, an old woman of sixty or seventy sat by herself against the wall. The room was lit only by a dim oil lamp on the table.

The serving woman greeted her as "Old Mrs. Filial Guo" and asked, "Where's the opium tray?"

"Still on the bed," Old Mrs. Guo replied.

The maid hastened to fetch a spill, went into the inner room, and lit the wall lamp. It was made of tin plate and had a reflector mirror in the glass dome. She turned it up high and invited the four men to come sit down. Then she lit the opium lamp.

"We don't want any opium. Go and fetch Second Wang," said Constant.

The woman answered yes and went.

Old Mrs. Guo groped her way into the room, her head wobbling, holding a foreign brass water pipe. "Which of you gentlemen will have a smoke?"

Constant Blessing accepted the pipe, saying, "Never mind this routine of politeness."

She went back to sit in the outer room.

"What kind of a place is this?" Longevity asked. "I must say you people know your way around."

"What kind of a place does it look like to you?" said Constant Blessing.

"Well, it looks like nothing to me. A streetwalker house? Not really. A place for moonlighting housewives? Doesn't seem right. Opium den with girls? Doesn't look like that, either."

"It is an opium den with a girl," said Constant Blessing. "But they have guests inside, so they borrow this place for us to sit here a while. Got it?"

As they were talking, they heard the door creak. Constant Blessing looked out quickly and saw that it was indeed Second Wang. The minute she came in, she greeted him, "Master Constant." She then asked for the names of the others and apologized, "Sorry, you've come at a bad time. If you don't mind the squalor, sit here for a while and have a smoke, all right?"

Constant Blessing looked at Verdure Xu to see what he thought. Xu, seeing that Second Wang was rather outstanding for an opium den girl, decided that it was all right to wait for a while, so he nodded his agreement. Second Wang then went to the outer room herself to fetch a pipe and two boxes of opium; she also told Old Mrs. Guo to have the serving woman make tea. Longevity saw that there was just one bed in this inner room; the space was so cramped, there wasn't even room for a table. He called out: "Talisman, we'll go on ahead."

Verdure Xu could not very well detain them further, so Longevity took his leave and went back with Talisman to Snow Scent's house in East Co-prosperity Alley. The party was over by then.

"Where have Mr. Zhu and Mr. Wang gone?" he asked.

Everybody said they had no idea. Longevity hurried away to look for Amity Zhu, while Talisman went searching for Lotuson Wang at Little Rouge's in West Floral Alley. He saw Wang's sedan chair at the door and hurried in to ask the bearers, "When did the party break up?"

"Not long ago," they replied.

Talisman was relieved to hear that. Just then, the maid, Pearlie, happened to be carrying a water kettle upstairs. He went up to her to ask a favor, "Please mention to my master that I'm here. Much obliged."

Pearlie did not answer but beckoned for him to come up. He tiptoed up after her and sat down in the middle room while Pearlie went into the bedroom. It was a long wait, and he got impatient. He turned his head to listen carefully; there wasn't a sound, but he dared not go downstairs. He was at the point of dozing off when he heard Lotuson cough and then the sound of footsteps. A moment later, Pearlie lifted the door curtain and beckoned to him. He went in and saw that Lotuson was sitting by himself on the divan yawning, saying nothing. Pearlie was busy preparing a hot towel. Lotuson took it, gave his face a wipe, and finally told Talisman to get the sedan chair ready to go home. Talisman answered "yes, sir" and went downstairs, shouting for the sedan-chair bearers to light the lanterns. When Lotuson came down and got into the chair, Talisman followed it back to Wang's residence on Fifth Avenue. Only then did he report:

"I've been to Constance's and spoken with them."

Lotuson acknowledged this with a nod but said nothing, so Talisman helped him prepare to turn in for the night.

The fifteenth was an auspicious day for moving house. Lotuson was up by half past ten. After having a wash and some breakfast, he went to return Elan Ge's call. Talisman followed him to High Honor Bank in Eternal Peace Alley and delivered his master's card. A servant came out to tender his regrets, saying, "Sorry, sir, my master is not at home."

Lotuson then ordered the sedan chair to turn to East Co-prosperity Alley. When they got there, he saw from his sedan chair a black lacquer plaque hung high over the door, with the words "Constance Zhang's residence" written in gold on it. He got down from the chair and walked into the courtyard. Some musicians were there, and a small stage had been set up, decorated in gold, green, vermilion, and blue; it was all very bright and gay. On seeing him, a new manservant rushed forward to offer his formal greetings, bowing down with one knee on the ground. A new serving woman standing on the staircase invited Mr. Wang to come up. Constance also came out from her room in welcome. She was dressed in brand-new clothes from top to toe, and it seemed to Lotuson that she looked more attractive than ever. Embarrassed by the way he stared at her, she suppressed her laughter, pulled at his sleeve, and pushed him into her room. Inside, everything was in perfect decorative order, which pleased Lotuson enormously. The only thing he could fault with was that the calligraphy and painting scrolls had just been bought from a store and were not very artistic.

Constance hid her mouth with a handkerchief and offered him watermelon seeds on a plate.

"So ceremonious!" he teased her.

She almost laughed out loud. Then she turned abruptly around, pushed open the panel of a folding door, and stepped out.

Lotuson saw that the folding door opened onto a corner balcony right above the entrance and overlooking the alley. Snow Scent's house was directly opposite. Seeing her plaque, Lotuson called out, "Talisman, go and see if Mr. Ge is there. If he is, ask him to come over."

Talisman went to deliver the message, whereupon Elan Ge immediately ambled over to greet Lotuson. Constance came up to offer watermelon seeds.

"Is this your lady love?" Elan asked, scrutinizing her, and then sat down.

Lotuson mentioned how he had just called to see Ge, and then they chatted about other things. Just then Snow Scent's maid, Little Sister, came to tell Elan Ge lunch was ready.

Hearing this, Lotuson suggested to him, "Since you haven't had lunch either, let's eat together."

"Good." Elan told Little Sister to bring his lunch over, while Lotuson told the maid to order a couple of dishes from the Garden of Plenty. In a moment, the food was all delivered and set out on the table by the window. Constance came up and poured two cups of wine, saying, "Please have some."

Little Sister also helped for a while. "Enjoy your meal, sir," she said. "I'll go now and do our maestro's hair. We'll come over after that."

"Please ask your maestro to come and visit," Constance said.

Little Sister answered yes as she left.

Having had a cup or two of wine, Elan Ge felt a little dispirited. It so happened that someone was singing a tune from a Kun opera on the stage downstairs, and Elan beat time on the table with his fingers.[1] Seeing he was out of sorts Lotuson suggested, "Let's play a few rounds of the finger game."

Elan stuck out his fist and drank a cup at every round. After seven or eight rounds, they suddenly heard Constance call out at the upstairs parlor window, "Do come up, Snow Scent, my peer." Lotuson looked downstairs, and, seeing it was indeed Snow Scent, he said smiling to Elan, "Your lady love has come looking for you." This was followed by the sound of bound-feet shoes tripping up the stairs and Snow Scent's voice saying, "Hi, Constance, my peer."

Constance invited her into the room. Elan had just lost another round, so he called out to her, "Come over here; I want to tell you something."

Snow Scent was leaning on the end of the table for balance. She asked, "What is it? Do tell."

Elan knew she would not come over. He waited till she was off guard and reached for her wrist. With just one pull, she lost her balance and toppled into his arms.

"What d'you think you're doing!" she cried out desperately.

"Nothing," he said smiling. "I just want you to drink a cup of wine."

"Let go; then I'll drink."

He would not let go but instead brought a cup of wine to her lips. "Drink this first." She had no choice but to gulp it down from his hand. Then she quickly struggled to her feet and ran off.

He resumed the finger game with Lotuson while she went to look at herself in the mirror, turning this way and that and then reaching her hands to the back of her head to feel her hairdo. Constance hurried over to help tighten her chignon, removed a narcissus blossom, tidied her hair, put it back, and then looked her over again. Seeing the smoothness of Snow Scent's elaborate chignon, she asked, "Who does your hair for you?"

"It's just Little Sister," replied Snow Scent. "She'll never learn."

"I think she's quite good. This style is rather shapely."

"Look, it's so puffed up. Isn't it ugly?"

"It's a bit puffed up, but it looks fine. She's used to doing it this way and probably finds it hard to change, don't you think so?" said Constance.

: :

1. Kun opera was a type of regional opera originating from Jiangsu province that achieved a fairly high status nationally.

"Let me look at your chignon."

"At first, my old grandmother did my hair; it wasn't bad. Now I have the maid do it. Does it look all right to you?" She turned her head to Snow Scent.

"It tilts too much to one side. Though there is a style called the lopsided look, if it tilts too much, it doesn't look right."

The two of them got on so well that Elan Ge and Lotuson Wang stopped their finger game and drinking to listen to them. When they heard the bit about the lopsided look, they both laughed.

"How is it you two aren't playing anymore?" Constance asked with a smile.

"We forgot to, listening to the two of you chat," replied Lotuson.

"I'm not playing anymore. I've had more than ten cups," said Elan Ge.

"Do have a couple more," said Constance as she picked up the wine pot to pour for him.

"Please don't, Constance," Snow Scent broke in. "He loses his wits when he drinks. Why don't you offer Mr. Wang some instead?"

"Would you like some?" Constance turned to Lotuson, smiling.

"Five more rounds, and we eat. It won't hurt, will it?" said Lotuson. He then turned to Snow Scent, "Don't worry, I won't let him drink too much."

Snow Scent could not very well stop them. She looked on as they played five more rounds. Constance poured the wine and then handed the wine pot to the maid, who took it away.

Lotuson also called for rice to be served. "We'll drink again in the evening," he said with a smile. So they ate, wiped their faces and left the table after it was cleared.

Snow Scent immediately urged Elan Ge to leave with her. But he said, "Let's rest a while."

"Why rest? I won't have it!"

"In that case, why don't you go back first?"

She stared at him. "You're not coming?"

He just smiled and refused to move. She got in a huff and pointed a finger at his face. "Watch out if you do show up later!" Turning around, she said to Lotuson, "Do come by, Mr. Wang," and then, "Come and visit sometime, Constance."

Constance promised and hurried off to see her out, but she was already on her way downstairs. When Constance came back to the room, she looked at Elan Ge and let out a titter. He felt fed up and ill at ease. It was Lotuson who said, "You'd better go over there. Your lady love is a bit upset."

"Nonsense. Who cares if she's upset or not."

"Come on! She only asked you to go back with her because she's fond of you, so why not do as she asks?"

Only then did Elan get up. Lotuson saluted him. "Please come early tonight."

Elan smiled and took his leave.

CHAPTER 6 :: *A playful belle calls her client her son, and a phenomenal girl dominates her madam*

Elan Ge sauntered over to Snow Scent's house. When he walked into her room, he found it deserted and dead quiet, so he lay down by himself on the divan. Then the maid Little Sister came in, her rice bowl in her hands, and said to him, "Please sit a while. The maestro is having lunch." While she was there, she emptied the cup of tea that had stood there since morning, put in new tea leaves, and shouted for the manservant to bring hot water.

In a moment, Snow Scent drifted in. Seeing him, she said loudly, "Didn't you say you'd sit in that house across the way? What are you doing here now?" So saying, she pulled him up from the divan and tried to push him out the door. "Back you go. You can sit over there. Who asked you to come?"

Unable to make her out, he stood there, nonplussed. "Constance across the way has nothing to do with me. Why should you be jealous?"

Snow Scent was stumped. "You must be joking! Why should I be jealous of Constance?"

"Why are you telling me to go to her place if you aren't jealous?"

"Just now, you sat there and refused to budge, so I'm suggesting you go back there now. What's it got to do with jealousy?"

Only then did he understand what had upset her. He gave her a smile, sat down, and asked, "You mean you want me to sit with you all day long. You don't want me to go to other houses, is that it?"

"If you do as I say, you can go anywhere. Why won't you ever listen to me?"

"When have I *not* listened to you?"

"When I told you to come over just now, you refused."

"That was because I had just finished lunch. I wanted to sit for a bit before coming back. Who said I wasn't coming?"

Still unconsoled, she sat in his lap, took his hand, and kneaded and squeezed it hard, grumbling all the while, "I won't have it! You must give me your promise."

"What promise?" He lost his patience.

"Next time, no matter where you are, if I tell you to come, you have to come at once. And no matter where you want to go, if I say don't go, then you're not to go. Do I have your promise?"

Seeing he was no match for her, he had to give her his promise. Satisfied, she let go of his hand and walked away.

"Even my wife never says anything about my comings and goings, and now you want to control me!" he said smiling.

"You're my son," she laughed. "Why shouldn't I control you?"

"The things you say! Is there any sense to it? You're shameless!" he said.

"I've brought up a son who's now old enough to go to dinner parties and tea parties in sing-song houses. I'm quite proud of myself. Why d'you say I'm shameless?"

"I'm not talking to you anymore."

It happened that Little Sister had just finished her lunch and was getting changed in the back room. Snow Scent called out, "Little Sister, come and have a look; is this son of mine any good?"

"Where is he?" asked Little Sister.

Snow Scent pointed to Elan Ge, laughing, "There."

"What nonsense!" Little Sister said. "How old are you yourself to have such a fine big man for a son?"

"What's so fine about him? When I do have a son, he'll be more presentable than him."

"Then have a son with the young master. That'd be a wonderful thing," said Little Sister.

"If my son went to sing-song houses like he does, I'd beat him to death."

Little Sister burst out laughing. "Did you hear that, young master? It's a good thing you have nostrils for ventilation, otherwise you'd be sure to explode."

"She's gone crazy today," he said.

Snow Scent rolled into his lap and put her arms round his neck, chortling like a child. He fooled around with her for a while. They only separated when a manservant came in with the water kettle to make tea. Elan stood up as if to go.

"What are you doing?" Snow Scent asked.

"I need to do some shopping."

"Not allowed."

"I'll be right back."

"Says who? Sit still for me." She pressed him back on the seat and whispered, "What is it you want to buy?"

"I'm going to Hope Brothers to get some odds and ends."

"Shall we go together in a horse carriage?"

"Fine by me."

So Snow Scent called out for a carriage. A manservant answered and went to fetch one.

"Would you like to wash your face?" Little Sister asked. "You just had lunch."

Snow Scent took a look at herself in a hand mirror and said, "Never mind." She just wiped her mouth with a napkin and dabbed on some lip rouge and then went and got dressed.

"The carriage is here," the manservant came back to report.

"I'll go out first." Elan got up to go.

Snow Scent hastened to stop him. "One minute. Wait for me."

"I'll wait for you in the carriage."

She stamped her feet in protest. "I won't have it!"

He had no choice but to come back. "Look at her," he said to Little Sister, smiling, "she behaves like a child herself yet talks of having a son."

Snow Scent retorted, "You're the child, no sense whatsoever! What right do you have to lecture me?" She turned her profile toward him, nodded twice, and said in a low voice, giggling, "I'm your real mother, don't you know?"

"Hurry up!" he snapped at her, smiling. "Stop babbling."

After this, she finally finished dressing. Little Sister carried her silver water pipe, and the three of them went out together. They got into the carriage at the entrance to the alley and instructed the driver to go first to the Hope Brothers Company on First Avenue. Once past the Bowling Alley junction, they did not have far to go. When they had alighted, the driver pulled the carriage aside to wait for them, while the three of them wandered into the foreign store. They were greeted with such strange and fantastic things that their eyes were dazzled and their heads spun. They looked briefly at item after item, most of which they could not name and had no time to inquire into. The salesclerks in the store put on a free display of clockwork toys: toy birds that beat their wings and chirped and toy animals that danced rhythmically. There were even four or five bronze foreign figures sitting in a row, blowing the trumpet, playing the lute, and beating on various brass and wood instruments to perform a set of tunes. As for the ships, carriages, dogs, and horses that could move or walk, they were too numerous to mention.

Elan Ge just picked the things he needed. Spotting a bracelet watch, Snow Scent said she wanted to have it, so Elan Ge bargained over the total price and made a deposit with a bank draft. He also wrote a slip and told the store to send the things to High Honor Bank and collect the rest of the bill there. Having made these arrangements, they left together. In the carriage, Snow Scent took off her bracelet watch to show Little Sister.

"It's only a pretty gewgaw. There's not much to it," said Elan.

It was five o'clock by the time they got to Luna Park by the Bubbling Well Temple. Though most visitors had gone and the horse carriages were thinning out, Elan Ge ordered a pot of tea on the ground floor of the foreign-style building. Resting her hand on Little Sister's shoulder, Snow Scent took a turn around the winding corridors and pavilions and then said she wanted to go home. Elan, not in the mood to linger there, was agreeable. As they turned from the Bund into Fourth Avenue, the gas streetlamps were already burning bright. Back home, the menservants at the door reported, "Invitations from across the way have come twice already."

Elan sat for a moment before he took his leave from Snow Scent and walked across the alley. Lotuson Wang welcomed him into Constance's room where several guests had gathered. Aside from Amity Zhu, Cloudlet Chen, Benevolence Hong, and Whistler Tang, there were two young men from a local official family. They were the Tao brothers, named Cloud and Jade. Both of them were under thirty and were close family friends of Elan Ge. After deferring to one another in terms of seating order, they all sat down. A moment later, Prosperity Luo also arrived.

"Who else is coming?" Cloudlet Chen asked.

"There're my two colleagues from the bureau, said to have gone to Sunset's place first," said Lotuson.

"Then let's send someone to remind them," said Cloudlet.

"I already did. Let's not wait for them." Lotuson told the maid to set the table and asked Whistler Tang to write out the call chits. Since each man was calling his usual girl, Whistler got it all done without having to ask. Prosperity Luo took the tickets to look them over and withdrew the one for Green Phoenix.

"Why?" Lotuson asked.

"Didn't you notice yesterday that she came late and left after only a little while?" said Prosperity Luo. "Who feels like calling her!"

"Don't be angry with her," Whistler Tang replied. "She probably had to go to another party."

"What other party! She was just living up to her name!" said Prosperity Luo.

"Don't you enjoy making them go green with jealousy?" was Whistler's answer.

In the course of this conversation, the man sent to hasten the guests had come back to report that there was another party at Generosity Alley. "They say please go ahead."

So Lotuson Wang called for hot towels to be brought up. The maid answered and took the call chits down with her. Meanwhile, Whistler had written another one for Green Phoenix and slipped it in with the rest.

Lotuson invited everybody to go into the middle room, where three square tables had been set end to end to make a big dining table. The men removed their jackets and sat around anyhow, leaving two high-back chairs in the middle vacant. Constance poured wine for everyone and offered them watermelon seeds. Benevolence Hong raised his cup to her, saying, "Maestro, my congratulations."

Constance was so shy, she pursed her lips to suppress a smile and said, "What for?"

Benevolence imitated her in falsetto, "What for?" Everybody laughed.

The singers submitted a handwritten folder of opera titles, asking them to indicate their choices. Lotuson Wang offhandedly picked two: "The Broken Bridge" and "In Search of a Dream." The singers went downstairs and began the performance. A manservant wearing a formal silk fez served the first course, shark's fin. Green Phoenix was already there in answer to the call.

"Look, she's the first to arrive," Whistler Tang said to Prosperity Luo. "How she's trying to please!"

Prosperity Luo made a sign with his lips. Whistler turned his head around and saw Snow Scent sitting behind Elan Ge.

"She's like a girl from the same house, coming from just across the way. You can't compare her with the others," said Whistler.

Green Phoenix's maid, Mama Zhao, was just getting the water pipe out to fill it. She was a little taken aback to hear what Whistler said. "We always hurry to answer a call," she said. "It's only when there are other parties that we're sometimes a bit late."

Displeased, Green Phoenix snapped at Mama Zhao, "What're you going on about? Early or late, what's the difference? Who needs you to do all this talking?"

Whistler Tang heard all this but just ignored it with a smile. Prosperity Luo, however, was beginning to lose his patience. Lotuson Wang quickly changed the subject, saying, "Let's play the finger game. Prosperity, you start a bank of fifty cups."

"Fifty it is then. No big deal!" Prosperity responded.

"Come, twenty will do," said Whistler Tang.

"He's got all these people to drink for him," said Lotuson Wang. "It'll have to be thirty cups at least. I'll be the first challenger." So saying, he started a finger game with Prosperity Luo.

"Have you sung a song yet?" Green Phoenix asked Snow Scent.

"I'm not going to. You go ahead," Snow Scent replied.

Mama Zhao gave Green Phoenix the *pipa*. She tuned it and sang a prelude, which was followed by an allegro section from the Beijing opera "Breaking All Ties." Mama Zhao drank five penalty cups in a row for Prosperity Luo and flushed crimson in the face, yet Prosperity still would not let her off. Lute happened to arrive just then. She reached over and took the cup.

Mama Zhao took the opportunity to fill the water pipe twice. She then said, "Our maestro has to go now. Would you like to us to drink a couple of penalty cups as reserve?"

This fueled Prosperity's rage. He took three of the large drinking bowls and filled them to the brim for Mama Zhao. She picked up one of them but was reluctant to drink it. Green Phoenix's temper flared. She told Mama Zhao to give her the cups and then poured all the wine into a big glass bowl and downed it in one gulp. "Please drop by later." So saying, she went straight off without looking back.

"See?" Prosperity Luo said to Whistler Tang. "Wouldn't it have been better not to have called her?"

"It's your fault, really," Lute put in. "They couldn't drink anymore, and you still made them."

"Childish tantrums, that's all," said Whistler Tang. "Just drop her, and that's that."

"I *will* call her again!" Prosperity Luo said loudly. "Maid, bring ink and writing brush."

Lute pulled at his sleeve. "Why call anybody! You . . ." she choked back the rest of what she wanted to say.

"Don't tell me you're also turning green," Prosperity said, smiling.

Lute turned away holding back her laughter. "Go ahead then. I'm leaving as well."

"If you do, I'll also call you again."

At this, Lute could not help breaking into a smile. The maid, holding the inkstone and writing brush, asked, "Do you still want them, sir?"

"Give them to me. I'll write the chit for him," said Lotuson Wang.

Prosperity Luo saw Lotuson writing with his head bent and wondered what he had put down. Cloudlet Chen, who was sitting near Wang, glanced at the chit and smiled but said nothing.

Cloud Tao asked Prosperity Luo, "When did you start seeing Green Phoenix?"

"Just a fortnight ago. At first she seemed all right."

"You have Maestro Lute here. What d'you want Green Phoenix for? That girl does have quite a temper," said Cloud Tao.

"A courtesan with a temper, how is she going to get any business?" said Prosperity.

"The thing is, once a client gets to know what she's like, no one can compare with her for fondness and devotion. The only trouble is that she throws these tantrums in the beginning," said Cloud.

"But Green Phoenix was sold to the house," said Prosperity. "How is it that the madam allows her to throw tantrums instead of keeping her under control?"

"How would the madam dare control her? She's the one who controls the madam. The madam has to consult her in all matters great and small, and whatever she says goes. Even then the madam fawns on her now and again."

"This madam is too good-natured," said Prosperity.

"Is there such a thing as a good-natured madam? Have you heard of one called Second Sister Huang? That's Green Phoenix's madam. She started as a maid and rose to be madam. Having owned seven or eight girls, she counted as quite somebody in these foreign settlements. But when she ran into Green Phoenix, even she had to do a turnabout."

"Why, what powers does Green Phoenix have?" said Prosperity.

"If you want to know, she's a real hard case! When she was still a virgin courtesan, she quarreled with the madam and was given a beating. During the beating, she just clenched her teeth and never made a sound. When the maids pulled the madam away, she went straight for the jar of raw opium on the divan and swallowed two handfuls. The madam was terrified when she learned about it and sent for a doctor right away. But Green Phoenix refused to take medicine. It was no use cajoling or threatening her; she just refused. What could the madam do? She knelt down and kowtowed to the girl and then made her this promise: 'From now on, I won't dare offend you in any way.' Only then did Green Phoenix bring up the opium and let the matter rest."

Prosperity Luo's heart was beating fast as Cloud Tao told the story. He was lost in thought while the others at the table all expressed their admiration and sympathy for Green Phoenix. Even the courtesans and maids listened stunned. Lotuson Wang, still busy writing, was the only one who did not hear it. When he had finished and handed the note to the maid, Prosperity Luo took it to read. It turned out to be the sedan-chair bearers' dinner allowances, so he set it aside.

"Why aren't you people drinking?" asked Lotuson Wang. "Is your bank broken yet, Prosperity?"

"Ten more cups to go," replied Prosperity.

Lotuson told Whistler Tang to challenge the bank.

"Jade hasn't played either," said Whistler. The words were scarcely out of his mouth when there were footsteps on the stairs and two men rushed straight in, shouting:

"Who's banker? Here we come; to the attack!"

Everybody knew these were the two friends Lotuson Wang had invited from his bureau. They all stood up to offer them seats, but neither of them bothered to sit down. One stood in front of the table with his sleeves rolled up and a fist extended, shouting wildly into space the set phrases for the finger game. Another grabbed White Fragrance's younger sister, Green Fragrance, by the waist and tried to kiss her on the mouth, murmuring, "My little baby! Give us a cheek-to-cheek."

Green Fragrance covered her face with her hands and hid behind Whistler Tang, crying out desperately, "Leave me alone!"

"Don't go and make her cry," Lotuson Wang intervened quickly.

"Oh, she won't cry," White Fragrance said smiling and then turned to lecture Green Fragrance. "What's wrong with a little cheek-to-cheek? It won't hurt, will it? See, you've made your hair come loose now."

Green Fragrance struggled free, took her nutmeg box, and looked in the mirror as White Fragrance tidied up her hair. Fortunately, the two courtesans who came along with the two men arrived soon afterward. They dragged the two away and made them sit down in the vacant chairs.

"Whose party was it at Sunset's?" Lotuson Wang asked.

"Mallow Yao's—who else?"

"No wonder you both got drunk," said Lotuson.

The two of them started shouting again. "Who says we're drunk? We're going to play the finger game."

Seeing the state they were in, Prosperity Luo dared not give them further encouragement. He played them for the last ten cups just anyhow, saying, "As to the wine, anyone who wants to can substitute." Lute also drank several cups for him.

By the time the game was over, the Lin sisters had left, and Lute had also said her farewell. Prosperity Luo took the opportunity to leave the table and quietly asked Whistler Tang to come with him to the inner room, where they put on their jackets, slipped out through the door behind the bed, and went downstairs, the first ones to leave. Seeing them, the steward, Promotion, hastened to shout for the sedan chair. Prosperity Luo gave the order for the sedan chair to be taken to Generosity Alley. Whistler Tang realized he was going to Green Phoenix's because of what Cloud Tao had said and was secretly amused.

When the two of them got outside, they found that the alley was packed full of carriages and sedan chairs. They had to walk sideways. Just then, their way was blocked by a servant girl who had squeezed herself through the gaps between the various vehicles. She looked up and greeted them with a smile, "Aiyo! Mr. Luo," and quickly drew back to let them pass.

Prosperity Luo took a good look and saw that it was Goldie, Little Rouge's servant girl. He asked, "Are you here at a party?"

Goldie answered yes casually and went on her way.

Whistler Tang followed Prosperity Luo to Green Phoenix's. The menservants announced them, and the servant girl Little Treasure welcomed them upstairs, saying with a smile, "Mr. Luo, you haven't come for quite a few days now." She propped up the curtain and invited them in. Then Green Phoenix's two younger sisters, Pearl Phoenix and Gold Phoenix, came over from the room opposite to greet them, warmly addressing Prosperity Luo as "Brother-in-law." Both girls served them watermelon seeds.

Whistler Tang took the initiative to ask, "Is your elder sister out at a party?"

Gold Phoenix nodded and said yes.

Little Treasure, who had just come in with the teacups, broke in quickly, "She's been gone for a while now, so she should be coming back any minute."

His enthusiasm dampened, Prosperity Luo threw Whistler a glance, ready to leave. They got up together and went down the stairs. Little Treasure cried out in alarm, "Don't go," and rushed after them, but it was too late.

CHAPTER 7 :: *One girl casts a spell and lays a vicious trap, and another meets a good mate but can't escape her fate*

When Green Phoenix's little sister, Gold Phoenix, saw that they could not make Prosperity Luo and Whistler Tang stay, she leaned out of the upstairs window and called out loudly, "Mother, Mr. Luo is leaving!"

Hearing this, the madam, Second Sister, rushed out of her small room and bumped right into the two men at the foot of the stairs. She grabbed Prosperity Luo by the sleeve, saying, "You mustn't go."

Prosperity said repeatedly, "I can't hang around."

"If you have to go, at least wait till our Green Phoenix is back," she said loudly. Then she turned to Whistler Tang. "And you, Mr. Tang, you're in such a hurry, too! Why don't you sit down and chat with our Mr. Luo for a bit?" Brooking no protest, she dragged Prosperity Luo upstairs and told Little Treasure to see to it that Whistler Tang also came back into the room.

"Do take off your jacket and make yourself comfortable. Have a little rest," she said, reaching out to unbutton Prosperity's jacket. Gold Phoenix, seeing this, also asked Whistler Tang to remove his jacket. Little Treasure put a pinch of tea leaves in the cups and took

Whistler's jacket from him. Second Sister also passed her Prosperity Luo's. They went up on the clothes rack.

Second Sister turned around and saw Pearl Phoenix standing to one side. Angry that she had not come forward to help entertain, she glared at her. Frightened, Pearl Phoenix backed away, fetched a water pipe in a hurry, and filled it for Prosperity.

Prosperity held up a hand to stop her. "Give it to Mr. Tang."

"Had too much wine? Why not lie down for a bit?" Second Sister suggested.

Prosperity lay down nonchalantly on the opium divan. Little Treasure handed him a hot towel, put a cup of tea on the opium tray, and then turned to offer Whistler tea. Whistler sat on a high-back chair against the wall with Pearl Phoenix filling the water pipe for him by his side. Second Sister told Gold Phoenix to fetch another water pipe and then sat down on a low stool by the divan, took a puff herself, and turned sideways to whisper placatingly to Prosperity, "You're angry, aren't you?"

"What for?" said Prosperity.

"If you're not angry, why didn't you come the last few days?"

"I had no time."

"Humph." After a long while she said smiling, "That's true. You're at your old love's day and night, how would you have time for us?"

He smiled without answering.

She took another puff on the water pipe and said slowly, "Our Green Phoenix does have a temper. I don't blame you, Mr. Luo, for being angry. But the fact is her temper also depends on the client. Actually, she's never lost her temper the least bit where Mr. Luo is concerned. Mr. Tang here knows more about her. When she serves a client, she wants him to be constant, to be with her for the long run, and then she grows fond of him. Once she grows fond, of course she'll never get in a temper. It's only when she runs into a fickle client that her temper gets the better of her. When that happens, she not only won't try to please; she'll pay you no attention whatsoever. Isn't that so, Mr. Tang? You, Mr. Luo, are angry now because our Green Phoenix doesn't seem to be out to please. What you don't know is that in her heart she is quite taken with you. It's you, Mr. Luo, who are holding back, so she can't be all over you. She knows Mr. Luo has been seeing Lute for four or five years now. Sometimes, she has talked to me about it, saying, 'Mr. Luo shows constancy. If he's been going to Lute's for four or five years, could we fare much worse with him?' I said, 'Since you know Mr. Luo is not fickle, why don't you try harder?' What she said is true, too. She said, 'Mr. Luo has his old love; I'm afraid I'll never please him. I'd just get laughed at by Lute and her people.' That's how she feels. It'd be unfair to say she just won't make up to you, sir. The way I see it, you've just started seeing her, and you don't know her temperament yet. After one season, you'd have a rough idea. When our Green Phoenix knows that you truly want to see her, she'll also gradually try to please."

Prosperity sneered.

Second Sister just laughed. "You don't quite believe me, do you? Ask Mr. Tang; he knows. Just think, Mr. Tang; if she doesn't care for Mr. Luo, would she have answered the dozen party calls from him? In her heart, she cares, but she'd never admit it. Even the maids don't know what goes on in her heart; only I can make out some of it. If I'd let Mr. Luo go just now, she'd blame me when she comes back. I tell you frankly, Mr. Luo: it's been about five years now since she's done grown-up work. Altogether, she's only had three clients. One lives in Shanghai; the other two only come a couple of times a year. I'd like her to choose another client and bring me more business, but she makes it *so* hard! We can forget about all the clients who are run-of-the-mill, but she'll fault even outstanding clients for lacking real commitment and just refuse to establish a relationship. What am I to do? That's why when I see that she gets on so well with you, I hope you'll become a regular, Mr. Luo, and bring in more business for me. To be perfectly honest, if it weren't for this, we have plenty of clients of comparable standing to yourself who are left to come and go as they please. Do I ever go out of my way to entertain them? Why is it that I'm here to keep you company, Mr. Luo?"

Prosperity remained silent, while Whistler Tang just smiled. Second Sister continued, "You've been coming to us for a fortnight now, and you've been treating Green Phoenix well enough. But to her, you, sir, are someone who already has a regular girl, and she feels she can do little except fill in the gaps. I gave her this advice, 'You should try harder to please him. What's this talk about old love or new love? D'you think Mr. Luo would treat you badly?' But she replied, 'Let's wait a couple of days and see.' Then the day before yesterday, she told me after she had returned from a dinner party, 'Mother, you said that Mr. Luo is fond of me, but he was having a dinner party at Lute's place.' I told her a party or two meant nothing, but Green Phoenix is a good one for worrying. She said, 'Since Mr. Luo is sweet on his old love, how can he be fond of me?'"

Hearing this, Prosperity cut in, "That's easy! I'll host another dinner party here."

Mama Huang put on a solemn expression. "Mr. Luo, if you do want to come to Green Phoenix, it's not a matter of hosting dinner parties. If you have a party here just because of what I've said, and later Green Phoenix were to find out that your arrangements remain unchanged, she'd blame me for playing tricks on you. If you want Green Phoenix, you must make her your only girl. Then she will try her very best to please you without fail. It's just not a good idea to see Green Phoenix for a while and then to seek out Lute again. That way, you won't please either of them. If you don't believe me, give it a try, see what style my girl has, see if she aims to please or not."

Prosperity smiled and said, "That's easy. I'd stop seeing Lute then."

Second Sister bowed her head smiling, took another puff from her water pipe, and then said, "I see you're quite a tease, Mr. Luo! A lover of four or five years' standing, and you're going to drop her just like that? How could you say such a thing? 'Easy' you say! You're kidding us, aren't you?" So saying, she put down her water pipe and went into the next room to attend to some business.

Prosperity Luo now realized what Cloud Tao had said was true. Full of admiration for Green Phoenix, he wanted to consult Whistler Tang but could not very well do that. He mulled it over by himself, sat up, and took a sip of tea. Pearl Phoenix hastened to bring the water pipe over. He again refused it with a wave of his hand. He saw Little Treasure and Gold Phoenix were bent over the dressing table to get closer to the lamplight. Heads together and arms round each other's neck, they were looking at something and giggling away.

"What is it?" he asked.

Gold Phoenix snatched the object from Little Treasure's hand to show him, grinning. It turned out to be half a walnut shell with an erotic scene inside enacted by figures of painted paste.

"Look!" she pulled the thread outside the shell, showing how the figures inside could rock to and fro.

Whistler Tang also ambled over to glance at it. "D'you understand what it is?" he asked her.

"It's just a lady on a swing. What's there to understand?" she said.

Little Treasure hastily intervened, laughing, "Don't talk to him; he's making fun of you."

As they were talking and laughing, Second Sister came back into the room. "What're you all laughing at?"

Gold Phoenix showed her.

"Where did you get it? Put it back for her. If you ruin it, she'll give you another dressing-down," said Second Sister.

Gold Phoenix immediately gave the toy to Little Treasure to put away.

Prosperity got up, signaling Second Sister with his eyes, and they went out to the upstairs parlor. Nobody knew what they spoke of in the dark. They whispered for a long while, and then she called out of the window.

"Is Mr. Luo's steward here? Tell him to come up."

Meanwhile, Prosperity Luo went back into the room, told Little Treasure to fetch ink and writing brush, and asked Whistler Tang to write out invitations to the men who had been at the last dinner party with them, as they were at hand. Second Sister went to light a paraffin table lamp herself and watched as Whistler dashed the invitations off. Little Treasure then took them downstairs for the menservants to deliver.

"Your steward is waiting," Second Sister said to Prosperity. "Have you any instructions for him?"

"Tell him to come in."

Promotion, who was waiting outside, hastened to lift the curtain and came in to take his instructions. Prosperity took a bunch of keys from his pocket. "Go home and open the third trunk behind my bed. There's a document box inside; fetch it."

Promotion took the keys and left.

"Shall we set the table?" Second Sister asked.

Prosperity looked up at the clock on the wall: it was already half past one. "Yes, let's do that. It's getting late."

Whistler Tang said smiling, "What's the hurry? We have to give Green Phoenix time to get back from her dinner party."

Alarmed, Second Sister said, "I sent to hurry her. Theirs is a mah-jongg party. Unless she's substituting at the mah-jongg table, why would it take this long?" She then shouted, "Little Treasure, you go and hurry her up; tell her to come right back."

Little Treasure answered yes and was about to go downstairs when Second Sister stopped her, "Wait a minute, I'll tell you what . . ." She rushed out to the landing and whispered some instructions into the girl's ear. "Now don't forget."

When Little Treasure was gone, Second Sister supervised the menservants who were rearranging the tables and chairs and setting the cups and chopsticks for a party. The messengers were also reporting back. Except for Amity Zhu and the Tao brothers, who said they were coming right away, the others had either gone home or gone to bed and had declined with their thanks. Prosperity Luo had to leave it at that.

Suddenly, there was the sound downstairs of a sedan chair coming through the front gate. Thinking it was Green Phoenix, Second Sister hastened to look down from the window. It turned out to be a guest: Amity Zhu was here. Prosperity Luo welcomed him in and asked him to take a seat. Seeing that Green Phoenix was not even at home, Amity Zhu could not puzzle out the reason for the party and had to ask Whistler Tang in an undertone.

The three men chatted and waited until nearly two o'clock. Only then did they see Little Treasure run into the room, panting. "She's coming! She's coming!"

"What're you running for?" said Second Sister.

"I was in a hurry! The maestro was *so* worried," Little Treasure replied.

"What took her so long?" asked Second Sister.

"She was substituting at the mah-jongg table."

"Just as I thought," said Second Sister.

Then came the clop-clopping up the stairs of high-heeled shoes for bound feet. Second Sister hurried out of the room. Mama Zhao was the first to come in, holding the *pipa* and water pipe bag. "Mr. Luo," she greeted him with a smile. "Have you been waiting for long? It just happened we were called to a mah-jongg party. We wouldn't have been back yet if we hadn't been told to hurry."

Then Green Phoenix came in very sedately. After offering watermelon seeds to all the guests, she looked over her shoulder at Prosperity Luo and broke into a lovely smile. Prosperity had never seen her treat him like this. His joy at the unexpected boon could well be imagined.

After a while, Cloud Tao also arrived.

"Only Jade is missing now," said Prosperity Luo. "Let's go ahead and sit down at the table." Whistler Tang wrote a note to hasten Jade Tao and handed it to Mama Zhao together with a call chit, saying, "Go first to Water Blossom's in East Prosperity Alley, both the guest and the girl are there."

"Will do," Mama Zhao answered.

Everybody then moved over to the dining table. Green Phoenix poured wine for all the guests before she sat down behind Prosperity Luo. After attending to the routines of etiquette, Pearl Phoenix and Gold Phoenix sat around casually, while Second Sister slipped away at the first opportunity. Green Phoenix told Little Treasure to bring a fiddle and gave her own *pipa* to Gold Phoenix. Not bothering with a prelude, she just picked her best piece—the entire aria of "Boating on the Lake"—and sang in duet with Gold Phoenix. Their singing cast such a spell over the guests that no one got round to drinking. Prosperity Luo listened transported, as if in a daze. He never even heard Mama Zhao announce, "Second Young Mr. Tao is here." Only when Jade Tao came to the dining table did he stand up hastily to greet him.

One after another, the girls who had been called all arrived. Since Jade Tao had brought his girl, there was no need to issue another call. Surprisingly, the girl he brought was not Water Blossom but a virgin courtesan of twelve or thirteen with delicate regular features and childish manners. Clinging to Jade Tao, she seemed unwilling to let go. Prosperity Luo asked who she was.

"This is River Blossom. We may say she's Water Blossom's little sister. Water Blossom is not feeling well. She had just lain down after sweating a little, so I told her not to get up. River Blossom has come in her place," Jade Tao explained.

As they were talking, Green Phoenix had finished her song. She now busied herself seeing to the guests, saying, "Do please try some of the dishes." She then gave Prosperity Luo a nudge, "Why don't you say something?"

"I'll start with a round of the finger game." Prosperity smiled and stuck out his fist at each guest in turn, beginning with Amity Zhu. There were no big winners or losers to speak of until it came to Jade Tao, who kept losing. When River Blossom saw him start on the finger game, she covered his wine cup with her hands and would not let him drink a drop. Every penalty cup was given to the maid. Jade lost five times in a row, and when he reached out for a cup himself, River Blossom grabbed it, pleading desperately, "I'd thank you not to. Don't make it hard for us, all right?" Jade Tao had to leave it at that.

Prosperity Luo was so surprised by what River Blossom had said that he turned around to ask her what it was all about. But just then he saw Second Sister peeping in from beyond the bamboo curtain. He guessed what she wanted and, instead of questioning River Blossom, left the table and went out into the room opposite. Second Sister brought his steward, Promotion, in after him, and Promotion handed over a document box. Second Sister turned the foreign table lamp up high. Prosperity produced a bunch of small keys, opened the box, took out a pair of gold bracelets weighing almost ten taels, and gave them to Second Sister. He then locked up the box again and gave it to her for temporary safekeeping. He put away his keys, saying, "I'll tell Green Phoenix to come and see if she likes the design." He returned to the table and whispered to Green Phoenix, "Your mother wants you."

Green Phoenix pretended not to hear. After a long delay, she stood up abruptly and went off.

Prosperity Luo saw that it had gone quiet at the table. "Isn't any of you going to be the banker?" he asked.

Cloud Tao said, "We'll play a couple more rounds, but you let Jade go first. Since they won't let him drink, what's the point of keeping him here? Just because of him, several maids and servant girls are running endlessly back and forth, and somebody else is worrying over him. Later, if he should get a fright and be taken ill, we'd be held accountable. Better let him go so we can relax, don't you think?" At this, everyone roared with laughter.

Prosperity Luo looked and sure enough there were two servant girls and three maids hovering behind Jade. He said, "Looks like I shouldn't keep you."

Jade Tao could hardly wait for the word. Taking River Blossom with him, he said good-bye rather shamefacedly and left. Having seen him off, Prosperity Luo commented, "So, Water Blossom is terribly in love with him."

Cloud Tao said, "You get some people in love with their girls; it's common enough. But I've never seen such love as theirs; it's indescribable. No matter where he goes, she sends a maid to accompany him, and they have to go out together and come back together. If by any chance she hasn't seen him for a day, she'll have her maids and menservants look everywhere for him, and if they can't find him, she'll make such a row. One day, I went to her place purposely to take a look at them. I never thought the two of them would just sit staring at each other, not saying a word. I asked whether they had gone dopey but couldn't get an answer from them."

"It must be in their stars," said Whistler Tang.

"What stars?" Cloud responded. "I call it a debt from the last life. You see how Jade often looks a bit dazed lately; that's because they have him so hemmed in, he can't walk a step away. Sometimes, I tell Jade to go to a show, but Water Blossom says, 'The music in the theater is too loud. Better not go.' I tell Jade to take a drive, but Water Blossom says, 'Horse carriages jolt you so hard when they speed up. Better not go.' The funniest thing was that time he went to have his photograph taken. She said they'd taken the light from his eyes, so every day at dawn before they got up she licked his eyes for him. According to her, his eyes healed only after half a month of licking."

At this, everybody again laughed uproariously. Cloud Tao turned around, pointed to the courtesan he himself had summoned, Belle, and said with a smile, "Now, lovers like the two of us may not be terribly in love, but we do all right. Come and you're not a nuisance; go and you're not missed. We do just as we like; isn't that much more comfortable?"

Belle spoke up, "You were talking about them; why drag us into it? If you want to be as much in love as they are, you're welcome to go to her, too!"

"I was praising you; did I say anything wrong?" he said.

"Oh, you can insinuate all you like," she said. "But I'm made the way I am. Can't be better if I try; can't be nasty if I try, either."

"That's why I said you were nice. Why do you have to get funny ideas and accuse me of insinuation?"

Amity Zhu said in earnest, "I know you were only joking, but there's something in what you said. It seems to me the more one is in love, the less it lasts. It's those who behave the way they are that go on year after year, staying together."

White Fragrance, who was sitting behind Amity, did not say anything to that, but she, too, was making faces. Seeing this, Prosperity Luo quickly changed the subject.

"No more talking. Amity, you be the banker. We'll play the finger game."

CHAPTER 8 :: *Second Sister retains a treasure box with dark designs, and Green Phoenix refuses a carriage ride with ready wit*

Prosperity Luo was just about to start a finger game with Amity Zhu as the banker when he heard Second Sister whisper his name. Not bothering with the game, he just stood up and walked out of the room. Second Sister, who was waiting for him in the outer room, asked, "Would you like Gold Phoenix to stand in for you?"

He nodded, so Gold Phoenix went in to join those at the table, while Luo went over to the room opposite. He saw Green Phoenix seated by the table, with the pair of gold bracelets set out in front of her.

"Come," she said smiling as he approached and, taking both his hands in hers, made him sit down on the divan. "My mother was taken in by you; she was *so* happy to hear what you said. But I knew right away you weren't serious about it. After all, you already have Lute; why would you deign to show me such favors? My mother even went so far as to show me these bracelets, but I told her, 'What's so special about bracelets? Who knows how many of them he's given to Lute! Even I have a couple of pairs, all put away because I never use them. What do I want another pair for?' Please take them back. If, in a couple of days, you really make up your mind not to go to Lute's anymore and to favor me instead, then that would be the right time to give them to me again."

To Prosperity, these words were like cold water poured right over his head. He remonstrated, "I've given my word that I'll not go to Lute's again. If you don't believe me, I'll have a friend go and settle my bills there tomorrow, all right?"

"There's nothing to prevent you from going there again after you've settled your bills," she said. "You're an old patron of Lute's, you've been together for four or five years now, and she's quite affectionate, too. Now you say you're not going, but if you ever want to see her again, how can I stop you?"

"I've said I won't go, so how could I be going there again? D'you think my words are not worth a fart?"

"You can say what you like, but I don't believe it. Just think about it: even if you say you won't go, won't they go to your house and invite you? She'd ask you if she had offended you in any way or made you angry. What're you going to tell her? Won't it embarrass you to say that I told you not to go?"

"If she invites me, I just won't go. What can she do?"

"You make it sound so easy! D'you think they'd just give up if you don't go? What would you do if she were set on dragging you there?"

He pondered over it and then asked, "Why don't you tell me what *you* want me to do?"

"Well, if you really favor me, I'll have you come live with us for two months. During that time, you're not to go out alone. If you want to go anywhere, I'll go with you. Lute's people couldn't very well come to our place to invite you. What d'you say?"

"I have a lot of business to attend to. How can I not go out at all?"

"In that case, you should give me something as a guarantee. With that in hand, I won't be afraid of your going to Lute's."

"But I can't very well put something like that down in writing, can I?"

"What's the use of a written guarantee? Bring me some things that are important to you and leave them here; they'll serve as your guarantee."

"Things that're important? Well, there's money."

Green Phoenix sneered. "In your eyes, I must be pretty nasty! So you think I'm scheming for your money, do you? Well, money might be a good thing in your eyes, but it's of no importance to me."

"Then what sort of thing do you want?"

"Don't get the idea that I want anything from you; I have your interests at heart. The whole point is, if you leave your things here, then even if you wanted to go to Lute's, you'd think twice about it because you'd know you have things in my hands. That'd put a stop to any ideas about Lute. Don't you think so?"

Prosperity suddenly thought of something. "I've got it. The box I fetched here just now happens to be an important thing."

"The box will do. You're not worried about leaving it here, are you? I've got to warn you first: You go one more time to Lute's, and I'll take everything out of your box and burn it all."

He stuck his tongue out and shook his head. "Aiyo! You're a tough one."

She replied with a smile, "If that's what you think, you've judged me wrong. I may be a courtesan, but I can't be bought. Even ten pairs of bracelets are nothing to me, not to say just one pair, so please take your bracelets back. If you want to give them to me, any day will do. But tonight I won't let you look down on me and think that I have taken a fancy to your bracelets."

So saying, she picked up the bracelets on the table and put them round his wrists.

Prosperity could not push her further and had to go along with her. "Then I'll put the bracelets in the box for now and give them to you again in a couple of days. But I've got several warehouse receipts and bank drafts in the box; what if I should need to take them out sometime?"

"When you need them, you just take them out. Warehouse receipts, or bank drafts, or whatever, you can come for them whenever you need them. They're yours after all. Are you afraid I'll embezzle them?"

He again reflected for a moment and then said, "I want to know why you won't accept the bracelets."

She smiled. "It's hard for you to figure out how I think. You should know that if we're together, you mustn't set too much store by money. When I have need for money, I may ask you for a thousand or eight hundred, and you shouldn't think of it as too much. But when I don't need it, I won't even ask you for a cent. If you want to give me presents, say, give me bracelets, I'd accept them as a token of your feelings. But even if you go and get me a brick, I'd appreciate it just as much. Once you've figured me out, everything will be fine."

Prosperity could not help being visibly shocked by these words. He stood up and said, "You're a rare one indeed!" and then bowed deeply to her with the greatest respect. "I've really come to admire you today."

She hastened to tell him to stop bowing and then said with a smile, "What if they should see you like this? Won't you be embarrassed?" She then held him by his hand again and said, "Let's go next door." Hand in hand, they walked to the room across the way. At the door, she steered him to go in before her, and they joined those at the table. By then, the girls called to the party from other houses had all gone, and Second Sister was helping Gold Phoenix and the others entertain the guests. When she saw Prosperity came in, she announced immediately, "Mr. Luo is here."

Amity Zhu said, "We're already going to have our congee, and you've only just come."

"Let's have a couple more rounds of the finger game," said Prosperity.

"While you were having fun, Amity and I were having too much to drink," said Cloud Tao.

Prosperity, all smiles, apologized for his absence and called for congee to be served. In fact, everyone at the table was already full; they just ate a little of it as a matter of habit. The party then broke up, and everybody took his leave. Prosperity saw them off at the stairway. Whistler Tang was the last to go, and Prosperity said to him, "I have a small matter to ask you to see to. I'll tell you about it when we get together tomorrow."

Whistler assented to that arrangement. He waited till the sedan chairs bearing Cloud Tao and Amity Zhu had gone out the door before he went home on foot.

When Prosperity Luo came back to the room, the menservants had taken off the tabletop. Mama Zhao swept the floor cursorily with a broom and together with Little Treasure cleared away the teacups and left. Prosperity sat around and watched as Green Phoenix removed her jewelry.

Before long, Second Sister came in again to chat with him. Green Phoenix then told her to get the box out and give it to Prosperity, who took off the bracelets and put them in the box. Not knowing what this meant, Second Sister stared first at Prosperity, then at Green Phoenix, her eyes like a hawk's, but Green Phoenix ignored her. Prosperity locked the box up again, and Green Phoenix told Second Sister to put it in the trunk at the back of the room. Only then did she understand. As she took the box, she turned around to ask Prosperity, "Shall I tell them to send your sedan chair home?"

"Go and fetch Promotion," he said.

Second Sister went and summoned Promotion upstairs. Prosperity gave some orders and told him to go home with the sedan chair. A while later, Little Treasure came in to ask Green Phoenix to go over to the room opposite.[1] Green Phoenix was about to leave the room when she saw Prosperity would be left alone. She asked, "Where's Pearl Phoenix?"

Little Treasure answered, "Mama Zhao told her to go to bed." Green Phoenix looked at the wall clock; it had struck four, so she couldn't very well fault anyone. Instead, she just called out the window, "Hey, where has everyone gone?"

Mama Zhao answered the call at once and came up to see to Prosperity. She asked, "Retiring for the night, Mr. Luo?"

He nodded his assent, so Mama Zhao made the bed, blew out the lamp, and closed the door as she left the room. But Prosper-

: :

1. [Obviously Green Phoenix's favorite client, Vigor Qian, has come to spend the night as well. She is entertaining two men in the same night, one in her own room and one in the spare room. E.H.]

ity had to wait until Green Phoenix returned before going to bed with her.

The next morning, Prosperity woke up to see the red glow of the sun shining at the window. It was still early. Little Treasure was dusting the furniture with a cloth. He had no idea where Green Phoenix had gone.[2] He heard some noise in the middle room and figured that she was probably at her morning toilet by the window. He tried to sleep again but could not.

After a time, Green Phoenix, her hair done, came into the room to get some clothes out of the wardrobe and change. Prosperity sat up, put on his clothes, and got off the bed.

"Get a little more sleep," said Green Phoenix. "It's not yet ten o'clock."

"When did you get up?" he asked.

"I couldn't sleep anymore," she replied with a smile, "so I got up shortly after seven. You were sleeping so soundly just then."

Mama Zhao, having learned that Prosperity was up, came to wait on him as he washed his face and cleaned his teeth. Then she asked him about breakfast.

"Don't feel like any," he said.

"Then we'll just wait for lunch," said Green Phoenix.

"Lunch will be a while yet," said Mama Zhao.

"That suits me fine," said Prosperity.

"You can tell them to hurry up a bit," said Green Phoenix.

Mama Zhao went to pass the word on, but Prosperity called her back to ask, "Is Promotion here?"

"He's been here a while now. I'll go get him," said Mama Zhao.

Hearing the summons, Promotion presented himself. He handed Prosperity a note and a roll of foreign banknotes and then asked, "Shall I get the sedan chair ready, sir?"

"No, it's Sunday, and there's not much for me to attend to. I don't need the sedan chair." Prosperity then turned to Green Phoenix. "Shall we go for a drive?"

"All right. We'll have two carriages," she said.

Prosperity did not comment on that but turned his attention to the note. It was an invitation from Benevolence Hong for a dinner party at Twin Pearl's that evening. He tossed it aside. Promotion, seeing that there weren't any more instructions, went on his way.

Prosperity suddenly remembered something and said to Green Phoenix, "I saw you one night last summer in a carriage with a tall

: :

2. [She sneaked off early in the morning to be with Qian and to see him off. *E.H.*]

thin client at Luna Park.[3] I didn't know your name, or else I'd have called you last year."

For a brief moment, she looked a bit dazed, and then she replied, "Of course it doesn't matter much for us to ride with a client in the same carriage. It's just that shortly after Chinese New Year a Cantonese client asked me to go for a drive, and I didn't feel like sharing a carriage with him, so I said, 'Let's have two carriages.' Those were my exact words, I didn't say anything else. And you know how he responded? He said, 'That'll be all right as long as you never share a carriage with a client, but if I ever see you do that, I'll come and ask you about it to your face, and it's not going to be pleasant.'"

"And what did you say to him?"

"Me? I said, 'I seldom go for carriage rides, not even once a month. I only agreed to go today because it was the first time you asked me, and yet you say such unpleasant things! I'm not going, and I won't keep you.'"

"That must have put him in a pickle."

"Well, there was nothing he could do about it."

"No wonder even your mother says you have a temper."

"Cantonese clients are so uncouth. Frankly, I didn't feel like seeing him, so why should I have played up to him?"

While they were still talking, noontime came round. Mama Zhao came in with a big tray, and Little Treasure followed with a wine pot. They put them down on the square marble table by the window with wine cups and chopsticks for two and invited Prosperity to have some wine. Green Phoenix filled a huge porcelain wine cup and offered it to him, while she took a small silver cup and sat down facing him to keep him company. Second Sister also came in to help serve him.

"This is our own cooking. Do try some and see what you think of it," she said.

"Home cooking is always better than restaurant food."

"We have our own chef here," said Second Sister. She then pointed out that the small bowl of ham and a bowl of steamed duck's feet were from last night's dinner party.

"Come and have some yourself," Green Phoenix said to her.

"No, thanks, I'll eat downstairs. I'll go get Gold Phoenix to come and keep you company."

"Just a minute." Prosperity took out the roll of banknotes and handed it to Second Sister for expenses and tips to the maids and servants.

: :

3. [The client would have been Vigor Qian. Now Green Phoenix has to find an excuse for asking for a separate carriage where Prosperity is concerned. E.H.]

"Thank you," she said as she took the money.

"No need."

"I thanked you on their behalf. There's nothing wrong with that." All smiles, she went off to distribute the money.

Now that there was no one else in the room, Prosperity pretended to be a little tipsy and walked over to Green Phoenix's side to fondle her. She pushed him away, saying, "Don't! Mama Zhao is coming!"

He looked around and saw no one, so he climbed all over her, protesting, "You little liar! Mama Zhao is also having fun with her husband. How would she have time to look in on us?"

Green Phoenix ground her teeth in exasperation. Fortunately, Gold Phoenix came in at this moment. Seeing her, Prosperity loosened his grip slightly. Green Phoenix took advantage of it to give him a push with all her strength, and he almost fell down.

Gold Phoenix clapped her hands laughing. "Why does Brother-in-law kowtow to me?"

He turned around to embrace Gold Phoenix and tried to kiss her.

"Stop horsing around!" Gold Phoenix cried out desperately.

Green Phoenix stamped her feet. "Is there no end to your horseplay?"

Prosperity let go hastily. "No more horseplay, no more horseplay. Don't be angry, my maestro." He made a great show of respectfully saluting her. At this even Green Phoenix let out a giggle.

Gold Phoenix pushed Prosperity into his seat. "Please have some wine." She took the wine pot to pour for him, but nothing came out. When she looked into the pot, she smiled, "The wine's all gone." She then called out for Little Treasure to bring some more.

"Don't give him any more," said Green Phoenix. "If he gets drunk, he'll be acting silly again."

He pleaded, "Just three more cups, and I promise I won't horse around."

When Little Treasure brought another pot of wine, he reached out for it, but Green Phoenix grabbed it first, saying, "No more for you."

Prosperity kept begging. Little Treasure, who watched from the side, laughed and said, "No more wine for you. Come on, have a good cry!" At this, Prosperity actually made the sound of mournful weeping.

"Oh, do let him have some," said Gold Phoenix, "I'll pour." Taking the wine pot from Green Phoenix, she filled a cup to three-quarters full.

Prosperity bowed to her with his hands joined together. "Thank you. Please fill it right up for me, if you don't mind."

Green Phoenix could not suppress her laughter. "How is it you're so thick-skinned?"

"I said I'd just have three more cups. If I ask for more, I'm an animal. Don't you believe me?"

She looked away, ignoring him. Both Little Treasure and Gold Phoenix were rolling about with laughter.

When Prosperity was drinking his third cup of wine, Second Sister came in with the rice in a covered dish. She told Little Treasure, "Go and have lunch downstairs. I'll take your place."

Knowing that Second Sister had had her lunch, Prosperity said, "Let's have some rice now."

"Have another cup of wine," Second Sister said.

At this, Prosperity jumped up, pointed a finger at Green Phoenix, and yelled, "Did you hear your mother tell me to drink? Do you dare tell me not to?"

Green Phoenix glared at him. "It seems that being told off only makes you all the chirpier." She handed the wine pot to Little Treasure and told her to take it downstairs; she then called for rice to be served.

Second Sister brought three bowls of rice to the table. Gold Phoenix took a pair of ivory chopsticks for herself and sat down to keep Prosperity and Green Phoenix company.

Presently, Mama Zhao and Little Treasure both came in to wait on them. After they had finished, the table was cleared, and everybody sat around to drink tea. Even Pearl Phoenix came mincing in and offered to fill the water pipe for Prosperity. He took it from her and helped himself.

It was almost three in the afternoon when Prosperity instructed Little Treasure to tell the menservants to summon two carriages. Mama Zhao poured hot water in a basin for Green Phoenix to wash her face, while Green Phoenix told Gold Phoenix to dress up and go out with them. Gold Phoenix said yes and went with Little Treasure to another room, where she also washed her face and put on makeup. Green Phoenix just powdered and rouged herself very lightly, giving full play to her natural beauty and air of elegance. When she had finished, she went behind the bed curtains for a pee. Mama Zhao, having put away the toiletries, took a change of clothes from the wardrobe and laid it on the bed for Green Phoenix. She also took out her silver water pipe and then hurried off herself to get changed.

Gold Phoenix, the first to be ready, came over to wait. Prosperity saw that she had changed into a pale pink jacket with narrow sleeves and loose green trousers, topped by an embroidered sapphire-blue sleeveless jacket trimmed with dark blue satin. Her hair was tied up in a double chignon on either side of her head, each with a tassel trailing down, in the style of the Tartar Princess Yelu in the opera *General Yang Visits His Mother*. He smiled and said to her, "Forget about binding your feet. You can pass yourself off as a Manchu—could do worse."

"That'd be wonderful! With a pair of big feet, I'd have to be given away as a servant girl," said Gold Phoenix.

"If you were given away, it'd be as a wife, the lady of the house. Where d'you get that about a servant girl?" he said.

"If we pay you any attention, you just talk drivel, don't you?" said Gold Phoenix.

Hearing the exchange, Green Phoenix came out, still doing up her trousers. As she washed her hands, she asked Prosperity, "How would you like it if she were given to you as a concubine?"

"Let alone a concubine, she'd do very well for a wife." Then he turned to Gold Phoenix with a smile, "What d'you say?"

Gold Phoenix was so embarrassed, she covered her face and bent over the table, ignoring Prosperity's repeated questions. Yet Prosperity persisted, set on getting some answer.

She finally waved her hand and said, "I don't know, I don't know."

"That means you're willing," he said.

Green Phoenix brushed her own cheek with a finger to shame her. Pearl Phoenix, who was observing them from a high-back chair against the wall, let out a chuckle. Prosperity pointed to her, "There's another wife, and she's so tickled, she laughs to herself."

Green Phoenix was annoyed at the sight of Pearl Phoenix. "Look at her; isn't she a pain!"

Pearl Phoenix was so alarmed, she immediately sat up straight and assumed a serious expression.

This only enraged Green Phoenix all the more. "Are you angry because I put you in your place?" She walked over to pull Pearl Phoenix down by her ear. Pearl Phoenix fell facedown from the chair, quickly scrambled to her feet, and stood to one side. She pressed her lips together and swallowed hard but dared not cry.

Fortunately, Mama Zhao came to hurry them up, announcing, "The carriages are here."

Only then did Green Phoenix leave Pearl Phoenix alone. She picked up the clothes on the bed and said with a frown, "I'm not wearing this." She told Mama Zhao to open the wardrobe and picked for herself a padded silk jacket of pale bamboo green woven with golden peonies and matched it with a pair of lined trousers of pale pink crepe with wide satin pipings and lace trimming. The combination was eye-catching yet in good taste. Prosperity stared at her, bewitched.

After Mama Zhao had folded away the other suit of clothes, she turned to him, "Would you like to put your jacket on?"

Suddenly feeling self-conscious, Prosperity took his jacket, draped it over his shoulders, and said, "I'm going down first." He slipped downstairs right away, telling Promotion to come along.

Two carriages with leather tops stood at the entrance to the alley. He got into the one in front. Then Mama Zhao came out carrying the silver water pipe, followed by Green Phoenix and Gold Phoenix, who sauntered hand in hand to the second carriage. Promotion also got on the footboard at the back of Prosperity's carriage. The wheels started rolling, and the carriages dashed off at great speed.

CHAPTER 9 :: *Little Rouge fells Constance with her fist, and Green Phoenix engages Prosperity in a battle of words*

As the two horse carriages came to the turning at First Avenue, they saw an old-fashioned hard-top carriage dashing westward in their direction. It happened to fall in alongside Prosperity's carriage. He turned to look and saw through the window Lotuson Wang and Constance sitting together. Seeing each other, the two men nodded and smiled. When they drew near Mud Town Bridge, the driver of the hard-top applied the whip and charged ahead to cross the bridge. The other horse, seeing there was a carriage in front leading the way, followed in like fashion and raced forward, gaining momentum from the downhill slope of the bridge to gallop toward Bubbling Well Temple. In no time at all, they had arrived at Luna Park, where the carriages filed in and stopped by the steps in the outer courtyard.

Prosperity Luo and Lotuson Wang alighted, exchanged greetings, and, together with Constance, Green Phoenix, Gold Phoenix, and Mama Zhao, went upstairs. Promotion, knowing there wouldn't be anything for him to attend to, remained behind. Lotuson Wang preferred the front terrace, which was light and airy, so the two men each took a table by the balustrade to admire the distant views, drink tea, and chat. Lotuson Wang asked Prosperity Luo why he had given another party the previous night at Green Phoenix's. Prosperity gave a brief account of things. Then he asked how Lotuson had got to know Constance and where she had come from, and Lotuson filled him in.

"You've got some nerve, I must say! What if Little Rouge gets to know about this?" asked Prosperity Luo.

Lotuson said nothing, just smiled and made a face.

Green Phoenix, trying to lighten things up, said, "What you say of Mr. Wang is not like him at all! If he had such fear of his girl, what would he be like in front of his wife?"

"Have you seen the two plays about henpecked husbands called *In the Boudoir* and *Kneeling by the Pond*?" asked Prosperity.

"Maybe it's because you're used to kneeling, that's why it's always uppermost in your mind," she retorted. This made both Lotuson and Constance laugh.

Prosperity Luo also laughed. "That's enough nonsense for now."

They sat or stood around admiring the scenery. In the garden, the lawn was like embroidery, and the peach blossoms had just started to bloom. The song of the yellow linnets seemed to tease out the essence of spring unique to the area south of the Yangtze. To top it all, this was a clear, bright Sunday with a mild breeze, perfect for outings. The garden was full of people who had come to take a walk and show themselves off or to shake off the pall of winter and admire beautiful women. There was a constant noise of rolling wheels and neighing horses. Some thirty or forty carriages came one after another, their occupants filling the tables in the various pavilions and terraces. The finest hairpins and hats were on display, and men and women behaved freely in mixed company. Where the wine fumes had melted away, the aroma of brewing tea wafted in the air. Not even the gatherings in Buddhist paradise could rival such gaiety.

A handsome young man suddenly appeared on the scene. He had on a sleeveless jacket with a cutout cloud pattern and heavily embroidered slip-on leggings with broad pipings. He headed straight for the front terrace, where he stood staring at Constance and then smiled to himself. Constance, a little annoyed by this, turned and looked away. Lotuson recognized the young man as Little Willow, the young martial male lead of the Panorama Theatrical Troupe, and so paid him no attention. After a while, Little Willow went away.

Green Phoenix walked arm in arm with Gold Phoenix over to the railing, where they leaned forward to look at the incoming carriages. After a while, she suddenly beckoned to Prosperity Luo, "Come and look."

Prosperity looked down and saw none other than Little Rouge getting out of a carriage in the front courtyard. She was dressed in casual old clothes, her hair not even done up. He hastily signaled Lotuson and whispered, "Little Rouge is here."

Lotuson hurried over to see for himself, asking, "Where is she?"

"She's coming up," Green Phoenix replied.

Lotuson turned around, thinking he'd go down to meet her, but Little Rouge had already come upstairs. With her eyes glaring straight ahead and her forehead all greasy and sweaty, she was panting for breath as she charged toward the front terrace, followed by her maid, Pearlie, and the servant girl Goldie. Colliding with Lotuson Wang head-on, she did not say anything, just pointed a finger at his temple and jabbed him hard. Lotuson half turned to fend off the attack, and this gave Little Rouge her opportunity. She stepped forward, seized Constance by the front of her clothes, and started to pummel her with her fist.

Completely taken by surprise, Constance could neither give her the slip nor ward her off. All she could do was grab hold of Little Rouge and fight back, shouting, "Who are you lot? How can you beat up somebody with no reason at all?"

Little Rouge said not a word, just kept pummeling Constance in complete silence. The two women were twisted together like a knot. Seeing the fury of the onslaught, Green Phoenix and Gold Phoenix retreated to the room behind the terrace; Mama Zhao could not very well come forward to make peace either. All Prosperity Luo did was to bawl at Little Rouge, "Let go. We can talk things over peacefully."

Would Little Rouge let go when she had the upper hand? She pushed Constance from the center table all the way to the western end of the terrace. What was more, Pearlie and Goldie were secretly helping her, getting in a blow here and a blow there. People who were drinking tea downstairs all came up to watch when they heard there was a fight.

This was too much for Lotuson. He went forward, hooked an arm around Little Rouge, and tried to pull her away, but it didn't work. Then he wedged his body between the two women and gave Little Rouge a violent push. Little Rouge staggered backward several paces and just managed to keep her balance when her back hit a partition wall. Free at last, Constance stood in the middle of the room weeping and cursing at Little Rouge. Little Rouge tried to make a rush at her, but Lotuson pinned her against the wooden partition and tried to reason with her in a torrent of words. "If you have anything to say, say it to me. It's got nothing to do with her. What did you hit her for?"

All this fell on deaf ears. Little Rouge started biting and pinching him, while Lotuson continued to beg and reason with her despite the pain. Just then, Pearlie made a surprise attack from one side, pulling at Lotuson and shouting, "Whose side are you on? Shame on you!"

Goldie rushed up and held Lotuson round the waist. She also shouted, "So you're taking someone else's side against our maestro! Are you disowning her?"

With her two serving women tackling Lotuson, Little Rouge broke free and flung herself after Constance, resuming the fight. Lotuson, pinned down by the two servants, could do nothing to separate them.

Constance was no match for Little Rouge even under normal circumstances; now that Little Rouge was going at her for all she was worth, every blow was aimed to kill. In no time at all, Constance was stretched out on the floor with blood on her face and one of her lotus shoes fallen off. She still managed to keep up a stream of tears and curses. Spectators now packed the front terrace like swarming bees, but not one person lifted a finger to intervene.

Lotuson realized this would not do. In desperation, he flung aside Pearlie and Goldie, parted the onlookers, and went downstairs to call for help. It happened that the cashier of Luna Park was standing at the door of his office peering around. Lotuson knew him and said hurriedly, "Quick, call a couple of waiters to separate them, or else somebody's going to get killed!" Having said this, he pushed his way back onto the front terrace. He saw that Little Rouge had actually got Constance spread-eagled on the floor, and was sitting astride her, pummeling her furiously. Pearlie and Goldie, one on either side, held Constance's arms down so she could not move. Constance could only kick her feet about, yelling, "Help! Murder!" The spectators also shouted in unison, "Stop! You'll kill her!"

Lotuson's anger flared up. He gave Goldie a kick in the chest. It sent her yelling and rolling all over the floor. Pearlie quickly scrambled to her feet and rushed at him, shouting, "Shame on you! How dare you beat us, you animal!" She rammed her head against his chest, shouting repeatedly, "Come beat me! Come on!"

Lotuson lost his balance and fell backward, landing head first right on top of Goldie. Pearlie, who was ramming at him, also lost her balance and toppled forward, sprawling over him. The five of them thrashing about on the floor in a tangle sent the spectators clapping and roaring with laughter.

Fortunately, three or four waiters now came up with a foreign policeman, who barked at them, "Stop fighting!" Pearlie and Goldie immediately scrambled to their feet. Lotuson was helped up by a waiter, while another waiter pulled Little Rouge aside and then helped Constance sit up on the floor.

Frustrated by the waiters' intervention, Little Rouge finally started wailing in the most grief-stricken manner, stamping her feet on the floorboards as if they were a drum. Both Pearlie and Goldie joined her in name-calling. Lotuson, paralyzed by anger, could not get a word out. It was left to Mama Zhao to look for Constance's shoe and put it back on for her. With a waiter's help to prop her up, she slowly walked her to the room behind the terrace for a rest. The policeman waved his truncheon threateningly to disperse the bystanders. He then pointed to the staircase, indicating that Little Rouge should leave. She dared not defy him, and together with Pearlie and Goldie wept and cursed all the way down. They got into their carriage and went home.

Too busy to bother with Little Rouge, Lotuson hurried into the room behind the terrace to see Constance. He found the cashier, Prosperity, Green Phoenix, and Gold Phoenix huddled together in conversation. Constance lay stretched out stiffly on the couch, while Mama Zhao tried to do up her hair for her. Lotuson hastened to ask how she was.

"She's lucky. Just minor injuries to the ribs; nothing serious," Mama Zhao replied.

"Though it's not serious, it was risky enough," the cashier commented. "Why didn't she bring a maid with her? With a maid there, she'd have had some protection when she was cornered."

This gave Lotuson something else to worry about. After a moment of hesitation, he begged Green Phoenix to lend their maid Mama Zhao as an escort to take Constance home.

"Mr. Wang, you really should take her home yourself," said Green Phoenix. "Think about it: when she goes home in such a state, will her maids and menservants let it go at that? If they gather up a dozen people and rush over to seek revenge at Little Rouge's, they may cause real trouble, and it'll all end up on your plate, Mr. Wang. If you go back with Constance now, you can explain things to them first. Don't you think so?"

"That's right. It's best if you take her home yourself," the cashier chimed in. Yet Lotuson did not want to take Constance home, and he couldn't come up with a good reason. He just pleaded with Green Phoenix to let Mama Zhao do it.

Finally, Green Phoenix had to agree. She then instructed Mama Zhao, "You go and tell them: Mr. Wang will see to this business. They're not to take things into their own hands." Then she added, "Isn't that so, Constance? You should put in a word, too."

Constance nodded in agreement.

"Shall I call the carriage?" Promotion asked at the door.

"Get all our carriages while you're at it," said Mama Zhao.

Promotion went out at once to do so. Mama Zhao handed the silver water pipe to Green Phoenix and went to help Constance off the couch. Constance looked at Lotuson and tried to speak but couldn't find the words.

Lotuson said hastily, "Please don't be upset about this. You should go home in a good mood and think of this as nothing more than getting bitten by a mad dog. If you let it upset you and fall ill, that won't be worth it. I'll come round later; don't worry."

Constance nodded again and, supporting herself on Mama Zhao's shoulder, struggled down the stairs step by step.

"Take her jewelry along," said the cashier.

Lotuson saw there was a heap of broken ornaments on the table and realized they had been damaged during the fight. "I'll put them away for her."

Then a waiter brought Constance's silver water pipe, saying, "This fell downstairs and got dented."

Lotuson Wang wrapped it up in a towel with the jewelry.

"Let's go, too," Green Phoenix hurried everyone up and, taking Gold Phoenix by the hand, led the way out.

Lotuson saluted the cashier and thanked him. "All the damaged furniture will be paid for according to usual practice. I'll show my appreciation of your men's help separately."

"Oh, please don't mention any damages; they're nothing, really," the cashier replied.

Prosperity Luo also took his leave from the cashier and went downstairs with Lotuson. They found out from Promotion that Constance and Mama Zhao had already left, while the Huang sisters were still waiting in their carriage. Lotuson rode with Prosperity back to Generosity Alley, where Prosperity invited him into Green Phoenix's. When they reached her room upstairs, Prosperity lit the opium lamp and invited Lotuson to smoke.

Green Phoenix, who was changing into an at-home outfit, said, "Mr. Wang, you haven't smoked for a few hours now. It must be getting to you, right?" She then turned to Little Treasure, "After you've prepared the hot towels, get Gold Phoenix to fill the pipe for Mr. Wang."

"I can do it myself," said Lotuson.

"We've got some ready-made pellets, will they do?" asked Green Phoenix. She then told Little Treasure to have Gold Phoenix fetch them.

Gold Phoenix had also changed her clothes. She now came over to greet Lotuson and, as soon as she saw him, said with a smile, "Aiyo, Mr. Wang! The whole thing frightened me to death. I was so afraid I hung on to Elder Sister and said, 'Let's go home. What if they should start beating us as well?' Weren't you frightened, Mr. Wang?"

Even Lotuson could not help smiling at this. Prosperity and Green Phoenix both laughed.

Gold Phoenix picked up from the opium tray a box of water buffalo horn shaped like a crab apple blossom. The box was filled with opium pellets, and she offered them to Lotuson. He heated a pellet and started smoking. After he had smoked several pellets, he heard Mama Zhao's voice downstairs and sat up to listen.

Seeing his anxiety, Green Phoenix hastened to call out for Mama Zhao.

When Mama Zhao saw Lotuson, she reported, "I took her home, saw her all the way upstairs. Her people said, 'Since there's Mr. Wang to see to things, that'll be for the best. Please ask Mr. Wang to come over as soon as he's back.' They thanked me, too, and told me to come back and thank our maestro. Very nice and warm they were."

On hearing this, Lotuson felt that half his burden had been lifted. Then his steward Talisman came looking for him. Lotuson called him in to ask what the matter was.

"Little Rouge's maid came just now to say that Little Rouge is coming to the house," said Talisman.

This made Lotuson extremely uneasy again.

Green Phoenix said to him, "It seems to me Little Rouge is not the same as Constance. It may be all right for you to see Constance tomorrow instead of today, but as far as Little Rouge is concerned, you should go and see her straightaway. And what's more, you'll be in for a good chiding as well."

Lotuson hesitated, his forehead creased with a deep frown. He said nothing.

"Mr. Wang, you mustn't be afraid to see Little Rouge," Green Phoenix said pleasantly. "If there's anything you want to tell her, say it loud and clear. If you're afraid of her, you won't be able to say anything."

Lotuson still procrastinated. He told Talisman to fetch his sedan chair, saying he'd decide what to do later. But he gave Talisman the package of jewelry for safekeeping. Talisman took it and went home.

"I'd never have thought that Little Rouge could be so fierce!" said Prosperity Luo.

"What's so fierce about Little Rouge?" asked Green Phoenix. "In her place, I wouldn't have gone and beaten Constance up. For one thing, you tire yourself out with the beating, and all that jewelry that gets smashed will go on Mr. Wang's account, so it's Mr. Wang who ends up the loser. What's the point?"

"What would you do if you were her?" asked Prosperity.

"Me? I don't feel like telling you now. You might like to drop in on Lute, though, and then you'll see for yourself. How about that?"

"What if I do go, what can you do?" Prosperity said smiling. "If you act up I'll tell Lute to come and give you a beating, too!"

Green Phoenix gave him a fleeting glance out of the corner of her eyes and then said with a faint smile, "Aiyo, well said! I wonder whose benefit that's meant for? Are you showing off in front of Mr. Wang?"

Lotuson, who was inhaling a puff of opium as Green Phoenix spoke, nearly choked with laughter.

In his embarrassment, Prosperity felt he had to say something to hold his end up. He said, "You people are so unreasonable! Think about this: as a courtesan, how many clients do you entertain? And yet you won't let your clients see another girl. Is that reasonable? It's a wonder you people can say something like that and not feel ashamed of yourselves."

Green Phoenix responded with a smile, "But why not? We're in this business so we can't help it. If you're willing to secure my business for a whole year, all three seasons of it, then I'd drop all other clients. I can assure you that'd make me very happy."

"Ah, so you want to milk me alone!" he said.

"If I see no one else, who else can I milk? Who's being unreasonable now?"

Prosperity was stumped for a reply. After a while, Green Phoenix said, "If you have reason on your side, out with it. Why are you so quiet?"

"What's there to say? I've had enough of your barbed tongue," he said light-heartedly.

"It was you who didn't do your case justice, so don't blame it on my barbed tongue!" Green Phoenix was all smiles.

In the course of the conversation, the lamps had been lit. Little Treasure came in with a printed slip for Prosperity Luo. He looked at it and passed it on to Lotuson Wang, who took it rather nervously. It was Benevolence Hong inviting Prosperity to a party, so he paid no attention to it. But then he saw another line added at the end: "If the esteemed Mr. Lotuson Wang is there, his company is also requested." Lotuson said with a frown, "I'm not going."

"Benevolence seldom gives a party, so it's best if you go and mingle for a while. You don't *have* to call any girls," Prosperity said.

Green Phoenix also gave him her advice. "Mr. Wang, I think you should go to the party. If you don't, you'll be laughed at by Little Rouge and her people. I suggest that you act as if nothing has happened and just go to the party as usual. And then you can arrange with a couple of friends at the party to go with you to Little Rouge's afterward. What'd you think?"

Lotuson knew she was right and decided to follow her suggestion. He hastily smoked a couple more opium pellets before his departure. Meanwhile, Talisman had come with his sedan chair as well as an invitation from Benevolence Hong.

"Let's go together," said Prosperity.

Lotuson gave his assent, and Prosperity called out to summon Promotion. "Your sedan chair is waiting, sir," Promotion reported.

So Lotuson and Prosperity went in their sedan chairs to Twin Pearl's in Sunshine Alley. Benevolence Hong welcomed them upstairs and, seeing that everyone had arrived, told the maid Golden to call for hot towels and then invited them into the room. The guests who had already arrived included Elan Ge, Cloudlet Chen, Whistler

Tang, and two strangers—Rustic Zhang and Simplicity Zhao. Introductions were made, and they all saluted each other and urged each other to take the seat of honor. Meanwhile, the menservants had come with the hot towels.

"Who are you calling?" Whistler Tang hastened to ask Lotuson Wang.

"I don't want a girl," said Lotuson.

"Why not?" Twin Pearl broke in.

"Perhaps you should call a virgin courtesan," Benevolence Hong suggested.

"I'll introduce one to you, guaranteed to be excellent," said Whistler Tang. He pointed, "Look."

Lotuson Wang turned around and saw there was a virgin courtesan sitting next to Twin Pearl. The girl lowered her head shyly and did not look up again.

Prosperity Luo walked over to take a look at the girl. "I thought it was Twin Jewel, but it isn't."

"She's called Twin Jade," said Twin Pearl.

"A girl from the house is good. Let's put her name down," said Lotuson.

Benevolence Hong waited for Whistler Tang to finish writing the call chits and then asked everyone to come to the table.

The servant girl Clever Baby, who was standing beside Twin Jade, asked, "Would you like to go and get changed?" At this, Twin Jade got up and turned to leave the room.

CHAPTER 10 :: *A new girl is given strict instructions at her toilet, and old debts are lightly dismissed by a hanger-on*

After Twin Jade had gone to her own room, Clever Baby came in after her, asking, "Did Mother give you party clothes?"

Twin Jade shook her head.

"I'll go and ask for you. Now you comb your sidelocks." Clever Baby then hurried downstairs to consult with Orchid Zhou.

Twin Jade moved the paraffin table lamp to the dressing table but, instead of attending to her sidelocks, sat down on the bed and inclined her head to listen. Her room was directly above that of the madam's, while the room that Twin Jewel had moved into was under Twin Pearl's.

Now she heard Orchid Zhou tell Clever Baby to hold the lamp while she opened the wardrobe and the trunks. After a lot of rummaging and murmuring, they left the room and headed for Twin Jewel's. Twin Jade had no idea what that was about, and she couldn't hear anything at all. Only then did she give up and settle herself in front of the mirror. She found that her sidelocks had come loose, so she picked up a small brush and smoothed the hair down with a few light strokes. Now Clever Baby came in with the party clothes in her arms, followed by Orchid Zhou. Twin Jade put down the brush, ready to get changed.

"Wait a minute," said Orchid Zhou. "Your hair's no good. It looks all fuzzy!" She put down the nutmeg box she was holding to fix Twin Jade's hair for her. She twirled and pulled at Twin Jade's sidelocks and then sank the hairbrush into a basin of water soaked in wood shavings and worked it through her hair and bangs. The water from the brush dripped down Twin Jade's neck, and her forehead glistened with water marks. Twin Jade reached a hand up to wipe them off, but Orchid Zhou stopped her at once, saying, "Don't." She then lightly pressed a towel on Twin Jade's face and neck and told her to turn around. After careful scrutiny, she said, "That'll do."

Clever Baby held the clothes up and helped Twin Jade change into them. The padded silk jacket had a pale turquoise background and pipings with a woven pattern of gold potted orchids.

"I don't think I've seen this one before," Clever Baby said.

"How could you have seen it? Now you mention it, this was the eldest maestro's," replied Orchid Zhou. "My three girls are all a bit odd. Be it clothes or jewelry, they only wanted things bought with money they'd earned and would never touch anything that had belonged to someone else. Twin Pearl has a good collection of jewelry, but if we just look at clothes, there's no way she can compare with her two elder sisters. They had so much more! When they got married, they only took the things they liked best, and what was left was enough to fill several trunks. I packed them away and never had any use for them, for who else was there to wear them? I did give a few things to Twin Jewel to wear, but that didn't even scratch the surface. There's still a lot that Twin Jewel hasn't seen, let alone you."

Twin Jade put on the padded jacket, walked a few steps toward the full-length mirror, and held up an arm to see whether the jacket fit. Orchid Zhou went over to smooth out the crinkles on the side and began nagging again, "You should aim high and work hard to please your clients, understand? In my eyes, there's no difference between my own girl and an adopted girl; they're all my daughters. If you follow the example of your elder sister Twin Pearl, all these clothes and jewelry left by Eldest and Second Maestro are yours to pick and choose from. But if you end up like Twin Jewel, even if you were my own daughter, I wouldn't give you anything."

Twin Jade listened to this silently, so Orchid Zhou asked her, "Did you hear what I said?"

"Yes."

"Then answer me. Why didn't you utter a sound?"

Clever Baby could hear that the outside girls called to the party had all arrived. She hastily took the nutmeg box, hurried them up, and managed to cut Orchid Zhou short. Holding Twin Jade by the arm, she was about to go when she suddenly remembered that the girl needed a silver water pipe. "Let's just get one of Third Maestro's," she said.

"No," Orchid Zhou said. "Go and get Twin Jewel's. Let her use that. I'll get another one for Twin Jewel."

Clever Baby rushed off to get the water pipe, while Orchid Zhou continued to instruct Twin Jade about rules and manners at the dinner table. "If there's anything you don't know, ask your elder sister. You should pay attention to everything Elder Sister says. If you don't, it's you who'll suffer for it, and it'll all end badly for you. Don't say I haven't warned you in advance."

Twin Jade made an affirmative noise to everything she said. Shortly, Clever Baby came back with the silver water pipe, and Orchid Zhou went downstairs. Clever Baby hurriedly took Twin Jade to join the guests in the other room. They saw that one girl was already there; it was Cloudlet Chen's girl, Clever Gem, who lived by the entrance of Co-security Alley. Since she only had to cross Third Avenue to come over, she came on foot and was early. As they walked in, Clever Gem had just started singing an aria from Beijing opera. This put Prosperity Luo in excellent spirits, and he started a finger game with himself as banker. Simplicity Zhao and Rustic Zhang, who did their best to get into his good book, showed much energy and gaiety. The others went along with them, except Lotuson Wang, who was so restless he could hardly sit still. Twin Pearl knew he was bored. "Would you like to go and sit a while in the other room?" she asked.

It was exactly what he wanted, so he left the table instantly. Clever Baby led the way over to Twin Jade's room, lit the opium lamp, made him some tea, and said, "I'll go get Twin Jade."

She was gone before Lotuson could stop her. Now Twin Jade came unobtrusively back into her room, changed her top clothes, and sat down solemnly a long way from him, keeping him company in silence. Naturally, he did not try to engage her in conversation. In a moment, Clever Baby rushed in to see to things, told Twin Jade to entertain him, and then went away again.

He smoked a couple of opium pellets and was somewhat irritated by the noise of the finger game and singing in the next room. The way that Twin Jade just sat there quietly, with her head bowed, her feet tucked under her skirt, and her hands playing with her hand-kerchief seemed most appealing to him. He sighed and couldn't help but admire her sensibility.

He suddenly heard the maid Golden come out to the landing and call loudly for hot towels. In a moment, there was the patter of men and women walking around, the sound of curtain hooks, and the voices of guests and host taking leave of each other, all mixed up together. He had no idea who had left, but it certainly became a lot quieter. Then Whistler Tang ambled over to the room, his face bright red from drinking. Picking his teeth with a toothpick made from willow, he lay down casually on the humbler side of the divan to watch Lotuson heat up the opium.

"Is Prosperity gone?" Lotuson asked.

"They've got another engagement; he's gone with Elan and Cloudlet."

So Lotuson asked Whistler and Benevolence Hong to go to Little Rouge's with him. Whistler understood and promised to go. They did not return to the table until Clever Baby came to invite them to have rice. Whistler Tang whispered something in Benevolence Hong's ear, whereupon Benevolence smiled.

Twin Pearl also nodded and smiled. "I have some idea of what this is about."

"Do tell; let's see if you're right," said Whistler.

Twin Pearl jerked her head toward Lotuson. Everyone smiled, and they finished their rice. Rustic Zhang knew they had something afoot, so he and Simplicity Zhao said good-bye and left.

"Let's go, too," said Lotuson Wang.

Whistler Tang and Benevolence Hong answered in the affirma-tive, so Twin Pearl hastened to call Twin Jade over and they saw the guests off at the head of the stairs.

The three men walked leisurely ahead, and Talisman told the sedan-chair bearers to bring the empty chair in their wake. They came out of Sunshine Alley and went down Co-security Alley into West Floral Alley. Here, they were spotted by the maid Pearlie's son. The boy ran off to report it, and Pearlie came out the door in wel-come, saying with a grin, "I was just saying Mr. Wang should be here soon, and here he is."

Lotuson led the way in, followed by Whistler Tang and Benevolence Hong. Pearlie brought up the rear, and they all filed up the stairs. As they came up, they heard the sound of high-heeled bound-feet shoes making a racket in the room. When Lotuson came through into the middle room, Little Rouge, with unkempt hair and a dirty face, rushed out and sprang at him like a monster possessed. He backed away, flabbergasted. The servant girl Goldie dashed forward and put her arms round Little Rouge, restraining her from behind and yelling, "Maestro, don't!"

Thoroughly alarmed, Pearlie rushed forward to pin down Little Rouge's arms, also yelling, "Maestro, not so quick, wait and see!"

Little Rouge gnashed her teeth. "Let go of me! I want to die! What's it got to do with you?"

Pearlie tried to calm her down. "Even if you die, it shouldn't be like this. Now that Mr. Wang is here, you should at least hear him out. If you don't like what he says, there'll be time enough to kill yourself."

But Little Rouge, set on having it out with Lotuson, was not about to give up. Seeing her make such a scene, Whistler Tang and Benevolence Hong couldn't very well say anything, so they just smiled ironically. Lotuson, a prey to shame, anger, and fear, became quite desperate. The pressure actually brought out his temper. He sneered and said, "Fine, just let her die!" Then he turned around to leave. Whistler Tang and Benevolence Hong could only follow him.

This looked bad to Pearlie, who immediately let go of Little Rouge to try and detain Lotuson. With a fling of his arm, Lotuson freed his sleeve from Pearlie's grasp and went down the stairs.

Suddenly there was a loud banging against the partition wall in the middle room. The noise shook the house. Goldie could be heard shouting desperately, "Oh, no! The maestro is battering herself to death!"

That alone was enough to rouse three or four menservants downstairs. Thinking some disaster had struck, they ran upstairs, blocking the way for Lotuson and the others. Pearlie pulled and hauled at Lotuson with all her might, dragging him back. Whistler Tang and Benevolence Hong realized that there was no getting away, so they, too, urged Lotuson to go back upstairs. There, they saw Little Rouge still trying to knock her head against the partition wall, while Goldie held her across her chest from behind to pull her away, but to no avail. Nearly frantic, Pearlie grabbed Little Rouge around the waist and lifted her off the ground.

"Little Rouge, what d'you mean by this?" Whistler Tang and Benevolence Hong said in unison. "Whatever you want to say, just say it. Acting like this is beneath you, you know that."

Pearlie felt Little Rouge's head and found she wasn't really hurt. One side of her forehead was scratched by a nail on the wall, but it was a mere scrape, and she wasn't bleeding. Goldie rubbed it with her palm, saying, "That was close! What if the nail had hit your temple?"

Lotuson just stood on one side, at a loss. Pearlie gave him a contemptuous look and said, "Mr. Wang, if anything happens, you'll be in it too. Don't take this lightly."

The menservants, seeing that it was nothing serious, all smiled. "You surely scared us to death. Quick, help the maestro into her room."

Pearlie carried Little Rouge in her arms, while Goldie dragged Lotuson, Whistler Tang, and Benevolence Hong along, and they all went in. Pearlie lay Little Rouge down on the divan. Goldie set out the teacups and told the menservants to make tea.

"Now be careful, you two," the menservants said to Pearlie before they went downstairs, smiling sheepishly.

Lotuson, Whistler, and Benevolence sat down in a row of chairs along the wall. Little Rouge turned to the wall, covered her face, and wept. Pearlie sat down beside her and said to Lotuson in a measured voice, "Mr. Wang, it really is your fault; you figured it out wrong. If you had told our maestro right from the start, it wouldn't have mattered even if you were to take up with ten Constances. But you kept it from her, and that did it. When our maestro learned that you were with Constance, she said, 'I just know Mr. Wang won't come to us ever again. Constance's people have dragged him off... .' "

Benevolence Hong cut her short. "Mr. Wang only gave a party at Constance's last night, and now he's back here at your place."

Pearlie stood up, walked over to Benevolence Hong, and said in a low voice, "Mr. Hong, you're a most understanding person. Our maestro is not to blame really; she's at the end of her tether. When Mr. Wang first started to see our maestro, we had several long-term clients. But when she fell in love with Mr. Wang, some of them got angry and stopped coming. We wanted to invite them to come back, but Mr. Wang said to our maestro, 'If they want to stay away, let them. I'll keep your show going by myself.'—Mr. Wang, wasn't that what you said?—Having got Mr. Wang, our maestro's heart was at ease; she never even bothered to ask the others to come back, so one client after another left us. By now, there's no one except Mr. Wang. Now, Mr. Hong, do you wonder why our maestro got desperate when she learned that Mr. Wang has taken up with Constance?"

Whistler Tang took it up from there. "Don't let's talk about it now. Constance has been humiliated, and Mr. Wang is still here, so it doesn't look so bad for Little Rouge after all. Let's say no more, all right?"

Little Rouge, with tears streaming down her face, felt she had to speak up when she heard this. "Mr. Tang, why don't you ask him and see what he says? It was he who told me to get out of the business, to take my nameplate down from our door. I listened to him and turned down all the party invitations. He also said to me, 'Whatever debts you've run up, I'll pay them off for you.' I was so happy to hear that, I had eyes only for him, thinking he'd settle my debts, and I'd finally see some good days. But he has been deceiving me all along! And now he's actually cast me off and taken up with this Constance!" At this she drummed her feet in fury, pushed herself up, and started rocking her body and wailing her heart out. After a while, she said, "It's all right for him to take up with Constance, but I can't help thinking about myself: my clothes are all worn out, my jewelry pawned. With not a client left and loaded with debts, I'm left stranded. What am I to do?"

Whistler Tang replied light-heartedly, "There's nothing for you to do. Mr. Wang is still here. If you need clothes and jewelry, tell Mr. Wang to get them. If you have debts, have Mr. Wang pay the lot. Isn't everything all right?"

Little Rouge replied, "Mr. Tang, to tell you the truth, Mr. Wang has been coming here for two-and-a-half years, and everything he's ever given me is here right in front of your eyes. But with Constance, he's not been there ten days, yet he's decked her all up from head to toe. Then there're his lickspittle friends and cronies who eagerly bought her furniture and had it delivered to her new rooms. Oh, Mr. Tang, you've no idea!"

At this, Benevolence Hong cut in. "Mr. Wang certainly handled things badly. It's only right that anyone who sees a courtesan should pay the bills. But what have the courtesan's debts got to do with the client, and why should he pay them off for her? Frankly, a courtesan doesn't depend on just one client, nor does a client see just one courtesan. If one feels like it, one comes frequently; if not, one comes less often. There shouldn't be so many complications."

Little Rouge was about to retort when Pearlie hurriedly cut in, "Mr. Hong is of course right. A courtesan doesn't just depend on one client. Our maestro had several, so how come you, Mr. Wang, are keeping the show going by yourself? And even then, if you hadn't mentioned paying our maestro's debts, would she have asked you to pay them even if her debts amounted to ten thousand? It was you, Mr. Wang, who spoke to our maestro about it; *you* wanted to pay her debts for her. If only Mr. Wang had paid up, would our maestro be making any complications? Even if you take up with Constance, a client doesn't just see one courtesan—can our maestro say anything? But you, Mr. Wang, still haven't settled any of our maestro's debts, and now you've taken up with Constance. Think about it, Mr. Wang, is it our maestro who's making complications, or is it you, Mr. Wang?" Having said that, she fixed Lotuson Wang with a basilisk look. Lotuson turned his face up and said nothing.

Benevolence Hong said with a smile, "Their complications have nothing to do with us. We're going," and so saying he stood up with Whistler Tang.

Lotuson wanted to leave with them, and Little Rouge pretended not to see. It was left to Goldie to hold him in his seat, exclaiming loudly, "Uh? Mr. Wang, how can you go?"

Pearlie barked at Goldie to let go and then said to Lotuson, "Mr. Wang, go if you want to; we can't very well make you stay. We'd just mention this to you: last night, me and Goldie sat up all night with our maestro; we didn't sleep a wink. Tonight, we're going to bed. We're just maids, after all, and our responsibilities are limited. Even if anything happens, it has nothing to do with us. Now that we've said this in advance, Mr. Wang will know not to blame us."

These words put Lotuson in a dilemma. He didn't know what to do.

Whistler Tang said to him, "We'll go first; you stay a while."

So Lotuson asked him in a whisper to go and give a message to Constance. Whistler agreed, and left with Benevolence Hong.

Unexpectedly, Little Rouge got up and took a couple of steps to see them out. "You have been put through a lot of trouble. Tomorrow, we'll prepare a double-table banquet to thank you," and so saying, she laughed at her own joke.

Lotuson also felt like laughing. But Little Rouge turned around and jabbed a finger at his face several times, saying, "You . . ." She checked herself and heaved a sigh. After a long pause, she went on, "Were you afraid if you came by yourself, we'd bully you? I suppose you brought your two friends to help you, to argue on your side. It makes me so angry, it's killing me."

Ashamed of himself, Lotuson pretended to ignore her.

Pearlie sneered. "Mr. Wang is all right; it's his friends who think up these schemes for him, and Mr. Wang listens to them. Even taking up with Constance must have been his friends' doing. How else would he have met her?"

Little Rouge said, "His friends have nothing to do with Constance. He himself must have picked her up in the streets."

"But now she's a streetwalker no more; now she's passing herself off as a high-class courtesan. Hired a band for the housewarming, so grand!—Mr. Wang, how much did you spend on her these several days? Must be over a thousand," said Pearlie.

"Oh, don't talk nonsense," said Lotuson.

"It's not nonsense, though," Pearlie said as she cleaned and tidied the opium tray. "Have a smoke, Mr. Wang. Don't get any fresh ideas now."

So Lotuson went to the divan and lay down to smoke, while Pearlie and Goldie went downstairs one after the other.

Little Rouge sat silently on the humble side of the divan as Lotuson lay smoking next to her; there was no one else in the room. Almost an hour passed before she started weeping again. At a loss as to how he could reason with or console her, he decided to let her be. But then her weeping got more and more distressing and seemed most unlikely to stop anytime soon. He had no choice but to edge up close and plead with her, "I quite understand what you were getting at, so I'll do as you say. Please don't cry anymore, all right? If you go on like this, you'll break my heart."

"Don't you give me that!" Her voice was choked with tears. "You've been cheating me all along, and you're still at it now! You won't be satisfied till you've cheated me out of my life!"

"No matter what I say now, you wouldn't believe me, you'd say I was lying to you, so don't let's talk about it now. Tomorrow, I'll go and get you a bank draft to pay your debts, what d'you say?"

"Good idea. Once you've done that, you won't be coming anymore, will you? You can then take up with Constance, can't you? How clever of you! Since you're not offering to pay my debts willingly, I don't want you to do it, either." So saying, she turned away again, choking back her tears.

"Who said anything about taking up with Constance?" he said desperately.

"You mean you won't?"

"No, I won't."

She hissed in his face and shouted, "Go on, lie away! Tomorrow, I'll go and kill myself at Constance's place; you just wait and see."

Perplexed by this, Lotuson didn't know what to say and just sat there trying to figure her out. It so happened that Pearlie had come up with a water kettle to freshen up the tea. He stopped her and told her in detail what had been said and then asked, "What does Little Rouge mean?"

"I'm sure Mr. Wang understands quite well," Pearlie said smiling. "How would the likes of us know about any of this?"

"You may very well say that, but I'm asking you because I don't get it."

"Mr. Wang, you're a wise man; there's nothing you don't understand." She smiled. "Just think, our maestro has always been quite warm and loving toward you, but you have never paid her debts. Yet today, after the row, you offer to do so. Doesn't it look like you're doing it out of anger? Now if it's anger that makes you say you're going to pay her debts, d'you think she'll let you?"

He jumped up and stamped his foot in frustration. "I'd be much obliged if *she* stops being angry. How can she turn around and say *I'm* angry?"

She said smiling, "Our maestro is not angry either, except on account of Mr. Wang. Just think, does our maestro have another client? If you, Mr. Wang, should stop coming, what is she to do? As long as you do right by her, it doesn't matter even if you're also seeing Constance. You, Mr. Wang, will be the one who'll settle our maestro's debts sooner or later, so it's entirely up to you when you want to do it. Your feelings toward our maestro don't depend on this, right, Mr. Wang?"

"But it still doesn't make sense. If I don't pay her debts, naturally I'm said to be at fault. Yet when I offer to do so, she still says I'm at fault. What would she have me do to show my feelings for her?"

"Now you're joking, Mr. Wang. You don't need me to teach you that, do you?" She went downstairs carrying the water kettle, pretending to laugh all the way.

After a moment of reflection, he knew he had no choice but to soften her with tender words and a show of affection, so he waited on her with the greatest care. Seeing that Lotuson really would settle her debts for her, Little Rouge realized this was as good an ending as any and gradually stopped weeping. At last, he felt that a burden was lifted from his mind.

As Little Rouge wiped her tears with a handkerchief, she went on muttering, "You just blame me for being angry. Put yourself in my place for a moment; if you were me, wouldn't you blow up?"

"Yes, of course," he hastened to answer with a smiling face. "You have every right to blow up. If I were you, I'd be blowing up till the sun rises."

Little Rouge almost burst out laughing at this, but she managed to hold it back. "Shameless! Who's listening to you?"

She had scarcely finished speaking when a bell rang out over the city. She was the first to hear it. "Is that the fire bell?"

At this, he quickly pushed open a window to shout down, "Fire bell!"

Pearlie took up the cry downstairs, "Fire bell! Quick! Check it out!" Several menservants rushed out the door at once.

When the fire bell had stopped ringing, Lotuson had counted

four rings.[1] He went to look out from the back balcony. The moon was high up in the sky, all was quiet, and he saw no flames. When he returned to the room, one of the menservants had come back to report, "It's on East Chessboard Street."

Lotuson immediately stepped on a high-back chair and opened a window facing southeast. He saw flames through a gap between the buildings.

"Talisman!" he called out, alarmed.

"Master Talisman and the sedan-chair bearers have all gone to check it out," reported the manservant.

Lotuson's heart was beating fast.

"Why should you worry about East Chessboard Street?" asked Little Rouge.

"Why, East Chessboard Street is across the way from my house."

"There's Fifth Avenue in between," she said.

While they were talking, Talisman had come back and was calling for his master in the courtyard, reporting, "It's at the eastern end of East Chessboard Street, not far away. The police have taken charge, and we couldn't get past."

Lotuson dashed off the minute he heard this.

"You're going?" asked Little Rouge.

"I'll be back."

Taking only Talisman with him, Lotuson ran straight out of Fourth Avenue and hurried in the direction of the fire. At the entrance to South Brocade Alley, he saw Cloudlet Chen standing there alone watching the fire. Lotuson wanted to drag him along, but he replied, "What's the hurry? You're insured; what are you afraid of?"

Only then did Lotuson slacken his pace. At the street corner, they saw a foreign policeman heading up a group of people getting the leather fire hoses out, joining the sections up, and laying them flat on the ground. Then someone turned on the water hydrant and fitted a nozzle to the end of the hose. Noiselessly, the hose swelled up. They followed the line of the fire hose but were stopped by the police near Fifth Avenue. Only after Lotuson had spoken to them

: :

1. [The number of rings indicated the location of the fire. The fire services were originally made up of volunteers and financially supported by insurance companies. The first fire engine was introduced in 1863. Until the last decade of the nineteenth century, members of the fire brigade had to run the hose reels and ladder trucks to fires. In was not until 1890 that ponies were used to draw the reels. E.H.]

briefly in a foreign language were he and Cloudlet allowed to pass. The fire still seemed quite some distance away, but they could already hear loud explosive noises like thousands of firecrackers going off, and sparks rained down on them.

Lotuson and Cloudlet covered their heads with their sleeves and, together with Talisman, made a dash for the house. They saw Lotuson's nephew, the cook, and an odd-job man standing in the sheltered walkway, all eager to be the first to report: "The insurance people came to take a look. They said everything's all right and not to worry."

Cloudlet said, "Things should be all right, but you should have the insurance paper on you anyway. The silver dollars should go in the iron box, and the account books, contracts, and other papers should be tidied up and given to one person to keep. Everything else should be left as it is."

"My insurance papers are with a friend," said Lotuson.

"That's the best," said Cloudlet.

Lotuson asked Cloudlet to go upstairs and help with the packing. There came a sudden crashing noise. Lotuson knew it was the sound of a house collapsing and rushed to the window to look. The flames had leapt even higher, by well over ten feet, and were roaring in the wind. Thoroughly alarmed, Lotuson turned back to resume packing but was too unsettled to do it properly so he just threw things together anyhow. He then asked Cloudlet, "Did I forget anything?"

"Nothing that I can think of. Don't worry, I guarantee it'll be all right."

Lotuson made no reply and went back to look out the window. Suddenly, he saw balls of black smoke mixed with sparks rolling upward to the sky.

"It's all right now!" people at the door said in one voice.

Cloudlet also came to look. "The fire hose is working. The fire's going down."

Sure enough, the flames gradually subsided, and even the smoke had begun to lessen. Only then did Lotuson go back to his seat, relieved.

"What's there to worry about when you're insured?" Cloudlet asked light-heartedly. "Even your insurance company isn't alarmed enough to rush here, yet you yourself got all worked up. It's as if you weren't insured at all."

Lotuson smiled. "I knew it'd be all right, but it was still worrying to watch, wasn't it?"

Soon afterward, they heard cart wheels rolling away and the sound of air being let out of the pumps—now that the fire had been put out, the fire engines were leaving. Now Lotuson's nephew, Talisman, and the others all came back to the house, chatting along the way. Lotuson told Talisman to make tea, but Cloudlet stopped him, saying, "I'm going to bed now."

"I'll walk you out," said Lotuson.

"Where are you going?" Cloudlet asked.

"Little Rouge's."

Cloudlet asked no more questions. As they came out of the house, Lotuson's sedan-chair bearers had just brought his chair home, so Cloudlet said, "You take the chair. I'll go ahead."

Lotuson agreed and bade him goodnight.

Cloudlet looked east and saw that the scene of the fire, which had at first been belching smoke, was now enveloped in a whitish pall. He wandered over to take a look, but the hosed-down ground was dripping wet and littered with bricks and tiles. He stood downwind at one end of Chessboard Street and could feel a gush of hot air coming toward him; it was dusty, with a disagreeable smell. He hastened to turn westward and saw Talisman running after Lotuson Wang's sedan chair a long distance away. There was not a sound in the street. The full moon lent its light to the electric streetlamps,[2] making the place as bright as a crystal palace.

Strolling around by himself, Cloudlet suddenly saw an eerie figure standing bolt upright in a dark corner. He was about to give a yell when the figure walked into the light and revealed itself to be a red-turbaned Indian policeman. He felt a little ridiculous and headed back to his upstairs room in the Auspicious Luzon Lottery Store in South Brocade Alley, where his man, Constant Blessing, waited on him and saw him turn in for the night.

The next day, Cloudlet got up a little late and felt rather listless. When lunch was over, he thought he'd have a puff of opium. But where should he go? Though Amity Zhu lived nearby, he was said to be busy accompanying Script Li of Hangzhou around town and probably would not be home. Perhaps it'd be better to go to Clever Gem's, which was just as convenient. Having made up his mind, he ambled downstairs. Bamboo Hu handed him an invitation, saying it had just arrived. Cloudlet saw it was Lichee Zhuang inviting him to a dinner party at Jewel's at the Hall of Beauties. Cloudlet remembered Lichee was seeing a courtesan called Woodsy. So why would he be giving a dinner party in Jewel's room? He figured that Lichee must be acting for someone else.

Cloudlet tossed the invitation aside and went out. Instead of riding in his private ricksha, he just walked through a narrow lane hemmed in between double walls and cut across to Clever Gem's in Co-security Alley.

: :

2. [Electricity was first introduced into the International Settlement for use in the street lighting of the main roads in 1883. E.H.]

When he entered the house, Clever Gem was having her hair done in the middle room upstairs. The servant girl, Big Silver, invited Cloudlet into her bedroom and fetched the water pipe, but he told her to light the opium lamp instead.

"Would you like a smoke of opium? I'll fill the pipe for you," said Big Silver.

"Just a few small pellets will do."

By the time Big Silver had heated up the opium for him, Clever Gem's hair was done, and she came into the room to get changed. "If you're not doing anything today, I'll go for a drive with you. How about that?" she asked.

"You're still interested in carriages, are you?" he said teasingly. "Don't you know that Constance got a good beating from Little Rouge just because she went for a drive?"

"Well, they're a bunch of wimps; that's why they let themselves get beaten up by Little Rouge. Now if it were *us*, anyone who beat us up would see we're no pushovers!" she retorted.

"How is it you're in such good spirits today that you want to go for a drive?"

"It's not really a ride that I want. Last night, my sister was so frightened she came here and cried all night and didn't go back until dawn. I want to go and see if she's all right."

"Your sister is at the Hall of Spring, isn't she? The fire was so far away, what was she frightened of?"

"You sure make it sound like a breeze. If it wasn't frightening, why did all those people move out?"

"So, you want to go and see your sister and have me wait in the carriage, is that it?"

"It won't hurt if you come along to see my sister, too."

"What would I be doing there?"

"You can order some nuts and sweetmeats, same as a tea party."

Cloudlet thought that would be all right, so he said, "Let's go then." Clever Gem told her maid, Ocean, to get the menservants to hire a carriage at once. Shortly, the carriage arrived at their alley's entrance. Cloudlet and Clever Gem got in, taking Ocean with them. They told the driver to go via the Bund to East Chessboard Street, and the driver made an affirmative noise. It was no great distance, and soon they found themselves in front of the Waterscape Teahouse by the river. Ocean led the way, followed by Cloudlet, and Clever Gem walked slowly behind him. The first house in the alley was the Hall of Spring.

Cloudlet followed close behind Ocean all the way upstairs. She raised the curtain for him to enter. They saw Clever Gem's elder sister, Love Gem, sitting by the window with a needlework book open in front of her, embroidering the silk uppers of a shoe. The minute she saw Cloudlet, she smiled and said, "Mr. Chen, it's a rare pleasure having you here."

Following him in, Ocean replied in his stead, "Our maestro is here to see you."

"Oh, do come in," said Love Gem.

"She's coming," said Ocean.

Love Gem hurried out of the room to welcome her sister. Ocean asked Cloudlet to take a seat and then also went out. But now a bevy of courtesans with greasy hair and powdered faces swarmed in. They thought Cloudlet was a client who had taken the room for tea and so surrounded him, each behaving in a flirtatious and provocative manner, hoping to get his custom. Cloudlet knew exactly what they were up to but couldn't very well say anything.

Love Gem's maid happened to come in to prepare the teacups, so Cloudlet told her to order some nuts and preserves. A little taken aback, the maid then smiled and said, "Mr. Chen, you mustn't stand on ceremony."

"That's the rule for a home visit," he said, "so go and get them."

Only then did the courtesans realize they had no hope, and they all left. In a moment, Love Gem and Clever Gem walked in hand in hand, together with Ocean. The minute Clever Gem saw the needlework book on the table, she went to leaf through it, found the shoe uppers tucked inside it, and examined them in detail. After offering Cloudlet nuts and preserves, Love Gem wanted to prepare some opium for him.

"No need to be polite. I'm not smoking," he said.

She then took out a small bowl of rose jam from a drawer in her dressing table, removed a silver hairpin from her hair, put it in the jam to serve as a spoon, and invited him to eat. He felt rather overwhelmed.

Clever Gem, sensing this, said, "Sister, don't pay him any attention. He can sit by himself. Come, let's have a nice talk."

Love Gem called her maid over to keep Cloudlet company. As she put away the embroidered uppers and needlework book, she said smiling, "I'm no good at this."

"Oh, but you are. I haven't done it for three years now, so I've lost it completely. Last year, I sketched out a pattern for a pair of uppers and didn't touch it for half a month. I ended up having somebody else make them. But shoes made by others are never as good as those you make yourself."

Love Gem went and lifted the hem of Clever Gem's trousers, and Clever Gem stuck out a foot to show her the shoe.

"These shoes of yours look quite shapely," said Love Gem.

"Well, even this pair is no good. They keep poking ahead when you walk. If you were a little careless, you'd fall to your death."

"If you don't have time to do them yourself, you can have them done by others and then give them to your own shoemaker to sole. Then they'd be fine."

"I'd still like to make them myself. They'd be so much better that way."

The sisters then chatted about other things. Suddenly, they dropped their voices and whispered into each other's ear secretively. Afraid that Cloudlet would hear what they were saying, they consulted each other about going into the empty room next door.

"You wait here a moment," Clever Gem told him.

Love Gem asked, "What would you like for tea?"

"We only just had lunch," he hastened to say. "Please dispense with the formalities."

"Do have a little something."

"Sister, what's this supposed to mean?" Clever Gem put in, frowning.[3] "Would I stand on ceremony with you? If he wanted anything for tea, I'd tell you, but he's not going to eat just now."

Love Gem could not press the matter, but she signaled her maid with a glance before she went with Clever Gem into the next room.

Shortly afterward, the maid brought four kinds of snacks, set out three pairs of ivory chopsticks on the table, and invited Cloudlet to take the seat of honor. He couldn't help doing as he was bidden. Then she went to the next room to invite Clever Gem over. Clever Gem remonstrated with her sister for going to such trouble and refused to come to the table. Love Gem dragged and pulled her into the room.

Seeing there were four dishes, Clever Gem said again, "Sister, I won't have it! What's this supposed to be?"

Love Gem smiled without answering and made her sit down in the chair facing Cloudlet and then picked up a pair of ivory chopsticks to serve them.

"If you go on treating me like a guest, I won't eat any of it," said Clever Gem.

"Then you should help yourself." And she started to serve Cloudlet instead.

: :

3. [Clever Gem is a first-class courtesan, while Love Gem works in a second-class house. This explains the slight uneasiness and deference shown in Love Gem's behavior despite the fact that she is the elder sister. The way the other women in the Hall of Spring behave is typical of second-class courtesans, who have to try hard to get new customers. The scene they make is embarrassing for Love Gem. E.H.]

"I *have* been helping myself, so there's no need to serve me," he said.

"Well, you're really making yourself at home, aren't you? Aren't you a bit too forward?" said Clever Gem.

"Your sister is just like my sister. There's no need to stand on ceremony, is there?" he said laughingly.

Love Gem also laughed, "Mr. Chen does have the gift of the gab."

"Have some of this yourself, sis," Clever Gem said to her. "Or would you like us to serve you?"

Hearing this, Cloudlet immediately picked up a steamed pork dumpling with his chopsticks and gave it to Love Gem. She stood up in alarm, saying, "Oh, you mustn't, Mr. Chen!"

Clever Gem looked away and smiled. She said, "If you don't eat, then I'll join in and serve you as well."

Love Gem put the dumpling in the dish and picked up a piece of steamed cake to keep them company. Clever Gem just took a bite of a cupcake and set it down. Cloudlet, though, sampled all four dishes.

"Sometimes, I make you take tea, and you won't eat, but today you've had such a lot," Clever Gem commented.

"That's because Elder Sister took the trouble to buy us snacks. It seems we should feel guilty if we eat too little, isn't that so?"

"Mr. Chen, the way you put it embarrasses me," Love Gem said smiling. "These things are all rough and ready; they're not really very presentable."

After the maid had offered them hot towels, Ocean came in to report, "The driver has hurried us several times now. It really annoys me."

"Well, we ought to be going, now that we've had tea," said Clever Gem.

"Now you're the polite one, aren't you? And you'd go without even saying thanks for the tea. Shame on you," he said, teasing.

"So you don't want to go? Are you staying for dinner then?" Clever Gem asked with a smile.

"I can certainly afford a casual dinner, but I'm afraid Mr. Chen will never deign to accept," Love Gem said pleasantly.

Thereupon Cloudlet and Clever Gem thanked her and took their leave.

CHAPTER 12 :: *A peacemaker is dispatched behind the beloved's back, and trickery provides cover for an adulterous woman*

Clever Gem and Love Gem strolled out of the house together, chatting along the way. Cloudlet went ahead and got into the carriage while Ocean stood to one side to wait for Clever Gem. Love Gem saw them out all the way to Chessboard Street. She watched as Clever Gem was helped into the carriage by Ocean and waited till the driver set the carriage going with a flick of the whip before she turned back. Seeing it was getting dark and there was no time to visit Bubbling Well Temple, Cloudlet explained to Clever Gem and told the driver to take another turn around the Bund before going home. They came out of Fifth Avenue, turned onto First Avenue, and then went via Fourth Avenue to the entrance of Co-security Alley, where they got down and went home.

After sitting for a little while in Clever Gem's room, Cloudlet was just about to return to his shop when his ricksha man, who had brought his ricksha along, handed him two invitations. One was from Lichee Zhuang, urging him to go over soon, with two lines added at the end: "Benevolence is also coming. Please do not turn this down—much obliged." The other was from Lotuson Wang asking him to a dinner party at Little Rouge's.

Cloudlet figured that Benevolence was bound to be on the guest list at Little Rouge's, so the logical thing to do was to go to Lotuson's party first, where he could consult with Benevolence about the next step. He told his ricksha man to take the ricksha to West Floral Alley, while he himself headed for Little Rouge's on foot.

When he arrived there, he saw that aside from the host, Lotuson, there were only two guests in the room. Both were colleagues of Lotuson's at the government bureau; they were the two drunks who had brought their girls with them to Constance's party two nights before. One was named Yang, Willow to his friends; the other was Eminence Lü. Though no great friends of Cloudlet's, these two were well acquainted with him. They all greeted each other and took their seats. Shortly afterward, Talisman came back from delivering invitations and reported to Lotuson, "All the guests except Mr. Zhu say they're coming right away. Mr. Zhu is with His Excellency Script Li of Hangzhou. He sends his thanks and apologies."

Since Lotuson Wang had nothing further for him, Talisman put down the guest list and withdrew. Lotuson instructed Pearlie to have the menservants set the table. When Cloudlet looked at the guest list, he saw there were over a dozen people.

"Are you having a double table?" he asked.

Lotuson nodded in the affirmative.

Little Rouge said with a smile, "Originally we didn't know there was such a thing as a double table, but we live and learn, and now we're having a double table, too. You might say we've come up in the world."

Cloudlet Chen could not help smiling. He read the guest list from beginning to end and, to his surprise, found that it was identical to that for the party at Constance's two nights ago. He asked Lotuson Wang what this all meant, but the latter just smiled.

"I suppose it's Maestro Little Rouge's idea, don't you think so?" Willow Yang and Eminence Lü said in unison.

Only then did it dawn on Cloudlet Chen.

"That's nonsense," Little Rouge said, smiling. "When we invite friends to my place, we can only ask a few close friends to help make a good showing. We're not like other people who're important enough to get everybody to come. Take Mr. Zhu now; he's not coming, is he? That's because he looks down on me."

As they were joking, Elan Ge, Prosperity Luo, and Whistler Tang had arrived one after the other, with the Tao brothers, Cloud and Jade, following at their heels.

"Why is Benevolence not here yet?" asked Cloudlet Chen. "Maybe he's gone to another engagement first."

"No, I ran into Benevolence earlier on and sent him somewhere on an errand. He'll be here shortly," Lotuson Wang replied.

He had scarcely stopped speaking when the menservants downstairs announced, "Mr. Hong coming up." Lotuson made him welcome outside the room, and they talked in whispers for quite a while before they came in.

The minute Little Rouge saw Benevolence Hong, she got up hastily, all smiles. "Mr. Hong, please don't be angry. I haven't learned to weigh my words and so will speak out of turn. Sometimes, guests are offended and get angry, and I still don't realize it myself. Last night, I was puzzled: why did Mr. Hong leave so soon? Mr. Wang said you were offended. I said, 'Aiyo, I had no idea! Why would I want to offend Mr. Hong?' Early this morning, I wanted to send Pearlie to see you at Twin Pearl's. But Mr. Wang said, 'We'll invite Mr. Hong over later.' Do make allowances for me, Mr. Hong, out of regard for Mr. Wang."

Benevolence Hong laughed heartily. "Why should I be angry? You didn't offend me in any way, so don't make a fuss over nothing. I'm just a friend, so it doesn't matter even if I'm a bit offended. The important thing is you don't offend Mr. Wang, for if you do, it'd be no use even if I put in a good word for you."

"I'm not asking you to put in a good word for me, Mr. Hong, nor do I fear that you'd speak ill of me. But since you and Mr. Wang are friends, if I offend you, Mr. Wang would be embarrassed, too, as if he'd let a friend down. Isn't that so, Mr. Hong?"

Lotuson Wang cut in, "Let's drop that. Please take your seats."

Everybody smiled. They went out together to the middle room, and, after deferring to each other, all were seated. Cloudlet Chen asked Benevolence Hong, "Lichee Zhuang has sent you an invitation to Jewel Lu's. Are you going?"

"I didn't know about the invitation," Benevolence said, astonished.

"Well, Lichee sent me one and said you were going, too. Since Lichee is seeing Woodsy, this party at Jewel's is probably being done on somebody else's behalf."

"There's my nephew, Simplicity Zhao. He gave a dinner at Jewel Lu's before. Perhaps he's following up with another dinner tonight."

In a moment, the girls called to the party arrived one after another. Twin Pearl did bring an invitation from Jewel at the Hall of Beauties for Benevolence Hong. Simplicity Zhao was named as the host.

"Are you going?" Benevolence asked Cloudlet.

"Not me. What about you?"

"It's rather awkward for me. It's perhaps best if I don't go either." Having said that, Benevolence put the matter aside.

Seeing that several girls had arrived, Prosperity Luo wanted to be banker and start the finger game.

"You two like to get rowdy over wine," Lotuson said to Willow Yang and Eminence Lü. "We've got one here, too, of the same inclination—Prosperity—so go ahead and make a row."

"Oh, I forgot to hire a band today. Things would have been merrier with a band," said Little Rouge.

Whistler Tang said with a smile, "Is it already the yellow plum season? It's only the second month of the year; how come so many people sound so sour?"

"By the time the plums turn yellow, it won't be so bad; it's the green plums that are much more sour than yellow ones," Benevolence Hong joked, at which all the guests and courtesans burst out laughing.

To change the subject, Lotuson asked Willow Yang and Eminence Lü to hold out their fists and attack Prosperity Luo's bank. And so the feasting began, each man accompanied by his girl. Wine cups flew under the bright moonlight, and the music was heart-rending and exhilarating in turn. Everybody relaxed, so much so that the men's hats were askew and the women's hairpins fell out. In the midst of all this, the sly jokes and acid traces of jealousy were finally left behind.

When the drinking came to an end, the lamps were burning low, and the guests rose to take their leave. Lotuson saw them out one after the other but kept Benevolence Hong back and took him into the bedroom. When Benevolence asked what the matter was, Lotuson produced a package of jewelry and told him to go to the Galaxy

Jewelry Store the next day to exchange the old ones for new and then send them over to Constance. Benevolence, having promised to do that, opened the package to count the pieces and then tucked it away in his pocket. In fact, Lotuson had meant Little Rouge to see all this, but she just turned a blind eye and, after sitting around for a while, left the room and went downstairs. This suited Lotuson fine.

Left alone with Benevolence, he took out a detailed list and said in a low voice, "There are several other things on this list; just get them and have them sent over with the jewelry. Don't let Little Rouge know." Then he added, "Go and see her tonight. Ask if there's anything else she wants and just add it to the list. Please don't forget that. I'm much obliged to you."

Benevolence promised to do all that and put away the list. At this point, Little Rouge returned to the room.

"What were you doing downstairs?" Lotuson asked pleasantly.

She was a bit taken aback. "I wasn't doing anything. Why are you asking? D'you think I have somebody down there?"

"I was just asking," he said smiling. "How is it you're so super-sensitive?"[1]

She said seriously, "I thought there might have been things you didn't want to say to Mr. Hong if I sat around; that was why I went out to let the two of you talk. Didn't I do right?"

"Very thoughtful of you!" He saluted her with a smile, and she let it go at that.

Benevolence Hong figured that was all for the night and took his leave. Lotuson saw him out as far as the landing, where he repeated his instructions again and again. Benevolence went directly to Constance's in East Co-prosperity Alley and headed straight upstairs. Constance welcomed him into her room, where he took a seat and told her all about Lotuson's instructions to replace her old jewelry and get her other things. He then asked, "Is there anything else you want?"

"No, not really. Except the two rings on the list should have my name on them and should weigh an ounce each."

He told the maid to fetch an inkstone and writing brush and made a note of it on the list.

"Mr. Wang is truly good to me, but I just don't know what feuds I had with Little Rouge in my previous incarnation," she added. "What good did it do her to humiliate me?" So saying, she covered her face and wept.

::

1. Obviously, Little Rouge's lover, Little Willow, has come to the house, hence her nervous reaction.

He sighed. "You have good reason to be angry, but if you take it philosophically, the whole thing's no big deal. So you ended up on the losing end this time, but among us friends everybody sings your praises. You just keep working, and business will be good for you. Little Rouge, on the other hand, has ruined her own reputation, and no one but Mr. Wang is still close to her. Besides Mr. Wang, is there anybody who thinks well of her?"

"Some may think Mr. Wang muddle-headed, but in his heart he's quite discerning, too. Little Rouge should ask herself whether she has done right by Mr. Wang. As for me, I won't say anything about her. If Mr. Wang is to stay close to her forever, then all the more credit to Little Rouge."

He nodded in agreement. "That's the spirit, my girl." He then stood up and said, "I'm going. You take care of yourself. Don't let this ruin your health."

She saw him out, walking in graceful measured steps. "I was thinking to myself, it's not worth it to be upset by Little Rouge and die at her hands. If I just thicken my skin a little, there's nothing to be upset about—and here I am, quite happy."

"Good for you," he said as he left.

Out on Fourth Avenue, he saw the lights were getting sparse and the traffic had become quiet. It was past one in the morning. Thinking it would be more convenient to spend the night at Twin Pearl's, he turned back and walked northward to Sunshine Alley. Unexpectedly, all the houses there had already turned off their door lamps, and the alley was pitch-dark. He felt his way to the door, where a faint light shone through the gap between the panels.

He pushed the front door open and headed straight for Twin Pearl's room. She was sitting with her back against the window, playing solitaire with a set of ivory dominoes, while Twin Jade stood by the table and watched. He sat down in a high-back chair.

Twin Pearl paid him no attention. After a while, she suddenly asked, "The party broke up some time ago. Where did you go?"

"I went to Constance's," he said and told her light-heartedly how matters stood between Lotuson Wang and Constance. He then put the package of jewelry on the table.

"I thought you'd gone home. Golden and the others waited for quite a while before they went," she said.

"If they're gone, I'll wait on you," he said.

"Would you like some congee?"

"No, thanks."

Her game of solitaire was not successful, so she left it and walked over to open the package of jewelry. She looked through it before putting it away temporarily in the cupboard. Twin Jade sat down in

Twin Pearl's chair, shuffled the tiles, and started a game of solitaire herself. Suddenly there came the sound of someone at the front door and a child's voice asking, "Where's my mother?"

"She's gone home," a manservant answered from the parlor.

Hearing this, Twin Pearl hurriedly came to the window and called out, "Eldest, come up here."

The child came up at a run. Benevolence recognized him as Worth's son, called Eldest. He was only thirteen years old, and his eyes roamed the room ceaselessly, taking in everything.

Twin Pearl told him, "I sent your mother to the Qiao residence to see a client. It'll be a while before she gets back. You can wait here a bit."

Eldest made an answer and stood by the table to watch Twin Jade play solitaire. Although she did not say anything, Twin Jade immediately looked displeased. She pushed the tiles around, put them back into the box, and returned to her own room.

"Twin Jade has been here several days now. Does she ever say anything to you?" Benevolence asked.

"You've put your finger on it," Twin Pearl said with a smile. "My mother has spoken of this several times now. If you ask her a question, she'll give a brief answer; otherwise, she just sits there all day long and makes not a sound."

"Well, is she clever?"

"She's quite clever. After watching me play solitaire a couple of times, she could do it, too. Now all we need to know is how she does in business."

"It seems to me that her being so quiet makes her interesting. She'll do better than Twin Jewel at least."

"As for Twin Jewel, let's not even mention her. She's of little use herself, and yet she goes around putting other people down. And when it's time for her to speak, not a word comes out of her."

As they were chatting, Eldest moved his feet about listlessly, and when they were not looking in his direction, he slipped out and ran downstairs. When Twin Pearl turned around, he was gone. Furious, she shouted for him repeatedly. Eldest promptly reappeared.

Displeased, she barked at him, "What's the hurry? Wait for your mother and go home with her."

Eldest dared not disobey but was so embarrassed he wanted to hide himself. Yet that was not possible in the room. Fortunately, Golden came back almost immediately.

"Your son has been waiting for quite a while," Twin Pearl called out. "You'd better be off home."

Golden came upstairs and whispered a question in Twin Pearl's ear. Twin Pearl just gestured to her. Only then did Golden take her leave from Benevolence and go home with Eldest in tow.

"You with your playacting; it's so transparent," Benevolence said with a smile. "Only a child would be taken in. D'you think Worth'll be fooled? Not likely!"

"That kind of trick does smooth things over. Otherwise, when she got home, there'd be a terrible row."

"Which client did she see at the Qiao residence? Her client is in the Zhu residence. I'm afraid that was where she called on him."[2]

She snickered. "Oh, have a heart; don't talk about her now."

He smiled and let the matter drop. A night of love passes quickly, and pleasant dreams are hard to transmit, so we will not attempt to capture them in our narrative.

The next day, Benevolence Hong was going to wind up Lotuson's affairs after lunch, so Twin Pearl took the package of jewelry out of the cupboard and returned it to him. He bade her good-bye and strolled out of Sunshine Alley. As he passed through Fourth Avenue, he ran into Whistler Tang, and they saluted each other.

"Where're you off to?" Whistler asked.

Benevolence told him briefly and then asked, "What about you?"

"I'm on the same kind of errand as you. I'm to pay Prosperity's bills for him at Lute's."

"It seems the two of us have turned into peacemakers. What a joke!" Benevolence said, seeing the funny side.

Whistler laughed, and they went their separate ways. Benevolence headed for the Galaxy Jewelry Store, where the manager invited him in. After weighing the jewelry in the package, he selected the various pieces required from his stock. Everything on the list could be had ready-made except for one of the pair of rings. The one that was supposed to have a double joy—double longevity pattern he had in stock, but the other, which required the words "Constance of the Zhangs" set in a cutout square, had to be made to order and called for another day. So the ready-made ring and all the other new pieces were put into paper boxes, wrapped, and tied up. Benevolence then wrapped up everything in a handkerchief that he tied up crossways into a small bundle. He then waited for the manager to work out the total cost after deducting the value of the old jewelry. The sums were clearly written down on a sales slip, and Benevolence was asked to check it. He, however, had no time for such details and just put the slip away together with Lotuson's list, took the small bundle, and walked out the store. Thinking it was still early, he thought he'd rest a little somewhere else before delivering the jewelry to Constance.

As he was wondering where to go, he saw Simplicity Zhao come

::

2. Golden's lover, Longevity, is the steward of Amity Zhu.

running down from the north. His eyes fixed on the road, he dashed past Benevolence without seeing him.

"Simplicity!" Benevolence called out loudly.

Seeing it was his uncle, Simplicity came up in a hurry to greet him. They stood shoulder to shoulder by a white wall to talk.

"Where's Rustic Zhang?"

"Rustic and Pine Wu are together all the time. I have no idea what they're doing." Simplicity replied.

"Why do you keep giving parties at Jewel's?"

He hesitated a long while before he finally answered, "The way Lichee Zhuang and the others spoke, I could hardly refuse to play along, so I gave another dinner party there."

Benevolence sneered. "A party or two matters little, but you're not getting swindled by them, are you?"

Stumped for an answer, Simplicity just said vaguely, "It's nothing, no swindle there."

"What's the point of keeping it from me? I'm not going to lecture you," Benevolence smiled and said. "In the end, it's best if you have a mind of your own."

Simplicity dared do no more than express his agreement again and again.

"Where're you off to now?"

He had no answer to that, either.

Benevolence laughed. "What if you're going for a cup of tea at a sing-song house, what's so unmentionable about it? I'll come with you."

Afraid that Simplicity was infatuated with Jewel, Benevolence wanted to go and see how things were. Simplicity had no choice but to fall in with him.

"Coming to this international city of Shanghai and having a bit of fun is OK even if it means spending a little money," Benevolence said slowly. "Only this is not the time for you to have fun. If you have a business and are spending your own earnings, that's up to you. But that's not the case now, is it? You have nothing except what little you brought from home. It won't get you very far in sing-song houses. What if you use up your money and still have no way of making a living? How are you going to account for yourself back home? Even I wouldn't be able to face your mother."

Chilled with fear, Simplicity listened respectfully in silence.

"The way I see it, it's no easy task finding a job in a place like Shanghai. Living in an inn, your expenses can't be low. It makes no sense for you to muddle along like this. Now that you've had quite a few days of fun, you'd better go home. I'll look out for you, and if there's any job available, I'll write to send for you. What d'you say?"

Would Simplicity dare demur? He just expressed his agreement all the way, saying he should indeed go home. As they talked, uncle and nephew found they had arrived at the Hall of Beauties on West Chessboard Street. Benevolence set the matter aside for the moment and went upstairs with Simplicity.

CHAPTER 13 :: *At the deflowering of Jewel, someone waits in the wings,*[1] *and on the mah-jongg table, a trap is set for Crane Li*

When Benevolence Hong and Simplicity Zhao entered Jewel's room, she had already finished doing her hair and had just changed her clothes. The minute she saw Simplicity, she asked, "Why did you get up so early this morning?"[2]

Simplicity gave her a look to stop her from saying any more. She pooh-poohed this. "What's all this sneakiness? Others are a bit smarter than you, you know," she said, to his embarrassment.

She then turned around to make a little conversation with Benevolence. Seeing him put a parcel on the table, she snatched it, tore it open, and took out the smallest box on top to see what it was. It happened to be the ring with a double joy—double longevity pattern. She put it on without asking for permission and ran over to Simplicity, yelling, "You said there weren't any. Look, isn't this a double joy—double longevity ring?" She thrust the ring right under his nose to make her point.

"This is from Galaxy, and you wanted one from Lucky Dragon. They said they didn't have any," Simplicity answered with a smile.

::

1. [The Chinese expression literally means "waiting by the city gate." In old Chinese walled cities, all the gates were closed at night, but if an important personage needed access, a gate would be opened for him. Commoners who wanted to enter the city after curfew gathered at the gate and rushed in after the VIP. This expression was then transferred to brothel parlance to describe arrangements made to take advantage of the deflowering of a virgin courtesan. The brothel would line up several clients, making each of them believe he was being given the virgin's first night, for which they each paid a hefty sum. *E.H.*]

2. [Obviously, Simplicity spent the night with Jewel. Since she was a virgin courtesan, he must have paid for her deflowering, a fact that he is trying to keep from his uncle. His departure early in the morning suggests that Jewel had probably succeeded in frustrating his advances the night before. *E.H.*]

"How can that be? Didn't Lichee Zhuang get one from Lucky Dragon? That was the day of your first party—he said there were more than a dozen. And just a couple of days later, they're all gone? Who are you trying to fool?" she retorted.

"If you want it, you tell Lichee Zhuang to get it," said Simplicity.

"Give me the money then."

"If I had the money, I'd have got it yesterday. Why would I be saying Lichee Zhuang should get it?"

She pulled a long face. "Aren't you a sly one!" She plumped her buttocks down squarely on his thighs and rocked with all her might, demanding, "Are you going to be sly?"

Meekly, he begged to be let off.

"Get me the ring, and I'll let you off."

He just smiled, not committing himself either way.

She turned her head around, hooked an arm about his neck, and murmured, pouting, "This won't do! You go and get it." She said this several times, but he still kept silent. Getting angry, she shouted at him, "D'you dare refuse?" Simplicity got a bit irritated, too, but she just would not let go and kept wriggling her body against his as if she wanted to squeeze molten silver out of him this instant.

Just when they had reached this impasse, she suddenly heard the servant girl calling outside, "Second Miss, come quick, Young Mr. Shi is here."

She turned pale and dashed out of the room. Simplicity and Benevolence were actually left without anyone to keep them company. Benevolence took the opportunity to ask Simplicity, "What ring does Jewel want? Are you going to get it for her?"

"It was all because of Lichee Zhuang letting his tongue run away with him. At first, they wanted a pair of rings for her. I refused, so to fool them Lichee said, 'There aren't any ready-made ones. You can place an order for them in a couple of days.' That's why now she goes on and on about ordering rings."

"It's really your own fault, so don't blame it on Lichee. He's an old client of Woodsy's, so naturally he takes their side. You said Lichee was fooling them; in fact, he was fooling *you*. Don't fall for his tricks anymore, understand?"

Simplicity grunted in agreement but did not reply. Mama Yeung happened to come in to take the teacups out. Benevolence stopped her and said, "Tell Jewel to bring the ring, we're leaving."

Mama Yeung had no idea what it was about, but she said yes anyhow and went down to find Jewel. When Jewel came in and saw the expression on Benevolence's face, she hastened to say, "I'll put it back into the box for you."

"Leave that to me." He reached out for the ring, and she dared not tangle with him. Instead, she pulled Simplicity aside and said many things to him secretively. When Benevolence had repacked the parcel, he just said, "Let's go," and then turned around and walked out. Simplicity hurried out on his heels in a fluster. Jewel did not detain them, either, just made an appointment with Simplicity, "Come back later," and kept reminding him all the way to the staircase landing.

Out in the street, Benevolence asked, "Are you going to get her the ring?"

"I'll see in couple of days."

Benevolence snorted. "That means you *are* going to get it. I know what you think: you've spent a couple of dollars at Jewel's, and you don't want that to go to waste, so you figure that if you spent more, she'd warm up toward you, right? Let me tell you frankly: Jewel will never grow fond of you. You'd better put it out of your mind before it's too late. Even if you do get the ring, she'll just take you for a pushover. D'you think she will warm toward you?"

Simplicity listened and thought about it all along the way. When they were going to part at Treasured Merit Street, Benevolence stopped to say, "Even with those friends of yours, in a place like Shanghai, you have to be on guard all the time. Lichee Zhuang, for instance, doesn't really count as a friend. As for Rustic Zhang and Pine Wu, though they're from your hometown and should be reliable, they can't be depended on now they're in Shanghai. First you've got to have a mind of your own. Whatever other people say, the less you listen to them the better."

Simplicity dared not risk a single comment. Benevolence nagged him a little more and then went off by himself to deliver the jewelry to Constance.

Having bade good-bye to Benevolence, Simplicity didn't know where to go. The advice Benevolence gave him meant that he could not very well ask him for a loan. If he wanted to amuse himself in Shanghai, he had to think of a way to tide things over. Since he was at a loose end, why not look up Pine Wu for a chat? Perhaps he might run into some opportunity, one never knew. So he called a ricksha and headed for the Bund. Seeing from afar the words "The Righteous Company" on a white wall, he told the ricksha man to stop there and paid the fare. People were just laying in stock at the company's entrance, and an endless stream of coolies carrying shoulder poles filed in and out. A bespectacled man wearing a padded jacket, who looked like the bookkeeper, stood by the door staring at the Whampoo River. A coolie rested one end of his carrying pole on the ground, talking to him. Simplicity went up and saluted the man, asking, "Is Pine Wu here?"

The man made no reply, just smirked, turned his nose up, and ignored him. Embarrassed, Simplicity was about to walk away when the coolie was good enough to point him in the right direction. "If you're looking for someone, go and ask at the bookkeeper's office. This is the warehouse; there's nobody here."

Simplicity looked in the direction indicated. Sure enough, there was a low wall with another door displaying a small black lacquered sign with gold characters written on it. When he went in, he saw it was a huge foreign-style house. This was no place for him to wander about, he thought, so he just hung around, not daring to make his inquiry. Luckily, some coolies, dragging their carrying poles by one end, dashed in through a side door. He followed them and saw another small plaque with the words "The Righteous Company: Bookkeeping Office," under which was a sign of a hand with its index finger pointing inside the door.

Simplicity summoned up his courage and walked in. Inside the bookkeeping office, he saw tall counters on both sides of the room, with more than two dozen people hard at work. He approached a young apprentice and explained what he had come for. The apprentice looked him up and down and then tugged at a rope on the wall. A handyman came promptly to answer his call.

"Go and get Wu. Tell him somebody's looking for him."

After the handyman was gone, Simplicity made himself inconspicuous on one side of the room and was kept waiting until he nearly lost patience. Only then did Pine Wu dash into the office, looking very businesslike in a body-hugging Chinese suit of unbleached imported wool. When he saw Simplicity, he was a bit taken aback and then said, "Let's go sit for a while upstairs."

He led Simplicity through the bookkeeping office, around a couple of corners, and up a flight of stairs, urging him to tread lightly. Once they were upstairs, he pushed open one of a row of doors. Simplicity saw a narrow foreign-style room rather like a blind alley, piled full of various brass, iron, and glass utensils, with just a side table and a leather stool by the window.

"Have you seen Rustic?" Simplicity asked.

Pine Wu quickly held up a hand to silence him and then whispered, "You sit here a while. When I'm done, we'll go to North End together."

Simplicity nodded and sat down. Pine Wu closed the door quietly and hurried off. On the other side of the door, foreigners were coming and going all the time. The sound made by their leather shoes frightened Simplicity so much he sat bolt upright, held his breath, and broke out in a sweat.

Presently, Pine Wu pushed open the door and came in with two empty foreign bottles that he tossed on the ground, telling Simplicity, "Wait a little longer, I'm about finished." Then he shut the door again and hurried off.

It was fully an hour before he came back, already changed. He was wearing a fashionable padded jacket; even his shoes and small hat were brand new. Murmuring "Sorry to have kept you waiting," he invited Simplicity to walk ahead of him; then he locked the door, and together they went downstairs. They passed through the bookkeeping office, out a side door, and followed the road to the Bund.

"I arranged to meet Rustic in Nobility Alley. Let's go by ricksha," Pine Wu said and called two rickshas.

The ricksha men, eager to please, ran hard all the way. In no time at all, they had arrived at the entrance to Nobility Alley. Pine Wu paid the ricksha men the two stacks of coins he had counted out and led Simplicity into White Orchid's house. The maid, Sister Gold, welcomed them on the stairs, inviting them to sit in the little mezzanine room. She told Pine Wu, "Zhou and Zhang were here a while ago. They said they'd go and take a turn at the Splendid Assembly Teahouse."

Pine Wu told her to bring ink and a writing brush, and asked Simplicity to write the invitations: Mr. Crane Li at Grace Yang's. Simplicity copied this out in a neat hand according to the set form. He was just coming to the second slip when they heard the menservants shout downstairs, "Young Mr. Wu's friends are here."

Pine Wu got up abruptly and said, "No need to write anymore. They're here."

As Simplicity Zhao threw down the brush, he saw a tall bearded man with a square face and big ears walk into the room; he was followed by none other than Rustic Zhang. Simplicity saluted the stranger and asked for his name. He learned that the man was Clement Zhou, a manager in an ironworks.

"Honored," Simplicity murmured.

Everybody took a seat. Pine Wu handed the invitation to Sister Gold and told her, "Send it quick."

From her room, White Orchid heard the sounds of merriment and, thinking that all the guests had arrived, came over to entertain. The minute she saw Simplicity, she asked, "Was he the one who gave the party at the second-class house last night?"

"He's given two parties already. You were at the first one, remember?" Pine Wu replied.

White Orchid nodded. She sat with them for a while and then returned to the main room to entertain her clients.

In the mezzanine room, they chatted and waited until after the lamps were lit. Crane Li's man, Second Kuang, came to say, "Our

Eldest Young Master is having a Western meal with Fourth Master. He asked if there's anyone who can stand in for him for a while?"

"Do you play mah-jongg?" Pine Wu asked Simplicity Zhao.

"No."

"We can wait a while," said Clement Zhou.

"Would you like to have dinner first?" Sister Gold asked.

"Since they're having a Western meal, we might as well go ahead with dinner," said Rustic Zhang. So Pine Wu called for dinner.

Soon Sister Gold came in and asked everyone to go and have wine in the middle room, where a table had been handsomely laid out. The four of them deferred to each other in seating order and left the seat of honor for Crane Li. White Orchid, who had just changed into party clothes, came out of her room to pour wine for everyone at the table, but Pine Wu stopped her hastily.

"You be on your way. Don't get your clothes dirty."

And so she left it at that, saying offhandedly, "Have a good time. I'm sorry I have a dinner call." With this, she went out.

Pine Wu raised his cup and urged his guests to drink.

"If we drink, we can't play mah-jongg later. Let's just eat," said Clement Zhou.

Pine Wu urged Simplicity Zhao to drink. "You're not playing mah-jongg, so you should drink more."

"I'll have a cup or two," replied Simplicity. "Let's not be too formal."

"I'll have one to keep you company," said Rustic Zhang.

The two of them drank up and showed each other the bottom of their cups. But just when Simplicity Zhao had got into the mood for wine, Crane Li arrived. Everybody rose and invited him to take the seat of honor.

"I've had dinner. Have the four of you started playing yet?" Crane Li asked.

Pine Wu pointed at Simplicity Zhao and said, "He doesn't play, so we're waiting for you."

Clement Zhou asked repeatedly for rice to be served, and they hastily finished their meal, wiped their faces with hot towels, and returned to the mezzanine room. The square rosewood table by the window had already been moved to the center; four animal-fat candles were burning bright. The table was neatly set up with ebony mah-jongg tiles inlaid with ivory, and four lots of chips. Pine Wu asked Crane Li, Clement Zhou, and Rustic Zhang to draw lots for the seating order. Sister Gold put their teacups and the high-stemmed candy dishes on small tables to their right and left. Crane Li called for the party chits to summon girls with, and Clement Zhou wrote for him: Grace Yang of Generosity Alley.

"Anybody else?" Clement asked.

"Not me, thanks," said Rustic Zhang.

"Now Simplicity will call one," said Pine Wu.

"Since I'm not playing, why call any girls?" said Simplicity.

"Would you like to go in with me?" asked Rustic.

"That's a good idea," said Crane Li.

Rustic Zhang said, "Then write this down: Jewel, Hall of Beauties, West Chessboard Street."

Clement Zhou wrote it all down and handed the chits to Sister Gold.

"Let him take a smaller share. Otherwise, it'd be embarrassing if you lost too much." said Pine Wu to Rustic.

"Make it twenty percent," said Rustic Zhang.

"How much would that be?" Simplicity Zhao asked.

"Very little. You lose ten dollars at the most," said Clement Zhou.

Simplicity had to let it go at that, but he sat behind Rustic Zhang and watched him play one round as banker. He couldn't make head or tail of the game and so went off by himself to lie on the divan and smoke.

After a while, Grace Yang arrived, followed shortly by Jewel. "Where do I sit?" she asked Simplicity.

Pine Wu replied, "Go and sit on the divan for a while. He wants to play 'darling pairs' with you."

Jewel Lu sat down on a stool by the divan while Mama Yeung took the water pipe out of her bag and filled it. Simplicity Zhao sat up cross-legged, took the pipe, and smoked.

"Aren't you playing mah-jongg?" Jewel asked.

"I have no money, so I'm not playing," Simplicity answered.

She glanced sideways at him and sneered. "You're wasting your breath. Who's listening to you?"

He grinned. "All right, don't listen."

She pulled a long face. "Are you going to get me the ring or not?"

"Don't you see I haven't got the time?"

"You're not playing; what have you been doing all this time?"

"I have things to do, too. How would you know about them?"

Again she pouted and muttered, "I won't have it! Are you going to get it or not?"

He grinned in silence.

She poked a finger at his face and said, "If you don't bring it round later, I'll jab at your mouth with a silver hairpin; see if you can stand it."

"Don't worry, I won't come. You sound too scary." He smiled.

Hearing this, she asked in a panic, "Who said you're not to come? Let's have this out." While pressing for an answer, she clenched her teeth and pinched his thigh with all her might. He could not help calling out, "Aiya!" On hearing this, the mah-jongg players all laughed. She let go quickly.

Clement Zhou called Sister Gold over. "So you people keep a crowing cock under the table! I'd like to borrow it tomorrow." At this, everybody, including Grace Yang, laughed again.

Frustrated, all Jewel could do was curse in a whisper, "You'll die young!"

Simplicity Zhao turned his head slightly to take a peek at her. Her eyes were shiny with tears as she sat sedately, her face devoid of expression, not speaking anymore. He wanted to comfort her, but there was nothing to say. Suddenly, he saw somebody beckon to Mama Yeung through the gap in the door curtain. She went to find out what it was and then filled the water pipe for Simplicity again. He waved his hand to decline it.

"We're called to another party. Please excuse us for leaving early," said Mama Yeung.

But then Jewel whispered with her for quite a while. She then turned to Simplicity and said, "Young Mr. Zhao, you think it's Jewel who wants the rings from you. Don't you realize she'll be scolded by her mother over this?"

Jewel took over. "Think about it, yesterday you promised my mother, 'All right, go and order it.' Can I tell my mother that you're refusing to do it now? If you don't want to order it, it's fine by me, but you've got to come round later and tell my mother face-to-face. D'you hear?"

Afraid that the others would laugh at him, he said, "You'd better go; we'll leave this till later."

She couldn't very well say anything more and went away leaning on Mama Yeung's shoulder.

Crane Li said, "These second-class courtesans really have tactics of their own. They're so used to it, they aren't aware of the way they act."

Grace Yang snapped at him, "What's it got to do with you? Who're you to find fault with them?"

Crane Li smiled and dropped the subject.

Ashamed and annoyed, Simplicity Zhao went over to look at Rustic's game. As it happened, they had won a little, which pleased him. Just then, the players had finished four rounds, and they swapped seats for the next four. Crane Li wanted a smoke, so he told Grace Yang to stand in for him. However, after just playing for one round, she called out, "I'm no good, either. You come and play yourself."

"You carry on," he replied.

"I had a good hand, but no win," she said.

Simplicity Zhao peeked at their side of the table and saw that Crane Li's chips were almost gone. By the time Grace Yang finished another round, not one chip was left, and she insisted on playing no more, so Crane Li had to take over. He borrowed half a set of chips from the winner, Clement Zhou. Now Grace Yang took her leave.

Soon the game came to an end. Crane Li was the sole loser and was down by over a hundred dollars. Rustic Zhang had some winnings, so Simplicity had six dollars coming to him. Clement Zhou made an appointment for another game the next day with the same people and asked Simplicity Zhao, "Feel like coming along?"

Rustic Zhang stopped him. "He doesn't play, let's leave him out." Clement Zhou said no more.

Pine Wu asked Crane Li to smoke.

"No, thanks. I have to be going."

Sister Gold hastened to say, "At least wait until the maestro comes back."

"Your maestro is really busy, isn't she?" said Crane Li.

"She has five or six party calls today," said Sister Gold. "I'm afraid we haven't served you well today, Young Mr. Li."

"No need to apologize," Pine Wu replied pleasantly.

So the party broke up. The men left Nobility Alley together, bade one another good-bye, and went their separate ways. Simplicity and Rustic Zhang returned to the Welcome Inn for the night.

CHAPTER 14 :: *A lone whoremonger meets rough company, and a gang of conspirators runs a crooked game*

As Rustic Zhang and Simplicity Zhao approached the door of the Welcome Inn, the latter said, "I'll just look in over there. Be right back."

Rustic assented with a smile and returned to the inn alone. The inn attendant lit the lamp and brought him hot water for his tea. Rustic set out the opium tray himself to smoke his fill. But before he had taken two puffs, Simplicity Zhao was back. Surprised, Rustic asked what had happened.

Simplicity sighed. "Don't even speak of it." He then told Rustic in detail about Jewel's demand for the ring. "Just now I took a look at them on Chessboard Street, and I could see there was a party going on in her room. Clients were playing the finger game, and girls were singing. I suppose it's that man Shi."

"It seems to me there's more to it than that," Rustic said with a smile. "Think about it: You were together one day, and she's got another client lined up already? Has he been waiting in the wings? It's too much of a coincidence. You've been swindled, and so has the man Shi. Don't you see it?"

The truth suddenly dawned on Simplicity. The more he thought the whole thing over, the more likely it seemed. He was filled with regrets.

"Don't let's talk about it now. Just don't go there anymore," said Rustic. "There's something I have to tell you, too. I've got a job, right here at the Vitality Rice Shop, south of Sixteen Capes.[1] I'm moving there tomorrow. With me gone, it makes no sense for you to stay in an inn by yourself. It's best if you go home first and ask your friends to look for a job here for you. Otherwise, you may want to stay at your uncle's shop. You'll at least save on rent and meals that way, right?"

Simplicity reflected for a long while and sighed again. "You've got a job now, while I have spent all that money and haven't got a thing done."

"It's difficult to find a job in Shanghai, you know? Even if you stay here for six months or a year, there's no telling whether you'll succeed. You've got to have ideas of your own. Otherwise, when you've used up your money, you won't be able to get by, and you'll be lectured by your uncle. That wouldn't be much fun, would it?"

Simplicity realized there was much truth in that. He asked, "When you play mah-jongg, how much do you win or lose each time?"

"If the hands are no good, you could lose two or three hundred; that's common enough."

"Do you pay up if you lose?"

"Of course, you have to."

"How do you find all that money?"

"There's a lot you don't know. In a place like Shanghai, once you've made a name for yourself, everything's all right. These people whom you see socially seem to have money to throw away, but actually they're not much different from you and me; they're just better known. Without a name, there's no way of doing business, not even if you have a lot of money at home. Look at Pine Wu; he's quite penniless. But as he's not entirely unknown, it's nothing for him to see two or three thousand dollars come and go. As for me, I can't compare with him, but if I go to the bank, four or five hundred is also mine to take. You just don't know about things like that."

::

1. [Sixteen Capes and Little East Gate were two areas in Shanghai with the largest concentration of entertainment and business activities. *E.H.*]

"What's taken from the bank has to be repaid, no?"

"That you have to figure out for yourself. You can borrow some from your business, or you may run into some opportunity and make a profit. A bit here, a bit there, and it's paid up."

It sounded reasonable to Simplicity. He went on thinking about it but made no more comments. Shortly afterward, they both went to bed.

The next morning, Simplicity woke up and saw that Rustic had finished packing and had told the inn attendant to hire a pushcart. Simplicity hastened to get up and see him out to the front door, saying repeatedly, "If there's any job, do put in a good word for me." Rustic readily agreed to do so.

Simplicity did not return to the inn until Rustic and the pushcart had gone a long way away. After lunch, he was about to go out to kill time and dispel his melancholy when a manservant from the Hall of Beauties arrived with Jewel's card. Still resentful, Simplicity just handed him her fee for last night's party, but the man dared not take it. Simplicity tossed the money down and walked out. The man picked up the money and caught up with him, pleading and cajoling, but Simplicity turned a deaf ear and went off by himself. He went to Fourth Avenue and had tea on the top floor of the House of Floral Rain. After four or five refills, he felt there was not much point in staying on. Since Jewel is so heartless, he thought, it'd be better if he just amused himself with Second Wang. Thereupon he left the House of Floral Rain and headed south past the Beaten Dog Bridge to New Street in the French Concession. Here, he located Second Wang's door and went straight upstairs.

There was no one in the room. Simplicity hesitated. He was about to withdraw, but as he turned around he saw Second Wang had followed him upstairs on tiptoe and was at the head of the staircase. Delighted, he made a show of bending down to look at her, saying, "Trying to scare me, eh?"

Second Wang clapped her hands and laughed. "I was next door at Old Mrs. Guo's when I saw you walk past with your head down. I *knew* you were coming to us, so I followed and saw you come in and peer all around. It was so funny, I almost burst out laughing."

"I had no idea you were right behind me. You gave me quite a turn."

"Why didn't you see me? What're your eyes for?"

As they were talking, the old maidservant served the two usuals, tobacco and tea. Seeing Simplicity, she said with a smile, "Congratulations, Mr. Zhao!"

He asked in astonishment, "What's there to congratulate me for?"

Second Wang took it up. "Are we supposed to be kept in the dark? It happens that we know all about it."

"What do you know?" he said.

Instead of replying, she turned and said to the maid, "Listen to him. Isn't it exasperating? Does he think I'm going to be jealous, so he has to keep it from me?"

The maid guffawed. "Mr. Zhao, it's all right to tell. We can't compare with the sing-song houses, so even if you go and deflower ten girls, it's none of our business. Are you afraid our Second Miss would get jealous? If we were to get jealous, we wouldn't know where to begin."

Now he understood what they were talking about. "So it's about Jewel! I thought you were congratulating me for getting some job or other."

"How would we know whether you have a job or not?" Second Wang replied.

"Then how did you know about me and Jewel? It must be Mr. Zhang who told you."

"Mr. Zhang only came with you that one time. He hasn't been here since," said the maid.

"Mr. Zhang is not coming anymore," Second Wang said. "I'll tell you frankly: we hired a detective; that's why we know everything."

"Then do you know who stayed at Jewel's last night?" he asked.

Second Wang jerked her mouth sideways at him. "There! It was a dog."

He pooh-poohed this. "If I were there, I wouldn't be asking you."

Second Wang snorted. "Don't talk nonsense to me. Whoever heard of a deflowering client staying just one night? Who are you trying to fool?"

He heaved a sigh and replied satirically. "Is your detective deaf? Tell him to get a barber to clean out his ears before he goes to work."

Upon hearing this, she knew he was telling the truth and hastened to ask, "You weren't at Jewel's last night?"

He then related briefly to her the whole story, what Jewel suggested, how he got cheated, how the deal fell through and how they broke up.

The maid put in, "Mr. Zhao, I must say you have a good head on your shoulders. You actually saw through them. D'you know, the deflowering of courtesans in the sing-song houses is just talk. It's all fake! They do it three, four, sometimes five or six times! You don't just waste your money; you're swindled. It's not worth it."

Second Wang said, "If I'd known you'd fall for their trick, I could have claimed to be a virgin courtesan myself. I'd probably have been more convincing than Jewel."

He said with a grin, "Not with your front door, you wouldn't. Let me open a back door for you, more convenient, all right?"

Even Second Wang could not help laughing. "You! What you want is a good slap in the face."

The maid then said, "Mr. Zhao, you're partly to blame, too. If you'd listened to Mr. Zhang and just dropped in on us rather than gone anywhere else, you wouldn't have got swindled by them. Look at us, do we play any tricks on you?"

"I don't have any other place to go, as it happens," he said. "Now that I don't go to Jewel's anymore, I'll just drop in here sometimes. I wanted to come the last few days, but I thought it'd be embarrassing if I ran into Mr. Zhang. But now that he's not coming, it doesn't matter anymore."

Second Wang asked immediately, "Has Mr. Zhang found a job?"

So he told her all about Rustic Zhang having moved to the Vitality Rice Shop, south of Sixteen Capes.

The maid broke in again, "You're really too timid, Mr. Zhao. Leaving aside the fact that Mr. Zhang doesn't come here, even if he did and happened to run into you, what would it matter? Sometimes our clients come in groups of three or four. They're all friends and all our clients; it's the more the merrier for them. If you saw it, you'd be embarrassed to death!"

"Oh, you're such a coward!" Second Wang exclaimed. "Even if Mr. Zhang picked a fight, aren't you a match for him? What's there to be afraid of? If you talk about embarrassment, then we'll just have to stop doing business."

Ashamed of himself, he lay down on the divan, took the opium pipe that Second Wang had filled, and brought it to the lamp. But he did not smoke it right, and the opium flamed up and started to burn. Looking on, Second Wang found it funny. Suddenly, Old Mrs. Guo called out loudly next door, "Second Miss!"

In alarm, Second Wang said to the maid, "Go and see who's there."

The maid hurried downstairs. Simplicity paid no attention to this, but Second Wang cocked her ears to listen carefully. All she heard was the maid speaking to some people right at their own door. She talked at length but to little effect and finally called out, "Second Miss, please come down."

Second Wang clenched her teeth in vexation and cursed under her breath. She had no choice but to leave Simplicity and rush downstairs.

He did not finish the pipe but instead sat up to listen to what was going on. All he heard was Second Wang calling out in a jovial voice from the stairs, "So it's Master Constant! I was wondering who it was!" This was followed by murmured conversation that he couldn't make out, and then he heard the old maidservant calling out desperately, "Master Xu, listen to me!"

Before she could finish speaking, footsteps came up the stairs, and two burly men burst into the room. One still had a sneer on his face, while the other bared his arms and waved his fists and took over the divan in a show of manliness. He picked up the opium pipe and prodded the tray wildly with it, shouting, "Bring me opium."

Second Wang went up to him quickly with a smile. "The maid is getting it. Master Xu, please don't be angry."

Simplicity saw that they did not mean well. Although he was indignant, he knew he couldn't take them on, so he sneaked off in the midst of the hubbub. Second Wang dared not even see him out, but the maid who had gone out to get opium happened to meet him on the street. She grabbed him to tell him, "There're too many people in the daytime. Come after one o'clock at night. We'll be waiting." He took her meaning and nodded.

The sun was gradually going down then. Simplicity did not return to the inn but instead had his dinner in some restaurant and then went on to a Suzhou music hall specializing in storytelling to pass the time. He managed to hold out till past midnight before going back to Second Wang's house, where, sure enough, he got full satisfaction in a night of love.

The next day, when he returned to the inn before noon, the attendant came up to tell him, "Last night, a maid came looking for you several times."

He knew it was Mama Yeung of the Hall of Beauties and was determined to ignore her. Afraid she would come again to pester him, he decided to give her the slip. He hurried out right after lunch but was at a loss where to go. He headed north from Pebble Road onto First Avenue, where he entered Bowling Alley and took a turn, thinking how best to kill time. He suddenly thought of Pine Wu's mah-jongg party. There'd be no harm in inquiring at White Orchid's. With this in mind, he turned and crossed Fourth Avenue, heading straight for White Orchid's in Nobility Alley. He asked at the parlor, "Is Young Mr. Wu here?"

"He didn't come," the menservants answered.

He was about to leave when the maid, Sister Gold, happened to see him. As he had been at the mah-jongg party two days before, she decided to point him in the right direction. "Are you looking for Young Mr. Wu? He's playing mah-jongg at Grace Yang's in Generosity Alley. Go look for him there."

Hearing this, he made his way down Co-jubilation Alley, which linked Nobility Alley to Generosity Alley. Here, he found Grace Yang's nameplate, lifted up the hem of his robe, and walked in. A game of mah-jongg was in progress, and the man who sat facing the door happened to be Rustic Zhang. Simplicity waved to him through the window and sauntered in. Rustic Zhang and Pine Wu were obliged to exchange a few pleasantries with him. Crane Li just said, "Take a seat," while Clement Zhou completely ignored him.

After watching the game quietly for a while from behind Pine Wu, Simplicity felt quite out of place and took his leave in some confusion.

"What kind of business does he do?" Crane Li asked Pine Wu.

"He's come to town for a bit of fun; he's not in any business," Pine Wu replied.

"He's looking for a job," Rustic Zhang said. "Can you help him?"

Pine Wu snickered. "So he's looking for a job, eh? What kind of job d'you think he can do?"

Everybody laughed and brushed the matter aside.

By the time they had finished eight rounds and counted the chips, Crane Li had again lost about a hundred dollars.

"My my, you're good at losing, aren't you?" Grace Yang commented. "I've never heard of you winning."

"It doesn't matter how much you lose at mah-jongg, as long as you make a clean sweep four or five times at dominoes as the banker," Pine Wu replied.

"There's not much to sing-song house parties. You might as well go to Lucky You's and win it back," said Clement Zhou.

"I'll do that tomorrow," Crane Li said with a smile.

"Who's inviting you to dinner tonight?" Rustic Zhang asked.

"None other than Script Li. Otherwise, why would I be going to a sing-song house party?" said Crane Li. "He's not inviting anybody else either; just me and my fourth uncle. If I were to stand him up, he'd go through the roof."

"The old man is in really good spirits, isn't he?" said Pine Wu.

Crane Li said earnestly, "Well, you've got to hand it to him. Just think, how many concubines does he have at home? Then there're the courtesans and the women from respectable families he keeps outside; altogether, they must amount to a few hundred!"

"D'you have any idea how much he has in terms of cash?" Clement Zhou asked.

"Who's counting? Even he himself doesn't know for sure. When he does business, though, he's like a man possessed. He'll lay out millions and stop at nothing!"

Everyone listened agape and shook their heads in astonishment and admiration. After that, they departed one after the other. Crane Li lay down on the divan, stretched himself, and yawned.

"Would you like a puff of opium?" Grace Yang asked.

"No. I was up all night last night and haven't slept properly today. I'm tired."

"How much did you lose yesterday?"

"It wasn't too bad. I stopped after playing all the bets twice, but I lost about a thousand even then."

"I say, you really shouldn't gamble so much. It's not just the money; you're ruining your health as well. You may think you'll win back what you've lost, but it seems to me these people happily take your money when they win, but when they lose they're not likely to give it back to you."

"There you're talking nonsense," he said smiling. "You've got to pay for the chips, so where there're chips, there's always money—how can they refuse to part with it? The only trouble is that when the banker's luck turns a bit, they may stop betting. In that case, there's nothing you can do, and there's no way to win the money back."

"That's what I mean. If you go to Lucky You's tomorrow, you should have a good idea how much you want to win or lose and go all out just one last time. If you can win back what you've lost, fine; if not, you should just let go."

"You're right. If I can't win it back, I'm definitely going to stop gambling."

"It's of course best if you really stop, but even if you go on doing it, you should take more care. Losing tens of thousands may not matter to you, but others might get worked up when they hear about it. If the fourth master of your house asks me why I don't try to dissuade you and puts the blame on me, there'd be nothing I could say."

"Now that won't happen. Why would Fourth Master lecture you if he doesn't even lecture me?"

"Well, one can't be sure. People like to stir things up, you know. Of course, you were the one who felt like a game or two here at our place, but the way other people put it, it's as if we get a hefty cut out of it. We sing-song houses don't run gambling dens; we don't get any cuts, either."

"No one's running you down. Don't be so sensitive."

"From now on, if you want to gamble, you do it at Lucky You's. Then if there's any talk it'll be none of our business."

By now, Crane Li's eyes were drooping, and his mouth dry, so he smiled and did not respond. Grace also fell silent. Drowsiness overcame him, and he dozed off. Knowing he had not slept much, she did not wake him, just quietly covered him with a woolen blanket. He slept until after the lamps were lit, when the maid, Thrive, brought dinner into the room. The tinkle of bowls woke him up.

"Would you like a bite to eat before going to the party?" Grace asked him.

He replied after a moment of reflection, "I'm not hungry really, but a snack is all right."

"There isn't anything to go with the rice, though," said Thrive. "I'll go and tell them to add a couple more dishes."

He signaled with a wave of his hand to stop her. "Don't bother. Just dish out a mouthful of rice for me."

"He likes preserved eggs," Grace said, "go and get some."

Thrive immediately went to get everything ready. Grace and Crane Li ate together. When they had finished, his man. Second Kuang. had arrived from the inn to see him, reporting, "Fourth Master has gone to the party. He's asking you, sir, to go early, too."

"Wait until the invitation card comes. You'll still be on time," said Grace.

"I'll go early and have done with it and then go home early for a good sleep," Crane Li replied.

"If you're not feeling so well, come back to us here. It's more comfortable here than at the inn," she said.

"I haven't been back there for two days now. Fourth Master seems a bit worried. I'd better go back tonight."

She said no more. He then told Second Kuang to accompany him to the dinner party.

CHAPTER 15 :: *Bright Pearl attends a party at Civic Peace Alley, and Pragmatic Li smokes opium at the House of Floral Rain*

Where was Script Li actually holding his party, anyway? It turned out to be at the house of Lute, Prosperity Luo's old flame. Crane Li was in the know, so he led Second Kuang straight to East Civic Peace Alley. Second Kuang rushed ahead to announce him, and the servant girl, Tigress, welcomed him in and lifted the curtain for him to enter. He saw that there were only two men in the room: Fourth Master and a hanger-on at the Lis' named Yu, whom his friends called Old Merit. Fourth Master, named Pragmatic, was Crane Li's uncle, his father's first cousin. The three of them greeted each other, but the host, Script Li, had not yet arrived. Crane Li was about to inquire when Yu explained, "Script is at a party at the commissioner's. Lute has also been called there. He said the three of us are to start dinner first."

Tigress was then told to shout down the stairs for the men to set the dinner table and prepare hot towels. It happened that Lute came back from the party just then, holding four chits for calling girls in her hand. "His Excellency will be here shortly," she said. "He sent word that you should all call a couple more girls and to write out the four for the girls he's calling."

Old Merit went to write the chits. Knowing Script Li was in good spirits, he set an example by calling four girls as well. Crane Li had no choice but to follow suit, but Pragmatic Li refused to play the game; he only called two. After the chits had been issued, they sat down for dinner.

Soon afterward, Script Li arrived, bringing Amity Zhu with him. Deferring to one another as to seating order, they finally settled down. Script Li called for chits so Amity Zhu could call his girls. Amity wrote down the names of the Lin sisters, White Fragrance and Green Fragrance, but Script Li insisted that he fulfill the quota of four. Then he asked Old Merit, "How many girls are the three of you calling?"

When Old Merit told him, Script Li cast a glance at Pragmatic Li. "Goodness! You're calling *two* girls? It must be quite a strain for you. This will cost you six dollars, you know, sheer madness."

Pragmatic Li smiled in embarrassment. "I just don't know where I can get anybody else."

"You're supposed to be an old playboy, yet now there's not even a girl you can call to a party! The things you say; doesn't it show a lack of pride?" Script Li said.

"The ones I knew well are too old now. What's the point of having them here?"

"Don't you know the novices like to play with the young ones while the veterans prefer the old ones? The older the more fun."

Hearing this, Crane Li said, "Here, I've thought of one." Script Li had ink and a writing brush sent over to Crane Li to write out the chit. Pragmatic Li watched and saw he had written the name of Bright Pearl. He hesitated and then said, "She probably doesn't answer calls anymore."

"She couldn't very well refuse if *we* called her, could she?" Crane Li replied.

Script Li took the chits and looked them over. Seeing that Pragmatic Li was still summoning only three girls, he frowned. "I wonder what you want to salt so much money away for. Do you *have* to be miserly at my party?" And he urged Crane Li, "Call another girl, just to shame him." Pragmatic Li couldn't do anything but smile in embarrassment.

"But who else can I call?" Crane Li responded. After thinking for a moment, he reluctantly added one name: White Orchid. Script Li thought of two more girls for himself and told Old Merit to add them on and issue all the chits together.

The dinner was a double table made up of two square tables set end to end. Since host and guests altogether only numbered five, there was lots of room at the table, and Script Li told the courtesans to sit side by side with their clients. Only when all the seats at the table had been taken were they seated behind. Altogether, there were twenty-two courtesans, accompanied by twenty-two maids and serving girls. The room was jam-packed. Old Merit did a head count: only Bright Pearl was missing.

"Shall we send to hurry her up?" Lute asked.

"No, don't," Pragmatic Li replied quickly. "Even if she doesn't come, it's all right."

Crane Li turned around to see White Orchid sitting beside him. He said to her, "I asked you here as a favor, to grace the table."

"You're all politeness," she replied with a smile. "In fact, you're bringing us business, too."

Grace Yang also exchanged a couple of pleasantries with White Orchid, which pleased Crane Li even more.

White Fragrance and her younger sister, Green Fragrance, tuned their *pipa* and consulted over what to sing, but Amity Zhu, guessing that Script Li was in no mood to listen to singing, signaled them with his hand to desist.

Script Li, ignoring his own girls, looked instead at those the other men had called and talked to them. After a long while, Bright Pearl finally arrived. He knew her from way back and made conversation, asking this and that before getting on to the old days with her. He was full of reminiscences from a decade ago. To please him, Pragmatic Li said, "Let her switch over to you, all right?"

"Why switch? Though it was you who called her, I can still talk to her, right?" Script Li responded.

"Then sit over here to talk; it'd be easier," said Pragmatic Li.

Before Script Li could protest, Bright Pearl had already moved over to sit at his side, her shoulder pressing against his. Her maid, Second Sister, a quick-witted woman, immediately filled the water pipe for him. He took a puff but, feeling a bit awkward, said playfully, "Don't you try to suck up to me by filling my pipe. If this causes Fourth Old Master to lose his temper and get jealous, a frail old man like me is no match for him in a fight."

Bright Pearl chuckled. "Don't worry, Your Excellency. If Fourth Old Master picks a fight, I'll come to your aid."

"So, you've got your eyes on my three dollars, have you?" Script Li responded in like spirit.

"Is it because you begrudge three dollars that you won't even smoke the water pipe?" she asked. "Give it here, Second Sister; don't let him have it, or else he'll stay awake all night bemoaning the loss of his three dollars." So saying, Bright Pearl snatched the water pipe the maid had just refilled. The maid could not help laughing, covering her mouth with a hand.

"How can you bully a frail old man like me? It's a sin! Aren't you afraid that heaven will strike you down?" Script Li protested.

Bright Pearl, who had just taken a puff of the water pipe herself, nearly choked. She blew out the smoke hastily and said smiling, "Look! His Excellency is on the verge of tears. There, there, I'll let you have a puff." So saying, she put the pipe to his lips.

He stretched his neck out, sucked in all the smoke in one breath, and then cheered, "Aiyo! It smells so sweet!"

Even Second Sister broke out laughing. "His Excellency is such fun!"

Old Merit said to Bright Pearl, "Now you've been tricked by His Excellency. He got to smoke your pipe, but the three dollars will not be forthcoming."

Script Li clapped his hands and sighed. "Oh! Now that my trick has been exposed, I suppose it'd be too embarrassing for me to have another smoke." This sent everyone at the table into loud laughter.

Lute sat quietly to one side, unable to put a word in. When she saw Amity Zhu leave the table to lie down on the divan for a smoke of opium, she took the first opportunity to slip away unnoticed and went over to ask him in a low voice, "Have you seen Mr. Luo?"

"Not for the last three or four days," Amity Zhu replied.

"Mr. Luo has settled his bills at our place and isn't coming anymore. D'you know that?" she said.

"Whatever for?" he asked.

"It's a joke around town now. Green Phoenix forbids him to visit us, so he doesn't dare come anymore. I've worked in sing-song houses ever since I was a child, and I've never heard of a client acting like Mr. Luo."

"But is it true?"

"He sent Mr. Tang to pay his bills, and Mr. Tang told me."

"Did you people go and invite him back?"

"We'll just leave him be. Whether he comes again or not is entirely up to him. He's been seeing me for four or five years now, and I do have some idea of his likes and dislikes. Since he's fallen for Green Phoenix, even if we go and invite him now, he won't be coming. We'd just be called meddlers. That's why we'll let things be. You just wait, Mr. Zhu, and we'll see whether he'll keep up with Green Phoenix for four or five years. In the end, he'll still be coming to us, and we won't have to invite him, either."

Listening to Lute's words and line of reasoning, he felt this was a woman of interesting qualities. He was about to ask her for more details when he heard the others calling out repeatedly for Mr. Zhu, so he had no choice but to return to the table. It turned out that Script Li had just made Bright Pearl challenge all the guests to the finger game. Pragmatic Li, Crane Li, and Old Merit had all played, and it was Amity Zhu's turn.

After Amity had played, her challenge was done. Now all the courtesans who knew how to play held out their hands asking for a game. All of a sudden, everyone was playing: sleeves danced, bracelets tinkled, lamps swayed, and flowers quivered. One could not quite make out the numbers called or see the gestures. A little annoyed by the din, Script Li called out, "Serve the congee; we want it now." Only then did the courtesans give up the game and gradually disperse. Bright Pearl, unlike the others, stayed until after congee had been served.

Since Crane Li wanted to go to bed early, he took his leave together with Pragmatic Li the minute dinner was over. Second Kuang accompanied them back to the Long Peace Inn on Pebble Road. Once back in their room, Pragmatic Li lit the lamp on his bed to get himself a smoke, while Crane Li told Second Kuang to make his bed.

"What's the matter, aren't you going to Grace Yang's?" Pragmatic Li asked in surprise.

"Not tonight."

"Don't give up having fun just because I'm around. Go there, it's all right," said Pragmatic Li.

"I didn't get any sleep last night, so I'll turn in early tonight."

After a long interval, Pragmatic said slowly, "The one thing you mustn't do in these foreign settlements is to gamble. If you want to gamble, go back home and do it there."

"I wasn't really gambling; it was just a few mah-jongg parties in the sing-song houses."

"True, mah-jongg parties don't count as gambling. Well, as long as you don't gamble . . . Just don't go and get yourself into money problems."

Crane Li could not very well say anything to that, so he undressed and went to bed.

Pragmatic Li told Second Kuang to scrape the ashes out of his pipe. As he did so, Second Kuang asked with a smile, "What's the name of the old courtesan you called, Fourth Master?"

"Bright Pearl. D'you think she's any good?"

Second Kuang smiled but said nothing.

"What's the matter with you? Surely you can tell me what you think."

"I can't see anything in her," Second Kuang replied. "But His Excellency clung to her as if she was a treasure. Fourth Master, next time, don't call her. Might as well let His Excellency have her."

Pragmatic could not help smiling at this. Second Kuang also smiled and said, "Well, Fourth Master, what do *you* think of her? She's going bald at the forehead and has lost most of her teeth, even her cheeks are sunken. When she was talking to His Excellency, she looked terrible when she laughed—her mouth opened, and all the skin on her face pulled together like the ruffles of a dress! Even I felt a bit embarrassed on her behalf, and yet she put on such airs. She should really take a good look at herself in the mirror—what does she think she is?"

Pragmatic laughed out loud. "Bright Pearl is really out of luck today! You may not know this, but she was terribly famous, and she has some twenty thousand silver dollars in hand, too. Lesser clients still fawn on her."

"If I were a client, even if Bright Pearl were to give me money, frankly I wouldn't feel like it. Now the girl at whose place His Excellency gave the party—was her name Lute?—she's the steadier type, didn't even put on any powder, and wore a plain off-white cotton blouse, with no ornaments in her hair. She can't be much younger than Bright Pearl, either. There's nothing much to her, but she's neat and clean, rather like a maid."

"I must say your taste is not bad. You said she's like a maid, but in fact she has too many clothes and jewelry, and that's why she doesn't wear them. Did you see the size of the pearl on her headband? That alone costs five hundred dollars."

"I wonder how they get so much money."

"Why, their clients give it to them, of course. Take tonight, for example; we were only there a little while, but the bill came to over a hundred. It may not matter to His Excellency, but it's so unfair on us. The two of us had to come up with over twenty dollars. Next time we're invited to a sing-song house party, I'm not going. Let Eldest Young Master go on his own."

"Fourth Master is joking again. On a trip to Shanghai you must have some fun, so it's only right to spend a little money. If you don't have it, there's nothing to be done, but in the case of Fourth Master, just your annual surplus will last you forever."

"I'm no miser, but there's fun to be had in lots of places, so why go to the sing-song houses? Is it because they have a better name? Real suckers those punters are!"

Second Kuang chuckled at this. To their surprise, Crane Li was still awake and now laughed under his quilt. Hearing him, Pragmatic Li said, "I'm sure there's no way you'll take the advice I give. No wonder you're laughing. Your Grace Yang, for instance; she's somebody to reckon with, too, quite a celebrity in the foreign settlements."

Intent on getting some sleep, Crane Li made no answer. Having cleaned out the ashes, Second Kuang handed the pipe back and withdrew to the outer room. Pragmatic Li smoked his fill, put away the opium tray, and also went to bed.

Although an opium smoker, Pragmatic Li made it a rule to get up at eight every morning. Crane Li, on the other hand, followed no fixed hours. The next day, Pragmatic had lunch alone in the room. Seeing that Crane Li was still soundly asleep, he did not wake him but just told Second Kuang, "You keep an eye on things. I'm off to the House of Floral Rain." He headed for Fourth Avenue, and as he approached Generosity Alley, he suddenly heard somebody calling, "Mr. Li." He looked up and saw it was Amity Zhu coming out of the alley. They greeted each other.

"I was just going to send you an invitation," said Amity Zhu. "Dinner tonight for Mr. Script Li. We're having it at Bright Pearl's place, where it's roomier. It'll still be the five of us. I'm counting on you to keep His Excellency company, so I beg you not to refuse."

"I'm afraid I must give my apologies. Later, I'll tell my nephew to come and wait on you," Pragmatic replied.

Amity Zhu pondered. "I really shouldn't press you, but it seems the guests are too few. Would you do me this favor, please?"

Pragmatic could not very well turn down such a request, so he just made a vague promise, after which Amity Zhu saluted him and took his leave. Pragmatic made his way to the House of Floral Rain. He went all the way up to the third floor and saw the tables in the outer room and the opium couches inside had all been taken, it being the peak hour. A waiter who knew him realized he had come for a smoke of opium and invited him in, saying, "There's room inside."

Pragmatic Li saw that the smoker on the center couch was paying his bill and washing his face, so he sat down on the humble side of the couch to wait for him to leave and then moved to the head of the couch after the waiter had tidied things up. Within a short time, the tide of tea drinkers and opium smokers had risen even further, and there was not a seat left. Added to their numbers were peddlers of food, toys, and utensils, who carried their wares in their hands, or over their shoulders, or in trays at their chests, all ducking in and out of the crowd.

Pragmatic paid them no attention, for he was on the watch for game. The House of Floral Rain was a vast hunting ground for game birds.[1] They flocked there in countless numbers to joke with and tease potential clients, making spectacles of themselves.

The sight of this did not appeal to Pragmatic. After he had smoked a couple of pellets, he sat up cross-legged. The waiter brought him a hot towel. He wiped his hands and face and then switched to smoking a water pipe. Just then, he saw a game bird of sixteen or seventeen, her face blotched with face powder and her neck rimmed with a layer of dark grease left from some distant past. She had on a padded jacket of pastel pink Suzhou silk with a smear of grease on the lapel that had turned the color of green tea. The pale turquoise silk handkerchief she carried in her hand was comparatively new, and, afraid people would not see it, she swished it energetically as she walked in.

The sight of her made Pragmatic smile. The game bird, thinking he was interested, stood in front of him and fixed her eyes on him, waiting for him to make conversation so she could take the first opportunity to lie down. Unfortunately for her, he did not show the least sign of interest despite her respectful vigil, so she had no choice but to go away. It happened that a waiter was leaning on the screen doors looking after the smokers, so she chatted with him. Something he said made her laugh and curse him, and she flapped her handkerchief in his face. He hastily backed away, and the momentum pushed him against a peddler of foreign and top-class local goods. There was a loud crash, and all the peddler's wares ended up on the floor. Everybody crowded around to look. Seeing that trouble was afoot, the game bird made herself scarce.

Just then, two servant girls walked in with their arms around each other's shoulders. Absorbed in their own chit-chat and laughter, they stepped unwarily on a leather-backed mirror. One of them heaved herself off with a desperate push on one foot and managed to jump over it, but the other girl lost her balance and stepped on a thermometer, reducing it to powdered glass. How could a mere peddler sustain such loss? The man naturally demanded compensation from the servant girls.

But the girls insisted it was unfair. "Why did you throw your things on the floor in the first place?" Each side held to its own argument, and a shouting match almost ensued. The waiter had no choice but to take things into his own hands. He barked, "Go! Go! Say no more." The two girls went away, still muttering. The waiter then

::

1. For the different categories of prostitutes, see "The World of the Shanghai Courtesans."

fished a ten-cent coin out of his pocket for the peddler. The peddler dared not argue any more, just tidied up and left. The waiter, still enraged, cursed and swore. Pragmatic smiled and comforted him, which put a stop to the swearing.

Next, an old woman came in. Feeling her way along the wall, she got really close to the smokers and squinted at them. Seeing that Pragmatic Li was alone, she did not take her eyes off him. He was puzzled by this. Then the old woman faltered for a long while and finally asked, "Want to have some fun?" Only then did he realize she was a pimp. He smiled and ignored her. The waiter, carrying a water kettle to freshen up the tea, was annoyed that she was standing in his way. He glared at her and shouted, "Hey!" It gave the old woman such a fright she lowered her head and left without a word.

Pragmatic smoked two more pellets, scraping the ivory opium box clean with the toasting pick. It was approaching five in the afternoon, the teahouse was beginning to clear. Even the game birds had flown off to who knows where. Pragmatic told the waiter to put away the opium pipe and have the usual receipt made out. Then he fished out a dollar and added a ten-cent tip. The waiter took it to the cashier's and called his assistant to bring hot water for Pragmatic to wash his face.

After washing himself, Pragmatic stood up, straightened his clothes, and got ready to go as soon as the waiter brought his receipt. At this point, however, he saw another game bird glide gracefully in, and his soul was enslaved.

CHAPTER 16 :: *A bargain for a rich patron carries hidden consequences, and a game of dominoes serves as a pastime*

Pragmatic Li saw that the game bird was wearing a simple smooth-woven off-white cotton blouse under a satin-trimmed black crepe sleeveless jacket. An old maidservant walked behind her as she slowly approached the screen doors, looked inside, and stood still. When he got up close, her radiant complexion and limpid eyes really did seem quite appealing. He was just about to chat her up when the waiter came back from the cashier's, and the old maidservant asked him, "Has Chen been?"

"No, he hasn't," the waiter replied. "Not for several days now."

The maid, a little disconcerted, had nothing further to say. She took the game bird to the front terrace, where they leaned against the railing and looked at the carriages passing to and fro on Fourth Avenue.

"D'you know her name?" Pragmatic asked the waiter.

"She's Perfection Chu. She lives nearby."

"She looks rather like a respectable woman."

"Respectable women are just your type. Perhaps you'll go over and sit for a while, have some fun?"

Pragmatic smiled and shook his head.

"It's no big deal. If you like her, drop in now and then. If not, you've wasted a dollar, that's all."

Pragmatic smiled but made no reply. The waiter guessed that he was willing, so he hastily set down the opium lamp he had been polishing and went out to beckon to the maid and whispered into her ear for a long while. After that, the maid came in, all smiles. She asked for Pragmatic's family name and said, "Let's go together now."

This made Pragmatic rather uncomfortable. The waiter sensed it and said, "You two go first and wait at the alley entrance. What's this nonsense about going together?"

The maid hastened to answer, "Then come right away, Mr. Li. We'll wait for you in Great Prosperity Alley."

Pragmatic nodded in assent, and the maid turned around to go. But the waiter called her back to tell her, "Now, be more refined. This gentleman is used to first-class houses. Don't make fools of yourselves."

"I understand," the maid answered, all smiles. "As if you need to tell me!" So saying, she hurried to the front terrace to take Perfection Chu downstairs.

Pragmatic put away the opium sales slip and then left the House of Floral Rain and headed westward down Fourth Avenue for Great Prosperity Alley. From a distance, he saw the maid standing at the alley entrance, waiting. As he drew near, she walked into the alley; he followed. When they came to a turning, she pushed open both panels of a front door and showed him into a tiny courtyard with high walls. He saw that it was a very airy terrace house. Perfection was keeping watch at the upstairs window, but when she saw him come in, she drew back in haste.

He went upstairs into the room. Perfection, all shyness and timidity, offered him watermelon seeds and then returned to her seat in silence. After the maid had brought tea and lit the opium lamp, Perfection finally lay across the divan to fill the pipe for him. He went and lay down on the right-hand side. After some desultory attempts at conversation, the maid withdrew. As he watched Perfection toast the opium, Pragmatic chatted to her casually. When he mentioned the maid, she referred to her at once as "Mother." It turned out that the maid was indeed Perfection's mother, known by the name of Third Sister. A moment later, Third Sister came up again to light the foreign lamp and close the window. She then said, "Mr. Li, you might as well have some supper here."

It occurred to him that if he went back to the inn, Amity Zhu would certainly invite him to the party. It was better for him to keep out of reach. So he named two small casseroles and fished out a dollar to have them ordered from the Garden of Plenty. After a token gesture of declining the money, Third Sister took it and went out for the food.

Soon the food was delivered, accompanied by an additional four plates of cold cuts. Third Sister put two sets of cups and chopsticks on opposite sides of the table and addressed Perfection encouragingly, "Come and keep Mr. Li company."

Only then did Perfection come to the table, pour him a cup of wine, and sit down facing him. He took the wine pot to pour for her.

"I don't drink," she pleaded.

"Have a little," Third Sister Chu urged her. "Mr. Li won't mind."

They were about to commence with supper when they heard some noise downstairs. Somebody had just come through the door. Alarmed, Third Sister went down to ask the man into the kitchen. A while later, she called for Perfection to go down. Pragmatic thought it was a client and stole over to the staircase to eavesdrop, but the man's voice sounded like the waiter at the House of Floral Rain, so he paid no attention and went back to his seat to drink. He had drained five or six cups of wine in succession when Third Sister and Perfection finally came back upstairs, followed by the waiter. Pragmatic invited him to have a cup of wine.

"I've had some," said the waiter. "Please go ahead."

When Third Sister invited him to sit down, he declined again. He just stood there for a while and then said "See you tomorrow" and left.

Perfection solicitously urged several more cups of wine on Pragmatic. He felt a little tipsy and called for rice to be served, and she ate with him. After they had finished, Third Sister brought him a hot towel and then cleared the table and went off to the kitchen. Perfection again filled the opium pipe for him. When he talked to her, she answered less than half the time, but he still found her interesting. By the time he had smoked his fill, he fished a watch out of his pocket and saw it was already past ten, so he threw two silver dollars in the opium tray and stood up.

"Where are you going?" she asked at once.

"I'm leaving."

"No, please don't go!"

He had already walked out of the room before she caught up with him. In her agitation, she clutched his clothes with one hand and shouted, "Mother, come quick!"

Hearing this, Third Sister ran upstairs in alarm and held on to him.

"Our place here is nice and clean. Why d'you have to go? What's wrong?"

"I'll come again tomorrow," he said.

"In that case, don't bother to go tonight," argued Third Sister.

"I have to, but I'm definitely coming tomorrow."

"Then stay a little longer. What's the hurry?"

"It's getting late. I'll see you tomorrow," he said as he went down-stairs.

Third Sister, afraid of spoiling everything, could not very well insist. She just said repeatedly, "Mr. Li, we'll expect you tomorrow then." As for Perfection, she only managed to utter "come tomorrow" once.

He promised casually and walked out of Great Prosperity Alley in the dark, heading straight back to Long Peace Inn on Pebble Road. Second Kuang happened to have returned to the inn at the same time. The minute he saw Pragmatic, he said, "Where have you been all day, Fourth Master? Aiyo! We had such a gathering tonight! Mr. Zhu hired an all-girl opera troupe, as did His Excellency. Our Eldest Young Master was told to hire one, too. Altogether, there are just three all-girl troupes in Shanghai, and we had them all! There were about a hundred and ten people. A lesser house would have collapsed under the weight. Why didn't you go, Fourth Master?"

Pragmatic smiled. Instead of replying, he asked, "Where's your Eldest Young Master?"

"He was in a hurry to go to Lucky You's. He didn't stay for dinner but left right after the show."

Pragmatic had figured that would be the case. He made no comment, just smoked by himself and then went to bed.

The next day, he went again to the top floor of the House of Floral Rain after lunch. Since it was still early, there were not many smokers. The waiter, having nothing to do, toasted opium for him. The conversation turned to Perfection. The waiter said, "She had never worked before; not until this year did she go into the business. As far as looks go, there's little to find fault with. Her only weakness is that she's not good at entertaining. But you like respectable women, so that's all right."

Pragmatic nodded in agreement. He had just smoked a couple of pellets when other smokers drifted in one after the other. The waiter went to look after them.

Pragmatic sat up to smoke a water pipe and saw the squinting old woman of the day before come groping her way in. When she got to the divan across from Pragmatic where three people were smoking, her eyes crinkled up in a smile as she said, "Master Constant, Second Miss is missing you so. She's wondering why you didn't come and told me to come here and have a look. Isn't it fortunate that you happen to be here?" Seeing that the three men all wore blue cotton gowns and black silk sleeveless jackets, Pragmatic knew they were probably servants. The three men did not pay much attention to the garrulous old woman, so she said, "Master Constant, be sure to drop in later. The other gentlemen will please come over together." After that she left, groping to find her way out.

When the old woman had gone, Third Sister Chu turned up alone, without Perfection. Seeing Pragmatic, she said immediately, "Mr. Li, do come over to our place."

Slightly irritated by this, he said to her a little pertly, "I'll come later. You go first."

She sensed his displeasure and hastily walked away. To distract attention, she took a turn in the restaurant before she left.

He did not finish smoking until after five. When he left the House of Floral Rain, he went again to Perfection's in Great Prosperity Alley for a casual supper. This time, they were on familiar ground. He chatted with her and found that they got on very well. As for the pleasures of the flesh and the gratification of erotic desires, those are details we need not go into.

The next morning, he heard in his sleep the sound of suppressed weeping. When he opened his eyes, he saw Perfection lying facing the wall, whimpering. Startled, he asked at once, "Why are you crying?" But despite his repeated questioning, she did not answer. He sat up, draped his clothes over his shoulders, and thought up the most fanciful explanations for her behavior. Unable to solve the puzzle, he bent down to put his cheek against hers and asked, "Have I offended you in some way, or are you upset because I'm too old for you?"

She waved a hand from side to side to indicate "no."

"Then why? Do tell me." He frowned in puzzlement. His repeated questions only brought a brief answer from her, "It's got nothing to do with you."

"Even so, you can tell me about it."

But she still would not speak. Not knowing what to do with her, he got dressed and got out of bed. Third Sister Chu heard him downstairs and fetched water for him to wash and then lit the opium lamp. As he washed, he stopped her to find out why Perfection was crying.

Third Sister sighed before she answered, "Well, you can't blame her, really. There's something you don't know, Mr. Li. I raised her from her birth till she was eighteen and never dreamed of letting her go into the business. Last year, she got married to a shopkeeper's son. His family was not badly off; they had a jewelry store in Hongkou district, and the young couple got on very well, so she was doing all right, wasn't she? But then something happened in the first month of this year, and because of that she still ended up in the business! Now don't you think she's got cause to feel aggrieved, Mr. Li?"

"Well, what happened?"

"Let's not talk about it. It won't help anyway, and it may humiliate her husband. Better not say anything."

As they talked, he had finished washing, and Third Sister took the basin downstairs. He, however, felt uneasy and mystified by what she had said. He lay down on the divan to smoke and puzzle over the matter.

In a moment, Third Sister came in to inquire about breakfast. He again asked her, "What was it? Do tell me. I might be of some help to her, you never know. Tell me and we'll see."

"Mr. Li, if you're willing to help her, you'd be doing a good deed, but I'm too embarrassed to tell you. If I did, it'd seem like we're out to swindle you, Mr. Li."

He lost his patience. "Oh, for heaven's sake! If you have anything to say, just say it!"

She sighed again and then told him the story from the beginning. "I have to put it down to her bad luck! She went to a wedding at her maternal uncle's in the first month. Her husband, eager to put up a good front, let her take a set of jewelry from the shop with her. At night, she put it beside her pillow, but when she got up the next morning, it was gone! Lots of people went searching for it up hill and down dale, all to no avail. Her uncle and his family were scared to death. They said if it couldn't be found, they'd kill themselves by taking raw opium. Since her parents-in-law are still alive, how could she face them? They were really at the end of their wits. Then someone said perhaps she could go into the business. If she met a good client who took pity on the ill-fated girl, he might be willing to help her cover up this affair and in the process save seven or eight lives. I was at my wit's end, so I agreed to it. Now, Mr. Li, since her husband's family is not badly off and she gets on with him all right, if it weren't for this why would she have to make a living as a prostitute?"

Perfection, who was lying in bed, started weeping heartrendingly when she heard this. Pragmatic, all uneasy, scratched his ears and cheeks, unable to comfort her.

"You know, Mr. Li, this business is hard. Even the first-class houses only take in three or four hundred a season. For a respectable woman who's just come out, things are of course even tougher. Would it be easy to earn enough to replace a set of jewelry? Sometimes when we talk and the subject of business comes up, she bursts into tears. She says if she doesn't get enough business, she might as well die, for she'll never find happiness again."

"She's too young to talk about dying!" he said. "We'll discuss this later. There must be some way out. Go and talk to her; tell her not to cry."

Third Sister immediately clambered onto the bed and whispered something in Perfection's ear, after which the sound of weeping gradually subsided, and she got dressed and got up. Only then did Third Sister get off the bed. She said jovially, "The first guest she's had since she came out happens to be you, Mr. Li. It's probably not in her stars to die just yet. You're like a savior who's come to her rescue, don't you think so, Mr. Li?"

Pragmatic bowed his head deep in thought and said not a word.

Third Sister suddenly thought of something. "Aiyo! I kept chatting away and forgot to ask: what will you have for breakfast, Mr. Li? I'll go get it."

"A couple of rice balls will do."

She dashed out at once to buy the food.

Perfection's cheeks, flushed scarlet, were clear and smooth as a mirror, and her jet black eyes had puffed up from crying. Pragmatic, moved to love and pity, stared fixedly at her. Overcome by shyness, she got off the bed with her head lowered, stepped into a pair of slippers, and hurried off to the back half of the room. A while later, Third Sister returned with the rice balls, and Perfection also came in to wash her face and comb her hair. Pragmatic smoked another couple of pellets of opium and then got up to put on his jacket, taking five dollars out of his pocket to put in the opium tray.

"Are you going?" Third Sister asked.

"Yes, I am."

"And you won't be coming back again?"

"Who said so?"

"Then what's the hurry in paying?" Third Sister took the five dollars from the opium tray and put it back in his pocket.

A bit taken aback, he asked, "Does that mean you want me to get you a set of jewelry?"

"Oh, it's not that!" she said pleasantly. "If we have money in hand, we might spend it, and then we'd never save up enough. It's better to leave it with you, Mr. Li. You can give it all to us in a few days, right?"

Only then did he nod in agreement and say, "Fine."

"Come again later," Perfection urged, and he gave her his promise. Then he put on his jacket, went downstairs, and returned to Long Peace Inn on Pebble Road. Unexpectedly, his nephew Crane had already returned. Upon seeing him, Crane could not help smiling, which rather embarrassed Pragmatic. Second Kuang, also grinning, submitted an invitation. It was Mallow Yao asking him to a dinner party that night at Sunset's in Generosity Alley.

"Are you going?" Crane asked.

"No, not me. You go ahead."

Soon the inn attendant brought them lunch. When they had finished eating, Pragmatic Li went by himself to smoke at the House of Floral Rain, while Crane Li went to Grace Yang's in Generosity Alley. When he walked into the room, the maid, Thrive, was doing her own hair at the table by the window, while Grace was still in bed. Crane Li drew back the bed curtains and stretched a hand out to fondle her, but she had already woken up with a start and turned around to grasp his hand. He sat down on the edge of the bed.

"When did you get back from gambling last night?" she asked.

"We broke up at nine this morning. I haven't slept at all."

"Well, did you win?"

"I lost."

"You're a fine one! All this time, I've never heard of you winning once, and yet you still want to go and gamble with them."

"Say no more. Get up quick, and we'll go for a drive."

She draped some clothes around her shoulders, sat up, and buttoned up her undershirt, saying to Crane in some annoyance, "Go away!"

"My sitting here doesn't bother you, does it?" he said teasingly.

She replied with a smile, "I won't have it!"

It happened that a manservant came in with the water kettle just then, so Crane Li walked away to light the opium lamp and smoke. Now Thrive had finished doing her hair and busied herself with preparing tea and hot towels. By the time Grace had finished her coiffure and had taken some lunch, the sky had suddenly turned dark and threatened to rain.

"Let's forget the carriage ride. Why don't you sleep for a while?" she said.

He shook his head.

"Let's play a game of dominoes then! Does Eldest Young Master feel like it?" suggested Thrive.

"All right. Who else is there?" he said.

"Laurel Zhao from upstairs is quite fond of dominoes, too," said Grace.

Thrive hurried off to ask Laurel, who came downstairs at once. Grace said smiling to Crane Li, "The minute she hears of dominoes, she rushes in. Now I know why you're still so keen after you've lost twenty or thirty thousand."

Laurel gave Grace a pat and said jovially, "You make it sound as if it's all true."

Crane Li looked at Laurel. She was about twenty-five or -six, with the word "opium —smoker" written all over her sallow face. As she made casual conversation with him, Thrive had pulled the table to the middle of the room and produced the bamboo tiles and ivory chips. Crane Li, Grace, Laurel, and Thrive each cast the dice to determine their seating positions and then started to shuffle the tiles. Crane saw two fingers as black as charcoal on Laurel's right hand and knew she must be heavily addicted to opium. Who would go with a courtesan like that? he wondered. To his surprise, before they had got to the fourth round of the game, a client had come for her. This was followed by an invitation for Crane Li from Sunset's, so everybody decided to call it a day. When they counted the chips, Crane Li turned out to be the winner.

"You went out and lost twenty or thirty thousand and then came here to win two or three dollars from us. Isn't it infuriating?" Grace laughed at him.

Crane Li thought it was funny, too. At this point, Laurel went upstairs by herself, and Thrive started to tidy up.

Crane Li did not set off for Sunset's until after the menservants had lit the lamps. As he walked up to the door, he ran into Amity Zhu, so they went upstairs together. Mallow Yao welcomed them in and asked them to sit down, after which Sunset offered them watermelon seeds.

Crane Li said to Mallow Yao, "My fourth uncle sends his apologies."

"The Tao brothers can't come either. They're visiting their ancestral graves," said Amity Zhu.

"Then we're too few," Mallow Yao said. He went and wrote out two more invitations and handed them to the maid, Clever. She took them downstairs to show to the bookkeeper.

"Mr. Hong at Twin Pearl's in Sunshine Alley," the bookkeeper read out the first invitation. He was getting on to the next one when Amity Zhu's man, Longevity, who had been sitting to one side, suddenly pushed forward and said, "I'll take this to Mr. Hong." So saying, he snatched the invitation and went off.[1]

::

1. This is a heaven-sent excuse for Longevity to go to the Zhou house, where his lover, Golden, works.

Longevity took the invitation slip and headed straight for Twin Pearl's in Sunshine Alley. When he came through the front door, he saw Worth sitting in the parlor with one foot on a chair and a long pipe in his mouth. Longevity had no choice but to approach him and put the invitation on the table, saying, "It's for Mr. Hong."

Worth did not bother to look at the invitation. He just said, "He's not here. Just leave it here."

Longevity had to withdraw. But before he went, Worth sneered and said loudly, "So, we've got a new fashion now. Sing-song houses won't need menservants anymore!"

Longevity, pretending not to hear, left quickly with his head bent. He had just reached the mouth of the alley when he came upon Benevolence Hong, so he stood to one side and told him about the invitation from Mr. Yao. Benevolence Hong promised to go, whereupon Longevity left.

Benevolence Hong dropped in on Twin Pearl first. He asked for the invitation and looked it over in the parlor and then went upstairs. The madam, Orchid Zhou, was having a tête-à-tête with Twin Pearl. When he came in, Orchid Zhou greeted him and got up right away, saying to Twin Pearl, "It's best if you have a word with her. She'll listen to you." After that, she went downstairs.

"What was that about?" he asked.

"She said Twin Jade is not feeling well."

"But why did she tell you to have a word with her; what about?"

"It's all because Twin Jewel wags her tongue too much. That girl is just no good. She wants to do well, but she hasn't got what it takes, and yet she still tries to put on airs. And she happens to run into this Twin Jade, who won't stand for being second in anything. These two will never get along."

"In what way did Twin Jewel put on airs?"

"This was what she said: 'Twin Jade had no silver water pipe, so they got her one from my room. As for her party clothes, I've worn them, too.' Twin Jade happened to hear it, so she refused to wear those clothes anymore and also refused to take the silver water pipe. She's spent the whole of today in bed, refusing to get up, saying she's unwell. Because of that, Mother gave Twin Jewel a tongue-lashing, and now she wants me to speak to Twin Jade and tell her to get up."

"What are you going to say to her?"

"I really don't feel like speaking to her. In fact, I find Twin Jade exasperating. She's just had a few more party calls, and she acts like a grand dame, scolding and beating Twin Jewel as if she's the madam who owns that girl."

"Twin Jade is a shrewd one. It's a good thing you're not a girl sold to the house, otherwise she'd look down on you, too," he said.

"Well, with me she's all lovey-dovey. Whatever I tell her, she agrees to. I'm even more effective than Mother."

Just as they were talking, they heard Worth call out downstairs, "Maestro Twin Jade called to a party." Clever Baby answered from the room opposite, "Coming." So Benevolence said to Twin Pearl, "There's no need for you to talk to her. Now that there's a party call, she has to get up."

"The way I look at it, if she won't get up, that's her lookout. The worst she can do is stop working. If you let her have her way while she's still a virgin courtesan, in the future she'll think she owns the world."

She had scarcely finished speaking when they heard the voice of Orchid Zhou downstairs cursing all the way into Twin Jewel's room. Then there was the sound of slapping, followed by the weeping of Twin Jewel. From this they knew Orchid Zhou had given her a beating.

"Mother is unfair as well," said Twin Pearl. "If beatings are in order, then Twin Jade should get one, too. The fact that she does slightly better business shouldn't put her above the rules. Why is life so hard on girls whose business is not good?"

He was just about to speak when he saw Clever Baby come in from the room opposite. Twin Pearl asked her, "Hadn't they had one row already? Why was there another beating?"

Clever Baby whispered, "Twin Jade is refusing to answer party calls. Do talk to her, Third Maestro. If she'd just go, everything will be all right."

Twin Pearl sneered and just sat there. Benevolence stood up abruptly and said, "I'll talk to her. She's sure to go."

He walked over to Twin Jade's room at once. She was lying in bed. The room, only lit by a tall bedside lamp, was enshrouded in half darkness.

"I heard you're not feeling quite well," he made conversation cheerfully. She was obliged to greet him: "Mr. Hong."

He sat down on the edge of her bed and asked, "I heard you're going out on a party call."

"I'm not feeling well, so I'm not going," she answered.

"It's of course best not to go if you're not well. But if you don't go, your mother will have no choice but to send Twin Jewel in your stead. If that's the case, won't it be better to go yourself?"

The minute she heard that Twin Jewel would go instead of her, Twin Jade naturally became agitated. She thought for a moment and said, "You're right, Mr. Hong, I'll go." So saying, she sat up.

He was happy to have effected this change and hastened to call Clever Baby over to light the lamp and help Twin Jade get ready. Then he went back to Twin Pearl's room and told her about the new development. Twin Pearl praised the way he had handled it. Just then, Golden brought in supper and set it on the square table in the middle room. Benevolence said to Twin Pearl, "You better have dinner. By the time you get ready, it'll be time for you to answer calls, too."

"Would you like a bite before you go to the party?" asked Twin Pearl.

"No, thanks. I'll go now."

"Then send for me right away. It won't take me long to finish supper and wash my face."

He promised to do so and then left for the dinner party at Sunset's in Generosity Alley. Twin Pearl sat down in the middle room and told Golden to relay a message to Twin Jade: "If you feel like eating, come and have supper with me."

When Twin Jade had heard about Twin Jewel's beating, most of her anger had melted away. Now that Elder Sister took the trouble to send the maid to ask her to supper, she was eager to grab this opportunity to please and immediately agreed to come. She sat down cheerfully opposite Twin Pearl, while Golden and Clever Baby took the other chairs around the table.

During the meal, Twin Pearl said to Twin Jade in a casual manner, "Twin Jewel is not a girl who talks much sense; she just babbles on and on. I, too, get annoyed at the sight of her. Now, you're different; your business is good, and Mother likes you, so don't take what she says to heart. If she should say anything that jars on your ears, just come and tell me; don't go and tell Mother."

When she heard this, Twin Jade did not utter a word.

"Do you think I'm siding with Twin Jewel?" Twin Pearl went on with a smile. "That's not true. The way I look at it, now we're courtesans in a sing-song house but in a couple of years we'll all get married. As courtesans, no matter how popular we are or how good a show we put on, there's not much substance to it. If you look at it this way, it's best not to take things too seriously, right?"

Twin Jade put on a smiling face as she answered, "Now it's you, Elder Sister, who're being supersensitive. I may be stupid, but I haven't got to the point when I can't tell good advice from bad! You're speaking to me for my own good, so how can I possibly blame you for it?"

"As long as you understand, I'm glad."

During this conversation, they had finished eating. Clever Baby immediately hurried Twin Jade off to get ready for the parties. Twin Pearl also went to wash and powder her face. Benevolence Hong's call chit did not come until after nine o'clock. There was also a chit for

Twin Jade, sent by a client named Zhu at the same party at Sunset's. Instead of waiting for Twin Jade, Twin Pearl was going to leave first. But just as she was getting into the sedan chair at the door, Twin Jade came back from another party, so Twin Pearl told her to turn the sedan chair around, and they went together. At Sunset's, Benevolence Hong pointed at a youth and said to Twin Jade, "It's Fifth Young Master Zhu who called you." Twin Jade went to sit down behind him.

Twin Pearl saw that there were seven men seated at the table. Besides the host, Mallow Yao, there were Crane Li, Lotuson Wang, Amity Zhu, Cloudlet Chen, and others whom she knew well. Only this boy looked unfamiliar. She asked Benevolence Hong surreptitiously and learned that he was Amity Zhu's little brother, whose informal name was Modesty. He was only sixteen and not yet married. Twin Pearl thought him very handsome. With his well-defined eyebrows and fine eyes, he looked rather like Amity Zhu, but he was shy and timid and just sat there looking ill at ease. Clever Baby went up and presented him with the water pipe, but he would not smoke, so she gave the pipe to Lotuson Wang.

Just then, Mallow Yao challenged Amity Zhu to a round of the finger game. Amity Zhu was sitting next to Modesty. During the game, the latter took the opportunity to steal a glance at Twin Jade. As it chanced, she was also looking stealthily at him. Their eyes met. She smiled ever so slightly, but he looked away in embarrassment.

After Amity Zhu had had five rounds, Mallow Yao wanted to play against Modesty. But the latter excused himself by saying he didn't know the game.

"Nonsense! Everybody knows the finger game!" said Mallow Yao.

"Just give it a go," Amity Zhu said encouragingly.

Modesty Zhu had no choice but to stick out his fist. He won the first three rounds but lost twice in the end. He had just taken up a penalty cup when Twin Jade pulled at his sleeve from behind and said, "I'll drink it." Taken by surprise, he gave a violent start and dropped the cup. It went spinning off the table, spilling wine all over her. In desperation, he grabbed a napkin to wipe her off. She covered her mouth and said laughing, "It doesn't matter." Clever Baby hastened to pick up the cup, which, fortunately, was made of silver and therefore not broken. Everybody at the party laughed out loud. At this, Modesty flushed crimson to his ears. His penalty wine was left undrunk, and he just bowed his head and tucked his hands into his sleeves, trying to be inconspicuous but finding nowhere to hide.

"Would you like us to drink the two penalty cups?" Clever Baby asked, but he didn't even hear her. Twin Jade took one cup from her and drank it for Modesty; Clever Baby drank the other, so he was clear.

By the time all the girls had arrived, Twin Jade had to leave for some other party, but Twin Pearl stayed behind. Knowing that Mallow Yao was always keen on getting others drunk, she waited until after Benevolence Hong had taken his turn as banker before she went home.

After she left, Mallow Yao was still in great spirits and refused to stop. Already a little tipsy, Benevolence Hong heard that it was pouring outside. He decided not to get drunk and made his escape from the party when people were not looking. He headed due north out of Generosity Alley and then took a ricksha back to Twin Pearl's in Sunshine Alley. Arriving in her room, he saw Twin Pearl sitting alone playing solitaire with a set of ivory dominoes. He took off his jacket, shook the water off it, and gave it to Golden to hang up on the clothes rack.

He sat down casually and saw that it was still dark in the opposite room. Obviously, Twin Jade had not yet come back from her round of parties. But Twin Pearl said to Golden, "You can go home when you're ready."

Golden made an affirmative noise and hastened to prepare tea and opium; she then made the bed and blew the lamp out.

"It's still early; Twin Jade's not back yet. What's the hurry?" he said with a smile.

"Worth has been asking for her to go back," Twin Pearl said. "I kept her here because it's been raining and I knew you'd come. If she doesn't go back now, there's going to be another row."

He could not help smiling at this.

Twin Jade did not return until after Golden was gone. After that, a group of guests dropped in and crowded into her room for a tea party. There was a lot of noise and laughter.

Twin Pearl, who had finished her game of solitaire, felt she should not go to bed right away, so she came over to lie down opposite Benevolence on the divan and chatted to him as she toasted the opium.

"So Mr. Wang is seeing this Constance. Does Little Rouge know about it?"

"Of course she does," he replied. "But as long as she gets the money, why should she be jealous?"

"As far as personality goes, Little Rouge is not dissimilar to our Twin Jade."

"Who is Twin Jade jealous of?"

"I don't mean getting jealous. They both think very highly of themselves and want to steal the show. It's as if they're going to be courtesans all their lives and never get married."

As they were talking, Twin Jade suddenly walked in to show Twin Pearl a silver water pipe.

"What d'you think of this design?" she asked.

Twin Pearl saw the brand of the Galaxy Jewelry Store and knew it was a new gift from a client of hers. She asked, "How much did it cost?"

"He said it cost twenty-six dollars. Is that expensive?"

"That's about right for such quality. Not bad at all," Twin Pearl replied.

Hearing this, Twin Jade was even more pleased. She took the water pipe and returned to her room to entertain her guests. Twin Pearl commented, "Look at her, what a show-off!"

"If she's good at doing business, that's for the best. Otherwise, everything would fall on your shoulders, and you'd surely feel the burden, right?" he said.

"Of course you're right. I wish her the best of business, for everybody's sake."

As they were talking, the guests in the opposite room had noisily dispersed. Now it was quiet all round. Twin Pearl took off her jewelry and was about to go to bed when they heard Twin Jewel talking to somebody downstairs in a low voice. The conversation was interspersed with the sound of sobbing.

"Is that Twin Jewel crying?" Benevolence asked.

Twin Pearl sniffed. "If she's going to cry like this, she shouldn't have wagged her tongue so much."

"Who is she talking to?"

"A client."

"So Twin Jewel has a client here, too?"

"He's not bad, and he's really quite fond of her. But Twin Jewel is always a bit silly and doesn't manage things properly."

He asked for the client's surname.

"It's Ni. His father owns the Great Prospects Grocery Store at the Great East Gate."

He asked no more questions but just closed the door and went to bed with Twin Pearl. Yet downstairs, Twin Jewel's complaint to her client and her weeping continued. Although the words were muffled, the sound of her intermittent sobbing and sniffling carried a sense of overwhelming sadness that made Benevolence toss and turn, unable to sleep. He did not doze off until the clock had struck four and the noise downstairs gradually subsided.

At eight the next morning, Benevolence was still roaming the kingdom of dreams with its golden princess when unexpectedly Golden pushed the door open and came into the room, calling softly, "Mr. Hong."

Twin Pearl woke up first and asked, "What is it?"

"Somebody to see Mr. Hong," Golden replied. Twin Pearl shook Benevolence awake to tell him.

"Who is it?" he asked. Golden had no idea. Puzzled, he got dressed hurriedly and got out of bed, dragging his shoes along as though they were slippers, and told Golden to bring the man upstairs.

Golden took the man into the upstairs parlor. Benevolence saw that it was a stranger and asked, "Why are you looking for me?"

"I'm from the Welcome Inn on Treasured Merit Street. There's a certain Simplicity Zhao; is he related to you?"

"Yes, he is."

"Last night, Mr. Zhao had a fight on New Street. His head was broken, and he had blood all over him. The police sent him to Hope Hospital. This morning, I looked in on him, and he told me to come and find Mr. Hong."

"What was the fight about?"

"I've no idea," the man said with a smile.

Benevolence had a fairly good idea of what had taken place. After a moment of reflection, he said, "All right. It's nice of you to take the trouble. I'll go there later."

The man immediately withdrew. Benevolence returned to the room to wash his face.

Twin Pearl asked from behind the bed curtains, "What is it?"

"Nothing."

"If you're going, have some breakfast first."

He told Golden to order ten steamed dumplings. After he had eaten, he said to Twin Pearl, "You get a little more sleep. I'm going now."

"Do come back early this evening," said Twin Pearl.

He gave his promise and then put on his jacket and left.

The sky had just cleared after prolonged rain. The morning sun was dazzling, and the weather mild. He went straight to Hope Hospital and asked for Simplicity Zhao. A man took him upstairs and pushed open a screen door. It was a huge foreign-style room with seven or eight iron beds arranged in two rows. Several patients were lying in bed. They had the mosquito nets gathered up and thrown over the bed rail. Simplicity Zhao occupied the last bed in a row. His head bandaged and his arm in a sling, he sat there cross-legged. The minute he saw Benevolence, he got up and greeted him, shame written all over his face.

Benevolence sat down on a rattan stool by the bed, and Simplicity told him the whole story: how he had been beaten by the two gangsters Xu and Zhang and had got injuries to his head and face. He tried to make out he'd had a rotten deal, but his gibbering did not make much sense.

"Surely, it was your own fault," said Benevolence. "What were you doing in New Street? If you hadn't gone there, would they have come to your inn to beat you up?"

This silenced Simplicity.

"Now there's nothing else to say; wait till you're a little better and then go home quick. And don't you come to Shanghai again."

Simplicity hesitated a long time before confessing that he owed the inn for his room and board and they were holding his luggage. Benevolence gave him another scolding and then worked out the amount for his room and board and his traveling expenses back home. He gave Simplicity five dollars and told him to go straight home and not to tarry on any account. How could Simplicity dare to object? He just kept saying "yes."

Benevolence repeated his admonitions several times before saying good-bye. As he walked out of Hope Hospital, he thought he should attend to some business matters, so he headed south. Near Beaten Dog Bridge, he saw someone walking straight toward him. To his surprise, it was Cloud Tao's younger brother, Jade. The latter was in such a hurry that he kept his head down and never even noticed Benevolence.

He grabbed Jade by the arm. "How come you're walking down the street all on your own? Where're your sedan chair and your servant?"

When Jade Tao saw it was Benevolence, he saluted him hastily.

"Are you on your way to East Prosperity Alley?" Benevolence asked.

Jade nodded, smiling.

"Then take a ricksha!" Benevolence called one over. "Have you got no change?"

Jade nodded again with a smile, so Benevolence fished a handful of copper coins out of his pocket and gave it to Jade. Seeing how solicitous Benevolence was, Jade could not very well refuse. He got on the ricksha as he was told. Benevolence also got himself a ricksha to go back to Flourishing Ginseng Store on Salt Melon Street in South End.

After Jade Tao had parted company with Benevolence Hong, he went straight to Fourth Avenue, stopping at the entrance of East Prosperity Alley. He gave all the copper coins to the ricksha man and went into Water Blossom's house.

The maid, Big Goldie, happened to be washing and starching clothes in the courtyard. Seeing him, she exclaimed, "So here you are, Second Young Master! Did you see Laurel Blessing?"

"No, I didn't."

"He went to look in on you. Where's your sedan chair?"

"I didn't take the sedan chair."

As they talked, Big Goldie propped up the bamboo curtain with a stick for him to enter.

He took care to walk noiselessly into the room, where he saw Water Blossom lying in bed. The pale turquoise summer silk bed curtains were hanging down.

The servant girl, Beckon, was dusting the furniture. Thinking that

Water Blossom was still asleep, he signaled her with a hand to keep quiet and sat down in a high-back chair. But Beckon told him in a whisper, "She had another sleepless night last night. She insisted on getting up after she had gone to bed, and each time she did she had a fit of coughing. She didn't really go to sleep till dawn."

"Is she running a fever?" he asked at once.

"Not really."

"Quiet. She needs to rest some more." He signaled Beckon to keep silent.

But just then Water Blossom started coughing in bed again.

CHAPTER 18 :: *A lined jacket conveys Jade Tao's deep love, and an expensive banquet allays White Fragrance's wrath*

Hearing Water Blossom cough, Jade Tao dashed over to her bedside in alarm and lifted the bed curtain to look at her face. She turned her head around, glared at him for a long time, and then sighed.

"Aren't you feeling well?" he kept asking her.

She did not answer him directly but said, "You're a fine one! How many times did I tell you to come as soon as you got back yesterday? You just won't do as I say. No matter what I tell you, you treat it like a breeze that brushes past your ears."

He explained hastily, "That's not true. Yesterday, we got back late, and there were relatives at home, so Elder Brother said, 'What's so important that you have to rush out of the city at night?' What could I have said to that?"

"Humph, don't talk nonsense to me. It's not as if I know nothing about your character. It'd be unfair to accuse you of seeing another woman. It's just a case of out of sight, out of mind, let live or die, nothing to do with you, right?"

He forced a smile. "Even if it was out of sight, out of mind, it was only for one night. Didn't I think of you and come here first thing this morning?"

"It's all right for you. You fall soundly asleep, and when you wake the night has passed. D'you know that for someone who can't sleep and just sits there, one night seems longer than a year?"

"It's all my fault. I made you suffer. Please don't be angry."

She coughed a little more and then said slowly, "Last night, the weather made me nervous, too; it rained endlessly. River Blossom was out on a party call, and Beckon was filling the opium pipe for Mother, which left just Big Goldie here, dozing in a chair, so I told her to tidy up and go to bed. After she was gone, I sat by myself on the divan for a bit, and it rained harder than ever. Gusts of wind hit the window pane, making a clatter like someone was banging on it. The curtains even blew up and flew right into my face. It nearly scared me to death. There was nothing I could do but go to bed. Yet once in bed, how could I sleep?

"A party had just started next door, the noise of the finger game and singing gave me a terrible headache. When the party was finally over, that clock on the table went tick-tock, tick-tock; I wasn't listening to it, but it just burrowed into my ears. Then I got up again to listen to the rain, and it was falling ever so merrily; I looked at the sky, and it was never going to be dawn. I didn't shut my eyes until half past two, but the minute I did, I heard you come. A sedan chair came all the way into the parlor, and I saw you get out, but you paid me no attention and just ran straight out of the house. I shouted out at once and ended up waking myself. As I woke, I heard that there really was a sedan chair in the parlor. From the sound of metal-heeled boots walking on the wooden floor, I could tell there were several people there. I scrambled out of bed at once, didn't even put on more clothes, and opened the door to ask, 'Where's Second Young Master?' The menservants replied, 'There's no Second Young Master.' I said, 'Then where did the sedan chair come from?' They answered, 'It's River Blossom coming back from the parties.' They all laughed at me for being groggy with sleep. I went back to bed, but there was no way I could sleep. I never stopped coughing till dawn."

Jade frowned, worried by what she said. "Why did you act like that? You must take better care of yourself. The wind was so strong last night, yet you got up in the middle of the night without putting on more clothes and went outside your room; didn't you feel cold? If you don't take care of yourself, it's no use even if I keep a daily watch over you."

"But would you really watch over me every day?" she replied, smiling. "It's easier said than done. I know my fate is not a happy one. All I ask is for you to keep me company for three more years. If you'd agree to that, I'll die content. And in case I don't die and you decide to marry somebody else, I won't interfere either. I'm just asking for three years, and you won't even agree to that, so why talk about keeping watch over me every day?"[1]

::

1. [While the characterization of Water Blossom is based partly on Lin Daiyu in the Qing dynasty novel *Honglou meng* and her relationship with Jade Tao on that between Lin and Jia Baoyu, this particular conversation can be traced to the Tang dynasty story "Hou Xiaoyu zhuan," in which the courtesan Huo Xiaoyu asked her lover Li Yi to spend eight years with her, after which he could marry someone respectable. *E.H.*]

"The minute you talk, you come out with something unlucky. You have a widowed mother whom you can't leave. In three or four years' time, when your brother is married and can take over the house, you and your mother can come live with me. Then I'll really keep watch over you every day, and you'll be happy."

"You're born to have a happy life, but mine is not a blessed fate." She smiled again and said. "I was just thinking, you're twenty-four now; in three years, you'll only be twenty-seven. If you take a wife then, you'll still have decades to grow old together. I'm just asking for three years, so even if you think I'm unfair to you, you should be able to bear with me."

"What's all this nonsense you're talking?" he answered with a smile. "You'll be the wife I'll grow old with."

She said no more. Now River Blossom entered the room through the back door, her hair still uncombed. Rubbing her sleepy eyes, she asked Jade, "Brother-in-law, why didn't you come yesterday?"

With a jolly smile, he pulled her over by the hand. She stood leaning against the dressing table.

Water Blossom noticed that her young sister was wearing nothing but a tight undershirt of pale pink Huzhou silk. She asked, "How is it you didn't even put on any clothes?"

"It's hot this morning," she said.

"Nonsense! Go and put some clothes on quick."

"No! It's terribly hot as it is."

Just as they were talking, Beckon came in with a lined magenta jacket and said to River Blossom, "Mother is scolding, too. Quick, put it on."

But she still refused, so Jade took the jacket and draped it over her shoulders, saying, "Just put it on for now. If you feel hot later, you can take it off, all right?"

River Blossom had little choice but to obey. Beckon then went and fetched hot water for her to wash her face and comb her hair. Water Blossom also wanted to get up.

"You get a little more sleep. It's still early," Jade interposed.

"I don't want to sleep anymore."

He helped her sit up in bed but still tried to dissuade her, saying, "Why don't you just sit in bed for a while and chat with me?"

Yet Water Blossom still insisted. When she at last got off the bed, she felt that her nose was blocked, her voice hoarse, her head giddy, and her legs weak. The coughing, though, was a bit better. Supporting herself on some chairs and tables all the way, she walked to the divan and sat down, where he followed her and lowered a curtain. Now Big Goldie came in with some bird's nest soup for Water Blossom, but after a sip or two, she just told River Blossom to eat it. As River Blossom finished her toilet, Water Blossom got up to wash her face.

"Your hair looks fine. There's no need to do it again," said Beckon. Knowing that she couldn't sit up for long, Water Blossom agreed. Big Goldie dipped a narrow brush into the toilet water and gently brushed her hair a few times, after which Water Blossom attended to her sidelocks herself. That was enough to exhaust her, and she lay down on the divan, panting.

The sight of Water Blossom's frailty worried Jade, but he put on a smiling face. River Blossom, however, stood in front of him and stared at her sister.

"What are you looking at?" Water Blossom asked.

River Blossom was speechless. She just smiled.

Big Goldie, who was putting away the mirror box, responded. "She sees that Elder Sister is not well. She's not in such good spirits, either, don't you know?"

River Blossom took it from there. "My sister was quite well yesterday. It's all Brother-in-law's fault! I won't have it!" So saying, she dived into his arms in protest.

He smiled and comforted her immediately, saying, "They're fooling you. Your sister is not unwell. She'll be all right a little later."

"If she isn't, then you'll have to give me back a healthy Elder Sister!" demanded River Blossom.

"You have my word. I'll give you a healthy Elder Sister later."

Only then was River Blossom reassured. Lying on the divan, Water Blossom gradually closed her eyes, as if about to doze off.

"Why don't you go back to bed?" Jade suggested.

She held up a hand to indicate she wouldn't, so he took a woolen blanket from a rattan chair and put it over her.

"It's heavy!" she said, annoyed, and pushed it off.

Not knowing what to do, he went to lower the other window curtain. Still afraid that Water Blossom would catch cold if she fell asleep, he tried to keep her awake with small talk and started telling her about the scenery he saw on his visit to his ancestors' graves. River Blossom listened with the liveliest interest, but Water Blossom said with distaste, "Why d'you have to be so tiresome? I don't want to listen to this."

"Then promise me you won't fall asleep," he said.

"I won't, don't worry."

He sat cross-legged on the edge of the divan to watch over her. That left River Blossom extremely unsettled; whether sitting or standing, she could not keep still. Yet when Water Blossom told her to go outside and amuse herself for a while, she refused. A moment later, Big Goldie came in with their lunch.

"How's your appetite?" Jade asked Water Blossom. "Do try and have a bite."

"I don't want any."

Seeing that her sister would not even eat, River Blossom thought she must be seriously ill. Agitation made her flush red in the face, and she was on the verge of tears. This made Water Blossom smile.

"What're you acting like this for?" she scolded. "I'm not dead yet. I don't have any appetite now, so I'll eat later."

Knowing she had overreacted, River Blossom tried her best to control herself. To set the young girl's mind at ease, Jade pleaded with Water Blossom to eat a little, so Water Blossom told Big Goldie to buy her some congee and took half a bowl of it. River Blossom did not have much of an appetite, either, and only had one bowl, while Jade Tao was never a big eater anyway. When they had finished, lunch was cleared away and they washed their faces. Jade was about to send River Blossom away on some excuse when Beckon came in to report, "Mother is up."

As River Blossom dawdled, Jade told her to hurry up. "If you don't go to her quickly, Mother is going to scold."

Only then did she leave, her reluctance to go tinted by a little embarrassment.

Jade and Water Blossom were alone in the room; not a sound was heard. Unexpectedly, Jade's brother, Cloud Tao, came in a sedan chair to look for him shortly after four. He was invited into the room, where they greeted each other and sat down.

"Are you unwell?" Cloud asked Water Blossom.

"'fraid so," she replied.

Big Goldie busied herself with the teacups, but Cloud stopped her. "I'm just here to have a brief word with him. Don't bother about the tea." He then said to Jade, "The third of the third month is Script Li's birthday. Amity Zhu has sent a circular around saying he has reserved the Panorama Garden for a day's performance and dinner, but Script is wary of disturbing the government officials and has turned down the invitation. That's why Amity has asked a few others to club together for another party at Bright Pearl's. It's a small affair, but both of us are included. I've come to tell you ahead of time: on the day, you don't have to go to the Panorama Garden, but you must turn up at Bright Pearl's."

Although Jade Tao promised repeatedly to go, he stole a look at Water Blossom. Cloud Tao happened to notice and addressed her with a smile, "Would you let him go and mingle for a while?"

Embarrassed, she answered pleasantly, "Eldest Young Master, I'm surprised by your question. This is a matter of propriety, so of course he should go. Why would I stop him?"

Cloud nodded. "That's right. I've always said Water Blossom is a sensible girl. If she clings to him despite the demands of propriety and refuses to let him go, then what love is there to speak of?"

She couldn't very well say anything to that, so she just smiled, whereupon Cloud Tao said, "I'm going."

Jade hastily got to his feet, and Water Blossom saw Cloud Tao off as far as her own door.

Once Cloud got onto the street, he told his sedan-chair bearers to take him to the Zhu residence. The bearers, who knew the place well, took the chair along East Prosperity Alley and then turned eastward into Middle Peace Alley. As they approached the Zhu residence, Amity Zhu's man, Longevity, had already seen him and came up to report, "My master is at the Lins' in Generosity Alley."

At this, Cloud Tao ordered the sedan chair to turn around. They went down Fourth Avenue to White Fragrance's in Generosity Alley. He saw Amity Zhu's sedan chair standing at the door, so he got off and went in.

When he arrived upstairs, Amity Zhu welcomed him into the room and said immediately, "I was just going to ask you here. I can't do everything myself. Why don't you take care of the arrangements at Bright Pearl's?"

Cloud then asked for the details of the arrangements.

Amity Zhu took a rough list out of his pocket. "There'll be the two of us and our brothers, plus Pragmatic Li and his nephew; the six of us will be hosts. We'll get Old Merit Yu to come along to keep our guest company. Lunch will be Western, dinner will be a complete Manchu-and-Han feast. We'll have three all-girl opera troupes, one in the daytime starting at eleven o'clock, two in the evening starting at five. What d'you think?"

"Sounds good to me."

Seeing that they had finished their consultation, White Fragrance came up to offer Cloud Tao some watermelon seeds. Cloud, having put away the list, got up and said, "I still have something else to attend to. I'll see you around." Amity Zhu did not detain him but just saw him off at the stairs with White Fragrance.

When they were back in her room, she asked, "What was that about?"

After he had explained everything, she said, "So, you're giving a party, but instead of doing it here, you're going to suck up to Bright Pearl. You're infuriating!"

"It's not my party. There're six of us clubbing together."

"Wasn't it your party the day before yesterday?"

He had no answer to that, so he just laughed.

"Mine's a small place; naturally it's not fitting to invite His Excellency here. I'm afraid you, too, must have found this place lacking. Now that you've found a large place, you're going to be more comfortable."

"Now this is really a surprise," he said smiling. "It's not as if I've been seeing Bright Pearl, so why are you jealous?"

"If you want to see Bright Pearl, it's your business. I haven't exactly tied you down, have I?"

"All right, I'll shut up. You can say whatever you like." He smiled.

"Humph!" She went on muttering, "You go ahead and suck up to Bright Pearl, but d'you think she'll show you any affection?"

"And who wants her affection?" he asked with a smile.

But she wasn't done yet. "Even if you give ten double-table dinners at her place, it's nothing to her. All my affection has been wasted on you. It seems you'd rather go and be a creep of a guest. You're certainly one of a kind in Shanghai!"

"Don't be angry. I'll give a double-table dinner here tomorrow night," he said, smiling.

She remained poker-faced and made no reply. He went over to pull her by the hand to the divan, pleading, "Won't you fill a pipe for me?"

"I'm too clumsy. I can't do it as well as Bright Pearl." But as she was saying this, she had lain down on the divan and started to toast opium. He sat down at her knees and bent over to whisper into her ear, "You've always been very affectionate, so why is it that you're so angry on account of this Bright Pearl? D'you think I'm going to take up with her?"

"Perhaps you are. One never can tell."

"Well, I might take up with somebody else, but you can be sure it won't be Bright Pearl. Even if she took the initiative I wouldn't be tempted."

"What has it got to do with me, whether you see her or not? I don't want to hear about it."

So he smiled and let it go. When she had filled the pipe, she set it down and walked away. As he smoked, he realized that she still bore a bit of a grudge, so he took ink and a writing brush from a drawer and wrote out a few invitations and an order for some dishes. She pretended not to notice. When he had finished writing, she asked, "Since you're ordering, would you like a couple of dishes first for supper?"

He hastened to comply and added two small dishes to the order. She told the maid to take it downstairs for the menservants to place at the restaurant.

Lamps had just been lit when the dishes were delivered, and the house sent up four extra plates of cold cuts. Amity and White Fragrance sat drinking and chatting, and soon the subject turned to Bright Pearl again.

"All there is to being a courtesan is fashion," said White Fragrance. "When you're in fashion you'll have lots of clients making a big fuss of you. Now, our clients are a sickening lot: if they want to spend a thousand dollars, wouldn't it be nice to give the business to a courtesan not too much in demand? If you spend it on a fashionable one, she won't even notice it. And yet the clients *will* go to the fashionable courtesans, they *will* waste money just to suck up to them."

"But it's not just the clients," he said. "The courtesans are sickening, too. When business is poor, they do their best to please whatever client they have, but when business is a little better, they take up with actors and keep lovers—the whole works. Is it any surprise that they end up with nothing?"

"Those who take up with actors are rare cases, so we needn't talk about them. But it seems to me that the fashionable courtesans don't come to a good end, either. If, while they're in fashion, they pick a reliable client and get married, then they should do all right. The problem is, none of them wants to get married. And come the time they're a bit older and their business declines, they're in for it!"

"Marriage is no easy matter for a courtesan. It goes without saying that she'd want to marry a good client, but when she comes across one, he's sure to have several wives and concubines at home. Even if she married into the house, she'd never be happy. If there isn't any wife or concubine, the client is unreliable. He may take her clothes and jewelry and pawn them all, and then she'd have to work again as a courtesan. This happens quite frequently in the foreign settlements."

"It seems to me that the most important thing is whether you're suited to each other," she said. "If you find a client compatible, even if he's sort of hard up, as long as there's food on the table, it's all right. But if the client is just so-so, then you'd do better to pick one who has a bit of money."

"If you're looking for a man with money, it will never be my turn," Amity said teasingly.

She replied with a smile, "Aiyo! You're too modest! You, poor? Who are you trying to fool?"

He responded, "Even if I do have money, I won't be considered compatible, so I still won't find favor in your eyes."

"Listen to the way you carry on; you've gone off the subject," she said as she picked up the wine pot to pour for him.

"I've had enough to drink; let's have some rice," he said. She called for the maid to bring the rice and also asked for her sister, Green Fragrance, to join them. "Green Fragrance has had dinner," the maid answered.

Just when the two of them had finished dinner, a group of clients dropped in for a tea party and were taken into the vacant room across the way. After that came party calls for White Fragrance, so Amity took the opportunity to leave. Knowing he would not be detained, she saw him off at the door. He went downstairs, got on his sedan chair, and went straight home. Come the next evening, he had to invite all his friends to a double-table dinner at White Fragrance's. But there is no need to go into the details here.

On the third of the third month, Amity got up at ten o'clock and went in his sedan chair to Panorama Garden, where the front door was decorated with lanterns and colorful silk banners. Here, Longevity Zhang, wearing a formal hat, reported to him, "Mr. Chen, Mr. Hong, and Mr. Tang have just arrived."

Amity went in to greet them, inquired about the arrangements, and found that everything was ready. Delighted, he said, "Then I'll go over there, and leave you three gentlemen to take care of things here."

Cloudlet Chen, Benevolence Hong, and Whistler Tang all said, "We'll do our best," upon which Amity set out for Bright Pearl's in Tripod Alley in his sedan chair.

CHAPTER 19 :: *Deceived by love, Modesty Zhu misreads a hidden motive; plagued by illness, Water Blossom puts on a brave face*

Amity Zhu went by sedan chair to Bright Pearl's and then told the bearers, "Take the chair back to fetch Fifth Young Master here." After that, he went upstairs. He was met by the maid, Second Sister Bao, who invited him to go into Bright Pearl's room.

"I'll just sit in the study," he replied.

Bright Pearl's house had five rooms on each floor. The two west rooms were the main ones. Of the three east rooms, the parlor was in the middle. On the right was the Western dining room. With its whitewashed walls, white curtains, an iron bed, and mirrors, it looked like a crystal palace. The room on the left was used as a waiting room for guests when the main rooms were occupied. Since it was furnished with paintings, calligraphy scrolls, books, and chess sets, it was called the study.

As Amity Zhu entered the east rooms, he saw the partitions between them had all been taken down. The parlor led straight to the little mezzanine room at the back. There, a small stage had been set up, with rows of tasseled lanterns suspended from the overhang. The screens and curtains onstage were made of beautifully embroidered silks and satins of a variety of colors. The foreign dining set had been moved to the center of the parlor. The table was covered with a tablecloth, on which were placed two condiments sets, cutlery, and eight drinking glasses, each displaying a linen napkin folded into the shape of a flower.[1]

At the sight of this, Amity said, "Excellent." When he went into the study on the left, he could see Bright Pearl doing her hair at the window on the other side of the house. Given the distance, they just nodded at each other in greeting. Second Sister Bao presented him with a water pipe and tea. The four or five girls owned by Bright Pearl all came out to entertain him, and the little girls in the all-girl theatrical troupes also came to sit with him.

Soon the five other hosts, Cloud and Jade Tao, Pragmatic Li, Crane Li, and Modesty Zhu had all shown up. Having finished her toilet, Bright Pearl also came over. They were just going to send a message to hurry Script Li up when Old Merit appeared, saying, "There's no need. He's on his way."

On hearing this, Cloud Tao went off to make the arrangements. Sixteen kinds of imported fruits, nuts, candies, and cream cakes displayed in high-stemmed glass dishes were set out on the table. The players and musicians were all on standby, waiting to start as soon as Script Li arrived.

In a moment, a steward rushed upstairs to report, "His Excellency is here."

They all stood up. Bright Pearl welcomed Script Li at the head of the stairs, where she took his hand and walked with him into the parlor. Script Li said in mock vexation, "You've gone to so much trouble. It's quite uncalled-for."

Everybody came up to greet him. Since this was Modesty Zhu's first meeting with Script Li, the latter looked him up and down and then said to Amity, "If you don't mind my saying so, he's one better than you."

Everybody covered his mouth and laughed. They all crowded with Script Li into the study.

Bright Pearl, who was standing to one side, asked, "May I take your jacket, Your Excellency?" So saying, she reached out to unbutton his jacket for him. He took it off and handed it to her, saying, "Much obliged." She replied with a smile, "Your Excellency is courtesy itself!" The jacket was passed on to Second Sister Bao, who hung it on the clothes rack while Bright Pearl made Li sit down on a high-back chair.

The maid of the theatrical troupe submitted a list of operas asking

::

1. [This is in contrast to Chinese custom, which leaves such preparations until after the arrival of the guests. *E.H.*]

for their choices. Bright Pearl answered on behalf of Script Li, "We should ask Mr. Yu to pick the plays."

Old Merit chose two short plays and told Second Sister Bao to bring the call chits. Amity Zhu pointed at Jade Tao and Modesty Zhu, "What about these two? There aren't that many girls they can call."

"Never mind," said Script Li. "They can call as many as they like or just call one. It's up to them."

Amity Zhu gave the names while Old Merit wrote them down. They were calling all the girls everybody had ever summoned before. In Jade Tao's case, he could summon Water Blossom as well as her younger sister, River Blossom. But Modesty Zhu had no one to call but Twin Jade.

After the chits had been written, Cloud Tao asked them to take their seats at the table.

"It's too early," Script Li said.

"We can have some appetizers first," Cloud Tao replied.

Script Li again complained to Amity Zhu, "It's all your fault. You're the one who started all this."

Everybody proceeded into the parlor. There, they saw that eight foreign rattan chairs had been set out in a row in front of the dinner table and facing the stage, with a set of teacups for each person.

"Let's sit wherever we like. Anyone who feels like eating can just help himself."

As he said this, Script Li picked up a cream cake, pulled out a rattan chair, and sat down against the wall, so the others had to follow his example, dispense with ceremony, and sit around informally.

Private performances always started with the routine "Dance of Official Promotion." After this came the two auspicious short plays they had picked, *A House Full of High Officials* and *Beating the Princess.* They bored Script Li, so he said to Modesty Zhu, "Come, let's have a chat." He took the young man by the hand and went back into the study. Amity Zhu followed them but was told off by Script Li. "You go and watch the play. Forget about this silly fuss of keeping me entertained, all right?" Amity had to obey. Script Li told Modesty Zhu to sit across from him on the divan and asked him his age, what books he was studying, and whether he was betrothed. Modesty Zhu answered all his questions.

Soon, Bright Pearl came in with a handful of imported hazel nuts, pine nuts, and walnuts she had shelled and presented them to Script Li. He took them and offered half of them to Modesty, saying, "Try some." Modesty picked up a few but did not eat them. Script Li again asked him about all sorts of things. This went on for a long time. Bright Pearl, who was watching and listening to one side, got some idea of what Script Li had in mind.

They chatted until noon, when Second Sister Bao came to get the call chits. Bright Pearl realized it was time for lunch to be served, so she invited Script Li back into the parlor. Everybody stood up, ready to toast him and decide on the seating order, but Script Li would not permit it. Instead, he made Modesty Zhu sit beside him. The others could not very well insist, so, with the exception of Old Merit, they took their seats according to their age. The first course was oyster soup, after which came the fish. Bright Pearl hastened to bone it for Script Li with her knife and fork.

By then, the girls summoned to the party were arriving one after another. Onstage, they were performing the Kun opera *Catkin Pavilion,* in which the gongs and drums were silent and only stringed instruments played. That made it quiet and peaceful. Script Li looked around him and found that he was already surrounded by girls called to the party, yet more were still coming. He asked Amity Zhu, "How many girls did you call for me?"

"A very limited number," Amity Zhu answered smiling. "Less than twenty."

Script Li frowned. "You really don't have any sense of proportion!" Then he looked at the others. Some had called two or three girls, some four or five, but Modesty Zhu had just one. Script Li learned it was Twin Jade. He looked her up and down and nodded in approval. "They do make a perfect couple."

Everybody echoed his praise in chorus.

Script Li then turned to Amity Zhu. "You're the elder brother. Don't you play the fool! You should bring them together—seriously."

On hearing this, Modesty Zhu was overcome with embarrassment. Even Twin Jade lowered her head.

"No need to be so formal, you two," said Script Li. "Sit over here and chat, so I can listen in, too."

"If you want to hear these two talk, I'm afraid you'll be disappointed," said Amity Zhu.

Script Li was taken aback. "Is she a mute?"

The others could not suppress a smile.

"A mute she's not; only they don't talk," Amity Zhu replied.

Script Li urged Modesty Zhu, "Come on, show them. You must say a few words for everyone to hear. Don't let your brother triumph over you."

Modesty Zhu was more embarrassed than ever. Then Script Li turned to Twin Jade and tried to get her to speak. She just smiled. Finally, pressed hard by Script Li, she said with a smile, "There's nothing to say, though. What should I say?"

This sent everybody exclaiming: "Well done! She's broken her golden silence."

Script Li lifted his cup for a toast, "All of us should drink a cup to congratulate them." He drained his in one draught and then showed Modesty Zhu the bottom of his cup. Everybody drank up. Modesty Zhu was so embarrassed even his ears turned red. He just would not drink. Fortunately, a new play, *Tianshui Pass*, had just started. The noise of its battle cries cut short Script Li's badinage.

Seeing that the eighth course, curried chicken rice, was about done, most of the summoned girls took their leave. Twin Jade also made to go, but Script Li spotted her and said, "Don't go just yet. I want a word with you." She thought he still was teasing, but when Amity Zhu joined in to detain her, she had to return to her seat. Her servant girl Clever Baby whispered something in her ear. She just replied she'd be back directly. Clever Baby then left ahead of her.

At the end of the feast, everybody drank a cup of coffee with milk. Then they wiped their faces, rinsed their mouths, and dispersed. The theater troupe happened to have finished its main performance just then, and the maid came to ask for further choices.

"Would somebody just pick something?" said Script Li.

Amity Zhu knew that Script Li needed his afternoon nap. He thought it best to stop the show for now and have both troupes play together that night. Without even consulting Script Li, he just dismissed the troupe.

Taking Modesty Zhu in one hand and Twin Jade in the other, Script Li walked away from the others, saying, "Let's go over here." He walked slowly into the dining room and sat down on an air cushion on the sofa against the wall. He told them to sit on either side of him and then asked Twin Jade how old she was, where she lived, and whether her mother was still alive. She answered his questions one by one. He then turned to Modesty Zhu, "When did you start seeing her?"

Modesty Zhu looked lost and bewildered. She answered for him, "Only at the end of last month, when the elder Mr. Zhu called me to a party for him. He hasn't been to our place yet."

Script Li immediately pulled a long face. "You're really not a nice person," he chided Modesty Zhu. "Someone's been longing for your visit day in and day out, so why disappoint her?"

Modesty Zhu got quite a turn. Only when Twin Jade let out a giggle did he realize what Script Li meant.

Then Script Li consoled her, "Don't be angry. I'll come with him tomorrow. Tell me if he's not nice to you, and I'll give him a beating."

She turned sideways to hide a smile. "Thank you."

"Don't thank me yet. Wait till I've really played matchmaker for you, then say your thanks in one go."

At this, even Twin Jade ceased smiling and said nothing.

"What is it? Don't you want to marry him?" said Script Li. "Look, such a nice young fellow, what's wrong with marrying him? If you refuse, you'll be missing out on a great opportunity!"

"I'm afraid such blessings are not my lot." she said.

"You can count yourself blessed if I speak up for you. Just say yes, and with a word from me it's done."

She still said nothing.

Script Li kept urging her, "Speak up. Are you willing?"

She replied in vexation, "Your Excellency, is it reasonable to ask me about something like this?"

"Am I to ask your mother then? You have a point there. Once you've agreed, naturally I'll go and ask your mother."

She remained silent, her head still turned away.

Second Sister Bao happened to come in with tea, so Twin Jade changed the subject and said playfully, "Do have some tea, Your Excellency."

He reached out for the teacup and asked Second Sister Bao, "Where's everybody?"

"They're chatting in the study. Shall I ask them to come over?"

"Don't bother." He handed her the teacup and lay down on the sofa. Once Second Sister Bao was gone, it was quiet in the room. Before he knew it, everything grew blurred; his mouth fell open, and his eyes closed.

Taking this in from the corner of her eye, Twin Jade tiptoed off. Modesty Zhu remained seated there, afraid to leave. As he hesitated, he heard Script Li starting to snore. He coughed deliberately, and the noise did not wake Li, so Modesty also slipped out of the room. He wanted to find Twin Jade and talk to her. When he walked over to the study, he saw the younger men were seated around Old Merit, deep in conversation. Bright Pearl put in a word from time to time, but Twin Jade was not there. He was just going to withdraw when Bright Pearl spotted him and asked, "Is His Excellency alone in there?" He nodded. She rushed over, all flustered.

Modesty took the opportunity to retrace his steps. He stood at the door trying to figure out where Twin Jade had gone. As he chanced to look that way, he caught sight of someone leaning at a window on the east wing. On looking more closely he found it was none other than Twin Jade. Overjoyed, he made bold to skirt round the back. When he entered Bright Pearl's own chamber, he tiptoed up behind Twin Jade, but she had sensed his approach and just pretended not to notice. As he slowly reached out a hand for her wrist, she suddenly snatched her hand away and shouted, "Don't horse around!"

Never expecting such a reaction, he got a real shock and stumbled back a step or two. Cowering before the divan, he stood in a daze, his face frozen.

She waited a moment. Seeing that nothing was happening, she turned around to find out what he was doing. To her surprise he seemed to be in a state of shock. Realizing she had been too brusque, she felt quite apologetic. But how was she to console him? She could not come up with an idea, so she just shot him a sidelong glance with the flicker of a smile.

Reassured, he sighed. "You're a fine one! You almost scared me to death!"

Holding back her laughter, she said in a low voice, "If you have enough sense to be scared, why don't you keep your hands to yourself?"

"How would I dare do otherwise? I just wanted to ask you something."

"What is it?"

"I wanted to know where Sunshine Alley is. How many people are there in your place? Would it be all right if I came?"

She did not answer. He repeated his questions, and finally she said in vexation, "I don't know!" Then she stood up and walked out of the room. Modesty just stared after her, bewildered, and could not very well stop her.

When she got to the door curtain, she turned around and asked him with a smile, "Are you close to Benevolence Hong?"

He thought for a moment. "Benevolence Hong? No, not really. But he and my brother are old friends."

"Just go and find Benevolence Hong."

He wanted to ask her why, but she had walked out of the room. He followed her back to the study. Clever Baby had just come to fetch her, so she made ready to say good-bye.

"Go and tell His Excellency," Amity Zhu said.

"Never mind. His Excellency is asleep," said Bright Pearl.

After a moment's reflection, Amity Zhu said, "In that case, you can go now. We'll call you again later."

Twin Jade had just left when a maid came peeping around the edge of the curtain. Seeing her, Jade Tao hurried outside, and they talked for a while in undertones, after which he returned to the study to sit with the others. When Cloud Tao saw the expression of uncertainty on his brother's face, he asked, "More trouble?"

"No," Jade Tao mumbled. "It's just that Water Blossom is not feeling well."

"She was fine just now," Cloud Tao said.

"With her, it's hard to say," Jade replied glibly.

Cloud sneered. "If you want to go and look in on her, do it now when we're free. Come back early."

This was just what Jade had been hoping for. He immediately excused himself, went downstairs, got into the sedan chair, and made straight for East Prosperity Alley. As he walked into her room, he saw Water Blossom lying in bed, hugging the quilt. Only her younger sister, River Blossom, was there, propping herself up on the bed by the elbows, keeping Water Blossom company. He reached out to feel her forehead, which was slightly feverish.

"Sister, Brother-in-law is here," River Blossom called out repeatedly.

She opened her eyes and saw him. "You shouldn't have come right away. Won't your brother scold?"

"It's all right, he told me to come."

"Why would he do that?"

"He told me to come here first and then go back there early tonight."

After a long pause, she said, "Your brother is a nice man. Don't be stubborn with him, just do as he says."

He did not reply, just bent down, put her hands under the quilt, and tucked it up firmly around her neck and shoulders, leaving a little gap for air circulation. Then he suggested that she take off her earrings. But she refused, saying, "I'll be all right after I get a little sleep."

"Just now, you were perfectly all right. Did the wind get at you in the sedan chair?" he said.

"No, it was just that awful play, *Tianshui Pass*. It made such a racket, my head was bursting."

"Then why didn't you leave early?"

"The girls hadn't all arrived. How could I leave first?"

"That doesn't matter really."

River Blossom broke in, "Brother-in-law, you should have said something. If you did, then Elder Sister could have left first while I stayed a little longer. That'd have been all right, wouldn't it?"

"Then why didn't you say so?" he asked.

"But I didn't know Elder Sister was unwell."

"So you didn't know, but I was supposed to know?" he said with a smile. At this, River Blossom also smiled.

Jade Tao sat down on the bed, and River Blossom leaned against his knees. Neither of them spoke. Water Blossom remained wide awake, unable to sleep. By the time the lamps were lit, Cloud Tao's sedan-chair bearers came with a message: "The table is set. Second Young Master is requested to go over right away."

Jade Tao answered in the affirmative. Water Blossom happened to hear this, so she said, "Hurry up, or else your brother will lecture you again."

"There's ample time."

"It's not that. If go early, you can come back early. That'll also give your brother a good impression, won't it? Otherwise, he'll go on about your being bewitched and say you won't even attend to serious matters."

After a moment of reflection, he turned to River Blossom, "Then you keep your sister company. Don't go away."

"No," Water Blossom said quickly. "Let her go and have supper. After that, she'll have to answer party calls."

"I'll eat here," said River Blossom.

"I have no appetite. You go and eat with Mother."

"Have something, all right?" he tried to persuade her. "If you don't eat, your mother will worry herself sick."

"All right, now off you go."

Thereupon he went by sedan chair to Tripod Alley for dinner at Bright Pearl's, while River Blossom lingered by the bed, asking questions about this and that.

"Go and tell Mother I want to sleep for a while. I'm not feeling unwell, but I don't want dinner," Water Blossom said.

At first, the young girl refused to go, but finally Water Blossom made her.

A moment later, Water Blossom's mother, Fair Sister Li, pushed open the back door and came in. Seeing there was no one with her, she asked, "Why isn't Second Young Master here?"

"I told him to go. He's the host today so he should go and entertain."

Fair Sister Li walked up to the bed to look at Water Blossom's face and touch and feel her all over.

"Don't, Mother, I'm all right," she said smiling, trying to stop her.

"D'you feel like eating anything special? I'll tell them to make it. The cook is not doing anything just now."

"I have no appetite."

"There's some five-spiced pigeon. I'll tell them to make a little congee, and you can have it later."

"You eat it yourself, Mother. Just the thought of it makes me unwell, so how could I get it down?"

Fair Sister gave her some more advice and then turned up the lamp on the dressing table and lowered the wick of the paraffin lamp in the side chamber. She also let down the curtains before she went out through the backdoor to go to supper. Water Blossom was alone in the room.

As Water Blossom was ill, she preferred to rest in peace and would not even let Beckon and Big Goldie wait on her. She lay in bed with her eyes wide open, all alone. After lying like that for a long time, she wanted to relieve herself, so she pulled a jacket over her shoulders and got up. She stuck her feet into a pair of slippers and, holding on to the railings of the bedstead, groped her way to the area behind the bed. She had just sat down on the chamber pot when she heard the back door to her room creak open a little.

"Who is it?" she asked quickly.

No one answered. She became anxious and made haste to get up. Just then, she saw a dark ball roll in through the slightly opened door and go under her bed. Water Blossom was so flustered by this that she even forgot to tie up the sash of her trousers but just stumbled back into the room, only managing to steady herself when she reached the round marble table at its center. She was about to strike a match to see what had come in when a big black cat with white fur on its belly crawled out from under the bed. It gave a yowl and stretched itself in front of her. In anger and frustration, she stamped her foot. The cat bolted toward the door but then turned round to stare at her out of luminous, tigerlike eyes.

There was nothing she could do about it. When she got back to her bed, her heart was still pounding. She wanted to call for somebody to keep her company but was afraid to alarm her mother, so had to give up the idea. Instead, she just sat on the bed, hugging the quilt. It happened that Jade Tao's call chit came just then for River Blossom. The young girl came in dressed in party clothes and said to Water Blossom, "Elder Sister, I'm off. Have you got any message for Brother-in-law?"

"Nothing. Tell him not to drink so much and to come back as soon as dinner is over."

The young girl answered yes and made to leave, but Water Blossom stopped her to inquire, "Who is going with you?"

"Beckon."

"Tell Big Goldie to go along, too. She can do some of the drinking for him."

She promised and left.

Water Blossom felt she could not bear up anymore and had to lie down. She had not foreseen that the black cat was a real troublemaker: it sneaked back into her room. Lying facing the wall, she was unaware of it. The cat quietly jumped on to the dressing table from a high-back chair and sniffed endlessly at every object on the table:

mirror, lamp stand, teapot, clock, and so on. Water Blossom saw a black shadow like a man's head flicker across the bed curtain. This so frightened her that a chill went through her and her hands and feet trembled uncontrollably. She could not even manage to call out. By the time she sat up, supporting herself by her arms, the cat had leapt away. She gnashed her teeth and cursed, "The damned beast! It deserves to die!"

After a moment's reflection, her mind settled somewhat. She picked up a hand mirror from the dressing table to look at herself. The thin sallow face was flushed like a Fuzhou tangerine. She heaved a sigh, put down the mirror, and turned to lie down facing the door, her eyes wide open, waiting for Jade Tao to return from the dinner party. The hours passed, but there was no sign of either him or River Blossom.

Just as she was consumed with anxiety, her mother came in to ask her, "The congee is ready. Would you like a sip?"

"Mother, I'm all right. I'm not hungry just now; I'll eat later."

"Then tell me when you feel like it, for they'll never think of it after I've gone to bed."

She promised and asked her in return, "River Blossom has been gone for a while now; hasn't she come back yet?"

"She has to go on from there to another party."

"In that case, you might have sent a manservant to go and look in on Second Young Master."

"The men have all gone out. Big Goldie is over there with Second Young Master."

"When the men are back, tell them to go there right away."

"Who knows when they'll be back! I'll tell the cook to go." So saying, Fair Sister went out to the parlor to summon the cook and instructed him to "go and look in on Second Young Master Tao."

The cook was about to go when Jade Tao arrived in a sedan chair, with Big Goldie in tow. Fair Sister was overjoyed. "He's here! He's here! You don't have to go now."

Jade came straight to Water Blossom's bed and asked solicitously, "I kept you waiting a long time. Are you bored?"

"It's all right. Is the party over?" she said.

"Not yet. The old man was in such good spirits, he picked a dozen operas to be performed. The whole thing will go on till dawn."

"So you left early. Did you tell them you were leaving?"

He answered with a smile, "I said I had a slight headache and I wasn't up to drinking either. They said, 'If you have a headache, you should go home.' So I left."

"Did you really have a headache?"

"It was real all right. I did have a headache when I was there, but as soon as I left, it was gone," he replied.

"You're a crafty one. No wonder your brother scolds you," she said lightheartedly.

"Well, he just smiled at me and didn't say anything."

"Your brother was so angry, he was at a loss for words; that's why he smiled."

He responded with a smile and then sat down at the edge of her bed, felt the palm of her hand, and asked, "Feeling better?"

"Just about the same."

"How much did you eat at supper?"

"I didn't have any. Mother made some congee; d'you want some? If you do, I'll have some, too."

He was going to call for Big Goldie when she happened to come in on orders from Fair Sister. She asked, "Would you like some congee?"

He told her to bring it at once. Then he turned around and said to Water Blossom, "Your mother has a difficult time getting you to eat the smallest morsel. You'd make her very happy if you'd just eat a little more!"

"You make it sound so easy. I'd like to eat, too, but what can I do when I've got no appetite?"

Big Goldie brought in a large tray, which she put on the dressing table; she then lit a second paraffin table lamp. Jade helped Water Blossom sit up in bed and just sat on the edge of the bed himself. They each picked up a bowl of congee and started eating. He saw there were four very nice vegetarian dishes on the tray, together with a small bowl of spiced pigeon that was very light, so he tried to persuade her to have some. But she shook her head and just had a little salted vegetable to go with the congee.

As they were eating, River Blossom came home from the other party. She came in to ask after her elder sister even before she got changed. Seeing Jade Tao, she said joyfully, "I knew Brother-in-law would have been here for a while. What are you eating? I want some, too!" She turned to call for Beckon, "Quick, fill a bowl for me."

"You should get changed first. What's the hurry?" Beckon responded.

River Blossom hastily took off her party clothes, handed them to Beckon, and repeatedly urged Big Goldie to hurry up and give her a bowl of congee. She ate leaning against the dressing table and as she did so started laughing at herself. This made Jade and Water Blossom laugh, too.

Soon, everybody had finished eating and had cleaned their faces.

Big Goldie came in again to say, "Second Young Master, Mother requests a word with you."

He had no idea what it was about, so he told River Blossom to keep Water Blossom company and went out by the back door for Fair Sister Li's room.

Fair Sister greeted him and asked him to sit down. She then said, "Second Young Master, her illness doesn't look good to me. If it was just a fever, I wouldn't worry, but this illness of hers doesn't seem like fever. She's been ill since the first month, and she's completely lost her appetite. She's wasted away so much that she's just a bag of bones now. Second Young Master, could you please persuade her to see a doctor and take a couple of doses of medicine?"

"This illness of hers should have been tended to by a doctor last winter. Actually, I've spoken to her about it several times, but she's set on refusing treatment. There's nothing I can do."

"She's always been like this. When she's ill, she won't tell you, and if you ask her, she always says she's better. If you do get a doctor and prepare the medicine for her, she gets upset about it. But I've been thinking, this illness is not like any other; if she still refuses to take medicine, Second Young Master, I'm afraid she may succeed in doing away with herself!"

He hung his head in silence.

"You go and talk to her. You don't have to go on about it; just tell her to see a doctor and take a couple of doses of medicine so she'll get well faster. If you told her the truth, she'd get worried, and if the worry brought on some other complications, she'd end up even worse. And don't you worry about it, either, Second Young Master, for no matter how much you worry, it won't help her. After all, this illness of hers will not last long. A couple of doses of medicine will see it ease off."

He frowned. "Though it's not serious, she should take better care of herself. She gets easily upset if things are just a tiny bit amiss. That being the case, it's hard to see how she'll recover."

"Well, you know what she's like, Second Young Master. If she was wise enough to take better care of herself, she wouldn't be ill at all. This illness all started because she was unhappy. That's why you have to be the one to speak to her, Second Young Master. She'll take it better from you."

He nodded silently. She then spoke of something else. After that, he took his leave and returned to Water Blossom's room.

"What did Mother say to you?" she asked.

"Nothing really. She asked about the affair at Bright Pearl's; whether she was hosting the party in honor of the money gods," he said.

"That wasn't it. Mother was talking about me."

"Why would Mother talk about you?"

"Don't try to fool me. I can guess what it was about."

"If that's the case, why ask me?" he replied with a smile.

She was silent. River Blossom pulled him over to the bed and made him sit down. She then clambered all over him and asked, "What did Mother really say?"

"She said you're no good."

"And why am I no good?"

"She said you won't listen to your elder sister. That makes your sister unhappy and that's why she got ill."

"What else did she say?"

"What else? She said your sister is also no good."

"Why is Elder Sister no good?"

"Well, your elder sister won't listen to Mother. If she had, and had taken some opium to cheer herself up, she wouldn't have been ill, would she?"

"You're talking nonsense! No one would tell Elder Sister to take opium! Once you start taking opium, you'll only get worse."

As they were talking, Water Blossom reached out for tea. Jade Tao hastened to take the teapot and raise it to her lips. After drawing at it twice, she said calmly, "I'm my mother's only child. When I'm unwell, she may not say anything, but in her heart she's dead worried. I, too, want to get well as soon as possible, so she'll be happier. Who'd have thought I'd be ill for *so* long! When I look at myself in the mirror, I see a face so thin it's not even human. Seeing a doctor and taking medicine are all very well if they can cure me, but I know this illness won't be cured! Ever since I got ill last year, Mother, needless to say, has been worried to death, and even you haven't had a single easy day. If, on top of it all, I'm to see a doctor and take medicine, the whole household will have no peace. The maids and servant girls are run off their feet as it is; how can I make them brew medicine for me all day long? Though they wouldn't say anything, I'd feel bad about causing all the fuss and not seeing any improvement in my illness. You see what I mean?"

"Oh, you're far too sensitive," he replied. "Who would say anything against you? The way I look at it, it's all right if you don't want to take medicine, but it'll take you longer to get well. With a couple of doses of medicine, you'll get well sooner. Don't you think so?"

"If Mother insists on getting a doctor, I'll just have to let her have her way. But suppose I don't get well even after taking medicine, won't she be more worried than ever? I was thinking, ever since I was a child, Mother has always made much of me. I always get whatever I want, and I've never given her anything in return. Instead, I make her worry her heart out. I just haven't done right by her, have I?"

"Your mother is worried just because you're ill. Once you get well, she'll be fine. It's not a question of whether you've done right by her."

"I'm the one who's ill, so I should know about this illness of mine. It won't kill me right away, but it won't be cured easily, either. I never talked about it because I was afraid Mother and the others would be worried, but I guess now I have to. As for you, I'm afraid we've known each other in vain. All the promises we've made, let's not mention them anymore. If we meet again in another life, I'll try to make it up to you. I was thinking, there's nothing I can't let go of really; all I worry about is my mother. But even then, I've still got a brother, after all, and if you help her a bit, she won't be too badly off, so I can die with an easy heart. Besides Mother, there's just her," she pointed to River Blossom. "Although she's not my real sister, she's always been as close to me as any true sister could be. She'll be the first to suffer when I die. That's why I have nothing else in my mind except this one thing I want to beg of you. If there's a place in your heart for me, then promise me this: as soon as I'm dead, you should marry River Blossom; it'll be just the same as marrying me. In the future, if she remembers that this elder sister had treated her well, she'll put out some sacrificial food for me, and even as a ghost I'll belong somewhere. With that taken care of, my business in this life comes to a full conclusion."

During Water Blossom's long monologue, River Blossom, who had been standing beside them, had at first listened in a daze. But as she heard Water Blossom's final words, she burst out crying uncontrollably. Jade Tao rushed to soothe her, but she pulled her hand free and ran weeping all the way to Fair Sister Li's room, calling, "Mother, Elder Sister is in a bad way!"

Startled, Fair Sister blurted out, "What's the matter?" River Blossom couldn't put anything into words; she just pointed, "Mother, you go and see for yourself!"

Just as Fair Sister was about to go, Jade came over to reassure her, saying repeatedly, "It's nothing, don't worry." He gave a brief account of what Water Blossom had said and chided River Blossom for getting worked up.

Fair Sister also told the girl off. "How is it you have no sense at all? Your elder sister said those things just because she's not well. How could you say she was in a bad way?" Thereupon she took River Blossom by the hand, and all three of them went back to the front room and stood in front of Water Blossom's bed. Seeing that Water Blossom looked all right, everybody felt relieved.

"The little silly," Fair Sister said laughingly, "She's naturally worried sick to hear you sound so miserable, and she certainly gave me a fright, too!"

Water Blossom saw that River Blossom's face was still wet with tears. She smiled at her and said, "If you want to cry, you can cry all you like when I'm dead. What's the hurry?"

"Oh, do stop talking like that. If you go on, she's sure to have another outburst," said Fair Sister. She then took a look at the black marble clock on the dressing table. "It's midnight already. Come and sleep in my room." So saying, she made to go, taking River Blossom by the hand.

But the girl did not want to go. "I'll just sleep in the rattan chair here."

"How can you sleep in a rattan chair? Come on."

Feeling desperate, River Blossom was again on the verge of tears when Jade Tao intervened. "Let her sleep here with us. This bed will accommodate three quite comfortably."

Fair Sister gave in and, after telling River Blossom not to cry, left the room. Then Big Goldie and Beckon came in to help them prepare for bed. Before the two women withdrew, they blew out the lamp, closed the door, and called out "Good night." Jade Tao told River Blossom to go to bed first. She took off her outer garments and went and curled up at one end of the bed, next to Water Blossom's feet. Jade Tao, in his tight undershirt and underpants, sat side by side with Water Blossom for a long time before they both lay down.

Worried about Water Blossom's illness, he was unable to sleep. She, though, fell sound asleep fairly quickly. He felt a bit hot and would have liked to turn over. But she was sleeping with one arm across his chest, and in order not to disturb her, he just reached a hand out to peel off some clothes that he had draped over his body and flung them toward the inside of the bed where River Blossom was lying. River Blossom showed no sign of movement and made no noise, so she, too, must have fallen soundly asleep. Jade Tao looked around: seen through the bed curtains, the lamplight on the dressing table was weak and shadowy. He figured that it was around two in the morning. All was quiet in the neighborhood except for the occasional sound of passing carriage wheels coming from the main road. He felt calmer and was finally ready for sleep.

Just as sleepiness was overcoming Jade Tao, Water Blossom suddenly called out: "I'm not going! I'm not going!" As she shouted, she clutched at his undershirt as if holding on for dear life and tried to bury her head in it.

He was wide awake at once and comforted her, "I'm here, don't be frightened." He sat up hastily and held her in his arms and rocked and patted her. Only then did she wake up, still maintaining the grip on his undershirt, staring at him, panting.

"Was it a dream?" he asked.

She said after a long pause, "Two foreigners were trying to drag me away!"

"You must have seen some foreigners in the daytime and got a fright."

Her breathing calmed down gradually, and she let go of him and sighed. "My back aches so!"

"Shall I massage it for you?"

"I want to turn over."

Jade Tao turned sideways to let her turn to face the wall. She curled up her body under the quilt and laid her head against his chest, telling him to hold her in his arms. Their movement woke River Blossom, who called out, "Brother-in-law." He answered, and she sat up, rubbing her eyes, and asked, "Where's Elder Sister?"

"Elder Sister is sleeping; you go back to sleep. Don't get up."

"Where's she sleeping?"

"Here, right here."

She did not believe him until she had crawled over and pulled up the quilt to see for herself. After that, he told her to go back to sleep. As she lay down, she again called out, "Brother-in-law, don't fall asleep yet. Wait till I've gone to sleep first." He promised offhandedly.

In a moment, all three of them had entered the land of sweet slumber, and they remained soundly asleep till nine o'clock the next morning, when Big Goldie called in a low voice through the bed curtains, "Second Young Master."

Both he and Water Blossom woke up. Big Goldie handed him a note. He saw it was his brother's handwriting. After reading it, he said, "Tell them I'll be there."

Big Goldie went out with the message.

"What is it?" Water Blossom asked.

"Script Li received a telegram last night. He said it's urgent business, and he's going home today. Brother told me to go with him to see Li off."

"Your brother is certainly on his toes," she said.

"You stay in bed. I'll be right back."

"You hardly slept at all last night. Come back early so you can get a little more rest."

He had just put on his clothes and got off the bed when River Blossom also woke up. She clamored, "Brother-in-law, how is it you're up? Why didn't you call me first?" So saying, she climbed out of bed. He hastily took her clothes and draped them over her shoulders.

"You should put on more clothes, too. It's windy on the Bund," Water Blossom said.

He changed into a padded jacket and also got River Blossom a padded sleeveless jacket. They were barely ready when Cloud Tao arrived in his sedan chair. Jade Tao quickly lowered the bed curtains and invited him into the room.

CHAPTER 21 :: *A prostitute lies about consulting the gods to find a missing article, and a henpecked husband throws a party behind his wife's back*

Jade Tao invited his brother, Cloud, into Water Blossom's room. Having inquired after her health, Cloud told Jade to wash his face and braid his hair quickly. After a little dim sum for breakfast, they got on their sedan chairs and left East Prosperity Alley for the Bund. At the wharf of the foreign hongs, they saw a little steamer. A mandarin's sedan chair and a carriage were already standing alongside it. The Tao brothers sent in their visiting cards and were welcomed by Script Li into the main cabin, where they saw Pragmatic Li and Crane Li, who had also come to bid Script farewell. After the usual greetings, everyone sat down. The conversation was, naturally, about Li's departure.

Before long, Old Merit and Amity Zhu arrived together in their sedan chairs. The minute Script Li saw them, he asked, "How did it go?"

"It's all settled. The total comes to eight thousand dollars," Amity Zhu replied.

Script Li saluted him, saying, "Thanks for your trouble."

Pragmatic Li asked what it was about.

"Oh, I bought a couple of old things," replied Script Li.

Old Merit said, "The things look all right, but the price is high enough, too. The five-foot Jingtai porcelain vase alone costs three thousand."

Pragmatic Li stuck out his tongue in shock and shook his head. "You shouldn't have bought it. What d'you want it for?"

Script Li smiled and said nothing.

Everyone lingered for a little longer, until the boat was about to sail, when they took their leave and went ashore. Script Li and Old Merit saw them off at the bow. The Tao brothers and Amity Zhu left in their sedan chairs, while Pragmatic and Crane Li got into the carriage in which they had come. The driver knew them well and drove straight to Fourth Avenue, stopping at Generosity Alley. Pragmatic Li knew his nephew was going to Grace Yang's, so he said he had some business to attend to and declined to go in. Knowing him, Crane Li just bade him good-bye and walked into the alley.

Pragmatic Li actually had nothing to do. Since it was still early, he wondered where he should go. Perhaps it would be best to get a casual meal at Perfection's, he thought. So he headed due west for Great Prosperity Alley. As soon as he stepped into the house, he saw an old woman sitting in the parlor. She was none other than the squinting crone he had seen at the House of Floral Rain. What a surprise!

Third Sister Chu came forward exclaiming loudly, "Aiyo! Mr. Li is here!" So saying, she rushed out into the little courtyard, grabbed him by the sleeve, and dragged him into the parlor. The old woman sensed she was in the way and got up to take her leave. Third Sister did not detain her but just said, "Drop in again when you have time." The old woman thanked her and left. Having shut the door, Third Sister turned around to say, "Do go upstairs, Mr. Li."

He went up to find that there was no one in the room. As she lit a match to light the opium lamp, Third Sister apologized to him, "Sorry, Mr. Li, please sit for a while. Perfection has gone to the temple and will be back soon. Please have a smoke. I'll go and make tea."

Before she could leave, however, he stopped her to ask who the old woman was.

"She's called Old Mrs. Filial Guo, a sort of elder sister of mine. D'you know her, Mr. Li?"

"Not personally, but I've seen her a few times at the House of Floral Rain."

"Mr. Li, though you don't know her, when I tell you, you'll realize you've heard of her. She's the eldest among us seven sisters. There used to be seven of us. We were so close to each other that we became sworn sisters. We worked together and played together, and in Shanghai we were pretty well-known, though I say it myself. Have you seen photographs of the Seven Sisters in the photo studios, Mr. Li? That's us."

"Oh, so you are the Seven Sisters! How come you've never mentioned this before?"

"You see, the minute I spoke of the Seven Sisters, you remembered us. But these days the Seven Sisters aren't what they used to be. Some are married, some are dead, now there're just the three of us left. Old Mrs. Guo is the big sister, and she's come to this. I'm third. Between us comes Second Sister Huang. She's turned out best among us three; she owns several girls and has her own house. Her business is not bad, either."

"What is Old Mrs. Guo doing now?" he asked.

"Speaking of our big sister, it couldn't be more unfair. She was the most capable of the lot, but she had no luck. The year before last, she found a new girl for her business, but after just two months she got arrested by the new yamen and was accused of abduction, of all things! She was thrown into prison for over a year and wasn't let out till the end of last year."

He had more questions, but just then the doorbell chimed downstairs.

"Perfection is back," she said and hurried downstairs to meet her.

He looked out the window and saw Perfection had come in, followed by a handsome young man in a lined gown of black crinkled crepe, topped by a padded jacket of pale gray Nanjing silk. He thought it must be a new client she had picked up, so he cocked an ear to listen to them. He heard Third Sister taking them into the downstairs parlor and then whispering to the young man, but he couldn't make out what was said. After they had spoken, she went to the kitchen to make tea. When she brought the tea upstairs, he took the opportunity to take his leave.

She grabbed hold of him and whispered, "Don't go, Mr. Li. Who d'you think that is? That's her husband. They've come back from the temple together. I told him there's a lady caller upstairs, so he won't be coming up. He'll go soon. Please, Mr. Li, sit for a while. Sorry about this."

"That's her husband? No kidding?" He was astonished.

"There you have it."

"What if he insists on coming upstairs?" he asked after a moment of reflection.

"Don't worry, Mr. Li, he won't dare come up. Even if he does, with me here it won't matter."

He returned to his seat in silence. Third Sister went downstairs again to see to things, and after a while the young man did leave. Perfection saw him to the door and then returned to the kitchen and talked in whispers with Third Sister. Only after that did she come upstairs to keep Pragmatic company.

"Was that your husband?" he asked.

She smiled but said nothing. He pressed the question. "Why would you want to ask about him?" she said, vexed.

"What's wrong with asking you about your husband? No one's going to snatch him away, so why are you so upset?"

"I don't want you to ask!"

"Aiyo! So you have a husband, and he's so precious no one's allowed even to ask about him!" he said teasingly.

She reached out and pinched him on the thigh. He cried out in pain.

"D'you dare say that again?"

"No, I'll say no more, I promise," he said repeatedly. She finally let go after that.

He went on grinning, as if nothing had happened. "This husband of yours is excellent though: he's young, he's got a handsome face; even his clothes look nice and spruce. You're *so* lucky!"

Hearing this, she jumped on him and, with the full weight of her body, pressed him down on the opium divan and started tickling him, scratching and poking his armpits with both hands. He laughed until he choked, his mouth dribbling saliva, but there was no getting rid of her. Fortunately Third Sister came in just then to ask about lunch. Perfection retreated in some confusion.

Third Sister Zhu helped him to sit up and said smiling, "So, you're ticklish, too, Mr. Li? It so happens her husband's the same."

"Here you go speaking of her husband again. It's because I mentioned him that she got angry and horsed around with me."

"What did you say about her husband that made her angry?"

"I said he's nice, nothing else."

"That's what you said, but she probably thought you were being sly and were making fun of her, right?"

He nodded smiling and stole a glance at Perfection. She was sitting perfectly upright by the window, her head lowered and her lips pouting. She pretended to be cleaning her nails but was so embarrassed that her face was flushed red and shiny as a mirror. He dropped the subject.

"What would you have for lunch, Mr. Li?" Third Sister asked. "I'll go and order it."

He named two dishes offhand. She went to order them right away.

Having smoked a couple of opium pellets, he told Perfection to sit near him and chat. She fished out a slip of paper from her pocket; it was a fortune-telling poem.[1] She handed it over for him to see and then asked him to interpret it.

"D'you want to know if your business will be good?" he asked.

"You really are sly. What business? We're not in business," she berated him.

"Then is it about your husband?"

She stood up abruptly, arms akimbo. He hastily left his seat to get away from her, begging to be let off. She took the opportunity to snatch back the poem. "I don't want you to interpret it anymore."

He held out a hand for it, grinning shamelessly. "Don't be angry. Let me read it for you."

::

1. Little bamboo sticks stand in a jar at the altar of a temple. The worshiper with a problem shakes the jar until a stick falls out and then gets a printed poem that matches the number on the stick that answers the question.

At this, she threw the poem down on the table and turned her face away, saying, "I won't listen."

Pragmatic Li was rather put out by this. After a moment of reflection, he said earnestly, "Though this is marked 'middling,' the message given in the poem sounds good. Even the most auspicious stick will say no better."

Hearing this, she turned around to look at the poem; it was indeed marked "middling." He took the opportunity to come over and point things out.

"Look at this, doesn't it sound good?"

"What does it say? Read it out for me."

"OK, I'll do that." He picked up the poem and, leaving out the four lines in the beginning, just read the four lines of commentary:

Come the matchmaker and the marriage is made,
Come the physician and the illness is cured;
Though the traveler is not yet home,
The missing article's safety is assured.

When he had finished, she was still bemused. He then explained it to her line by line.

"What's 'come-the-physician'?" she asked.

"It means getting a doctor. Once you get a doctor, the illness is cured."

"Where do I find the doctor?"

"That it doesn't say. What illness do you have that you need a doctor?"

"Nothing," she said evasively.

"If you want a doctor, ask me. I have a friend who's a really wonderful doctor. Even with the rarest and strangest cases, he only needs to feel your pulse, and he'll know all about it. Shall I ask him to come?"

"What do I want a doctor for? I'm not sick."

"Well, you asked about where to find the doctor, so I wondered if you wanted to see one. I wouldn't have mentioned it if you hadn't asked in the first place."

She saw the joke was on her and made no reply. Just then Third Sister came back with the food and served lunch, so his intention of questioning Perfection further had to be shelved.

He decided to go to the House of Floral Rain after lunch for a smoke. Instead of pressing him to stay, Perfection urged him, "Come back early and have supper here. I'll be waiting." He promised as he went downstairs. Third Sister repeated the invitation a couple of times as she saw him out.

Leaving Great Prosperity Alley, he strolled eastward along Fourth Avenue. At the junction with Generosity Alley he saw four of his friends sauntering toward him. They were none other than Prosperity Luo, Lotuson Wang, Amity Zhu, and Mallow Yao. Before he had time to greet them, Mallow Yao had grabbed hold of him, exclaiming, "Wonderful! Come along."

Pragmatic's attempts at refusing were brushed aside. He was dragged by Mallow Yao into Sunset's house in Generosity Alley. He saw hanging in the parlor a painting depicting some deities, and four groups of Taoists were seated facing each other, reciting treasured scrolls.[2] The incense smoke that filled the room and the sound of cymbals and drums told Pragmatic Li half the story. Mallow Yao invited everyone upstairs, and Sunset welcomed them into her room. As soon as they were seated, Mallow Yao told the servant girl, Clever, "Shout down the stairs: 'set the table.'"

"I've just had lunch. I'm too full to eat," said Pragmatic Li.

"We've all just had lunch! If you're too full, just sit for a while and chat," Mallow Yao replied.

"I suppose Pragmatic is in need of a smoke, no?" said Amity Zhu.

"We do have opium here," said Sunset.

Pragmatic Li yielded priority to the others.

"Please go ahead. We were all smoking just a while ago," said Lotuson Wang.

Pragmatic knew there was no getting away, so he went over to the divan and started smoking.

Mallow Yao went to write the call chits, starting with the two girls for Prosperity Luo and Amity Zhu. He then asked Lotuson Wang, "Are you going to call both of them?"

Lotuson hastily signaled the negative with a wave of his hand. "Just call Little Rouge."

When it came to Pragmatic Li's turn, everybody said in unison before he could speak, "It's Bright Pearl, naturally!" He was going to stop them, but Mallow Yao had already written and dispatched the chit. Yao then gave orders for hot towels to be served immediately.

Pragmatic Li, who had only consumed three pellets of opium, was far from satisfied. He asked Mallow Yao, "If you want to drink, you've got the whole night ahead of you. What's the hurry?"

"Well, there's no hurry at all," Prosperity Luo put in smiling. "It'll just be a little hard on his knees, that's all. Otherwise he can be as late as he wants."

::

2. "Treasured scrolls" are religious stories recited by Buddhist nuns or Taoist priests as a ritual.

Pragmatic Li did not understand the joke, but Mallow Yao was embarrassed and tried to explain his hurry, "It's because of the occasion. There's a religious ceremony here today. If we finish dinner early, later, when the other guests come to give their party, the room will be available, right?"

Sunset broke in, "Who wants you to vacate the room? If you want to dine later, you're free to do so." She immediately turned around to give instructions to Clever, "Go tell them downstairs not to send out the call chits just yet. Dinner won't start till later."

Clever, who had no idea what it was about, made an affirmative noise and turned to go. Mallow Yao stopped her hastily, saying, "Never mind. The table is already set."

"Well, the table can wait," Sunset responded.

"Actually, I'm starving, so we might as well eat now," said Mallow Yao.

"But you said you just had lunch. What about getting some dim sum to tide you over?" She told Clever to get the dim sum.

Mallow Yao was at the end of his wits. He pleaded in a low voice, "Don't make things difficult for me. Let me off this time, please."

Sunset snickered. "Then why did you use me as your excuse? Did I tell you to have dinner early?"

"No, no, you didn't."

Only then did she drop the subject, but she still muttered, "Lots of people are afraid of their wives, but never to this extent. You're a rarity indeed!"

At this, everybody burst out laughing. His cover blown, Mallow Yao had no choice but to put on a brave face and grin. Fortunately, at that moment the menservants came in with hot towels, so he invited everyone to take their seats for dinner.

After the wine had gone three rounds, Green Phoenix, Little Rouge, and White Fragrance arrived one after the other. Bright Pearl was the last to come. Amity Zhu pointed at Pragmatic Li and said, "He's jealous of His Honor, Mr. Li. Just now he didn't want to call you."

Bright Pearl replied, "Why would he be jealous of His Honor? The reason he wouldn't call me was not jealousy. He must have found someone who suits him. He wanted to call somebody else—understand?"

"Who did I want to call then?"

"How would I know?" Bright Pearl retorted.

Pragmatic Li just smiled in embarrassment.

Lotuson Wang said with a smile, "Clients are in such a difficult position. If you don't call a girl for three days, she'll talk nonsense and say you've been seeing somebody else. They're all like that."

Little Rouge, who was sitting behind him, put in an icy rejoinder, "It's not all nonsense, though."

Prosperity Luo laughed uproariously. "Come, of course it's non-sense! The clients talk nonsense and the courtesans talk nonsense. Let's start drinking and forget all this nonsense!"

Mallow Yao cheered and told Clever to fetch big cups, whereupon they started the finger game and made a racket. It was sundown when the drinking came to an end and the girls left.

Knowing that Mallow Yao had to go home early, Prosperity Luo did not dare drink his fill. He turned his cup upside down and pleaded intoxication, so Mallow Yao called for congee to be served. But Pragmatic Li took his leave without having any. Lotuson Wang and Amity Zhu had a token mouthful and then said good-bye, hur-rying off to get a smoke. Prosperity Luo was the only one who took two bowls of congee. After that, he wiped his face, rinsed his mouth, and made to go. Mallow Yao wanted to leave with him, but Sunset held on to him, saying, "My guests for the party haven't come yet. Why are you vacating the room already?"

"They'll be here soon," he answered with a smile.

"Even then they can sit in the little mezzanine room. You just sit here. There's no need for you to vacate the room."

He saluted her, bowing deeply in apology. After that, he followed Prosperity Luo downstairs. The sedan-chair bearers were already waiting at the door. He said good-bye and got into his sedan chair to go home.

Instead of riding in his sedan chair, Prosperity Luo decided to walk and told the bearers to follow him. They turned south toward Green Phoenix's. As he headed upstairs, he saw the door of the little room by the stairs was open. It was the room of the madam, Second Sister, and an old man was squatting in the doorway. Luo paid him no attention. When he got upstairs, he found that Second Sister was there. Green Phoenix sat in a corner of the room smoking a water pipe. Her face drawn and her mouth in a pout, she looked clearly displeased.

Second Sister stood up to greet him, "Mr. Luo, is the party over?"

He answered briefly and sat down. Green Phoenix just concen-trated on her water pipe and said not a word. Since he did not know the cause of all this, he, too, kept quiet.

After a long silence, Green Phoenix spoke abruptly, "Think about it yourself, how old are you? Going after lovers at your age, d'you have no shame?"

Second Sister was too ashamed to defend herself. With Prosper-ity there, Green Phoenix could not say much more. After another pause, during which she finished smoking her water pipe, she asked him, "D'you have money on you?"

"Yes," he answered hastily and fished out a slim leather purse from his pocket.[3] He handed it to her.

She opened it and saw a lot of banknotes tucked in the compartments. She just pulled out a ten-dollar bill and handed the purse back to him. She then tossed the bill at Second Sister and shouted at her, "Now go and give it to those men again."

Second Sister was so embarrassed she didn't know where to look. She put the banknote away and said with a forced smile, "I won't."

"I won't lecture you again. When you have nothing left, let's see who you're going to borrow from next."

"Don't worry, I won't borrow from you, all right?" Second Sister said smiling. "Oh, thank you, Mr. Luo. Sorry to trouble you." So saying, she went downstairs, smiling shamefacedly.

Green Phoenix was still muttering, "If only you know what it means to be sorry!"

"What does she want money for?" he asked.

She frowned. "This mother of mine is really the limit! I don't mean to speak ill of her, but when she's got money, she gives it to her lovers, and when she needs money herself, she comes to ask me for it. If you tell her off, she plays dumb. Scold her, beat her if you like, she'll forget it all in a couple of days and act the same way as before. I really don't know what to do with her."

"Who's her lover?"

"There're so many of them, you just lose count. Leaving aside the old ones, she took on several new ones just recently. And at her age, too! Is there no sense left in her?"

"There's an old man in the little room; is he her lover?"

"That old man is the tailor, Master Zhang. How could he be her lover? Just now, she came to me because she didn't have enough money to pay the tailor's bill."

He brushed the matter aside with a smile. They chatted for a while, and Mama Zhao brought supper. When he said he had had dinner, Green Phoenix called in her younger sister Gold Phoenix to eat with her. Before they had finished, the menservants downstairs announced, "Summons for the eldest maestro to a party!"

"Where?" Green Phoenix called out.

"Avenue Road."

"Coming," she answered.

::

3. Such slim purses had many compartments and were designed to be slipped into a boot. All well-to-do men wore such boots until Manchu influence declined toward the end of the dynasty.

Having received the call to a party, Green Phoenix finished her supper in a hurry and then called for Little Treasure to bring hot water for her to wash her face, after which she put on makeup in front of the mirror.

"Where in Avenue Road are you going?" Prosperity Luo asked.

"It's still the Qian residence," she said. "Theirs is a mah-jongg party, and once I get there, I have to play as a substitute. If I don't have another party call, I have to keep playing; they won't let me go. Sometimes I have to sit there for two or three hours. It's terribly boring."

"If it's boring, then just send your apologies and don't go," he said.

"It's a party call, how can I refuse to go? Mother will scold."

"Your mother wouldn't dare."

"Of course she would. I've never done anything wrong, that's why Mother doesn't say anything against me. If I step the least bit out of line, I'll never hear the end of it."

In the course of the conversation, Mama Zhao had taken party clothes out. As Green Phoenix got changed, she said to him, "You sit here; I'll be back in no time." She then told Gold Phoenix, "You stay here," and ordered Little Treasure to get Pearl Phoenix to come and sit with Prosperity as well. Then Mama Zhao went ahead carrying the *pipa* and the water pipe bag. Green Phoenix followed her downstairs, got into the sedan chair, and went straight to the Qian residence on Avenue Road. The parlor was ablaze with lamps and candles, and she could hear the loud voices of people playing the finger game, so Green Phoenix thought it was a drinking party. As she went in, however, she saw there were only four men seated at the table: Willow Yang, Eminence Lü, Cloud Tao, and Vigor Qian, the host. She realized it was just an informal supper and a mah-jongg party.

The minute Willow Yang saw her, he shouted, "Perfect timing! I offer you two cups of wine." He brought an oversized wine cup to her lips.

She turned her head aside. "I'm not drinking." But he went on pestering her. She ignored him and sat down in a high-back chair against the wall.

Vigor Qian got up quickly and said to Willow Yang, "You go back to the finger game. I'll drink this wine." He took the cup from him. Willow Yang went back to his seat to play against Eminence Lü.

Still holding the wine cup in his hand, Vigor Qian told Green Phoenix, "The four of us are playing Catch the Winner. I lost ten times in a row and have drunk eight penalty cups. There're two left. If you can, drink a cup for me, all right?"

Hearing this, she took the wine cup, drained it, and handed it back. "Bring me the other one as well."

"There's just the one left. Let Mama Zhao take it for me."

Mama Zhao took a cup from the table and drank it.

Cloud Tao goaded Willow Yang, "You really count for nothing. It's just the same wine, but when Mr. Qian tells her to drink it, she complies right away."

Green Phoenix responded, "You certainly have the gift of the gab; that's a lot to say about a cup of wine. They're both your friends, but you take Mr. Yang's side to lecture me. Isn't it the same as lecturing Mr. Qian? Well, talk away, it's got nothing to do with me."

Eminence Lü said, "Now I've lost, you should take a cup for me, too. Then he won't be able to pick on you."

"Mr. Lü, I would have drunk it for you. But now that he's lectured me, I'm certainly not going to do it," Green Phoenix replied.

Willow Yang hurried Eminence Lü, "Oh, just drink up! After that we'll play mah-jongg."

"Have you started?" she asked.

"We finished four rounds. There're four more to go," said Vigor Qian.

Eminence Lü drank up and pointed at Cloud Tao. "It's your turn to Catch the Winner." So Cloud Tao turned to play against Willow Yang.

Afraid of having to take more wine for the losers, Green Phoenix pretended to inspect her surroundings and disappeared into the study to the left of the parlor. She saw that the tables and desks had been moved to the center of the room and chips and mah-jongg tiles were scattered on them. The four mutton-fat candles had been blown out, however, and only the opium lamp on the divan was burning bright. She sat down on the humble side of the divan. Presently Vigor Qian also came in and lay down beside her to smoke.

She asked, "Did my mother borrow any money from you?"

"Not exactly," he replied. "But the night before last when I was chatting with her, she said expenses were high and money was tight, that she couldn't make ends meet. It seemed that she was going to ask for a loan. Then we got talking about something else, and she didn't mention it."

"My mother is a deep one! You'll have to watch out for her. The last time you had a pair of bracelets made for me, she said to me, 'Mr. Qian hasn't been doing much business recently. I wonder where he got all this money?' I said, 'What do you care where the clients get their money from?' She said, 'We're really short of money. I wonder where it's all gone to.' This so enraged me that I just had to let it go. What d'you think she meant by that?"

"You said I should watch out; are you worried that she'd borrow money from me?"

"If she tries, don't you lend her any. And don't you ever buy anything for me, either, for whatever you give me will sooner or later end up as hers anyway. People like that have no idea what gratitude means. It's as if you're to blame for having such a lot money because it makes them green with envy. If you don't buy me anything, there won't be any trouble."

"She's always treated you quite kindly, though. What's got into her now that makes her suspicious of you, I wonder?"

"You're right about that. These days, she deliberately makes things difficult for me. At the end of last month, a client left town, and before he went he settled his bills. It was a hundred dollars. When she got her hands on it, she lent it all to her lovers, ten dollars here and twenty dollars there. Today when the tailor came for his fees, she didn't have it, and she actually turned around and cadged off me. I said, 'How would I have any money? It's your responsibility to pay for party clothes. You knew the tailor had to be paid today, so why did you give all the money to your lovers?' I made such a big deal of it that she got scared and held her tongue."

"So did you give her anything today?"

"Because it's the first time, to keep up appearances for her, I borrowed ten dollars from Luo. But in her heart she doesn't want it from Luo. She wants me to come to you for a loan, the more the better."

"If that's the case, she'll never be satisfied until she gets at my money. If she does ask me for a loan, I can't very well say no, either."

"It's all right for you to refuse her; why shouldn't you? Just say, 'I haven't been doing much business recently, so I haven't got any money.' That'd be quite nicely put, don't you think? By the time the festival comes round, all you have to do is promptly settle your bills for the party calls. Then she'll have no excuse to bad-mouth you."

"Then she'd hate me. The way I look at it, if all she wants is to borrow some money, then just lend her a little. It won't come to much. Just play along for a couple more seasons, until you've redeemed your freedom."

"No, I won't! What's she to you that you're so keen on lending her money? Are you really flush with money? If so, wait till I've got back my freedom; then lend it to me."

"Are you going to redeem yourself soon?"

She silenced him with a gesture of her hand and then peeped outside and caught sight of a shadowy figure standing behind the green gauze screen. "Who is it?" she demanded. On hearing her, the man came out, clapping his hands, laughing. It turned out to be Eminence Lü.

Vigor Qian put down his opium pipe and sat up smiling. "You're trying to scare us."

"I'm here to catch the adulterers. Shameless, the two of you! Even if you want to have a rendezvous, you can at least wait until we guests have left and then go to it in comfort. How come you can't even wait a moment?"

Green Phoenix muttered, "Ivory certainly never grows in a dog's mouth!"

Before Eminence Lü could retort, Vigor Qian had dragged him back to the dinner table in the parlor.

Willow Yang said, "We lost at the finger game, and there was no one to drink for us, while you, the host, went off to have fun."

"You're welcome to have fun now. Later, you're bound to lose heavily at mah-jongg,"[1] said Cloud Tao.

Vigor Qian did not protest but just asked about the finger game and the wine. The four of them immersed themselves in the game and the drinking before they had supper. After the meal, they went to the study, lit the candles, and played mah-jongg.

As Vigor Qian had to smoke his fill, he asked Green Phoenix to play in his stead. After two rounds, she had won a tidy sum. Delighted at this, she called Mama Zhao over and whispered some instructions to her. Mama Zhao then walked home by herself and headed straight upstairs to look for Prosperity Luo. To her surprise, he was not in the room; there was just Pearl Phoenix bent over the table, dozing. Mama Zhao pulled her up by the ear. "Where's Mr. Luo?"

Pearl Phoenix, having been woken abruptly, was still dazed and unable to answer. After being questioned repeatedly, she finally said, "Mr. Luo is gone."

"Where to?"

"I don't know."

In anger, Mama Zhao jabbed a finger at her temple and then went downstairs to ask Second Sister, who told her, "Mr. Luo was invited to a friend's party at Snow Scent's. Go and tell the eldest maestro to come back earlier for the other party."

::

1. [This alludes to the belief that sex brings bad luck to a gambler. *E.H.*]

"I'll wait till Mr. Luo's call chit comes and then take it to her. She won't come back just yet anyway," said Mama Zhao.[2]

Second Sister agreed. After a long wait, they finally received Prosperity Luo's call chit, and it was indeed sent from Snow Scent's at East Co-prosperity Alley.

Chit in hand, Mama Zhao returned to the Qian residence on Avenue Road. As she went in, she saw all the lights had gone out in the study. She realized the mah-jongg party was over and the guests had left, so she headed for the room on the right. Here, she saw Vigor Qian's wife and greeted her, "Madam."

Mrs. Qian was all smiles. "Are you here to fetch your maestro? She's upstairs. Just wait a while here."[3]

Mama Zhao had no choice but to sit down. Gradually, she got round to mentioning the call to another party.

"In that case, the maestro mustn't delay. It won't do for her to be late," said Mrs. Qian. "Why don't you give a shout at the bottom of the stairs?"

Mama Zhao hurried off to the back and shouted in a loud voice, "Eldest Maestro!" No answer came from upstairs. She called again twice, saying, "There's another party call!" The silence remained undisturbed.

Mrs. Qian stopped her. "Don't call anymore. I'm sure the maestro heard you."

Mama Zhao could only return to the front room to chat with Mrs. Qian. After a while she heard Green Phoenix coming down. She hastily collected the *pipa* and water pipe bag and went up to meet her.

"What's so urgent that you had to make such a racket?" Green Phoenix said in a huff.

Mrs. Qian interceded pleasantly, "You might say she did right, too. That call chit came a while ago, so she was afraid you'd miss the party. That's why she asked you to go earlier."

Green Phoenix could not very well say much after that. She exchanged a few words with Mrs. Qian, thanked her, and took her

::

2. [Obviously, everyone in the Huang house knows that Green Phoenix is not just playing mah-jongg in Vigor Qian's house, and no one wants to irritate her by telling her to leave early. E.H.]

3. [This can mean only one thing: Green Phoenix is in bed with Vigor Qian in his house. In doing so, she causes the brothel to lose income, as Qian only pays three dollars for a party call to get her to his house. He would have had to pay a lot more (including tips for all the servants) if he had gone to the brothel. That Mrs. Qian and the brothel maid tacitly concur with this arrangement makes the case even more interesting. E.H.]

leave. Mrs. Qian walked her out all the way beyond the parlor and watched her get into the sedan chair.

Mama Zhao walked behind the sedan chair, and they went straight to Snow Scent's in East Co-prosperity Alley. Green Phoenix leaned on her as she made her way to the table. They saw that guests, courtesans, maids, and servant girls had crowded around it; there was no space left. Prosperity Luo's seat was right next to the dressing table, and Mama Zhao found it impossible to squeeze in. He happened to be sitting next to Lotuson Wang, whose companion that night was Constance. Seeing Green Phoenix, she moved her own stool over and called out, "Green Phoenix, my peer, come over here." She gave Mama Zhao a very warm greeting as well.

Green Phoenix saw the glitter of Constance's jewels and realized that they were new. She took Constance by the hand and had a look and then said, "These name rings are getting a bit out of fashion."

Seeing the pair of green jade hairpins in the shape of lotus pods that Green Phoenix was wearing, Constance wanted to look at them. Green Phoenix pulled one out and handed it to her. "Not a bad coloring," said Constance.

It happened that Lotuson Wang was sitting next to the host, Elan Ge. His girl, Snow Scent, seated behind him, heard Constance's praise and poked her head over for a look.

"How much did you pay for this?" she asked.

"Eight dollars," replied Green Phoenix.

Snow Scent hastened to pull out her own hairpin for a comparison. Seeing it was all green, Constance said, "That's not bad either."

Snow Scent retorted angrily, "Not bad either, eh? Mine are worth forty dollars. 'Not bad either,' is it?"

Hearing this, Green Phoenix took it from her and examined it carefully and then asked, "Did you get it yourself?"

"It was a client who got it for me, at the teahouse in the city god's temple. Everyone said it was a good price. The jewelry stores would have charged a lot more," said Snow Scent.

"I can't really tell the difference," said Constance. "Compared to hers, this does seem a bit better."

"With green jade, it's hard to tell the value," said Snow Scent. "A little difference in quality makes a piece really rare. These hairpins of mine are very special; nothing can compare with them. Forty dollars is about the right price."

Green Phoenix smiled, remained quiet, and handed her back the hairpin. Constance also gave Green Phoenix's back to her. Elan Ge, engaged in the finger game, did not hear everything that Snow Scent was saying. When he had finished playing, he turned around to ask her, "What cost forty dollars?" She handed him the jade hairpin.

"You've been taken for a ride! How would that come to forty dollars? It's only worth about ten," he said.

"What d'you know? You're no expert, so stop criticizing. I'd like you to go and get something like this for ten dollars," she retorted.

"Give it here. I'll have a look," said Prosperity Luo as he snatched the hairpin.

"You're no expert either. What d'you want to see it for?" Green Phoenix interceded.

Prosperity Luo laughed. "It's true I'm no expert!"

He passed the hairpin to Lotuson Wang, who said to Constance, "It's much better than the pair you're wearing."

"But of course. How could mine compare?"

"Oh, so you have a pair, too?" Snow Scent cut in. "Let me see if they're any good."

"Mine are no good at all. Now I want to get another pair," Constance said as she pulled one out of her hair and handed it to Snow Scent.

"How much did this cost?" Snow Scent asked.

"For what you paid for yours, I can get ten pairs of these," Constance replied pleasantly.

"Four dollars! Naturally, you won't get anything nice at that price. If you get another pair, you should go for the expensive ones. High prices mean high quality," said Snow Scent.

Smiling, Constance took the hairpin from Lotuson Wang and handed it back to Snow Scent in exchange for her own.

It was Prosperity Luo's turn to be the banker. The loud cries of the finger game rang out like spring thunder and managed to cut short Snow Scent's discourse on hairpins.

Aside from Prosperity Luo and Lotuson Wang, everyone at the gathering was a friend of Elan's in the money shop business. Knowing that Elan Ge's heart was more preoccupied with Snow Scent than with the wine, they tried their best to make things easy for him; none of them indulged to his full capacity. For the sake of form, they took turns playing against Prosperity as banker and then hastily wound up the party.

Snow Scent waited until all the guests had left before she set upon Elan Ge again. "When I say something, you should take my side and put in a word or two to support me; that's how you show your affection. But just now you actually picked on me—wasn't I surprised! I said the hairpins cost forty dollars, and that was the truth; I wasn't fooling you. If you don't believe me, ask Little Sister. But you were so worried that I'd make you come up with the forty dollars, you said at once they were just worth ten. Even if they cost no more than ten dollars, did you buy them for me? Even that foreign copper bracelet watch that you bought me was said to have cost thirty odd dollars, so why is it that when it comes to my own things they must be common? In your heart, you think of me as a cheap courtesan, so I can't possibly afford forty-dollar hairpins. I'm only good enough for a copper bracelet but not a gold one, is that it?"

Her incoherent nonsense amused him. "What's all the fuss about? Even if the hairpins cost forty dollars, it has nothing to do with me," he said.

"Then why did you say they're only worth ten? Since that's what you said, you go and buy me a pair exactly like this for ten dollars. It so happens that I want to buy another set of jewelry. I'll pay for it myself. You go and get it for me."

"Say no more. Consider it done," he said smiling.

"You're just playing for time. I want it tomorrow, no later."

"I'll go and get it tonight, all right?"

"Yes, fine."

He actually took his jacket and put it on. Little Sister happened to come in just then and asked in alarm, "What are you doing, Second Young Master?" She was about to stop him when Snow Scent signaled with her eyes for her to desist.

Elan put on his thumb ring, hung his watch on his jacket, picked up his folding fan, and said to her smiling, "Well, I'm off."

Snow Scent grabbed him. "Where're you going?"

"You told me to go shopping."

"All right, I'll go with you." She took his hand and made for the door.

He stopped at the door curtain, while she struggled to pull him out the door. Little Sister clapped her hands laughing behind them, saying, "A fine thing if you get hauled off by the police." The menservants in the parlor, puzzled by all this, came in to find out what was going on. Little Sister had to cajole and scold to get Elan and Snow Scent back into the room. She removed his jacket for him.

Snow Scent sat down to one side pouting in silence, while Elan smiled awkwardly. Little Sister said cheerily, "The two of you are just like children, crying and laughing all the time, and for no good reason at all. Isn't it a joke?"

"Sorry, it must be hard on an old lady like you—aggravating," he said.

"Exactly. I'm so aggravated, it's killing me." So saying, she walked out of the room.

He went over to Snow Scent and said gently, "Did you hear? They take us for a joke. A silly row over nothing at all. What d'you suppose we look like?"

She could not suppress a giggle. "Are you going to be stubborn with me again?"

"You win. You're in luck this time."

Only then did she make up with him. He heard the sound of the menservants shutting the door and looked at his watch; it was already past one o'clock. "It's getting late; let's go to bed."

"Would you like some congee first?" she asked.

"No, not really."

She called for Little Sister to come and tidy up. Little Sister came in with hot water for the washbasin and then made the bed. In the midst of the bustle, a servant girl suddenly pushed the door open and ran into the room. At the sight of Little Sister, she called out "Aunt," and covered her mouth with a sleeve, ready to burst into tears. Little Sister saw it was her husband's niece, named Clever, a live-in girl at Sunset's.

"Why are you here at this hour of the night?" she asked at once.

Clever wanted to reply, but the words would not come.

CHAPTER 23 :: *A young girl overhears things said behind her back, and a jealous wife courts insult in a brothel*

Seeing that her niece, Clever, was about to cry, Little Sister was taken aback and exclaimed, "What's the matter?"

"I'm not going back!" Clever said in tears.

Little Sister did not understand. She stared blankly at the girl and then asked, "Did you quarrel with somebody?"

Clever shook her head. "No, it's not that. This morning when I was polishing an opium lamp, I broke the glass lampshade. Their madam said I had to make up for it. I went and bought one at an imported goods store, but she said it wasn't good enough. I had to buy another one from another store, and I asked for a good one. But when I took it home, they said it was still no good and told me to go and change it and to take the broken one along to get a match. The store said it would cost twenty cents, and they wouldn't take the other one back either. As their servant girl, I only get one dollar a month. Since I started working there in the first month, I've earned less than three dollars, and I sent all that back home long ago. Where am I going to get the twenty cents?"

Hearing this, Little Sister laughed. "Why make such a to-do about this? I've never seen such a silly child as you. Leave the lampshade here; I'll go and get one for you tomorrow."

"Aunt, no!" Clever said at once. "I can't cope with the work there. The minute I get up in the morning, I have to clean three opium lamps and eight water pipes. Then there're the three rooms: sweeping the floor, dusting the furniture, emptying the spittoons; I get all the chores. In the afternoon, there's the laundry, all those clothes, and I have to wash them on my own. I don't get a minute off day or night. Sometimes, guests play mah-jongg, and I have to stay up all night. By the time the game is over at dawn, they all go to bed, but I have to clean the rooms."

"They have two other servant girls. Don't they do anything?"

"Would those two take on any work? I wake them up at noon for lunch, and they do the maestro's hair, that's all. When that's done and they're at leisure, they lie down on the divan, put up their feet, and smoke opium. If a client comes along, they laugh and joke with him and just enjoy themselves. As for me, I have to prepare the hot towels, fill the water pipes, and get run off my feet. By the end of the month, I watch them share the tips; sometimes it's three or four dollars, sometimes five or six. That certainly makes them happy, whereas I never even see a little copper coin." At this, she burst into tears again.

Little Sister said earnestly, "You just do your duty; don't take them as your example. As for the tips they get, you shouldn't envy them for it, either. It's only natural that you get a bad deal now, but once you've learned to dress hair, you'll do all right. If you don't listen to me, I can tell you what'll happen. You've just come from the countryside, and if you walk out of the first house you work for, what will you do after that? Who's going to take you on?"

Clever said sobbing, "Aunt, there're some things you don't know. I don't mind the work, but while I'm working, they horse around with me. If I don't play along, they're displeased and tell Mother I'm sulky when I work. And if some rowdy clients come along, they gang up with them and have fun at my expense. One client held down my hands, another pinned down my feet, and the two of them pulled off my pants."

So saying, she started weeping again. But Elan Ge and Snow Scent thought it funny.

Little Sister also laughed. "Did they actually pull them off?" she asked quickly.

"Of course they did!" Clever replied in tears. "In the end, it was the maestro who couldn't put up with it and helped me up. When their madam heard about it, she said I was a little baby and she was fed up with me and my moods."

Snow Scent cut in, "Those clients were really out of order! Pulling a servant girl's pants off, how could they do it!"

Elan Ge said, "At a dollar a month, d'you have to worry that nobody will take you on? Don't work for them anymore."

Little Sister, however, said nothing. When she had tidied up the room and Elan Ge and Snow Scent were ready to retire for the night, she said to Clever, "Even if you want to quit, wait until I've found another position for you. Go back now and carry on for a couple of days."

"You will look for a job for me, Aunt, won't you?"

"All right. Now go."

"Do I have to replace the lampshade?"

Little Sister told her to leave the broken one behind. "I'll go and get one tomorrow," she said. "Now take more care when you're working."

Clever promised and then took her leave and returned to Sunset's in Generosity Alley. The Taoist priests in the parlor were chanting the story "Luoyang Bridge," attracting a crowd of idlers to watch and listen. She paid no attention to any of it but went straight to the little back room to see the madam, Sister Wei, and reported, "The imported goods store refused to make an exchange. My aunt will get one tomorrow."

"You've been to see your aunt?" Sister Wei asked.

"Yes."

"So, a little thing like that sends you running to your aunt," Sister Wei said in vexation. "Did you think if you told her, you wouldn't have to make up for it?"

Clever did not dare answer back. She went upstairs and saw that the second party in Sunset's room was not quite over yet. The guests were Manager Zhai of Northern Fidelity Pawnshop and several clerks who, as it happened, were precisely the rowdy ones. Since she was going to quit anyway, she thought, there was no need to go and fawn on them. Instead of going into Sunset's room, she went into the mezzanine cubicle and, groping in the dark, lay down on an opium divan. But with the waves of laughter coming from the party, how could she sleep? A while later, she heard tables and chairs being moved, followed by the clatter of ivory tiles, and she knew they had started playing mah-jongg. She was just going to get up when she heard the two servant girls coming out of the room to call the men-servants for hot towels and to look for her downstairs.

"Clever is upstairs. She's probably gone to bed," said Sister Wei.

"So she's taking it easy. Go and get her," said one of the girls.

"No, not me," said the other. "If she doesn't feel like working, we'll take over. It's not as if we can't do without her."

This sent Clever back to the divan feeling hopeless and despondent, and soon she fell asleep. When she woke up, the sun was shining high in the sky. She sat up on the divan rubbing her eyes and then listened carefully. All was quiet downstairs: the chanting had ended. The only noise came from Sunset's room, where the menservants had brought in breakfast after the mah-jongg party and the guests were still fooling around with the two servant girls. She decided to stay out of their way. After going to the kitchen to clean her face, she saw to tidying the empty rooms first.

A while later, Little Sister came. Clever thought the cleaning could wait and concentrated on eavesdropping. She heard Little Sister going into Sister Wei's room to give her the replacement lampshade, asking, "Will this one do?"

Sister Wei laughed merrily. "My! You got taken in by the child and actually went and bought it! It was only because she was careless when she worked that I said she had to replace it, so she'd learn to be more careful. D'you think I was serious about it?" So saying, she gave Little Sister two ten-cent coins for the lampshade, but the latter refused them adamantly. Sister Wei had no choice but to thank her and then insisted that they sit down and chat for a while.

"This child is not a bad worker, but she's a bit of a loner," Sister Wei said. "In a sing-song house, what does it matter if a couple of clients horse around with her a bit? But *she* gets terribly upset about it."

This made Clever angrier than ever. She did not want to listen anymore and went back to cleaning the room. After Little Sister had taken her leave of Sister Wei, Clever caught up with her and followed her all the way to a corner of the lane before asking, "Aunt, you will look for a place for me, won't you?"

"Don't be so impatient! Even if there's an opening, you'll have to wait till the season's over. Where can you get a position now?"

Clever pleaded with her repeatedly before returning to the house.

Little Sister was gone for several days without news, and Clever was too busy to visit her at Snow Scent's. On the fourteenth of the third month, Clever got up early. She was polishing water pipes in the parlor when a sedan chair came to the door. A maid lifted its curtain and helped a lady out. Though middle-aged, she was still handsome and carried herself with confidence. The way she dressed was somewhat old-fashioned. Clever guessed that she must be a wealthy housewife. Her face suffused with anger and her chest thrust out, the lady came through the front door and demanded in a loud voice, "Is this Sunset Wei's?"

"Yes, ma'am," Clever answered.

Without further questions, she headed upstairs, maid in tow. An astounded Clever questioned the sedan-chair bearers at the door and learned that the lady was Mallow Yao's wife. She dashed into Sister Wei's room to tell her the news. Wondering what it was about, Sister Wei rushed upstairs with Clever and followed Mrs. Yao into Sunset's room.

Sunset was sitting primly in front of the window, still at her toilet. The minute Mrs. Yao saw her, she demanded loudly, "Are you Sunset Wei?"

Sunset started as she looked up. She took the measure of Mrs. Yao before replying coolly, "I am Sunset Wei, and who may you be?"

Mrs. Yao sat down proudly in a high-back chair and shouted at her, "I don't have time to bandy words with you. Where's Second Young Master? Tell him to come out."

Sunset had guessed what the visit was about. Again she responded coldly, "Which Second Young Master do you mean? And how is he related to you?"

Mrs. Yao roared, pointing a finger at Sunset's face, "Stop playing the fool! Second Young Master is my husband and you've cast a spell on him. Do you know who I am?" So saying, she glared ferociously at Sunset, looking as though she was ready to spring at her. At this sight, Sunset could not help laughing out loud, but she did not reply to the question.

Clever, being timid, wanted to smooth over any unpleasantness. She hastily fetched a teacup and some tea leaves and called out for the menservants to bring hot water. Then she said, "Please have some tea, Mrs. Yao." After that, she offered her a water pipe, asking, "Would you like a smoke, Mrs. Yao? I'll fill it for you."

Meanwhile, Sister Wei tried to keep Mrs. Yao from standing up and offered a torrent of explanations. "Second Young Master seldom visits us. He hasn't been for ages now. He sends the occasional party call once in a blue moon but has never given a dinner party here. You mustn't be misled by gossip, Mrs. Yao."

Just as everybody tried to put in a word to make peace, Sunset Wei stopped them, barking, "Silence! Enough of that claptrap!" Then she spoke to Mrs. Yao in a voice loud and clear, "If you want to find your husband, you should look for him in your own house. Did you ever entrust him to our care, so as to give you the right to come and look for him here? This sing-song house has never sent someone to your residence to invite our client over, yet you're here now in search of your husband; isn't that a joke? We're a house open for business; anybody who walks in is a client. What do we care whose husband he is? Is there a rule saying that if it's your husband, we're not allowed to see him? Let me put it to you straight: Second Young Master may be your husband at home, but when he is here, he's our client. If you're smart, you should keep a close eye on your husband. Why did you let him out to have fun in sing-song houses? When he's already in a sing-song house, d'you think you can drag him out? Go and ask around; is there such a rule in these foreign settlements? It so happens that Second Young Master isn't here, but even if he were, would you dare scold him or box his ears? You can bully your husband all you want, but be careful you don't bully a client of ours. Second Young Master may be afraid of you, but we don't know you, lady."

This little speech left Mrs. Yao flabbergasted. She flushed crimson to her ears and almost burst into tears of desperation. While she was still trying to think of some argument, Sunset spoke again, "Now you're a lady. Perhaps you're so bored with being a lady, you have come to a sing-song house to have some fun, too? It's a pity we don't have clients for a tea party just now. Otherwise, I'd tell them to hold you down and rape you. How would you face people back home then? Even if you sue us at the new yamen, sex in a sing-song house is nothing out of the ordinary."

Just as Sunset was getting into her stride, the menservants downstairs gave a sudden shout, "A guest coming up."

"Perfect timing. Do ask him in," said Sunset.

Sister Wei lifted the door curtain and a man of forty-odd years walked in. He had three strands of whiskers and was very plump: it was none other than Manager Zhai of Northern Fidelity Pawnshop. Mrs. Yao was so frightened that her heart was in her mouth. She didn't know whether to remain seated or to leave. Shame and anger had left her speechless.

When Zhai came into the room, he did not take a seat but just looked Mrs. Yao up and down, unable to make out who she was. Sunset asked him jovially, "Do you know her? She's the missus of Second Young Master Yao; Mallow Yao, that is. She's come to our house today to settle his hash."

Zhai looked lost. Only after Sister Wei had gone over to whisper the gist of it in his ear did he understand. "Then it's Mrs. Yao who has been ill advised," he said with a frown. "I've dined with Mallow a few times and so count as a friend. It seems to me that your coming here doesn't reflect well on him, Mrs. Yao."

"But why? *I* think it's great!" said Sunset. "Second Young Master hasn't been doing well in business all this time, but with such a wife he's bound to get rich."[1]

He held up a hand and signaled her to be quiet and then turned to

::

1. [It was a common saying that henpecked husbands would get rich. *E.H.*]

Mrs. Yao. "Please return to your residence now, Mrs. Yao. If there's anything you want said, tell Mallow to come and say it."

Unable to do or say anything and with pent-up rage driving her to the point of tears, Mrs. Yao rose hastily and, taking her maid, made for the stairs.

Sunset sneered, "Do stay a little longer, Mrs. Yao. If Second Young Master comes round, I'll send the maid to invite you back."

When Mrs. Yao got downstairs, she could not control her tears anymore. She started wailing and moaned and cursed in a muffled voice as she got into her sedan chair to go home.

With Mrs. Yao gone and her own toilet finished, Sunset thought back on what had taken place and found it increasingly funny. "Second Young Master cuts quite a figure; now let's see if he can live this down. A married lady coming to a sing-song house to drag a client off, well, she beats even the streetwalkers."

Sister Wei also sighed. "She's a lady, what more does she want? Yet she had to walk in here and ask for a slap in the eye. What rotten luck!"

"You can hold your tongue. Count yourself lucky you didn't get a mouthful from her," said Sunset.

Sister Wei smiled and went away.

"Why should your mother get a mouthful from her?" asked Manager Zhai.

Sunset told him smiling, "My mother is just too nice. Now even if Second Young Master comes to us every day, there's no reason we should deny it. But my mother insisted he hadn't come for ages, as if we should be afraid of her. As for this girl, Clever, she was even more exasperating. The other day when we had the religious chanting, the whole house was filled with guests, both upstairs and downstairs. When we called for her to make tea, she couldn't be found, and guests moving to another room didn't get fresh teacups, either. But today, when Second Young Master's wife got here, you should have seen how hard she tried to please. Without waiting to be told, she went ahead and made a cup of tea for her and then wanted to fill a water pipe for her. It was Mrs. Yao this, Mrs. Yao that. She skives off work, but she sucks up to Mrs. Yao! Unfortunately for her, Mrs. Yao wasn't in the least aware of it, so all that fawning was completely wasted."

Clever happened to come in with a basin of hot water for Sunset to wash her hands. Hearing this, she answered back, "Mrs. Yao is a guest, too. Why shouldn't I have made tea for her?"

Sunset smiled at Zhai. "Listen to her. Isn't it infuriating? Mrs. Yao a guest! Is she a client of mine?"

"Client or not, it's none of my business. You were the one who had a shouting match with her, and now you blame me for fawning on her!"

Sunset glowered. "Why d'you have to be so contrary? If you don't like working here, then leave. I'm sure Mrs. Yao likes your fawning."

Clever went downstairs pouting. She made short work of her cleaning and had lunch. She waited till the sun began to set and then snatched a free moment to go once more to Snow Scent's in East Co-prosperity Alley. Here, she told Little Sister what had happened and said in tears, "If I don't work, I get scolded; but if I do, I still get scolded. Whatever it is, it's always my fault. You told me to put up with it for a couple more days, Aunt, but I can't put up with it anymore."

"In that case, where would you go?" said Little Sister.

"Anywhere. I don't mind if there're no wages."

Little Sister thought about it but said nothing.

"Come here and help your aunt. You can look for a place later; how about that?" Snow Scent suggested.

"That'd be nice," Clever replied.

Little Sister decided to go along with it. That night, she settled Clever's wages at Sunset's and took her bedding out.

As it turned out, Clever only spent one night at Snow Scent's. The next morning, Snow Scent took out a pair of green jade hairpins after lunch and told her to return them to Constance at Big Feet Yao's across the way. She was to say, "The green is a good shade, and they look rather similar to mine. Sixteen dollars is not at all expensive."

Clever delivered the message to Constance very clearly, so Constance asked her, "Are you a new girl?" Clever told her the truth.

"We're just looking for another servant girl. If the maestro doesn't need you, come and work here," said Constance.

Clever was overjoyed. "That couldn't be better." She hurried back to tell Little Sister, who took her over personally the very same day. So Clever stayed at Constance's.

It happened that Lotuson Wang and Benevolence Hong were having a casual supper at Constance's. She showed Lotuson the pair of jade hairpins and asked, "Is sixteen dollars too much?"

Benevolence Hong valued them at only ten dollars.

"Offer them ten dollars and don't go any higher than twelve," said Lotuson.

Constance told him about getting another servant girl. Lotuson found Clever's face familiar. Upon questioning her, he realized that he had seen her several times at Sunset's.

By the time supper was over, Constance had already toasted seven or eight opium pellets and put them in the tray. Lotuson Wang wiped his face with a hot towel and lay down on the divan. She passed him the pipe, and he sucked in the contents in one breath. She took the pipe from him, cleaned the bowl, and filled it with another pellet.

"If you want to buy jade, ask Mr. Hong to get it at the teahouse in the city god's temple. It's cheaper there," he said to her.

She wanted a green jade jewelry set, she told Benevolence Hong. He promised to get it for her and then took his leave and returned to the Flourishing Ginseng Store in South End.

CHAPTER 24 :: *Constance protects a fellow courtesan to keep the peace, and Simplicity Zhao, a ruined man, feels no regret*

After getting his fill of opium while lying on the right-hand side of the divan, Lotuson Wang moved to the left-hand side to lie next to Constance and smoked three more pellets. Gradually, his eyebrows relaxed, and his eyes closed, as if he were far gone. Constance filled the pipe again, put the mouthpiece to his lips, and held it for him over the flame, but he held up a hand to show that he had had enough. She set the pipe down gently and was about to sit up, but he put a hand over her chest and held her down. "You have a smoke too."

"I don't want any. How can I work once I get hooked?" she said.

"But why would you get hooked? Little Rouge has always smoked it, and she's not hooked."

"Little Rouge is different. She's smart and good at the business. It doesn't matter even if she gets hooked. I wish I were like her!"

"You say Little Rouge is good at doing business, then why is it that she doesn't even have any clients anymore?"

"How d'you know she has no clients?"

"I saw her account books for the last season. Aside from me, there were just twenty or thirty party calls from a few old clients."

"She should do all right with you and twenty or thirty party calls."

"You don't understand. Little Rouge can't get by. Her expenses are very high. There're her parents and brother; she has to support all of them on her own."

"The parents and brother would be in a separate house, not much in the way of costs there. It's probably her own expenses that are a bit high."

"She herself doesn't spend much except for taking a carriage ride every couple of days."

"Carriage rides don't come to much either."

"Then what else?"

"How would I know?"[1]

He did not ask any more questions, just toasted and smoked the two remaining opium pellets till he had finished the lot. Then he supported himself on the arm of the divan and sat up. She knew he wanted the water pipe and got up at once to fetch one and then sat down on the divan, leaning against him, and filled the pipe for him.

After two pipes of tobacco, he asked again, "You said Little Rouge's own expenses are high. Now can you tell me what they are?"

She was slightly taken aback. "I was just talking. What other expenses would Little Rouge have? You mustn't go blabbing to her. If you do, she'll think I spoke ill of her, and she'll be cursing me again."

"Just tell me. I won't let on to her," he said smiling.

"What d'you want me to say?" she answered loudly. "You have been lovers for three or four years. Is there anything you don't know that you have to come and ask me?"

He sighed with a smile. "You're a real coward. Considering all the things Little Rouge has said about you, isn't it enough that you don't pay her back in kind? Why d'you have to cover up for her?"

She also sighed. "I'm not covering up for her! Why are you so obsessed by this? Little Rouge has got her parents and her brother to support, and she rides around in carriages, so naturally her expenses are higher than mine."

He laughed ironically and dropped the subject. After he was through with the water pipe, she remained seated shoulder to shoulder with him. In mutual delight and tender caresses, they spent their time, until the clock struck midnight, when the maid was called in to tidy up before they went to bed.

When they were in bed, she tried again to talk him round, "Though Little Rouge has a ferocious temper, she gets on quite well with you, all things considering. Now that she's as good as without any clients, and you're the only one keeping the show going for her, who else would she love besides you? That time at Luna Park, when she went at you hammer and tongs, well, that was because she was afraid that

::

1. [Though the chapter heading claims that Constance tries to keep the peace, it is obvious from this conversation that she is stirring things up in a very shrewd and understated manner. Once she has planted the seed of doubt, she sits back and allows it to grow in its own time. As this chapter progresses, the reader sees how her reasonable and considerate behavior pushes Lotuson Wang to a harsh assessment of Little Rouge. *E.H.]*

you'd drop her once you started seeing me. If you did that, wouldn't she have been desperate? The way I look at it, you should have some idea of what she's like after three or four years together. If certain things displease you, see if you can't let them pass. And if she's not quite up to standard sometimes, don't tell her off for it. Though she couldn't very well blame you for saying anything, she'd say I put you up to it, and you'd be making an enemy for me. I don't mind being run down behind my back, but if we met at a dinner party and she forgot about manners and rowed with me openly, wouldn't it be embarrassing?"

"You say she loves me, but it's hard to see how that can be the case. When she and I first came together, she said to me, 'A courtesan's life is hard, and the worst thing is if one doesn't have good clients. Being with you is the best thing that's happened to me. Now if some stranger comes along and wants me to take him on, I certainly won't do it.' I replied, 'If that's the case, just marry me.' She *said* that would be nice and all that, but she was just playing for time. At first, the excuse was that she had to pay off her debts before she married, but when the debts were paid she said her parents wouldn't let her go. It looks as if she just doesn't want to marry. I can't figure her out."

"Well, it's not that hard. She's used to the life of a courtesan and can't abide by all the rules in a family, so she doesn't want to get married. In a couple of years, when she's older, she'll marry you all right."

He waved that argument aside. "Even if Little Rouge agreed to marry me, I couldn't afford it now. The last couple of years, her three seasons of expenses came to about two thousand. This year, it's even more outrageous. After settling her debts, her shopping, and the party bills, I've spent over two thousand on her, and the season's not over yet. Just think, where would I get all that money to spend?"

She sighed again. "Well, if I get a thousand a year, I'll be very happy."

Lotuson was about to say more when he heard Clever coughing in her sleep in the middle room. This cut him short.

The next morning, Lotuson Wang and Constance had just got out of bed when his steward, Talisman, came to report, "The maid at Little Rouge's came to invite Master to drop over, saying there's something to discuss."

Constance hastened to ask what it was.

"It's nothing," said Lotuson. "I haven't been there for a couple of days, so naturally they've come to invite me over."

She reflected for a moment and then said, "I think Little Rouge probably has something to say to you. Think about it, no matter when you come here, they learn about it the minute you arrive. Obviously, they sent someone to invite you just now because they knew you were here. So even if there's nothing to say, they'd think of something, just to make a fuss and make you uncomfortable. Don't you think so?"

He did not reply. Only after he had finished lunch and satisfied his appetite for opium did he think of going over to Little Rouge's.

Constance told him repeatedly, "When you get there, if Little Rouge asks where you came from, just tell her you were here. If she raises matters that're not of much importance, just meet her halfway. Even if you don't want to do that, you should tell her nicely rather than play tough. Little Rouge is all right as a person; she's just a bit stubborn. If you make things clear to her, she'll take it all right. You'll remember this, won't you?"

Lotuson answered in the affirmative and went downstairs. Instead of riding in the sedan chair, he took Talisman with him on foot. As they left the house, he saw a child dashing off southward; it looked like Pearlie's son. He wanted to call him back, but it was too late. Lotuson headed north out of East Co-prosperity Alley and cut through a side lane into West Floral Alley. Pearlie was waiting for him at the door and went upstairs with him into Little Rouge's room.

Little Rouge was seated languidly by the window, playing with a pair of jade hairpins shaped like lotus pods. When she saw him, instead of getting up, she just sneered, "You never think of coming to our place if we don't send someone to invite you. How much official business could there have been these couple of days that kept you so busy you couldn't come at all?"

He put on a smiling face and sat down. A smiling Pearlie picked up the conversation. "Well, Mr. Wang came the minute he was invited. You might say he gave us face; we weren't humiliated. You should thank me for this, my maestro!" So saying, she wrung out a hot towel, put a cup of tea in the opium tray, and lit the opium lamp. "Please have a smoke, Mr. Wang."

He went and lay down on the honored side of the divan and started to smoke. Little Rouge said, "You suffer so, coming here! We're all so clumsy, there's nobody fit to fill the pipe for you."

"Who's asking you to fill the pipe?" he replied with a smile.

Pearlie, having performed her duty, made herself scarce. Lotuson had already sated his appetite for opium before he arrived, so after just one pellet he sat up and changed to the water pipe. Little Rouge showed him the pair of jade hairpins.

"Did the jeweler bring these to show you?" he asked.

"That's right. I bought them at sixteen dollars. Is that more expensive than those at the teahouse?" she said.

"You've got several pairs of jade hairpins already. What d'you want another pair for?"

"You can buy a pair for someone else, but when I buy one, I'm in the wrong, is that it?"

"I don't mean it that way. You really don't need more hairpins; just buy something else."

"I certainly shall, but that can wait. I may not need another pair of hairpins, but I was so angry I *had* to buy them to make you come up with another sixteen dollars."

"Then just take sixteen dollars and buy anything you like. These hairpins aren't particularly nice, so don't buy them. Fair enough?"

"*I'm* not particularly nice, either, so how would I get to buy nice things?"

He affected a hushed voice. "Aiyo! How modest our maestro is! Who doesn't know the maestro Little Rouge of Shanghai? Not particularly nice, you say!"

"How can I count as a maestro when I can't even compare with a streetwalker? Why, being called maestro overwhelms me!"

Knowing he was no match for her in this verbal contest, he dared say no more but just resumed his position on the divan and started to toast opium in silence. As he did so, he stole a look at her. She sat against the windowsill pouting, with her head hanging down, holding the pair of hairpins in her hands and carefully counting the number of lotus seeds on them with the tip of her fingernails. He felt very sorry for her but did not know what to say to comfort her. Just then, the menservants announced, "Mr. Wang's friend is here."

Lotuson stood up in welcome. It was Benevolence Hong. The minute he came into the room he said, "Just now I went to look for you in East Co-prosperity Alley. When they said you were gone, I knew you'd be here."

Little Rouge offered him watermelon seeds and said smiling, "Mr. Hong, you're certainly good at finding your friends. Mr. Wang has only just got here, and you've found him already. Mr. Wang seldom comes here, you know, he's at East Co-prosperity Alley most of the time. Today, it's just because we invited him that he condescended to drop in. He'll be going back to East Co-prosperity Alley later. Next time you want to look for Mr. Wang, you should just go there. If he's not there, then it's hard to tell where he might be. Just wait at East Co-prosperity Alley, and you'll be sure to see him, for when Mr. Wang finishes his business he always goes back there. That place is just like Mr. Wang's residence."

As she went on and on about this, Benevolence Hong cut her short with a laugh. "Oh, stop that! Every time I'm here I hear you going at it. It's enough to bore even me to death."

"You're right, Mr. Hong. I'm not born to be good at chit-chat," she replied. "So whenever I speak people are upset. I'm not like those who know how to talk and smile and make the client happy. That's why even for a tea party the client prefers to go to them. It's so cozy to go there with friends and have a chat, but if he comes here, he gets an earful of exasperating nonsense from me, and even his friends get upset. What would possess Mr. Wang to think of coming here?"

Benevolence said in earnest, "Little Rouge, don't be like this. Even if Mr. Wang is seeing Constance, he's still affectionate toward you, so just let things be. If you insist that Mr. Wang should stop seeing Constance, it won't mean much to him. He'll just listen to you and not go there anymore. But it seems to me Constance is having a hard time, too, so if you let Mr. Wang look after her a bit, it's charity on your part."

These words calmed her towering rage and left her without an answer. Benevolence Hong and Lotuson Wang talked about other matters. When dusk approached, Benevolence wanted to take his leave, but Lotuson stopped him and then went and whispered in Little Rouge's ear. She said in response, "Then go. Who's holding you back?"

He said something more.

"Whether you come here or not is entirely up to you," she said.

So Lotuson went out with Benevolence, both saying "after you." Little Rouge took a couple of steps to see them out, murmuring, "Constance is waiting. You've got to look in or you'll feel out of sorts."

"I'm not going there," he said smiling as they went downstairs and out the door.

"Where to?" Benevolence asked.

"To your girl's place."

The two of them went north heading for Twin Pearl's in Sunshine Alley via Co-security Alley. As Lotuson had once summoned Twin Jade to a party, Clever Baby led him into her room. Benevolence Hong followed him in and saw Twin Jade lying in bed. He walked over to her and asked, "Are you not well?"

Twin Jade patted the side of the bed and said with a smile, "Do sit down, Mr. Hong. Sorry about this."

He sat down to chat with her. Twin Pearl came over from the opposite room to exchange a few words of greeting with Lotuson and invited him to smoke opium, while Clever Baby filled the water pipe for Benevolence.

Benevolence saw it was a silver one and then spied a row of five water pipes displayed on the dressing table, all silver. "How come Twin Jade has so many silver water pipes?" he asked in surprise.

"That's because my mother fawns on Twin Jade," Twin Pearl said teasingly.

When Twin Jade heard this, she protested in mock vexation, "Elder Sister always talks nonsense! Mother fawning on me, indeed; what a joke!"

Smiling, Benevolence asked for the story. Twin Pearl said, "You remember the incident of the silver water pipe last time? Well, Twin Jade told a guest to get her one, so Mother took all the silver water pipes left by Eldest Sister and Second Sister and gave them to Twin Jade, while Twin Jewel didn't even get one."

"If that's the case, why are you feeling unwell again?" he said.

Twin Jade answered, "I'm running a fever. I had guests playing mah-jongg here the night before last, and I didn't get any sleep, that's how I got this fever."

As they were talking, Lotuson Wang had toasted himself an opium pellet, but the bowl of the pipe was clogged up. Twin Pearl was the first to notice. "Come and smoke in my room. There's an old pipe over there," she said.

They all went over to Twin Pearl's room. Only then did Benevolence tell Lotuson which pieces of green jade jewelry he had bought and how much they cost and that everything had already been handed over to Constance in person. After that, Lotuson asked him, "Some people say Little Rouge has a lot of expenses herself, do you know what they mean?"

After some pondering, Benevolence answered, "Little Rouge hasn't any great expenses, except for taking carriage rides, which might add up."

Hearing that it was just carriage rides, Lotuson did not dwell on it any further.[2] They chatted until the lamps were lit, when Lotuson took his leave hastily to keep his appointment with Little Rouge. Benevolence stayed for supper in Twin Pearl's room. As an old client, he usually had casual meals there together with Twin Pearl and Twin Jade, and no extra dishes were ordered. But Twin Jade did not come over this evening.

"Why is Twin Jade unwell every couple of days?" he asked.

"Don't you believe her! Running a fever indeed! It's because Mother is too fond of her that she fakes illness."

"But why would she do that?" he asked.

"The night before last, there wasn't any call for Twin Jade to begin with, but just after Twin Jewel and I had gone out to parties, four

::

2. [Obviously everyone except Lotuson Wong knew that Little Rouge went on carriage rides with her lover, Little Willow. E.H.]

chits came for her. There weren't any menservants or sedan chairs at hand, so they went to call back Twin Jewel in a hurry. It happened that Twin Jewel was asked to follow her client to another party, so the menservants were told to take Twin Jade to her party in the sedan chair and then go and fetch Twin Jewel. By the time they had brought Twin Jewel back here and gone again to Twin Jade, it was getting late. When she got to her fourth party, it was over, and the client had left. When Twin Jade came back, she complained to Mother. Since she doesn't like Twin Jewel, she said it was Twin Jewel who held things up and that Mother should scold her. Mother didn't say anything because the client who wanted Twin Jewel to follow him to another party was in her room just then. That upset Twin Jade, and she went back to her room and started throwing things, making a real clatter! Then it happened that some guests came and played mah-jongg, and she didn't get any sleep all night, so the next day she said she was unwell."

"Poor Twin Jewel! She seems to have run into an enemy from her last incarnation."

"At first, Mother didn't like Twin Jewel because she wasn't good at business, so she scolded her now and then. But since Twin Jade got here, Twin Jewel has had several beatings, and all because of Twin Jade."

"Is Twin Jade still pally with you?"

"She's pally all right, but she's a bit scared of me. Mother lets her have her way in everything, whereas I don't care whether her business is good or not; if I spot anything wrong, I always speak out. If she gets offended, it's fine by me."

"It doesn't matter if you tell her off. She won't dare take offense."

A while later supper was over. With nothing to do, Benevolence decided to return to his store right away. Twin Pearl did not press him to stay, either. Coming out of her house, he exited the south end of Sunshine Alley and headed eastward. Suddenly, he heard somebody call out "Uncle" behind him. He turned round to see that it was none other than his nephew, Simplicity Zhao, dressed in a ragged blue cotton short jacket. The only mark of respectability was a pair of pale turquoise silk leg warmers worn over his trousers. His Peking-style shoes were so tattered that one of his toes was sticking out.

Startled, Benevolence demanded at once, "Why aren't you wearing a robe?"[3]

Simplicity hesitated before he replied, "When I came out of hos-

::

3. The robe was a mark of gentility not worn by laborers.

pital, I stayed a couple of days at the inn. Because I was short of several hundred copper coins for board and lodging, they took all my clothes and bedding as collateral."

"Why didn't you just go home?"

"I wanted to, but I had no money. Uncle, could you lend me the boat fare?"

Benevolence spat at him in disgust. "How dare you come to see me? You've come to Shanghai just to humiliate me! If you call me Uncle again, I'll slap your face!" Having said that, he turned to go. Simplicity followed at his heels, imploring miserably. After they had walked some distance, Benevolence reflected that since this would affect his reputation, he had no choice but to settle the affair. He barked at Simplicity, "Take me to the inn."

Simplicity answered yes repeatedly and rushed ahead to lead the way. Instead of going to the Welcome Inn, he went to a small inn on Sixth Avenue. Pointing at it, he said, "This is it."

Benevolence suppressed his anger and went in to inquire at the counter.

The manager smiled and said, "There isn't any bedding. All he had was a robe that's been pawned for four hundred copper coins."

Benevolence turned to question Simplicity, who hung his head in silence. Benevolence again spat at him and then took some small silver coins from his pocket to redeem the robe and pay for another night's lodging at the inn. He barked at Simplicity, "Come to my store tomorrow."

Simplicity dutifully promised and saw him out. Ignoring him completely, Benevolence called a ricksha to go back to the Flourishing Ginseng Store. He sighed and groaned but could not figure out what to do.

The next morning, Simplicity duly turned up wearing a robe. Benevolence told a salesclerk to take him to the boat and only gave him three hundred copper coins to buy food on the way. Taking his leave from Benevolence Hong, Simplicity Zhao left with the salesclerk.

CHAPTER 25 :: *A fond lover's chiding revives old memories, and the time of the month delays a tryst*

Benevolence waited until the salesclerk came back to report that Simplicity Zhao had been put on the boat and his fare paid. Still uneasy, he wrote a detailed letter to Simplicity's mother advising her to keep her son under strict control and not let him come to Shanghai again. He told the salesclerk to take it to the post office before he finally settled down to attend to his business at the store.

By afternoon, his work was done. On his way out, he received a note from Lichee Zhuang inviting him to dinner at Woodsy's in the Hall of Beauties on West Chessboard Street, so he left instructions for the clerk at the counter and went out, heading north. As it was still early, he took a ricksha and told the puller to take him to the midsection of Fourth Avenue. There, he went looking for Lotuson Wang, first at Constance's in East Co-prosperity Alley and then at Little Rouge's in West Floral Alley. But both of them said Lotuson wasn't there, so he walked via Brocade Alley to the Auspicious Luzon Lottery Store. After exchanging salutes with Bamboo Hu, he asked for Cloudlet Chen.

"He's upstairs," said Bamboo Hu.

Benevolence went upstairs, where Cloudlet Chen greeted him and invited him to sit down.

"Lichee Zhuang is giving a party at a second-class house. Are you invited?" Cloudlet asked.

"Yes, it's at Woodsy's, isn't it? Let's go together later," Benevolence replied, and Cloudlet readily agreed.

"Last time Lichee Zhuang came up with a long list of stuff; did you sell any of it for him?"

"Script Li chose a few things, but there're still lots left. You can ask some of your customers if they're interested."

Benevolence promised to do so. They soon ran out of things to say and sat together in boredom. After conferring with each other, they decided there was time to take tea at a sing-song house before proceeding to dinner. They went downstairs together, bade Bamboo Hu good-bye, and threaded their way through a narrow lane with high walls on both sides. It led them to Clever Gem's in Co-security Alley. Cloudlet Chen took Benevolence Hong directly upstairs. When they entered her room, Clever Gem got up to welcome them. The two men sat down.

"An invitation came for you from West Chessboard Street. Is it a dinner party?" Clever Gem asked.

"It's just Lichee Zhuang inviting the two of us," Cloudlet replied.

"Mr. Zhuang has already given several dinner parties this season," she said.

"The last one was done on behalf of a friend; it wasn't his party. Tonight, it's probably in honor of the money gods, either that or it's the treasure scrolls."

"That's it. We're having treasure scrolls on the twenty-third, so you should have a dinner party here, too," she said.

Cloudlet reflected. "That's fine; I'll come. But if you have other clients coming on that day, I can have my party a day later, on the twenty-fourth."

"There aren't other clients, or else I wouldn't have asked you. It's because there isn't anyone else that I have to."

Cloudlet said teasingly, "So, you tell me to give a dinner party here simply because there isn't anyone else. If there were, it wouldn't be my turn, right?"

Hearing this, she wanted to pinch his lips, but she could not do it in front of Benevolence, so she just answered with a smile, "Picking on me again, aren't you? But did I say anything wrong? You're a client of long standing, so if you don't give a party during the recitations, you'll lose face, won't you? If you don't help me put on a good show, what's the point of being a long-term client? If someone else is having a party here, then whether you want one or not is up to you. As a long-term client, you can have your party any day. Am I wrong there?"

"Oh, don't get excited. I didn't say you were wrong," he replied with a smile.

"Then what's this nonsense about whether it's your turn or not? You really make me see red."

Benevolence Hong, seated to one side, chuckled. At this, Clever Gem said, "Now Mr. Hong is laughing at us. You've been coming for four or five years now, and you're still talking silly. Anybody'd think you'd just started seeing me."

"Isn't it nice for us to talk and have a laugh? It'd be so boring if we didn't talk," Cloudlet replied.

"Did I tell you not to talk? But the minute you open your mouth, you say something irritating, and you call it joking! Look at Mr. Hong, he's been seeing Twin Pearl for longer than you've been coming here, and does he ever make a remark that's out of place? You're the only one who comes up with all sorts of sneaky stuff."

Smiling, Benevolence broke in, "You were supposed to be quarreling between yourselves. Why make me the butt of your jokes?"

"You don't know what he's like, Mr. Hong," she said pleasantly. "If you go by appearances, he seems quite easygoing, but when he's disagreeable, he can be truly exasperating. There was this time when he happened to come when there was a client in my room, so he was asked to sit for a while in the room across the way. Without a word, he just walked out. I asked him, 'Why did you leave?' And he put it so sweetly; he said, 'You had your favorite client here. I didn't feel like being a drag.'"

Before she had finished, Cloudlet cut her short with a smile, "That was quite a few years ago. Why bring it up now?"

She shot him a sideways glance and then said half in vexation and half in joke, "With you, things are no sooner said than forgotten, but I don't forget, and I *will* tell Mr. Hong about them. Mr. Hong is so good as to visit us, and we don't have much to entertain him with, so what's wrong with a little amusing chatter to make up for it?"

Anxious to put a stop to her chatter, Cloudlet stretched out his arms, rushed over, and embraced her in protest.

"What're you doing?" she shouted.

When the maid, Ocean, and the servant girl, Big Silver, heard this, they both came into the room. Only then did he let go. Clever Gem struggled free and patted her hair into place and then pulled a long face and barked at him, "Go and sit down over there."

He struck a pose of obedience, saying repeatedly, "Sure! Sure!" and backed away, returning to his seat.

Ocean and Big Silver, looking on, said in unison, "Mr. Chen has always been very well-behaved. How come he's so merry today?"

Benevolence nodded. "I've never seen him horsing around like this either."

With this little drama over, they suddenly realized it was long past lamp-lighting time. Cloudlet's steward, Constant Blessing, had come to look for him, bringing a note from Lichee Zhuang hurrying him to the party.

Benevolence stood up and said, "Let's be off," and went out with Cloudlet.

Clever Gem saw them to the head of the staircase, saying, "Call me right away."

Cloudlet made an affirmative noise, went out the door, and left word with Constant Blessing, "I'm going with Mr. Hong. You go home and tell the puller to bring my ricksha to West Chessboard Street." Constant Blessing left to carry out his instructions.

Arm in arm, Cloudlet Chen and Benevolence Hong walked at a leisurely pace down Fourth Avenue and Treasured Merit Street toward the Hall of Beauties. When they got there and went upstairs, they saw two other guests were already in the room: Pine Wu and Rustic Zhang. They introduced themselves to Cloudlet, and everybody casually took a seat.

Lichee Zhuang immediately wrote out two notes and handed them to Mama Yeung, saying, "You can set the table while reminders are sent to the guests."

By the time the table was set, the menservants had come back to report, "The guest at Sunset's in Generosity Alley wasn't there. The one at Grace Yang's is coming right away."

"Are you inviting Mallow Yao?" Benevolence Hong asked.

"No, it's Old Zhai," Lichee Zhuang replied.

"The other day, Mrs. Yao went to pick a row at Sunset's, have you heard about that?" asked Benevolence.

Aghast, Lichee immediately asked what it was all about. Before Benevolence could tell him, the menservants announced again, "Young Mr. Zhuang's friend is here." Lichee hurried out to meet him, and everybody stood up waiting to salute the newcomer.

It was Crane Li. As everybody had met before, there was no need for introductions. Lichee Zhuang told Mama Yeung to go to Jewel's room next door to ask Young Mr. Shi over. A handsome young man, splendidly dressed, walked in, holding Jewel by the hand. Nobody knew who he was. Lichee Zhuang introduced him as Shi, Fortune to his friends. Having expressed their eagerness to meet him, they were ushered to the table. Lichee Zhuang put Crane Li in the seat of honor and Fortune Shi next to him. The others sat as they pleased.

By then, Jewel, who had changed into party clothes, came over to sit behind Fortune Shi. Seeing Benevolence Hong, she asked, "Have you seen Young Mr. Zhao?"

"He's gone home today," replied Benevolence.

Rustic Zhang put in, "No, he hasn't. I saw Simplicity just now on Fourth Avenue."

Benevolence was greatly astonished but could not very well clarify the matter there.

"Oh, I meant to ask you, where d'you buy double joy—double longevity rings?" Fortune Shi asked Lichee Zhuang.

"At Lucky Dragon. They've got plenty of them."

Fortune then turned to Woodsy to look at the design of her rings, which he returned to her right away.

"Did you play mah-jongg the last couple of days?" Pine Wu asked Crane Li.

"No, I didn't."

"Feel like playing later?"

Crane Li frowned. "There aren't enough people for a game."

Pine Wu turned to ask Cloudlet. "Do you play?"

"I only do it to appease the courtesans. Not much money is won or lost," replied Cloudlet. Hearing this, Pine Wu fell silent.

At that moment, Clever Gem, Twin Pearl, Grace Yang, White Orchid, and Cassia Ma arrived one after the other. Cassia secretly tugged at Rustic's sleeve. He turned around. She opened her fan, hiding half her face behind it, and whispered to him. He nodded and immediately walked over to the opium divan, signaling surreptitiously for Pine Wu to join him. He whispered in Wu's ear, "There're treasure scrolls at Cassia's, too. She told me to go and show support. Would you tell Crane Li we'll play mah-jongg with him later?"

"Who else is there?"

"If there's nobody else, let's just ask Cloudlet Chen. What d'you think?"

Pine Wu said after a moment of reflection, "I'm afraid Cloudlet won't play. Since there're treasure scrolls at Cassia's, you should host a dinner party there. If you take this party over to her place and then mention mah-jongg during the meal, it'd be a lot easier."

Rustic considered the proposal. "I don't feel like having a dinner party, and there's no fun having it at Cassia's either."

"Now there's something you don't understand: It's far better to have dinner parties at second-class houses. The first-class girls are so much in demand that even a double table means nothing to them. But in a place like Cassia's, if you favored them with a dinner party and a game of mah-jongg, how they'd fuss over you!"

"Then why don't *you* host the party? I'll contribute a couple of dollars toward the tips," said Rustic.

"She's *your* girl, so it's not right for me to give a party there. Still, if I win at mah-jongg, I'll foot half the bill."

Rustic thought for a minute and then stood up and saluted everybody, explaining why he was taking the party over to Cassia's and pressing the others to honor him with their company. Everybody said he would indeed impose on Rustic's hospitality. Jubilant, Cassia immediately told her maid to go home and get things ready.

At the table, a finger game was under way. Lichee Zhuang, as the host, was the first to play. He offered everybody three shots to show his hospitality, and when he had finished, he invited the others to take over. Crane Li, neither a good drinker nor a good player of the game, saluted everyone and begged off. Fortune Shi was fooling with Jewel, his mind not on the wine. Rustic Zhang dared not get drunk as he was taking the party elsewhere, so he teamed up with Pine Wu just to do his bit. Cloudlet Chen and Benevolence Hong were the only ones in their usual good spirits. After some merry-making, Clever Gem and Twin Pearl each drank two cups of penalty wine for them and then left together with Grace Yang and White Orchid, each going her own way. Jewel, after having changed out of her party clothes, came in again to help entertain. At this point, Rustic told Cassia, "Go on ahead and set the table."

Before she left, Cassia urged him, "Please come over right away." After her departure, the party broke up.

Jewel had already pulled Fortune Shi into her own room. She made him lie down on the opium divan while she leaned over him, whispering, "Are you going to the party?"

"They want to take the party somewhere else, but I don't feel like going," he replied.

"Since you were drinking together, naturally you should go over there with them. It's not nice if you drop out on your own," she said.

"It only means one less party call for you. What else is not nice about it?"

She sneered. "When you called Third Treasure to parties, it was three dollars per call, and how many times in a row did you call her? With me, you're already making a saving."

"Third Treasure is a virgin courtesan. She doesn't cost three dollars."

"A virgin courtesan at first, but virgin no more once you started seeing her."

He guffawed. "You're speaking of yourself. That only applies to Jewel. She was a virgin courtesan at first, but virgin no more once I started seeing her."

She broke out in silly giggles and reached a hand inside his sleeve to pinch his arm. He took the opportunity to hug her and was just going to feel her up when the spoilsport Mama Yeung came in with the message, "Young Mr. Zhang asks you to go over."

He sat up, but Jewel pushed him down again. "What's the hurry? Just let them go on ahead."

He had to answer, "Ask Young Mr. Zhang to go ahead. I'll be there shortly."

Mama Yeung assented, all smiles, and went out. Locked in an embrace, Fortune and Jewel kept quiet and listened carefully to what went on outside. After Mama Yeung had delivered his message, they heard Rustic say, "Let's go then." Crane Li and Cloudlet Chen, who had their ricksha and sedan chair there, were the first to leave. Rustic Zhang then led the way for Benevolence Hong, Pine Wu, and Lichee Zhuang. The three proceeded slowly downstairs, talking and laughing all the way.

"They're all gone," Fortune whispered in Jewel's ear.

She pretended to be offended. "So what?" She had scarcely finished speaking when unexpectedly Woodsy came in after having seen the guests off. Her desire now kindled, Jewel hated this intrusion. She clenched her teeth and pushed Fortune Shi away with all her might and then stamped her feet and dashed over to the dressing table, her bound-feet shoes making a rickety noise. She stood in front of the foreign mirror to tidy up her hair.

"Young Mr. Zhang told me to tell you it's the third house in Auspicious Cloud Alley, in case you don't know the place," Woodsy said to Fortune.

"Got it, got it," he said repeatedly, his eyes glancing sideways at Jewel. Woodsy turned around and saw that Jewel was all red in the face. She said no more and withdrew in haste.

He lay down on his side on the opium divan and beckoned to her slyly, calling in a low voice, "Come here."

She cast a fleeting glance at him but then stamped her foot and said in a pet, "Not coming."

Taken aback, he sat up cross-legged, patted his thigh, and pleaded, "Don't be like that! I'll kowtow to you on behalf of your sister. Don't be angry, for my sake."

Hearing this, she almost laughed, but she suppressed it. Her little mouth pouting, and balancing first on one tiny foot then the other, she shimmied and swayed as she moved reluctantly toward him. When she was only three or four paces away from the divan, she suddenly launched herself at him. Unable to block her, he fell back spread-eagled. She pressed her head tightly against his chest, lay on top of him, and held his body down so he could not move. Despite a thousand protests from him, she refused to budge. Helpless, he managed to free his right hand, which gradually felt its way along her midriff under her blouse. Suddenly, it came across the knot of the sash of her trousers. He meant to pull it undone, but she became aware of what he was doing and gave a screech like a whistle. At the same time, she gripped his hands and looked up, staring at him eyeball to eyeball.

"Why are you still resisting?" he whispered. Despite his repeated questions, she would not answer.

After a long while, she finally murmured, "You're going to the party. When the party's over, come back early, all right?"

"We've got nothing to do now. Why does it have to be later?"

Hard-pressed and unable to find the words to explain the situation, she just pointed at her own bosom. He was still puzzled.

Getting desperate, she let him go and got up from the divan, frowning. "You! How can anyone make you understand?"

He thought for a moment and then sighed helplessly, grumbling, "All right, I'll let you off now. Later, if you still resist me, I'll show you who's boss."

She pulled the corners of her mouth down. "You reckon you've got what it takes?"

He said smiling, "Nothing spectacular, but I can make you die."

"Aiyo! You certainly can talk. Let's hope it won't turn out later to be all talk."

"Why not try it now and see."

Hearing this, she backed off in a hurry. He pulled a long face. "Running away before I've even touched you, huh? You little tease— I've never seen the likes of you!"

She was about to answer back when the menservants called out, "Mama Yeung, an invitation and a party call!"

Jewel said, "They're asking for you." When Mama Yeung brought the invitation in, it was indeed from Rustic Zhang.

"Shall we say you'll be there right away?" Jewel asked.

"Since you don't want me, naturally I'm going," he said.

"Oh, goodness! You're such a —" she exclaimed loudly but did not finish what she wanted to say.

Seeing this, Mama Yeung laughed foolishly in sympathy and then called down the stairs without being instructed, "The guest is coming right away."

Fortune did not react, while Jewel went and got herself ready. Seeing that he was still lying on the divan, she asked, "Aren't you going to the dinner?"

He said coldly, "I'm not going. I'm already filled up with empty words and have lost my appetite."

She at once hit the roof, stamping both feet on the floor and heaving a sigh. At last, she climbed onto the opium divan and whispered in his ear.

He finally saw the light. "Then why didn't you say so before?"

She walked away without explaining herself. He stood up and straightened his clothes, preparing to go, but then turned to her and said, "I'll be frank with you, too. Since you're not well yet today, I'll come tomorrow. After the dinner party, I'll go home."

She glared at him "What are you saying?"

He said appeasingly, "Well, I'm just consulting with you. I'll definitely come tomorrow."

"Who's asking you to come tomorrow?" she shouted. "If you want to go home, just go!"

Having no time to argue, Fortune turned his head away and, in imitation of her, stamped his foot on the floor and heaved a sigh. Even Mama Yeung was tickled by this.

He turned around and begged Jewel's pardon and then took out her party clothes and obsequiously draped them over her shoulders. She pretended to ignore him and arranged to go together with Woodsy. The two women went downstairs by themselves. Fortune followed them to the door, where he watched them get into their sedan chairs. He followed them on foot with Mama Yeung.

Just as they walked past the Galaxy Jewelry Store, a young maidservant dashed toward them and grabbed Mama Yeung, saying, "Grandma, wait!"

Fortune could not wait for Mama Yeung as the sedan chairs had gone far ahead. He hurried after them. When he reached Auspicious Cloud Alley, he saw the sedan chairs were standing in front of Cassia's door, and the girls were looking for Mama Yeung. He explained how a maid had stopped her on the way. Woodsy, enraged, got off the chair and went in by herself. He asked Jewel, "Would you like to take my arm?"

"No, you go in first," she said at once.

He followed Woodsy in. When they entered Cassia's room, the others were already seated, leaving the seat of honor vacant. Fortune Shi could not very well refuse, so he reluctantly took it.

After a long wait, Jewel finally came in, leaning on the arm of Mama Yeung. The minute Woodsy saw Mama Yeung, she lashed out, "Have you taken leave of your senses? You're supposed to follow the girls to a party. Where did you make off to?"

Mama Yeung explained with a smile, "The young kids get scared stiff if the least thing happens. I told them not to worry, but they won't believe me. They're asking me to go back."

Woodsy was still going to complain when Fortune Shi interrupted, "What happened to them?"

Mama Yeung took her time in telling them the story.

CHAPTER 26 :: *Nocturnal sounds show a couple's real prowess, and a lustful look betrays a woman's false modesty*

Mama Yeung said, "It's none other than Aroma Su. She's said to have been arrested by the new police."

Cloudlet Chen said, suddenly alert, "Aroma? Is that the runaway concubine from a Ningbo family?"

"That's her, but she's no runaway. The wife of that family couldn't get on with her, so her husband let her out and told her to marry again but forbade her to return to the business. Since she's now back in the business, her husband is on her trail. It so happens that my granddaughter has just become a maid at her place. Now isn't it rotten luck?"

"Did your granddaughter pay her a premium?" Lichee Zhuang asked.

"You've put your finger on it," replied Mama Yeung. "It's a bit awkward for somebody who's got money invested. For someone like me, what would it matter? Would I be afraid that the new police would arrest me?"

"Aroma has always been too big for her boots. Now she's going to suffer," said Crane Li.

"She'll be all right. I heard that His Excellency Qi is in Shanghai," said Mama Yeung.

"Is it Harmony Qi of Pinghu?" Benevolence Hong asked.

"That's the one. In the Su house, only Aroma and Essence, Mr. Qi's concubine, are real daughters of the family. All the other girls are just bought by the house."

Lichee Zhuang suddenly thought of something he wanted to ask, but Pine Wu and Rustic Zhang, who had their minds set on mah-jongg, deliberately started the finger game to cut short the conversation. As soon as the summoned girls had all arrived, Rustic Zhang urged Cloudlet Chen to play mah-jongg. Cloudlet asked how much they were playing for, and Rustic told him that each player would start with a hundred dollars' worth of chips.

"That's too high," said Cloudlet.

Rustic pleaded hard for him to play along just the once, and Pine Wu joined in to persuade him. Cloudlet Chen then asked Benevolence Hong, "I'll be partners with you, all right?"

"What partners, when I don't even know how to play?" said Benevolence. "Perhaps you could team up with Lichee."

Lichee turned to Fortune Shi. "Why don't you take a share as well?"

Fortune had something more important than this on his mind. He hastily held up a hand to indicate his lack of interest and refused to join in. That being the case, Cloudlet Chen and Lichee Zhuang agreed to take equal shares in a hand and to play four rounds each.

"Since we're going to play mah-jongg, don't let's drink any more," said Crane Li.

Fortune Shi took the opportunity to say good-bye and left with Jewel. Rustic Zhang, not knowing what they had in mind, was very apologetic. Afraid also that Benevolence Hong would feel let down, he hastily filled several large tumblers with wine and offered Hong five shots at the finger game, after which Pine Wu also offered to play Benevolence Hong five shots on behalf of the host. When the ten tumblers of wine were gone, so were the girls, except for Grace Yang, who stayed on on a mah-jongg party call. After everybody had had a little congee, the table was cleared and the mah-jongg game began. Rustic Zhang asked Benevolence Hong, "Feel like playing a couple of games?"

"I really don't know how."

"Look on and you'll learn," said Pine Wu.

So Benevolence Hong pulled over a stool and sat between Rustic Zhang and Pine Wu, looking at both their hands. Grace Yang naturally sat behind Crane Li. Lichee Zhuang was in a hurry to smoke and asked Cloudlet Chen to play first. A throw of the dice decided that Cloudlet should be banker.

Cloudlet grunted the minute he looked at his hand. "How come I got such a hand?" The other three kept pressing him to discard a tile. He finally did. But after he had taken his turn, picking up three or four new tiles, he again hesitated and suddenly called out to Lichee Zhuang, "Come and have a look, I have no idea how to deal with this."

Lichee got up from the opium divan and ran over to the table. He saw the fourteen tiles were all of a kind and there were many possible winning formations. After shifting the tiles around to check the different formations, he finally picked up a six-circle, telling Cloudlet to discard it. The others immediately guessed they had an all-circle hand.

"They're fishing for either four- and seven-circle or five- and eight-circle. Be on the lookout everybody," said Rustic Zhang.

It happened that Rustic had a one-circle. Since an identical tile was already lying in the discarded pool, he threw it out without much thought.

"Game!" Cloudlet exclaimed. When his winning hand was laid out, the triplet formations pushed the total points to eighty. The other three paid up in chips.

Lichee Zhuang commented, "With this hand, it was right to discard the six-circle, wasn't it? When he did that, he could win the game by going either for one-, four-, seven-circle or two-, five-, eight-circle. There were so many tiles that could complete his hand."

Pine Wu pondered. "I think he should have discarded the seven-circle. In that scenario, every circle tile except for seven and eight would have made him a winner, and the same one-circle would have given him three more triplets, meaning a hundred and seventy-two extra points. Figure it out yourself."

"You're right. Cloudlet made the wrong move," said Rustic Zhang. Lichee Zhuang was also full of admiration.

"You people make so much of it! Who's got the patience for all this calculation!" said Crane Li, who started shuffling the tiles for the next game.

Seated to one side, Benevolence ruminated over the winning hand. He felt there was something to everybody's remarks and came to realize that mah-jongg was no easy game. It was better to plead ignorance and remain a nonplayer. He lost interest in watching them and took his leave with his spirits a bit dampened. After sitting for a while, Grace Yang also left.

By the time the eight rounds of the game were finished, it was past two o'clock. Pine Wu and Rustic Zhang were both pressed to stay by Cassia Ma. The other three took their leave before congee could be served. Crane Li's sedan chair and Cloudlet Chen's ricksha went their separate ways, and Lichee Zhuang walked alone at a leisurely pace back to the Hall of Beauties on West Chessboard Street. He groped in the dark to find the door and knocked. When he had done so a dozen times or more, it was Woodsy who heard him. She pushed her window open and called out for the menservants downstairs to get up and welcome him in.

Seeing it was Lichee Zhuang, the man hastily lit a match to light the foreign lamp and show him upstairs. At the bottom of the stairs, they met Mama Yeung, who had tottered out from her room, squinting her eyes and dragging her feet along in a pair of old shoes. The manservant handed her the foreign lamp, and Lichee said to him, "Never mind about bringing hot water. Go to bed." The man withdrew.

After Mama Yeung had seen Lichee into Woodsy's room, he told her to go to bed as well. She hovered around a bit and left. All the paraffin lamps in the room had been put out except for a long-stemmed lamp on the dressing table. Woodsy had removed her jewelry and makeup and was sitting idly, smoking a water pipe. On seeing Lichee, she asked, "Did you win at mah-jongg?"

"A little." Then he asked her, "Why aren't you in bed?"

"I was waiting for you."

He smiled and thanked her and then took off his jacket and hung it on the clothes rack. She handed him the water pipe and lit the opium lamp. He followed her to the divan and was delighted to see a boat-shaped glass container already filled with toasted opium pellets. The water pipe was immediately put aside, and he lay down to satisfy his craving. She moved a teapot with its hexagonal Suzhou-embroidered tea cozy toward him, asking, "Would you like some tea? It's still nice and hot."

He shook his head. After he had finished two pellets of opium, he handed her the pick, so she lay down on the left side of the divan and filled the pipe for him.

Lichee Zhuang got up and went behind the bed to relieve himself. There, he heard the faint sound of panting from the next room. He suddenly remembered that Fortune Shi was staying the night. Having finished his business, he tiptoed out of the room to peep in through the window along the corridor. Unfortunately, in the dim, flickering lamplight he could not see anything behind the pale turquoise bed curtains. All he heard was a low voice saying, "Are you still resisting?" It sounded like Fortune Shi. Jewel said something in reply, but her voice was even lower, and he could not make out what she said. Fortune Shi said again, "You talk tough, don't you? Such a little thing like you, d'you really want to die?"

At this, Lichee Zhuang could not repress a chuckle. They heard him in the room. There was a whisper, "Quick, stop. Somebody's looking in."

But Fortune Shi responded loudly, "Let them look!" He then shouted toward the door, "What's there to look at? If you want to look, just come in!"

Lichee Zhuang did his utmost to suppress his laughter and turned to go. Woodsy, who had filled his pipe and had guessed from his long absence what he was up to, tiptoed out of the room just then. She pulled at his ear and dragged him back into her room and then gave him such a hard shove he almost fell down. She slammed the door shut. He was still laughing hard, his body bent over and a hand covering his mouth.

She scowled and scolded him, "You unlucky wretch—it would be hard to find your likes again!"

He just grinned all over his face and drew her to him with both hands. Sitting beside her on the opium divan, he repeated in detail what he had heard, reconstructing the imagined scenes and imitating the action. She turned her head away in fake anger. "I don't want to hear."

At this rebuff, he lay down to smoke opium. Putting frivolity aside, he composed his face and chatted with her. Gradually, the subject turned to Jewel. He happened to praise Fortune Shi, "He can count as a good client."

She made a dismissive gesture. "Shi's disposition is no good. He's just like a sack of lime that leaves its mark everywhere. Now he shows considerable affection because he has just started seeing her. When they're better acquainted, he get bored and stop coming."

"That's hard to say. I think the two of them are so well matched, they're inseparable. Even if Shi wanted to get another girl, a lesser courtesan wouldn't be able to take it from him."

She glared at him and said in vexation, "There's just no stopping you, is there?" Then she walked away to get a water pipe.

He smoked two more opium pellets and then blew out the lamp. He put the teapot and tea cozy back on the dressing table, took off his shoes, and sat on the bed with legs spread out. When he looked at the clock, he saw it was about to strike four. He beckoned to her, but she pretended to ignore him.

"Give me the water pipe. I'd like a smoke," he rapped out.

Caught off guard, she started and then hastily brought him the water pipe and said to him earnestly, "You know, I had just fallen asleep when you made all that racket and got yourself cursed at."

He smiled without defending himself, put an arm around her shoulders, and spoke into her ear. Though she laughed, she still told him off, "You're raving mad, aren't you?" So saying, she tossed the water pipe at him and struggled free and then went behind the bed.

He had not quite finished his smoke when he heard her giggling to herself. "What's so funny?" he asked.

She did not answer. A moment later, when she was done, she came out and stood in front of the bed, grinning ear to ear. He put down the water pipe and tried to tease out the reason for her mirth. She was about to tell him when another burst of laughter caught her. Finally, she said in a low voice, "You didn't hear them earlier on—that was what I'd call scandalous. After I came back from the party in Auspicious Cloud Alley, I sat here chatting with Mama Yeung. Then I heard something thumping by the window over in Jewel's room. I thought she was downstairs, so I said urgently, 'Mama Yeung, quick, go and see what that is.' When she came back, Mama Yeung said, 'Rotten luck! Even the door to that room is closed.' I said, 'Did you go in to have a look?' Mama Yeung said, 'What for? If anything's broken, make him pay for it.' I had no idea what it was until then. After a while, Mama Yeung went downstairs and went to bed, and I started a game of solitaire and then toasted seven or eight opium pellets, which took a long time. After I had finished, I listened again, and the thumping noise was still there. Oh how I hated it! I wished I could tear my ears off!"

He burst into laughter as he listened. When she had finished, the two of them rocked with mirth and collapsed in a heap. He suddenly whispered into her ear again. She told him off in a laughing voice, "Now I'm not going to talk to you anymore." He hastened to beg her pardon. As it was almost dawn, they got ready for bed.

The next morning, Lichee Zhuang woke up at about seven because there was something on his mind. Telling Woodsy to get more sleep, he got up first. When the servant girl brought hot water, he asked why Mama Yeung wasn't there.

"Her granddaughter came to call her away," the servant girl replied.

Lichee asked no more questions. He gave his face a quick wipe, left the Hall of Beauties, and walked round to the Auspicious Luzon Lottery Store in Brocade Alley. Surprised he was so early, Cloudlet Chen, who had just got out of bed, invited him upstairs.

"I have a favor to ask of you. I heard Harmony Qi is here," said Lichee.

"Though I've dined with Harmony Qi, I don't know him well. I've no idea if he's in town," said Cloudlet.

"Can you ask somebody you know well to make the approach and ask if he's interested in a small deal?"

Cloudlet pondered. "There're Elan Ge and Crane Li. They're family friends of his. I can write them a note."

Delighted, Lichee thanked him. Cloudlet immediately wrote out two informal notes and told his steward. Constant Blessing, to take one note to Great Virtue Money Shop and the other to the Long Peace Inn and, if they were not at home, to take the notes to Snow Scent's and Grace Yang's, respectively.

After Constant Blessing had received his orders, he left with the notes and decided to head for the nearest place: Snow Scent's in East Co-prosperity Alley. Here, he asked for Second Young Master Ge, who was indeed there, still in bed, so Constant Blessing handed over the letter and left. He was on his way to Generosity Alley when he met Crane Li's steward, Second Kuang, on Fourth Avenue. He explained about delivering the letter.

"Just give it to me," said Second Kuang.

He produced the letter and handed it over. "Where're you off to?"

"I'm at a loose end so I thought I'd take a walk."

"Shall we pay Third Pan a visit?"

Second Kuang hesitated. "It's a bit embarrassing."

"Verdure Xu won't be going there. And even if he does, there's nothing embarrassing about it."

Second Kuang consented and turned around to go with him. When they came to the corner of Pebble Road, they saw Pragmatic Li walking alone, heading west. Second Kuang exclaimed in astonishment, "What's Fourth Master going there for?"

"Probably to see a friend," replied Constant Blessing.

"Not likely."

"Let's follow him and see for ourselves."

The two of them tailed Pragmatic at a distance of only a dozen paces, taking cover as they walked along. When Pragmatic Li went straight into Great Prosperity Alley, Constant Blessing and Second Kuang peeped in at the alley entrance and saw him stop in front of a small terrace house by a bend. He knocked, and an old woman, all smiles, welcomed him in and shut the door after him. Constant Blessing and Second Kuang went into the alley and looked appraisingly at the house but could not tell what kind of a household it was. They tried peeping through the gap in the door but saw nothing. Then they drew back and looked up, across the wall, but could not see anything clearly behind the green windows.

Just as they were lingering there, a young streetwalker with a pretty face pushed open an upstairs window and bent forward as if she were talking to someone in the courtyard below. Right behind her was Pragmatic Li. Seeing this, Second Kuang grabbed hold of Constant Blessing and turned to go. Then they heard a door open and somebody coming out.

When Constant Blessing and Second Kuang got to the entrance of the alley, they waited there for a moment and saw it was the old woman who had come out. Second Kuang was wary of engaging her in conversation, but Constant Blessing asked boldly, "What's the name of your Miss?"

The old woman looked the two of them up and down and then

put on a sullen look. "What's this about Miss or not-Miss? Don't come bothering me. Stop talking nonsense!" Having said that, she went off.

Although Constant Blessing did not answer back, he grumbled something to himself.

"She might be a respectable woman," said Second Kuang.

"I'm sure she's a streetwalker. If she were respectable, the old one would've been ruder."

"If she is a streetwalker, what's wrong with calling her Miss?"

"Unless she's now kept by your fourth master and doesn't walk the streets anymore, right?"

"Well, that's none of our business! Let's go to Third Pan's."

The two of them turned back eastward to Security Alley, where they found the door at Third Pan's house standing wide open. A maid was squatting in the courtyard close to the doorway, washing and starching clothes. When the two walked in, the maid, who only knew Constant Blessing, got up to welcome him. "Master Constant, do go upstairs."

This told Second Kuang that there was company, so he said, "Let's come back later."

Upon hearing this, the maid hastily shook off the water on her hands, wiped them on her blouse, and grabbed hold of the two of them, positively refusing to let go.

"Is the guest Verdure?" Constant Blessing asked in a whisper.

"No, and he'll be going soon. Please sit upstairs for a while."

"What d'you say?" Constant Blessing asked Second Kuang, who reluctantly agreed and went upstairs with him. Second Kuang saw that the room was quite adequately furnished, so he asked whose room it was.

"Third Pan is the only one here. There're several who don't live here and are only summoned when there're guests," replied Constant Blessing. Second Kuang realized only then that this was something like a knocking shop.

In a moment, the maid brought tobacco and tea. Constant Blessing stopped her to ask, "Who's the guest?"

"He's from Hongkou, name of Yang. He came at seven, so he'll leave soon. He's a busy man and comes only once every seven or eight days."

"What's his trade?" he asked.

"I've no idea what business he's in."

During their conversation, Third Pan had sauntered upstairs. Her hair still disheveled, she was just wearing slippers and a tight undershirt. She told the maid to go downstairs and then lit the opium lamp herself and invited them to smoke.

Second Kuang lay down on the opium divan, but Constant Blessing just stared at Third Pan, grinning. Embarrassed, she asked, "What's so funny?"

He put on a serious expression and said, "There's a bit of dirt on your face, that's why I laughed. When you wash your face later, remember to clean it off with foreign soap."

She turned her head away and ignored him. Second Kuang, being a simple soul, got up to look. Constant Blessing pointed his finger at her face. "Look! There it is. I wonder how this muck got on to her face. Very strange."

To back him up, Second Kuang guffawed.

"So, even Master Kuang is fooled!" she said. "That mouth of his, is it a mouth or some other hole?"

Constant Blessing jumped up. "Go look at yourself in a mirror, then tell me it's nonsense!"

Second Kuang said, "Maybe the color came off the knitting wool you use to braid your hair."

She was taken in and was on the point of going downstairs to wash when they heard the maid calling loudly, "Please come and sit downstairs." Constant Blessing and Second Kuang followed Third Pan to the room downstairs. She picked up a hand mirror at once to look at her face, only to find that there was not the slightest mark on it.

"Master Kuang, I thought you were a good man, but you've learned to play tricks, too. You fooled me!"

At this, Constant Blessing and Second Kuang clapped their hands and stamped their feet in mirth, laughing so hard they almost fell down. She could not help laughing as well.

"I wasn't talking nonsense though. Your face is filthy enough, though it doesn't show," said Constant Blessing when he had stopped laughing. "Give it a good scrub with the towel—seriously."

"Your mouth should be scrubbed, too," she said.

"*We* are quite clean," said Second Kuang. "As for *you*, a filthy face goes with a filthy mouth."

"Master Kuang, why would you want to follow their example? People like them are the worst sort. Granted, they know how to wag their tongues, but tongue wagging isn't that rare, is it?"

"Listen to her!" Constant Blessing retorted. "Lucky I have nostrils, otherwise I'd burst from getting steamed up."

The three of them went on bickering and laughing. After some time, the maid brought in a kettle and poured hot water into a basin. Only then did Third Pan wash her face and tidy her hair.

It was almost noon, and Constant Blessing wanted to go home for lunch, so Second Kuang had to leave with him. On their way out, Third Pan tugged at Second Kuang's sleeve and said, "Come back later." Constant Blessing did not see this tug. He made a vague promise and left with Second Kuang.

CHAPTER 27 :: *The drunk who disrupts a tryst empties his stomach, and a whore's burning hands prove her randy nature*

Together Constant Blessing and Second Kuang walked to Generosity Alley on Fourth Avenue, where they parted company. Constant Blessing went back to the Auspicious Luzon Lottery Store to report on his mission, while Second Kuang went into Grace Yang's. Here, he learned that his master, Crane Li, though out of bed, had not yet washed. He dared not disturb him. The menservants invited Second Kuang to a casual meal in the bookkeeper's office at the back, next to the kitchen. They warmed a pot of Shaoxing wine in his honor, and there was a big fish and lots of meat on the table. After he had eaten his fill, he saw Thrive carry a plate of fine food into Grace Yang's room, and he hurried forward to entreat her to report his presence.

In a little while, he was summoned. Crane Li and Grace Yang were having a tête-à-tête over some wine. Second Kuang submitted Cloudlet Chen's letter. After he had read it, Crane Li put it aside, and Second Kuang withdrew promptly. After lunch, Li's sedan-chair bearers came to await orders. Second Kuang asked Thrive what was afoot, and the latter replied, "I heard they're going for a carriage ride."

Second Kuang could only sit around and wait. Little did he realize that he would be waiting till three in the afternoon for the order to summon a carriage. By then, he had seen Mallow Yao arriving in a sedan chair to see Crane Li. Li knew there had to be a reason for this visit and invited Yao into Grace Yang's room so they could chat at leisure. Mallow Yao, however, kept beating around the bush. This made Crane Li impatient. He asked Yao if he had anything particular in mind. Mallow Yao said evasively that there wasn't anything and asked him in turn, "What about you?" When Crane Li answered in the negative, Mallow Yao said, "Then perhaps we can go to Sunset's for a cup of tea. What d'you think?"

Crane Li, unaware of the reasons for Yao's suggestion, agreed quite readily. Grace Yang, who was sitting by their side, was quick on the uptake. She chuckled. Mallow Yao just let her laughter pass and urged Crane Li to put on his jacket. As they did not have far to go, neither of them took a sedan chair; they just made their way on foot to Sunset's.

The minute they came through the door, a servant girl welcomed them with a smiling face. "What's kept you away these last few days, Second Young Master?"

Mallow Yao smiled without answering and went straight upstairs with Crane Li.

Sunset also welcomed them with a big smile. "Why, it's Second Young Master! You've been held in the police station for several days. How come you've been let out today?"

Mallow Yao smiled awkwardly. Crane Li, puzzled by her words, asked what she meant. She pointed to Yao, smiling. "Just ask him whether it's true that he was hauled off by the police and shut up for several days."

Crane Li, who had heard about the business with Mrs. Yao, now realized what this was about. He smiled and dropped the subject.

When they had all taken their seats, Sunset leaned close to Mallow Yao and asked in a whisper, "Your wife is cursing me, isn't she?"

"Who says so?" he asked.

"Humph! Don't you give me that nonsense. I can't blame her if she does a bit of cursing, but you actually help her to bad-mouth me! You see, I know all about it."

"Now *you're* talking nonsense. If you know it all, tell me what she said in cursing you."

"She was cursing all the way when she left here, so why wouldn't she curse me when she got home?"

"She didn't come here to pick a quarrel, in fact. I went to Wusong for three days on some important business, and they didn't know about it at home. They thought I was here and called in to ask. When I got back and told them where I had been and that it had nothing to do with you, she didn't say anything."

"You say she didn't come here to quarrel, but the minute she came in she looked black as thunder and made a real racket even before she had come upstairs, now if that wasn't quarreling what was it?"

"Don't let's talk about it anymore. She had a real dressing-down from you and couldn't get a word out herself. That should have made you feel better."

"Honestly, since she's a lady, I wouldn't have gone out of my way to offend her. But when she turned up here to find fault with me, I had to give her a piece of my mind. Did I do wrong?"

"No, it was a good thing you did that, and I ought to thank you for it. If it weren't for you, she'd have thought nobody dared offend her, and the next time she found out where I was giving a party, she'd butt in again. That'd be embarrassing, wouldn't it?"

Sunset had meant to give him a thorough tongue-lashing, but the way he talked about the incident as well as the presence of Crane Li made her decide to be lenient with him. After a long pause, she said sarcastically, "Second Young Master, it seems to me you're far too considerate. At home, you have to please your lady by saying bad things about me, and when you're here, you have to say it was your lady's fault, that she deserved to have been told off. It's such hard work, doesn't it make you feel miserable?"

Her words touched a sore spot, and he could find no answer, so he let them pass in silence. Crane Li tactfully changed the subject by asking, "Do you know Harmony Qi?"

"I've dined with him several times, so I claim a slight acquaintance. But I don't know whether he's in town."

"He's said to be here, but I haven't run into him," said Crane Li.

At this point, Sunset asked what they would have for tea. Mallow Yao named a couple of things offhand and kept Crane Li company at tea, after which Sunset invited Crane to smoke opium. Before they knew it, it was getting dark, and Second Kuang brought the sedan chair to fetch his master and handed him a party invitation. Crane Li saw that it was Clement Zhou asking him to Lucky You's in Sunshine Alley. He knew it was a gambling party.

"Feel like a little amusement?" he asked Mallow Yao.

Mallow Yao excused himself, saying he did not play. Crane Li then told Second Kuang to go back to the inn and keep watch there. "If Fourth Master asks about me, just say I'm at Grace Yang's." Second Kuang promised to do as bade.

So Crane Li took his leave from Mallow Yao and left Sunset's place. Second Kuang followed him to the door, saw him get in the sedan chair, and watched the chair go off before he returned to the Long Peace Inn on Pebble Road. After supper, he took advantage of Fourth Master's continued absence, locked the door, and sneaked off to Third Pan's in Security Alley off Fourth Avenue. Here he knocked lightly on the door three times with the brass knocker. The maid called out in answer and opened the door. He learned that Third Pan was home and without company. Overjoyed, he ducked his head and dived into the room.

Third Pan was lying on the couch smoking opium. Knowing it was Second Kuang, she closed her eyes and pretended to be fast asleep. He went up quietly, lay on top of her, and kissed her on the mouth. She still ignored him. So he put out a hand to feel her all over, touching every inch of her body. This made Third Pan impatient. She opened her eyes and said smiling, "You! What're you up to?"

Feeling pleased, he made no excuses. Instead, he pushed the opium tray aside, pressed his cheek against hers, and asked, "Is it true that Verdure Xu doesn't come here anymore?"

"Whether he comes or not is none of your business. Why d'you ask about him?"

"I told you, it won't do!"

"Listen, my original client was a man named Xia. He brought Xu here, and then Xu brought you along. It's all the same to me. Why won't it do?"

Just as his hand was led to its target, and the squeezing and rubbing made way for the real entrance, suddenly there was a loud banging at the door.

"Who is it?" the maid shouted from within.

The man outside answered, "It's me."

It sounded like Verdure Xu. Alarmed and flustered, Second Kuang got up to hide himself.

Third Pan grabbed him. "What d'you think you're doing?"

He held up a hand in protest, saying, "It won't do! It won't do!" and managed to struggle free and tiptoed upstairs. It was pitch-dark there. He groped around and found a high-back chair, where he sat down, cocked his ears, and listened. He heard the maid open the door. Verdure Xu was alone and already dead drunk. He threw up copiously right at the door and then staggered into the room. Third Pan said in an angry voice, "Where did you go for a binge? Now that you're drunk, you think you can come here to throw a fit?"

Verdure Xu dared not say anything. The maid tried to smooth things over and got him a cup of hot tea. He wanted to smoke opium.

"We do have opium here. Help yourself," said Third Pan.

"You fill a pipe for me."

"You know where to go to get drunk, and you don't know how to fill a pipe?"

He jumped up and shouted, "Have you taken up with an actor? Is that why you're tired of me?"

She shouted back at him, "Who's tired of you? And even if I take up with an actor, who are you to say anything?"

At this, he couldn't help laughing.

Upstairs, Second Kuang guessed that Xu would not be leaving anytime soon and thought he'd better make himself scarce. He tiptoed down the stairs and on second thought went to the kitchen at the back and whispered to the maid, "I'm going."

Taken by surprise, the maid grabbed the lapel of his jacket, saying, "Don't go!"

"I'll come tomorrow," he said, agitated.

Still she would not let go. "No! If you go, Miss is going to scold me later."

"Then go and call Miss here. I have something to say to her."

Not knowing it was a ruse, the maid went to call Third Pan. He took the opportunity to dash into the little courtyard, slide open the door bolt, and bound out of the house. By mischance, he trod in the vomit of wine and food Verdure Xu had brought up, lost his balance, and fell. Scrambling up, he did not even turn to look back but made his way directly back to the Long Peace Inn.

The attendant at the inn presented him with two invitation cards. He saw that it was Cloudlet Chen inviting his two masters to dinner the next day at Clever Gem's in Co-security Alley. Since it was not urgent, he just put them away. He figured that as Eldest Young Master would gamble all night and Fourth Master was engrossed with his new love, neither of them would be coming back, so he just shut the door and went to bed.

Lying there, he thought of Third Pan. With consummation so near, what rotten luck it was to have it all spoiled by an archenemy! Now there was nothing left for him but desolation all night long. Then he thought of Eldest Young Master spending all that money on Grace Yang, and she was not even as affectionate as Third Pan. Then his thoughts turned to Fourth Master, who had picked up a streetwalker. That was a real bargain, and there was no knowing what fun he was having just now! With his mind jumping from one thing to the next, how could Second Kuang sleep? His brooding led to resentment, and his resentment to jealousy. A fine thing Fourth Master has done, and keeping it from everyone, too! Why, I'll blow his cover and see how he's going to face me.

His mind made up, the next morning Second Kuang got up and washed, braided his pigtail, had breakfast, and then waited till nine o'clock before he took Cloudlet Chen's invitation to Great Prosperity Alley west of Fourth Avenue. He walked up to the terrace house and gave it another looking over before he emboldened himself to knock on the door. The same old woman he had seen the day before opened the door. The minute she set eyes on him, she demanded imperiously, "What're you doing there?"

"Is Fourth Master here?" he said in a ringing voice. "Eldest Young Master told me to come and look in on him."

At the words "Fourth Master," the old woman was stopped in her tracks. She dared not be rude, just told him to wait, and then hurried upstairs to tell Pragmatic Li in a low voice. Pragmatic was on the opium divan, his morning appetite not yet sated. Astonished at Third Sister Chu's report, he came downstairs to see for himself.

"Fourth Master," Second Kuang greeted him and submitted Cloudlet Chen's invitation.

With shame written all over his face, Pragmatic, instead of looking at the invitation, asked Second Kuang with a smile, "How did you know I was here?"

Before he could answer, Third Sister clapped her hands and laughed. "Why, he came yesterday with you, Fourth Master. Didn't you know that?" As she said this, she pointed at Second Kuang, chuckling. "T'was a good thing I didn't give you a mouthful yesterday. The questions you asked were so strange, I thought you probably knew something about us; otherwise, I'd have boxed your ears for you."

Pragmatic, smiling sheepishly, took the invitation card and went upstairs again. Second Kuang was about to withdraw when Third Sister Chu said gushingly, "Now that you're here, why be in such a hurry to leave? Please come in and rest for a while." She took him by the arm and steered him into the parlor. Having installed him in a high-back chair, she presented him with a water pipe and poured him a cup of ready-made tea. Then she questioned him about all manner of things, showing the most friendly concern. In turn, he asked how their business was. At this, she drew close to him and told him a long story in a low voice, "We weren't in business originally, you know. But something happened earlier this year, and things became difficult for us. That was why we got into the business. And for the first guest we were so lucky to run into Fourth Master. He's a respectable man, and he doesn't like things that are just for show. A place like ours, honest and clean, suits Fourth Master very well. But now that we have Fourth Master's patronage, other people are envious of our good fortune, and they say a lot of bad things about us to Fourth Master. We're really an honest place, but they say we're cheats; we're a clean place, but they say we're filthy. Such rumors make me mad! Though Fourth Master doesn't listen to them now, we're still a bit uneasy. What if he should listen to them one day and stop coming here? We haven't got another client; aren't we going to starve to death, mother and daughter? That's why I'd like to ask you, Master Kuang, to put it to Fourth Master that he shouldn't listen to gossip. Coming from you, Master Kuang, it'd carry more weight."

As he had no idea what the true situation was, he readily agreed. They had a long talk before he finally got up to say good-bye. She saw him to the door and said, "Do come and visit when you're free." He blandly assented and left.

Third Sister closed the door, went upstairs, and as usual asked Pragmatic Li for his choice of dishes for lunch. Although Perfection Chu ate with him, she was on a diet for reasons of health. She did not eat restaurant food but kept him company on vegetable dishes.

After dinner, he went as usual to smoke opium at the House of

Floral Rain. The waiter had reserved a divan for him and filled a pipe in advance. After he had been smoking for a while, other customers arrived. The place was soon full, but an endless stream of new customers kept coming in. Suddenly, he saw Old Mrs. Filial Guo come groping in again, her eyes in a tight squint. Having met him once, she had found out all about him. Groping her way to the divan, she asked, all smiles, "Been to Perfection's place?"

He just nodded. The waiter, seeing that she was striking up a conversation with Pragmatic, dashed over, sat down on the humbler side of the divan, and fixed her with a beady eye. She snorted at him and walked away with her head bent. The waiter lay down to toast opium for Pragmatic and asked, "How did you get to know this Old Mrs. Filial Guo?"

"I saw her at Third Sister Chu's."

"Then Third Sister Chu's at fault," said the waiter. "Why would she still want to be friends with such vermin? You may think she's harmless because she's old and her eyes have gone blind, but she's still quite an operator. This woman is bad news."

Smiling, Pragmatic asked why.

"Only the year before last, she managed to talk a young lady from a Ningbo family into leaving home and going into the business in the foreign settlements. She was arrested by the county officials, charged with abduction, and given two hundred lashes of the cane and a life sentence. But somebody put in a good word for her, and she was let out."

Pragmatic had no idea that she was such a hardened criminal; he could not help sighing over it. The waiter finished preparing his pellets, handed him the pipe, and went to attend to other customers. By the time Pragmatic had finished the opium in his box, he saw that the customers were thinning out, so he joined the departing stream. Instead of going to dinner at Clever Gem's or returning to the Long Peace Inn, he headed straight to Perfection's.

Ever since he had started seeing Perfection, he had stayed for the night every five days and kept it a secret. Now that he had been seen by Second Kuang, there was no need for concealment, and he went so far as to tarry for ten days without returning to the inn. Second Kuang, who paid him a daily visit, sometimes came across Perfection with her face flushed pink and dark circles under her eyes.[1] He became suspicious and told his master Crane Li of his worries, but Crane Li did not give it much credit.

One day early in the fourth month, the weather suddenly turned

::
1. [Signs that she is suffering from sexually transmitted diseases. *E.H.*]

warm. Pragmatic Li had just come back from the House of Floral Rain and had barely sat down when he heard the sound of the front door opening again. It was Second Kuang, who came in and announced, "Eldest Young Master is here."

Alarmed, Third Sister Chu was just going to ask Pragmatic for instructions when Crane Li strolled in without further ado. She had no choice but to welcome him with a smiling face. "Fourth Master is upstairs."

Crane Li told Second Kuang to wait in the parlor and went up himself to see his uncle. Perfection also got up and greeted "Eldest Young Master". She then stepped to one side, standing there awkwardly and ill at ease. Pragmatic asked Crane Li where he had come from.

"I've been for a carriage ride," Crane Li answered.

"Then where's Grace?" asked Pragmatic.

"They went home first."

During the conversation, Third Sister brought tea for Crane Li in a lidded cup. She then took a high-stemmed glass dish, wiped it clean, scooped a handful of watermelon seeds from a clay jar under the bed, and handed the dish to Perfection. Perfection had no choice but to offer it shyly to Crane Li. He had decided to take a good look at her, and his close examination made her cringe. As there was nowhere for her to hide, she blushed intensely, all the way down to her neck. Sensing this, Pragmatic tried to distract Crane Li by making conversation.

"Have you been busy on the social circuit the last couple of days?" he asked.

"It hasn't been too bad. But with the end-of-season rituals starting now, there'll be dinner parties at every house."

Perfection took this opportunity to sneak out into the anteroom, but Third Sister dragged her back and made her keep the others company. Third Sister then went behind the bed, fished out a string of coins, and started counting them. Seeing this, Pragmatic asked, "What's that for?" To which she did not reply.

"Are you going to buy dim sum for tea?" he asked.

"Please don't bother; I just had tea," Crane Li hastened to say.

"It's only right that I get something for you," a smiling Third Sister said and turned to go.

Pragmatic stopped her, saying, "Wait, there's really no need to get anything for tea. Why don't you get two packs of cigarettes instead?"

Third Sister made an affirmative noise and went downstairs.

"I've got my own cigarettes," Crane Li said.

"I know you do, but just let her buy some more. She'd feel uneasy if she weren't allowed to get you anything at all." The remark made Perfection more ashamed than ever.

By the time Third Sister Chu came back with the cigarettes, it was lamp-lighting time. Having run out of things to say, Crane Li got up and took his leave.

"Where're you off to?" Pragmatic asked.

"To dinner at East Co-prosperity Alley. It's Lotuson Wang's party."

Hearing this, Perfection hurried forth to help press him to stay longer. Crane Li took this opportunity to touch her hand, and sure enough her palm was burning hot.[2] She and Pragmatic saw him out to the head of the staircase.

When he got to the ground floor, Third Sister dashed out of the kitchen, all flustered, pleading, "Please don't go, Eldest Young Master! Do stay for a simple supper here."

"Thanks, I'm going out to a dinner party."

Knowing she could not detain him, Third Sister saw him out, with Second Kuang following behind. At the door, she was still apologizing, "I'm afraid we haven't served you properly, Eldest Young Master."

"Don't be so modest," Crane Li said with a smile. With Second Kuang behind him, he walked out of Great Prosperity Alley and headed eastward. At the junction with Pebble Road, he told Second Kuang to summon the sedan chair. Second Kuang went off by himself while Crane Li walked on alone to Constance's in East Co-prosperity Alley, where the guests had all arrived. The host, Lotuson Wang, ordered hot towels to be brought to them.

CHAPTER 28 :: *A policeman mounts the roof of a gambling den, and a whoremonger shames his family by pulling a ricksha*

The dinner party at Constance's in East Co-prosperity Alley was hosted by Lotuson Wang, and it was given to mark the rituals honoring the money gods. There were parties that night in all the rooms in Big Feet Yao's house. Lotuson's, being a double-table affair, created more hustle and bustle than others. As nobody felt much like drinking, they finished early. Lotuson Wang had surreptitiously

::

2. [Another good indication that Perfection suffers from venereal disease. E.H.]

made an appointment with Benevolence Hong. As soon as the guests had gone, he asked Benevolence to leave with him.

"Where're you going?" Constance asked in alarm. Lotuson was unwilling to tell her. Thinking he was leaving out of anger, she held on to him and would not let go.

Benevolence Hong said with a smile, "Mr. Wang is in a hurry to complete an assignment. Don't get silly and make him late for official business."

Although Constance did not understand what "complete an assignment" meant, she sensed it had to do with Little Rouge and so did not dare press Lotuson to stay. Lotuson told Talisman and the sedan-chair bearers to go home, while he strolled with Benevolence to Little Rouge's in West Floral Alley. Pearlie welcomed them in the parlor and followed them upstairs.

It was dark in the room. Little Rouge was lying on the bed fully dressed. Pearlie went up to her quickly and whispered, "Maestro, Mr. Wang is here." She did so four or five times.

"I heard you," Little Rouge replied in a huff.

Pearlie drew back smiling, but she muttered, "So I did wrong to call you! When business is bad, it can't be helped. What's the use of envying other people?" So saying, she turned up the hanging paraffin lamp and went to prepare tea and tobacco.

Little Rouge sat up slowly and got off the bed. After dawdling for a long while, she sauntered toward them and sat down on a highback chair. But her face was turned to the wall, and she remained silent. Lotuson and Benevolence, sitting on the opium divan, did not speak either.

Pearlie asked Little Rouge, "Would you like some supper?" She shook her head.

Hearing this, Lotuson said, "We didn't have supper either. Go and order a couple of dishes, and we'll eat together."

"You've just come from a dinner party. How come you didn't eat?" Pearlie asked.

"Well, we really didn't," Lotuson replied.

Pearlie turned to Little Rouge, "Then I'll order something so you can eat together, OK?"

"I don't want any," Little Rouge replied loudly.

Pearlie smiled and stood still. "Mr. Wang, do order something if you yourself feel like it. Our maestro won't eat restaurant food anyway. She'll have a bit of congee later."

Lotuson had to give in. Benevolence Hong knew there wouldn't be anything he could do, so he got up and took his leave. Lotuson did not press him to stay. As Benevolence was a close friend of Lotuson's, Little Rouge did not even see him out, and neither did she bother to make any polite farewell. Pearlie, though, saw him all the way downstairs.

Lotuson waited until Benevolence was gone before he went over and sat down by Little Rouge's side, took her hand in one of his, and hooked his other hand round her neck to turn her face toward him.

"What d'you want?" she said in annoyance.

"Don't be like this!" he pleaded. "Let's go and lie down for a bit on the divan. I have something to tell you."

She struggled free. "If you have anything to say, say it here."

"It's nothing special, just that I want you to be happier. No matter what time of day I come, you never show the least hint of a happy face. You've no idea how miserable I feel when I see you unhappy. Do me a favor, don't be like this, all right?"

"I was born to be unhappy. If you feel bad, just go somewhere else where you'll feel good."

He could not help heaving a sigh. "I talk to you like this, but all I get from you is an unreasonable retort." His voice choked, and he could not carry on. The two of them sat side by side in complete silence.

After a long time, she answered, "Just now I hadn't either told you off or offended you, but you said I was unhappy and called me unreasonable. In fact, you're the one who tells other people off, and you don't even notice it. Would anyone be happy when they've been told off?"

He knew she was coming around and she was saying all this as a way out. He immediately put on a smiling face and said, "It's all my fault. I made you unhappy because I didn't put things the right way. Let's forget it. The next time I behave badly, you can hit me or scold me. It doesn't matter as long as you're not so unhappy." As he spoke, he steered her toward the divan. She could only lie down with him, each taking one side of the divan.

"There's something else I want to consult you about," he said. "I *have* asked my friends to come here, but it'll be on the ninth. Round about now, there're just too many feasts in honor of the money gods. There's one on the seventh at Twin Pearl's, another on the eighth at Green Phoenix's. They said since you don't have the money god ritual here, we can come on the ninth. I've agreed to that. What d'you think?"

"Well, just as you like."

Seeing that she raised no objections, he was still more pleased. After smoking just a few pellets of opium, he urged her to have some congee.

"We have some homemade congee with ham. Would you like some?" she asked.

"That'd do very nicely."

She called for Pearlie to bring the congee. Goldie also came in to wait on them. After they had finished, Lotuson smoked his fill of opium and then went to bed with Little Rouge.

The next day was the seventh. Talisman brought the sedan chair to fetch Lotuson at noon. After lunch, Lotuson left in the sedan chair to attend to some official business. When evening came, he reported back at Little Rouge's before going to dinner at Twin Pearl's in Sunshine Alley. Elan Ge, Mallow Yao, Amity Zhu, and Cloudlet Chen had all arrived there before him, as had the host, Benevolence Hong.

As the party in Twin Jade's room across the way had started very early, Benevolence Hong said, "Let's have the hot towels, too."

"Who else is coming?" Lotuson Wang asked.

"Crane Li isn't, so that only leaves Prosperity Luo," Benevolence replied. Everybody then sat down, leaving a place empty.

After offering watermelon seeds to everyone, Twin Pearl asked Lotuson Wang, "Will you be calling a girl from this house?"

"She has a party in her room. Let's forget it," replied Lotuson.

After the first course, sharks' fin, was served, Clever Gem arrived ahead of all the other summoned girls. Then Prosperity Luo came with Green Phoenix. Already a little tipsy, Prosperity was extremely high-spirited and called at once for large wine cups so he could be banker of a finger game. He picked on Mallow Yao as his opponent, saying he had lost to Yao last time and had been looking forward to getting his own back. Yao, for his part, was already pushing up his sleeves, eager to meet the challenge. Luck was not on Prosperity's side, and he lost the first three rounds. Green Phoenix wanted to drink the penalty wine for him, but he would not allow it. Downing the wine in one gulp, he stuck his fist out to play again. This time, Mallow Yao lost two out of three rounds. By then, the summoned girls, White Fragrance, Snow Scent, Little Rouge, and Sunset, had all arrived, so Sunset drank a cup for him.

"Substitutes don't count," Prosperity Luo shouted.

Sunset said, "Says who? Our rules allow for substitutes. Whether you want them or not is up to you."

Green Phoenix snatched the wine cup from Prosperity and gave it to Mama Zhao, saying, "Oh, big silly, why d'you insist on drinking it yourself?"

Prosperity Luo caught sight of a huge glass on the dressing table. He grabbed it and, pointing his finger at Mallow Yao, said, "Let's give our pledge now: we'll do our own drinking, no substitutes!" He took the wine pot and started to fill the glass, but the pot was emptied before the glass was full. He told Clever Baby to refill the wine pot while he started the game with Mallow Yao again. Mallow, rising to the challenge, proved a tough opponent. Their contest made the onlookers even more nervous than they were themselves.

The two were just coming to grips when they heard Clever Baby shouting in panic from the middle room, "Quick! There's somebody there!" Everyone at the table was startled. Thinking it was a fire, they fought to be first to get out of the room and see. Clever Baby was pointing wildly out of the window, shouting, "There! Over there!" When they turned to look, they saw that it was not a fire but a foreign policeman standing bolt upright on top of the pitched roof of the storied house opposite. He was in a black uniform and had a steel sword in his hand that glittered in the electric light.

Benevolence Hong had a good idea what this meant. He immediately tried to put everybody at ease by saying, "It's nothing serious. Don't worry."

Cloudlet Chen tried to summon his steward. Constant Blessing, to find out what was going on, but the small crowd gathered at the door made quite a hubbub, and Cloudlet called out to no effect. Longevity took this opportunity to dash upstairs and report, "It's a gambling raid at Lucky You's in the alley. Nothing to worry about."

Just when everybody felt reassured, they suddenly saw a casement window open in the house opposite. A man crawled out and climbed onto the balcony, intending to escape via the shed next door. But his luck was out: a policeman pursuing him leaped out across the balcony to the shed, raised the truncheon in his hand, and caught the man on the ankle with his blow. The man lost his balance and, toppling headfirst, fell from the wall into the alley, bringing down two tiles with him. The tiles shattered loudly on the ground.

Twin Jade came out of her room badly shaken. She whispered to Twin Pearl, "A man in the alley has been killed in a fall." Everybody exclaimed in surprise.

Seeing that Twin Jade's party guests had all left, Benevolence Hong went into her room to peep out the window. Sure enough, the gambler who had taken the fall was lying motionless by the wall, looking as if he were indeed dead. The others also crowded into the room, jostling to have a look. Snow Scent, being timid by nature, was frightened by what had happened. Pulling at Elan Ge's gown, she said, "Let's go home."

"If we go out now, we'll get hauled off by the police," Elan replied.

She would not believe him. "Nonsense!"

Twin Pearl intervened. "It's not nonsense, though. The police are at our door. We're not allowed to go out."

Snow Scent had no choice but to wait. Benevolence Hong suggested that they should resume their party. "Let's have a drink and leave the policemen to make their arrests. There's nothing interesting to see."

Twin Pearl went to the stairs herself to call out for Clever Baby to bring wine, but Clever Baby, standing at the front door taking in all the excitement, did not hear the summons at all. Twin Pearl then called out for Golden, but she didn't answer, either. When her summons became urgent, however, Golden slipped out of the mezzanine cubicle with her head bent and went straight downstairs without a word. Twin Pearl looked toward the mezzanine room; it was pitch-dark, unlit by lamp or candle.

"What's this supposed to mean?" She said, furious. "Do we still have any rules or manners here?"

Golden was in no position to answer back. The minute Twin Pearl turned her back, Longevity emerged from the mezzanine room and sneaked downstairs. Twin Pearl, pretending not to have seen him, walked back into her own room.

By the time Golden brought the wine pot and handed it to Benevolence Hong, the others were all too eager to watch the gambling raid to care about drinking. Shortly there came the sound of footsteps in the alley, sweeping from west to east like a storm. Benevolence Hong, too, took a look. He saw that the gambler who had taken the fall was being carried out of the alley on a door plank under the escort of a large number of Chinese and foreign policemen. They were followed by a crowd of spectators, all gesticulating and joking. Even the menservants and the housekeeper downstairs joined the crowd. Soon all was quiet at the door.

The spectacle over, everybody walked away from the window. Benevolence Hong finally succeeded in gathering them back to the table, where fresh wine was poured. The interlude had allowed Prosperity Luo to sober up, and he refused to drink anymore. Mallow Yao, seeing that his curfew was approaching, withdrew from the finger game. Everybody called for rice and congee to be served. Snow Scent was the first girl to leave, and she was quickly followed by the others.

In the hustle and bustle, Longevity came upstairs again to report on what he had found out about the gambling raid and take credit for his diligence. He said, "Everyone at Lucky You's has been arrested, including twenty or thirty guests. The house has been sealed up as well. The man who fell off the wall didn't die; he's just broken a leg."

Everybody sighed and expressed regret over the incident. Just then, Worth brought in the rice and congee, so a downcast Longevity had to leave.

When dinner was over and the guests had gone, the host felt a little weary. Shortly afterward, a double-table party commenced in Twin Jade's room, followed by another party downstairs in Twin Jewel's. The house was again in a bustle.

Benevolence Hong, feeling a little off-color, bade Twin Pearl good night, and returned to spend the night at the Flourishing Ginseng Store. The next day, at dusk, he headed back into the International Settlement and made straight for Green Phoenix's in Generosity Alley. Prosperity Luo came up to greet him and asked right away, "Crane Li has gone home, d'you know that?"

"Why, he didn't mention it when I met him the night before last," said Benevolence Hong.

"Just a while ago I sent him an invitation and was told he'd got on the boat home with Pragmatic," said Prosperity.

"Something must have happened," said Benevolence.

Just then, Elan Ge, Lotuson Wang, Amity Zhu, and Whistler Tang arrived one after another. When Crane Li was mentioned, they all said there must be a reason for his sudden departure. Cloudlet Chen was the last guest to arrive, and when he did, Prosperity Luo told Mama Zhao to hand out the hot towels.

Cloudlet asked Prosperity, "Did you invite Crane Li?"

"He's said to have gone home. D'you know on what business?"

"It's got nothing to do with business," replied Cloudlet. "Last night, Crane Li was caught in the raid in Sunshine Alley. He was hauled into the new yamen and fined fifty dollars. As soon as he was released, he headed straight for the boat. I went to look in on him but just missed him."

"Was it Crane who had the fall?" Benevolence asked anxiously.

"No, it was a gangster. Originally, he had bought the right to wear the hat of a third-grade official and traveled around in an official-style sedan chair, all very grand! But after a brush with the law in Suzhou, he ended up running a gambling den and taking his cut. He should count himself lucky that he wasn't killed by the fall yesterday," said Cloudlet.

"Why, that must be Clement Zhou! How come Crane got mixed up with such an unsavory character?" said Prosperity Luo.

Cloudlet replied, "It was Crane's own fault. He's addicted to gambling and lost thirty thousand in less than a month. If this had gone on, he'd have been in serious trouble."

"Pragmatic was negligent then. He should have spoken to Crane," said Prosperity.

"Pragmatic is something of a family man. Even on his trips to Shanghai, he refuses to party at sing-song houses. He's very respectable," said Cloudlet.

Benevolence said with a smile, "You call Pragmatic a respectable family man, but that may not be a good thing either. A friend in South End told me that Pragmatic has caught a little ailment because of his 'family' inclination."

Cloudlet Chen was just going to ask what the ailment was when Clever Gem, summoned to the party, sat down behind him and surreptitiously tugged at his sleeve. He turned around, and she whispered in his ear. He could not quite hear her and said smiling, "Aren't you busy! Last time it was the treasure scrolls, and now it's the feast of the money gods."

"It's not for me," she said and whispered in his ear again.

He thought for a moment and assented readily enough. The friends at the table were invited to accompany him to another party, to be held at the Hall of Spring. Everybody promised to go but wanted to know where the Hall of Spring was.

"On East Chessboard Street. It's the place of Clever Gem's sister. They're having the ritual for the money gods, too, and we're to go and lend our support."

Clever Gem took the opportunity to ask, "Shall I tell Ocean to go over and set up the table first? Then everybody can bring their girls over later."

Everyone agreed, and the maid Ocean left to carry out her orders.

Now Prosperity Luo started a bank and to everybody's surprise turned out to be a big winner at the finger game. He had barely downed ten of the twenty cups he had set up when the others had lost as many as thirty. They consulted among themselves and decided to take turns challenging him and to share out the penalty wine. Only then did they manage to finish the game.

By then, they had come to the last four courses of the dinner. Ocean was back to report that everything was ready, and Clever Gem reiterated the invitation. Green Phoenix still had two other party calls in the house, so she explained to Prosperity Luo that she would be a little late and there was no need to send her another call chit. Prosperity Luo, Elan Ge, Lotuson Wang, Amity Zhu, and six courtesans went together in ten sedan chairs, while Cloudlet Chen walked with Benevolence Hong and Whistler Tang to the entrance of Generosity Alley, where his private ricksha was waiting, and told Constant Blessing to call two more rickshas.

Benevolence Hong was about to step into the ricksha when he saw that the puller was very young and that his face was familiar. He took a good look and started violently, exclaiming, "Why, you're Simplicity Zhao!"

The puller turned around and, seeing it was Benevolence Hong, ran off westward with the empty ricksha as if fleeing for his life. Benevolence waved and shouted, but the puller did not come back. This so enraged Benevolence Hong that he just stood in the middle of the street, his eyes popping, lost for words. The rickshas bearing Chen and Tang had gone far away, and he was left on his own. Fortunately, the ten sedan chairs came out of the alley just then, and he was spotted by those walking along with the chairs. Golden and Ocean came up to him to inquire, "Mr. Hong, what are you doing here?"

Only then did his mind clear. He hailed another ricksha and followed the sedan chairs to a corner of East Chessboard Street, where he got off and went into the Hall of Spring with the others.

Love Gem was welcoming everybody at the head of the staircase. They saw the table was set in the upstairs parlor, but first they went to sit in Love Gem's room for a while. Love Gem hastened to offer each of them watermelon seeds and to toast opium at the divan.

"Elder Sister," Clever Gem said, "Don't bother to fill the pipes. Just tell your people downstairs to bring the hot towels. Everybody here's in a hurry."

Love Gem said smiling, "Which of the honored guests will kindly have a smoke?"

Nobody spoke up, only Cloudlet said, "Thank you."

Love Gem smiled coyly, saying, "Mr. Chen, you're far too polite."

Her patience taxed, Clever Gem left the room to stroll around. Finally, Love Gem told the menservants to bring the hot towels, and everybody, including the courtesans, settled down at the dinner table. Love Gem and Clever Gem sat down side by side behind Cloudlet Chen, and Love Gem tuned her *pipa* to sing a duet with her sister.

"You go ahead. I'm not singing," said Clever Gem.

"No songs, thanks," said Cloudlet Chen. But Love Gem would not listen and started tuning up her *pipa* again. At this, Clever Gem intervened, "Please don't, Elder Sister. One song is quite enough." Only then did Love Gem lay down her *pipa*. No other courtesan offered to sing after her.

At this point, Green Phoenix arrived from her other parties, and Prosperity Luo asked for a large cup in preparation for the finger game. The maid was gone for a long time and came back with a huge glass.

"That won't do!" Love Gem said and hurriedly told the maid to get another cup.

Prosperity Luo was overjoyed at the sight of it. "That glass is just fine. Give it here."

Love Gem offered it to him at once and then pushed up her sleeves to lift the wine pot and fill the glass.

Prosperity pounded the table with his fist. "I'll start a bank with five glasses."

Seeing the enormous vessel, nobody dared stick out a hand. Cloudlet Chen consulted Elan Ge. "Let's share one glass, all right?"

"Good," replied Elan.

Cloudlet played the first round against Prosperity Luo and promptly lost. Love Gem offered to drink for him, so he gave her a small cup as her share and another to Clever Gem.

"Since you're the one who wanted to play, you should drink it yourself. I'm not substituting," Clever Gem objected.

"I'll drink it," Love Gem said pleasantly and reached for the cup.

But Clever Gem stretched out an arm to block her, saying loudly, "No, Elder Sister!" Startled, Love Gem let go. Cloudlet smiled and without further ado took the cup and drained it. Elan Ge also took half a glass and drank his share.

Amity Zhu and Whistler Tang were the next to attack the bank, followed by Lotuson Wang and Benevolence Hong. Each team had to repeat the challenge three times before the game was over. After downing five glasses of wine, even Prosperity, who took pride in his capacity, was on the point of collapse. All the others were drunk, too. No longer in the mood for wine, they were just waiting for the girls to leave. Nobody wanted any congee, and the guests took their leave soon afterward. The only ones who remained were Benevolence Hong and Clever Gem. Cloudlet Chen and Love Gem invited the two of them to go and sit in her room.

CHAPTER 29 :: *Second Treasure and a friend go in search of her brother, and an adopted relative takes the girls sight-seeing*

Cloudlet Chen and Clever Gem led the way into Love Gem's room, with Benevolence Hong and Love Gem following them. The menservants came in with nuts and sweetmeats that Love Gem offered to everybody. She then went to toast opium on the divan. Cloudlet lay down on the honored side of the divan and said, "I'll fill the pipe."

"No, Mr. Chen, please let me do it," said Love Gem.

"There's no need to be so formal." He smiled and took the toasting pick from her.

Love Gem turned to Benevolence Hong and said, "Mr. Hong, do come and lie down for a bit."

Benevolence lay down on the humble side of the divan. As Love

Gem put two cups of tea into the opium tray, she saw Clever Gem smoothing her sidelocks in front of the dressing table mirror. She immediately hurried over, picked up a small comb, and smoothed Clever Gem's hair, after which they gossiped and shared each other's secrets.

Over on the divan, Benevolence took the opportunity to tell Cloudlet about Simplicity Zhao and to consult him about what to do. Cloudlet first asked him what he had in mind.

"I thought perhaps you could report it at the police station,[1] tell the detectives to find his ricksha, and have him shut up in my store. What d'you think?" Benevolence said.

Cloudlet mulled it over. "I don't think it's a good idea. Why keep him in your store? Isn't it humiliating to have a relative who pulls a ricksha there? I suggest you write to tell his mother and leave things up to them, so you can wash your hands of the matter."

This was a revelation to Benevolence. Feeling that all his troubles had lifted, he got up right then to take his leave.

"Let's go, too," said Clever Gem to Cloudlet, who immediately put down his opium pipe.

Afraid they would really leave, Love Gem detained Cloudlet on the divan with one hand, saying, "Please don't go, Mr. Chen!" With her other hand, she held on to Clever Gem, complaining. "Why are you in such a hurry? Is it because our place is small, so you won't stay a minute longer than necessary?"

Clever Gem shifted her weight impatiently from one foot to another and persisted. "I'm going." But Love Gem clasped her around her waist and threatened, "Go then! If you do, I'll never look in on you again."

Cloudlet laughed a little awkwardly. At this, Benevolence said, "You two stay a little longer; I'll go ahead." He then took his leave from Cloudlet and walked out of the room. Love Gem immediately let go of Clever Gem to see him off at the stairs, saying repeatedly, "Do come tomorrow, Mr. Hong."

Benevolence assented offhandedly. After he left the Hall of Spring, he headed toward the Three Huts Bridge, where he called a ricksha and told the puller to take him to Lu Stone Bridge at Little East Gate. From there, he strolled back to the Flourishing Ginseng Store on Salt Melon Street. He wrote a letter that very night to his sister, relating the circumstances of Simplicity Zhao's vagrancy and destitu-

::

1. [Hong's store is in an area under Chinese jurisdiction while Chen's is in the International Settlement. That is why Hong cannot go directly to the foreign police. *E.H.*]

tion, and told the young clerk to take it to the post office early in the morning and have it sent to the country.

Simplicity Zhao's mother, née Hong, was just fifty years old. But she was already going deaf and blind and lacked both strength of character and ability. Fortunately, Simplicity's younger sister, with the pet name Second Treasure, was a good housekeeper. When they received Benevolence Hong's last letter, they thought Simplicity would soon be home. They looked forward daily to his return, but a fortnight passed without any news of him. Now suddenly another letter arrived. They asked their next-door neighbor, Juvenity Zhang, to read it to them.

When Juvenity explained the contents of the letter to them, mother and daughter burst into tears out of shock and shame. The sound of their crying reached Juvenity's elder sister, Flora, who came over to find out what it was about and to comfort them. Mother and daughter dried their tears, thanked her, and they all discussed what should be done. Juvenity Zhang thought it best that they go to Shanghai to bring Simplicity home and keep him under strict control.

"I don't know anything about the foreign settlements in Shanghai. How can I go there?" said Mrs. Zhao.

"And even if Mother goes there, how is she to find him?" said Second Treasure.

"In that case, ask somebody reliable to search for him. It won't matter if you have to pay a little money as long as he's found," suggested Flora Zhang.

"But there's no one we can ask, except their uncle, perhaps," said Mrs. Zhao.

"Their uncle sounds very angry in the letter. He thinks Simplicity has humiliated him," said Juvenity. "D'you think he'd go and look for him?"

"Uncle was unreliable to begin with. And it's no use asking other people to look for him, either. I'd better go with Mother," said Second Treasure.

Mrs. Zhao sighed. "Those are brave words, Second Treasure, but you're a girl, and you've never been away from home. What would I do if in Shanghai a trafficker in women abducts you?"

"But that's nonsense, Mother! All that talk about traffickers in women is just to scare children. Do they really exist?" said Second Treasure.

"Not in Shanghai, but it's still best to go with somebody you know," said Juvenity.

"You said you're going to Shanghai after the festival," said Flora to Juvenity.

"But I'm going straight to the store once I get there. How would I have time for anything else?" he replied.

Second Treasure took this in but did not say anything. Since no decision was reached, Juvenity Zhang took his leave. Second Treasure asked Flora to stay and invited her into the bedroom. Flora, nineteen, was a bosom friend of hers. There was nothing they did not talk about. She asked Flora, "Why is Juvenity going to Shanghai?"

"Mr. Zhai sent for him to be a clerk at his store," Flora replied.

"Will you be going?"

"I have no business there; what would I be going there for?"

"I suggest you and I go to Shanghai together. I'll look for my brother, and you can have a good time in the foreign settlements. Wouldn't that be nice?"

Flora liked the idea but was afraid of what people might say. She replied hesitantly, "It won't do!"

Second Treasure then whispered in her ear, telling her how to go about it. Delighted with the scheme, a smiling Flora went home right away. When Juvenity asked about the matter, she said with a frown, "They racked their brains and couldn't think of anything; then they started blaming our cousin. They said our cousin Rustic went to Shanghai with Simplicity and shared his money. Now that the money's gone, he can't face anyone, so they want us to go with them and look for our cousin Rustic."

Before Flora had finished speaking, Second Treasure walked in. "Flora, stop playing the innocent fool," she said. "It's only right that you take responsibility for what your cousin did. If you come with me to find your cousin Rustic, then you'll have discharged your duty."

"Rustic is in Shanghai. You can go and find him yourself," said Juvenity.

"I don't know Shanghai, so I have to go with her," said Second Treasure.

"She can't go. I'll go with you, all right?" he said.

"You're a man, how can we travel to Shanghai in your company? If she refuses to go, I'll make sure that she won't hear the end of this matter, and it won't be pleasant."

He looked at Flora and asked for her answer. She said, "I've got nothing to do there; what would I go to Shanghai for? When people hear of it, they'll think I just want to have a good time. Wouldn't I be laughed at?"

"You don't want people to laugh at you, and my brother pulling a ricksha has nothing to do with you, right?" demanded Second Treasure.

Juvenity appealed to Flora, "Elder Sister, it may be best if you go with them. It won't take more than a few days to find him and bring him back."

At first, she still refused, but at his persistent urging she reluctantly agreed. It was decided that they should commence their journey on the seventeenth of the fourth month. Mother Wu, the wife of their neighbor, Old Wu the barber, was asked to look after their houses.

Second Treasure went home and told her mother, who thought it an excellent arrangement. That night, Old Wu came to see both their families, first to promise someone would keep an eye on the houses and then to say that he had heard his son Pine was doing extremely well and could he get a ride in their boat to go and visit him. Both families readily agreed.

On the appointed day, they hired a boat with a cabin from Wusi. Mrs. Zhao, Second Treasure, Juvenity Zhang, Flora Zhang, and Old Wu settled in with their luggage, and they set sail for Shanghai. It took more than a day to reach the Zhaoyang pier in Shanghai. Old Wu, who had no bedding, carried his bundle on his back and went ashore to go his own way. Since Simplicity Zhao had stayed at the Welcome Inn, Second Treasure told Juvenity Zhang they should go there, too. Their luggage was handed over to the men from the Welcome Inn. Juvenity then hailed four rickshas to take them to the inn on Treasured Merit Street. The coolies who brought their luggage by carrying poles arrived at the same time as they did. Having chosen a very spacious room in the inn, they unpacked and got ready for their stay.

Seeing that the women had temporarily settled in, Juvenity Zhang went first to the Northern Fidelity Pawnshop on First Avenue to see his master, Manager Zhai, and was given a job in the Southern Fidelity Pawnshop. When he returned to the inn to get his bedding, he asked Second Treasure, "D'you want to come along and look for my cousin Rustic?"

Second Treasure declined with a wave of a hand. "Even if we do find your cousin, it'll be no use. Please go to the Flourishing Ginseng Store on Salt Melon Street and ask my uncle to drop in here."

He did as she asked. That night, Flora Zhang went to the theater by herself and saw a Beijing opera, while Second Treasure and her mother sat facing each other morosely and did not venture out.

Early the next morning, Benevolence Hong came to see them at the inn. After he had greeted Mrs. Zhao, his sister, Second Treasure came forward to do her obeisance. Benevolence talked briefly about their several years' separation and then came to the subject of his nephew Simplicity. Having told them frankly of the young man's degrading behavior, he said, "I'll send someone to find him now, but I won't be able to help if anything happens in the future."

Second Treasure interrupted, "It'd be best if Uncle finds him.

You can rest assured, Uncle, that in the future we won't dare disturb you again."

To make conversation, he asked about the harvests in the country, after which he took his leave. As Flora Zhang was still in bed, she did not meet him.

Sure enough, somebody escorted Simplicity Zhao to the door after lunch. The inn attendant knew him and made the announcement. Mrs. Zhao and Second Treasure hurried out in welcome. Simplicity stood there with black smudges on his face, and the hair on the front part of his head had grown to well over an inch.[2] He was wearing a patched and darned short jacket and trousers, so grubby that they couldn't tell what their original color was. He stood there in his bare feet, without shoes or stockings, just like a beggar. Second Treasure's sisterly feelings were aroused, and, intensely pained by this sight of him, she started to weep.

His mother, whose eyesight was poor, was still asking, "Where is he?" The inn attendant pushed Simplicity forward, telling him to kowtow. Mrs. Zhao started violently, stamped her foot, and wailed, "Oh, why has my son come to this?" She then choked and almost collapsed. Fortunately, Flora Zhang propped her up from behind and tried to console her.

Embarrassed by the crowd of hotel guests looking on, Second Treasure, assisted by Flora, hastily helped her mother back into their room. They beckoned to Simplicity to come in and then closed the door and took from a leather trunk a suit of clothes, shoes, and stockings. They told him to go for a shave and a bath in a neighboring bathhouse and to come back at once after that.

Soon Simplicity returned as instructed. He had changed into his new clothes and, except for looking a bit thin in the face, was like a new man. Flora asked him to sit down, and Mrs. Zhao and Second Treasure gave him a sound rebuke. He listened with his head bowed and tears running down his face, not daring to utter a word. Second Treasure insisted that he tell them why he did not want to come home. She questioned him a dozen times, but he remained tongue-tied.

Flora answered for him with a smile, "It was too embarrassing to go home, right?"

"That wasn't it. If he knew what embarrassment meant, he'd have gone home," said Second Treasure. "I'd say it was because he couldn't bear to leave Shanghai. Pulling a ricksha, he could take in the sights all around him. That made him *so* happy!"

::

2. Under the Manchus, men wore pigtails with the front part of their heads cleanly shaven. No respectable person would let his hair grow there.

Mortified by this remark, Simplicity turned his face to the wall. Mrs. Zhao, suddenly moved by pity and affection, stopped reproaching him. She turned to confer with Flora and Second Treasure about going home.

"Tell the servants at the inn to hire a boat; we'll leave tomorrow," said Second Treasure.

"You told me to come to Shanghai and have a good time, but now you want to go home before I have been anywhere. I object!" said Flora.

"Then let's stay for one more day for some sight-seeing, all right?" Second Treasure pleaded.

"We'll stay one more day first, then we'll see," said Flora. Mrs. Zhao had to agree.

After supper, Flora wanted to go to a storytelling performance. Second Treasure said to her, "Let's get this clear first: I'll pay. If you won't accept that I'm not going."

Flora thought for a moment and glossed it over with a smile. "All right, then you'll be my guest tomorrow night."

With Flora and Second Treasure gone, only Mrs. Zhao and Simplicity were left in the room. Mrs. Zhao, all tired out, went to bed early. Simplicity sat there alone, the sound of rickshaw traveling on Treasured Merit Street hitting his ears like a tidal wave. On top of that, there was the music of the *pipa* coming from afar. It seemed to be a virgin courtesan singing an aria from a Beijing opera, but he had no idea which house it came from. Though his heart was as restless as a monkey, he dared not go out on his own. The inn attendant had set up a bed for him in the little anteroom, so he went in, lit the clay oil lamp, and lay down fully dressed. Unfortunately, two men next door were smoking opium and talking with great relish about the night life and the fun they had had in Shanghai. Their talk stirred up Simplicity's desire, making it impossible for him to sleep. He waited wide-eyed for Flora and Second Treasure to come back from the storytelling and then got up and came out to ask, "Did you enjoy it?"

Second Treasure sighed. "I might as well not have gone. We ran into a relative of hers named Shi, and when I went in to order tea, Shi paid for the tickets and bought a lot of cakes and fruit for us. It was so embarrassing! He has also invited us to go for a carriage ride tomorrow. I'm definitely not going."

"What does it matter in a place like Shanghai? Since he's asked us, I don't see any harm in going," said Flora.

"Well, you would say that, wouldn't you? You even brought your summer silk blouses along, so of course you can go. But I look like a beggar; it's so humiliating!" said Second Treasure.

Her unintentional admission brought a chuckle from Flora. Embarrassed, Simplicity was about to make himself scarce when Second Treasure called him back. He hastened to ask what it was. She opened a small parcel wrapped in a handkerchief and gave him some of the cakes and fruit from the storytelling theater. She also asked Flora to have some.

"Let's have another pipe of opium," said Flora.

"Don't be silly. A fine state of affairs if you get the habit," said Second Treasure.

Flora smiled but would not listen. She took an opium tray set from a bamboo basket, lit the lamp, and started toasting opium. But she did not do it right, and the pipe bowl was blocked. Trying to please her, Simplicity asked, "Shall I do it for you?"

"So you've learned to fill the opium pipe, too? Do go ahead." She let him take her place.

He took the pellet that was burned hard, spread it out, and then put it back into the bowl, kneading it till it was smooth and glossy. After that, he turned the mouthpiece around and offered it to Flora. She deferred to him briefly and then inhaled the opium in one breath and marveled over and over again, "You made a brilliant job of that! Where did you learn to do it?"

He smiled but did not reply. He filled the pipe again, and Flora insisted that Second Treasure take it. Second Treasure, unable to resist, smoked it. The third pipe he smoked himself. Then the opium tray was packed up, and they bade each other good night. He went back to the little back room to sleep.

The next afternoon, a driver turned up at the inn, announcing, "This is the carriage Young Mr. Shi called. Madam and the two young ladies are invited to go together."

Second Treasure had no intention of riding in his carriage, but Flora, requesting Simplicity to guard their room, dragged Mrs. Zhao and Second Treasure along for a visit to Luna Park.

Simplicity had nothing to do in the inn. He discovered that the opium tray set was not locked up and actually stole a smoke and toasted two more pellets. It happened that Rustic Zhang got the news of his cousins' arrival and had come to see them. He was surprised to see Simplicity looking so presentable. Recalling how Rustic had taunted him when he was down and out, Simplicity was not very friendly and abruptly put the opium tray away. Rustic, feeling put down, took his leave. Too embarrassed to show his face outside, Simplicity did not see him out.

By dusk, the carriage had not returned. Getting impatient, Simplicity slipped into the courtyard and stood on tiptoe to look out for them. Just then, Flora and Second Treasure were helping Mrs. Zhao get down from the carriage, and they came in together. He went up and told them about Rustic's visit. Second Treasure was silent, but Flora said, "Our cousin is not a good man. You shouldn't have anything to do with him anymore."

He expressed his compliance and followed them into the room. Second Treasure fished a bottle of perfume out of her pocket to show him. He could not tell the quality and asked how much it cost.

"It's said to be two dollars!" she said.

He stuck his tongue out in amazement. "What did you want to buy it for?"

"I didn't want it, but her brother Fortune insisted on getting it. He bought three bottles, one for himself, one for Flora, and this one he gave to me."

Simplicity held his tongue.

Flora and Second Treasure started recounting the many views they saw in Luna Park. Then they progressed to the looks and clothes of the courtesans and their servant girls, commenting on them in detail. Flora said, "It's a pity you didn't go up to the photographer's studio. It wouldn't have been a bad idea for all of us to take a picture together."

"With your adopted brother Fortune in the picture as well? We'll be the butt of everybody's joke," said Second Treasure.

"We're relatives, so there's no harm in being a bit familiar," said Flora.

"This brother Fortune is quite an easygoing person, though. He doesn't seem to have a temper at all," said Second Treasure. "When he heard us say Mother, he called her Mother, too. He asked Mother to tea and took Mother to see the peacock; he was just like Mother's own son."

"Mind that your chattering doesn't get out of hand!" Mrs. Zhao barked to stop her.

Second Treasure chewed a nail to hide her laughter. Flora also laughed. She asked, "He's inviting us to the opera tonight at Panorama Garden. Are you going?"

Second Treasure pouted, affecting modesty. "I still feel a bit embarrassed. Brother can go."

"Yes, it'd be nice to go with brother," said Flora.

"He didn't invite me. What would I be doing there?" said Simplicity.

Second Treasure said, "In fact, he did. Just now, on the way back, he said, 'Why didn't he come along for the ride?' We replied that there was nobody else at the inn. He said straightaway, 'Ask him to come to the show later.'"

"It's already half past six; they'll probably be asking for us soon. Let's have supper now," Flora said.

The inn attendant was told to hurry with the supper, and the four of them ate around the table. Soon they had finished. Just then, a man carrying a lantern marked Panorama Garden and holding high an invitation came up the steps and shouted, "Invitation!" Simplicity hurried out to take it and read it out: "Madam, the Young Master, the two young ladies." It was just signed with one word: Shi.

"Now what are we going to tell him?" Second Treasure asked.

"We'll of course say we're on our way," said Flora.

Simplicity raised his voice to relay the message, and the man who delivered the invitation left immediately.

Second Treasure pretended to be vexed. "Why did you say we're on our way? I don't feel like going to a show."

"Oh, you and your tricks! In life, it's best to be straightforward, so stop this playacting." Flora repeatedly pressed her to get changed.

"Give me a minute; what's the hurry?" Second Treasure looked at herself in the mirror and put on a little rouge and powder. Then she chose an off-white Huzhou crepe blouse. When she was dressed, the party was ready to leave. But then Simplicity said, "Please send my apologies."

Flora broke out laughing. "Are you following your sister's example?"

He lamely tried to defend his decision. "It's not that. I saw the Panorama Garden's program sheet; I've seen the operas before, and they're not very good."

"He reserved a box, and there're just the few of us. Even if you don't go, there'll be no savings made, so why not come along whatever you think about the operas?" said Flora.

In fact, Simplicity was keen to go. All the while he gave his apologies, he was watching the expressions of his mother and sister. Second Treasure said to him, "Since Flora tells you to go, you should. Isn't that right, Mother?"

Mrs. Zhao also said, "Naturally, you should do as Flora says. You should all come back together after the show. Don't go anywhere else."

Then Flora turned to ask Mrs. Zhao to go as well, but the latter declined. Simplicity cheered up, asked for a lantern marked "Welcome Inn," and led the way. As it was no great distance, Flora Zhang and Second Treasure just walked behind him to Panorama Garden.

CHAPTER 30 :: *The Zhaos move to new quarters that come with hired help, and an old barber complains about his worthless son in a teahouse*

Simplicity Zhao led his sister, Second Treasure, and Flora Zhang to a reserved box on the first floor of Panorama Garden. The host, a young man, was dressed in a robe of pale mauve crepe de chine and a lined jacket of sapphire blue gauze. He was seated at one side, waiting. Simplicity recognized him as Fortune Shi although they had not met before. The latter was overjoyed to see them. He stood up immediately, put on a smiling face, and led Flora and Second Treasure by the arm to the best seats by the railing. Then he showed Simplicity to a front seat as well. When Simplicity retreated to the back row after he had put down the lantern, Fortune insisted on dragging him to the front. Ashamed by the contrast between him and Shi, Simplicity felt extremely ill at ease. Luckily, Fortune started whispering in Flora's ear, and Flora in turn whispered to Second Treasure, so Simplicity was left alone to watch the show in peace.

Panorama Garden boasted the largest number of first-rate actors, among whom the best was a leading man called Little Willow, whose acting and singing were in a class of their own. That night his number, *The Green Screen Mountain*, in which he played Shi Xiu, came last.[1] When it came to the scene of Pan Qiaoyun cursing him and her aged father trying to make peace, Little Willow gave his songs all he had. Then, in the wine shop scene, his lightning maneuvering of a sword turned it into a flashing streak of electricity. The performance certainly lived up to his reputation.

When the play was over, it was midnight. The audience made a mad rush for the exit, blocking the way out.

"We'll take our time," said Fortune Shi. He asked Simplicity to walk in front and light the way for the girls, while he himself brought up the rear. Together, they returned to the Welcome Inn. Second Treasure dashed forward and opened the door to their room, calling "Mother." Mrs. Zhao, who was reclining on the bed, got up instantly.

"Why didn't you go to bed, Mother?" Simplicity asked.

"I was waiting for you. If I had gone to bed, who'd get the door?"

"It was a very nice show. It's a pity you missed it, Mother," said Flora.

"They have the best show on Saturday nights. It's Wednesday today; we'll go with Mother in a couple days," said Fortune.

::

1. An episode from the novel *Shuihu zhuan*, or *The Marshes of Mount Liang*, in which Shi Xiu rejects the advances of Pan Qiaoyun, his adopted brother's wife. Naturally, she accuses him of attempted seduction. Episodes from this novel—one of the four fiction classics of traditional Chinese literature—are the basis for a large number of short operas.

Mrs. Zhao could tell it was Fortune by his voice. She greeted him and invited him to sit down, thanking him for his hospitality. Second Treasure called for the inn attendant to make tea, while Flora set the opium tray on the bed, lit the lamp, and invited Fortune to smoke. Simplicity, being socially awkward, kept in the background.

Mrs. Zhao said, "Eldest Young Master, I'm afraid we have imposed on your hospitality; you have taken us out many times these last two of days. We really should go home tomorrow."

Fortune said quickly, "You mustn't, Mother. Don't keep saying this. You rarely come to Shanghai, so naturally you should enjoy yourself for a few more days."

"To be honest, Eldest Young Master, board and lodging for four in this inn cost eight hundred copper coins a day. Our expenses are too high. It's best if we go soon," said Mrs. Zhao.

"That's not a problem. I have an idea: you'll find it more economical than living in the country," said Fortune. As he talked, the opium he was toasting started dripping. He did not notice it, but Flora saw and hastened to lie down on the other side of the divan, take the pick from him, and toast the opium for him.

Second Treasure took a string of copper coins from under her own bed, quietly handed it to Simplicity, and told him to buy some snacks. He went first to the kitchen to ask for a big bowl and, instead of calling for the inn attendant, went shopping himself on Treasured Merit Street. Unfortunately, it was late at night and the shops were closed. He only managed to get six bean curd dumplings, which he divided into three small bowls and took into the room.

Second Treasure frowned. "You're a fine one, Brother. Why did you buy that of all things!"

"But this is the only thing available!"

Fortune sat up, took a look, and then said, "Bean curd dumplings are nice. I happen to like them." Dispensing with any formality, he picked up a pair of bamboo chopsticks and manfully swallowed one down. Second Treasure offered Mrs. Zhao one bowl and called out to Flora, "Come and keep us company, Elder Sister."

But Flora felt embarrassed. "I don't want any," she said disagreeably.[2]

"Then you can eat it up, Brother," Second Treasure said smiling. Simplicity finished all the dumplings at one go and told the inn attendant to clear away the empty bowls.

Fortune smoked a couple more pellets of opium and took his

::

2. Apparently, the shape of the bean curd dumplings carried sexual connotations.

leave. Only then did Simplicity ask Flora how she was related to Fortune Shi.

She said with a smile, "Indeed, you wouldn't know anything about these relatives of mine, would you? Fortune's mother is my adopted mother.[3] I was only two or three when I was adopted. Last year we ran into each other in Longhua and had no idea who the other was. It was only when we started talking that things fell into place, so I was asked to stay at their house for three days. That's how we're related."

Simplicity fell silent and asked no more questions. The night passed quietly.

When Fortune came to the inn the next afternoon, it was just after lunch. The dishes had yet to be cleared away.

"Hurry up, we're going shopping today," Flora told Second Treasure.

"I don't want to buy anything; you go ahead," Second Treasure replied.

"We're not buying anything either. Do come along just for fun," said Fortune.

Flora said, "Don't plead with her. I know her ways. In the end, she's sure to come along."

Hearing this, Second Treasure sneered and lay down on the bed.

"Are you angry because of what I said?" Flora said.

"Who's got the time to get angry with you?" Second Treasure retorted.

"Then let's go," said Flora.

"I wouldn't have objected to going out, but now that you've read my mind for me, I'm definitely not going," said Second Treasure.

Knowing how stubborn Second Treasure was, Flora knew she could not turn her around, so she signaled for Fortune to take over. He sat down on the side of the bed with a jolly smile on his face and, addressing Second Treasure as "Younger Sister," patiently made conversation with her before finally trying to persuade her to go out. Second Treasure still refused.

"Though I have offended you, won't you make a little allowance for our brother Fortune's sake?" said Flora.

Second Treasure smiled sarcastically and made no reply.

Mrs. Zhao, sitting on the other bed, did not catch what was said. She called out, "Second Treasure, don't act that way. Your brother Fortune is speaking to you; get up quickly."

::

3. [This is similar to having a godmother in the West, though there is no religious dimension to the Chinese practice. The child stays with his/her own parents and only visits the adoptive one occasionally. *E.H.*]

"Keep quiet, Mother! What d'you know about it?" Second Treasure said in a pet.

Fortune sensed they had got to an impasse. He laughed and made light of it and then changed tactics, saying, "In that case, we won't go, either. It's nice to sit here for a while and chat." As he stood up, he happened to see Simplicity sitting at the window, his head buried in a newspaper. "Any news?" he asked. Simplicity offered him the paper with both hands. He took it and picked out one paragraph, which he read out aloud to them, gesticulating and explicating as he did so. Flora and Simplicity played up to him and rolled around in laughter.

At first, Second Treasure ignored them, but Fortune was so funny that soon she could not hold back anymore. She suddenly got off the bed and went into the anteroom to relieve herself. Flora covered her mouth with a hand and laughed, but Fortune held up his hand to stop her. When Second Treasure came out, he tossed the newspaper aside and told a very funny joke instead. Even Second Treasure could not help laughing at it. Flora turned on purpose to steal a glance at her to see her reaction. Second Treasure, now feeling awkward, went and sat down close to Mrs. Zhao and buried her head in the latter's bosom, whining, "Mother, look! They're teasing me."

"Who's teasing you? Let's hear it," Flora said loudly.

"Would Elder Sister tease you? Don't talk such nonsense," said Mrs. Zhao.

Fortune clapped his hands and laughed uproariously; even Simplicity joined in the laughter. Their little quarrel, which had started out of thin air, finally came to an end.

By and by, Fortune resumed persuading Second Treasure to go out. She, finding it hard to climb down from her earlier stance, pretended not to hear. Guessing that she was willing, he took an off-white jacket and wrapped it around her shoulders. Flora had already got ready. With Mrs. Zhao's permission, the three of them went out, leaving Simplicity to keep his mother company. As she had not slept well, she took this opportunity for an afternoon nap. To relieve his boredom, Simplicity strolled out into the common parlor with a water pipe in his hand. He sat down on a high-back chair, putting one foot up on the seat, and chatted with the bookkeeper. They carried on till the lamps were lit, but there was still no sign of the three who had gone out.

"Shall I serve supper now?" the inn attendant asked. Simplicity went to consult his mother, who told them to bring dinner for two.

In the middle of the meal, mother and son suddenly heard the sound of laughter at the main entrance. Then they saw Flora coming in with a bundle of clothes and Second Treasure holding a paper bag. Their faces flushed from eating and drinking, they came into the room in a peal of laughter and giggles. Mrs. Zhao asked them whether they had had supper.

"We did. We had a Western meal," replied Flora.

Second Treasure darted forward, saying, "Mother, try this!" She took a shrimp roll from the paper bag and held it out for Mrs. Zhao. After just one bite, Mrs. Zhao was put off by the strange taste and passed it to Simplicity.

He asked about Fortune Shi. "He's busy, so he just saw us to the door and then left in a ricksha," Flora said.

When Mrs. Zhao and Simplicity had finished supper, Second Treasure opened the bundle of clothes and showed Simplicity a pale turquoise gauze blouse, asking him to guess the price. He saw it was trimmed with a wide satin cloud-patterned border that was at the height of fashion. He stuck out his tongue and said in awe, "It must have cost at least ten dollars!"

"It costs sixteen dollars!" she said. "I didn't want it. It was Elder Sister who said she'd have it, but then she thought it was a bit too short for her and just right for me, so she told me to buy it. When I said I had no money, Elder Sister told me to take it first and talk about the money later."

Simplicity said not a word. When Second Treasure took from the bundle three or four summer silk garments and said these were all Elder Sister's purchases, he was quieter than ever.

That night, none of them went out. With nothing to do, Simplicity went to bed early. Flora and Second Treasure talked in a low murmur in the front room, but he took no notice of them. As he was sinking into sleep, he heard his sister call "Mother" repeatedly. This woke him, and he called out to ask what the matter was.

"Nothing," Second Treasure answered evasively.

Mrs. Zhao woke up and joined the murmured conversation, which Simplicity just disregarded. He slept soundly until the sun was shining in the window. Flora and Second Treasure were already doing their hair in the front room. He knew he had overslept and hurriedly came out with his clothes draped around his shoulders. But then he saw his mother was still in bed hugging the quilt around her and realized it was still early. He called for the inn attendant to bring hot water for him to wash his face.

"We've had breakfast. What would you like, Brother? Just tell them to get it for you," said Second Treasure.

He had no idea what he wanted, so Flora suggested, "Why not have a couple of soup dumplings as we did?"

"All right," he said. The inn attendant took the money and went out.

With the girls' toiletries set out on the table, there was little space left, so Simplicity picked up the water pipe and went out to the parlor, where he ate the soup dumplings and chatted again with the bookkeeper. A long while later, Second Treasure suddenly called out "Brother," saying, "Mother wants you." He went in immediately.

Flora and Second Treasure had finished dressing and were seated side by side on the bed. Mrs. Zhao had got up and was sitting in a chair. Simplicity sat down to one side, waiting for instructions. The four of them looked at one another, but no one said a word.

Finally, Second Treasure got impatient. "Mother, do tell Brother."

"Ah, well!" Before she spoke, Mrs. Zhao sighed. "Their brother Fortune is really most kind. He told us to have a couple more days' sight-seeing. When I mentioned that it was expensive living at an inn, he said, 'I have a house in Tranquillity Alley that is standing vacant.' He told us to move there so we could live more cheaply."

Flora cut in quickly, "It's Fortune's house, so there'll be no rent to pay. If we cook for ourselves, it'll only cost us two hundred copper coins a day. That's a lot cheaper than staying in the inn, isn't it? Well, I told him yesterday that we'd take up his offer. What d'you say?"

Second Treasure backed her up. "Board and lodging for four in this place come to eight hundred a day. If we move, we'll save six hundred. There's nothing wrong with that, is there?"

How could he object? Simplicity just bowed his head and agreed.

After lunch, Fortune Shi brought a manservant to the inn and asked, "Are you all packed?"

Flora and Second Treasure both laughed and said, "We don't have that much to pack, do we?"

Fortune told the manservant to carry their things out. Simplicity helped to tie up the trunks and baskets and roll up the bedding. Then he called a pushcart and, together with the servant, went to Tranquillity Alley to set up the rooms.[4] He saw the two-storied house had two main rooms on each floor. The windowpanes were crystal clear, and the wallpaper brand-new. The kitchen was fully equipped with pots and pans, and the two rooms upstairs were furnished with brand-new furniture from Ningbo. The beds, divans, tables, and chairs were neatly arranged; the rooms even boasted paraffin lamps and full-length mirrors. All that was lacking were paintings and calligraphy scrolls, curtains and drapes.

::

4. [The phrase "setting up a room" is the technical term for a courtesan furnishing a room to set up her own establishment. Tranquillity Alley is of course part of the brothel district. This is made clear in chapter 31, which states that all the houses there have lamps hanging at the entrance. *E.H.*]

A short while later, Mrs. Zhao, Flora Zhang, and Second Treasure arrived in the company of Fortune Shi. Mrs. Zhao walked all around the house, marveling, "Down in the country, we've never seen houses like this! Eldest Young Master, you've really been far too kind to us."

Fortune responded with the greatest humility. After some consultation, it was agreed that Flora and Second Treasure would each occupy one of the main rooms upstairs, Mrs. Zhao would take the little mezzanine room, and Simplicity and the manservant would live downstairs.

Soon evening came, and a banquet was delivered from the Garden of Plenty. Fortune had it laid out in Flora's room, saying it was for housewarming. Mrs. Zhao again thanked him profusely. Everybody sat around the table, uninhibited and carefree, drinking to their heart's content.

When they were all slightly tipsy, Flora suddenly said, "Oh, we forgot! We should have called a couple of courtesans here for fun. That wouldn't have been a bad idea."

"Do call them now, Fortune. We want to see what they're like!" said Second Treasure.

"Stop that, Second Treasure," Mrs. Zhao barked at her. "No more tricks from you. Your brother Fortune is a respectable man. He doesn't go to sing-song houses. How can he summon courtesans here?"

Simplicity had something to say to this, but guilt and embarrassment stopped him.

Fortune said smiling, "It won't be much fun if I call them by myself. Tomorrow I'll invite a couple of friends to have dinner here and ask them to summon some courtesans here on a party call. That'd be much better."

"My brother can call one, too. I'd like to see if they'd come," said Second Treasure.

Flora patted her on the shoulder, saying, "I'll call one, too; I'll call Second Treasure."

"There's never been a courtesan with the name Second Treasure. Your case is different, though, for there're three or four Flora Zhangs, all fashionable courtesans who are called to parties all the time."

Riled by this remark, Flora tried to pinch Second Treasure on the mouth. The latter laughed and ran away. Fortune got up from his seat to stop Flora and make peace, and the two of them went over to the divan to smoke opium. Seeing that the last four courses had been put on the table, Mrs. Zhao told the manservant to bring rice. Simplicity, who had sought relief in drinking, was now feeling the effect of the wine. He had some rice to keep his mother company and then saw her into the mezzanine room and went downstairs himself. After he had lit the lamp and loosened his clothes, he stopped worrying and went to bed. When he woke up, the effect of the wine had worn off, but he felt very thirsty. Draping some clothes around his shoulders, he put on his shoes slipper-fashion and groped his way into the kitchen. There, he found a big yellow clay teapot, lifted it with both hands, and drank his fill from the spout. The manservant was sitting bolt upright on the covered water jar, dozing. Simplicity woke him and found out from him that, though dinner was over, Fortune was still there. Simplicity went back to his own room, where he could hear whispers and the sound of laughter coming from upstairs, mixed with the wheezing of the water and opium pipes.

Simplicity trimmed the lamp and went back to sleep. This time, it was the sleep of oblivion. He was dead to the world until the manservant woke him. Startled, he asked the man, "Did you sleep at all?"

"It was dawn by the time Eldest Young Master left. Couldn't very well go to bed then, could I?"

After he had washed in the kitchen, Simplicity tiptoed upstairs. Mrs. Zhao was alone in the mezzanine room, combing her hair. In the front room, where the opium lamp was still burning, Flora and Second Treasure were sleeping on the divan fully clothed. Simplicity lifted the curtain and entered the room. Flora woke up first. She sat up and took out a guest list from her inner pocket, telling Simplicity to write the word "Seen" to acknowledge the invitation. Simplicity saw that Fortune Shi was borrowing their place that night to invite Cloudlet Chen and Lichee Zhuang to dinner. Simplicity and Juvenity Zhang were to keep them company.

After pondering for a while, he said, "Tonight, I really have to beg off."

"Why?" Flora asked.

"It'll be too embarrassing for me."

"D'you mean seeing my brother will be embarrassing?" she asked.

"No."

"Then what is it?"

He would not tell her the truth. It happened that Second Treasure had been wakened by the sound of their conversation, so he turned to her and whispered his reasons in her ear. She nodded, saying, "That makes sense."

Flora could not very well put pressure on him. She summoned the manservant, gave him the guest list, and told him to deliver the invitations.

Simplicity hung around the house until two in the afternoon and then picked up his courage and asked his sister for thirty cents. With his mother's permission, he left the house. First, he took a turn on Fourth Avenue, going back to Treasured Merit Street, where he dropped in at the Welcome Inn, thinking he would have a chat with the bookkeeper. But as he approached the entrance, a man charged out right in his path. The man was wearing a Chinese shirt and trousers of old blue cotton and was carrying a little bundle on his back. His short whiskers seemed to be standing up in anger, and his face was contorted in rage. Simplicity was startled to find that it was Old Wu, the barber.

The minute Wu saw Simplicity, his expression turned joyful. "I came looking for you. Where have you moved to?" he asked.

Simplicity gave him a brief account of events. Old Wu took his arm and, standing by his side, embarked on a long harangue.

"Let's go for a cup of tea round the corner," Simplicity said.

Old Wu was agreeable to the suggestion, and Simplicity led the way to the Wind in the Pines Teahouse at the corner of Pebble Road. They walked up the stairs and ordered light lotus tea. Old Wu put down his bundle and sat across from Simplicity. They each took a small cup and poured the tea out for each other as politeness required.

Suddenly anger flared in Old Wu's eyes, and he rolled up his sleeves as if getting ready for a scrap. "There's something I want to ask you: have you been going around with Pine?"

Taken by surprise, Simplicity had no idea what Old Wu wanted. His heart started beating wildly.

Old Wu pounded the table with his fist, his face in a deep frown. "Don't worry! I'm just worried that a young man like you, alone in Shanghai, might have been swindled by him. It's best if you don't take up with vermin like Pine."

Simplicity still stared in silent incomprehension.

"Humph! I'll tell you this: he won't even acknowledge me, his own father. D'you think he'd do anything for you, who's just a friend?"

This began to make sense to Simplicity. He smiled and asked what had happened.

Old Wu spoke more calmly. "I'm his father. Now, I may be poor, but I still manage to earn a bowl or two of rice to eat, if not much else. I came to Shanghai not because I wanted anything from my son but because he's made a fortune and I thought it'd be right and proper to look in on him. I didn't know he's such a rat! I went to his shop three times, but the accounts office said he wasn't there. Well, that was all right. But the fourth time I went, he *was* there, and he didn't come out. He just took four hundred copper coins from the accounts office and had them handed to me, telling me to take the ferry boat home. Was I desperate for his four hundred copper coins? If I wanted to go home, I could have done so even if I had to go begging all the way. Did I have to depend on his four hundred copper coins?"

As Old Wu told his story, he started wailing bitterly. Simplicity comforted him as best he could and tried to find excuses for Pine Wu. After a long time, Old Wu controlled his tears. "I'm partly to blame as well, for telling him to come to work in Shanghai. These foreign settlements are really no good."

Simplicity expressed admiration for Old Wu's sentiments and hid his real opinion. After their tea had been freshened up with hot water five or six times, Simplicity settled the bill, which came to ten cents. Old Wu thanked him as a matter of course, put his bundle on his back, and parted company with him outside the teahouse. Old Wu headed for the pier in search of an inland riverboat to go home, while Simplicity Zhao wandered down Treasured Merit Street wondering what to do about supper.

CHAPTER 31 :: *An uncle's reproaches lead to the severing of family ties, and a difference in taste frustrates a would-be matchmaker*

With only two ten-cent pieces and some copper coins on him, Simplicity Zhao had little option other than to dine in a small restaurant on Pebble Road, where he had a piece of yellow fish served with soup and rice. He then went to Panorama Garden on Treasured Merit Street, where he saw an opera, sitting in the cheap section behind the center tables. When he walked home after the show, it had struck midnight. The door of every house in Tranquillity Alley was illuminated by a glass lamp. His door, however, was pitch-dark and tightly shut. He knocked a couple of times, and the manservant let him in. He asked, "Is the party over?"

"It's been over for a while now. Only Eldest Young Master has stayed behind," the manservant replied.

Simplicity saw that at the stairway a new tin-plate wall lamp was shining brightly. He walked upstairs at a leisurely pace and, hearing voices in the mezzanine room, lifted the curtain and went in. His mother was sitting up in bed, with Flora Zhang and Second Treasure sitting side by side on the edge of the bed chattering away.

Seeing him, Mrs. Zhao asked, "Have you had supper?"

"Yes," said Simplicity. "Is Fortune gone?"

"Not yet, he's asleep," said Flora.

Second Treasure broke in, "We've just hired a servant girl. See what you think of her." She called out loudly, "Clever!"

Clever came over from Flora's room and stood to one side. Simplicity scrutinized the little servant girl. She looked familiar, but he could not place her right away. Then the name Clever jogged his memory. "Have you just left Sunset's place?" he asked her.

"I worked at Sunset's for a couple of months, but I've just come from Constance's. Where have you seen me before? I don't remember you."

Instead of telling her, he dismissed the matter with a smile. Flora and Second Treasure did not try to get to the root of the matter, either. Everybody went back to talking about the party. "How many girls did they call?" he asked.

"One each. But it seems to us none of them was much good," said Flora.

"I think the two from the second-class house weren't so bad," said Second Treasure.

"Did Juvenity call a girl?" he asked.

"Juvenity was busy, so he didn't come," said Flora.

"Who did Fortune call?" he asked.

"Jewel Lu," Second Treasure replied. "She wasn't so bad."

"Was it the Jewel from the Hall of Beauties on West Chessboard Street?" he asked, startled.

Flora and Second Treasure exclaimed in unison, "Exactly. How did you know?"

Simplicity smiled awkwardly. How could he dare tell?

"It seems that after a couple of months in Shanghai, you've got to know quite a lot of courtesans and servant girls," Flora commented with a smile.

"Huh! Knowing a few courtesans and servant girls is nothing to brag about!" Second Treasure jeered.

Embarrassed, Simplicity unobtrusively withdrew from the mezzanine room. Then he sneaked into Flora's room, where he saw Fortune Shi sprawled on the divan, snoring. His drunken face was damp from the effect of too much wine. The two paraffin lamps had been turned up high and looked dazzling against the new wallpaper. The large shiny round tabletop placed on the square table had not yet been removed. Beside the door lay a big heap of watermelon seed shells and chicken, fish, and meat bones. Without disturbing Fortune, Simplicity went back downstairs to his own room. The manservant had long since stretched out stiff on a plank bed. Having trimmed the wick of his bedside lamp, Simplicity undressed and retired for the night.

By the time he woke up, it was past noon. He made haste to get up. As soon as the manservant had ladled a basin of water for him to wash his face, Clever came in and said, "You're wanted upstairs."

Simplicity followed her up to Flora's room, where Fortune Shi lay smoking opium. Although he did not get up, he did nod at Simplicity. Flora and Second Treasure were both doing their hair in the outer room.

In a moment, Mrs. Zhao was also invited over. Clever placed five sets of cups and chopsticks on the round table, while the manservant brought in a huge tray on which were placed all the leftovers from the party: pig's knuckles, stuffed duck, Yunnan ham, and fish were on four big dishes, while all sorts of appetizers and vegetables were served up in a large bowl. Fortune, Mrs. Zhao, and Simplicity sat down informally. Flora and Second Treasure, their toilet not yet finished, were both dressed in blue sleeveless cotton jackets, their hair held in place with two bone hairpins. When they came in, Fortune lifted his cup and said, "Have some wine." But Flora and Second Treasure adamantly refused to drink. They told Clever to bring rice and started on the meal with Mrs. Zhao. Only Simplicity poured some wine to keep Fortune company.

Simplicity took a sip of wine and frowned. "It's too hot."

"I seem to have a bit of a cold. Hot wine suits me quite well," said Fortune.

"It's your own fault," Flora said. "Clever came to call you and ask you to sleep in the proper bed. Why didn't you listen to her?"

"The two of us sleeping in the outer room heard you coughing till daylight. What were you doing all by yourself?" said Second Treasure.

Fortune smiled but said nothing.[1]

Mrs. Zhao nagged, "Eldest Young Master, your constitution is on the frail side, so you should take better care of yourself. Take the night before last, for example. You insisted on going home at dawn. Wasn't it cold? It'd have been quite all right for you to have stayed here."

Fortune straightened his gown and put on a solemn expression. "Mother is of course right. I should take better care of myself. If only I knew how!"

"If you have a cold, you shouldn't drink so much," said Flora.

"Brother should stop drinking as well," said Second Treasure.

Naturally, Fortune and Simplicity complied.

::

1. [Though the two girls have already been seduced by Fortune Shi, they still try to maintain a facade of respectability. *E.H.*]

After lunch, the manservant and Clever came in to tidy up. Simplicity had slipped downstairs already. He wiped his hands and face with a wet towel and then picked up a water pipe and sauntered out into the parlor, where he sat down majestically with legs crossed. Bored with the solitude, he tried to find some excuse to go out and look around.

Just as he was racking his brain, suddenly somebody came knocking on the door. He shouted, "Who is it?" and as he did not quite catch the answer, he had no choice but to put down the water pipe and go to take a look. The visitor was none other than his uncle, Benevolence Hong. The color drained instantly from Simplicity's face. He greeted his uncle, at the same time retreating to a safe distance.

Benevolence paid him no attention. He bellowed angrily, "Tell your mother to come out."

Simplicity assented repeatedly and then went upstairs in a fluster to announce him. Flora and Second Treasure had both changed into very fashionable clothes and were sitting with Mrs. Zhao helping her entertain Fortune. When Simplicity told them the state Benevolence was in, Fortune and Flora, beset by guilt and fear, dared not show their faces. Afraid that her mother would be indiscreet, Second Treasure followed her downstairs to meet Benevolence.

Benevolence did not even observe the rules of normal greeting. He asked Mrs. Zhao in a huff, "Has old age robbed you of your senses? Aren't you supposed to have gone home? D'you have any idea what kind of a place Tranquillity Alley is?"

"But we *are* going home," said Mrs. Zhao. "There's nothing I'd like better than to go back right away, but Miss Flora wants to have a couple more days' holiday, see a couple more shows, ride around a bit in a horse carriage, and do a bit of shopping . . ."

Second Treasure, seeing that her mother was getting nowhere, stepped up hastily and cut her short, "Uncle, what Mother is trying to say—"

Before she could finish, Benevolence pounded his fist on the table and barked at her, "I'm talking to your mother—you've no right to speak. Go look at yourself in the mirror. What have you turned into? Shameless little hussy!"

The tongue-lashing made her cheeks burn. She withdrew to one side and started sniveling.

Mrs. Zhao heaved a sigh and then picked up where she had left off, "Then there's that brother Fortune of theirs, who's got very attached to us—"

At this, Benevolence violently stamped his feet and thundered at her, "You have the nerve to speak of 'brother Fortune'! He's ruined your daughter, d'you realize that?" He repeated this several times, thrusting his face down at hers. This so frightened Mrs. Zhao that she just stared at him, dumbfounded. No one uttered a sound.

Flora, who was upstairs, heard the uproar and sent Clever to find out more. Seeing Simplicity peeking behind the door, Clever, too, stood there and listened. It was completely quiet in the parlor.

After a long while, Benevolence's anger somewhat subsided. He said in a clear loud voice to Mrs. Zhao, "Just tell me this: do you still want to go home or not?"

"Why wouldn't I want to go home?" said Mrs. Zhao. "But how am I to go home now? My wastrel of a son has scattered what little money I'd managed to save up in the last four or five years. And when we came out here, we had to spend some more. Now we haven't even got the fare home."

"I'll give you the fare. Go hire a boat and leave right away."

That stopped Mrs. Zhao dead in her tracks. She hesitated. "Of course it's best to go home, but even if we have the fare, we still owe Miss Flora thirty dollars, and once we get back home, we'll have no resources for the greater part of a year, no oil, salt, rice, or firewood. Who can we turn to then?"

Benevolence sighed heavily. "All that you've said amounts to only one thing: you're not going home. Well, I haven't got enough of a fortune to take care of a nephew. You can do whatever you like, but leave me out of it. From now on, don't come looking for me and give me a bad name. Just don't think of me as your brother!" Having said that, he stood up and strode off without so much as a backward glance.

Faint with anger, Mrs. Zhao collapsed in a chair while Second Treasure covered her face with her handkerchief and sobbed ceaselessly. Simplicity and Clever waited until Benevolence was at a safe distance before they came out from behind the door. Simplicity stood loyally by, wishing to comfort them but not knowing how.

Clever said in surprise, "Why, that was Mr. Hong! Why was he so angry?"

Mrs. Zhao told her to shut the front door and then called Second Treasure over and said, "Let's go upstairs."

Simplicity followed behind. They went up together and sat down with Flora and Fortune as before.

Flora asked Mrs. Zhao, "Are you going home?"

"We really should," Mrs. Zhao said. "Your uncle was right after all. But I just can't figure out how we're going to manage."

Second Treasure exclaimed tearfully, "Mother, how can you still say Uncle was right? All he did was reproach us. As soon as money was mentioned, he washed his hands of us and went off!"

Simplicity chimed in, "Uncle spoke very strangely, too. Sister's sitting right here, looking perfectly well, yet he said she was ruined. Whatever did he mean?"

Fortune sneered. "Maybe I shouldn't say this, but that uncle of yours is really outrageous. Even among us friends, we look out for each other when we're in need, yet your uncle wants nothing to do with your problems! If you ask me, you're better off without an uncle like that!"

When everybody had expressed their opinion on the matter, it was put aside. Fortune spoke again to console Second Treasure and comfort Mrs. Zhao and also promised to find Simplicity a job. After that, he took his leave. Knowing she could not detain him, Flora simply enjoined him, "Come back for dinner later."

He promised and left the house. Before he had walked pass a couple of doorways, he suddenly heard a seductive voice call out "Eldest Young Master Shi." He looked up. It was Third Treasure calling from her window and beckoning, "Come sit for a while."

Not having seen Third Treasure for a long time, he now discovered that she had developed a curvaceous figure. He thought this would be a good opportunity to have a cup of tea at her place and go in for further exploration. But it so happened that two other men walking toward him went into Third Treasure's house just then and headed straight upstairs. Fortune checked himself, while Third Treasure turned her attention away from him to greet her two guests.

Only one of them—Vigor Qian—was known to her. She asked the name of the other guest and was told it was Gao. She offered tea, a water pipe, and watermelon seeds. The routines over, as they sat talking, Vigor Qian kept calling Gao "Brother Second Bai." Reminded of a character in the Beijing opera *Rehearsal for a Wedding*, Third Treasure chuckled. When Vigor asked her for the reason for her mirth, she covered her grinning mouth and did not reply. Second Bai Gao did not seem interested in this.

After a brief stay, Second Bai Gao and Vigor Qian got up to leave. Third Treasure saw them out to the staircase. Walking shoulder to shoulder, the two men strolled leisurely out of Tranquillity Alley and turned into Fourth Avenue, where they stopped at the Western restaurant Sky in a Wine Pot. Vigor Qian offered to treat Second Bai to a Western meal there, and the latter accepted. They went in and chose a room of moderate size, after which the waiter brought inkstone and writing brush.

"I'll ask a friend to come and keep you company," Vigor said after a moment of reflection. He filled out an invitation slip and gave it to the waiter.

Second Bai saw that he had put down the name of Thatch Fang. "Is it the gentleman known as Old Fisherman?" he asked.

"That's the one. How did you come to know him?"

"I don't know him personally, but he writes poems, so I have often come across his name in newspapers."

Before long, the waiter came back to report, "Your guest will be here right away."

Vigor then turned to the business of calling girls to the party. He asked Second Bai, "Who'd you like to call?"

"Just anyone will do," Second Bai said with a frown.

"Is it possible that not one of Shanghai's numerous courtesans appeals to you? What kind of a girl have you set your heart on?"

"I really have no idea. But since they're courtesans, the words 'chaste' and 'elegant' wouldn't apply; perhaps the carefree behavior of Madame Wang or the gay abandon of the young widow Zhuo Wenjun would be more their style."[2]

"You're far too fastidious for a place like Shanghai," Vigor said with a smile. "I for one have no idea what you're talking about."

"Not to worry," Second Bai said, smiling as well.

Just then Thatch Fang arrived. Second Bai saw that he had a graying beard and cut quite a handsome figure in a boxy gown and vermilion shoes. When he learned Second Bai's name, he laughed loudly and raised a thumb to signify number one, saying: "So here's another great scholar from the south of the Yangtze![3] Delighted to meet you. Delighted!"

Second Bai looked away without replying.

Vigor wrote out two call chits, one for Laurel of Generosity Alley, who was Thatch's girl, and another for Green Phoenix, his own girl. Second Bai then said, "The three girls we've visited today, let's call all of them." So Vigor wrote three more chits respectively for Third Treasure, River Blossom, and Twin Jade. After that, they looked at the menu and each ordered a few of their favorite dishes.

"I see that our friend Second Bai is a practitioner of universal love," Thatch said with a smile.

"Not at all," replied Vigor. "His book learning is so thorough that no courtesan appeals to him, so he's calling just anyone."

::

2. Madame Wang was the wife of the famous fifth-century calligrapher Wang Xizhi and a calligrapher in her own right. She was noted for her talent and self-confidence. Zhuo Wenjun was a widowed heiress of the second century who eloped with the writer Sima Xiangru after listening to a song he played on the zither. It comes as no surprise that soon Second Bai was to be introduced to two courtesans named after Zhuo Wenjun.

3. [The name Second Bai means second only to the Tang dynasty poet Li Bai who was well known for his prodigious talent. E.H.]

Thatch asked, "Why didn't you say so earlier? I know of one who'd definitely do the trick."

"Who is it? We'll get her here and see," said Vigor.

"It's Jade Wenjun of Prosperity Alley. Because she set her sights too high, your average client dares not approach her. It's as though she's reserved for a connoisseur like our friend Second Bai." As this sounded rather appealing to Second Bai, he let Vigor add another call chit to the rest.

Not long afterward, when they had finished the first two courses—soup and fish—the girl last summoned was the first to arrive. Second Bai carefully appraised this Jade Wenjun. Though she was only twenty, she had the emaciated look of a heavy opium smoker. There was little to recommend her, and Second Bai could not understand why Thatch admired her so much.

"Later, when you go to Jade Wenjun's place, you'll see her study," Thatch said to Second Bai. "Now that's decor for you! One wall is lined with bookcases and another wall features four hanging scrolls, and all the poems her clients have written to her are framed in brocade. Where else would you find its like in the sing-song houses of Shanghai?"

As the reason for Thatch's admiration of Jade Wenjun dawned on Second Bai, he felt a pang of disappointment.

Jade Wenjun picked up the subject. "There're two poems dedicated to me in today's newspapers. I don't know who wrote them."

"Nowadays there isn't any good poetry in Shanghai. Why don't you ask Mr. Gao to write a couple of poems for you? He'll make you famous, much more so than anyone else can," said Thatch.

Second Bai shouted, "Enough! Let's play the finger game!" Vigor responded immediately, and the two were locked in combat. Thatch sat to one side, holding himself very upright. With his eyes closed and his head wagging, he mumbled on and on. Second Bai knew that the man was suddenly seized by poetic inspiration and so ignored him. After ten rounds of the finger game, Vigor, who was the loser, was about to ask Thatch to take on the winner. Just then Thatch burst out laughing. Having reached out for the inkstone and writing brush, he dashed something off and presented it to Second Bai with both hands, saying, "Such an artistic gathering as this calls for a poem. I have written a few vulgar lines, and I respectfully await your instruction."

Second Bai took the piece of paper and saw that it was a red card for writing out invitations; the poem was written on the back, which was white. He said, "That's a nice invitation card. It's made of foreign paper, isn't it? What a waste!" He then tossed it on the table.

To save Thatch from his embarrassment, Vigor took the poem and read it out loud. As he did so, Thatch slapped the table to mark the rhythm. Second Bai said impatiently to Vigor, "Didn't you invite me to drink? Now I'm afraid I'm so nauseated I won't be able to keep the wine down."

Smiling to cover his embarrassment, Vigor said, "I'll play another ten rounds with you."

"Fine."

This time, Second Bai was the loser, but as the summoned girls had all arrived and each reached out a hand for a cup of penalty wine, he himself ended up not getting any to drink. After taking one cup for him, Jade Wenjun was the first to leave.

Seeing that Second Bai did not take to Jade Wenjun, Thatch consulted with Vigor. "The two of us have to find him a more congenial girl. Otherwise we don't do justice to his talent and sensibility."

"You go ahead. Matchmaking for him is beyond me," said Vigor.

Green Phoenix put in, "What about the new girl at our place, Gold Flower?"

"Even I don't think much of Gold Flower. How would she suit him?" said Vigor.

"I disagree," Second Bai responded. "Whether a girl suits me or not has nothing to do with whether she's good."

"All right, then let's go and see," said Vigor.

After they finished the Western meal with a cup of coffee, the guests and courtesans went their separate ways. Thatch, who had a date with Laurel, walked with Second Bai and Vigor as far as Generosity Alley, where they parted company. Thatch Fang went into Laurel's, while Second Bai and Vigor Qian headed for Green Phoenix's. Green Phoenix herself had gone on to another party, so Pearl Phoenix and Gold Phoenix both came to keep them company. Having been told by Vigor to fetch Gold Flower, Little Treasure went downstairs to carry out her order.

Vigor first told Second Bai how Gold Flower had come to be there. "Well, Gold Flower was sold to Green Phoenix's maid, Third Sister Chu. Third Sister's own daughter, Perfection, managed to borrow three hundred dollars from a guest named Li, so they bought Gold Flower and put her here temporarily. She will go to a second-class house when the new season starts."

Before he had finished speaking, Gold Flower came in. After presenting them with watermelon seeds, she sat down to one side. Second Bai saw that she had a sluttish look about her that made her fine second-class material. Nor was she good at entertaining; though she sat there for a long time, she was completely silent. Second Bai felt he had had enough and rose to take his leave. Vigor wanted to go with him, but Gold Phoenix barred his way in a panic and pleaded, "Brother-in-law, please don't go! Elder Sister will scold us if you do!"

Vigor had little choice but to see Second Bai on his way. Gold Phoenix then asked him to lie down on the divan while she sat down on the humble side and toasted opium for him. He talked to her as he smoked. After he had had a few puffs, he heard a sedan chair come in from the street and go straight into the parlor. He knew that Green Phoenix had come home.

Green Phoenix came into her room, changed out of her party clothes, and then picked up a water pipe and sat down by the window. Through all this, she uttered not a word. Gold Phoenix, being intelligent, immediately pulled Pearl Phoenix into the opposite room, but Gold Flower just sat there with a blank face, like a wooden puppet.

CHAPTER 32 :: *Gold Flower gets a whipping for imitating her better, and Twin Jade leaves a handkerchief as a token for her lover*

It was only natural that Green Phoenix would want to talk to Vigor Qian in private, but Gold Flower just sat there, not realizing she was a nuisance. Green Phoenix stared at her for a long time and then saw the funny side of it. She asked, "Why are you sitting here?"

"Young Mr. Qian called me upstairs," replied Gold Flower.

Only then did it dawn on Green Phoenix. With a sigh, she said, "Young Mr. Qian called you upstairs to make a match for you! Didn't you know that?"

Bewildered, Gold Flower answered, "Young Mr. Qian didn't say."

Green Phoenix smiled ironically. "That's wonderful!"

Vigor held up a hand and said, "It's not her fault. Second Bai is like that. I told him before we came that she wouldn't suit him. Then when he got here, he kept fidgeting, so how was she to entertain him?"

Green Phoenix looked away. "If I had bought a girl like her, I'd certainly break her neck and be done with it."

He said soothingly, "Why not try and teach her a thing or two? She's new to the business, so naturally she doesn't know what to do."

"Humph! When I saw my maid beating her, it seemed like a sin. But even after the beating, she still never takes in anything you tell her. Wouldn't you be angry, too?"

Gold Flower answered hastily, "I remember everything Elder Sister says, only it takes time to learn. Isn't that so?"

Green Phoenix turned to her and laughed. "And what have you learned?"

Gold Flower was stumped. Vigor Qian couldn't help smiling.

After taking two puffs from the water pipe, Green Phoenix said to him slowly, "The girl's a lowlife by nature. It's not as if she's not scared of beatings, but will she try harder to please? No. She has to be told to make even the slightest move." Then she turned to address Gold Flower, "I'll be frank with you: if you go on like this, you're going to get a couple of good thrashings yet."

Hearing this, Gold Flower started weeping quietly, not daring to answer back. Green Phoenix was moved to pity, too, and said with a sigh, "As a girl sold to the house, you should consider yourself lucky. Just imagine running into someone like my mother. You know Pearl Phoenix is quite a bit smarter than you, but leaving out the beatings she's had, just the footbinding made her lose three of her toes."

Gold Flower still said nothing.

Green Phoenix went on smoking. After a long pause, she turned to Vigor again, "Look at it this way: our madams buy us girls to have us do business so they can earn a living. Wouldn't they starve to death if we didn't know how to do business? Naturally, they'd beat us. If our business were a bit better, would they dare beat us? Of course not; they'd turn around to fawn on us. Only stupid courtesans like her would do business for the madam and still get beaten. I never could understand why they make themselves so cheap."

As she was talking, they heard another sedan chair come in, and then the menservants announced, "Mr. Luo is here." Gold Phoenix was already at the stairs welcoming him, saying, "Brother-in-law, over here." Prosperity Luo went straight into the room opposite.

Vigor Qian wanted to take his leave, but Green Phoenix held him back and barked at Gold Flower, "Go and make yourself useful in the other room."

After Gold Flower had gone, he asked Green Phoenix in a whisper, "Have you spoken to your mother?"

"Not yet. If I do it now and it turns out badly, things can be awkward. I'll wait till after the festival and see. Don't bother yourself with things here; I'll speak for myself. Luo will pay my ransom; you just get the clothes and jewelry and furniture ready for me."[1]

Vigor gave his promise and left. She did not see him off. Instead, she put down the water pipe and called out at the door curtain, "You

::

1. [The total honesty between Green Phoenix and Vigor Qian is a clear indication of the strength of their relationship. In contrast, though Prosperity Luo knows about the existence of another client, he is never allowed to know who the man is. E.H.]

can come over now." And so Gold Phoenix brought Prosperity Luo over, holding him by the hand. Pearl Phoenix walked behind them, and Little Treasure came in last with the teacup and Luo's jacket. Gold Flower was the only one who went downstairs to keep Second Sister company.

When the clock on the wall struck ten, Prosperity told Green Phoenix he had business to attend to the next morning and wanted to go home for an early night.

"You can go to bed early here as well," she replied. "I have something to say to you; don't go home."

Naturally, he obeyed. Promotion was told to go home with the sedan-chair bearers. Green Phoenix called for Mama Zhao to come in and tidy up and then sent Prosperity to bed. Mama Zhao, Gold Phoenix, Pearl Phoenix, and Little Treasure left one by one. Green Phoenix figured there would not be any more party calls, so she, too, went to bed. She consulted with Prosperity in low whispers under the quilt for a long while, but there's no need for us to go into the details.

Knowing that his master had to attend a wedding in a certain official's family and that the wedding banquet was to be held at the Garden of Plenty, Promotion came back with his sedan chair early the next morning. By the time Prosperity got ready and went by sedan chair to the Garden of Plenty, the place, sumptuously decorated with lanterns and draperies, was already filled with guests dressed for the occasion.

When the feast was over, Prosperity did not leave by sedan chair but arranged to take a leisurely walk with the brothers Cloud and Jade Tao and Amity and Modesty Zhu. They happened to run into Benevolence Hong, and, after a brief greeting, everybody stood talking. It suddenly occurred to Amity Zhu that Whistler Tang had said something about Benevolence taking his younger brother, Modesty, to tea at Twin Jade's. Afraid that Modesty was too young to know how to control or protect himself, he wanted to see how he had got on, so he said to Benevolence, "We haven't seen your lady love for quite a few days, shall we go and look in on her together?"

Benevolence guessed his intentions and gladly led the way.

"We won't come along," Cloud Tao said. "There're so many of us, it's bound to be awkward."

"It's all right, I'll make it an occasion," replied Amity.

With Benevolence Hong leading the way, the six men headed for Twin Pearl's in Sunshine Alley. Twin Pearl was puzzled by this group visit. After greeting them and inviting them to sit down, she called for Twin Jade to come over.

The minute Amity Zhu saw Twin Jade, he said to Modesty,

"Though you've called her a couple of times, you've yet to give a party at her place. Since all our friends are here today, I'll throw a party on your behalf and treat them all to dinner."

Modesty Zhu had no idea how he should respond, and the embarrassment made him flush completely red in the face. Prosperity Luo, on the other hand, was delighted, saying repeatedly, "Excellent, excellent." He told the servant girl, Clever Baby, "Hurry up, go place the order!"

Modesty became agitated. He stood up to stop it. "Let's have the dinner party in a restaurant. We can send call chits from there."

Prosperity shouted, "We don't want to go to a restaurant. It's nice here." Brooking no protests, he told Clever Baby to order dinner. "Set the table right away."

Cloud Tao said to Amity Zhu, "You're all right as elder brothers go, but it's a pity Modesty is not as good at having fun as you are. If our Jade were your brother, then you'd really have some great times together."

Jade Tao was a bit embarrassed to hear himself mentioned. But Amity Zhu said in all seriousness, "Since we live in the foreign settlements, it's just as well to let them have some fun. If you're used to it from a young age, it's no great shakes. On the other hand, someone shut in the schoolroom all the time may seem well behaved, but once they're let out, they just throw themselves at it, and then they're in trouble."

Benevolence Hong chipped in. "What you say is true, but it depends on the person, too. With Modesty, you don't have to worry. But somebody who has a taste for the fun really mustn't be indulged."

All this made Modesty Zhu so uneasy he could not sit still. Pretending to look at calligraphy and painting scrolls, he walked to a corner of the room and stood facing the wall. Even Twin Jade slipped out of the room.

Twin Pearl said smiling, "The two of them are cut from the same cloth. They never have a word to say, but deep down they're both clever."

At this, everybody laughed, and the conversation came to an end. They waited till Golden came in to report that the table was set before they walked across to Twin Jade's room. The call chits were immediately issued and hot towels produced. They sat down casually, without the routine of giving one another precedence. Although Modesty Zhu was host, he did not ply his guests with wine and food. Instead he sat there mutely, his hands folded together and his head bowed. Twin Jade, sitting beside him, only managed to say, "Please help yourselves." When everybody lifted his cup to thank him for dinner, Modesty's bashfulness prevented him from responding. Worth brought the first course, shark's fin. After everybody had tasted it, Modesty still had not lifted his chopsticks.

"What kind of a host are you? D'you want your guests to invite you to partake?" said an amused Prosperity Luo, lifting his own ivory chopsticks. "Please, please!"

Modesty was so embarrassed that he just looked away.

"The more you speak to him, the more bashful he gets. It's best to leave him alone for a while," said Amity Zhu. That gave Modesty Zhu license to sit back. Fortunately, the resident girl, Twin Pearl, was there to entertain on his behalf, so things were not too quiet at the table.

Presently, Green Phoenix, White Fragrance, Belle Tan, and Water Blossom all arrived. Prosperity Luo was the first to be banker. Though there were just six at table, spirits were still high. Modesty Zhu caught an opportunity to look back at Twin Jade from the corner of his eye and saw that she was also sitting bolt upright and in silence; a black summer silk handkerchief was hanging out of her sleeve. Taking advantage of the noisy finger game, he reached out a hand to pull at her handkerchief. She felt the pull and quickly tucked it back inside her sleeve, paying him no attention. That move having failed, he unfastened a fan pendant from his belt. It was a green jade monkey, and he put it furtively in her lap. She quickly drew back her hands. He had thought she was sure to accept the gift and so had let go; the monkey slid onto the floor.

Twin Pearl heard the sound. "Did you drop something?" she asked and then told Clever Baby to look under the table. Alarmed, Modesty tried to pick it up himself. To his surprise, Twin Jade put her foot on the monkey and kept it hidden under the flared bottom of her trouser leg, saying, "It's nothing." She then diverted Clever Baby by giving her the wine pot to fill and so managed to cover up the matter.

Now it was Modesty's turn to challenge the bank. Prosperity Luo extended a fist, waiting. Modesty hastily obliged and lost five rounds in a row. He had just taken the penalty cup when he heard Twin Pearl calling loudly, "Twin Jade, come and substitute for the drinking." He turned around, and sure enough Twin Jade had left the table; the green jade monkey on the floor had also disappeared. Only then was he reassured. Clever Baby, who had come back with the wine, took two cups for him, and then Twin Jade was told to drink the rest. After drinking his penalty wine, she sat down primly behind him. He peeked at her and saw she had another handkerchief in her sleeve, this time of pale turquoise summer silk, also hanging out. Now he understood. He stealthily reached out a hand to pull it. Her attention on the finger game, her face blank, she did not feel it at all, and he succeeded. Overjoyed, he tucked the handkerchief in his gown. He wanted to leave the table to admire the handkerchief in private but for fear of being noticed had to be patient for the moment.

Prosperity Luo's high spirits were undiminished; he insisted that everybody take turns as banker after him. Later, Jade Tao succumbed to the wine and had to leave early with Water Blossom. They were followed by White Fragrance and Belle Tan. Finally, Green Phoenix removed Prosperity's wine cups, took him in hand, and forbade any further horseplay. Only then was the party over, and Green Phoenix hustled her patron home with her.

Amity Zhu and Cloud Tao went to lie down on the divan to smoke and chat, while Benevolence Hong went over to Twin Pearl's room. Left alone, Modesty Zhu sneaked out into the parlor and took out the handkerchief. As he shook it out, he seemed to sense a warm fragrance, but when he sniffed at it, the fragrance was gone. He looked at the handkerchief: it was brand-new, made of pale turquoise summer silk and embroidered with a tea-green blanket stitch border. Perhaps it was Twin Jade who embroidered it? After a moment's foolish thoughts, he folded it up and hid it in a silk purse. Just as he was about to turn around, he saw Twin Jade standing behind the screen door peeping out, smiling. Bashful as ever, he was going to avoid her, but she nodded and beckoned him. Overjoyed, he came up to her in a hurry.

Now she looked displeased and grumbled, "Don't you know how to get here by now? Why did you come with so many people?"

He apologized in a low voice, "Then I'll come by myself in a couple of days."

"Are you so busy that you have to wait a couple of days?"

"Sorry," he apologized again. "I'll come tomorrow. Definitely tomorrow."

She said no more, and he went back into the room.

When Amity Zhu and Cloud Tao each had had a couple of smokes, it was already time to light the lamps. They called Benevolence Hong over and arranged to leave together along with Modesty Zhu. Twin Pearl and Twin Jade saw them to the stairs, bidding them good-bye. After that, Twin Pearl returned to her room, and Twin Jade followed her. Twin Pearl was perplexed. They sat facing each other on the divan. Twin Jade smiled bashfully and then took out the green jade monkey to show Elder Sister. Twin Pearl saw that it was green all over except for its head, which was pure white, and the peach of immortality hugged to its chest, which was red. Then there were two black spots cleverly carved as the eyes. Her guess was that, though not a rare treasure, it would not have come cheap.

"Did Fifth Young Master give it to you?" she asked. Twin Jade did not answer, just nodded. "That's a token for you. Put it away and keep it safe," she said smiling.

Twin Jade's face suddenly crumpled, as if she were about to cry. "Elder Sister," she pleaded, "Don't let Mr. Hong know."

"Why?"

"Mr. Hong will tell their family."

"Why would he want to do that?"

Twin Jade had trouble getting her words out.

Twin Pearl pointed two fingers at her and laughed, "You're a real amateur. Why, you've just started seeing Fifth Young Master, and by taking Mr. Hong into your confidence, you can ask him to help. If Fifth Young Master doesn't come, you can have Mr. Hong go and invite him. Wouldn't that be good for you? Why would you want to keep him in the dark?"

"Then will you please mention it to Mr. Hong, Elder Sister?"

Twin Pearl pondered. "I don't mind doing that, but you must tell me everything Fifth Young Master said. Then I'll speak for you."

"Fifth Young Master didn't say anything, just that he'll come tomorrow."

Twin Pearl pondered this silently.

Twin Jade took the green jade monkey and went merrily downstairs to Orchid Zhou's room to show her. She saw Orchid Zhou lying on the divan with her eyes closed, deep in an opium doze, while Twin Jewel was lolling on the divan, toasting opium. Not daring to disturb her, Twin Jade was about to withdraw when Orchid Zhou opened her eyes and called out to stop her, asking, "What is it?"

In Twin Jewel's presence, Twin Jade was vague and evasive, unwilling to produce her treasure. Orchid Zhou thought she wanted to complain about Twin Jewel again, so she sent Twin Jewel away on some pretext.

After Twin Jewel had gone, Twin Jade drew near and leaned against Orchid Zhou's thigh; she handed over the green jade monkey. Orchid Zhou held it in her palm and marveled at it.

Brimming with happiness, Twin Jade was just going to tell her about Modesty Zhu when she suddenly heard the sound of Twin Jewel's footsteps on the stairs. She hastily put away her monkey, took her leave from Orchid Zhou, and tiptoed upstairs after her.

Seeing Twin Jewel go straight into Twin Pearl's room, she stood quietly behind the door curtain to eavesdrop. She heard Twin Jewel complain tearfully: "I've run into an enemy from my last incarnation! We've only just had a scene, and now she's bad-mouthing me again. It's certain death for me."

"It's not about you," Twin Pearl said.

"Of course it is! Otherwise why was I told to go away?"

Hearing this, Twin Jade felt as if there were a charcoal fire burning in her breast. She flung aside the curtain and walked proudly in, sat down in a high-back chair by the wall, and said arrogantly, "So you won't let me have a word with Mother, is that it? I'll do as you say then. From now on, I'll never go to Mother's room or say a word to her. Does that satisfy you?"

Tired of their quarrels, Twin Pearl frowned and told them off. "What's the big deal?" She sent Twin Jewel away and quelled Twin Jade's anger. Since this was how her elder sister felt, Twin Jade had to let the matter rest.

After dinner, everyone was busy answering party calls. At some time after ten, Twin Pearl came back first, with a heavily drunk Benevolence Hong on her heels. She told Golden to make a cup of strong tea to quench his thirst and, as they were chatting, mentioned Modesty Zhu and Twin Jade.

Twin Pearl first laughed to herself and then said, "The virgin courtesans nowadays have more tricks up their sleeves than their seniors. You were there at the table, but you didn't notice anything, did you?"

Benevolence asked what she meant, so she told him in detail about Modesty's giving Twin Jade the green jade fan pendant.

He replied, "It seems Twin Jade is ready to do grown-up work. Let him come and light the big candles then."

"Good. You be the matchmaker," she said.

"I'll leave that to you and help you on the side."

She agreed, and they worked out a plan, after which they settled down for the night. The next day, they both got up around noon. After they had washed their faces and broken their fast, Golden submitted an invitation. Prosperity saw it was from Lotuson Wang, asking him to Constance's for consultations. He told the messenger to say he had got the note and made ready to go right away. Twin Pearl bade him, "Come back later."

"Later, Modesty will be here. It'll be awkward if I come." Twin Pearl knew he was right.

After leaving Twin Pearl's, Benevolence Hong walked out of Sunshine Alley, cut to East Co-prosperity Alley through Co-security Alley, and then went up to Constance's room. Constance had not yet had her hair done but was toasting opium for Lotuson Wang. Lotuson came up to greet him and sent the maid to place the order for a snack. When Benevolence had taken his seat, Lotuson handed him a shopping list and asked him to help. He saw that it was for a complete set of green jade jewelry, with a special note saying everything must be pure green.

"With green jade, it's best if you and I shop together," said Benevolence. "If you're willing to make do, a hundred-odd dollars will get you a set. But if you want a good set that's pure green, I'm afraid it will come to a thousand or so."

"I told you it'd be over a thousand," Constance put in. "It's easy to work out: just a pair of bracelets easily costs several hundred."

"Is it for you?" Benevolence asked.

She broke out laughing. "You must be joking, Mr. Hong. Do I deserve anything like this? I don't even have a complete set in gold yet, what do I want green jade for?"

He guessed it was for Little Rouge.

She went to do her hair at the parlor window, while Lotuson lay smoking on the divan. Benevolence moved over to the divan's humbler side and asked, "You've spent quite a bit at Little Rouge's this year. Is it necessary to buy her a green jade jewelry set?" Lotuson wrinkled up his forehead but said nothing. "It seems to me you can just say no."

Lotuson sighed. "Get her a couple of things first. We'll see about the rest."

Benevolence gathered it was no use advising him, so he held his tongue.

In a moment, the maid brought the four small dishes ordered from the Garden of Plenty and four cold plates prepared at home and then warmed a pot of wine. Lotuson asked Benevolence to sit opposite him for a simple meal.

CHAPTER 33 :: *Little Rouge is unhappy with the jade jewelry, and Lotuson Wang goes on a drunken rampage*

After drinking for a while with Lotuson Wang, Benevolence Hong went to relieve himself. On his way back, Constance beckoned to him in the parlor, so he walked over.

She whispered, "Mr. Hong, when you go and buy the jewelry, would you please just do as she says and get the whole set? Mr. Wang's fear of this Little Rouge really knows no limits. You haven't seen his shoulders and arms; they're badly cut all over because Little Rouge pinched him with her sharp fingernails. If you don't get her the full jewelry set, I don't know how she'll torture him, so please just get it for her. It doesn't matter if Mr. Wang has to spend a bit more."

He smiled without replying and returned to the table quietly. Lo-tuson Wang had caught the conversation faintly but pretended he had not heard. The two of them finished the pot of wine and asked for rice. Constance, who had now finished her toilet, sat down at the table's humble side to eat with them.

The meal over, Benevolence set out for the jewelry stores in the Old City, while Lotuson told Constance to toast more opium for him. After smoking a dozen pellets, his appetite was finally satisfied. Benevolence returned as the clock struck five. He had only bought two items, the bracelets and the comb, which cost over four hundred dollars. He could not find the right quality for the rest and so had left them until another day. Overjoyed, Lotuson thanked him for his trouble.

Benevolence had business to attend to at the Flourishing Ginseng Store, so he took his leave. Lotuson Wang also bade Constance good-bye and went by sedan chair to West Floral Alley to deliver the jewelry to Little Rouge.

"Where's Mr. Hong?" Little Rouge asked as soon as she saw him.

"He's gone home."

"Well, did he go and get it?"

"He bought a couple of things." He lifted the lid off the cardboard box, took out the comb and bracelets, and put them on the table. "Take a look. The bracelets are all right, but the comb is not quite as good. If you don't like it, we'll send it back and get another one."

She didn't even take a proper look at the jewelry. "That's not a whole set. Just put it there," she said indifferently.

He hastened to return everything to the box, which he then put in a drawer of the dressing table. "He couldn't find the right quality for the rest of the set. I'll go and make the choice myself in a couple of days."

"Well, since all I get are the leftovers, what quality is there to speak of?" she said.

"Whose leftovers are you talking about?"

"Why were these things taken to the other place first?"

In his agitation, Lotuson produced the sales slip to show her. "Look, it's all on the sales slip."

She pushed it aside. "I'm not interested."

He backed away dejectedly. Pearlie, who happened to come in to freshen the tea, guffawed. "Mr. Wang has had too much fun at Constance's, so it's right he comes here for a little talking to, no?"

He could only smile awkwardly and let it pass.

It was getting dark. Talisman submitted an invitation from Elan Ge, asking him to dinner at Snow Scent's. As Little Rouge was looking displeased, Lotuson took the opportunity to leave. She neither detained him nor saw him out.

Lotuson went by sedan chair to Snow Scent's. The host, Elan Ge, came up to greet him and asked him to be seated. Only two guests had come before him. When they introduced themselves, he learned that one was Second Bai Gao, the other Devotion Yin. Although this was their first meeting, Lotuson had long been aware of their reputation as talented poets of Zhejiang and Jiangsu provinces.[1] He saluted them, saying, "Delighted to meet you."

Then the attendants outside reported, "The guest at Sky in a Wine Pot said please take your seat first." So Elan Ge told them to set the table. Lotuson Wang asked who else was coming. "Iron Hua" was the reply.

This Iron Hua, the guest of honor, was a family friend of Lotuson's. Since he did not like crowds, Elan Ge only invited three guests to keep him company. After a moment's wait, he arrived with his girl, White Orchid. Elan Ge issued three call chits and asked everyone to come to the table.

"Have you met the woman of your dreams yet?" Iron Hua asked Second Bai. When the latter shook his head, he said, "You'd never expect a man of such sensibilities as Second Bai would be so hard to please."

"I quite understand his temperament," Devotion Yin said. "A pity I'm not a courtesan. If I were one, I'd make him thoroughly lovesick and die of longing for me in Shanghai."

Second Bai laughed. "Though you're not a courtesan, I'm still pining for you."

Devotion Yin also broke out laughing. "I suppose I brought the insult on myself."[2]

Iron Hua quoted: "'Everybody wishes to be the master's concubine. Marriage ties to be realized in the next incarnation.' This makes a good anecdote, too."

Devotion Yin insisted on punishing Second Bai for the insult and told Little Sister to get the large wine cups.

"With his capacity, drinking is no punishment for him," Iron Hua said.

The argument was still going on when the girls arrived. Second Bai had called River Blossom, and Devotion Yin Green Fragrance, both virgin courtesans, while Lotuson Wang just called Constance

::

1. Zhejiang and Jiangsu were the two provinces well known over the ages for producing literary talent.

2. Though homosexual relationships were not rare in dynastic China, it was still an insult to say that a man took on the woman's role in such a relationship.

from across the way. When the finger game started, the girls vied with one another to substitute for the penalty wine. Second Bai, set on getting Devotion Yin drunk, would not allow any substitutes for him. Lotuson, guessing what he was after, helped him to make fun of Devotion. But Devotion excelled at the game and actually got Lotuson drunk first.

Constance stayed until Lotuson was banker and, before she left, advised him repeatedly not to drink anymore. However, Iron Hua was as keen a drinker as Second Bai. When the finger game was over and the girls were gone, he wanted to play the drinking game Catch Seven, and the others had no choice but to keep him company. Lotuson Wang, who was less than alert, kept making mistakes and ended up drinking a lot more. At one point, he felt he could not bear up any longer, so he did not wait for the end of the game but just went to lie down on the divan. Seeing this, Iron Hua wound up the game hastily.

Elan Ge asked Lotuson Wang to have a little congee, but he waved it away and instead tried to toast some opium. Since he could not hold the pick steadily over the flame, the opium dripped on the tray. Snow Scent called at once for Little Sister to help fill the pipe, but Lotuson again waved her away. Then he suddenly got up, saluted everybody, and took his leave. Elan Ge could not very well detain him, so he saw him off at the door and told Talisman to attend to him carefully.

Talisman saw Lotuson into the sedan chair, hung up the chair curtain, fixed the hand rest, and asked, "Where to, sir?"

"West Floral," replied Lotuson. With Talisman running beside the sedan chair, they went straight to Little Rouge's in West Floral Alley, alighting in the parlor.

As Lotuson headed up the stairs, Pearlie hurried out from the kitchen and called out loudly, "Aiyo! Mr. Wang, watch your step!" Lotuson did not answer, just kept running. A smiling Pearlie followed closely behind him into Little Rouge's room, saying, "You gave me a fright, Mr. Wang. It's a good thing you didn't trip and fall."

He looked around and did not see Little Rouge, so he asked Pearlie.

"She's probably downstairs."

He asked no more, just collapsed onto the leather chair by the bed. Fully dressed and not even asking for opium, he dropped off. A manservant brought a kettle and a hot towel.

"Mr. Wang, would you like to wipe your face?" Pearlie whispered. He did not answer. She signaled the manservant with her eyes for him just to fill the teacup and go. Then she walked quietly out, tapped three times on door of the mezzanine room, and said, "Mr. Wang is asleep."

Perhaps these events were decreed by fate. Now although Lotuson was snoring loudly, he was not asleep and was greatly surprised by Pearlie's behavior. The minute she went downstairs, he got up and walked softly to the back of the parlor. There was some light in the mezzanine room. He pushed at the door to find it barred from the inside. He looked around and saw there was a hole the size of a pigeon egg in the partition wall, so he peeped in. There had always been just a divan in the mezzanine room, without bed curtains, so everything was visible at a glance. He saw two people lying on the divan in each other's embrace; one was definitely Little Rouge, and the other was a familiar face as well. He searched his memory: it was none other than Little Willow, the male lead of the theater troupe at Panorama Garden.

Lotuson was in a towering rage. He turned round, rushed into Little Rouge's room, and made for the dressing table by the bed. A violent shove brought it toppling to the ground, with lamps, mirrors, clock, vases, and all. As for whether the newly purchased jade comb and bracelets in the drawer were broken, we will never know. When the maid Pearlie heard the noise, she rushed upstairs, knowing things had gone wrong. The servant girl Goldie and a few menservants also came in a body. Lotuson was now at the divan. He picked up the opium tray and threw it at the center table, scattering all the equipment and ornaments in it across the room. Pearlie flung her arms around him from behind, holding on to him desperately by the waist. Though always timid and frail, at this moment Lotuson was as strong as a tiger. Pearlie was no match for him; he was rid of her with one hefty kick. Even Goldie backed away several steps.

Lotuson picked up the opium pipe and lashed out at everything around the room. Except for the two hanging paraffin lamps, everything made of glass—table lamps, wall lamps, glass frames of paintings, the wardrobe mirror, and the framed panel over the bed—was smashed to smithereens. Although there were three or four menservants present, the most they could do was put themselves between Lotuson and his target because they dared not lay hands on him. Talisman and the two sedan-chair bearers peeped in from behind the door curtain but did not enter the room. Goldie stood trembling to one side, stunned. Pearlie, unable to climb to her feet, merely kept shouting in panic, "Don't, Mr. Wang!"

He heard nothing, just kept hitting out wildly, battering his way to and fro across the room. In the heat of this uncontrollable rampage, a young man dashed into the room, threw himself on the ground, and started kowtowing, shouting, "Have mercy, Mr. Wang! Have mercy, Mr. Wang!"

Lotuson saw that it was Little Rouge's own brother. The sight of him kowtowing on the floor touched a soft spot in Lotuson's heart. With a sigh, he threw down the opium pipe, pushed his way out of the crowd, and rushed off. Startled, Talisman and the two sedan-chair bearers hurried after him. He did not take the sedan chair, though, just ran straight out the front door. Leaving the bearers behind, Talisman gave chase. He saw Lotuson going into East Co-prosperity Alley; only then did he turn back to fetch the sedan chair.

Lotuson ran to Constance's and burst into her room without waiting to be announced. He collapsed on the chair panting and gasping, trying to catch his breath. This gave Constance such a turn that she just stared at him, not daring to ask what had happened. After a long while, she tested the waters with a question, "Has the party been over for a while now?" He glared straight ahead without a word. She secretly sent her maid to find out from Talisman, who had just arrived with the sedan chair. On being told briefly what had happened, the maid came back and whispered into Constance's ear. Only then was she reassured. Failing to think of anything to say that would divert Lotuson, she went and filled a pipe of opium, asked him to smoke, and then unbuttoned and took off his summer silk gown for him.

He went through a dozen pellets of opium in silence. She waited on him attentively but did not attempt to talk to him. After about an hour, she asked quietly, "Would you like a little congee?" He shook his head. "Then let's go to bed." He nodded. So she passed on the order to Talisman to take the sedan chair home and told the maid to make the bed. Constance helped him out of his clothes, took off his socks, and lay down with him. As she drifted off to sleep, she could still hear him groaning and sighing as he tossed and turned.

By the time Constance woke up the morning, sun was shining on the window. She saw Lotuson lying there staring at the canopy of the bed. She could not help asking, "Did you get any sleep?" He still did not answer. She sat up, tucked up her hair a bit, and bent down to ask him, her face close to his, "Why are you like this? If you let this anger ruin your health, is it worth it?"

What she said suddenly gave him an idea. He pushed her aside, sat up in bed, and asked her huffily, "I want to ask you: will you help me get even?"

Failing to understand what he meant, Constance's face flushed red in agitation. "What are you talking about? Did I do you wrong?"

Seeing that she had taken it the wrong way, Lotuson actually broke into a smile. He hooked an arm around her neck and lay down with her, explaining at length about Little Rouge's scandal and his intention to marry Constance as a concubine. Would Constance show any objection? She was all willingness and obedience, and the matter was settled at once.

Presently, the two of them got up to wash. He told the maid to summon Talisman, who had been in attendance since early in the morning. He came in at once. Lotuson first asked whether there was any official business.

"None," Talisman replied. "But Little Rouge's brother and her maid came to the residence, crying, smiling, and kowtowing, saying to ask Master to call in."

Before he had finished, Lotuson barked at him, "I don't want to hear about it!"

He answered "yes, sir" several times, took two steps back, and stood stiffly at attention, waiting for orders. After a while, Lotuson said, "Ask Mr. Hong here."

Talisman went downstairs bearing the message, left word for the sedan-chair bearers, and went his way. He thought to himself: best to go first to Little Rouge's to report the news and get credit for it. So he turned to West Floral Alley from the northern end of East Co-prosperity Alley. Little Rouge's brother was overjoyed. Talisman was invited into the bookkeeper's room, where the brother respectfully presented him with a water pipe.

Talisman smoked as he said, "I don't have much of an idea except for putting in a good word for you. Now I'm told to go and invite Mr. Hong. I suggest you come with me and ask Mr. Hong to think of something. That'd be much more effective than anything I say."

Full of gratitude, Little Rouge's brother told Pearlie about it, and the three of them went on their way. They headed for Twin Pearl's at Sunshine Alley, only to learn that Benevolence was not there. So they each took a ricksha to Lu Stone Bridge at Little East Gate and from there walked to the Flourishing Ginseng Store. The apprentice at the store knew Talisman and hastened to announce him. The minute Benevolence Hong came out into the parlor, Little Rouge's brother went up and kowtowed to him, his face soon wet with crying and sniveling as he told of Mr. Wang's inexplicable anger and so on and so forth. After hearing him out, Benevolence had a pretty good idea of what had happened.

"What are you here for?" He turned to Talisman.

"My master asks you to drop in at Constance's, sir," said Talisman.

Benevolence bowed his head and thought for a moment and then told the two men to wait in the parlor while he and the maid Pearlie went into an inner room for detailed consultation.

Talisman and Little Rouge's brother waited in the parlor for a long time. When the maid Pearlie finally came out, she unexpectedly took Little Rouge's brother off with her. Talisman had to wait a little longer before Benevolence Hong came out to tell him, "They want me to put in a good word for them in front of Mr. Wang. Since I'm his friend, it's a bit awkward. What about this: I'll take Mr. Wang to their place, and they can do the talking themselves, what d'you think?"

Talisman was of course all for it. So Benevolence went to Constance's in East Co-prosperity Alley in a ricksha, with Talisman in tow.

Lotuson Wang had just ordered four small dishes and was drinking in glum solitude. When Benevolence came in, Lotuson invited him to sit down.

"Worn out from last night?" Benevolence asked, smiling.

"So now you're teasing me! I did ask you to find out about her, but you refused," Lotuson replied in mock vexation.

"What was there to find out?"

"When a courtesan takes up with an actor, aren't there many ways of finding out about it?"

"It was you who brought about all this by taking her on carriage rides; that was how the whole thing came about. Didn't I tell you Little Rouge incurred too much expense because of carriage rides? Too bad you didn't catch my meaning."

Lotuson held up a hand to stop him. "Say no more. Let's drink."

The maid brought another cup and a pair of chopsticks, while Constance came over to pour the wine herself. Lotuson said to Benevolence, "Forget about the green jade jewelry set." He produced another shopping list consisting, among other things, of a dark blue cape and a scarlet skirt—a bride's outfit—and asked Benevolence to see to it as soon as possible.

"Congratulations!" Benevolence smiled at Constance, who was so embarrassed she walked away.

Benevolence then turned to Lotuson and said earnestly, "Your marriage to Maestro Constance is a fine thing. But it'd be a bit awkward if you stop going to Little Rouge's just like that."

"Awkward or not, it's none of your business!" Lotuson retorted, losing his temper.

Somewhat embarrassed, Benevolence smiled and said mildly, "That's not what I mean. Since Little Rouge has no other client but yourself, if you stop going, she'll be at a loss. And with the festival approaching, she'll have to pay up her many bills. Then there're her parents and brother; the family needs food and money, too. What can she do about it? If she sees no way out, she just might take her own life. Now Little Rouge's life may not matter much, but if she dies because of you, it'd be a blemish on your karma, too. We come out to look for fun, not bad karma, so why push it?"

Lotuson pondered and nodded. "So—you, too, are speaking up for them."

Benevolence's face turned livid. "What d'you mean by that? Why would I want to speak up for them?"

"You're telling me to go to her place, isn't that speaking up for them?"

Benevolence heaved a long sigh, but then he smiled. "All the time when you were seeing Little Rouge, I told you it wasn't worth your while, but did you listen to me? No. You doted on her. But now that you're angry, you turn around and say I'm speaking up for her. That really leaves me with nothing to say."

"Then why d'you want me to go there?"

"I'm not suggesting that you should go on seeing her, just that you should go one more time."

"What for?"

"It's for your own protection, in case anything happens. If you go, they'll feel relieved, and you can also take a look at how things are with them. You've been seeing her for four or five years and must have spent some ten thousand dollars on her, so it doesn't make sense to withhold money for this last bill. Go settle the account with her so she can pay her expenses and get through the festival. Come the next season, whether you see her or not is up to you, right?"

Lotuson heard him out but said nothing, so Benevolence tried to encourage him. "I'll go with you later and see what she has to say. If there's half a word that jars on the ear, we'll just leave."

Lotuson jumped up from his chair, yelling, "I'm not going!"

Benevolence had to cut himself short with an awkward smile. After they had each had several cups of wine, they took lunch with Constance as usual. Then Benevolence had to see to Lotuson's shopping list, while Lotuson wanted to return to his residence. An appointment was made for Benevolence to meet him at Constance's again at sundown. Benevolence gave his promise and left.

Lotuson took a few more puffs of opium and then called out for his sedan chair. When he got back to his residence on Fifth Avenue, he went to his upstairs bedroom and wrote a couple of routine social letters, with Talisman waiting on him. Suddenly, they heard the doorbell chime. Somebody seemed to come in and start talking to Lotuson's nephew in the courtyard, and then a sedan chair came and stopped at the door. Thinking it was a visitor, Lotuson told Talisman to go and find out. Talisman did not come back to report; instead came the clickety sound of bound-feet shoes up the stairs.

Lotuson went to the outer room to see for himself. It was none other than Little Rouge, followed by Pearlie. He was outraged at the sight of her. "How dare you show your face here! Get out!" He roared, stamping his foot.

Little Rouge stood there silently, her eyes filled with tears. Pearlie came up and tried to explain, but Lotuson would not be calmed down. He kept shouting wildly and incoherently.

Pearlie simply sat down. When Lotuson's fury had slightly abated, she said in a ringing voice, "Mr. Wang, suppose you were the judge and we brought a complaint, you'd have to listen to the details of our case before you could pass sentence, be it a beating or some other form of punishment, right? Now we're not allowed to say a word. So if an injustice has been done, how are you to find out?"

"How have I done her an injustice?" he asked huffily.

"Our maestro has been wronged, sir, and she wants to tell you about it. Will you let her?"

"Since she's been wronged, she might as well go and marry the actor."

Pearlie gave a mock chuckle. "If her brother wronged her, she could tell her parents; if her parents wronged her, she could tell you. But when you wrong her, sir, there's really nobody for her to turn to." Then she said to Little Rouge, "Let's go. What else can we say?"

Little Rouge was sitting in a high-back chair, sobbing into a handkerchief. With another outburst, Lotuson ran into his bedroom, leaving Little Rouge and Pearlie to their own ends. All was quiet. He picked up his writing brush to continue with his letter, but the words would not come. His attention was drawn to the whispering in the outer room. A while later, Little Rouge actually came into the bedroom and sat down facing him across the desk. He buried his head in his writing.

She spoke in a trembling voice, "You can accuse me of all sorts of things, and I won't defend myself. I was indeed in the wrong. I didn't do right by you, so I'm willing to take whatever you mete out. But why won't you let me speak? Do you really want to drive me to an unjust death?" Having said this, she started choking and was about to cry again.

Lotuson put down his writing brush to hear her out.

"It's my own mother who's been my ruin. She was the one who

made me go into the business, and she was the one who insisted I renew my relationship with an old patron. I listened to her because she's my mother. I did it against my own will, and now you use that to accuse me of taking up with an actor!"[1]

Lotuson was about to retort when Talisman rushed upstairs to announce, "Mr. Hong is here." He got up and said to Little Rouge, "You and I have nothing to talk about. Please go; I have something else to attend to." He then walked away, leaving Little Rouge in the bedroom and Pearlie in the outer room, and went with Benevolence Hong to Constance's in East Co-prosperity Alley.

Constance showed Lotuson Benevolence's purchases, and Lotuson told her how Little Rouge apologized. They all laughed and sighed over it. Benevolence stayed for supper that evening.

As they got ready for bed, a smiling Constance asked Lotuson, "Will you be seeing Little Rouge again?"

"Let Little Willow be her patron," he replied.

"Even if you won't be seeing her, don't be nasty to her, either," she said. "If she asks you to go there, there's no harm in going as long as you act thus and thus." She then told him what he should do.

"At first, it seemed that Little Rouge suited me rather well. But now that she's no longer fierce, I actually look down on her. It's puzzling."

"Probably your fated affinity has come to an end," she said. After a leisurely discussion, they drifted off to sleep.

The next day was the third of the fifth month. Benevolence Hong came to consult with Lotuson in the afternoon. As they agreed that the arrangements were mostly ready, the conversation turned again to Little Rouge. Benevolence repeated his advice as before, and because of what Constance had said to him, Lotuson readily agreed to go.

And so Benevolence Hong and Lotuson Wang set off to see Little Rouge. As Constance saw them out at her door, she signaled Lotuson with her eyes, and he acknowledged it with a smile. When they arrived at Little Rouge's door in West Floral Alley, Pearlie came out to meet them. Delighted by this unexpected visit, she said guffawing, "We thought Mr. Wang would never come here again. It's a good thing our maestro hasn't worried herself to death." Her awkward laughter accompanied them all the way to the room upstairs.

::

1. [As a courtesan, Little Rouge is entitled to take on paying clients other than Lotuson Wang. That is why she claims Little Willow is a client. Had that really been the case, Lotuson, however jealous he might feel, would not be in a position to fault her. E.H.]

Little Rouge got up to greet them and then drew back and sat down mutely. Lotuson saw that she was wearing a plain off-white cotton blouse and no makeup, as if in mourning. Then he looked at the room: it was empty of all furnishings except for a full-length wall mirror, cracked at a corner. Struck by the contrast between such desolation and what he remembered of the past, he heaved a long sigh.

Pearlie made conversation while serving them tea. "When Mr. Wang accused our maestro of such and such wrongdoings, our people downstairs asked me where the rumor had come from. I told them, 'In his heart of hearts, Mr. Wang knows the truth. He's accusing her just because he is too angry now. It's not as if he really thinks she's taken up with an actor.'"

"Actor or no actor, what does it matter? Say no more," said Lotuson. Pearlie left after doing her chores.

Trying to break the ice, Benevolence said pleasantly to Little Rouge, "You pined for Mr. Wang when he didn't come, so why don't you say something now that he's here?"

With a forced smile, she took a pick to toast opium at the divan, prepared a pipe, and set it on the honored side. When Lotuson lay down to smoke, she said, "When I was fourteen, I used this opium set to fill the pipe for my mother, and since then it has been left untouched. Now it has come in handy."

Benevolence asked about this and that, saying whatever came into his head. Even before it was dark, Pearlie asked them to place their order for a casual dinner. Not waiting for Lotuson's response, Benevolence took the decision and ordered four dishes. Lotuson went along with it.

By the time dinner was over, Pearlie had already sent away Talisman and the sedan-chair bearers. Now that Lotuson was there, would they let him go? Benevolence took his leave and went home by himself, leaving Lotuson and Little Rouge alone in the room.

Only then did Little Rouge speak. "In the four or five years I've known you, I have never seen you so angry. I do know that your anger at me shows that you care. Oh, the way you blew up! It was my fault that I followed my mother's orders before I had talked to you about it. But if you accuse me of taking up with an actor, then even death will not put an end to my sense of grievance. Fashionable courtesans doing good business may want to amuse themselves with actors, but is my business good enough for that? I'm not an ignorant child, either. Don't I know that taking up with an actor would mean the end of my business? People are all jealous because you're so close to me. It's not just Constance; even your friends say bad things about me. So when you accuse me of having taken up with an actor, there's no one to speak up for me. The truth won't be known until I'm at the court of the king of the dead."

"If you say you didn't, you didn't. What's so serious about it?" he responded with a smile.

"My body was born of my parents, but everything else I own, be it a piece of cloth or a length of thread, has been a gift from you, so it's all right for you to smash them up. But if you want to cast me off, can you imagine what else I have to live for? There's no other way out for me but death. If I die, it won't be your fault; the blame's on my mother. But this concerns your interests, too: you're here in Shanghai on a posting, without your family for company. At your residence, there's no one but a clumsy and thoughtless valet to take care of you. You do have friends, but even those close to you don't always understand everything. I'm the only one who knows your temperament, who can guess what is on your mind and suit your wishes. Even in our casual conversation and jokes, we always get on well. It's true that Constance is keen to play up to you, but can she be like me? You're my only client; though I'm not yet married to you, I'm as good as yours, for I'm entirely dependent on you. As for you, I know no one else pleases you like I do. Now if you cast me off in a moment of anger, the worst that can happen to me is death. But I'm worried about you. You're in your forties now, with no son or daughter. Your constitution is frail to begin with, and you like to smoke a little opium, too, so you do need somebody to keep you company, to make sure that you'll have a happy life. Yet now you harden your heart toward the one person who pleases you. If your accusations drive me to death, who is going to take care of you when you're unwell? When you let drop a remark, who will be there to guess what you want? When you look around for someone close to you, who will be there to answer your call? By that time if you think of Little Rouge, even if I rushed through a reincarnation, it'd be too late for me to come back and wait on you." So saying, she started weeping again.

Lotuson smiled again and said, "There's no need to say things like that, is there?"

Little Rouge felt that he was a changed man, completely indifferent to her. She suppressed her tears and went on, "After all I've said, you still won't relent. What more can I say? Though my faults may be numerous, in the four or five years we've been together, I must have done some good. Just remember what's good in me and look after my parents. As to me, I've told them to put me in a charity house. If one day the injustice is cleared up and you know that I've had no liaison with actors, you should take me back. Don't forget that."

Before she had finished speaking, she was again in tears. Lotuson merely smiled. There was just no way Little Rouge could move him.

When they went to bed, there was again endless tenderness and soft words on the pillow, but we will not go into the details.

The next day, Lotuson got up after noon and prepared to leave. She held on to him and asked, "Once you're gone, will you come again?"

"I will." He smiled.

"Don't try and fool me. I've said everything I can; it's all up to you now."

He pretended to smile and then left.

Not long afterward, Talisman came with the silver dollars to settle accounts for the last season. Little Rouge took the money and gave him her card as a receipt. The next three days, she saw no sign of Lotuson Wang. Though she sent Pearlie and Goldie to invite him several times, they never got to see him.

On the eighth, Pearlie, who had gone to invite Lotuson again, came back greatly agitated. She told Little Rouge, "Mr. Wang is marrying Constance. Today is their wedding day."

Incredulous, Little Rouge sent Goldie to find out. When Goldie came back, she said loudly, "It's all true! They had performed the marriage rites and were having a feast. There were lots of people. I just asked; I didn't go in."

Little Rouge was in a towering rage. She stamped her feet and cursed, "It wouldn't have mattered if you married somebody else. Why marry Constance?" She wanted to go to his house and confront him, but further consideration dampened her courage. Pearlie and Goldie went away, dispirited. Little Rouge cried the whole night long, her eyelids swelling to the size of walnuts.

The next day was the ninth. Little Rouge had fallen ill from pent-up anger. Unexpectedly, after the clock had struck noon, Talisman delivered a call chit summoning her to Lotuson's residence. He said it was a drinking party. Pearlie tried to detain him to find out more, but he rushed off on the excuse that he was busy. Since it was a party call, Little Rouge dared not turn it down. She forced herself to get up and do her toilet and then had a little breakfast before she went to the party.

When she arrived at the Wang residence on Fifth Avenue, she saw the sedan chairs of other courtesans standing at the entrance. She walked up the stairs leaning on Pearlie's arm and saw two dinner tables set side by side in the outer room, while an all-girl theater troupe was playing in the mezzanine room, the present number being the Kun opera *Jump over the Wall to Play Chess*. Little Rouge recognized all the faces round the table and realized that Lotuson's friends were clubbing together to congratulate him on taking a concubine.

Seeing Little Rouge's swollen eyes, Benevolence Hong made a point of greeting her. His mild words, which could have been taken as consoling, served to stir up what was weighing on her mind. A teardrop fell, and she almost wept aloud. He hastened to change the subject. Those at the table were moved to pity and sighed to themselves. Iron Hua, Devotion Yin, and Second Bai Gao were the only ones who did not know the story, and they took no notice of her.

The girl Second Bai had summoned was Third Treasure of Tranquillity Alley. Elan Ge knew Second Bai had not yet found the woman of his desires, so he asked, "Shall I make the rounds of all the first-class houses with you?"

Second Bai held up a hand to decline the offer. "You couldn't be more mistaken. It's no use going on a search; one's mate will appear when the time is right."

"And meanwhile our Second Bai's chivalry and tenderness are left to cool. What a pity!" said Devotion Yin.

Reminded of what had happened, Second Bai turned to Prosperity Luo, "There's a girl called Gold Flower at your lady love's place. A friend recommended her to me, but she was truly disappointing."

"Gold Flower doesn't have what it takes. She's gone to a second-class house now," Prosperity replied.

Just then a new play, *The Green Screen Mountain*, came on. The girl who took the part of Shi Xiu had a good voice and good acting skills; her performance was convincingly heroic. Her swordplay in the wine shop scene was pretty good, too. Though it was not real swordsmanship, it showed considerable training and control.

This play was a poignant reminder for Little Rouge; she blushed.[2]

Second Bai shouted, "Bravo!" but he did not know the actress's name. Elan Ge, who recognized her, told him it was Wenjun Yao of Big Feet Yao's at East Co-prosperity Alley. Devotion Yin, seeing that Second Bai was quite taken with the girl, called the troupe's maid over as soon as she had come off the stage, saying, "Mr. Gao calls Wenjun Yao to the party."

The maid immediately took Wenjun Yao to a seat behind Second Bai, who, when he looked closely at her, saw an indomitable spirit shining in her eyes: quite a challenge!

By this time, all the girls called to the party had arrived. Lotuson Wang suddenly went into the bridal chamber and after a moment's consultation came out to ask Snow Scent, Green Phoenix, Twin Pearl, Wenjun, and Little Rouge to go and meet the bride. Little Rouge had no choice but to join the other four. A smiling Constance

::

2. [Wenjun Yao is playing a role in which Little Willow excels. *E.H.*]

stood up to greet them, inviting them to sit down and chat. Little Rouge's mouth was sealed by shame and anger. Each girl received a present when she left: for Snow Scent, Green Phoenix, Twin Pearl, and Wenjun Yao, it was a green jade lotus pod hairpin, and for Little Rouge something much more valuable: a pair of earrings and a ring, both of pure green jade. She had to accept them and say thank you along with the others. By the time they returned to the party, half the summoned girls had left. Second Bai picked another play featuring Wenjun Yao. At the end of this number, all the girls were gone, so both the performance and the party drew to a close.

CHAPTER 35 :: *Second Treasure, poverty-stricken, takes up the oldest profession, and River Blossom, falling ill, spoils everyone's fun*

As the party at the Wang residence came to an end, the guests took their leave one after another. Benevolence Hong, though, stayed till dusk to help oversee various chores. When he left, he made for Twin Pearl's in Sunshine Alley. Along the way, he thought about what had happened: who could have imagined that Little Rouge's ready-made position would have been so easily lifted by Constance? What was more, Lotuson had behaved with indifference toward Little Rouge, and Little Rouge looked forlorn; it was probably all over between them.

As he turned this over in his mind, Benevolence heard someone greet him as "Uncle." He stopped and saw that it was indeed Simplicity Zhao. In a long gown of fine white cotton, silk shoes, and white socks, Simplicity had a prosperous look about him. Benevolence acknowledged his greeting with a nod. Overjoyed, Simplicity exchanged a few polite words with him and then stood at one side with the gesture of a farewell salute and watched Benevolence Hong proceed on his way via South Brocade Alley.

When Benevolence Hong had gone a long way off, Simplicity Zhao headed toward Fourth Avenue to look for Fortune Shi in the opium den at Splendid Assembly Teahouse. Fortune gave him a wad of banknotes and said, "Take this home and give it to Mother. Don't let Flora Zhang know." There was no other message.

Simplicity answered in the affirmative and returned to their house in Tranquillity Alley. He found his sister, Second Treasure, and their mother sitting face-to-face in the mezzanine room. Mrs. Zhao seemed to be sighing, while Second Treasure was wiping away tears of anger. He had no idea what had upset her.

Second Treasure said suddenly, "We're not living in her house, and we're not spending her money, so why should I suck up to her? Even the thirty dollars that we owe don't come from her! How dared she ask me for it!"

Only then did Simplicity realize the reason for their falling out with Flora Zhang. Grinning, he took out the wad of money and handed it to his mother. Mrs. Zhao gave it to Second Treasure. "You put it in a safe place."

Second Treasure turned aside in annoyance and said petulantly, "What for?"

Simplicity could not make any sense of this. Then Second Treasure said to him, "If you have money to settle our bills, we'll just pay up and go back home. Otherwise, we might as well set up our own establishment and go into the business. It's all up to you. What's the point in our staying here?"

He murmured hesitantly, "How would I know what to do? I'll do whatever you say, Sister."

"Now you're putting everything on my shoulders, so in the future don't you turn around and say I've dragged you down!" said Second Treasure.

"Of course I won't." He tried to pacify her with a smile and then withdrew. As he could not see any other way out, he was content to go along.

A few days later, Second Treasure went by herself to find rooms in Tripod Alley and brought home three hundred dollars the sing-song house had advanced her. Only then did she inform Flora of her decision. Flora knew there was no dissuading her, so she just let her go. They decided to move on the sixteenth. The new rooms were furnished with rented rosewood furniture, and a lot of household items were speedily acquired. The servant girl Clever followed them to the new place. She was joined by a maid called Tiger and a manservant, both of whom were investing two hundred dollars.[1] Simplicity personally wrote out the words "Residence of Second Treasure" on scarlet paper and pasted it at the door. That night, Fortune Shi came to give the opening dinner. The guests he invited were none other than Cloudlet Chen, Lichee Zhuang, and their group, so the news quickly reached Benevolence Hong. He sighed copiously and then decided to ignore them.

As soon as Second Treasure set up in a sing-song house, her business flourished. Mah-jongg parties and dinner parties came back to

::

1. This arrangement means Second Treasure has to share her earnings with the maid and manservant as well as the sing-song house.

back, and she was riding high. Simplicity Zhao also put on a swagger and settled comfortably into his new profession. Since Fortune Shi single-handedly launched her career, Second Treasure gave him special treatment. This, however, made Flora Zhang so jealous that she took a sedan chair to his house in the Old City to tell her adopted mother about it. The old lady, ignorant of the true story, gave Fortune a scolding and told him off for all sorts of things. This so angered him that he broke with both Second Treasure and Flora and gave his patronage to the virgin courtesan Third Treasure instead.

There was no way Flora Zhang could manage without Fortune's support. The example of Second Treasure's triumphal success made her want to follow suit, so she moved to West Civic Peace Alley off Fourth Avenue. It was Belle Tan's house, and she took the room opposite Belle's. Their relationship turned out to be very cordial. When Cloud Tao happened to see Flora and praise her, Belle Tan immediately said, "She's new in the business. If you've got friends, why not make a match for her?"

Cloud Tao gave his promise offhandedly. Flora, who took pride in her good looks, went riding in a carriage daily to attract clients.

It was now the middle of the sixth month. The weather had suddenly turned hot, and even a hand-pulled punkah fan in the room was of little help. Cloud Tao decided to go for a carriage drive to catch the breeze, and he sent a manservant to ask his brother, Jade, if he'd come along. The man got to Water Blossom's house and sent in the message. Since Water Blossom's health was on the mend, Jade Tao thought visiting gardens and parks would be of benefit, but he had no idea whether she felt like going.

"Your brother has asked us several times before," she said, "So let's go just this once. I do feel a lot better now." When she heard this, River Blossom rushed out, demanding, "Brother-in-law, I want to go, too."

"Of course. We'll all go together. Let's call two closed carriages," he said.

"Your brother will laugh at you if you ride in a closed carriage. You better take one with a folding leather top," said Water Blossom. The manservant was told that they'd be going, and an appointment was made to meet up in the foreign building in Luna Park. Laurel Blessing, her own manservant, was told to hire two carriages, one closed and one with a leather top.

River Blossom, greatly delighted, changed into a new outfit. Water Blossom just tidied her hair and checked that her hairpins, earrings, and other ornaments were all right. She then went to tell her mother, Fair Sister Li, they were going out, and Fair Sister urged her not to stay out too long. When Water Blossom returned to her room,

Jade Tao and the servant girl, Beckon, had already gone to wait outside. She stood in front of the mirror for a long time, looking at her reflection, before taking the hand of River Blossom and walking out with her. When they got to the entrance of East Prosperity Alley, River Blossom insisted on traveling with Jade Tao in the leather-topped carriage, so Water Blossom rode with Beckon in the closed carriage. When they drove past Mud Town Bridge, the road ahead was lined with trees on both sides, and the overhanging branches blocked off much of the fierce sunlight. A refreshing breeze blew into the carriage, and they felt the summer heat melt away.

At Luna Park, they alighted and went up the storied building. Cloud Tao and Belle were already there, so Jade and Water Blossom sat down at a table across from them and ordered two cups of tea. River Blossom stood leaning against Jade Tao, unwilling to move even an inch. Though he told her to go downstairs and amuse herself for a while, she did not budge. Water Blossom said, "Off you go! Your clinging like that makes others very hot!" River Blossom had no choice but to go, leaning on Beckon's arm.

Cloud Tao noticed that Water Blossom still looked thin and sallow-faced. "Are you still unwell?" he asked.

"I'm much better now."

"You don't look so good, so you really should take care of yourself," he said.

"It's hard to find the right doctor for her," Jade put in. "The prescriptions she's been given just don't suit her."

"Hill Dou is quite a good doctor. Have you tried him?" asked Belle.

"Oh, don't even mention him! All those pills he prescribed, how could I possibly swallow them all?" said Water Blossom.

"I've heard Vigor Qian say that Second Bai Gao is a fine doctor, though he isn't practicing," said Cloud Tao.

Jade Tao was going to find out more about it, but just then River Blossom came back with Beckon. Shifting from one foot to the other, she asked with a smiling face, "Are we going home?"

"Why, we only just came. Let's enjoy ourselves a little longer," said Jade.

"There's nothing to enjoy here. Nothing for me!" So saying, she clambered onto Jade Tao's knees and rolled about restlessly in his arms. He leaned forward and put his cheek against hers to ask what the matter was. She whispered into his ear, "Let's go home."

Seeing she was getting out of hand, Water Blossom intervened. "Don't be silly! Come here."

Not daring to disobey her, River Blossom made haste to go over. Water Blossom suddenly gasped, "Why is your face all flushed? Did you drink any wine?"

Jade Tao saw that River Blossom's cheeks were indeed as red as rouge. He put his hand on her forehead; it was burning hot, as was her palm. He exclaimed in alarm, "Why didn't you tell us? You're running a fever!" She just laughed playfully.

"You're not a child anymore. How could you not know you were running a fever? Why did you insist on coming out in a carriage?" said Water Blossom.

Jade Tao lifted River Blossom in his arms and sat her down in a sheltered corner, while Water Blossom told Beckon to summon the carriages to take them home.

When Beckon had gone, Cloud Tao said with a smile to Water Blossom, "Both of you are always falling ill; you're really the best of sisters."

Belle had heard that Water Blossom was one who easily took offense, so she signaled Cloud with her eyes. Fortunately, Water Blossom was too preoccupied to answer. Shortly afterward, Beckon came back to report, "The carriages are here."

Jade Tao and Water Blossom bade Cloud and Belle good-bye. Beckon went ahead, helping River Blossom down the stairs. Water Blossom wanted the young girl to go in the closed carriage.

"I want to sit with Brother-in-law."

"Then I'll take the leather-topped one with Beckon," said Water Blossom.

When they were all seated, the carriages took off. River Blossom sat with her head buried in Jade's chest, and he covered her head and face with his sleeves so that not the slightest part was exposed to the breeze. They got off at East Prosperity Alley on Fourth Avenue and went home. Water Blossom immediately told River Blossom to go to bed. River Blossom, however, was reluctant to go and wanted to sleep in Elder Sister's room. "I'll lie down a bit on the divan," she said.

Knowing how stubborn she was, Water Blossom just told Beckon to get a light quilt and wrap it around her. When Fair Sister Li heard of it, she sent Big Goldie to find out what was wrong with River Blossom. Water Blossom answered, "She probably caught a bit of a chill in the carriage." Fair Sister was reassured. Water Blossom waved Beckon away and, together with Jade, watched over the young girl.

River Blossom was lying on the left side of the divan. As the room went all quiet, she lifted a corner of the quilt, poked her head out, and called, "Brother-in-law, come here."

Jade Tao walked over to the divan and bent down to ask, "What d'you want?"

She pleaded, "Brother-in-law, will you sit here, please? Sit here and watch over me as I sleep."

"All right. Now go to sleep." He sat down on the left-hand side of the divan.

For a while, she slept, but her mind was still uneasy, and soon she opened her eyes and said, "Brother-in-law, please don't go. I'm scared to be all by myself."

"I'm here. You just sleep."

But then she called for Water Blossom, "Elder Sister, would you like to come and sit on the divan?"

"You've got Brother-in-law there, you're doing fine," Water Blossom replied.

"But Brother-in-law won't stay put. If Elder Sister comes and sits here, then Brother-in-law won't go away," said River Blossom.

Water Blossom smiled and assented to her request. She pushed the opium tray aside and sat down, her thigh pressing against River Blossom's, and tugged the quilt tightly around her.

As they sat silently, dusk fell. Seeing River Blossom lying quietly in sound slumber, Water Blossom walked softly to the door and summoned Beckon. She whispered to her, "Bring a paraffin lamp."

Beckon got the paraffin lamp, put it in the lamp tray, and withdrew quietly. Water Blossom said to Jade Tao in a low voice, "The poor child! She's too young to be a courtesan. Clients think that she's cute and keep calling her to parties; they keep her awfully busy. She got this fever because the night before last she was taken out of bed to answer a party call. She didn't get back till dawn, so it wasn't surprising that she caught a chill."

He replied in an undertone, "Well, she's very lucky to be in your house. Even real daughters don't get any better treatment than this."

"I'm lucky to have her, too. Otherwise, I'd have had to entertain all these old clients, that would've been the death of me!"

During their conversation, Beckon had brought dinner and set it on the center table, where she placed another paraffin lamp. So Jade Tao, too, walked softly away from the divan and sat down for dinner with Water Blossom. Beckon waited on them and filled their rice bowls. Although they were careful, they still made some noise, and that was enough to wake River Blossom. Water Blossom immediately put down her rice bowl and went to soothe her.

River Blossom looked dazed. A moment later, she collected herself and asked, "Where's Brother-in-law?"

"He's having dinner. You wouldn't want him to go without dinner just to keep you company now, would you?"

"Why wasn't I called to dinner?" River Blossom demanded.

"You have a fever. Never mind dinner."

River Blossom became agitated and propped herself up. "I want to eat!" So Water Blossom told Beckon to help her over to the dinner table.

"Would you like to take a mouthful from my bowl?" Jade Tao asked. She nodded. He put the bowl to her lips and fed her one mouthful; she kept it in her mouth for a long time before finally swallowing it. When he offered her more, she shook her head.

"No appetite, right? I told you so. You've hardly eaten anything at all," said Water Blossom.

Soon Jade Tao and Water Blossom had finished their meal, and Beckon cleared the table and brought hot water for them to wash. She also brought a message for River Blossom from Fair Sister Li, "Mother says you should go to bed. If there're party calls, she'll tell the two girls upstairs to substitute for you."

River Blossom turned to Jade Tao. "I want to sleep in Elder Sister's bed. Will you let me sleep here, Brother-in-law?"

He agreed at once. Instead of objecting, Water Blossom wiped the young girl's face with a hot towel and then told her to go to bed. Beckon lit the bedside lamp and quickly made the bed. As Water Blossom did not use a summer straw mat, she just took away the thick quilts on the bed and spread out the light quilt that she had taken from the divan. She then put a little pillow at one end.

River Blossom did not go to bed right away after she had relieved herself. She looked at Jade Tao thoughtfully. He guessed what she wanted and said, "I'll keep you company." He walked over to the bed, unbuttoned her clothes, and helped her undress. She took the opportunity to plead with him in a whisper. He smiled but refused.

"What is it?" asked Water Blossom.

"She's asking you to come to bed as well."

"Enough of your tricks! Go to sleep now."

River Blossom got into bed and then said loudly from under the quilt, "Brother-in-law, please say something to Elder Sister, won't you?"

"What's there to say?" he asked.

"Anything at all."

Before he could answer, Water Blossom smiled and said, "All this is just to get me to come over to the bed, right? You and your tricks! You're a real pest!" So saying, she went and sat down beside Jade Tao on the edge of the bed. River Blossom pulled the quilt over her head and laughed out loud. Jade Tao laughed. too.

With both Elder Sister and Brother-in-law keeping her company, a delighted River Blossom drifted off to the land of sweet dreams. Since Jade Tao was unencumbered by any business, he and Water Blossom went to bed when the clock struck eleven. For a long time, Water Blossom just tossed and turned. Knowing she was worried about River Blossom, he tried gently to reassure her.

"She's a child, so her fever is nothing to worry about. You yourself have been feeling better just these couple of days so you should take care of yourself."

"I'm not worried, and I don't know why my mind is made this way. Once I start thinking about something, no matter what it is, I go on and on, unable to sleep. Even if I want to stop thinking, I can't."

"Well, that's the root of your illness. You should just put your mind at rest."

"In fact, I was thinking about my illness just now. River Blossom was the first to get upset when I became ill. Sometimes when you aren't here, she's my only companion. While other people are sick of the sight of me, she not only keeps me company but tries to cheer me up in all sorts of ways. I do know this illness of hers is nothing serious, that all she needs is rest, but my heart is still uneasy."

Before he could comfort her any further, they heard River Blossom turning over. Water Blossom sat up and called her name but received no response. She then reached out to touch her forehead: she was still running a fever and had pushed the quilt off her shoulders. Water Blossom pulled it up to cover her properly and then lay down again to sleep.

Jade Tao continued to reassure her. "However fond you are of her, you mustn't worry yourself unnecessarily. Even if you brood all night, it won't help her get well. Now suppose you yourself fall ill from lack of sleep, won't that make things worse?"

She heaved a long sigh. "She's a poor thing, too. I'm the only one who looks after her when she's ill."

"In that case, just take good care of her. There's no need to brood."

As they talked, River Blossom woke up and heard them. "Elder Sister," she called out in a drowsy voice.

Water Blossom hastened to ask, "Would you like some tea?"

"No."

"Then go back to sleep."

River Blossom made an affirmative noise. After a long pause, she called again. "Elder Sister, I'm afraid."

Jade Tao cut in, "We're both here; what is there to be afraid of?"

"There's somebody outside the back door."

"The back door is shut. You're just dreaming," he said.

After another long pause, she switched to "Brother-in-law," saying, "I want to sleep at your end, too."

Water Blossom answered at once, "No. Brother-in-law is kind enough to let you sleep here. You mustn't make any more trouble."

River Blossom, not daring to insist, fell silent. After another long pause, there came the sound of low moaning. Jade Tao said, "I'll sleep at that end to keep her company."

Water Blossom agreed, so he took a small pillow and turned around to sleep at the other end. Overjoyed, River Blossom folded her arms and legs close together and snuggled up into his arms. As Jade Tao did not much mind the heat, he just lifted a corner of the quilt. After she was settled, she looked up at him and asked, "Brother-in-law, what were you and Elder Sister talking about just now?"

He gave a vague answer.

"Were you talking about me?"

"Hush now. Elder Sister couldn't sleep because of you, so stop being a nuisance."

She finally fell silent, and the night passed uneventfully. The next day, Water Blossom was the first to wake up. Though she had had a long rest, she still felt lethargic and so remained lying in bed. By eleven o'clock, Jade Tao and River Blossom both woke up. Water Blossom immediately asked about the young girl's fever.

Jade Tao answered for her, "It's gone. Her temperature came down at dawn."

River Blossom did feel quite bright and cheerful. She dressed and got out of bed together with Jade. Then she washed her face, did her hair, and ate breakfast like the lively little girl that she was. Water Blossom, on the other hand, felt physically weak and mentally drained. She might have looked her usual self to other people, but Jade Tao knew that her illness got more serious every time it recurred. He was worried but had to keep it to himself.

When lunch was served at noon, River Blossom called out in concern, "Elder Sister, get up." Water Blossom felt too tired to answer. Though River Blossom kept calling her, she just turned a deaf ear. River Blossom shouted in alarm, "Brother-in-law, come! Why is Elder Sister not talking?"

Annoyed, Water Blossom managed to get this out, "Hush! I want to sleep."

Jade Tao quickly dragged River Blossom away, warning her, "Now don't kick up a fuss. Elder Sister is unwell."

"Why is that so?"

"It's all because of you. You passed your illness to her, and you got well."

Greatly agitated, she pleaded, "Then tell Elder Sister to pass it back to me. I don't mind being ill. With Brother-in-law keeping me company and Elder Sister chatting with me, I quite enjoyed it!"

Her words made him laugh. He said, "Let's go and have lunch." Though she did not feel like eating, she kept him company.

After lunch, Fair Sister Li came in to comfort Water Blossom. She was clearly worried. Jade Tao said, "Yesterday, we heard of a good doctor. I'd like to get him to have a look at her."

Hearing this, Water Blossom held up her hand to object. "Your brother jokes about me always falling ill. Don't ask him about doctors."

"I'll ask Vigor Qian directly," he said. As she did not object, her mother urged him to go and see Vigor Qian.

CHAPTER 36 :: *A strange love feeds on constant squabbling, and a miracle cure depends on the good doctor*

Jade Tao went by sedan chair from East Prosperity Alley to Vigor Qian's residence on Avenue Road. He sent in his visiting card and was invited into Qian's study, where tea was served and host and guest sat down. After the usual polite exchange, Jade brought his hands together in a salute and asked for Qian's help to invite Second Bai Gao.

Vigor Qian gave his promise, but he then said, "Second Bai is a bit of an eccentric; there's no telling whether he'll agree to it. It happens that he has invited me to dinner tonight at East Co-prosperity Alley. I'll take the opportunity to ask him in person and then send you an answer by messenger, OK?"

Jade Tao expressed his gratitude over and over again and then solemnly took his leave.

That evening, Vigor Qian waited until he had received the note to hurry him before he got into his ricksha and headed for Big Feet Yao's in East Co-prosperity Alley. Wenjun Yao's room was upstairs, where Constance used to be. As Vigor Qian went in, he was greeted by Elan Ge and the host, Second Bai. Taking advantage of this interlude before the arrival of other guests, Vigor Qian relayed Jade Tao's request. As predicted, Second Bai turned him down. Thereupon Vigor Qian spoke in detail about the devotion Jade Tao and Water Blossom had shown to each other. Even Elan Ge felt deeply moved. Wenjun Yao, who was sitting to one side, jumped up and asked, "Are you speaking of Water Blossom of East Prosperity Alley? She's deeply in love with Second Young Master Tao. I've seen them several times; they always come and go together. How come she's ill?"

"She's been ill for some time now. That's why they want to ask your Mr. Gao to have a look at her," said Vigor Qian.

Wenjun Yao said to Second Bai, "In that case, you've got to go and cure her. In the Shanghai brothels, clients and courtesans all cheat on each other; everybody's shameless. Now, these two are truly in love, yet she's got the rotten luck to fall ill. You must cure her so she can be held up as an example for all those shameless clients and courtesans."

Elan Ge could not help laughing. A smiling Vigor Qian turned again to Second Bai, who had in fact made up his mind to go but still made a show of shaking his head. This made Wenjun Yao so anxious that she ran over to him and held him by his wrists, asking, "Why wouldn't you take the case? D'you think she deserves to die?"

"I just don't want to. Do I need a reason for it?" he said with a smile.

She glared at him and shouted, "That won't do. If you refuse to go, you must give a reason."

Smiling, Elan Ge intervened. "He's fooled you, Wenjun! Once he knows about someone like Water Blossom, he's more than happy to treat her."

She let go of Second Bai's hands, but her eyes were still fixed on him as she grumbled, "If you refuse to go, I'll drag you there if I have to."

He clapped his hands, laughing his head off. "So I've come under your control now!"

"It's all because you were unreasonable," she responded.

Vigor Qian then asked Second Bai to make an appointment, and he proposed, "Tomorrow morning." Qian told his ricksha puller to deliver the message to Water Blossom's house. In no time at all, the ricksha puller came back with two of Jade Tao's visiting cards, on which was written: "Please honor me with your company at a tea party at noon tomorrow." Under that was the venue: Water Blossom's at East Prosperity Alley.

"Let's invite him over right now," said Second Bai. An invitation was immediately written out, and a manservant was told to deliver it. Jade Tao came right away. He happened to arrive at the same time as the other guests, Iron Hua and Devotion Yin. Second Bai called for hot towels to be served, and everybody moved over to the table.

Second Bai was a generous host who plied his guests with wine. Jade Tao was the only one who did not drink. Iron Hua and Devotion Yin both prided themselves on their capacity, while Elan Ge and Vigor Qian just consumed token amounts.

The minute the girls arrived, Second Bai called for the large wine cups and offered to play everybody at the finger game. Jade Tao, in the seat of honor, declined with an apology.

"You can have substitutes for the drinking," said Second Bai.

Jade Tao reluctantly complied. His penalty wine was given to Big Goldie by River Blossom.

When Devotion Yin's turn came, he raised objections, saying,

"You have a whole lot of people here drinking for you, but I've only got Green Fragrance. It's too much of a disadvantage."

"In that case, let's not have any substitutes," Second Bai replied.

"Fine," said Devotion.

Second Bai lost all three games and so had to drink three penalty cups in a row. The other three guests, however, had substitutes as they saw fit.

Second Bai put the large wine cups in front of Iron Hua. The latter said, "Your round as host doesn't count. You should play another round as banker."

"Later," Second Bai replied.

Iron Hua then started a bank himself with twenty cups. Devotion Yin, who only wanted to get at Second Bai, did not object when he saw White Orchid substituting for Iron Hua. Before long, the banker's twenty cups were knocked off.

"Who will be banker next?" Iron Hua asked. Everybody looked at each other mutely; none accepted. Second Bai suggested that Devotion Yin should go ahead.

"You go first. I'll be the challenger," replied Devotion Yin.

Second Bai followed his predecessor's example and poured out twenty cups. Devotion rolled up his sleeves and launched his challenge. He was on an unbreakable winning streak, and Second Bai lost game after game. Wenjun Yao tried to substitute for the penalty wine, but Devotion forbade it. After five games, Second Bai became extremely vigilant and finally won three. Devotion only drank two cups himself; the other one went to Green Fragrance. Second Bai sneered at him, but Devotion pretended not to notice. Wenjun Yao was so angry, she turned her head away.

After he had finished the penalty wine, Devotion Yin laughed and said, "I'll give somebody else a chance at you." Vigor Qian, who sat next to him, kept whispering to Green Phoenix about confidential matters and told Elan Ge to play instead. Elan, who thought that the wine cups were much larger than usual, gave half a cup to Snow Scent every time he lost. Devotion Yin did not seem to notice. But when Second Bai lost, Devotion immediately filled a cup and gave it to him, saying, "You're a good drinker; have it yourself."

Second Bai was about to take the cup when Wenjun Yao reached out a hand and covered it. "Just a minute. If they have substitutes, why not us? Give it here."

"I'll drink it myself. I feel like drinking just now," said Second Bai.

"If you want to drink, you can have a whole vat after the party. But now I *will* take this for you." So saying, she pulled at his sleeve. As

Second Bai was still holding on to the cup, it fell and got smashed, splashing wine all over him. This caught everybody at table off guard; even Vigor Qian and Green Phoenix stopped talking. The maids waiting at table picked up the pieces and brought a towel for Second Bai to wipe off his gauze gown.

Devotion Yin said nervously, "Drink for him, by all means. If the two of you should start fighting again, it'd be the undoing of me." So saying, he hastily filled another cup for Wenjun Yao, who drained it in one gulp. He cheered.

Vigor Qian was puzzled by what Devotion had said. The latter explained, "Don't you know that their relationship is built on fighting? At first, they just got on all right, but the more they fought, the closer they became. Now they're of course inseparable."

"But what do they fight over?" Vigor Qian asked.

"Who knows? They fight whenever they have the smallest disagreement, and neither of them will give in during the fight. But afterward they're all lovey-dovey again. They're just like kids; they drive you mad!"

Wenjun Yao snickered and looked at Devotion from the corner of her eyes. "Yes, we're kids, and you're a big boy, right?"

"I'm not all that big, but I do all right. Do you want to try?" he replied.

"Aiyo! I reared you until you were the little man, and now you've learned to tease me. Where did you learn to be so clever?"[1]

As they bantered, Vigor Qian managed to break Second Bai's bank, so Wenjun Yao drank two more cups for him. Vigor Qian, on a winning streak, only left three cups of wine for Iron Hua to deal with.

After Second Bai's bank was broken, the girls left together. Devotion Yin then cut his own bank by half, to just ten cups. After that, Elan Ge and Vigor Qian teamed up for ten cups as well. Seeing that Jade Tao did not drink, Second Bai refrained from indulging his full capacity and instead ordered the wine to be removed and dinner served. Before Jade Tao took his leave, their appointment for the next day was reconfirmed, and Second Bai saw him off at the stairs.

Jade Tao headed back to Water Blossom's at East Prosperity Alley, where he alighted from his sedan chair in the parlor and walked

::

1. [In the mutual teasing between clients and courtesan, men invariably go for sexual innuendo while women often claim to be their opponent's mother. Eileen Chang considered this a roundabout way of calling the man a son of a bitch. This is not necessarily true as such teasing is often friendly. Both this case and that between Snow Scent and Elan Ge show no malice. E.H.]

softly into her room. It was dark, lit only by a lamp on the dressing table. The pink bed curtains were hanging down. Fair Sister Li and Beckon were in the room to keep Water Blossom company. He asked in a low voice how she was doing. Instead of replying, Fair Sister just pointed to the bed.

He lit a candle at the lamp and then lifted the bed curtain. Water Blossom was panting feebly. This looked quite different from her previous illness. He raised the candle to examine her complexion. She opened her eyes and fixed them on him without a word. He touched her forehead and the palms of her hands: a slight fever.

"Feeling better?" he asked.

She took a long time to answer, "No."

"Can you tell me what's wrong?"

After another long pause she answered, "Don't worry, I'm all right."

He withdrew from the bed, blew out the candle, and asked Fair Sister, "Did she have supper?"

"I kept trying to tell her to eat a little congee, but she just had a mouthful of soup and nothing else at all."

They looked at each other in silence for a long time. Suddenly, Water Blossom called out from the bed, "Mother, you go and have your smoke."

"I will. You get some sleep," Fair Sister replied.

River Blossom happened to come back just then from a party and was eager to see Elder Sister. The fact that both Fair Sister and Jade were in the room made her think that Elder Sister was seriously ill. She turned pale. Jade Tao held up his hand to calm her fears, saying softly, "Elder Sister is asleep." Reassured, she went to her own room to get changed.

Water Blossom again called out, "Mother, do go and rest."

"All right, I'm going," said Fair Sister. She turned around and said to Jade Tao, "Won't you come sit a while at the back?"

Since there was not much he could do there, Jade Tao told Beckon to watch over Water Blossom and followed Fair Sister through the rear door to her room. After they had sat down, she said, "Second Young Master, I want to ask you something. When she first got ill, she herself was extremely anxious and would start crying as soon as we talked. But just now when I went in to see her, she spoke not a word, didn't even answer my questions. She looked like she wanted to cry, but there were no tears. What's happening?"

He nodded in agreement. "I also felt that this was different from before. Let's ask the doctor tomorrow."

"Second Young Master, one thing occurred to me. When she was little, we went to worship at the city god's temple. There, she got surrounded by beggars and had a bad fright. Perhaps we should hold three days' service for her there and ask for the city god's help. What d'you think?"

"That's fine."

As they were talking, River Blossom came running in to look for him. He asked, "Is there anybody in your sister's room?"

"Beckon is there," River Blossom replied.

"Why don't you go and keep her company as well?" Fair Sister said to her.

Seeing her hesitate, he stood up and asked to be excused. Taking River Blossom by the hand, he returned to Water Blossom's room. They tiptoed up to the leather chair by the bed and sat down in each other's arms. Beckon took the opportunity to sneak out for a while. All was quiet. River Blossom, with her thumb in her mouth, sat abstracted in his arms, worrying about something. He did not prompt her, just kept his eyes on her. Her eyes gradually reddened and filled with tears. He patted her shoulder and asked with a smile, "What grievance are you thinking of?" She laughed.

Beckon, who heard his voice, thought he was calling and came in promptly.

"It's nothing."

She turned to go. Actually, Water Blossom was still awake. "Beckon," she called out. "Go to bed when you're done."

Beckon promised she would and turned to ask Jade Tao, "Would you like some congee?"

Jade Tao declined, so she went to freshen up the tea instead.

"River Blossom," Water Blossom called out again, "you should go to bed, too."

Naturally, she refused, so Jade Tao made up a reason to send her off. "Elder Sister got ill because of all the trouble you made last night. If you sleep here again, Mother will tell you off."

Beckon happened to bring in the teapot just then. She also said, "River Blossom, Mother tells you to go to bed." The young girl had no choice but to follow Beckon out of the room.

Jade Tao wanted to stay up, but thinking that this would upset Water Blossom, he closed the door and lay down in bed beside her, pretending to sleep. But at her every toss and turn, he got up to attend to her needs. At dawn, she started snoring softly. Only then did he get some sleep. Not long afterward, he was wakened by the menservants walking back and forth outside. When Water Blossom tried to persuade him to rest a little longer, he insisted that he had slept enough.

He thought she seemed a little better, certainly not as irritable as yesterday. Taking advantage of their early-morning solitude, he asked lovingly, "What is it that makes you unhappy; why don't you tell me about it?"

She sneered. "How can I ever be happy? There's no need to ask."

"If there isn't anything else, when you're a little better, I'll rent a house in the Old City. You and Mother can move there and ask the bookkeeper to help your brother take care of the sing-song house. What d'you think?"

This went so completely against her wishes that she just sighed and looked more miserable than ever. He panicked, put on a smile, and apologized for saying the wrong thing.[2]

Yet this likewise brought a sullen retort from her. "Did I say you were wrong?"

Unable to think of anything else to say, Jade Tao went to open the door and call for the maid, Big Goldie. To his surprise, River Blossom had got up early and came out from her room in the back. She greeted him and was delighted to hear that Elder Sister was feeling better. Come the time Beckon was up and had helped Big Goldie tidy up the place, he told the menservants to take two of his cards to hurry the guests, Gao and Qian.

Toward noon, Vigor Qian arrived with Second Bai Gao. Jade Tao welcomed them into Water Blossom's room. After greetings were exchanged, everyone took a seat, and tea was served.

Second Bai was the first to speak. "I've newly arrived in Shanghai and have no intention of practicing medicine. But my friend Vigor told me of your command, and I appreciated your esteem too much to turn down your request. May I suggest we do the consultation first and chat after that?"

Jade Tao naturally agreed. Beckon hurried off to get things ready and then notified Jade, who told River Blossom to keep Vigor Qian company while he took Second Bai into Water Blossom's room. Water Blossom greeted them faintly and then put out her hand on a small foreign-style pillow. Second Bai sat down on the edge of the bed, carefully regulated his own breath, and then felt her pulse on both wrists. After that, he told them to lift the window curtains so he could look at her tongue.

The examination over, Jade Tao accompanied him back to the room opposite, where River Blossom had set out a writing brush, inkstone, and poetry writing paper on the table. Beckon rubbed ink stick on the stone to make ink. Vigor Qian moved to one side. Jade Tao asked Second Bai to sit down and then explained, "Water Blossom's illness goes back to the ninth month of last year when she caught a cold and ran a fever a few times. It was nothing serious. But

::

2.      [This arrangement would have made her his unacknowledged concubine while all the time she wanted to be his wife. *E.H.*]

by spring this year she had gone downhill. Every time she got better, she fell ill again, as if the illness were chronic. It wasn't fever, either. It started with her losing her appetite, so she ate and drank less and less, sometimes not eating for a couple of days. She got so thin, she was just a bag of bones. She did seem to get better in the summer, around the fifth and sixth months, but even then she still had a fever, though it didn't immobilize her. She herself thought that she was recovering and didn't take enough care. The day before yesterday she went for a drive to Luna Park, and she just stayed in bed all day yesterday, completely exhausted. When she's irritated, she gets short of breath, and if you ask her questions, she says not a word. She only eats about half a bowl of congee a day, and that just turns into phlegm. She can't sleep at night, and when she does, she breaks out in a cold sweat. She knows all this bodes ill, and she cries, which makes it even worse. I wonder if anything can be done about it?"

Second Bai replied, "This is consumption. If she had taken a concoction to strengthen her respiratory energy and improve her general condition when she first fell ill in the ninth moon last year, she'd have been all right. The fact that you mistook it for a fever led to a bit of a costly delay. This relapse has nothing to do with the carriage ride; it's more a matter of her poor condition. The root cause of her illness is a weakness in her circulation and respiratory systems. This is aggravated by poor digestion. But that alone wouldn't give you consumption. I take it that she is extremely bright and has overworked her mind, accumulating worries and sorrows over the years, thus doing damage to her digestive system. Such damage is evidenced in an emaciated appearance, physical feebleness, coughing and congestion in the chest, a sour acid taste in the mouth and hiccups, very little intake of food and drink, and an intermittent fever. This is what is called consumption. The problem is, the damage has gone beyond the digestive system to the heart and kidneys. Irritation and sweating are just some of the symptoms. In a few days, she'll experience many other problems, chills and aches in her back and knees, palpitations, and wild dreams."

Jade broke in, "You're right; she has these problems even now. She often cries out from fright in her sleep and on waking says it's a dream. As to her back and knees, they've been aching for a long time."

Second Bai picked up the writing brush and dipped it in the ink. After thinking for a moment, he said, "Given her poor appetite, she probably has trouble taking medicine, too."

Jade replied with a frown. "That's right. And even worse is her habit of covering up her illness to avoid seeing a doctor. If she sees one and gets a prescription, she stops taking the medicine as soon as she feels a little better. There's a prescription for pills that she never even touched."

Thereupon Second Bai dashed out a prescription, the writing brush moving swift as a hare. He began by detailing his diagnosis and then listed the herbs and their different methods of preparation. He handed the sheet to Jade Tao. Vigor Qian also came over to look at what he had prescribed. River Blossom, thinking there was something interesting, pulled at Jade's arm to have a look. When she saw it was just a sheet of paper covered with cursive writing, she lost interest.

Jade Tao had a quick look at it and saluted Second Bai, expressing his gratitude. Then he asked, "Another thing: when she first fell ill, she used to cry and fret, but now she doesn't do that at all. Does it signify complications?"

"Not really. Previously, her problem was restlessness; now it's weariness and fatigue. All this stems from the heart. If she could stop worrying, take the right nourishment, and rest well, she'll recover faster than by taking medicine."

Vigor Qian asked, "Is this illness curable?"

"There is no such thing as an incurable illness. But if an illness has dragged on for a while, the recovery will also take time. She'll be all right for the next couple of months. The autumn equinox is probably the critical time. After that, we'll be able to tell if she will completely recover."

Jade Tao, on hearing all this, was severely shaken. When he recovered, he asked Second Bai and Vigor Qian to make themselves comfortable while he took the prescription into Fair Sister Li's room. Fair Sister had just woken and was sitting up in bed. He read out the diagnosis and the list of herbs and then repeated to her what had just been said.

She, too, was shocked. "Second Young Master, what do we do now?"

Jade Tao had no answer; he stood there numbly. Only when the table had been set outside and Big Goldie repeatedly called out for "Second Young Master," did he toss the prescription down and go out to join his guests.

CHAPTER 37 :: *A willing apprentice is rewarded with torture, and a brothel hand is blackmailed into a loan*

Jade Tao came out to River Blossom's room and asked Second Bai and Vigor Qian to come to the table. The three of them drank and chatted; there were no other guests, and they did not summon any other girls. River Blossom tuned her *pipa* and prepared to sing, but Second Bai said, "Don't bother."

"Second Bai likes opera. Sing an aria; I'll accompany you on the flute," said Vigor Qian. Beckon handed him a flute; he played as River Blossom sang two sections of "Pale Sky, Light Clouds" from *A Small Banquet*.

This put Second Bai in a good mood, and he followed with "Sitting in a Southerly Breeze" from *Viewing Lotus Flowers*.

"Would you like to sing?" Vigor Qian asked Jade Tao.

"I've got a bad throat. I'll play the flute; you sing," Jade replied.

Vigor Qian passed him the flute and sang "South Creek":

*Parting brings endless sorrow*
*After two months together, I'm suddenly alone . . .*

He finished the whole aria. Second Bai cheered. Taking her chance, River Blossom poured a large cup of wine and urged him to drink. As Jade Tao was rather depressed, Second Bai ordered rice to be served as soon as he had drained his cup. Feeling apologetic, Jade pressed him to take three more cups of wine.

Soon the party was over, and the guests took their leave. After seeing them out of the parlor, Jade Tao hurried back to Water Blossom's room. As Second Bai walked shoulder to shoulder with Vigor Qian out of East Prosperity Alley, he asked, "Water Blossom's mother, brother, and sister, as well as Jade Tao, are all very affectionate toward her; there's nothing to make her unhappy. I don't understand why she should have such an illness."

Vigor sighed before he spoke. "Water Blossom should not have gone into the brothel business. It's really her mother's fault. Since she ran a sing-song house, Water Blossom had no choice. Even then, her only client has been Jade Tao, whom she wanted to marry. Now, if he were to have taken her as a concubine, she wouldn't have been unwilling. Unfortunately, Jade insisted on marrying her as his wife. This aroused the opposition of his uncles, his brother and sister-in-law, and all his relatives on the grounds that it'd be a disgrace for the family to take a courtesan for a wife. Water Blossom heard about it. Now, she had never wanted to be a courtesan in the first place and in reality had never worked as one, yet everybody called her a courtesan, and could she have denied it? Her illness came from the pent-up anger."

Hearing this, Second Bai also sighed. They had reached the entrance to Generosity Alley. As Second Bai had another engagement, he saluted Vigor Qian and went on his way. Qian walked into the alley alone, and as he approached Green Phoenix's house, he saw a courtesan in front of him staggering alongside the wall, leaning on a maid's shoulder for support. At first he paid her no attention, but at the door he recognized that it was Gold Flower.

"Mr. Qian," Gold Flower greeted him and then headed for Second Sister Huang's little back room.

Vigor Qian walked upstairs. Pearl Phoenix and Gold Phoenix vied with each other to welcome "Brother-in-law" and ushered him into the room.

"Where's Gold Flower?" Green Phoenix asked.

"Downstairs," he replied.

In case Vigor had anything confidential to say to Green Phoenix, Gold Phoenix used Gold Flower as an excuse and went downstairs, taking Pearl Phoenix with her.

After Green Phoenix had been talking with Vigor for a while, the grandfather clock struck three. Since he knew Prosperity Luo came every day, he wanted to take his leave.

"Sit for a little longer. What's the hurry?" she said.

He was still hesitating when Pearl Phoenix and Gold Phoenix came back with Gold Flower to see Green Phoenix, so he said good-bye and left.

The minute Gold Flower saw Green Phoenix, tears welled up in her eyes. "Elder Sister," she whimpered, "I wanted to come and see you a few days ago, only I couldn't walk. Today I made up my mind to come. Elder Sister, will you save my life?"

"What d'you mean?" Green Phoenix asked in bewilderment.

Gold Flower lifted her trouser legs to show her. Her calves were marked with long dark streaks—marks left by a whip. They were also covered in blood red dots that looked like stars in the sky—burnt marks left by a red-hot opium pick.

Green Phoenix was moved to pity. "I told you to try harder to please. Why wouldn't you listen to me? Look at the state you're in!"

Gold Flower said, "You don't understand! This mother of mine is different from the mother here. If you don't try hard, you naturally get a beating, but even if you do, you still get a beating. This time, it was because a client came three or four times, and then Mother said I was too eager to please him and beat me for it."

Green Phoenix said with a great upsurge of anger, "You have a mouth, why didn't you speak up for yourself?"

"I did! I said exactly what you taught me, Elder Sister. I said if she wanted me to do business, she had to stop beating me, otherwise I wouldn't do business. When she heard this, she locked me in my room and called Old Mrs. Guo over to help her. They pinned me down on the divan, beat me all night long, and then asked whether I dared not to do business."

"Then you should have flatly refused and let them go on beating you."

Gold Flower replied with a frown. "Elder Sister, it hurt so terribly, I just couldn't say no anymore!"

Green Phoenix said sarcastically, "If you can't stand pain, you should have been a lady in a mandarin's family. What are you doing as a courtesan?"

Gold Phoenix and Pearl Phoenix let out a giggle. Gold Flower hung her head and sat there in silent shame.

"Well, was there any opium?" Green Phoenix asked again.

"Yes, there was opium in a jar. I tasted a wee bit, and it was horribly bitter; how could you swallow it? Besides, I heard that raw opium would cause all your intestines to burst. Wouldn't that have been painful?"

Green Phoenix poked two of her fingers at Gold Flower's forehead, saying between clenched teeth, "You good-for-nothing!" Then she stopped herself.

It so happened that while they were talking, Second Sister and Mama Zhao were in the parlor, where the laundered and starched sheets had been spread out on two square tables for sewing. Hearing what Green Phoenix had said, Second Sister walked in and told her with a smile, "If you want to pass your own abilities on to her, you'll have to do it in another life. Just think, since she went over there the month before last, only an old client of Perfection's called Chen has given a dinner party there. It's been almost two months now, and she's only had one client, who ordered sweetmeats once and had a tea party three times. It turns out that this was none other than her lover who works in a hardware store. He went there after supper and stayed until midnight every time. That's why his boss complained and Third Sister Chu beat her."

"Well, if she had no dinner parties, what about party calls?" asked Green Phoenix.

"I told you she managed one dish of sweetmeats. What party calls are you talking about?"

Green Phoenix jumped up to confront Gold Flower. "So, you earn all of one dollar in a whole month! D'you want your mother to eat shit?"

Gold Flower dared not reply. Green Phoenix repeated her question several times and reached out to push Gold Flower's head up. "Speak up! D'you want your mother to eat shit while you have a good time with your favorite client?"

Second Sister tried to intervene. "What's the point of telling her off?"

Green Phoenix was so angry, her eyes popped out and her lips trembled. She shouted, "That Third Sister Chu is useless. If she has the energy to beat her, then she should beat her to death! Keeping her around just means losing more money."

Second Sister stamped her foot and said, "Enough!" She then pressed Green Phoenix back onto her seat. Green Phoenix slapped the table and gave an order, "Throw her out! Even the sight of her annoys me." Her hand came down so hard that a gold-trimmed tortoiseshell bracelet on her wrist was broken into three sections.

Second Sister cleared her throat and then said, "Now that's bad luck we don't deserve." She signaled Gold Phoenix with her eyes.

Gold Phoenix took Gold Flower by the hand and led her over to the next room, but Gold Flower, feeling she had lost face, wanted to go home. Second Sister did not detain her. Yet Gold Phoenix was very friendly toward her and saw her out to the courtyard. They happened to meet Prosperity Luo, who had just gotten off his sedan chair. Unwilling to come face-to-face with Luo, Gold Flower stepped aside and waited until he had gone in before saying goodbye to Gold Phoenix. Leaning on a maid, she walked slowly out of Glory Alley and then turned into Treasured Merit Street, where she headed eastward, back to the Hall of Immortals on East Chessboard Street.

Having no idea how to deal with her misfortune, Gold Flower could only hope that Third Sister would not check on her so she could somehow get by. Unexpectedly, the next day after lunch, when she was flirting with several menservants in the parlor, Old Mrs. Guo turned up at the door and beckoned for her. She hurried over in trepidation.

Old Mrs. Guo said, "I've found two nice guests for you. Now, you must try hard to please them, understand?"

"Where are they?" Gold Flower asked.

"Here they come!"

Gold Flower looked up to see a slim youth and an older man with whiskers who walked with a limp. Both wore a pale blue gown of mandarin gauze. Gold Flower welcomed them into her room and asked for their last names. The youth was named Zhang; the one with whiskers said he was Zhou. Both were strangers to Gold Flower, and Old Mrs. Guo only knew Rustic Zhang. The menservants brought nuts and sweetmeats that she offered them according to etiquette. She then went over to the divan to toast opium.

Old Mrs. Guo edged near Rustic Zhang and whispered, "The girl's my niece. Could you look after her a bit? Give what you like."

Rustic Zhang nodded.

"Shall I order a dinner party for you?" she asked.

Rustic Zhang firmly forbade it.

After dawdling for a while, Mrs. Guo tried again. "Why not ask your friend if he'd like to?"

"D'you know who this friend of mine is?"

She shook her head.

"This is Clement Zhou."

Upon hearing this, Mrs. Guo grimaced and sneaked out. Gold Flower filled a pipe with opium and offered it to Clement Zhou, who, not being an addict, invited Rustic Zhang to smoke first. Seeing that Gold Flower had little to recommend her in looks, singing, or conversation, Rustic just smoked his fill of opium and then left the Hall of Immortals together with Clement Zhou. They strolled about at leisure and then stood at Fourth Avenue to look at the horse carriages coming and going and finally drifted into Splendid Assembly Teahouse for a cup of tea to kill time.

The two of them had barely sat down when they saw Simplicity Zhao, also dressed in a pale blue gown of mandarin gauze, come in alone. With an ivory cigarette holder with a lighted cigarette in it stuck in his mouth and a pair of dark glasses adorning his ruddy and radiant face, Simplicity carried himself with a new air. He walked straight upstairs and looked right and left. Seeing him as a good connection, Rustic Zhang raised a hand in greeting, but Simplicity ignored him and instead walked around the opium den at the rear before strolling toward the tea tables. When he saw Rustic Zhang, he asked, "Have you seen Fortune Shi?"

Rustic rose to his feet. "Fortune isn't here yet. If you're looking for him, why not wait right here?"

Simplicity had meant to cut Rustic Zhang, but the chance to show off in front of Clement Zhou made him accept the invitation to join them. Rustic ordered the waiter to bring another cup of tea while Clement went to get a water pipe and a spill for him. Simplicity saw his limp and asked the reason for it.

"I had a fall and broke my leg," Clement replied.

Pointing to Simplicity, Rustic said to Clement, "He's the luckiest of us all. You and I have had rotten luck. You broke a leg, while I'm plain broke."

Simplicity asked how Pine Wu was faring.

"Pine has been unlucky, too. He was locked up in the police station for a few days and has just come out. His own father tried to borrow money from him and made a big row. Lucky the foreigners didn't know, otherwise he'd have lost his job, too," said Rustic.

"Did Crane Li come to town again after going home?" asked Clement.

"Old Mrs. Guo told me he'll be here soon. His uncle is coming to

Shanghai to see the doctors because he has syphilis, and Crane will be coming with him," Rustic replied.

"Where did you see this Old Mrs. Guo?" Simplicity asked.

"She found her way to my inn to say her niece is in a second-class house and asked me to look in. I went with Clement and ordered a dish of nuts and sweetmeats just now."

"So that was Old Mrs. Guo!" Clement said in astonishment. "I didn't even recognize her. Now *that* was an oversight. In a case I handled two years ago, I sentenced this Old Mrs. Guo for abduction."

"No wonder she was a bit frightened to see you."

"And she was right to be. If I want her imprisoned for life, all I need do is file a report," said Clement.

Something had just occurred to Simplicity, who tilted his head in thought. As he remained quiet, Clement and Rustic also stopped talking. The three of them drank five or six refills of their tea and saw that it was getting dark. Simplicity Zhao realized it was quite impossible to track down the wandering Fortune Shi, so he bade Clement Zhou and Rustic Zhang farewell and returned directly to Tripod Alley off Third Avenue to report to his sister, Second Treasure, that he could not find Shi.

"Then go to his house early tomorrow to invite him," Second Treasure said.

"If he doesn't come on his own initiative, why bother to invite him? We've got plenty of good guests."

Second Treasure looked displeased. "I'm just asking you to go and invite a guest, and you're refusing to do it. All you do is eat your fill and have fun. What else are you good for?"

He changed his tack in a panic. "I'll go, I'll go! It was just a thought."

This placated Second Treasure. By now she was extremely popular, with bookings for mah-jongg parties and dinner parties every night. The leftovers from the parties were sent over to Mrs. Zhao's room, where Simplicity was free to munch his way through all the delicacies. Stuffed to the gills with food and drink every night, he would fall on his bed and go out like a light, thinking that he was in paradise.

The next day, Simplicity went as instructed to the Old City to invite Fortune Shi, but Fortune was not home, and he just left a calling card. If he went home immediately, he thought, he was bound to be told off again. It'd be far better to go to Second Wang's and renew their friendship. When he got to New Street, he was specially careful because he had met with violence last time and had his head smashed. He went first to Old Mrs. Guo next door; with her as a go-between, there would be room for withdrawal. Old Mrs. Guo welcomed him joyfully, as if he had dropped out of the sky. She told him to wait there while she fetched Second Wang.

Seeing it was Simplicity, Second Wang minced over to him, all smiles, and said coaxingly, "Let's go to my room."

"It's all right here," Simplicity said as he took off his gown and hung it on the bamboo pole that held up the bed curtains.

Second Wang asked Mrs. Guo to have a word with the old maid-servant, while she made Simplicity sit down on the edge of the bed. She then settled herself in his lap with her arms around his neck. "I've missed you so badly, yet you never thought of me after you made a fortune. I won't have it!"

He took the opportunity to put his arms around her and asked, "Does Mr. Zhang come here?"

"Don't even mention him! He's down and out now. He owes us more than ten dollars, and we're yet to see a cent of it."

Simplicity told her everything that Rustic had said the day before. She jumped up at once, saying, "So he goes to a second-class house when he's got money! Tomorrow I'll see what he has to say about that."

Simplicity made her sit down. "If you go, don't mention me."

"Don't worry, this doesn't concern you."

As they were talking, the old maidservant brought opium and tea and then went back to keep an eye on the empty house next door. Old Mrs. Guo, hearing that all was quiet inside, figured that the ship was well docked. To prevent anyone from disturbing them, she stood at the front door to keep watch. After a long while, she suddenly heard a scuffling of feet in the rear room. Puzzled, she went in and saw Simplicity trying to put on his gown while Second Wang was snatching it away from him. The two were tangled together in a struggle.

"What's the hurry?" she intervened.

Second Wang complained in a huff, "I asked him nicely for a loan of ten dollars, which we'd count toward his opium bill. He told me he hasn't got it and then stood up to leave!"

"I really don't have it on me. When I have the money in a couple of days, I'll bring it over, all right?" Simplicity pleaded.

Second Wang would have none of it. "In that case, leave your gown here. You'll get it back when you bring me ten dollars."

Simplicity stamped his foot in frustration. "You'll be the death of me. What am I to say if I go home without my gown?"

Old Mrs. Guo assumed the role of the good guy and offered to be Simplicity's guarantor. Asked to fix a date for delivering the money, Simplicity said the end of the month. "That's all right, but you've got to keep your word," Mrs. Guo said.

Second Wang gave him back his gown and also told him emphatically, "If you don't bring the money at the end of the month, I'll be coming to Tripod Alley to have it out with you."

He made his promise repeatedly before finally getting away. On his way home, he bitterly regretted having gone there, but what was done was done. As he approached Tripod Alley, he saw two mandarin sedan chairs standing at his door and a white horse tethered there. When he entered the parlor, he saw a steward occupying a high-back chair, with four sedan-chair bearers seated on either side of him.

Simplicity went upstairs to make his report. Second Treasure was entertaining guests, however, so he dared not disturb them. Stealing a look through a gap in the door curtain, he saw two guests but only recognized Elan Ge. The one he did not know was handsome and well-built and had a distinguished air. Simplicity had never come across anybody comparable. He quietly went back downstairs and invited the steward to go sit in the bookkeeper's office at the back. Upon inquiry, Simplicity learned that his master was Third Young Master Shi, widely known for his wealth and connections. A native of Nanjing, he started his career as an official in a scholarly post in the capital. Now aged about twenty, he was known by the name Nature. He was visiting Shanghai for health reasons and had rented a grand foreign-style house at Big Bridge, which was cool and breezy. There, he spent his days conversing with a couple of close friends over a cup of wine. The only thing lacking now was a girl after his heart who could keep him company and add to his pleasure so that the romantic hours of the day would not be wasted.

When Simplicity heard this, he did his best to get on the good side of the steward. He found out that his name was Wang. Known to all as Little Wang, he was Third Young Master's personal steward and had responsibility for his money. Simplicity plied him with endless rounds of tea, opium, and snacks in order to please him, and sure enough Little Wang was delighted.

Soon it was time to light the lamps. The maid, Tiger, relayed the order for the menservants to send for dinner and deliver the invitations. When Simplicity heard this, he asked his mother's permission to order separately four cold platters and four main dishes for the steward. Mrs. Zhao readily agreed. By the time dinner was served upstairs, a table was also set in the bookkeeper's room, with Little Wang in the seat of honor and Simplicity at the humble end. The food and drink put them in excellent spirits, and they indulged their appetite without the least inhibition.

In contrast, the party upstairs had only two guests—Iron Hua and Amity Zhu—so things were on the quiet side. What was more, Third Young Master disliked the heat and was not inclined to stay long.

The departure of the summoned girls was the cue for hosts and guests to leave the table together. They gave orders for their sedan-chair bearers to light the lanterns. Little Wang had no choice but to take a little rice in a hurry and then rush out to stand at attention. After Third Young Master had seen the others off, Little Wang attended on him as he got into his sedan chair and then mounted the horse himself. They left in a file.

CHAPTER 38 :: *Second Treasure hopes for wedded bliss in the Shi family, and Harmony Qi hosts a party in Rustic Retreat*

Simplicity Zhao watched Little Wang flourish his whip and ride out of the alley and then returned to the house to tell Mrs. Zhao about Third Young Master Shi's background. Mrs. Zhao, delighted by the news, made no mention of his fruitless mission to find Fortune Shi.

Unfortunately, the next three days were unbearably hot, and Third Young Master Shi never turned up. The fourth day was the thirtieth of the sixth month. Simplicity got up at the crack of dawn and put together the money he had managed to save, which came to ten dollars. He took it to New Street, where he knocked at Old Mrs. Guo's door and counted it out for her, telling her to take care of things for him. After that, he returned home immediately, convinced that his mother and sister were still in bed and that he had covered his tracks. To his surprise, the servant girl Clever, a hard worker, was already standing in the parlor yawning, her hair uncombed.

"You're up early. You should go back to bed," he tried to make conversation.

"I've got work to do," she replied.

"Need some help?"

She thought he was flirting with her and turned away. Simplicity congratulated himself for having diverted her attention.

As noon approached, a wisp of dark cloud spread from the northwest across the sky, hiding the scorching sun. In the midst of thunder and lightening, the skies opened. The downpour lasted for two hours, after which the sun came out again. Second Treasure had just finished her toilet and was cooling herself in the breeze that came through the window when she saw a man, panting and perspiring heavily, rushing into the parlor holding a call chit. Then Simplicity came upstairs to formally announce that Third Young Master Shi was calling her to the Shi residence at Big Bridge. Delighted, Second Treasure proceeded there by sedan chair.

By nightfall, there was still no sign of her returning. Worried and agitated, Simplicity was on the point of going to fetch her himself when the maid Tiger and the two sedan-chair bearers returned by themselves. Simplicity turned pale and, staring wide-eyed at them, asked, "Where is she?"

Tiger was amused. She turned to Mrs. Zhao and said, "Second Miss is not coming back. Third Young Master has asked her to spend the summer at the house, at the rate of ten party calls a day. I'm to fetch her clothes and her toiletry set right now."

Mrs. Zhao had little to say in response, but Simplicity rebuked Tiger, "You're a bold one! How could you have left her on her own?"

"Second Miss told me to come back," she replied.

"Now be more careful next time. If something should go wrong, you, as the maid, would be held responsible, too."

Tiger looked displeased. "There's no need to get into a state. I have four hundred dollars invested in this, too, so would I be careless? I've been in the business since I was little, making my way up to be a maid. You go and ask around—what trouble did I ever get into?"

Simplicity had no answer to that and withdrew in silence. To make peace, Mrs. Zhao said, "Don't pay him any attention, just get the things and go."

Tiger went upstairs, grumbling all the way. She put everything onto two pieces of foreign wrapping cloth that she tied up into two bundles and then bade Mrs. Zhao good-bye and went out.

Feeling unsettled, Simplicity did not get any sleep all night. The next day, after consulting his mother, he bought a lot of fresh peaches and lichees that he put into two boxes and a tall basket and then set off to pay his sister a visit. A ricksha took him past Big Bridge to the door of the Shi residence. It was indeed a grand foreign-style house. Four or five hulking fellows were seated on the benches on either side of the door. Thickly built and wearing black leather boots, they looked like army officers. Simplicity hesitantly explained to one of them the purpose of his visit, but the officer just kept fanning himself and ignored him. Simplicity stood there, his body bending forward respectfully to await instructions.

Suddenly, another officer turned around and barked at him, "Wait over there."

Simplicity withdrew to one end of the wall, his face flushing in the full glare of the sun. Fortunately, he saw the man who had brought the call chit yesterday plodding toward him, leading a horse. He went up, saluted the man, and asked him to notify Little Wang. The man merely shot him a glance and continued on his way. A while later, a boy of thirteen or fourteen rushed out shouting, "Where's the man named Zhao?"

Not daring to answer, Simplicity peeped into the house. The officer glared at him and shouted again, "You're called!"

Simplicity picked up his basket and made to leave.

The boy seized him. "Is your name Zhao?"

"Yes, yes, it is," he answered.

"Follow me."

As he followed at the boy's heels and entered the first gate, he saw a courtyard of about an acre where rare flowers grew. The main building had three stories while the two wings had one. He walked along a multicolored cobblestone path that led to a covered walkway along one wing. He saw dimly through the window that there were many people in the room, all dressed casually, discoursing in a lofty manner.

The boy led him to a bungalow behind the main building, where Little Wang was standing at the curtained door to welcome him. Simplicity hastened to greet him, first setting down his basket, and then made a salute.

Little Wang invited him into his bedroom and said, "They haven't come downstairs yet. Take off your gown and have a smoke. There's time enough."

The boy served Simplicity ready-made tea in a lidded cup. Little Wang then sent him off to keep watch.

"Let us know as soon as they come down."

The boy made an affirmative noise and went off. Little Wang said to Simplicity, "Third Master is really fond of your sister, says she's like a respectable woman. If it works out, then you have it made."

Simplicity said "yes" repeatedly. Little Wang then taught him some basic etiquette for the meeting, which he took to heart. Just then the boy called outside. Little Wang knew that meant Third Young Master had come downstairs. He told Simplicity to sit for a while and then rushed off himself. A moment later, he rushed back, lifted the curtain, and beckoned for Simplicity. Carrying his basket, Simplicity followed him to the main building. At the door, Little Wang took the basket from him and led him in. Third Young Master was sitting on the lounge at the center of the room, all smiles, attended by two pages with shaven heads.

"Third Master," Simplicity greeted him, walking up sideways and then bending down on one knee to salute him formally.

Third Young Master just nodded. Little Wang drew near to report briefly. Third Young Master turned to Simplicity with a frown, "There's no need for presents."

Simplicity dared not utter a sound. Third Young Master glanced at Little Wang, who immediately brought a low stool, set it down on the humble side of the lounge, and told Simplicity to sit down.

Soon they heard the steps of bound feet coming down the stairs behind the parlor. Then Second Treasure walked leisurely in, leaning on Tiger's arm. Simplicity stood up with bated breath, not daring to look directly at her.

Second Treasure greeted him and then asked after Mother. That was all she said.

Tiger put in, "Isn't Second Miss quite well here?"

Simplicity had no choice but to bear with her.

Third Young Master gave orders to Little Wang, "Take him to sit outside for a while. See that he has lunch before he goes."

Hearing this, Simplicity withdrew, walking sideways. He then returned to Little Wang's bedroom.

"Make yourself at home. If you want anything, say so. I have something to attend to," Little Wang said. He then called in the boy to wait on Simplicity while he himself hurried off.

Simplicity paced the room. Not until the wall clock had struck one did a manservant bring in a tray of food and wine, which he set out on the table in the outer room. The boy asked Simplicity to take the seat of honor and drink alone. Simplicity just wet his lips and then made an excuse, but the boy urged him solicitously to drink more. Loath to refuse, he downed three cups in succession. Just then, Little Wang rushed in and insisted that Simplicity finish what was in the wine pot; he poured himself a cup to keep Simplicity company, so Simplicity had to do his best to comply.

Before they could start a conversation, one of the pages suddenly called Little Wang away on some unknown business. Simplicity finished lunch, washed his face, and waited until Little Wang returned. Then he thanked him and said good-bye, carrying his empty basket.

"Third Master is asleep. Second Miss wants another word with you," said Little Wang.

Simplicity readily complied and followed Little Wang to the bamboo curtain in front of the main building. Little Wang told him to wait while word was sent in. Then a page rolled up the curtain. Second Treasure, resting a hand on Tiger's arm, stood inside the threshold. She said, "Tell Mother I won't be back till the fifth. When the call chits come, say I've gone to Suzhou."[1]

Simplicity promised to do as she said and then was on his way out. Little Wang took the trouble to see him off at the front door and actually said, "Come and visit in a couple of days."

::

1. Since Suzhou women had the reputation of being great beauties, courtesans all claim to have come from there.

Simplicity got on a ricksha and returned to Tripod Alley, where he told his mother in detail what he had seen. Mrs. Zhao was both delighted and impressed.

On the fifth, Simplicity went to order choice teatime snacks from the Garden of Plenty, and then he proceeded to the foreign store Hall and Holtz to buy various imported candies, biscuits, and fruit. Not until afternoon did they see Little Wang come on horseback. He was followed by two official sedan chairs and one medium-sized sedan chair, all of which stopped at their door. Tiger came out of the medium-sized chair to assist Second Treasure into the house, walking behind Young Master Shi. Simplicity darted up to salute him, one knee on the ground. Third Young Master again just nodded in acknowledgment. When they got to Second Treasure's room upstairs, Third Young Master said, "Tell your mother to come out and meet me."

Second Treasure told Tiger to go and ask her. Despite her unwillingness, Mrs. Zhao could not find any way to excuse herself, so she changed into a blouse and skirt of black raw silk and came upstairs shyly. Her faced flushed red after she managed to say the words, "Third Master." He asked how old she was and whether she ate well. That was all.

Second Treasure said to him, "You sit here a while, I'll go downstairs with Mother."

"If there's nothing particular, let's go back soon," he said.

She made an affirmative noise before going downstairs into the little back room, taking Mrs. Zhao by the hand. Only then did Mrs. Zhao feel at ease. "Where are you off to now?" she asked.

"We're going home. Back to his house."

"How many days will you be gone this time?"

"It's hard to say. Mr. Qi of Rustic Retreat has invited him to visit on the seventh, and he wants me to go along. We'll see after staying a couple of days there."

Mrs. Zhao advised her earnestly, "Now, you look out for yourself. People like them are used to having their way. When they're in love, they seem ever so nice to you, but if you put a foot wrong, they show their displeasure."

At this remark, Second Treasure glanced outside. She shut the door, nestled against Mrs. Zhao, and spoke in whispers. She said this Third Young Master was heir to three branches of his family. In his own branch, he was married, but he did not have a son yet. His adopted mothers from the other two branches were consulting about his taking a wife for each branch, both of them to live in separate households. He was afraid that he might marry the wrong woman, so he was putting off making the decision.

Mrs. Zhao asked urgently in a low voice, "Did he say he'd marry you?"

"He said he'd first go home to talk it over with his adopted mothers. They have to settle on another one, and then he'll marry both women at the same time. He told me not to do business anymore but to wait for him for three months. He'll be back in Shanghai after getting things ready."

Mrs. Zhao was so happy, she could not close her mouth for grinning.

Second Treasure continued, "Now tell Brother not to come to the house again. It'll be so humiliating when he becomes a brother-in-law in the future. Don't buy them any fruit either; they have too much of it. If there're presents to give him, don't you think I'd know what to buy?"

Mrs. Zhao nodded silently at everything Second Treasure said. The girl had much to say but didn't know where to begin.

"It's been a while now. He's all alone. Go upstairs," Mrs. Zhao hurried her.

Second Treasure walked out of the little room slowly, balancing on her tiny feet. Halfway up the stairs, she peeped into the mezzanine room through the latticed window and saw Simplicity and Little Wang lying side by side on the divan smoking opium. The servant girl, Clever, was leaning close to the divan, making facetious conversation. Annoyed by this sight, she hastened back to her own room.

Third Young Master Shi waited till she came close and then pulled nonchalantly at her blouse and whispered, "Let's go home. There's nothing else, is there?"

She saw small meatballs, steamed buns, and other snacks set out on the table, so she said, "Aren't you going to eat some of our tea things?"

"You eat them for me."

She struggled freed, pretending she had not heard him, and told Tiger to instruct Little Wang to get the sedan chairs ready.

Behaving like a new son-in-law, Third Young Master told Second Treasure to say good-bye and tender his thanks to Mrs. Zhao on his behalf. Mrs. Zhao, too shy to come out, packed a basketful of the assorted candies, biscuits, and fruit and gave it to Tiger to take it with her. Second Treasure looked back and frowned.

Mrs. Zhao whispered into her ear, "There's no one to eat it if we leave it here. Why not take it with you and give it to their servants?"

Second Treasure did not have time to stop her. She hurried out the door and got in her sedan chair the same time as Third Young Master did. With Little Wang riding in front and Tiger bringing up the rear, the procession headed grandly back to the Shi residence at the north end of Big Bridge. The officers guarding the door stood at attention as the bearers carried the sedan chairs into the courtyard and set them down in front of the main building, where Third Young Master and Second Treasure got down, walked into the hall, and sat down shoulder to shoulder.

He saw Tiger bringing in the basket. "What is this?" he asked.

"Well, it's imported stuff. You can't find it anywhere else except in Shanghai," Tiger replied with a smile.

He lifted the lid to look and then laughed out loud.

Second Treasure picked out a pine nut, shelled it, and put it to his lips. "Try it. After all, it's a kind thought from my mother."

He immediately assumed a solemn countenance and held out both hands for it. This made both Second Treasure and Tiger laugh. Then he called to a page to remove the pomelos in the display bowls and replace them with these candies, biscuits, and fruit and to place the two bowls high on the small stands of carved tree roots. His sincerity made Second Treasure extremely grateful, but there is no need to labor the point.

Two days later, it was the seventh night of the seventh month, lovers' day. Third Young Master had Little Wang get everything ready early in the morning. Carefully made up and wearing her best clothes, Second Treasure looked more charming than ever. At ten in the morning, they received a note from their host hurrying them along, after which they got into their sedan chairs in front of the hall and, accompanied only by Little Wang and Tiger, went via First Avenue and Mud Town Bridge to the gate of the Qi residence, Rustic Retreat. The doormen begged to redirect them to the garden, so they threaded through another street to the main garden gate. The word on the plaque, written in clerical script, read "Conical Hat Garden."

The garden attendants invited them in. The sedan chairs were borne straight to the Phoenix Pavilion by the lake. Second Bai and Devotion Yin welcomed them on the covered walkway, and Nature Shi and Second Treasure went up with them to the pavilion, where Aroma, Wenjun Yao, and Green Fragrance all came up to greet them. Nature Shi was surprised the girls had come so early.

"The three of us have been here for two days," said Aroma.

Devotion Yin said, "Harmony is the leader of a true love cult. A couple of days ago, he gave a wedding party for Second Bai and Wenjun. Today, the guests of honor at this seventh night party are you and your lady love."

As they were talking, Harmony Qi emerged and walked toward them, tripping lightly. Nature Shi addressed him as Collegiate Uncle, saluted him with a deep bow, and asked after his health.

Harmony Qi made a few modest remarks, glanced around, and saw Second Treasure. "Is this your lady love?"

"Yes, sir," Nature Shi replied.

"Your Excellency," Second Treasure said in greeting.

Harmony Qi, smiling, came over to Second Treasure, took her hands, and looked her up and down. He then nodded at Second Bai and Devotion Yin, saying, "She certainly has the style of a girl from a good family."

Qi was over sixty. With his grizzled beard and air of innocence and sincerity, he made Second Treasure feel at ease. Everybody sat down and made light conversation. As she was still a stranger, Second Treasure did not say much. Harmony Qi told Aroma to show her the garden. Wenjun Yao and Green Fragrance, both in high spirits, also went along. The four of them walked down the steps on the left of the pavilion and came to a narrow winding path in the green shade of a bamboo grove. The path led to a stream, and they could make out on the other bank, hidden behind the trees, a cluster of gold and turquoise buildings of varying heights. They looked charming but inaccessible.

The four of them followed the stream into a crescent-shaped winding gallery. At both ends of the gallery, its name was inscribed in cursive script: Threshold of the Waves. Once past the gallery, it was curtains of pearls and painted pillars, turquoise tiles, and etched glass. Tall trees reached up to the clouds and brilliant red flowers shone in the sun. The building only had thirty-two chambers, but its visitors felt as if its eaves met up and its roofs were joined, that there were a thousand doors and windows, leaving them confused, not knowing where to go. Its name was Panorama Hall. In front of the hall, amid strange rocks and luxuriant foliage, a rugged peak rose abruptly: the Dragon Range. An octagonal pavilion on the range was called the Mid-sky Pavilion.

A palm arbor had been newly erected in the space between the hall and the hill. With about three hundred pots of jasmine blossoms displayed in the arbor, it did justice to the name Sea of Fragrant Snow. The four women were picking jasmine buds to wear in their hair when suddenly they heard someone calling from way up high. They looked up to find Aroma's servant girl, Greenie, standing alone in the pavilion. She had a lotus flower in her hand and was beckoning to them, smiling. Aroma shouted for her to come down, but Greenie did not seem to hear; she kept beckoning. How could Wenjun Yao stand the suspense? She flew up to the hilltop. When she got there, she waved her arms to beckon the others to join her even more urgently. They were baffled.

"Let's go and have a look," said Green Fragrance. She stepped out, lifting the hem of her skirt to lead the way. Reluctantly, Aroma followed. Holding Second Treasure by the hand, she kept to the stone steps, pausing along the way and panting delicately, quite overcome by exhaustion.

The fact was, the name Conical Hat Garden came from Conical Hat Lake, the circular shape of which symbolized heaven and evoked a conical peasant hat. It occupied a couple of acres and so qualified as a lake. This Conical Hat Lake was situated in the center of the garden. To the southwest was the Phoenix Pavilion, which backed onto the water; to its northwest was Dragon Range, from where one could look down and see the entire garden.

Having arrived at the Mid-sky Pavilion, Aroma and Second Treasure could see that in the distance a group of colorfully dressed women was crowding around the fishing bank in the southeast corner of the lake, and a stream of servant girls and maids were heading there. "What's going on?" they asked Greenie.

"A maid was picking a lotus flower when she saw a fish trap and gave it a pull, and up came a huge golden carp, so everybody has gone to have a look."

"And I thought they were looking at something wonderful! My feet are all sore from so much walking," said Aroma.

"Even with flat heels, I was tripping and falling," said Second Treasure.

But Wenjun Yao, dissatisfied with this distant view, was determined to have a closer look. As the others talked, she streaked off again. Green Fragrance wanted to follow suit, but how could she catch up with Wenjun? The three women sat for a while longer before slowly descending Dragon Range.

"I want to go and change," said Green Fragrance. So they parted company in front of Panorama Hall.

Aroma saw all the windows in Panorama Hall were open and the curtains were hanging low. Four or five menservants were busy arranging tables and chairs. She asked, "Are we having our meal here?"

"This is for tonight. Lunch will be served at the waterside pavilion," the men replied.

Aroma said nothing in reply and took Second Treasure back to the Phoenix Pavilion along the original route. They were greeted by the sight of beautifully decked-out women and could smell their fragrances in the breeze. Four more guests had arrived: Iron Hua, Elan Ge, Cloud Tao, and Amity Zhu. Their girls, White Orchid, Snow Scent, Belle Tan, and White Fragrance, were already seated. Only Wenjun Yao remained standing. She had removed her outer garments and was just wearing a narrow-sleeved blouse of mandarin gauze. Leaning at the window overlooking the lake, she tried to cool herself with a straw fan.

"Did you see it when you got there?" Aroma asked.

Unable to speak, Wenjun signed with her mouth. Aroma turned her head around and saw a medium-sized jar for planting lotus set on an ice-bucket rack. In the jar was a golden carp measuring over a foot long. Second Treasure also gave it a fleeting glance.

"We should catch another one to make a pair." Wenjun came over to them, gesticulating.

"*You'd* have to catch it then," Aroma said teasingly. This brought a smile to every face.

CHAPTER 39 :: *A drinking game sees ivory sticks fly at the pavilion, and golden carp draw fishing boats to compete on the lake*

Two square tables were set in the Phoenix Pavilion with a casual meal of sixteen dishes, eight of them hot appetizers and eight main dishes. The guests followed the usual rule, and each sat with his own girl. Iron Hua, Elan Ge, Cloud Tao, and Amity Zhu took one table, and Nature Shi, Second Bai, Devotion Yin, and Harmony Qi the other. Everybody raised his cup to toast one another, and conventional etiquette was put aside. Second Treasure, still shy, did not join in.

"Don't stand on ceremony when you're here," said Harmony Qi, "we all eat together and drink together. Just look at them."[1]

And indeed she saw Wenjun Yao pick up half a crab marinated in wine, shell it, and eat it. As she ate, she said to Second Treasure, "If you don't eat, nobody will serve you, and you'll be hungry later on."

Smiling, Aroma Su picked up a piece of pork belly with her own chopsticks and put it before Second Treasure. Only then did Second Treasure start eating.

"Since she's a free woman, why be a courtesan?" Second Bai suddenly asked.

"The usual story: to make ends meet," Nature Shi answered for her.

Harmony Qi heaved a long sigh. "This city of Shanghai is like a trap; too many people have fallen in."

::

1. This goes contrary to the rules of the sing-song houses, where courtesans have to sit behind their clients and are not supposed to partake of the food, hence Second Treasure's hesitation.

Nature Shi answered, "A relative of hers came to Shanghai with her and has become a courtesan, too."

"What's her name? Where does she live?" Devotion Yin asked immediately.

Second Treasure took it up. "Her name's Flora Zhang. She's in West Civic Peace Alley, in the same house as Belle Tan."

Devotion Yin called across to the other table to ask Cloud Tao about Flora.

"Oh, she's quite nice. She also looks like a respectable woman. Shall we call her here?" Cloud said.

"Later. We're going to do some drinking now," said Devotion.

Harmony Qi asked Nature Shi to start a drinking game. Nature thought as he ate the first dish—shark's fin—that since Cloud Tao and Amity Zhu did not like poetry and fine writing, this game had to have a broad appeal. He announced, "Well, I have an idea. Let's each pick an item on the table and use quotation from the *Four Classics* to 'stack a pyramid.'[2] How about that?"

"Your word is our command," everybody said.

The servants, used to attending such literary games, moved a small tea table over and opened a sandalwood stationery box that contained all the necessary equipment: writing brushes, inkstones, ivory sticks, and dominoes.

To take command of the game, Nature Shi first drank a cup of wine. "My key word is fish," he said. "Let's draw lots for our turn. The one who comes last will be the next commander."

"But there aren't many quotations in the *Four Classics* we can use for 'fish,'" said Harmony Qi.

"Let's give it a try and see," replied Nature Shi.

The eight men each drew an ivory stick and wrote down a quotation from the *Four Classics* on it, followed by his name. The servants collected all the sticks, meticulously copied out the quotations on colored notepaper, and then submitted it for their inspection. Both tables were vacated as they read it. They praised one another in unison and then each drank a cup to mark the end of round one.

Cloud Tao, being the next commander, chose the word "chicken." They drew lots again with the ivory sticks, after which they all remained silent. Some paced around with their eyes on the ground, while others did word counts on their fingers. Wenjun Yao found the game boring. The key word "fish" reminded her of something, and, after hastily downing two cups of wine, she dashed off. Think-

::

2. So called because each succeeding quotation has to be one word longer than the previous one.

ing she was just bored, Second Bai paid no attention. When everyone had written his quotation on the ivory stick, the servants again had it all copied out for their perusal and mutual admiration. It was then Iron Hua's turn to be commander.

"Now that we've used 'fish' and 'chicken,' things are getting harder," said Iron Hua.

"If you can't think of a word, just drink a tumbler of wine and pass up the command. Anybody who can think of a word can take over," said Nature.

Iron Hua stared silently ahead and then suddenly said, "Got it! What about 'meat'?"

"Good" was the general response.

"Now it's really getting difficult! I wonder who's going to have to take over after this," said Elan Ge.

Once more the servants copied the quotations out for them to read. It was now Second Bai's turn. But instead of assuming the command, he just poured himself a full cup of wine.

"Are you going to drink and pass?" asked Devotion Yin.

"What's the matter with you? Won't you even let me drink?" replied Second Bai. "If you want to take over, you're welcome."

Smiling, Devotion turned around and told the servant to spread out the ivory sticks.

When Second Bai finished his drink, he said loudly, "Let it be 'wine' then!"

Harmony Qi guffawed. "It's wine that we're drinking, so why didn't any of us think of it, I wonder?"

Without deliberation, everybody dashed off their quotations.

Devotion had written the last quotation. Having finished reading it, Second Bai said to him, "Now it's your turn. Go on."

After a slight pause, Devotion replied, "I will when you have drunk a large tumbler of penalty wine."

"Why's that?"

"You need a pointed top to make a pyramid. Now there are sentences beginning with the words 'meat,' 'fish,' and 'chicken' in the *Four Classics*, so the pyramids all have a tip. But you chose 'wine.' Is there a sentence in the *Four Classics* that starts with the word 'wine'?"

Harmony Qi was the first to applaud. "That makes sense."

Nature Shi nodded in agreement.

Second Bai had no choice but to accept the punishment. After that, he said to Devotion, "You're what is called the convict type. Your greatest talent lies in finding fault with others."

Devotion ignored him and proceeded with the game. "Let's use the word 'grain.' There seem to be many instances of it in the *Four Classics*."

Upon hearing this, Second Bai shouted loudly, "Now it's your turn to be punished! We're here to drink. Who wants anything to do with grain?" He snatched the wine pot and poured wine into a tumbler. Would Devotion submit to that? The argument that ensued made everybody laugh uproariously.

Just then, they suddenly heard three or four maids shouting together at the back of the pavilion. Alarmed, everybody approached the railings to look out on the lake. They saw that Wenjun Yao had got into one of the skiffs tied up by the bank and, fishing net in hand, set out to catch a golden carp. The maids, worried, were trying to call her back. But would she listen? Paddling hard, she swung out toward the middle of the lake.

Second Bai took one look and then dashed toward the river bank, where he picked up a bamboo pole and leapt onto another skiff. He freed the mooring ropes and, with a hefty kick, sent the boat off. It shot like an arrow straight toward Wenjun's skiff. When he got to the middle of the lake, he poked the bamboo pole at the stern of her skiff. One hard push sent it spinning round and round. Though she was agitated at having lost control of her boat, she did not beg for mercy.

"You want a fish? If you persist in this, I'll overturn your boat so you can take a bath. Don't you doubt it!" Second Bai said, laughing.

Cheeks flushed red, she waited silently until the boat had settled somewhat and paddled herself back to the shore. He turned around and followed her.

Back on shore, she fixed him with her beautiful eyes, now wide with anger. Her cherry lips in a pout, she leapt toward him like a gust of wind. He ran; she followed in hot pursuit. But when she got into Phoenix Pavilion, he had disappeared without a trace. She was about to press on, when Harmony Qi barred the way with outstretched arms. She tried to duck under his arms, but he took advantage of the move to embrace her. "That's enough. Now out of regard for this old man, just forgive him and be done with it," Qi pleaded.

"No, Your Excellency! He said he'd throw me into the water. I'd like to see him do it!"

"He was talking nonsense. Don't pay him any attention."

Still she would not desist. Seeing Second Bai peeking through the bamboo curtain, Qi called out, "Come here! How can you run away after you've made your girl angry?"

Second Bai edged into the pavilion, bowing to her and apologizing for his behavior. Fired up again, she struggled free. He panicked and rushed out of the pavilion once more. She pursued him for some distance but, surmising that she would not be able to catch him, returned in dejection.

Devotion Yin said, "Come, the two of us will play the game 'officers' roll call.'"

It was her favorite game, one that she never turned down. So guests at the two tables joined together to play the finger game, and the squabbling was forgotten. Soon the air was filled with the tinkling of jeweled bracelets. Having lost two rounds, Wenjun was getting tipsy. Besides, the others also wanted to save some of the gaiety for the night, so Harmony Qi told a servant to ask Second Bai to come for rice.

"Mr. Gao has already had lunch with Secretary Ma in the study," reported the servants.

Harmony Qi smiled and left it at that.

After lunch, they walked around in small groups of three or five. Some played with the cranes, others looked at the fish, yet others sipped tea or showed off plants they had found. They rested on stones washed by the stream and went in search of willows and flowers. Only the host, Harmony Qi, went back to his bed chambers for a nap.

Devotion Yin strolled idly along the lakeshore with Green Fragrance, Aroma Su, and Wenjun Yao. They happened to come round again to Panorama Hall, where they saw that the three hundred pots of jasmine had been moved to the corridors. Multicolored glass globes hung around the arbor. Thick ropes were tied around the palm beam at the center of the arbor, and a huge box of fireworks was suspended from it.

Aroma pointed at the fireworks and said, "They say they were ordered from Guangdong. I wonder if they're really as good as people say."

"What can be particularly good about them? They're just fireworks," said Devotion Yin.

"If they're no good, why would anyone pay so much for them?" Green Fragrance asked.

"I've never seen fireworks before. I'll take a look now and see what they're like," Wenjun Yao said. She strolled down the steps and scrutinized the box.

It so happened that Second Bai was coming this way. On seeing her in the distance, he smiled and saluted her with a bow. She simply ignored him. Second Bai walked surreptitiously toward the arbor but dared not go straight in. Green Fragrance could not suppress her titter. When Devotion Yin turned around and saw this, he said, "What is it with the two of you? When all the guests arrive later on, won't you be embarrassed?"

Aroma beckoned to Second Bai. "Come, Mr. Gao, it's all right. We'll help you."

Second Bai was just about to walk up the steps when he saw a man come running toward them. It was Qi's steward, Felicity Xia.

"The guests are here," Xia reported.

Second Bai held back and walked away to avoid the crowd; Devotion Yin also took off with Aroma, Wenjun, and Green Fragrance. As they strolled across the Bridge of Nine Twists, they saw in front of them the Lingering Clouds Lodge, which consisted of three rooms and was situated under an artificial hill. Nature Shi and Iron Hua were playing chess there, with Second Treasure and White Orchid leaning against the table watching the game. They filed in and stood about casually.

A note of a Kun opera song suddenly trilled in the air, accompanied by a flute. The music was carried to them on the wind.

"Who's singing?" said Green Fragrance.

"The theater troupe must be having singing lessons in Pear Blossom Court," Aroma replied.

"No, I don't think it's them. Let's go and find out," Wenjun said.

Following the music, she walked northward with Green Fragrance. They peeped through the bamboo fence and saw Elan Ge and Snow Scent singing a duet at the top of the steps beside the archery path, with Cloud Tao playing the flute and Belle Tan marking time on the wooden clapper. Wenjun Yao dashed across the straight path for archery practice and up the steps; Green Fragrance had no choice but to try and keep up, panting and perspiring. When she ran past the Right Target Hall, her elder sister, White Fragrance, called out, "What're you running like that for?"

Green Fragrance had no answer. White Fragrance told her to come near, checked her bracelets and hair ornaments, and gently rebuked her.

Green Fragrance saw Amity Zhu smoking opium on the lounge at the center of Right Target Hall. "Brother-in-law," she greeted him and then propped her elbows on the edge of the lounge and chatted with her sister. Before she knew it, it was nightfall. The servants lit the lamps in all the buildings. The three paraffin lamps at Right Target Hall shone brightly, illuminating the archery path.

Longevity Zhang came to report, "Secretary Ma is over there now."

Amity Zhu told Longevity to put away the opium tray, while he took the Lin sisters to the banquet. Paraffin lamps lit the way to Panorama Hall, which shone gloriously through the thin mist. The front part of the hall was surprisingly quiet; there were just seven or eight actresses getting dressed there. It turned out that the banquet was set in the center hall, behind a courtyard, with nine tables arranged in three rows. All the guests had arrived and were deferring

to each other as to seating order. Seeing there was still room at Devotion Yin's table, Amity Zhu sat down across from him while White
Fragrance and Green Fragrance sat next to each other. Of the girls
who had been summoned later, those who were willing to sit down at
the tables had room made for them, while those who wouldn't could
please themselves.

There was a stage in the hallway facing the courtyard on which
the girls of the home theater troupe gave a performance. Once the
gongs and drums sounded, everybody concentrated on drinking and
watching the show, for it was quite impossible to talk. Even the host,
Harmony Qi, could only apologize for not plying everyone with
food and drink by saying briefly, "Please excuse my rudeness."

As time passed, more girls arrived. By now, the hall was packed.
Some of the guests had called two girls; even Devotion Yin had summoned another girl, Flora Zhang. Seeing Second Treasure, Flora
nodded in greeting. Since Fortune Shi had stopped seeing her a
long time ago, Second Treasure was ready to let bygones be bygones
and did not mind talking to Flora, but the noise prevented them
from having a real heart-to-heart. By the time a dessert dish had
been served and two of the summoned girls had each sung an aria
from Peking opera, Second Treasure found it too hot to remain
with the crowd. She got up and gestured to Devotion Yin and then
took Flora Zhang with her. They went out by the corridor on the
left and headed toward the Bridge of Nine Twists, where they leaned
against the railings to talk at leisure.

"How's business for you?" Second Treasure asked.

Flora just shook her head.

"This guest named Yin is quite nice; just try harder with him,"
said Second Treasure. Flora nodded in assent. Second Treasure
then asked about Fortune Shi.

"How many times did he come to your place? He never came to
West Civic Peace Alley," Flora said.

"Guests like him are unreliable. I heard he's seeing Third Treasure now," said Second Treasure.

Flora was keen on getting more details, but just then somebody
approached, so they both stopped talking. When the person came
close, they saw it was Aroma. Aroma thought the two of them had
come out to answer a call of nature, so she asked Second Treasure in
a whisper. It turned out to be exactly what the latter wanted.

"I was just going to call on Pendant. Let's go to her place," said
Aroma.

Flora and Second Treasure followed Aroma down the bridge and
then headed northward. They came to a white wall with a black lacquered door. When they walked in, they saw an old woman mend-

ing clothes under an oil lamp. Aroma took them straight upstairs to Pendant's bedroom. Pendant, who was lying in bed, got up in a fluster to greet them, addressing Aroma as "Maestro." Aroma whispered something to her.

"But my place is filthy," Pendant said in response.

"I don't think you need to be so modest," said Aroma.

Second Treasure could not suppress a smile, and then she went behind the bed. Flora Zhang withdrew to the outer room to catch the breeze at the window. Aroma then asked Pendant, "Are you feeling all right?"

"It's nothing serious; just a sore throat. That's why I couldn't sing."

"His Excellency told me to come and ask after you and to say there's no need for you to sing if you can't manage it. Are you coming?"

"Since His Excellency is summoning me, how can I decline to go?" Pendant said with a smile. "You mustn't joke about coming here to invite me, Maestro."

"But it's true. His Excellency was afraid you were having a lie-down because you didn't feel well. I'm just here to ask you; it's all right if you don't want to go."

Pendant insisted she would. Just then Second Treasure finished and washed her hands, so Pendant made ready to go with them.

"Aren't you going to change at all?" Aroma asked.

Embarrassed, Pendant went to get changed.

Flora Zhang suddenly beckoned to them from the outer room. "Come out and have a look. It's fun here."

Second Treasure followed her to the window and looked out. She saw Panorama Hall at the southwest corner of the garden, surrounded by firelight. The light was reflected in Conical Hat Lake, where the ripples flickered and formed strange patterns of light and shadow. The sound of music and singing, soft and melancholy, seemed familiar but distant, as though it had come from high above the clouds. Second Treasure, entranced, agreed with Flora that it was fascinating. They did not leave until Pendant had changed and Aroma came out to invite them to go. They deferred to each other on their way out and returned along the same route. Halfway there, they met the head steward, Felicity Xia, who had a lantern in his hand and was heading in another direction. Seeing the four of them, he stood aside to let them pass and said pleasantly, "Maestro, do go and look at the fireworks."

Aroma asked as she walked on, "And where are *you* going?"

"I'm fetching somebody to set them off. They're said to work best when set off by the man who made them." He then went on his way.

The four women went back to Panorama Hall, where Second

Treasure and Flora Zhang rejoined their table. Aroma told a man-servant to place a stool beside Harmony Qi and asked Pendant to sit down.

The opera had just ended, and the musicians onstage had taken their instruments into the arbor to await instructions. Most of the guests were engaged in conversation. Pendant sat there silently with a pallid face, wearing no makeup and no jewelry, her head hung low as if weighed down by melancholy. Harmony Qi regretted his rashness in summoning her and said solicitously, "I didn't call you here to sing, just to watch the fireworks. After that, you can go back to bed." She stood up to answer yes.

In a moment, Steward Xia reported, "They're ready."

"This way, please," said Harmony Qi to his guests. One of the menservants in attendance then spoke in a sonorous voice, requesting Secretary Ma and the honored guests to walk over to the front of the building to watch the fireworks. Thereupon everybody left their tables.

CHAPTER 40 :: *A bridge of magpies joins two stars on Lovers' Day, and a witty pun is a stone that kills two birds*

Secretary Ma was known to his friends by the name Dragon. A native of Hangzhou, he was just in his thirties but was already well-known for his literary accomplishments. Descended from a long line of Confucian scholars, he was strong in his loyalty and unworldly in his aspirations. His friendly disposition and interesting conversation made him a magnet for learned scholars as well as women and children; there were none who did not delight in his company. Harmony Qi invited him home to stay and sought his advice every day.[1] Qi once said, "One word from Dragon is enough to set my mind thinking for three days."

As for Dragon, he found that Harmony was not one for flaunting despite his wealth, and, though amiable, he never drifted with

::

1. [The trusted personal secretary of a Chinese official was a personal adviser rather than a government employee. He was on the official's—rather than on government—payroll. It was a position often filled by men of talent who failed the civil service examinations. Dragon Ma's first name in Chinese—Longchi, or "the dragon in a pond"—suggests his abilities and ambition were higher and bigger than his situation in life. *E.H.]*

the tide. Since he stood as a pillar in the world of social entertainment, Dragon playfully gave him the sobriquet "Grand Leader of the Cult of Love." Whenever Harmony had a party, Dragon devised something special to enhance his enjoyment. The seventh night fireworks were one such example. He hired craftsmen from Guangdong, gave them verbal instructions, and, within a month, the work was finished.

If Dragon had a flaw, it was one shared by many: he was a henpecked husband. Though a resident of Shanghai, he dared not misbehave. Since Harmony insisted on calling a girl for him at parties, he could not very well refuse. At first, he just called any girl, but after a while he found that Sunset Wei's temperament was similar to his wife's, so he called Sunset regularly.

This night, Sunset and Dragon were placed at the head of the table. They now followed the others to the front courtyard of Panorama Hall to view the fireworks. All the windows there had been shut, and the lamps and candles had been blown out. They were enveloped in darkness.

As the craftsmen from Guangdong lit the fuse, the musicians played the marshal tune "General's Orders." The fuse burned into a hole, and the bottom of the hanging box fell off to the ground. Two long strings of firecrackers were the first to go off, each consisting of a hundred shots, making a deafening noise. That was followed by a shower of twinkling golden stars. Then a great brilliance radiated from the box, illuminating every tiny speck in its immediate surroundings. The music became soft and gentle, and the Cowherd and the Weaving Maid slowly descended, one on either side of the box. The Cowherd had his buffalo on a rope, and the Weaving Maid was leaning against her loom. They gazed soulfully at each other.[2]

As the music faded, drumbeats sounded. Countless fiery balls came spinning down to encircle a dancing blue dragon that hovered in the space between the Cowherd and the Weaving Maid. The tribal drums now took over, making a sound similar to popping beans; this was echoed by the brass gongs. Out of the dragon's mouth came dozens of moon rockets that fell to the ground like pearls of vary-

::

2. [According to myth, the Cowherd and the Weaving Maid (the constellations Altair and Vega) fell in love and became derelict in their duties. This angered the Emperor of Heaven, who had them separated by the Silver River, or Milky Way. They were only allowed to meet once a year, on the seventh night of the seventh month, when magpies formed a bridge over the Milky Way. E.H.]

ing sizes. Yellow smoke, heavy with fragrance, came out between the scales on the dragon's body and hung in the air for a long time. The spectators cheered.

A moment later, the music from the gongs and drums quickened. The dragon spun its head and tail to turn a hundred somersaults. Out of nowhere, there came sprays of firelight to envelop the dragon's entire body; it looked fierce and uncontrollable, ready to cause havoc in the great seas and rivers. The spectators' loud cheers went on and on.

When the sparks died down and the drums and gongs fell silent, the dragon hung still in the air, brightly lit from head to tail, every scale and claw distinct. A scroll unfolded from the little wooden box at its head, with these words written on it:

*The Emperor of Heaven has decreed*
*The Cowherd and the Maid may cross the river*

To the beat of the tune "Imperial Audience" played by the musicians, the Cowherd and the Weaving Maid bowed as if acknowledging the decree. As the spectators pressed forward for a closer look, they could see that the hands and feet of the figures were just attached to a thin thread. When the dragon's threads broke and it fell to the ground, the servant hurried over to pick it up. It turned out to be a little longer than the full height of a man, with sparks of fire not quite extinguished.

Just then, the Cowherd and the Weaving Maid, following the imperial decree, conjured up a shooting star that flew out of their palms. It went along a fuse into the box. Now all the brass instruments burst into music, and forty-nine black magpies flew out and took up their positions in formation to make an arched bridge. Their outstretched wings made them look truly alive.

This sight so amazed the spectators that they forgot to cheer. Instead they just pushed forward for a better look. The musicians now played on their bugles a tune resembling a wedding song, whereupon the Cowherd left his water buffalo and the Weaving Maid her loom, and they both ascended to meet beside the bridge. The two figures and the forty-nine magpies, together with the water buffalo and the loom, now burst into sprays of fireworks that looked very different from what had come before. These were in the form of bamboo leaves or orchid flowers. Flying in all directions, they were the very picture of the saying "Where fiery trees merge with silver blossoms, the bridge of the stars is unchained."

This was a sight that sent even the menservants jumping up and down with excitement, all their manners forgotten. The display took fully a quarter of an hour, at the end of which the two figures, the magpies, the buffalo, and the loom were clearly illuminated. Now they saw the fine features of the Cowherd and the Weaving Maid and the loving looks they gave each other as they stood together, loath to be separated.

The closing music was again "General's Orders." When the music came to an end, the Cantonese craftsmen let go of the threads, and everything fluttered to the ground. All lights were extinguished, and they were once more enveloped in darkness.

"We've never seen fireworks such as this!" everyone said. Harmony Qi and Dragon Ma were of course delighted. The servants opened the windows in the front court and invited everyone to return to the banquet. As the many girls summoned late to the party now took the opportunity to leave, Sunset Wei and Flora Zhang also said their farewells, and Pendant returned to her room, too. For fear of overtiring their host, many of the guests left without saying good-bye. As a result, only about a dozen people returned to the banquet. When Harmony Qi tried to summon his private theater troupe for a performance, they, too, pleaded intoxication. Since Pendant was not singing, Harmony Qi himself was not in high spirits. He told Aroma to offer each of the guests three more toasts. As she stood up, the menservants poured the drinks. Without waiting to be pressed, the guests drained their share and showed her the bottoms of their cups. After that, rice was served, and the banquet was over.

Harmony Qi said, "I was going to drink all night with you, but tonight is a night for lovers and should not be wasted. So why don't you retire at your pleasure, and we'll meet another day, all right?" He then laughed loudly. A steward was waiting for him, lamp in hand, and so he saluted everyone and excused himself.

Dragon Ma went back to the study by himself, and Elan Ge, Cloud Tao, Amity Zhu, and several relatives of Qi's were put up elsewhere. They were accompanied on their way by servants with lanterns. Nature Shi and Iron Hua had bedrooms furnished for them in Panorama Hall, near the rooms of Second Bai and Devotion Yin. A manservant led the way, and they went upstairs with their girls. They all went to sit a while in Nature Shi's room, where everything was brand-new. It was furnished to the last detail, including face powder jar and spittoon. Nature Shi noticed that Devotion Yin only had the virgin courtesan Green Fragrance for company. "Mr. Devotion will be lonely," he said with a smile.

Devotion gave Green Fragrance a pat on the shoulder. "Not at all. Our little maestro is no greenhorn." She laughed and ran off.

Hoping to find out more about Flora Zhang, Devotion turned to

Second Treasure, but Wenjun Yao kept pestering him for an explanation of how the fireworks worked.

"I don't know," he replied.

"Was there a man hiding in the box?" she asked.

"If there were, he'd have fallen to his death."

"Then how could it have looked so real?" she protested, and the others could not help smiling.

"It was probably puppetry," said Iron Hua.

It still eluded her, and after thinking for a moment, she asked no more questions. A manservant brought in eight kinds of pastries from which they chose what they liked. By then, it was past midnight. The red gauze lanterns hanging under the eaves swayed, their light on the point of going out. Iron Hua, Second Bai, and Devotion Yin all retired to their rooms. The maid Tiger made the bed and waited on Nature Shi and Second Treasure as they prepared for bed; then she, too, withdrew.

The next morning, Nature Shi woke to the chatter of sparrows in the woods. He hurriedly shook Second Treasure awake. They sat up and draped some clothes around their shoulders and then called for Tiger. Only then did they learn it was still early, but they could not very well go back to bed again, so they washed and had breakfast. Tiger spread out the toilet set to do Second Treasure's hair. Nature Shi, who had nothing to do, went out for a stroll. As he passed Second Bai's bedroom, he looked in only to find that neither occupant was in. He lifted the curtain and walked in. Except for the furniture, the room was quite empty; there were neither calligraphy scrolls nor ornaments. Only two items hung on the wall: a sword and a zither. The bed curtains, however, were of white silk and closely painted with plum blossoms. He could tell the work was by Devotion Yin. The blue silk panel across the front of the canopy bore calligraphy in white; it was clearly the work of Iron Hua.[3] He was just reading it when he heard someone call out, "Nature, come over here."

He turned around and saw Devotion Yin calling from his room across the courtyard, so he walked over. Devotion, who had just got up and needed to wash, asked him to make himself comfortable.

::

3. [The different styles in which the rooms are decorated reflect the character of their occupants. Second Bai's high opinion of himself is shown in the fact that his room contains only two choice pieces by his close friends—people comparable to him in talent. Though Iron Hua plays but a peripheral role in this story, he is presented as extremely well connected and talented. In Eileen Chang's opinion, Hua is a self-portrait of the author, Han Bangqing. *E.H.*]

This room looked quite different from Second Bai's. It was heavily decorated in gilts and brocades, with all the symbols of wealth on display. Nature Shi took no notice of this. His attention was caught by several roughly bound volumes on the desk by the window. He asked Devotion what they were.

"Last year, Harmony printed an anthology of poems and essays called *The Complete Works of Associates of the Conical Hat Garden*. Some exquisite short items were left out because they didn't quite stand on their own, you know, things like antithetical scrolls and inscriptions on the buildings, seals, short pieces on utensils, riddles posted on lanterns, compositions resulting from drinking games, and so on. It seemed a pity to throw away all of it, so he told me to make another anthology, an appendix, so to speak. Now the selection's half done, but it's yet to go to print."

Nature picked up the book and turned to a section that contained compositions from drinking games. "Will those from yesterday be included?" he asked.

"I've thought about that. Besides the four words 'fish,' 'chicken,' 'wine,' and 'meat' we used, there are three more possibilities: 'rice,' 'lamb,' and 'soup.' Altogether there can be seven words," said Devotion Yin.

"But does the *Four Classics* have 'rice', 'lamb,' and 'soup' in quotations with the required numbers of characters?"

"Well, I've got all the necessary quotations from the *Four Classics*," and he recited them all.

Nature Shi laughed after he heard the recitation. "I bet you couldn't sleep last night, so you spent the whole night thinking these up, right?"

"I had no trouble sleeping," Devotion quipped, "but I doubt if you found the time."

As they were talking, Second Treasure had finished her toilet. Hearing Nature's voice, she followed him out. Devotion looked her up and down and then said with a smile, "Now somebody definitely won't be able to sleep tonight."

Though she did not know what he was talking about, she knew it was directed at her, so she turned aside and murmured, "Say whatever you like." He immediately tried to explain his remark away, but would she believe him? Nature Shi just laughed.

A steward came to invite them to lunch, which was served in the center room of Panorama Hall. Harmony Qi and Aroma asked them to take the table of honor; the one on the humbler side was already occupied by several of Qi's relatives. Then they saw Wenjun Yao come in. She was wearing a short blouse and matching pants and had a bag of arrows hanging at her waist and a bow on her back.

Behind her came Iron Hua, White Orchid, Elan Ge, Snow Scent, Cloud Tao, Belle Tan, Amity Zhu, White Fragrance, Green Fragrance, and Second Bai. Wenjun put down her bow and arrows and sat down at the table of honor. Besides her, only Green Fragrance came over to sit by Devotion's side.

When all the wine cups had been filled three times and two sets of dishes had been served, Harmony Qi again asked for a drinking game.

"We haven't finished yesterday's game yet," said Second Bai.

"Oh, but we did," said Nature, who then repeated the quotations for "rice," "lamb," and "soup" that Devotion had taken from the *Four Classics*.

"Is it so impossible for us to come up with eight words?" Harmony Qi asked.

"Now, if it's a Western meal, we can have 'ox,'" said Devotion.

"Come now, the ox devotes its whole life to serving humans, why place it among all these other beasts?" Second Bai asked.

"Second Bai does have a sharp tongue, and it shoots straighter than Wenjun's arrows," Iron Hua said jokingly.

Devotion Yin applauded, "Wonderful! That's what you call 'killing two hawks with one arrow.'"

Nature Shi took it up: "Since we have chicken, fish, ox, lamb, all of those beasts, why don't we include 'hawk' as well?"

At first, nobody understood the joke, but after a moment's reflection they all burst into irrepressible laughter. "Why is everybody making fun of Second Bai and Wenjun today?" they exclaimed.

Harmony Qi stroked his whiskers and said, "Well, 'there's no holding back an arrow on a tightly drawn bow.'"

Second Bai nodded in agreement. "At least the jokes are not vulgar. Do continue, everybody, it helps me to down the wine." He poured a large cup of wine and gave it to Wenjun, saying, "You're a hawk, too, so you should drink a cup of penalty gift as well." At this, laughter broke out again.

"Let's all drink to keep her company. Consider it our punishment," said Nature Shi and Iron Hua, upon which the servants filled everybody's wine cups.

Sipping at his wine, Devotion asked Second Treasure, "Can Flora Zhang hold her wine?"

"Once you become her patron, you'll find out; why ask?" Second Treasure replied.

"Flora can probably match your capacity. Want to put her to the test?" Cloud Tao said.

"Devotion can't keep Flora Zhang out of his mind. I'm sure we're going there later," said Second Bai.

Since Devotion had indeed found Flora quite to his liking, he made no rejoinder. Instead he joined everybody in two drinking games, after which the party broke up, and they took a short rest.

It was soon dusk. Devotion invited everyone at the party to go and visit Flora Zhang. Qi's relatives declined, while Qi himself said, "I won't go this time. If she suits you, ask her to come back to the garden with you."

Devotion gave his promise. The seven men, together with their girls, each took a leather-topped carriage and went on their way. Green Fragrance managed to suppress her jealousy and rode in the same carriage with Devotion Yin. They traveled past Mud Town Bridge and headed for Fourth Avenue via the Bund. When the carriages stopped at West Civic Peace Alley, Cloud Tao and Belle Tan led the way into her house, and they all crowded into Flora Zhang's room upstairs. Taken by surprise, Flora went around trying to get things ready, all flustered. Second Bai restrained her, saying, "Don't bother with this pointless entertaining. Just order dinner quickly. We'll be going back after we've had a bite."

Flora Zhang immediately had word relayed to the menservants to order dinner and set the table. Amity Zhu took the opportunity to go over to Belle Tan's room to smoke his fill of opium with Cloud Tao, while Green Fragrance pulled impatiently at her elder sister, White Fragrance, and they walked away together.

Out of boredom, Second Treasure, who was sitting alone, went and opened Flora's wardrobe. She found something and beckoned to Nature Shi to come and look. It was several sets of erotic paintings. Nature handed them to Devotion Yin, who barely glanced at them before putting them down on the table, saying, "Not much good."

Iron Hua picked up one set that was ragged, opened it, and saw that although the colors had faded, the figures were lifelike. "This one is pretty good," he said.

Elan Ge, who was standing by his side, also said, "Yes, not bad at all." It was a pity that there were only seven pictures and no seal or signature to identify the painter.

Second Bai examined all the pictures. The first seemed to be a scene of welcome and the last a send-off. The five in between depicted one man and three women, showing the same faces in all five pictures. "These are probably scenes from some novel," he said.

"You're right," Nature Shi smiled and said. He pointed at one of the women. "Look, she looks a bit like Wenjun." Everyone laughed and put the pictures aside. The menservants brought in hot towels, and Devotion Yin asked them to step out to the parlor where the table for dinner had been set.

CHAPTER 41 :: *Harsh words in the boudoir kill old loyalties, and a re-union in the garden cures lovesickness*

Once the seven of them sat down around the table, a bank was set up for the finger game, and there was much noisy gaiety. Seeing how Flora Zhang tried to please Devotion in every way, Second Bai just waited until the desserts were served before he left with Nature Shi, Iron Hua, and Elan Ge, each taking his girl with him. Amity Zhu also took his leave and escorted White Fragrance and Green Fragrance home. Cloud Tao and Devotion Yin were the only ones to remain. Belle Tan and Cloud Tao knew each other so well that we need not dwell on them. Flora Zhang, taking Second Treasure's advice to heart, behaved in an easygoing and unaffected manner and managed to give Devotion Yin great satisfaction.

On the ninth, a servant of Harmony Qi's came to see Tao and Yin with two invitation cards, asking them to return to the garden with their girls.

"Please convey my thanks to Qi," Cloud Tao said to Devotion Yin. "Cloudlet Chen has asked me out tonight, and the venue is just nearby."

And so Devotion Yin set out with Flora Zhang in a leather-topped carriage for Conical Hat Garden.

Cloud Tao waited until dusk before going by sedan chair to dinner at Clever Gem's in Co-security Alley. He happened to arrive at the same time as Lotuson Wang. They greeted each other, and each pressed the other to take precedence at the door. It so happened that Pearlie's son was among the group of children playing at the head of the alley. When he caught sight of Lotuson Wang, he immediately ran home and rushed upstairs into Little Rouge's room to report, "Mr. Wang is drinking at Clever Gem's."

Little Willow, the actor, was in the room, locked in a tight embrace with Little Rouge. Startled by the sight, Pearlie's son tried to withdraw, but it was too late. Little Rouge's embarrassment quickly turned into anger, and she gave the boy a loud dressing-down. Not daring to argue, the boy went downstairs grumbling.

When Pearlie found out what had happened, she answered back in a loud voice, "He's a child, what does he know about anything? You used to send him frequently to go and see where Mr. Wang was, so when he saw Mr. Wang just now, he came to report back to you. Did he do wrong? Ask yourself this: Why isn't Mr. Wang coming anymore? What right d'you have to tell other people off?"

Would Little Rouge stand for such remarks? She blew her top, slapping the table and stamping her feet, making a terrible racket.

Pearlie sneered. "There's no need to make a row. I'm just a maid; if you don't like me, I can be discharged."

Furious, Little Rouge shouted, "If you want to leave, get out at once. D'you think I can't do without you?"

Pearlie did not bother to answer back. She just sneered and then made a bundle of her valuables, bade her colleagues good-bye, and left, head held high, with her son in tow. They spent the night in a place she rented. The next morning, she told her son to keep watch there while she went to find her guarantor for the job and took her bedding back from Little Rouge's. She told Little Rouge's parents and brother that nothing would make her stay.

When lunch was over, Pearlie strolled to the Wang residence on Fifth Avenue and rang the bell. She had to wait for a while before the door was opened by the cook. She gave no greeting and went straight into the parlor. The cook shouted for her to stop: "The master is not in. You have no business going upstairs!"

Pearlie had no answer to that and did not know what to do. Fortunately, Lotuson's nephew heard the noise and came down to investigate.

"Is there anything you want to say?" he asked.

Pearlie told him briefly what had happened. By chance, Constance heard her voice and summoned her upstairs. Pearlie went into her room and greeted her as "my lady concubine" and then stood to one side as etiquette required.

Constance was binding her feet. She insisted that Pearlie take a seat and then asked about Little Willow. Filled with resentment, Pearlie told her everything, lock, stock, and barrel. This was a crowning moment for Constance, who would not stop talking except to laugh heartily.

Before they had exhausted the subject, Lotuson had returned home in his sedan chair. He was greatly surprised to see Pearlie and asked Constance what was the cause of their mirth. Constance relayed in detail what Pearlie had said, laughing as she spoke. Being sentimental, Lotuson ignored her.

Pearlie knew better than to dwell on that again. Instead, she raised a matter that concerned herself. "Twin Pearl of Sunshine Alley is looking for another maid. Could you please recommend me, Mr. Wang?"

Lotuson wanted to refuse, but Pearlie pleaded with him again and again. He finally gave her his card and told her to ask Benevolence Hong instead.

Pearlie took the card, thanked Lotuson, and left. As it was not yet dusk, she headed for Sunshine Alley right away. Seeing two sedan chairs for summoned girls at Twin Pearl's door at this early hour, she could tell that business for this house was booming. She found Golden and asked, "Is Mr. Hong here?"

Thinking that Lotuson Wang had sent Pearlie here, Golden immediately led her to the dinner party in Twin Jade's room. There were only four guests at the table: Cloudlet Chen, Whistler Tang, Benevolence Hong, and Modesty Zhu. Pearlie knew them well and greeted everyone by name. She then produced Lotuson Wang's card from her sleeve, submitted it to Benevolence Hong, explained her predicament, and begged Benevolence to put in a good word for her.

Before Benevolence could speak, Twin Pearl said, "We need someone to look after this room here because Clever Baby can't manage on her own. Would you like to try it out?"

Overjoyed, Pearlie readily agreed and immediately lent Clever Baby a hand in the entertaining. After a while, she went out to refill the wine pot in the kitchen, but as she came to the last step of the stairs, a towel came flying out of the parlor door and covered her head and face.

"Who is it?" she shouted, startled.

The man who threw the towel apologized, looking startled. She saw that it was Modesty Zhu's steward, Longevity. She tossed the towel back to him and refrained from saying anything just then. When she returned to the party with the wine, the two summoned girls, Clever Gem and Green Fragrance, were both taking their leave. Twin Pearl also wanted to go back to her own room and called repeatedly for Golden. There was no answer; no one knew where she had gone.

"Allow me," Pearlie said at once. She picked up Twin Pearl's nutmeg box and followed her back to her room. After Twin Pearl had changed out of her party clothes, Pearlie folded them up carefully and put them in the wardrobe. Then she heard Clever Baby calling loudly for hot towels and, realizing that the party was over, hurried out to clear the table. Benevolence Hong excused himself, saying he had business to attend to, and left together with Cloudlet Chen and Whistler Tang. Modesty Zhu was the only guest who stayed behind. Twin Jade sat with him. They smiled at each other but made no conversation.

Pearlie tactfully followed Clever Baby downstairs, leaving the young lovers alone. Clever Baby took her to see Orchid Zhou, who told her what percentage she would share of the tips at the end of each season. Pearlie agreed to everything. Orchid Zhou then asked about how Lotuson Wang and Little Rouge used to get on, adding, "Recently, Mr. Wang has called our Twin Jade to a dozen parties."

Pearlie heaved a long sigh. "I don't mean to bad-mouth Little Rouge, but Mr. Wang was really a most loving patron to her."

As she spoke, a wailing noise was heard coming from the front door. It was Golden's son, Eldest. Clever Baby dashed out. Pearlie stopped talking and, together with Orchid Zhou, strained her ears to listen, but Eldest just cried and could not make himself clear. Then a manservant from next door came to tell them, "Worth is in a fight. Quick, go and restrain him."

As soon as Orchid Zhou heard this, she knew it had to do with Longevity Zhang. She immediately ordered Pearlie to get someone to stop Worth. Unexpectedly, when news of the fight reached upstairs, Modesty Zhu was so frightened that his face blanched. He snatched up his gown, draped it over himself, and rushed downstairs, paying no attention to Twin Jade calling after him.

He bumped into Pearlie, who was just coming out of Orchid Zhou's room and nearly fell over. Pearlie grabbed hold of him, babbling, "It's under control, Fifth Young Master. Please don't go."

Desperate, he shoved her off and ran straight out. As he headed toward the southern entrance of Sunshine Alley, he saw that his way was blocked by a crowd of spectators. It was indeed Longevity Zhang who had been seized by Worth. Amid the yelling of the spectators, Worth held Longevity by his pigtail and pummeled him till he fell down at the foot of a wall. Modesty turned around immediately and went out by the western entrance. He took a detour via Fourth Avenue to go home, and when he got there, his heart was still thumping hard. Longevity Zhang arrived soon after with bruises on his head and face and told some lie about falling off a ricksha. Modesty did not expose him. At the first opportunity, Longevity begged Modesty to cover up for him. Modesty gave his promise but also admonished Longevity in private. From then on, Longevity Zhang dared not go again to Sunshine Alley, and even Modesty Zhu dared not go and see Twin Jade.

Seven or eight days went by. Twin Jade then asked Benevolence Hong to relay her invitation to Modesty, after which he resumed his visits. Consumed by envy, Longevity Zhang turned Modesty's deflowering of Twin Jade into the talk of the town, holding forth on the subject to all and sundry.

The talk reached the ears of Amity Zhu, who then questioned his younger brother, "Is it true?" Modesty's face flushed bright red; he hung his head and made no reply.

Amity spoke to him kindly. "It's all right to have a bit of fun. I've always told you so, and I was the one who called Twin Jade to a party for you, so why would you want to keep me in the dark? I have my reasons for encouraging you to have a little fun, and you're wrong to try and keep it from me."

Modesty remained silent, so Amity did not go any further into the matter. However, Modesty felt such a strong sense of shame and abashment that he stubbornly kept to his study and did not venture out. At the same time, Twin Jade's looks, voice, and her every movement were replayed daily in his heart. He wrote poems about her, he dreamed about her, and finally he fell ill pining for her. Knowing only too well the reason for his illness, Amity was worried. He sought the advice of Benevolence Hong, Cloudlet Chen, and Whistler Tang. Since they had helped Modesty hide his relationship with Twin Jade, the three men felt guilty and awkward and could not come up with any ideas.

Devotion Yin, who happened to be there, made a sudden suggestion, "With affairs of the heart, Harmony Qi is the man to consult."

Realizing he was right, Amity Zhu immediately summoned a carriage and asked Devotion to go with him to Conical Hat Garden.

When they saw Qi, Devotion said solemnly, "I've brought you the best bit of business in the world. Now how are you going to thank me?"

Harmony Qi had no idea what he meant. It was left to Amity to explain to Qi his brother Modesty's natural shyness and the cause of his lovesickness and to ask him to think of a solution.

Harmony Qi chuckled. "What's so difficult about this? I'll invite him to come to my garden and have Twin Jade come for a couple of days as well, what d'you think?"

Devotion said, "Didn't I say I brought you business? I'm your broker."

"What broker? You're horning in for a cut," Harmony replied, and they all laughed uproariously. Harmony Qi settled on the next day to invite Modesty to convalesce in his garden. Amity could not thank him enough.

"You, Amity, should stay away. Modesty wouldn't feel at ease with his elder brother around," said Devotion.

"It seems to me you should see to his marriage as soon as he gets well," Harmony said.

Having acknowledged the wisdom of their comments, Amity saluted them and took his leave. He went home in a carriage alone and went straight into Modesty's room. Having asked about his illness, Amity said, "Second Bai says this illness calls for a change of air. Harmony Qi has asked you to spend a couple of days in his garden. That way, you'll be near your doctor as well."

Though Modesty was not keen to go, he accepted the invitation out of consideration for his brother's solicitude. Amity gave the order for Longevity Zhang to pack for Modesty.

The next day was the fifth of the eighth month. When the sun sank toward the west, an invitation was delivered to Modesty, who was then helped into a sedan chair in the center hall. He was met at the gate of Conical Hat Garden by Qi's servants, who led the way to the northeast corner of the garden where there was a cottage by the lake. Harmony Qi came out to welcome him and told him to dispense with any formal greeting. Modesty got off the sedan chair rather shakily, and Harmony walked with him into the bedroom, supporting him on one arm, and helped him settle down on the bed. The room was complete with medicine pot, incense burner, congee bowl, and ginseng jar. Modesty expressed his uneasiness at the trouble Harmony had taken.

"Just make yourself at home. You should take a nap now." Harmony told the servants to attend to Modesty's needs and then left without further palaver.

Modesty thought he might as well lie down and calm his spirits. As he did so, he caught sight of a beautiful woman in a silver summer silk blouse coming out of the bamboo grove and going round the lakeshore. She was the very likeness of Twin Jade, but Modesty thought it was just an illusion caused by dizziness. Having walked around the lake, the woman now came into his cottage. Modesty looked closely at her; it was indeed Twin Jade! A range of emotions swept over Modesty: astonishment and bewilderment were followed by understanding and great joy. All this was conveyed in one exclamation: "Oh!"

Twin Jade stood by his bed, her limpid eyes looking sideways at him, her face full of smiles. As she broke out in laughter, she covered her mouth with her handkerchief. He struggled to sit up and reached for her hand, but she stepped back to avoid him. Not knowing what to do, he sat up in bed and asked, "Did you know I was ill?"

She tried to suppress her laughter as she replied, "I've never seen the likes of you!" He asked what she meant, but she did not answer.

He begged her to come over, gesturing that she should sit down on the bed. Seeing that there were several menservants in the outer room, she pointed her chin in that direction and declined. He shook his hand to indicate that she should ignore them and then brought his palms together in a gesture of prayer. She hesitated and then picked up the teapot from the table, poured half a cup of almond tea, and offered it to him, taking the opportunity to sit down on the stool by the bed. The two of them engaged in tender whispering until dusk. Modesty was not the least bit tired; in fact, his illness was mostly over. A manservant came in to light the lamp, but neither his host nor any other guests showed up. That night, she made him a brew of the Great Tonic. Out came the perspiration of love and off went the little demon of illness. But for a slight weakness in his legs, Modesty was a new man.

After he had received the servants' report, Harmony Qi sent a sedan basket chair to fetch Modesty to the Phoenix Pavilion. Modesty saluted him formally before Harmony could stop him, so Harmony could only tell him not to be so ceremonious in the future. Modesty gave his promise and then greeted Second Bai and Devotion Yin. After that, they all took their seats.

Before they could start a conversation, Aroma Su had come in, holding Twin Jade by the hand. Harmony Qi asked Aroma, "Shall we call Wenjun Yao and Flora Zhang here to keep Twin Jade company?" Aroma naturally said that was a good idea. Steward Xia was summoned and told to write out the call chits. After Xia had withdrawn to carry out his order, Harmony Qi called him back to tell him to send out invitations to Nature Shi, Iron Hua, Elan Ge, and Cloud Tao. Steward Xia again departed with his orders.

Modesty Zhu asked Second Bai if he should keep to any special diet.

"Now that you've recovered, you should get some nourishment. If you have a good appetite, all the better. There's nothing you should avoid."

Devotion cut in, "You should ask Twin Jade. She's a better doctor than Second Bai."

Modesty blushed when he heard this, but there was nowhere for him to hide. Knowing how bashful he was, Harmony Qi quickly changed the subject.

Soon a servant announced, "The Eldest Young Master Tao is here."

Cloud Tao came in with Belle Tan and Flora Zhang. After he had exchanged greetings with everyone, Cloud Tao asked after Modesty's health, "Are you quite recovered now?" Afraid of being teased, Modesty answered vaguely.

Second Bai said to Cloud Tao, "Your brother's girl, Water Blossom, is in a bad way."

Startled, Cloud asked for details.

"I went to see her today. It's a matter of days now," Second Bai replied.

Cloud Tao sighed. But then it occurred to him that once Water Blossom died, Jade would be free from all the cares and worries, which might not be a bad thing for him. And so he dropped the subject.

Now Nature Shi, Iron Hua, and Elan Ge arrived one after the other, each bringing his girl. As Modesty Zhu had just recovered from a serious illness, Harmony Qi thought he needed strong flavors to stimulate his appetite, so a chef was hired especially for a Western meal, and the guests were invited to place their orders.

Three square tables were set up to make a long table in the waterside lodge, a tablecloth was laid, and everyone sat down. Each man had a small wine pot for his own use, and they all started drinking, each according to his own capacity. Despite this, Harmony Qi still felt that excitement was lacking. He asked Nature Shi, "The game you proposed last time was not bad. Can you think of another drinking game that draws from the *Four Classics*?"

Nature could not think of any.

"I have an idea," said Iron Hua. "We should each think of a word that can be pronounced four ways, each illustrated by a quote from the *Four Classics*." And he gave an example.

"Now if it were just three ways of pronouncing a word, there're plenty in the *Four Classics*," said Elan Ge, giving four examples.

"Well, I've thought of one that is pronounced in four different ways," said Modesty Zhu, who then gave four quotations to illustrate his point.

Everyone praised him in unison, saying, "It'll be hard to come up with another one."

Devotion Yin suddenly exclaimed triumphantly, "There're two more," and he rattled them off, together with the quotations. "That's all you'll get from the *Four Classics*. I don't think there's a fifth word that'd fit our requirements."

Stroking his beard, Harmony Qi said, "I've got one that's pronounced in five ways!"

There was astonishment and incredulity all around.

"Please drink a cup of wine, gentlemen, and then I'll tell you," said Harmony.

Everybody drank up and awaited enlightenment. But unexpectedly something came up to cut short their conversation.

CHAPTER 42 :: *Water Blossom, leaving her beloved, departs this world, and Cloud Tao, worried about his brother, faces the funeral*

Harmony Qi was just going to say his piece in the drinking game when a servant led a coolie straight to the table. Cloud saw that it was Jade Tao's sedan-chair bearer and asked him what the matter was. The man bent down to whisper into his ear, after which Cloud just said, "All right, I'll be there." The man withdrew.

"Is it bad news about Water Blossom?" Second Bai asked.

"No, it's Jade who's unwell."

"But there's nothing wrong with Jade," Second Bai said in surprise.

Cloud replied with a frown, "Well, he's made himself ill by staying at Water Blossom's bedside and looking after her day and night. He hasn't slept for several days now, so he's running a fever, too. Water Blossom's mother told him to get some rest, but he just refused. That's why she sent his chair bearer to ask me to go and talk to him."

Harmony Qi nodded in sympathy. "Jade and Water Blossom are an exceptional pair. Even Water Blossom's mother is quite admirable."

"The more in love they are, the worse their trouble! I suppose Jade owed them a huge debt in his last incarnation. He's now paying it back," said Cloud.

Everyone at the table sighed. Cloud Tao intended to leave Belle Tan there to keep the others company, but she refused. Instead, she ordered her maid to gather up her silver water pipe and nutmeg box. Cloud made his apologies to everybody, and Harmony saw him out the door.

He walked down the steps with Belle Tan, and they boarded their sedan chairs. Two servants of the Qi house led the way to the gate, each holding a lantern. Their sedan chairs left the garden in haste for Fourth Avenue, from where Belle returned to West Civic Peace Alley while Cloud made his way to Water Blossom's in East Prosperity Alley. When he got there, he went into River Blossom's room on the right. Big Goldie, who had caught a glimpse of him, followed him in with tea and was going to offer him the water pipe, too. He waved her off, telling her to get Second Young Master.

It took Jade Tao some seven or eight minutes to come over from the next room. He was followed by River Blossom. Having greeted his elder brother, Jade sat down in silence. Cloud immediately inquired about Water Blossom's condition. Too upset to speak, Jade shook his head as tears streamed down his face. Unable to get his handkerchief out in time, he wiped his tears on his sleeve. River Blossom, who was leaning on his knees, pulled away his hand to look up at him. Seeing his tears, she started wailing. Big Goldie's admonitions failed to make her stop. It was only when Jade told her not to cry that she tried to get a grip on herself.

Seeing how it was, Cloud Tao was also shaken. He spoke gently to Jade: "Poor Water Blossom! It's perfectly all right if you want to stay here and look after her, but you do need to use your common sense. I heard that you're running a fever, is that true?"

Jade stared at the floor silently, his face blank. Just when Cloud was about to speak again, he heard Fair Sister Li's voice calling softly at the door for "Second Young Master." Jade rushed off in a panic, followed by River Blossom. Cloud was left alone in the room. He wanted to find out how bad Water Blossom was so he, too, crossed over to her room. When he entered, he saw Water Blossom sitting up in bed, propped up by several quilts. Her face was as white as paper, her eyes were half closed, and her breathing was labored. Jade leaned against her bedside to massage her chest slowly while Beckon was kneeling on the bed with a cup of ginseng soup. Fair Sister Li stood at a corner with a candle lamp in hand. River Blossom pushed her way up to the bedside but was told off by Fair Sister; she had to be satisfied with standing behind Jade and peeking from there.

Realizing that the situation was grave, Cloud was about to walk away. Just then, Water Blossom coughed up some thick phlegm. Fair Sister brought a handkerchief to her mouth for her to spit in. After that, her breathing seemed a little easier. Beckon served her some of the ginseng soup with a silver spoon. She opened her mouth as if to drink it, but of the four or five spoonfuls fed her, she only swallowed half of them.

Jade asked her tenderly, "Does your heart still hurt?" Despite his repeated inquiry, she barely glanced at him before closing her eyes again. He knew she found this annoying, so he drew back and stood up.

Only when Fair Sister turned around to put down the candle lamp did she see Cloud standing there. "Aiya! So you're here as well, Eldest Young Master? It's filthy here, do please go and sit in the next room," she said, flustered.

And so Cloud turned and walked out of the room. Fair Sister told Beckon to get down from the bed but to stay in the room, while she went quickly into the next one with Jade and River Blossom. Nobody took a seat; they just stood around looking at one another. River Blossom stared restlessly from one face to another, not knowing what to do.

In the end, it was Fair Sister who started talking. "Well, it seems Water Blossom stands little chance of overcoming her illness now. We had hoped she'd get better, but now that looks unlikely, and there's really nothing we can do. Though she is ill, the rest of us have to carry on with life. Nothing says that we shouldn't live because of her illness; it just doesn't make sense. Isn't that so, Eldest Young Master?"

When Jade, who was seated by her side, heard this, he took a deep breath, his voice choked, and he almost burst out crying. To hide this, he made for the back door. Cloud pretended not to notice.

Fair Sister continued, "Water Blossom has been ill for more than a month now, and so many people have suffered because of it. First among them is Second Young Master, who has taken the strain all this time, keeping her company day and night. This morning, I felt Second Young Master's forehead and noticed that he had a little

fever, so I thought it best if you would talk to him, Eldest Young
Master. As I had said to Second Young Master, after Water Blossom
passes away, I'll be relying on him to look after me. To me, Second
Young Master is just like family. Now that Water Blossom is ill, what
am I to do if Second Young Master falls ill, too?"

Cloud listened to this with a frown. He hesitated for a long while
before sending Big Goldie to fetch Jade. She looked for him in
Water Blossom's room, but he was not there. She asked Beckon,
who replied, "He didn't come in."

What had not occurred to them was that Jade was sitting in Fair
Sister's room and crying his eyes out, trying his best not to make any
noise. River Blossom, who was also weeping, tugged at his sleeve,
pleading with him, "Brother-in-law, please don't cry."

When Big Goldie found him, she passed on the message: "Eldest
Young Master wants you."

Jade made an effort to hold back his tears and then waited a while
before going to join them. He sat down facing Cloud, with River Blossom by his side. Fair Sister sat on one side to keep them company.

Cloud tried to reason with him. "It makes no sense for a man to
give up his life at the death of his wife. Even if Water Blossom had
been your wife, according to etiquette, it'd only be right for you to
temper your sorrow with decorum, not to mention the fact that her
relationship with you has not been formalized."

Before he could finish, Jade replied, "Don't you worry, Brother.
Water Blossom will only live a couple more days. After that, I'll see
to it that her funeral is properly arranged, and then I'll go home
and never set foot outside again. If other people have anything to
say, don't pay them any attention. Poor Water Blossom, she hasn't
got anybody dear to her to look after her in her illness. This is too
much for me; I just need to speak out."

"You're an intelligent man, so you should have learned to take it
philosophically. What you propose to do is all right. But now you're
running a fever, so why do you refuse to sleep?" said Cloud.

"I couldn't sleep in the daytime, but I'm going to sleep now. Don't
worry, Brother." Jade gave his promise over and over again.

Having said all that he could, Cloud Tao prepared to leave. But
Fair Sister detained him, saying, "There's something else I'd like to
discuss. A couple of days ago, when Water Blossom didn't look so
good, I thought we should make the final preparations for her.[1] As

::

1. [This meant getting the coffin, burial clothes, and other necessities for
the funeral. This was often done as a last resort in the hope that the worst
omen would turn the tide. *E.H.*]

you know, it is believed that such preparations may very well pull the patient back from the brink. But Second Young Master forbade me to do it because he still hoped she'd recover. I'm afraid we must go ahead now, or else we won't be able to get things ready in time."

"Go ahead by all means. Even if she does get well, there'll have been no harm done." Cloud rose to his feet as he replied. Jade stood up to see his brother out. River Blossom, afraid that he would leave with Cloud, held on to him, refusing to let go. Cloud also told Jade to stay in the room, keep out of the draught, and have an early night. Fair Sister saw Cloud out.

"Jade is not thinking straight. If anything happens, send someone to West Civic Peace Alley to let me know. I'll come and give him a hand," Cloud said.

Fair Sister was deeply grateful. Cloud also ordered Jade's sedan-chair bearers to report to him at regular intervals. Fair Sister accompanied Cloud all the way to the front door and did not turn back until he had got into his sedan chair. But Cloud was still worried. As soon as he got to West Civic Peace Alley, he told one of his sedan-chair bearers, "Go to East Prosperity Alley and find out whether Second Young Master has gone to bed."

It was a long time before the man came back to report, "Second Young Master is in bed, but he's running a fever again."

Cloud sent the man off with another message: "Since he caught a chill, having a fever is not too much of a worry. Just keep him warm and make sure he sweats; that should help."

After the sedan-chair bearer had delivered the message, he again reported back. Then Cloud had some congee for supper and went to bed with Belle. The next morning, he was about to send someone over to inquire when Jade's sedan-chair bearer came to report, "Second Young Master is quite well. The maestro is also feeling a little better."

Somewhat relieved, Cloud got up to wash. It so happened the Flora Zhang's maid had come back from Conical Hat Garden to fetch some more clothes for her, and Harmony Qi told her to take a note to Cloud, inviting him to dinner that evening and also inquiring after Water Blossom. Cloud sent his card in reply, saying, "I'll be there if nothing happens."

Shortly after the clock struck twelve, Cloud was still having lunch when Jade's sedan-chair bearer dashed in to report that Water Blossom had passed away. Worried about Jade, Cloud put down his rice bowl and left at once for East Prosperity Alley. On the way, he tried to work out what to do, and as soon as he reached the house, he sent the chair bearers to invite Cloudlet Chen and Whistler Tang to come for consultation.

On entering the house, he saw all the windows in Water Blossom's room were wide open and the door curtain had been removed. Besides paper money for the underworld, they were also burning the clothes Water Blossom had worn. The smoke gushed up from the courtyard and scattered in the wind. The loud wailing indoors was ear-piercing. There were also a number of people shouting out orders as they went about tidying up. Cloud could not tell whether Jade's voice was among them. Just then, the manservant, Laurel Blessing, happened to come out carrying the bed curtains, now roughly rolled up. Seeing Cloud, he called loudly over his shoulder, "Eldest Young Master is here."

Cloud went into River Blossom's room and sat down to wait. He suddenly heard Fair Sister shout desperately, "No, Second Young Master!" The maids and servant girls dashed into the room, while the sedan-chair bearers gathered outside the windows to find out what had happened. A moment later, Jade came out of the room, surrounded by Fair Sister and the maid and servant girls, who had pulled and pushed to make him come out. Jade had cried himself hoarse. Still choking in his tears, he tottered into River Blossom's room like a blind man. Cloud saw the bump on his forehead, the result of his knocking his head against the bedstead.

"What d'you think you're doing?" Cloud stamped his foot in anger.

His brother's anger made Jade calm down a little. He turned around and stretched himself out stiffly on a chair. Just as Fair Sister was going to consult Cloud about the funeral, Beckon called out in the parlor, "Mother, come! River Blossom is still calling Elder Sister. She's on the bed trying to pull her up." Fair Sister rushed out to get River Blossom, who was dissolved in tears. After a few words of rebuke, Fair Sister placed her in Jade's care.

It happened that Cloudlet Chen had arrived just then, so Cloud went out to greet him. Cloudlet said, "Whistler has gone to Hangzhou on account of Modesty Zhu's betrothal. What did you want him for?" When Cloud Tao replied that he needed their help with the funeral, Cloudlet readily agreed.

Cloud turned around to address Jade, "Let's face it, she's dead now, and you know too little about practical matters to be of much help even if you hang around. I suggest we leave things to Cloudlet. You and I should keep out of his way."

Jade became desperate. "Why don't you just give me another four or five days, Brother?" That was all he managed to say before he was choked in tears again.

"You misunderstood me. We'll come back here later. I just want you to have a change of scene," said Cloud.

Fair Sister also urged him to go: "It's good to have a change of scene. In fact, it worries me a little having Second Young Master here."

Cloudlet also tried to smooth things over. "A change of scene is not a bad idea. If anything comes up, I'll tell them to send for you."

With the pressure piling up, Jade hung his head and said no more. Cloud immediately called out for the sedan chairs and took Jade by the arm to make him come along. "We'll go across the way to West Civic Peace Alley."

River Blossom heard him say "across the way" and thought they were going over to see Water Blossom. She ran ahead into the room before Beckon could stop her. She waited there but no one came. Completely at a loss, she ran out to the parlor and saw that Jade was just getting into his sedan chair. She rushed out of the front door crying and yelling and rammed her head against the sedan chair. Fortunately, Fair Sister reacted quickly. She grabbed River Blossom around the waist and lifted her off her feet. Even then, the girl still struggled stubbornly.

"Let her come along," Jade interceded.

Fair Sister consented and let her go. River Blossom took the opportunity to duck into Jade's sedan chair. He managed to soothe her.

The sedan-chair bearers bore them to Belle Tan's at West Civic Peace Alley. Cloud took Jade and River Blossom upstairs into Belle's room. Seeing the tears on the faces of Jade and River Blossom, Belle realized Water Blossom had died. When the menservants brought them hot towels, Cloud told them to get a couple more for River Blossom. Belle went further; she told the maid to fetch a basin of hot water and her own toilet articles and then combed River Blossom's hair for her and persuaded her to put on some rouge and powder. The young girl could not very well refuse. Jade settled on the opium couch but remained fidgety whether lying down or sitting up.

Soon Cloudlet Chen came to them with a question, "There're some ready-made coffins. One is made of Wuyuan wood; it's not bad really. The other is made of cedar and is more expensive. Which should it be?"

"Cedar," replied Jade. Cloud said nothing.

"They've made a list of the clothes. They want to use the bridal headdress and the wedding cape for burial.[2] What d'you say to that?" said Cloudlet.

::

2. [These were the bridal garments of a Chinese official's wife; customarily, these garments were also used in funerals. E.H.]

Jade had no answer to that; he turned to look at Cloud.

"That's all right. It'll just mean that Jade will have to spend a couple more dollars. This business is in the Li family, it has nothing to do with us Taos. Let them use whatever they want," said Cloud.

"The astrologer has picked noon on the ninth as the hour for the body to be laid out in the coffin and two hours later for the funeral procession. Burial will be at four in the afternoon on the tenth. The grave is in Xujiahui. The gravediggers should be sent there tomorrow; that's rather urgent."

Cloud and Jade said yes simultaneously. Cloudlet left as soon as these matters had been settled.

At dusk, Jade thought of something he had to see to. Unable to stop him, Cloud accompanied him back to the Lis'. River Blossom naturally went with them, again sharing Jade's sedan chair. When they reached the house in East Prosperity Alley, they saw that Water Blossom's body was already laid out in the parlor and blue cotton mourning curtains had been hung up. Four nuns sitting on either side of the bier were chanting Buddhist sutras. Water Blossom's room was brightly lit, and six or seven tailors had set up work tables there to make white mourning clothes. Cloudlet Chen was in River Blossom's room, helping Fair Sister Li sort out clothes for the burial.

At the sight of this scene, Jade's heart contracted with grief. He turned away from Cloud and went into Fair Sister's room, where he hammered the tables and chairs with his fist and howled. This sent River Blossom into loud wailing as well, and the noise rang through the house. Fair Sister wanted to rush in and talk to him, but Cloud stopped her. "Let him be. It's all right if he just cries. He needs to get it out of his system."

So Fair Sister told Big Goldie to get tea and hot water ready and to stand by when the clothes for the burial had been sorted out. The noise continued, except now it sounded more like shouting than weeping.

"Now go and talk to him," said Cloud Tao.

Fair Sister went in. Sure enough, Jade stopped crying as soon as she consoled him. He even came out to wash his face and rinse his mouth. River Blossom stayed glued to his side, not leaving him for an instant.

His mind now more at ease, Jade asked Fair Sister what jewelry would be used for the burial.

"There's quite enough jewelry for that. All that's lacking is some clothes."

"She didn't like any of the pearl combs or flower-shaped pearl hairpins. Her favorite was the large pearl on her hat," he said. "Use that as the center ornament of her hat band. Then there's a white jade pendant that she used to wear hanging on a button; make sure she takes it with her. Don't forget."

"I won't," Fair Sister replied.

There was much that Jade wanted to say, but he could not think of anything right away. Cloud said, "It's all right if you want to come here to have a good cry; just don't spend the night here. You should come with me to West Civic Peace Alley. It's nearby, so you can come over whenever you think of something, and they can go there to consult you. It's convenient for everybody, right?"

Jade did not have the heart to reject such kindness, so he agreed. Thereupon Cloud invited Cloudlet Chen to a casual dinner at Belle's. Fair Sister tried to press them to stay for dinner.

"We don't mean to turn you down," Cloud explained. "But we won't feel at ease eating here."

"It's our home-cooking. We'll send the dishes over when they're done, how about that?" she asked.

Cloud agreed. As they were leaving, River Blossom again barred Jade's way, refusing to let him go.

"Come with us then," Cloud said with a smile.

Keeping a tight grip on Jade's robe, River Blossom refused to ride in the sedan chair, so Cloud and Cloudlet walked with them, acting as a screen in front and behind so nobody could see her.

As soon as they arrived at Belle's, the Li's manservant, Laurel Blessing, delivered a lidded bamboo basket up to Belle's room. It contained four main dishes and four bowls of food. Cloud told Belle and River Blossom to join them at dinner and drink with them. Jade still wouldn't touch a drop. Cloudlet, who had business to attend to, did not feel like drinking, so when the wine had gone three rounds he excused himself and had rice together with Jade and River Blossom. Only Belle kept Cloud company, matching him cup for cup. Hoping to drown his sorrow in wine, Cloud did not desist till he was tipsy. Cloudlet left immediately after dinner.

Cloud arranged with Belle to clear out the mezzanine room for Jade to sleep there. Bereft of all hope, Jade had little to occupy his mind and actually slept very soundly that night. But River Blossom, who slept by his side, was plagued by nightmares and slept but fitfully. The next morning, she suddenly cried out tearfully in her dream, "Elder Sister, I'm going with you!" He woke her up hastily and held her in his arms. She kept sobbing, still looking dazed. He did not question her; they both dressed and got up. Word reached Cloud and Belle, and they, too, got out of bed earlier than usual.

After breakfast, Jade wanted to go to East Prosperity Alley to have a look. Still worried about him, Cloud accompanied him there. River Blossom, who would not leave Jade's side, went with him, too. He went back and forth three times that day, crying his eyes out each time. Cloud felt completely worn out at the end of the day.

CHAPTER 43 :: *An empty room is a potent reminder of lost love, and innocent words affirm that the dead will return*

Came the ninth day of the eighth month, Cloud Tao was wakened from his slumber by the sound of cannon, and he heard the sound of percussion and wind instruments coming from afar. Thinking he had overslept, he got up in a hurry.

"What's the matter?" Belle woke up, startled.

"I'm late," he said.

"But it's still awfully early."

"You sleep a little longer; I'll get up first." He called the maid in and asked, "Is Second Young Master up?"

"Second Young Master was gone at dawn. He didn't even take the sedan chair," the maid replied.

Cloud quickly washed and went over to East Prosperity Alley. When he got there, he saw two standing lanterns had been erected in front of the Lis' door and a group of children were jumping up and down, trying to see what was going on. He got out of his sedan chair and went into the parlor. A tablet wrapped in white silk had been set up on the offering table in front of the coffin. Two tea tables, one on either side, held oblong gold-lacquered trays. On one were a bridal headdress and a wedding cape, on the other gold and pearl jewelry. Several women guests from the countryside stood around examining the display. They were full of admiration for the family's "good fortune." There were also a dozen male guests in Water Blossom's room holding forth loudly. Some of them were rather uncouth, and Cloud figured that Jade would not be with them.

He walked into River Blossom's room. Cloudlet Chen was assigning duties for the funeral procession. The room was tightly packed. An old man with white whiskers sat at a newly installed desk against the wall. He was the bookkeeper and was now registering the mourners' gifts in the funeral record book. When Cloud walked in, the bookkeeper stood respectfully to one side, not daring to greet him. Cloud asked him where Jade was.

"Over there." The bookkeeper pointed.

Cloud turned around and found Jade bent over the round table, his head buried in his arms. He was completely silent, but occasionally his head and shoulders shook ever so slightly. Cloud realized he was quietly weeping and decided to ignore him. When the bearers had all left, he went up to greet Cloudlet and suggested that they should send Jade away on some pretext.

"He won't agree to go just now. We'll see when this business is over," said Cloudlet.

"And when will that be?"

"Soon. We'll start once lunch is over."

As there was nothing Cloud could do about it, he went over to the opium divan to smoke. Shortly afterward, lunch was announced. Three tables were set in Water Blossom's room; it was filled with the Lis' relatives as well as the announcers, musicians, and cannoneers hired for the funeral. In River Blossom's room, only one table was set; it was for Cloudlet Chen, Cloud Tao, and Jade Tao. They were just going to sit down when a manservant from Belle's came in. When Cloud asked him what his errand was, he said it was to deliver a funeral gift. So saying, he produced a box containing a packet of money for joss sticks as well as Belle's name card. Cloud thought it was a little laughable and paid it no attention. But right afterward came another bearer of gifts. The man was dressed formally in a summer hat with purple tassels, and he had a tray in his hands. Seeing that it was one of Harmony Qi's stewards, Cloud immediately inspected the tray. It held three portions of money for joss sticks and three white greeting cards in the names of Aroma Su, Wenjun Yao, and Flora Zhang.

"His Excellency is indeed too considerate. There's really no need for this." Cloud said to the steward, all smiles.

The steward politely acknowledged Cloud's comment and then told him, "His Excellency says that if Second Young Master feels unhappy, he is welcome to come and amuse himself in our garden."

"Please convey our thanks to His Excellency. In a couple of days, Second Young Master will go to the house to thank him personally," said Cloud.

The steward answered "yes, sir" and departed. Only then did the three of them take their seats for lunch. As there was an extra seat at the table, Cloudlet asked the bookkeeper to join them. But the bookkeeper felt it was too exalted a position for him and told River Blossom to keep them company instead. Not only did Jade abstain from wine, he actually refused all food and water. Cloud did not press him. Everybody else just had a little congee and then left the table.

Cloudlet went outside the house to see to everything. Fearful of ridicule, Jade hid himself in a corner. Cloud noticed that River Blossom in white mourning clothes looked lovelier than ever. Moved by pity, he took her hand and walked over to the opium divan, where he made small talk with her. River Blossom was usually quick on the uptake, but now she just stared dumbly, replying to his questions like an automaton.

As they were talking, a man suddenly pushed his way through the parlor, shouting orders, whereupon four men in red and black hats in the courtyard started to clear the way loudly. This was followed by three blasts of the cannon and nine strokes of the gong. River Blossom was so frightened, she ran off to the back of the room, while Jade was nowhere to be seen. Cloud stood up to watch. The parlor was jam-packed with people making an awful din, so Cloud could not tell whether the body had been laid out in the coffin. A moment later, there were again loud shouts to clear the street; the gongs sounded, and the cannon was fired as before. All those who wore mourning clothes as well as the hired women mourners started wailing. Cloud drew back and lay down to wait quietly. He heard drums and cymbals followed by bells and incantations and figured that they were performing the ritual cleansing after the body had been laid out in the coffin.

After the cleansing, all was quiet for a long time. Cloud was about to inquire once again when Cloudlet pushed his way through the crowd and beckoned for him. He rushed out to discover that Jade was holding tight to the coffin with both hands, with the upper half of his body actually in the coffin. Fair Sister tried her best to pull him out, all to no avail. Cloud approached him from behind and forcibly dragged him into the room. The noise of gongs and cannon instantly rang out, and the sound of wailing rose to the skies. The coffin was sealed, and the spectators gradually dispersed. The music for the final send-off now began.

Cloud kept watch at the door to stop Jade from going out. Water Blossom's adopted brother led the way in paying last respects. He was followed by River Blossom, Beckon the servant girl, and the two girls sold to the house. After they had performed their kowtows, it was the turn of her relatives and the male and female guests to do their obeisances.

Cloudlet hurried out of the front door to give instructions to the men, and the bearers swarmed into the parlor to remove the offering table and tie ropes round the coffin. At the report of a cannon, the coolies gave a shout and hoisted the coffin on their shoulders. The men in red and black hats sounded the gongs and shouted loudly to clear the way. They went with the drumming monks to the alley entrance and waited there. In the house, the coffin bearers slowly started moving. Fair Sister walked at the head of the family and followed the coffin, weeping. Some of the relatives would go with the coffin, others not. Everyone piled out of the house.

Taking advantage of the confusion, Jade ducked under Cloud's arm and got out, but Cloud dragged him back. Feeling helpless, Jade stamped his feet in frustration.

"There's no point in your going there now. I'll go with you to Xujiahui tomorrow. That'd be the sensible thing to do. Even if you send her off all the way to the boat, there won't be anything for you to do. What's the point?"

Knowing that Cloud was right, Jade gave up his struggle. Cloud wanted to take him to Civic Peace Alley right away, but Jade insisted on waiting until the funeral procession had returned. Cloud gave in, not realizing how long it would take.

Jade thought of the things Water Blossom had left behind and wondered whether Fair Sister had put them away. He sneaked off to her room to take a look. The sight shocked him. The room had been emptied of most of its contents. The wardrobes and trunks had all been padlocked, and two benches had been thrown on the bed. The pendant lamp, with its glass broken, dangled there forlornly. Many of the paintings and calligraphy scrolls on the walls had also gone. Chicken and fish bones littered the unswept floor. Water Blossom was but newly dead, yet her room was already in ruins. At this thought, Jade burst into bitter tears again. Since Cloud was in River Blossom's room, Jade could weep to his heart's content. He approached the bed in tears. Suddenly a fluffy black ball rolled out from under the dressing table. Before he could look closely at it, it had vanished. Startled, he wondered whether it could have been Water Blossom's spirit appearing in this strange guise to stop him crying, so he dried his tears.

Just then Cloudlet returned ahead of the party. Jade hurried forth for information.

"Everything is settled on the boat. It'll sail down tomorrow," said Cloudlet. "It's best if you have lunch first before you take a carriage to Xujiahui tomorrow."

Impatient to leave, Cloud did not wait for the sedan-chair bearers. He told Jade repeatedly that they should go. As Jade walked out into the courtyard, a cat with a black coat and a white belly was sitting on the lid of the water jar chewing noisily. Realizing that the black ball he had seen was this creature, he sighed and then followed Cloud on foot to Belle's in West Civic Peace Alley.

It was a gloomy day, and toward evening it started to drizzle. To overcome the sense of depression, Cloud ordered a few of his favorite dishes and asked Cloudlet over for a drink after his business was done. Cloudlet brought River Blossom with him. Surprised, Jade asked why she was there.

"She wants to see her brother-in-law. She has been pestering her mother for a while now," replied Cloudlet.

River Blossom leaned close to Jade and whispered, "Brother-in-law, d'you know that Elder Sister is all alone in the boat? We've all come back, even Laurel Blessing has left. If some stranger rowed it away, how would we find it?"

Cloud and Cloudlet both laughed at this, while Jade tried to console her kindly.

"It's sad for her to have lost her sister," Belle said.

"Are you trying to make her cry?" Cloud said in reproof. "She has only just stopped crying; d'you want to set her off again?"

Belle could see that River Blossom's eyes were indeed filled with tears, so she put on a smiling face, took the girl's hand, and drew her close. She then made conversation by asking her all sorts of questions: how old was she? who taught her to sing? how many arias had she learned? This tided them over till the meal was on the table. Cloud and Cloudlet had some wine. While Belle was able to drink a little with them, Jade and River Blossom had rice served early. Cloud noticed that Jade had only had about half a bowl of rice all day. He did not press him to eat more but said to him kindly, "You got up early today; d'you want to go to bed now? Go on ahead."

Jade, who felt sad and dreary, took the opportunity to excuse himself. He went to the mezzanine room with River Blossom and closed the door, saying they would go to bed. But once in the room he just sat there mutely like a puppet, looking at the table lamp. River Blossom nestled against him, but she, too, seemed preoccupied. After a long while, she suddenly said, "Listen, Brother-in-law, the rain has more or less stopped. Let's go to the boat and keep Elder Sister company for a bit. We'll come back later, all right?"

He did not answer, just shook his head.

"We can go if we keep it from them," she said.

Her foolish devotion aroused his grief. Sadness surged in his heart, and tears streamed down his face. At this sight, she cried out, "Why are you crying, Brother-in-law?"

He held up a hand to keep her quiet, saying, "Hush."

She turned around to embrace him. When he had dried his tears and stopped choking, she said, "Brother-in-law, I have something to tell you. You mustn't tell anybody else, all right?"

"What is it?"

"Yesterday, the bookkeeper told me Elder Sister is only going away for two weeks; she'll come back after that.[1] The astrologer has picked

::

1. It is a traditional belief that the spirit of the dead would return home for a final visit after a prescribed period, normally said to be the seventh day, the fourteenth day, or the twenty-first day after death.

the day. He said she's definitely coming back on the twenty-first. The bookkeeper is an honest man, so what he says must be true. He told me not to cry, for Elder Sister wouldn't come back if she heard me cry. He also said not to tell anybody for fear that they won't let her come back. So you shouldn't cry, Brother-in-law. You have to let Elder Sister come back."

What she said caused him to break down completely. He wept aloud. Scared, she stamped her feet and called aloud desperately for help. The noise brought Cloud and Cloudlet. When they pushed the door open and saw the state of affairs, Cloudlet chuckled.

Cloud frowned. "Don't you think you're overdoing it?"

With a tremendous effort, Jade controlled himself. Belle told her maid to bring a basin of hot water and then said to Jade, "Second Young Master, you'd better go to bed after you've freshened up. It's been a long day." Having said that, she left with the others.

The maid brought the water. Jade cleaned his face and then gave River Blossom's face a wipe, too. After the maid had taken the basin away, he helped River Blossom undress, and they went to bed, sleeping side by side. Though wide awake at first, he gradually dropped off and was not even aware of Cloudlet Chen's departure.

The next morning was sunny and bright. Jade thought he would sneak off to the quay to find the funeral boat. But as soon as he got out of the mezzanine room, the maid stopped him, saying, "Eldest Young Master has left word that Second Young Master is not to leave." Meanwhile, River Blossom rushed out to cling to him. He figured it was impossible to get away, so he went back into the room.

It was noon when he heard Cloud clear his throat. Belle came out of her room, her hair uncombed, to call for the maid. Seeing Jade and River Blossom, she greeted them, "We've just got up. Do come in."

They walked into her room to see Cloud. Jade wanted to tell the sedan-chair bearers to call a hackney so they could set off.

"It's too early. Let's have lunch first," Cloud said. Jade then turned to order lunch, but Cloud told him, "It's been ordered." Only then did Jade sit down on the divan. He looked at Belle as she dressed her hair in front of the mirror.

Belle said to River Blossom, "Your hair is a bit messy, too. It needs combing. I'll do it for you."

Bashful, River Blossom declined.

"Why not?" Cloud said. "Go look in the mirror yourself. Isn't it untidy?"

Jade also tried to persuade her, which made her more ill at ease than ever.

"Now that she knows you a bit better, she's become more self-conscious," Jade commented.

"It's all right; come on," Belle said, smiling pleasantly. She pulled River Blossom to her side and started combing her hair. She asked casually who used to do her hair.

"It used to be Elder Sister, but recently it's been anybody. The day before yesterday, because I had to change to a blue binding,[2] Mother did it for me."

Afraid that this would remind Jade of Water Blossom, Cloud changed the subject. Belle understood and said no more. Although Jade was sitting there sedately, his face expressionless, Cloud knew that his mind was in turmoil. Just then the menservants reported, "Lunch is here." Cloud told them to bring it upstairs. Since River Blossom's hair needed just to be tied into simple buns, it was a lot easier to manage than Belle's hairdo and was soon finished. They lunched together.

As soon as the meal was over, Jade told the chair bearers to call a hackney and have it wait at the mouth of the alley. Cloud had no choice but to set off at once with him and River Blossom. They headed southwest to a huge cemetery on a hill near the highway in Xujiahui. Toward its farther end, seven or eight diggers, sweating heavily, were working on a new grave. In front of it was a heap of bricks and tiles, and the hollow in the ground was lined with lime. They knew it was the right place and got off the carriage.

A manservant supervising the work came up to report, "Mr. Chen is here, too. They're on the boat over here."

Jade looked around. The boat was some twenty yards away. He asked Cloud to take River Blossom by the hand and walk over to the embankment. There, they saw three large Wuxi-style boats moored in a row. The largest carried the coffin and a group of monks, the second was occupied by Cloudlet Chen and the geomancer, and the last by Fair Sister and her family. Jade handed River Blossom over to Fair Sister and then went with Cloud to Cloudlet's boat to greet him and sat down for a friendly chat. Half an hour later, the geomancer announced, "It's time." Whereupon Cloudlet told Laurel Blessing to relay orders for the local cannoneers to take up their positions and for the undersupervisors to made sure that their coolies were ready for work. He also sent word to Fair Sister to tell River Blossom and the others to change into mourning clothes. With the geomancer leading the way, Cloudlet, Cloud, and Jade set off toward the grave.

::

2. White and blue are colors of mourning in China. Normally, women tied their hair with red knitting wool.

Soon afterward, the cannon was fired and the coffin taken off the boat. The monks at the head of the procession beat on their religious instruments, while the family walked behind the coffin, weeping as they went along. At the sight of this, Jade felt sick to his stomach. He struggled to control himself, but it was no use. Dizziness suddenly overwhelmed him. He saw nothing but blackness; his legs gave way, and he fell to the ground. Cloud and Cloudlet, greatly alarmed, reached out to hold him up, calling his name. Fair Sister was in a panic. She abandoned the coffin and rushed forward to undertake a series of folk remedies, including pinching his upper lip, calling on the deities, and what not. Fortunately, Jade gradually came to and opened his eyes. Everyone was somewhat reassured.

The geomancer pointed out that a foreign-style building to the left was a Western restaurant where they could rest for a while. And so Fair Sister and Cloud helped Jade walk over there. The autumn sun was fierce, no different from midsummer. Since Jade was suffering from the heat, once he was inside the building and had taken off his gown, he felt much cooler. Then he had some lemonade and was all right.

As soon as Cloud went out to stand on the porch, Jade tried to sneak out. But would Fair Sister let him go? He pleaded, "Let me go and take a look. I'm fine now. Let go of me!"

She tried her best to dissuade him. "Second Young Master, you've just got a bit better, so how can I let you go? It's too much of a responsibility for me."

Cloud heard them and said loudly, "Are you intent on scaring everybody to death? Now quiet down a bit."

Jade returned to his seat, dejected and restless. He took hold of a piece of white jade that he wore at his waist and cut it hard with his nails, wishing he could smash it to pieces.

Fair Sister consoled him gently, "I'll go and take a look, Second Young Master. You just sit here. When they're done, I'll tell Laurel Blessing to ask you over. How about that?"

"In that case, go quickly," Jade said.

Before she went off, Fair Sister asked Cloud to make sure Jade stayed in the restaurant. Jade looked through the window toward the burial mound. As it was only a short distance away, he could see everything clearly. All things necessary, including the steps leading up to the mound and the inscriptions on the tomb, were ready. Yet River Blossom could be seen circling round the grave, crying in great agitation; he did not understand why. Just then Laurel Blessing came to invite him over, so Cloud left the Western restaurant with him, and they headed for the tomb. River Blossom was still crying, and as soon as Jade arrived she rushed into his arms.

"Stop them, Brother-in-law!" she kept shouting.

"What's the matter?"

"Look! They've shut Elder Sister inside. How can she come out again?" No one except Jade knew what she meant. She pushed him, saying in tears, "Talk to them, Brother-in-law, tell them to open a door there."

There was nothing he could say to comfort her, so he resorted to white lies. River Blossom was not ready to leave it at that. She turned around, rushed up to the tomb, and tried to remove the plaster with her hands. The plasterers had no way of stopping her. In the end, it was Fair Sister who pulled her away. Fair Sister placed her back in Jade's charge and said, "Well, it's finally over. Please go back first, Second Young Master. We'll take care of things here."

Jade knew that there was no point in staying behind in this desolate place, so he left with Cloud in the hackney, with River Blossom squeezed between them. They headed back to West Civic Peace Alley, and River Blossom pestered them all the way. When they entered Belle's place, they heard many voices talking upstairs. The menservants told Cloud that Devotion Yin was at Flora Zhang's, and Second Bai Gao and Wenjun Yao were also there. Cloud was delighted. He took Jade and River Blossom upstairs to Belle's room, where he sat for a while before going over to Flora Zhang's.

CHAPTER 44 : *Wenjun tricks a rascal and gets off with a song, and Green Phoenix tackles greed by insisting on a low ransom*

As soon as Second Bai Gao and Devotion Yin saw Cloud Tao, they inquired about Water Blossom's burial. Cloud filled them in briefly. On learning that Jade Tao was in Belle's room, Devotion Yin sent the maid to invite him over, so Jade brought River Blossom with him to Flora Zhang's room. When greetings had been exchanged and everyone had settled down, Second Bai urged Jade Tao to take care of himself and eat properly, while Devotion Yin just said a few simple words of condolence. Jade dreaded nothing more than the mention of his loss; he was instantly overwhelmed by sorrow.

To change the subject, Cloud asked, "Did you continue with the *Four Classics* drinking game the night before last?"

"We've had so many good drinking games in the last few days, which one are you referring to?" Devotion Yin asked.

"Just yesterday we had a big gathering and Mr. Dragon Ma thought up a *Four Classics* drinking game that was quite neat. What's clever about it is it's neither too hard nor too easy and was exactly right for

the total number of guests: twenty-four guests seated at six tables."
Second Bai said.

Cloud asked what the rules of the game were. Second Bai pointed at Devotion. "Ask him. He's got the manuscript."

"I don't know if I have it with me; I'll have a look." So saying, Devotion took out his wallet and found that the manuscript, in the form of three sheets of poetry notepaper, was there. He took it out to show Cloud. While they discussed drinking games, Jade Tao took the opportunity to go back to the Belle's room with River Blossom and sat there in total dejection. Belle sent a maid to keep them company, while Second Bai said to Cloud in a low voice, "Your brother looks a bit off-color. You should really try and persuade him to take better care of himself."

"Why don't you spend a couple of days at Conical Hat Garden with your brother and get him to relax a bit?" Devotion Yin suggested.

"We intend to go tomorrow. Even I have been feeling depressed these few days," replied Cloud.

Devotion looked around him and came up with an idea. He told Flora Zhang to give orders for a dinner party, saying, "Today, I'll stand him dinner first. It's a rare coincidence that all our good friends are here. There're eight of us including our girls, just the right number for a table."

Before Cloud could object, Flora had already told the menservants to order the dishes. Wenjun Yao stood up and said, "There's an opera performance in our house. I'll go and do a show and then come right back."

"We'll be waiting," Second Bai said.

Wenjun left without more ado. It was the time of day when the sunset glow spread across the sky and the dusk gathered. She went in a sedan chair via Fourth Avenue and West Civic Peace Alley to East Co-prosperity Alley. When she entered the house and looked up, she saw the upstairs parlor was brightly lit and crowded with people. Loud music assaulted her ears. Upon asking, she learned that the client was Lai, the son of a powerful official. The news startled her, and she went into the back room to complain in a low voice to the madam, Big Feet Yao, that she should not have invited the attention of Lai the Turtle.

"But I didn't! He just showed up and asked for you, insisting on having a dinner show. Could we have refused him?" Big Feet Yao replied.

There was nothing Wenjun could do except to show up at the dinner table and play it by ear. As she ascended the stairs, the maid announced, "Our maestro Wenjun is back." Immediately, a tidal wave of Lai's hangers-on rushed out in welcome. They surrounded her, shouting and leaping about in joy. She stood there erectly and glared at them. They cowered back, and instead of pestering her, they simply said, "The Young Commander has waited for you for a long time. Come in quickly." One man walked ahead of her to clear the way; another put a stool behind Lai and asked her to sit down. Since Lai was completely surrounded by the eight or nine girls he had called to the party, there was no room for her, so she moved the stool farther away. Master Lai looked over his shoulder repeatedly to size her up. She sat there primly, with her hands in her lap, and he could not very well find fault with her.

Wenjun noticed that only two guests were seated with the host. They were Prosperity Luo and Lotuson Wang. This reassured her somewhat. The rest of the two dozen men there looked suspiciously like street hooligans. They were not seated at the table but were just hanging around. These were probably Lai's lackeys and hangers-on.

A hanger-on came up to her, bowed low with shoulders thrusting up, and asked, "Which play will you do? Make your choice."

She thought that after she had performed she could make an excuse about being called to another party, so she said she would play *Wenzhao Pass*. Delighted to have received this decree from her, the hanger-on immediately reported to Master Lai that Wenjun would play *Wenzhao Pass* and narrated for him the plot of the play. Another hanger-on urged her to hurry off and get changed.

When the play that had been going on was over, Wenjun went onstage in costume. Even before she had opened her mouth, one of the hangers-on shouted, "Bravo!" This triggered the others, who shouted "Bravo!" one after another. It was an avalanche that created havoc. Master Lai's guest Lotuson Wang was a quiet man, and the noise gave him a bad headache. Even Prosperity Luo, who was rather boisterous by nature, could not stand this nonsense. But Master Lai enjoyed all this and laughed uproariously. Halfway through the performance, he ordered a servant to give out the tips. The servant poured a packet of silver dollars into a small basket and submitted it for Master Lai's inspection. He then threw the contents onto the stage. There was a loud jingling noise, and then they saw shiny coins rolling all over the stage. The hangers-on gave another triumphant shout.

Realizing that Lai had obvious designs on her, Wenjun's desperation gave rise to a plan. She sang well during the performance, and once it was over, she called a maid to the backstage and laid out her plan. Then she changed out of her costume and joined those at the table, all smiles. Suddenly, Master Lai reached out his hand and pulled her into his arms. She pushed him away and stood up, pretending to be angry, but then she leaned on his shoulder and whispered into his ear.

He nodded and said repeatedly, "I get you." Thereupon she picked up the wine pot and poured wine for those at the table, starting with Prosperity Luo and Lotuson Wang. When she got to Master Lai, she held the wine cup to his lips, and he drained it in one gulp. She offered him another cup, saying it was to "make a pair." He drained that, too. Only then did she return to her seat. His lust aroused, Lai could not keep his mind on the performance but turned his backside toward the stage to leer at her. Fortunately, he kept his hands to himself. Wenjun slapped and cursed him flirtatiously, pretending intimacy. Prosperity Luo and Lotuson Wang were both surprised by this. The hangers-on, who knew little about her, thought she was trying hard to please and did not suspect anything.

Soon a manservant called out loudly, "A party call for the maestro."

"Where to?" the maid asked loudly.

"The Old Banner,"[1] the manservant answered.

"Whatever next!" The maid turned to Wenjun. "You've still got three parties to go to, and now there's the Old Banner as well."

"Drinking parties at the Old Banner last till dawn. It'll be all right if I'm a bit late," said Wenjun.

The maid called out loudly in reply, "OK, we'll come, but we have three other parties to go to first." The manservant assented downstairs.

Hearing this, Master Lai got worried. "Are you really going to all these parties?" he asked Wenjun.

"Are there such things as fake parties?"

He showed a hint of displeasure, but she pretended not to notice and whispered in his ear again. He nodded repeatedly and in an about-face actually told her to go early, saying, "Why don't you hurry up then?"

"There's time enough. What's the hurry?" she replied.

As she dawdled, the manservant brought a lantern and stood to wait by the bamboo curtain, while the maid got ready the *pipa* and silver water pipe and handed them to the man.

Master Lai told her to go again. She pretended annoyance, "What's the hurry? Are you tired of me?"

His heartbeat quickened. He wanted to hold her close and feel her up but was afraid that she'd take offense and so spoil everything. Before she left, she whispered a few remarks in his ear. He again nodded repeatedly. His hangers-on stared as Wenjun sailed off.

::

1. [A Cantonese restaurant-cum-brothel dating back to the times when Cantonese merchants, highly experienced in foreign trade, played a leading role in the commercial life of Shanghai. *E.H.*]

Prosperity Luo and Lotuson Wang knew only then that she had used a ruse to get away. They were full of admiration for her.

Master Lai remained in high spirits and continued to drink and watch the show, but several of his hangers-on put their heads together and discussed the matter in whispers. A moment later, they chose a representative to come forward and ask Master Lai why he had let Wenjun go.

"I was the one who told her to go. It's none of your business," he replied. The hanger-on withdrew, silenced.

Prosperity Luo and Lotuson Wang waited until the fourth course was served before they took their leave together. Master Lai, who had little idea of etiquette, let them go without even seeing them off. The two of them parted company downstairs, each getting into his own sedan chair. Lotuson Wang returned to his residence on Fifth Avenue, while Prosperity Luo went to Green Phoenix's in Generosity Alley, where the servant girl, Little Treasure, saw him into her room. Green Phoenix and Gold Phoenix were both out on party calls, so Pearl Phoenix, the awkward girl, was the only one to keep him company.

Soon the madam, Second Sister Huang, came upstairs to greet him, and they started chatting, so Prosperity did not feel lonely. Second Sister asked him, "Well, Green Phoenix is going to buy back her freedom. Did she tell you, Mr. Luo?"

"She did mention it, but it seems that nothing has come of it."

"That's not quite true. When the girls raise the issue of buying back their freedom, they always manage to get it done. Would I be the one to stand in her way? What I want is not her person but for her to do business. If she can't buy back her freedom, naturally she won't be keen on working for me. It's better to let her do it, right?" she said.

"Then why did she tell me nothing came of it?" he asked.

Second Sister sighed. "I don't mean to say anything against her, but Green Phoenix is a sly one. We who run brothels buy our girls when they're only seven or eight, and we have to bring them up till they're sixteen before they can do business. On top of food and clothing, we have to teach them everything to do with the trade. How much thought and care would you say goes into it, Mr. Luo? And we can't tell whether business will be good. If it isn't, we lose our capital and our time, and there's nothing we can do about it. If we're in luck and get a presentable girl, then business may look up. Suppose we own ten girls and nine of them aren't much good, the only one who does well naturally has to make up for our full investment. Don't you think that's right, Mr. Luo? Now Green Phoenix wants to buy back her freedom, and she tells me that since she was bought for a hundred dollars, even if she gives me ten times that, it'll only be a thousand. Now, Mr. Luo, would you say it's fair to use the original purchase price as a basis for reckoning?"

"If she says a thousand, how much are *you* looking for?"

"Heaven be my witness, I don't mind taking this to the teahouse for arbitration.[2] Just on party calls alone she brings in over a thousand dollars a season, and that's not counting her patrons' gifts and the pocket money they give her. Even if she pays me three thousand as her ransom price, it's only a year's party bills. After she leaves me, she'll continue to do booming business, right, Mr. Luo?"

He reflected in silence for quite a while. Pearl Phoenix took the opportunity to withdraw to one of the high-back chairs against the wall and start dozing. When Second Sister caught sight of her, she swung her arm and gave her a swipe. The girl fell down on the floor but did not wake up; her outstretched hands kept scratching on the floorboards.

"What are you up to?" Prosperity broke into a smile and asked.

"I've lost something," she managed to say.

Second Sister pulled her up and gave her another vicious blow. "It's your wits you've lost!" Finally wakened by the second blow, Pearl Phoenix got to her feet, grimaced, and stood in attendance on one side.

Second Sister turned again to Prosperity. "Take the likes of Pearl Phoenix, I'm just wasting food on her. Can she do business? Would anyone want her? I'll gladly let her go for just a hundred. Would I ever say that Pearl Phoenix can't go unless she matches Green Phoenix's ransom price?"

"Here in Shanghai the ransom price for a courtesan can be three thousand or a thousand; there're no set rules. I suggest you lower your expectations while I lend a hand, and we all do our bit to make it work. It counts as a good deed, after all," said Prosperity.

"You're right, Mr. Luo. I'm not insisting on three thousand, either. It was Green Phoenix who went into a lot of nonsense to begin with, so I wasn't in a position to say anything."

Having worked out the figures in his head, Prosperity hoped to take this opportunity to settle on a sum and get the matter settled. But just then Green Phoenix and Gold Phoenix returned from the same dinner party, so he held back. Looking slightly embarrassed, Second Sister took her leave and went to bed.

The minute Green Phoenix stepped into the room, she asked Pearl Phoenix, "You were dozing, weren't you?"

"No, I wasn't."

::

2. [An age-old way of settling dispute in the Jiangsu-Zhejiang area was for the parties involved to meet for tea at a teahouse, where one or more authority figure from the clan or the profession would pass judgment on the case. The practice was called "having arbitration tea." *E.H.*]

Green Phoenix pulled her over to make her face the table lamp for an examination.

"Look at your eyes, and you said you weren't dozing?"

"I was listening to Mother talking all this time; how could I be asleep?" Pearl Phoenix responded.

Green Phoenix did not believe her and turned to ask Prosperity. He said, "Your mother has given her a few knocks already, so just let her be. Why bother with her?"

Angry that Pearl Phoenix had lied to her, Green Phoenix thought she deserved a beating. But since Prosperity had interceded, she restrained herself. He shouted at Pearl Phoenix to leave them. Green Phoenix changed out of her party clothes into a sleeveless jacket worn at home. Gold Phoenix, who had also changed, came over to greet Prosperity and sat down. He repeated in detail what Second Sister had said about the ransom price.

"Humph!" Green Phoenix responded, "Just wait and see. Anyone who becomes a madam has no heart left in her. Mother was only a maid to begin with. She used the money she invested in her mistress to buy us girls; what capital could she speak of? In the last five years, I brought in more than twenty thousand all on my own; every cent went to her. The clothes, jewelry, and furniture come to another ten thousand or so. Can I take them with me? And on top of all that she wants another three thousand from me! Humph! Three thousand is no big deal. I'd like to see if she's capable of getting it."

Prosperity also recounted in detail his answer to Second Sister. The minute Green Phoenix heard it, she said in annoyance, "Who wants you to help out? I have my own plans for buying back my freedom. There's no need for any of your nonsense!"

This unexpected telling-off left Prosperity smiling awkwardly. Gold Phoenix, seeing that this was a serious matter, dared not cut in. Green Phoenix told Prosperity again and again, "Now don't go and prattle with Mother. Given what she's like, if you go along with her, you'll only come to grief."

He gave his promise, and then he thought of Wenjun Yao. "You know, that girl Wenjun Yao is a bit like you," he said to her, smiling.

"Not in the least bit. Since Lai the Turtle is such a terror, it's just as well that Wenjun didn't go along, but it seems to me she shouldn't have given him false hopes. She may be able to stay at the Old Banner tonight, but what will she do tomorrow?"

Prosperity thought this made sense, and he became worried for Wenjun. "You're right. Now Wenjun is going to be in trouble."

Gold Phoenix smiled and said, "Come now, Brother-in-law, Elder Sister told you not to talk nonsense, didn't she? Whether

Wenjun Yao is in trouble or not, what's it to you?" On hearing this, he smiled and brushed the matter aside. He stayed the night, but we need not go into the details.

The next day was the eleventh. Toward noon, Green Phoenix and Gold Phoenix were both doing their hair at the window in the center room. Alone in the bedroom, Prosperity felt a little enervated and thought he'd smoke some opium. He roasted a pellet for himself and fixed it onto the pipe, only to see it fall off, so he never got to smoke it. Second Sister happened to come in and saw this. She came up, took the pick, and toasted another pellet for him. And so they ended up lying facing each other on the opium divan, consulting in whispers. She asked about the idea of his helping out with the ransom price, and Prosperity told her Green Phoenix was adamantly against increasing the ransom or accepting his help.

"Green Phoenix does like silly talk!" Second Sister said in a low voice. "The way she acts now makes me quite angry, so much so that I'm tempted not to let her go even if she pays three thousand. But the two of us have talked, and if you're willing to help out a bit, Mr. Luo, it'll all be for the best. I'd just ask you to name a sum. I'll agree to whatever you say, Mr. Luo."

He hesitated. "That should be all right, except she's said she doesn't want my help, so it's awkward for me. I don't know what she wants."

"Well, that's Green Phoenix up to her little tricks. She wants to buy back her freedom, so does it make sense for her to reject help when it's offered to her? She says she doesn't want help, but in her heart she does. After you have helped out with the ransom price she'll also need your help with her expenses when she leaves here. Don't you think that's what she wants?"

Prosperity thought there was truth in what she said, so he rashly reached an agreement with Second Sister on a ransom price of two thousand, to which he would contribute half. Overjoyed at getting an unexpected bonus, Second Sister filled the opium pipe for him three times. Only when he had smoked enough did she leave the room.

CHAPTER 45 :: *The vile crone changes color when a settlement is over-turned, and the child courtesan gets jealous when left on the sidelines*

Second Sister left Prosperity Luo in the room and walked over to the center room, where Green Phoenix and Gold Phoenix had just finished their toilet and put on their hair ornaments. Second Sister told Green Phoenix delightedly about Prosperity's contributing a thousand dollars toward her ransom. Green Phoenix said not a word in reply. She washed her hands hastily and rushed into the room to tell Prosperity in a loud voice, "So, it seems you're flush with money. Well, I had no idea and was actually worried for you! Now, after I'm free, I'll need clothes, jewelry, and furniture in order to set up on my own, and the cost will come to three thousand. Taking into account the two-thousand ransom price, you should go and get me five thousand."

"But how would I have so much money?" he said, alarmed.

She sneered. "Surely there's no need for you to be so modest! The minute Mother talked to you, you came up with a thousand, so how can you say you don't have the money? If you really don't, am I to starve to death after getting my freedom?"

Only then did he grasp the full import of her words. "What you're saying is you don't want me to help out, is that it?" he responded in a loud voice as well.

"Well, of course everyone likes to be helped out! After you've seen to my clothes, jewelry, and furniture, you can help out as much as you like," Green Phoenix replied.

Prosperity turned to Second Sister. "Forget our agreement; it never took place. Whether she buys back her freedom or not is none of my business." Having said that, he lay down on the opium divan.

Second Sister had not expected such a showdown. Her face turned iron blue with anger, and she pointed at Green Phoenix, upbraiding her malevolently, "Don't you have any conscience? Think about it! You lost your parents at seven and were sold into a brothel. I felt sorry for you and treated you like my own daughter. I was the one who combed your hair and bound your feet, who's taken care of you all this time. Did I do anything to offend you that you've become my mortal enemy? Where's you conscience? Now, you're going to do well in the world when you get your freedom. I had hoped you'd look after me a bit in my old age if you did well. Is this the way you'll look after me? For one so young, you're really hard. You'll come to no good end, you know." She said all this between clenched teeth, crying and sniffling.

Green Phoenix immediately put on a smiling face and consoled her, "Don't be like that, Mother! It's nothing important, is it? I'm a girl you bought; it's up to you whether you allow me to buy back my freedom. Let's forget the whole idea. Otherwise, when the people next door hear our row, we'll be a real laughingstock."

Before Green Phoenix had finished speaking, Second Sister walked out of the room and wiped her face with a hot towel. Mama

Zhao, who was still putting the toilet articles away, offered her a few words of comfort. Second Sister said to her, "It's common enough for clients to help out when courtesans redeem themselves. Now, if Mr. Luo were unwilling, she should have talked him into it as a favor to me. After all, she counts as a daughter of mine, doesn't she? But now Mr. Luo is willing to help, and she actually forbids him to! Does she want to lay her hands on all his money?"

Green Phoenix was smoking her water pipe in her room, and when she heard this, she smiled and said, "Oh, do stop, Mother. All right, I'm not going to buy my freedom. I'll work another ten years for you. With a thousand or so a season of party bills, how much will it be in ten years?" She counted it out on her fingers and pretended to be startled. "Aiyo! The party bills will come to thirty thousand![1] Mother will be so happy then, she won't even want any money for my freedom, she'd just say, 'Off with you! Off with you!'"

Even Prosperity burst out laughing at this. Second Sister answered from the next room, "Don't you make me the butt of your silly jokes. If you want to be my enemy, it's up to you. It won't do you any good." Having said that, she went downstairs. Mama Zhao, having finished her chores, followed her.

Pearl Phoenix and Gold Phoenix came into the room together, both of them scared stiff by what had happened. Green Phoenix finally turned to Prosperity to tell him off, "Where's you common sense? Why would you want to make her a gift of a thousand dollars? There have been occasions when money needed to be spent, and I spoke to you about it, but you showed a lot more reluctance than this. Now that the need's not there, you actually agreed to a thousand!"

Feeling ashamed, he did not argue. The matter of redeeming Green Phoenix was dropped.

The next day Prosperity happened to read the newspapers and saw an item in the back pages: "The night before last, a Cantonese man called Mr. A was consorting with prostitutes at a party in the Old Banner. One of his guests, Mr. B, called Wenjun Yao of East Co-prosperity Alley to the party. The said Wenjun Yao offended B in a quarrel, whereupon B flew into a rage and swung his fists at her. Only after A's efforts at peacemaking did they go their separate ways. Rumors have it that B is still in a rage and has gathered a group of hooligans to seek revenge at Wenjun Yao's home. Wenjun Yao is now in hiding, and reportedly no one knows her whereabouts."

::

1. [As noted in "The World of the Shanghai Courtesans," there were three seasons in a brothel's fiscal year. E.H.]

Prosperity was greatly startled by this news and immediately told Green Phoenix about it. Green Phoenix, however, was skeptical. He told his steward, Promotion, to go to Big Feet Yao's house to find out what had happened to Wenjun and whether it had anything to do with Lai the Turtle.

Promotion left to carry out his instructions. Walking down Fourth Avenue, he saw a leather-topped carriage parked at the entrance to East Co-prosperity Alley. The courtesan sitting in it had the same build as Wenjun Yao. He quickly stepped up for a closer look. It turned out to be Belle. Promotion was rather surprised that she was going for a drive so early in the day. He glanced at her before turning into the alley and heading into Big Feet Yao's parlor to ask the menservants for news. The men just said it had nothing to do with Lai the Turtle but were vague about the rest of the story.

Promotion was about to leave when he saw Cloud Tao come into the parlor, accompanied by the madam, Big Feet Yao. Promotion stood to one side and greeted him, "Mr. Tao." Cloud asked why he was there.

"To find out about Wenjun," he replied.

Cloud bowed his head and thought for a moment and then whispered to Promotion, "Nothing happened really; it was just done to mislead Lai the Turtle. They put it in the papers in case he didn't believe it. Wenjun is in Conical Hat Garden now; she's quite well. Go back and tell your master, and don't let outsiders hear you."

Promotion gave his promise. After that, Cloud took his leave from Big Feet Yao, exited the alley, and got into the carriage waiting there. It took them all the way to beyond the gates of Conical Hat Garden. There, Cloud Tao and Belle alighted, and a servant came to lead the way. They headed east and then north along a curved path that led to a place that faced the lake and backed on to the hill. The building, called the Moon-worshiper's Chamber, had five rooms opening on to a hall. Here, the shadows of flowers played on bamboo curtains, and the smoke from making tea drifted under the eaves. But it was quiet inside; not a murmur of talk or laughter was heard. Cloud Tao went in with Belle. They saw Amity Zhu lying on the divan smoking opium, and Jade Tao and River Blossom sitting beside him. There was no one else around. Cloud was just going to ask where everybody was when the servant said: "All the masters are watching archery. They'll be here soon."

Before he had finished speaking, a gaggle of finely dressed men and women could be seen making their way round the hill at the back. At the head of the group was none other than Wenjun Yao. Dressed in close-fitting garments that complemented her nimble movement, she looked very different from the others. Twin Jade,

Flora Zhang, White Fragrance, and Aroma walked behind her, followed by Modesty Zhu, Second Bai Gao, Devotion Yin, Harmony Qi, and a large number of maids and menservants. They all drifted into the Moon-worshiper's Chamber, where they sat down casually.

Cloud Tao said to Wenjun Yao, "I've just been to your house myself. Your mother said Lai the Turtle was there again yesterday and was inclined to believe what she told him. But his hangers-on are still speculating about it. I think it should be all right."

Harmony Qi said to Cloud, "There's something else I need to tell you. Your brother said he wanted to go home today, so I asked him: 'Has anything come up? We're going to have some fun during the festival; why leave in such a hurry?' In reply, he said he'd go and then come right back. Then it occurred to me that tomorrow is the seventh day after Water Blossom's death, and that's probably the reason he has to go there. Now, Water Blossom's strong love and tragic fate deserve not just our pity but our respect, too. Tomorrow, the seven of us should go and honor her. This will be remembered as a romantic event."

"In that case, we'd better inform them beforehand," Cloud replied.

"There's no need. We'll leave directly after we've paid our respects and go for dinner at your lady love's place. That way, I'll get a chance to see your lady love's room and Flora Zhang's as well. We'll make a nuisance of ourselves at their place for a whole day," said Harmony Qi.

"Your Excellency is really too kind," said Belle. "Our place is small and untidy. If Your Excellency doesn't mind that, we'd be honored if you were to drop in."

A moment later, orders were give for lunch to be served. The menservants set up two round tables in the center of the Moon-worshiper's Chamber. The formality of giving each other precedence was dispensed with, and everyone just took his seat, with eight at the table on the left and six at the one on the right.

Harmony Qi counted the number of those present. "Where's Green Fragrance gone off to? I haven't seen her all day today," he asked in surprise.

"She went back to bed again after getting up," White Fragrance said.

Devotion Yin hastened to ask, "Is she not feeling well?"

"Who knows. She looked all right to me," White Fragrance replied.

Harmony Qi told the maid to ask her over, but after a long time the maid still had not reported back. Harmony suddenly remembered something. "The other day, I heard Green Fragrance and Hairpin singing a duet in Pear Blossom Court. It was the entire aria 'Receiving the Portrait.' It wasn't bad at all."

"It couldn't have been Green Fragrance. She does know a couple of arias, but she hasn't learned 'Receiving the Portrait,'" said White Fragrance.

"I'm sure it was Green Fragrance. She listened in at the singing lessons there and has learned several arias just like that," said Aroma.

"It's pretty hard work to have to sing 'Receiving the Portrait' and 'Weeping in Front of the Portrait' one after the other," said Cloud Tao.

Second Bai responded, "*The Palace of Eternal Youth* has evenly balanced roles for all other characters.[2] It's only the male lead who has a hard time with the two scenes 'Receiving the Portrait' and 'Weeping in Front of the Portrait.'"

These comments increased Harmony Qi's enthusiasm, and he sent another maid to summon Hairpin, who immediately came back with the maid. The others saw that her pretty round face was without the least touch of rouge or powder. A thick braid hung down her back, reminding them of black clouds surrounding a full moon. Harmony told her to sit at his side. A seat beside Devotion Yin was kept vacant for Green Fragrance.

By then, four small bowls of food had been served, each followed by dim sum. The menservants brought them cups of tea as well as ready-prepared water pipes, regular pipes, and cigars. Amity Zhu, the only one who preferred opium, left the table for the divan for a smoke.

Cloud Tao thought of drinking games and suggested, "Shall we have another go at Mr. Dragon Ma's four-tones drinking game?"

Devotion Yin waved his hand to signal his disagreement. "It can't be done. I've gone through the *Four Classics* in my head. You'll never get another twenty-four lines in the right tonal patterns."

As they were discussing drinking games at the table, Green Fragrance finally arrived with the maid in tow, approaching slowly along the flowery pathway shaded by willows. Her arrival was unnoticed, and she stood there quietly for a long time. When Devotion Yin heard some noise behind him, he turned to find Green

::

2. A play about the tragic love story of Emperor Xuanzong of the Tang dynasty (r. 712–755) and his favorite imperial concubine, Yang. The latter was executed by popular demand of the army when the emperor escaped the capital during an uprising.

Fragrance looking sad and desolate. Her hair had worked slightly loose, and her hairpins, earrings, and bracelets had not been properly arranged. Resting one hand on the back of Devotion's chair, she rubbed her eyes with her other hand. He smiled gallantly and invited her to sit down, but she ignored him. When he got up and tried to lead her to her seat, she shook her hands free and said with a frown, "Let go!"

Harmony Qi chuckled, and the others all burst into laughter. Devotion sat down a bit shamefaced. Green Fragrance, suspecting they were laughing at her, became even more angry and just looked away. As she was only a virgin courtesan, Flora Zhang did not mind this. She wished to make peace between the two of them, but no opportunity arose. Finally, at the beckoning of White Fragrance, Green Fragrance dawdled over to her. White Fragrance tidied her hair and took the opportunity to whisper a couple of remarks in her ear. Green Fragrance acted as if she did not hear. When her sister had finished tidying her hair, she walked slowly to a row of high-back chairs by the windows and sat down sideways. Holding a handkerchief against her face, she opened her little mouth and yawned.

Everyone at the table thought it was funny, but no one dared laugh aloud. A smiling Devotion Yin said softly, "Well, I guess it's just my rotten luck." So saying, he took a compact water pipe, walked over to the opium divan, lit the spill at the opium lamp, and then went and sat in another high-back chair by the window, one separated from Green Fragrance by a semicircular table. He knew that jealousy was taboo to virgin courtesans and therefore Green Fragrance would never admit to it. That being the case, there was no way he could console her. All he could do was try in a myriad ways to amuse her. But she just turned around to lean on the windowsill to look at a pair of white waterbirds swimming in the lake. However elaborate a performance Devotion put on, she would not even take a proper glance at him. Harmony Qi surmised that there was no chance of her coming around anytime soon and decided to order Hairpin to sing the aria "Receiving the Portrait" alone. Hairpin played the clappers herself and asked Aroma to accompany her on the flute. Those seated at the table now concentrated on the singing and no longer paid attention to the lovers' quarrel.

Amity Zhu got off the opium divan, and as he walked toward the table, he stopped at the window and urged Green Fragrance to come along and have some wine.

"I'm not feeling very well. The wine won't agree with me." She begged off so plaintively that Amity could only walk away.

At the end of his wits, Devotion Yin sat down by her side and put on a solemn expression. He called her name and then addressed her seriously and intimately. "If you're not feeling well, you should go and sit for a little while at the table; there's no need for you to drink. If you don't join them, I may know it's because you're unwell, but they'll insist on saying you're jealous. Think about it."

When she saw that he was still treating her the same as before, her anger began to melt away. Now, his remark went straight to the heart of the matter, and she was persuaded by it. But to turn around instantly would have been too demeaning. She bowed her head and did not speak. Devotion could tell from such small signs how she felt, and so he took the opportunity to hold her hand. She snatched it away in fake vexation, "Get away from me! Don't be a nuisance!"

"Come with me, all right?" he pleaded.

"If you want to go, just go. Why should I?"

"Just go and sit at the table for a little while. You can come back here later."

"You go first."

Afraid that it would arouse her displeasure, he dared not press her too hard, so he returned to the table after urging her to come soon. Hairpin had just reached the most melodious part of her aria, and everyone was listening to her in a respectful silence. After he had sat for a while, Devotion signaled White Fragrance with his eyes. White Fragrance again beckoned to Green Fragrance, who took the opportunity to totter over to her, "What is it, Elder Sister?"

White Fragrance pointed with her chin toward the chair beside Devotion, who half rose to offer her the seat. Green Fragrance pulled the chair a little away from him and sat down sideways, facing Hairpin.

Devotion waited until Hairpin had finished her song and then whispered into Green Fragrance's ear about Harmony Qi's original intention of asking them for a duet.

"But I don't know 'Receiving the Portrait,'" Green Fragrance responded.

He again told her in whispers that Harmony had heard her singing it.

"But I haven't learned the whole aria," she said.

Though she had turned him down twice, Devotion did not mind. He continued to plead with her to drink a little warm wine to lubricate her throat and then sing one of her best arias. She didn't have the heart to tell him off again, so she just pretended not to hear and turned deliberately to Hairpin with a question. Hairpin felt compelled to respond. Meanwhile, Devotion took the wine pot, filled a large wine cup, and brought it to Green Fragrance's lips.

"Just put it down!" she said loudly in displeasure.

He hastily withdrew his hand and put the wine cup on the table. She continued to make conversation with Hairpin as she reached out for the cup and drained the wine in one gulp, after which she threw the cup down and wiped her mouth with a handkerchief.

"Will you sing?" Hairpin asked.

She nodded, so Hairpin accompanied her on the flute, and Green Fragrance sang half of "Weeping in Front of the Portrait." Needless to say, everyone praised her. After that, rice was served, and then the table was cleared.

It was almost three o'clock. Without waiting for Harmony Qi to return to his room for his nap, everyone left the Moon-worshiper's Chamber. They walked in twos and threes all over the garden, going wherever their fancy took them. Green Fragrance grasped the first opportunity to leave unnoticed, dragging Hairpin with her. They walked northwestward toward Pear Blossom Court. When they got there, they saw the courtyard door wide open; on the luxuriant trees, a few swallows were darting about. A class was going on in the side chambers where young girls were having beginners' singing lessons. Hairpin led Green Fragrance upstairs to her own bedroom. Pendant from the next room heard them and came over. When she saw how badly the makeup on Green Fragrance's face had faded, she said, "You have to wash your face. You must have gotten into a fight to look like this."

"It wasn't a fight," Hairpin said in mirth. "It was jealousy."

"What d'you mean by jealousy? Now out with it!" Green Fragrance broke out in anger.

Instead of arguing with her, Hairpin just called an old woman to fetch a basin of warm water and then placed her own toiletry box in front of Green Fragrance. The latter sat down and redid her toilet. Pendant was still full of questions.

"There's no point in asking her," said Green Fragrance. "She heard them say it was jealousy, and she thinks she's learned something new. But does she know what jealousy is?"

Hairpin winked and shook her head at Pendant behind Green Fragrance's back to stop her from saying any more. Green Fragrance saw it all in the mirror, but instead of confronting them, she hurriedly tidied her hair and applied makeup to her face and then stood up and walked away. At the door, she turned around and said, "I'm leaving so the two of you can gossip about me in peace."

Pendant and Hairpin immediately tried to detain her, but she had turned and run down the stairs. After leaving Pear Blossom Court, she considered where she should go. As she came to a junction on the footpath by the white wall, she looked up and saw that in the distance a man was standing at the head of the steps leading up to Right Target Hall, hands clasped behind his back. It looked like Longevity. She surmised that her brother-in-law and elder sister must be there and that it would be a good idea for her to go and pass some time with them.

Having made up her mind, Green Fragrance meandered over to Right Target Hall, where Longevity lifted the curtain for her to go in. She saw her brother-in-law, Amity Zhu, lying on the divan smoking opium and her sister, White Fragrance, sitting beside him, chatting.

"Brother-in-law," Green Fragrance said in greeting, all smiles. Then she nestled against her sister's knees and turned sideways to look at them.

Recalling her misbehavior, White Fragrance gently rebuked her, "You shouldn't pick a quarrel over nothing, you know. Mr. Yin is quite affectionate toward you, so you should take it easy and chat cheerfully with him. They're in a relationship, so naturally they behave intimately. Since you're a virgin courtesan, there's no reason for you to be jealous."

Green Fragrance dared not answer back. Her face instantly flushed red, and she was close to tears.

"If you insist on lecturing her again, her anger will certainly kill her," Amity commented with a smile.

White Fragrance giggled. "She can't even tell right from wrong, so what's there for her to be angry about?"

Overwhelmed by shame and regret, Green Fragrance could not very well defend herself. It was a difficult situation. White Fragrance dropped the subject and went back to making conversation with Amity.

After a long while, Green Fragrance finally showed a slight smile. Seeing that, Amity immediately urged her to go out and have fun. Green Fragrance, who had been bored sitting there, was about to go when White Fragrance stopped her and said, "Now be sensible, won't you? If you go on pulling a long face, people will certainly laugh at you!"

Green Fragrance remained silent. As she walked listlessly down the archery path in front of Right Target Hall, her head bowed, her mind was still preoccupied with unruly thoughts, and, without thinking, she took a turn onto a flowery path that led to the Bridge of Nine Twists. A lane that led northwestward from the bridge was the main path to Panorama Hall, but there was a smaller path that forked southward toward layers of artificial hills. These hills were laid out in twists and turns, like a swimming dragon, so it was called Dragon Range. At the end of the range, past the dragon's head with its Mid-sky Pavilion, was another approach to Panorama Hall.

Green Fragrance had taken this narrow path inadvertently. With its sheer cliffs and deep valleys, it felt more and more secluded as she

walked along. She was just about to turn back when she saw somebody ahead. He was dressed in brand-new silk clothes and squatting
in front of a very damp cave.

"Who is it?" she blurted out.

The person did not turn round. When she came closer, she saw it
was Modesty Zhu. He was doubled over and tiptoeing about, scraping off moss and digging into the mud with a bamboo stick.

"Have you lost something?" she asked.

Modesty held up a hand to silence her. Moving sideways with his
ears cocked, he edged toward the cave.

"Look, you're getting your clothes dirty," said Green Fragrance.

Only then did he say in a low voice, "Hush. If you want to see
something interesting, go over there."

Not knowing what there was to see, she ventured in the direction
he indicated and saw three shallow chambers of white stone halfway
up the hill. Twin Jade was sitting alone on the stone parapet holding
a large blue-and-white porcelain bowl in her hands. She was peeping into the covered bowl through the slightly raised lid.

"What is it? Let me have a look," Green Fragrance shouted before
she got near.

"It's nothing," Twin Jade smiled when she saw it was Green Fragrance. She passed her the bowl casually.

Green Fragrance took it, lifted the lid, and discovered to her
surprise that inside was a cricket waving its two feelers spiritedly.
Alarmed that it would escape, Twin Jade reached out to cover it
with her hands, but Green Fragrance, thinking she was snatching it
back, jerked away, and the cricket landed on her lapel. She tried to
catch it, but it hopped into the grass. Desperate, she shouted wildly,
dropped the bowl, and ran in pursuit, with Twin Jade behind her.
When the cricket leapt into a crevice in a rock, Green Fragrance
caught up with it and trapped it in her palm. She walked back, grinning, "Got it! That was close."

Twin Jade picked up the bowl from the grass. Green Fragrance put
the cricket in and replaced the lid. When Twin Jade peeped in again,
she could not help smiling. "It's no use anymore; we might as well
let it go," she said.

Green Fragrance stopped her in alarm, asking, "Why is it no
use?"

"Why, it's lost a leg!"

"Oh, that doesn't matter."

Twin Jade did not want to be pestered by her, so she just smiled.
A delighted-looking Modesty happened to come toward them just
then, one of his hands smeared with mud and the other closed tightly. "Did you catch one?" Twin Jade asked at once.

He nodded. "It's not bad. Come and take a look."

"Now I *have* to let it go to make room for this one," Twin Jade said to Green Fragrance.

But Green Fragrance pressed the lid down, refusing to let go, shouting, "No, I want it."

Twin Jade left her with the bowl and went into the stone chamber with Modesty, but Green Fragrance followed at their heels. The room was furnished with only a long slab of agate that made a natural table. A big heap of things was piled on it, and there were many porcelain bowls of assorted colors. Twin Jade picked an empty white Ding-ware bowl with a gold pattern and put Modesty's new cricket into it. She peeped into the bowl and saw that indeed it was a "metallic wings" with a handsome head. "Not bad," she said, impressed. "It's even better than the shell blue one."

Green Fragrance tugged at her sleeve, begging to have a look, so Twin Jade taught her how. She held the bowl as instructed, peeped in, saw nothing but a cricket, and lost interest.

When Twin Jade mentioned how the shell blue had broken a leg just now, Modesty also wanted to release it. But would Green Fragrance give it up? She clasped the bowl in her arms and kept saying, "I want it."

"What d'you want it for?" he asked, amused.

Stumped, she turned around and said to him, "Well, I don't know. You tell me." Modesty was so amused, he just grinned at Twin Jade.

Twin Jade said to her, "If you pipe down, we'll show you something interesting, OK?"

Green Fragrance readily agreed. They spread a scarlet tiger-striped blanket over the stone-paved floor in front of the table and placed at the center a carved ivory cage set with precious stones. Porcelain bowls of assorted colors were then placed in a row on the outer edge. Modesty and Twin Jade sat down cross-legged, facing each other, and told Green Fragrance to take the south-facing position. First, they put the new cricket—Metallic Wings—into the ivory cage, and then they took out various crickets from the bowls and put them in turn into the cage to fight the newcomer. At first, the new cricket just stayed still, holding its head high, but teased by a blade of grass, it went into an instant rage and charged headlong at its opponent. The two crickets became completely entangled. Green Fragrance was so delighted she slapped her thigh and laughed wildly as she peered down at the fight. Then a sharp shrill came from the cage and gave her a shock. It turned out that one of the crickets—a sandalwood lion— had been bitten to death by Metallic Wings. The victor reared up and shook its wings in triumph. It fought five or six battles and won every time. In the end, even the oily wrestler was on the run. Modesty Zhu cheered, "Now this is a real warrior."

Suddenly, they saw the maid Pearlie poke her head in. "So here you are, my little maestro. I searched all over the garden for you. You'd better be off."

Green Fragrance got angry. "Why did you search for me in the first place? Did you think I was going to run away?"

Pearlie was displeased. "It's Mr. Yin who's looking for you. I have no business with you, Little Maestro."

Even as she spoke, they heard Devotion Yin talking and laughing on his way there. Modesty immediately got to his feet to greet him. Devotion stopped at the door. When he saw Green Fragrance, he said, looking pleased, "I see you've found some playmates."

"D'you want to have a look? Come here," said Green Fragrance.

"It's been doing all the fighting today, so don't overstrain it. Let's wait till tomorrow," Twin Jade intervened.

When she heard this, Pearlie went up to clear away the utensils. Modesty picked up the ivory cage, put Metallic Wings into a bowl, and marked it solemnly. Green Fragrance and Twin Jade gave each other support and stood up together.

"You shouldn't be sitting on icy stone, should you?" Devotion said to Twin Jade. "It's all right in the case of Green Fragrance, but you should take care."

"Why so?" Modesty asked.

Twin Jade darted a sideways glance at Devotion. "Don't ask him. Does he ever say anything decent or proper?"[1]

Devotion chuckled. He asked Green Fragrance to go with him, but the girl still had her eye on the crippled cricket and was reluctant to leave. Twin Jade said to her, "It's yours." Green Fragrance took the bowl with delight.

"Everybody is in Panorama Hall. Are you coming?" Devotion asked Modesty. The latter nodded in assent.

"You'd better clean your hands." Devotion said and then walked off with Green Fragrance.

Almost done with the tidying-up, Pearlie grumbled to herself, "That one's got quite a temper for a child."

"Well, you did say the wrong thing. Call her 'maestro' if you will, but why 'little maestro'?" Twin Jade commented.

"And what's wrong with 'little maestro'?" Pearlie asked.

"There was nothing wrong with it before, but when there's a grown-up maestro around, it sounds different," said Twin Jade.

::

1. [A cold seat is supposedly harmful to pregnancy. Devotion Yin is teasing Twin Jade here. *E.H.*]

Modesty lent Twin Jade his support. "That's right. We'd better be careful, too."

"Who'd bother with that! Just don't pay her any attention," Pearlie said.

Modesty and Twin Jade, taking Pearlie with them, left the stone chambers. Instead of following Dragon Range to its peak, they turned west through the dragon's chin, which was a tunnel that led to the western side of Panorama Hall. It was a slightly longer route but far less strenuous. When they arrived, they saw that though the smoke of making tea had not yet dispersed, it was all quiet. They figured that the others were probably taking walks nearby, so they told Pearlie to fetch water for them to wash their hands as they waited. A while later, the menservants on duty came up to the hall to light the lamps. It was not until twilight closed in that the others came back, couple after couple.

Amid talk and laughter, the evening banquet was served. It so happened that nobody was in particularly high spirits, so they parted early. Modesty Zhu, who had been staying with Twin Jade in the lake house for recuperation, was to move once he got well, but Amity Zhu and White Fragrance came to the garden just then and decided to stay there because of its spacious rooms, so Modesty decided to stay put. Although their bedrooms were not connected, they were just divided by one vacant room in between that served as a sitting area. Green Fragrance had previously stayed in Panorama Hall, with an extra bed installed behind Devotion's room. Now that Flora Zhang was there, Green Fragrance felt it was not a convenient arrangement, so she also moved into the lake house. The rear half of the sitting area was turned into her bedroom, and she went in and out through her elder sister's room.

That night, the Zhu brothers and their girls came back together to the sitting area, where they parted company. In his room, Amity Zhu smoked opium and talked desultorily with White Fragrance. He mentioned the mourners' group the next day and said they had to go to bed early. Seeing that Green Fragrance was not there, White Fragrance thought she was at Devotion's, so she told her servant girl, "Take a lantern and go and look in on them. The gaslights will go out later; how is she to walk back by herself?"

"She's right here in the courtyard," the servant girl replied.

"Then tell her to come in! What's she doing in the courtyard?"

The servant girl went out but did not report back. After a while, White Fragrance called out loudly and heard a faint reply from outside, "Coming."

It took another long while, during which Amity smoked his fill and blew out the opium lamp, before Green Fragrance hurried in to greet her brother-in-law and elder sister briefly and then turned to go.

White Fragrance saw something hanging out of her sleeve pocket; it looked like an abacus. "What's that you're carrying?"

Smiling, Green Fragrance airily waved her arm, "It belongs to Fifth Young Master." So saying, she walked into her own room and closed the door.

Amity undressed and went to bed first. When White Fragrance got into bed, she again called out to Green Fragrance, "You should go to bed, too. We need to be up early tomorrow."

Green Fragrance grunted assent. After that, White Fragrance lay down and did not bother about her. As she was afraid of oversleeping and being laughed at, she had to take extra care.

She was in a deep slumber when Amity suddenly turned over. He continued to sleep, but she was wakened. She opened her eyes and wondered what time it was and then lifted the bed curtain and got up softly. She turned up the oil lamp to look at the clock on the table and found that it was only two o'clock. Just as she got ready to go back to sleep, she heard a squeaking noise in Green Fragrance's room. She listened closely and realized it was not mice. "Green Fragrance?" she called out tentatively.

"Are you calling me, Elder Sister?" Green Fragrance asked.

"Why aren't you sleeping?" White Fragrance said.

"I'm going to sleep now."

"It's two o'clock; what are you doing staying up?"

Green Fragrance did not answer. She hastily put things away and went to bed.

White Fragrance had difficulty going back to sleep. Frogs were croaking noisily, and in the distance cocks were crowing, dogs barking, children crying—noises that shouldn't have been in the garden and should have been inaudible if they were outside the garden. She couldn't figure it out. Then the night watchman came round, striking his bamboo clapper. She listened to the beat and soon entered the land of sweet dreams.

Luckily, the next day she did not get up too late. Just when she had finished her toilet, a manservant informed her through her maid that all the masters and maestros were to meet in Phoenix Pavilion for breakfast. Amity Zhu answered, "We'll be there right away."

Modesty Zhu in the next room also came over to ask: "Are you ready?"

"Yes, we are," White Fragrance replied.

"Then we'll finish dressing and go together," suggested Modesty.

"Good," White Fragrance said.

Green Fragrance in the inner room heard Modesty's voice and called out, "Fifth Young Master!"

Modesty went in and asked, "What is it?"

Green Fragrance took the cage and the porcelain bowl and handed them back to him. "Take these. I don't want them anymore."

Modesty saw that there were two crickets in the cage, one was the shell blue with a broken leg, the other was an oil gourd.

"Where did you get that one?" he smiled and asked.

Green Fragrance sighed. "I don't even want to talk about it. Last night, I went through a lot of trouble to catch another one so there could be a fight, but this accursed creature would only run away. I tried my damnedest to make it fight, and it tried its damnedest to run away. Now *that's* infuriating!"

"I told you it wasn't any use, but you wouldn't believe me. If you like, I'll give you a pair to take home and play with," he said pleasantly.

"Thank you, but I don't want them. The mere sight of them makes me angry."

He smiled and hurried back to his room with the cage and bowl to tell Twin Jade to get changed and go. The two parties came out to the sitting area simultaneously. With their maids and servant girls in tow, they walked out of the lake house together and made for Phoenix Pavilion, where all the others were waiting. Greetings were exchanged, and they sat down for breakfast.

After breakfast, the steward, Felicity Xia, hurried forth to report, "All the funeral gifts and other necessities were dispatched quite a while ago. As to personnel, we have sent two ushers. Would a master of ceremonies be needed?"

Harmony Qi replied after pondering for a while, "No, just send an announcer."

Steward Xia went out to dispatch the order. In a moment, the menservants who would accompany them on the visit, led by an announcer wearing a summer hat with a feathered crown, were clustered outside, waiting for them.

Harmony Qi looked around and asked, "Are the carriages ready?"

"Yes, sir," the menservants reported.

Harmony then said to the others, "Let's go."

Upon hearing this, everybody stood up with his girl. Seven guests and eight courtesans, together with their entourage of menservants and maids, came down the steps of Phoenix Pavilion and made for the stone arch. Beyond this arch a driveway led straight to the avenue outside the garden; more than a dozen carriages were waiting there. They boarded the carriages and drove out of the garden gate in a single file.

Soon they were on Fourth Avenue. Jade Tao saw the three golden words "East Prosperity Alley" on the archway of the alley. The shops on either side looked the same as before. A fortuneteller's stall at the mouth of the alley had a picture showing the significance of different facial features; it was something he used to see in his comings and goings. The sight was unbearable. His heart contracted, and he burst into tears. That made River Blossom cry, too. Luckily, all the carriages soon came to a stop. The ushers stood waiting outside the alley, and the group alighted and walked in. Afraid of being laughed at, Jade Tao walked behind Cloud Tao on his way in.

When they got to the Lis' door, Jade was startled to see that not only had Water Blossom's name been stripped off but even River Blossom's had disappeared. A notice written on yellow paper was posted on the white wall opposite, and eight monks were chanting the *Sutra of Great Compassion* in the parlor—a rite to console and guide the dead. Smoke from the incense they were burning filled the room. The ushers asked the group to sit in River Blossom's room for a while. It happened that Cloudlet Chen was there, and his presence surprised Harmony Qi. Cloud Tao walked up immediately and made the introduction, recounting how he had asked Cloudlet to help out. Only then did Harmony Qi greet Cloudlet with a salute, saying, "Pity we haven't met before."[2]

Everyone sat down wherever they pleased. Presently the ushers invited them to do their obeisances. Harmony Qi wanted to perform the rites himself, but Cloud Tao tried to dissuade him.

"Don't worry; I have my reasons. Anyway, why should you be so modest on the Lis' behalf?" said Harmony. So Cloud said no more.

Harmony looked around and found that only Jade Tao was missing. After looking everywhere for him in vain, Cloud Tao suspected he had gone to the rear part of the house. Sure enough, he was found in Fair Sister Li's room. Harmony saw that the red circles around Jade's eyes were tinted with purple and swollen to the size of lichees. River Blossom, who walked behind him, had a tear-stained face and tear marks on the white mourning blouse she had just changed into. Deeply moved, Harmony nodded and sighed but could not very well say anything. Together with the others, they went past the platform for Buddhist chanting and swarmed into Water Blossom's room.

This room now looked completely different. All the furniture had been cleared away. An off-white curtain completely covering the paneled doors at the back of the room served as a backdrop in front

::

2. [Qi and Chen belong to very different social circles. Under normal circumstances, Qi would have been far beyond Chen's reach. *E.H.*]

of which three square tables had been put together as an altar. On the altar was a three-foot multicolored paper structure housing the tablet for the spirit of the deceased. Offerings set out in dishes were piled high on the table; major items such as dragon incense, candles for the night watch, and a paper pavilion for rice were all there.

Now, behind the white cloth curtain, Fair Sister and the other relatives started wailing. Fair Sister's adopted son was too shy and timid to come out, so River Blossom was the only one to kneel beside the altar. The announcer, holding a tray with three silver cups in it, stood facing sideways, waiting for the chief mourner to step up.

CHAPTER 47 :: *Cloudlet Chen has the good fortune of meeting a bene-factor, and Snow Scent gets predictions for a male child*

Harmony Qi went up to the offering table in ordinary rather than mourning clothes and bowed respectfully. The announcer waited on him as he made his offerings of incense and wine, after which he bowed again, stepped back, and told Aroma Su to kowtow on his behalf, which she did four times. The others followed suit. Second Bai Gao was next, and Wenjun did the kowtow. After she had stood up, she knelt down and kowtowed again four more times. He whispered to ask why.

"The first time was for you. I myself should do obeisance to her, too," she replied.

He smiled.

Devotion Yin was going to have Green Fragrance kowtow for him, but she refused, making the excuse, "I can't go before Elder Sister."

"You're quite right, too," Devotion smiled and then told Flora Zhang to do it for him.

When White Fragrance had kowtowed on behalf of Amity Zhu, Green Fragrance joined her to pay her respects. After that, everybody had a tacit understanding: when Modesty Zhu had bowed, Twin Jade kowtowed; after Cloud Tao had bowed, Belle Tan kowtowed. Finally, it was Jade Tao's turn. As he bowed, Harmony Qi commented loudly, "River Blossom is a member of the bereaved family and can't take on two roles. Jade will have to kowtow himself."

This was exactly what Jade wanted. He kowtowed after bowing, praying to the departed as he did so. Nobody could make out what he said. After he had finished praying, he kowtowed again and then stood up with tears in his eyes. The announcer then took a scroll from the offering table and unrolled it with both hands. It was an elegy in rhyme written by Second Bai, giving a sentimental and sad account of Water Blossom's life. The announcer knelt by the table and recited it in a sonorous voice, after which Harmony Qi bowed again and burnt it as an offering.

The ceremony over, Jade Tao took advantage of the bustle to slip away, taking River Blossom with him. The party returned to River Blossom's room. Cloudlet Chen stood facing sideways to welcome them in, but the din of bells and drums outside made conversation impossible. Belle Tan and Flora Zhang said, "Now that it's over, please move on to our place."

"Very well," Harmony Qi said and invited Cloudlet Chen to join them. When Cloudlet mumbled that he did not deserve the honor, Harmony appealed to Cloud Tao to persuade him. Only then did Cloudlet agree to go along. As they were leaving, they found that Jade Tao had gone missing again, so Big Goldie was sent to look for him, but she did not report back.

Harmony frowned. "Well, I give up!"

"I'll go get him," Cloud Tao said at once. He rushed to Fair Sister Li's room and saw River Blossom leaning against the door while Fair Sister and Jade stood inside facing each other, weeping as they talked. Cloud stamped his feet in frustration. "We're leaving! All the others are waiting for you!"

Fair Sister also told him to hurry. "Please go now, Second Young Master. We'll talk about it later."

Jade had no choice but to follow Cloud. When everybody saw him, they all said, "Here he is! Here he is!"

"Are we all here now?" Harmony Qi asked.

"There's still River Blossom," said Aroma.

As she spoke, River Blossom came into the room supported by Beckon. The girl walked up to Harmony, knelt down, and kowtowed to him once. Astonished, he asked what it was for. Beckon answered, "Mother tells her to thank Your Excellency and the masters, maestros, and misses."

Harmony waved her away, saying, "Don't be ridiculous. Thanks are not allowed."

Aroma, who was standing beside him, pulled River Blossom to her, helped her take off the mourning clothes, and then handed them to Beckon to put away. Meanwhile, Harmony had stood up and asked Cloudlet to walk ahead of him. But Cloudlet dared not take precedence; he backed away with his arms pressed against his sides.

"There's no need for politeness. I'll lead the way," Devotion Yin said with a smile and strode out of the room. One by one, the others followed him out. At the mouth of East Prosperity Alley, he heard an usher call behind him, "Mr. Yin!" Overtaking him, the usher reported: "The carriages are at South Brocade Alley, I'll go get them."

"There's no need for carriages. Go ask His Excellency," Devotion said.

The usher turned around to ask for instructions. Harmony also said, "It's no distance at all; we'll walk." The usher answered "yes, sir." Harmony told him to tell all the attendants to withdraw, leaving just two menservants. The usher answered "yes, sir" again and stood to one side.

The party straggled along the street in twos and threes and soon found they had arrived at West Civic Peace Alley. Wenjun Yao, who was at the head of the group, rushed upstairs. Devotion Yin was the next to arrive. Instead of going in, he stood at the door to wait for the others. When Harmony Qi led them there, Devotion stretched out his hand to invite them in.

"So, you're one of the family?" Harmony teased him.

Devotion smiled without protesting and followed them into the parlor. A manservant came up and submitted an invitation to Cloud Tao, who glanced at it and stuffed it in his pocket. No one paid this any attention.

Belle Tan was waiting behind the door to help Harmony Qi up the stairs, but Harmony pretended to be angry with her. "D'you think I can't walk? I may be getting on, but I'm as good as any young man." So saying, he lifted the hem of his robe and walked nimbly up the stairs. The maid raised the bamboo curtain and invited him in.

He looked around Belle's room and spoke a few words of praise.

"It's not much good. Please take a seat, Your Excellency," Belle replied casually.

Harmony asked Cloudlet to take precedence, and it took some time for both of them to sit down. The rest of the group came in one after another and just sat around informally. They filled the room. Her face shining with perspiration, Wenjun Yao picked up a corner of her jacket to fan herself. Second Bai commented, "If you're bothered by the heat, why did you rush in like that just now?"

"I wasn't rushing. I was just afraid to be seen by Lai the Turtle's lackeys; that's why I dashed in."

Seeing it was hot in the crowded room, Harmony Qi said to the others, "We have yet to see Flora's room. Let's pay our visit."

Everyone said, "Good." Flora got up to wait respectfully for them, saying, "Would everybody please come this way?" Cloudlet Chen did not stand on ceremony this time. He walked a step ahead of Harmony Qi, and they went over to Flora's room. Some of the others accompanied them, while the rest just strayed off, leaving Amity Zhu to smoke his fill of opium. Thoroughly downcast, Jade Tao and River Blossom remained in Belle's room. Cloud Tao told the maid to give the order for the menservants to set up the dinner table and then went over to Flora's room to entertain the others for a while. He took the first opportunity to return to Belle's room and ask Jade, "What was Fair Sister Li talking to you about?"

"River Blossom," Jade replied.

"In that case, why were you crying?" Cloud asked.

Jade hung his head in silence.

Cloud calmly gave his brother this advice: "Don't be preoccupied with your own grief to the exclusion of everything else. Why d'you think so many people came here today? This mourning for Water Blossom is but an excuse; they came for your sake. They're afraid that, had you come alone, the thought of Water Blossom would trigger another outburst of tears. They hoped that their presence would be a diversion, that it'd help you forget a little. Now, even if you can't forget, you should at least try and put on a happy face and talk and laugh a little so they'll know you appreciate their kindness. Think about it; isn't what I said right?"

Jade remained silent. The maid came in just then to report, "The table is ready." Cloud was about to ask Harmony Qi whether hot towels should be served, but Amity Zhu said, "Why ask? Just tell them to go ahead." The maid made an affirmative noise. Cloud wrote out a call chit for Cloudlet Chen and handed it to the maid to take downstairs for dispatching.

By the time the menservants brought the hot towels, the patrons and courtesans had gathered in the center room, seated at two tables. By consensus, Harmony Qi took the seat of honor, Second Bai came next, and Cloudlet Chen was in third place. The others had already settled in their seats. Taking advantage of this rare opportunity, Cloudlet did his best to please and flatter Harmony Qi, and conversation flowed congenially. In response to his brother's instructions, Jade also tried to join in occasionally.

Presently, Clever Gem, Cloudlet's girl, arrived. Everyone told her to sit next to Cloudlet. Clever Gem, being an adaptable person and seeing that other girls around the table partook of food and wine at their ease, followed their example when she joined them. Harmony noted her adaptability and remarked on it with approval. This made her want to show off more than ever. She played the clown with great success, bringing merriment to the entire gathering. The party was not at all dull.

Harmony suddenly thought of something and asked Second Bai Gao, "The elegy you wrote mentions the origin of Water Blossom's illness and says that there are lots of twists to the story. What's that about?"

And so Second Bai explained in detail how Water Blossom, as a courtesan, could not be a wife and how her frustration and sorrow made her ill.

Harmony could not help sighing aloud. Then he said, "A pity! A great pity! If I had been consulted, I'd have come up with an idea." Second Bai asked what it was. "Easy," Harmony said. "I'd have adopted Water Blossom as my daughter. Who could object then?"

Everyone was silent when they heard this. Only Jade Tao thought it was a wonderful scheme. He thought that when Water Blossom first became ill, such a scheme might have saved her life. But now this was just empty talk, and it was too late for regrets. At this thought, he could not hold back a flood of tears, and he hurriedly slipped into Belle Tan's room.

Second Bai said, "It was my fault. I got carried away and forgot about Jade's feelings."

Wenjun Yao cut in, "Water Blossom was too nice about it. Why can't a courtesan be a wife? That was just nonsense circulated by busybodies. If I were her, I'd have given any gossiper a good slap in the face."

Her words generated much merriment, but Harmony Qi put a stop to it, saying, "Let's not dwell on this anymore. Talk about something else."

Second Bai said abruptly, "There's something interesting here; I'll show you." He left the table and went swiftly into Flora Zhang's room, took out a tattered volume of erotic paintings, and handed it to Harmony.

Harmony looked through it carefully. "It shows good skills with the brush. A pity it's incomplete," he said and passed it around.

"It looks like the work of the Jade Vase Hermit, but I can't find any proof," Second Bai said.

"Well, would a well-known painter sign such pictures or put his seal to them?" Harmony commented.

"Harmony collects such items. D'you want to start your own collection with this?" Devotion Yin said to Second Bai.

"You're the owner of this, are you? From the way you welcomed us in just now, it seems you own this house, too," Second Bai said teasingly.

Devotion ignored the general laughter. "Seriously, you can have it. Flora has given it to me."

Second Bai knew Devotion would make it up to her in some way. "All right, I'll stand you dinner for this."

"It'll have to be at the Old Banner though. Hire a function hall," Devotion said.

"A function hall it will be, then."

When the raised voices reached Jade Tao next door, he thought there was an argument, so he quietly wiped away his tears and returned to the table.

"I suppose we're all invited, right?" Harmony said.

"Yes, we'll meet after the festival, on the eighteenth. That's settled. The seven of you here at the table will excuse me for not sending you written invitations," Second Bai said.

"We'll be there" was the unanimous reply.

Jade asked Cloudlet Chen in a low voice what it was all about. Cloudlet took the volume of erotic paintings and explained to him, but Jade was in no mood for something like that. He just leafed through it and pushed it aside. Harmony Qi saw that Jade was only trying to put up a cheerful front and that the darkening sky was threatening rain, so he suggested that the banquet end early. Everyone obeyed him. Seeing that the other girls did not disperse, Clever Gem hesitated about leaving. Cloudlet Chen told her surreptitiously, "Go." Only then did she leave.

After the party was over, Cloud Tao wanted to go home and see to his affairs. With Whistler Tang out of town, Amity Zhu had no helper and was busier than ever at such festival times. The two of them excused themselves to Harmony Qi. Harmony was going to invite Cloudlet Chen to the garden, but the latter also excused himself, pleading he was too busy.

"Then you must come at the Midautumn Festival," Harmony said.

Before Cloudlet could reply, Cloud Tao promised on his behalf.

"Are you coming back?" Harmony turned to Devotion.

"You go on ahead. I'll be back shortly."

So Harmony, Second Bai, Modesty Zhu, and Jade Tao, each taking his girl, saluted the others in farewell and returned to the garden in their carriages. Belle Tan and Flora Zhang saw them out all the way to the front door. After that, Amity Zhu got up to leave, and Green Fragrance went with her sister, White Fragrance, in their sedan chairs. Only then did Cloudlet Chen try to find out from Cloud Tao what the midautumn function in Conical Hat Garden would be like.

"It's not really a function," said Cloud. "We're supposed to be viewing cassia blossoms in the daytime and the moon at night, but seriously the fun is still the girls and the wine."

"I heard that after drinking one has to compose a poem, is that true?" Cloudlet asked.

Cloud gestured with his hand to indicate that was not true. "There's no such thing. No one would want to do it! If you feel like it, you're of course welcome to write a poem, but you'd never do it as well as their own people, so why parade your weakness?"

"Since it's my first visit, do I have to send in a formal visiting card?"

Cloud waved the idea off. "Once he's invited you, he'll leave word with the gatekeepers, and your name will be entered into their books. Just turn up at the garden gate in everyday wear and tell them who you are, and a manservant will show you in. When you see Harmony, salute him casually and don't ever put on airs. As you're in business, just act like a businessman."

Cloudlet had some more questions, but Devotion Yin came in just then from Flora Zhang's room to say that he was returning to the garden. After that, Cloudlet also rose to say he was going to East Co-prosperity Alley.

"It's Elan Ge's party, isn't it? I'll go with you and mingle for a while before returning to the Old City," Cloud said.

Cloudlet agreed to wait for him, so Cloud hastily put on a summer silk robe and a lined gauze jacket. Instead of seeing them out, Belle just said, "Send for me right away."

Cloud followed Cloudlet downstairs, and then each told his ricksha or sedan chair to go and wait at East Co-prosperity Alley. They crossed the street side by side, heading for Snow Scent's house. On entering her room, they saw a pair of tall red candles burning brightly on the dressing table. They asked in surprise what the occasion was. Elan Ge just smiled. Snow Scent replied as she offered them watermelon seeds, "It's nothing."

A moment later, three of their old friends, Prosperity Luo, Lotuson Wang, and Benevolence Hong arrived one after another.

"Neither Amity nor Whistler will be coming. It'll just be the six of us. Let's all sit down," Elan Ge said.

After checking the call chits, Little Sister said, "Mr. Wang's is missing." Elan asked Lotuson Wang whom he would call, and Lotuson went and wrote down the name "Gold Phoenix" himself. Then, giving precedence to one another, they sat down.

When Little Sister was filling the water pipe for him, Benevolence Hong took the opportunity to ask her softly, "Why the tall red candles?"

Little Sister told him in a low voice, "Our maestro is due for a happy event. We'll be calling in a midwife."

Benevolence immediately offered his congratulations to Elan Ge and Snow Scent. Upon hearing the news, the others all called out, "Congratulations! Congratulations! We'll borrow your wine to drink to you. Three cups, everybody!"

Elan just laughed, but Snow Scent pretended to be displeased. "There's no reason to congratulate me. Little Sister is talking nonsense."

This was taken in the wrong way, and they said to her in all seriousness, "It's a proper and happy event. There's nothing embarrassing about it."

Snow Scent heaved a sigh. "I'm not embarrassed. Lots of people lose their sons when they're all grown up; now in my case it's just been two months. How do we know whether he'll make it or not? It's too early for congratulations."

Hearing the way she put it, the dinner guests couldn't go on teasing her. Then she sighed again and said, "It's not just difficult to bring them up, some people have sons who turn out to be no good. No matter how happy they make you when they're born, they're exasperating when they grow up."

Before she had finished speaking, Elan shouted at her laughingly, "Oh, shut up! Don't you think it's also exasperating for them to listen to you go on and on?"

She reached out a hand to pinch his arm. "You're the one who's exasperating!"

He cried out, "Aiyo! Ouch!" This made everyone laugh uproariously. Even Little Sister and the girls who had been called to the party could not suppress their mirth.

Seeing that Green Phoenix and Gold Phoenix had come early, Prosperity Luo wanted to start the finger game right away. Just then, Belle arrived. She said to Cloud Tao, "It's raining. Do you *have* to go to the Old City?"

Cloud insisted on going because he had some important documents to see to. He turned to ask Prosperity to let him be banker first, to which Prosperity agreed. The other guests stretched out their hands to attack Cloud Tao's bank.

In her corner, Green Phoenix took the opportunity to ask Prosperity Luo, "Why didn't you come today?"

"I was afraid your mother would start nagging again."

"Oh, she's all right, and the ransom is settled. The price is still a thousand," Green Phoenix said.

Greatly surprised, Prosperity asked, "If it's still a thousand, why didn't she agree to it before? And why does she agree now?"

Smiling sarcastically, Green Phoenix replied after a long pause, "I'll tell you later."

His heart was pounding wildly, but he dared not press her.

As soon as Cloud Tao had served his term as banker, he was in a hurry to go home and took his leave together with Belle. Prosperity's mind was not on the wine. Although he took over as banker, it was just to keep his end up. He was waiting for all the called girls to leave so he could arrange with Lotuson Wang to go for a tea party. Cloudlet Chen and Benevolence Hong were quick to sense this, so they turned the wine cups upside down and asked for rice to be served. The host, Elan Ge, did not press them to drink either, and the banquet was hastily wound up.

Prosperity Luo ordered his sedan-chair bearers to light the lanterns. He got into his chair in the parlor, as did Lotuson Wang. When they left East Co-prosperity Alley, strong wind and pelting rain lashed into the sedan chairs. Promotion and Talisman, who were walking alongside them, lowered the blinds and helped to steady the chairs by lending a hand at the poles. When they arrived at Green Phoenix's in Generosity Alley, they alighted in the parlor, and Prosperity urged Lotuson to go ahead of him.

Green Phoenix welcomed them into her room. She invited Lotuson to sit on the divan and told Mama Zhao to light the opium lamp before she made tea. Gold Phoenix, who was in the room opposite, hurried over to greet "Brother-in-law" and then said, "Mr. Wang, do come and smoke in my room."

"It's just the same here," Lotuson replied.

"I've made lots of toasted pellets," Gold Phoenix said.

"Well, just go and fetch them," said Green Phoenix.

Gold Phoenix hadn't thought of that, so she rushed back to her room and brought over seven or eight opium picks, each with a pellet at its tip. Lotuson, who had been originally taken with her girlish charm and intelligence, was now touched by her eagerness to please him and felt that she was better than a mature courtesan. He accepted the pellets gladly, saying, "Thank you for all the trouble," and then pulled her down to sit beside him. She half sat and half reclined on the divan to watch him smoke.

Wriggling awkwardly and self-consciously, Pearl Phoenix filled the water pipe for Prosperity Luo, but Prosperity pushed it aside and asked eagerly about the matter of the ransom. Green Phoenix laughed and sighed over it as she recounted what happened.

CHAPTER 48 :: *Mistake after mistake bars the gates of the mansion, and swindle after swindle exemplifies the ways of the marketplace*

Green Phoenix told Prosperity Luo what happened right in front of Lotuson Wang. "My mother is a nice person, after all. If you listen to her talk, you may think she's got the gift of the gab, but in fact she's not particularly clever. Well, she was so angry with me, she couldn't eat for three days! Yesterday, after you had gone, she threw a tantrum in her own room. This morning when Mama Zhao went downstairs, Mother told her I was no good. She said, 'I bought clothes and jewelry for her worth ten thousand dollars. Originally, I thought I'd give her quite a lot of it when she ransomed herself, but now I won't give her any at all.' Now, I was upstairs and happened to hear that, and I was angered as well as amused, so I went to make myself clear to Mother. I said, 'The clothes and jewelry were bought with money I earned. When I'm here, those things are mine, and no one else should touch them. But when I buy back my freedom, I have no right to take them with me. I need to make this clear to you, Mother, even if you want to give them to me, I'll just say, "No, thank you." Let alone clothes and jewelry, I won't even take a hair yarn or a shoestring. I'll take off everything I wear and give it back to you, Mother, before I walk out of this house. You can put your mind at rest, Mother, for I don't want any of it.' Well, it turned out that she really meant to give me some of it, and when I made it clear I didn't want any, she was delighted. So she agreed to my ransom price of a thousand and picked an auspicious day for the event. The agreement will be signed on the sixteenth, and I'll move out on the seventeenth. It's all been finalized. Now isn't that quick? Even I didn't expect it to be so easy."

Prosperity was very happy for Green Phoenix, while Lotuson was full of admiration for her independent spirit. "There's this saying, 'A worthy son does not live on his share of the inheritance, and a worthy daughter does not wear the clothes in her trousseau.' It fits you to perfection!"

Green Phoenix replied, "As a courtesan, one has to work things out for oneself if one wants to do well. Now if I ransom myself and incur a debt of five or six thousand, then whether I do good business would be beside the point; I wouldn't count as someone who's done well. This time, I'm acting with a blueprint in hand. Several of my patrons are not in Shanghai, so they don't count; I only have two patrons who are here. If both of them look after me a bit, I'll do all right. Though I can cope with a debt of five or six thousand, I don't see any sense in taking clothes and jewelry from her. You've put it so well, Mr. Wang. 'Clothes in the trousseau' are gifts from one's own parents, but even then a worthy daughter wouldn't want to wear them, so why would I want anything from the madam? Even if I took them, they'd only be worth a thousand dollars or so. Would that be worth all the trouble?"

Lotuson was still full of praise for her. Prosperity, though aware that there would be extra expenses after her ransom and prepared to be especially considerate, had not expected the expenses to come to so much. He asked thoughtfully, "How come you'll be in debt for five or six thousand?"

"Well, work it out yourself: the ransom is a thousand; however hard I skimp, clothes and jewelry will be at least three thousand. Then there are three rooms to furnish, won't that take another thousand? And on top of this, there're some odds and ends, so all together won't it be five or six thousand? I've told Mama Zhao and a downstairs manservant whom I'm taking with me to go and borrow three thousand dollars. When the ransom is paid up, I'll just buy a few essentials and make the move. The rest can wait."

Prosperity fell silent. Lotuson, after smoking four or five opium pellets, sat up cross-legged. Gold Phoenix immediately went to fetch the water pipe for him, which he took from her and filled for himself.

There was a long pause, after which Prosperity asked about the move. Green Phoenix told him briefly that she had chosen three upstairs rooms in Prosperity Alley and would be renting jointly with Jade Wenjun downstairs. Aside from the maid and the manservant who'd come with her, she'd hire four others: a bookkeeper, a cook, a servant girl, and another manservant. The rosewood furniture would be rented for the time being, and if she found it suitable, she would discuss the purchase price.

"On the sixteenth, they'll draw up the papers while I'll get things ready to account for them to Mother, so we'll be busy. Why don't you give a dinner party on the fifteenth and get it over with?" she said.

Prosperity immediately invited Lotuson to the party. He also wrote out invitations to Ge, Hong, and Chen and told Promotion to deliver them at once.

Promotion rushed to Snow Scent's in East Co-prosperity Alley. Sure enough, Benevolence Hong and Cloudlet Chen were still there, held up by the rain. Upon seeing the invitation Elan Ge said, "I'm sorry, I can't make it. I have an appointment at Conical Hat Garden for that day."

Cloudlet also declined, citing the same appointment. Benevolence was the only one to say he'd definitely attend and wrote a return slip for Promotion to report back. Then he noticed the sound of rain was gradually lessening and the bamboo awning had stopped dripping, so he took the opportunity to slip away and left on foot.

"When a courtesan is called to Conical Hat Garden for a stay of several days, how many party calls does it count as?" Cloudlet asked Elan in a leisurely manner.

"It all depends. There're often three or four courtesans in the garden, and everybody pays in his own fashion. Then there's the courtesan who's her own mistress and who likes to have fun, so she makes an arrangement with the patron to spend the whole summer in the garden and takes that as a vacation. In that case, she'd of course be less exacting," said Elan.

"Will you be taking Snow Scent with you?" asked Cloudlet.

"Yes, if she's free. Otherwise, I'll just send her a call chit from the garden."

Cloudlet did some reckoning of his own and did not ask any other questions. He took his leave from Elan and returned to the Auspicious Luzon Lottery Store in South Brocade Alley.

The next day, Cloudlet Chen went to a ready-to-wear store he knew well in Bowling Alley and selected a new suit consisting of a light-colored jacket and a robe of stylish print.[1] Then he went to Clever Gem's in Co-security Alley to give her a message. When she saw him, she asked, "When did you get to know His Excellency Qi?"

"Just yesterday," Cloudlet replied.

"Now that you're friends with him, I want to see his garden," Clever Gem said.

"How would you like it if I took you there tomorrow?"

"But you're still so careful and polite around him, it's not a good time for me to go, is it?" she said.

"Tomorrow is the big midautumn do in Conical Hat Garden. It'll be a merry crowd. Now I'm going to the drinking party, so if you want to sightsee, get ready early and come as soon as you get the call chit."

She was naturally overjoyed. That night, Cloudlet and Clever Gem had a most satisfying time together.

The next day was the fifteenth of the eighth month, the Midautumn Festival. Cloudlet Chen got up extremely early and dressed and groomed himself to perfection. The clock had just struck eight when he woke Clever Gem to remind her of the arrangements, after which he rushed back to his shop, got into his private ricksha, and headed for Rustic Retreat.

When he reached the front gate of the Qi residence, his ricksha stopped beside the screen wall opposite the entrance. As he alighted, he saw that beyond the gate all the doors leading to the main parlor were open. The buildings were high, the distance long, and the way barred by fences and railings. Unable to enter, he withdrew and looked around him, but all was quiet. Then Constant Blessing pointed to the left, which seemed to be a small entrance for conducting daily business. Cloudlet found that it was still of fairly impressive proportions, so he went in. There in the gatehouse he saw

::

1. The best Chinese clothes were all tailor-made. The ready-to-wear stores apparently dealt in secondhand clothes as well as new ones.

a few handsomely attired porters sitting with their feet up, chatting. Cloudlet stood at the door ready to give his name, but one of the porters held up a hand to stop him, saying, "Whatever your business, go to the bookkeeping office."

Cloudlet politely acknowledged this instruction and went through an inner gate. On one side were three interconnected rooms with the signboard "Bookkeeping Office" over the lintel. He walked in and saw that, of the several desks set out in a row, only the desk marked "No. 1" was occupied. There, a bookkeeper sat, talking to a man seated beside him.

Cloudlet saw that the man was none other than Lichee Zhuang, so he had to go up and greet him. The bookkeeper took him for Zhuang's associate and just gave him a slight nod. Lichee asked Cloudlet to take the seat of honor. Cloudlet looked surreptitiously into the rooms on both sides and saw bookkeepers hard at work at the desks. None of them paid him any attention. Cloudlet felt there had to be some mistake, so he walked up to "No. 1," saluted, and smiled ingratiatingly at the bookkeeper, to whom he related the purpose of his visit. Upon hearing what he said, the bookkeeper responded immediately, "Pardon my rudeness. Please sit and wait for a moment." He called a handyman over and told him to notify the chief receptionist.

Reassured, Cloudlet sat and waited, but after a long time there was still no news. He saw there was a real bustle at the inner gate, with menservants going in and out on errands, but there was no sign of guests coming to the banquet. He suspected he had come too early and deeply regretted it.

Suddenly, he heard the sound of yelling approaching from the distance. Lichee Zhuang immediately rushed out. After that, some twenty or thirty coolies came in, carrying four huge packing cases. Lichee ran back and forth to make sure they did not bump into anything. The cases were brought to the passageway outside the bookkeeping office and set down lightly, whereupon Lichee opened one of them and asked the bookkeeper to inspect the contents.

Cloudlet took a brief look through the window and saw that the cases contained a total of sixteen panels of a cedar-and-poplar screen about half a man's height, on which were carved all the characters of *The Romance of the Western Chamber*.[2] The buildings, scholars and ladies, and flora and fauna were all set with coral, green jade, pearls, and other colorful precious stones.

He had only seen two or three of the panels when the handyman

::

2. [Originally a story about the romantic dalliance of a young scholar with a beautiful girl, this then became the basis for popular opera in many regions of China. *E.H.*]

came running back with the chief receptionist to ask the bookkeeper where the guest was. When told that he was in the office, the receptionist straightened his tasseled hat and walked in sideways. As he did not recognize Cloudlet, he stood respectfully and inquired the visitor's name. After Cloudlet told him, he asked, "Where is your honored residence?" Cloudlet told him that, too.

The chief receptionist thought for a moment and then asked with a smiling face, "Do you remember on which day the invitation was delivered, Mr. Chen?"

Cloudlet replied that it was an appointment made face-to-face at dinner at Belle Tan's the day before yesterday.

The chief receptionist again thought for a moment. "On that day, it was the announcer who went out with His Excellency," he said.

"That's right," Cloudlet said.

The chief receptionist turned around and told the handyman to summon the announcer at once. To make conversation, he asked, "Who will you call to the party, Mr. Chen? I'll get the call chit ready so it'll be sent out early."

Before Cloudlet could tell him, the announcer had come in, panting. He greeted Cloudlet and then handed a red piece of paper to the chief receptionist.

"You sure made a mess of things!" scolded the chief receptionist. "I didn't have any information, and Mr. Chen was made to wait all this time. I'm going to report this to His Excellency."

The announcer said, "I left word at the garden gate though I didn't send in the slip. That was because His Excellency said there was no need for a written invitation. I thought I could send you the slip later, but I had no idea Mr. Chen would use this door."

"Don't make excuses! Why didn't you send the slip over yesterday?" the chief receptionist retorted.

The announcer had no answer to that, so he stood in attendance slightly behind the receptionist, who, when he found out that Cloudlet had come by ricksha, ordered the announcer to take care of the ricksha puller. He himself then took Cloudlet through the house to the garden.

By then, the bookkeeper had finished inspecting the screen and was talking to Lichee Zhuang. Cloudlet Chen took his leave from both of them. Lichee Zhuang was full of envy when he saw the chief receptionist respectfully leading the way to show Cloudlet Chen to the banquet.

After Lichee and he had spoken, the bookkeeper went to the office to fetch a money order drawn on the Great Virtue Money Shop. Lichee pocketed it and took his leave right away. When he left the Qi residence, he walked a short stretch before calling a ricksha and heading to Avenue Road to cash in the money order for eight hundred taels of silver. He took out half in cash and half in another money order and then went alone to Fourth Avenue for a foreign meal at the Western restaurant Sky in a Wine Pot. After that, he went to the Hall of Beauties on West Chessboard Street.

When Woodsy saw the joyful look on his face, she asked, "Have you struck it rich?"

"Things are really unpredictable in business," Lichee replied. "Last time, I made two hundred out of a deal of eight thousand and had to work flat out for it. This time, I had no trouble at all, and out of a deal of eight hundred I got a profit of four hundred."

"Your lucky turn has come. This year, brokers aren't doing very well, but you're doing all right with a bit of business farmed out to you," she said.

"Speaking of luck, Cloudlet Chen is the one who's in luck." He related in detail how Cloudlet had gone to Qi's banquet.

"I don't see what's so great about it. With drinking parties, you need to call a girl, so you're spending money up front, and if nothing comes of it, that's too bad. *Your* business is more reliable," Woodsy commented.

Lichee said nothing. After smoking a couple of opium pellets, he settled on a plan and told Mama Yeung to fetch the inkstone and writing brush. He wrote an invitation for immediate delivery to Mr. Bao at Longevity Bookstore in Bowling Alley, requesting him to come over right away. Mama Yeung relayed the message instantly. Then Lichee wrote out invitations to Fortune Shi, Benevolence Hong, Rustic Zhang, and Pine Wu. He thought perhaps Cloudlet Chen would return to his shop that night, so he wrote an invitation to him, too. He handed the lot to Mama Yeung, who gave them to different menservants for delivery. The order for dinner was also placed.

When he had finished his brief instructions, he heard clear female voices laughing and clamoring, "This way, old bawd![3] Come on, old bawd!" They came all the way to the upstairs parlor. Lichee figured that Old Bao of Longevity Bookstore had arrived and hurried out to welcome him. To his surprise, Old Bao was besieged by courtesans and servant girls who were relentlessly pulling and tugging at him. Lichee beckoned and called out, "Old Bao!" whereupon the man pretended to be furious with those around him and wrenched himself free. Nonetheless, some of the sillier virgin courtesans followed him into the room and continued to give him a pinch or a pat. One said, "What about a carriage ride today, Old Bao?" Another

::

3. [A pun on Old Bao's name. *E.H.*]

said, "Old Bao, where's my handkerchief? You promised to give me one!" Outnumbered and overwhelmed, Bao kept muttering excuses to all around him.

Lichee pretended to be annoyed with Bao and told him off. "I asked you here on account of important business. Stop playing the fool!"

Old Bao rose abruptly to his feet, chastened. "Sorry. What's the business?" He put on a serious face to await orders from Lichee Zhuang. Seeing this, the courtesans finally scattered and left.

Lichee began: "The sixteen-paneled screen has been sold to Harmony Qi. I got the price up to a full eight hundred dollars. They've only paid six hundred now, in case they find some flaw, and will pay the rest in a fortnight. I like to keep things simple and straightforward when I do business. Why count the pennies when it's not a big deal anyway? I'll pay you the full amount up front, and in a fortnight I'll go and collect the rest so you won't have to be bothered about it. What'd you think?"

Old Bao kept saying, "Wonderful!"

Lichee fished out a money order for six hundred dollars from his pocket and gave it to Old Bao and then handed over one hundred and twenty in cash and explained, "That's less the forty dollars for me. I'll give you your forty dollars later. The net price should be seven hundred twenty. Now go and settle with the seller, then come right back."

Old Bao assented, wrapped everything up in a handkerchief, and took his leave.

"Where should we send you your invitation slip?" Woodsy asked.

"I'll come right back. There's no need for an invitation." So saying, Old Bao peeped around the edge of the curtain. The coast was clear, so he hared off through the parlor. Just then, Mama Yeung came in from the opposite direction, and they bumped into each other.

"Old Bao! You're not leaving, are you?" Mama Yeung shouted.

This brought the courtesans and servant girls swarming out from all directions. Working together, they tried to capture him, clamoring, "Old Bao, don't go!" Without even replying, he made his escape down the stairs and out the door. The women, knowing they could not catch up with him, muttered a few curses, but Old Bao just pretended not to hear. He walked out of West Chessboard Street and headed for the Complete Imported and Cantonese Goods Store in Bowling Alley, whose owner, Third Shu, was the seller of the screen.

Third Shu lived on the top floor of a three-story Western-style house. Lying on the opium divan, he was wearing nothing but a tight underblouse and slippers, the bottom of his pants untied. On the honored side of the divan, a boy servant called Extravagance was preparing the pipe for him. When he saw Old Bao, Third Shu simply said, "Please sit down." There was no attempt at the usual etiquette.

Knowing his ways, Old Bao just untied his handkerchief, put the money order and the cash on the table, and asked Third Shu to check them. Then he said, "Lichee Zhuang said he spent a lot of effort on this small deal. He had to talk to them for several days and go there several times. What was more he had to sweeten their bookkeepers and porters, so Zhuang says he'll keep all of the eighty dollars. I told him, 'Just as you like.' It's not much anyway, so I don't mind."

"But it's not right if you get nothing out of it," Third Shu said and gave him twenty dollars.

Old Bao refused to accept it. "There's no need for that. If you want to do me a favor, just give me some business."

Third Shu did not press him, so Old Bao said, "I'm going." Third Shu did not see him out.

Old Bao returned directly to Woodsy's room in the Hall of Beauties. Fortunately, the courtesans and servant girls were all engaged in tea parties and did not bother him. Lichee Zhuang had four ten-dollar banknotes ready for him and paid him right away. Then a number of virgin courtesans heard that there was a dinner party at Woodsy's and came over to surround Old Bao, clamoring, "Call me, Old Bao! Call me, Old Bao!" Seeing that he just grinned and ignored them, they became even more pressing. One of them pulled at his ear and shouted, "Old Bao, d'you hear me?" Another pinched and shook him with all her strength, saying, "Say something, Old Bao!" The older girls did not handle him physically, but they all joined in the persuasion. "Naturally, you'll have to call one of us. How can you not do that when you're at a party here?"

"Who says there's a party?" Old Bao said.

"Isn't Young Mr. Zhuang inviting you to a party?"

"Take a look at Young Mr. Zhuang. Is he having a party?" Old Bao countered.

One of the girls did not get it and turned to ask Woodsy, "Is Young Mr. Zhuang giving a party?"

"Who knows?" Woodsy answered offhandedly.

Upon hearing this, the girls looked at one another in bewilderment. Just then, a manservant came in to report to Lichee, "We looked in at all the smoking dens and teahouses on Fourth Avenue, but we couldn't find any of the invited guests. We don't know where else to look for them."

Before Lichee had time to respond, the courtesans had started shouting in a chorus against Old Bao, "How dare you play tricks on us! Now you must call one of us." They pushed forward to grind the inkstone, wet the writing brush, and look for the call chits to force Old Bao to call them. Old Bao was at a loss what to do.

At the end of his patience, Lichee shouted at them angrily, "Where did this lot of urchins come from to offend my friend? Get me the owner of the house so I can ask him if he knows the rules of a brothel or not?"

Sensing trouble, the manservant vaguely acknowledged Zhuang's demand as he signaled with his mouth for all the virgin courtesans to make themselves scarce.

Woodsy tried to make peace and said with a smile, "Be off with you and stop pestering them. Our guests for the party haven't even arrived yet, so how can we call the girls in advance?"

It was pretty mortifying for the virgin courtesans, who walked off in embarrassment.

Lichee said to Old Bao, "I know what. Call a girl of the house, but definitely not anyone you've called before."

"Then there's just Woodsy; there's no one else."

"There's Jewel, too," Woodsy suggested.

Brooking no protests, Lichee wrote a ticket for Old Bao calling Jewel Lu. He wrote out three other invitations, two for people in the same trade who were sure to come and one for Bamboo Hu. The manservant took them and had them delivered right away.

CHAPTER 49 :: *What's returned to the owner becomes a target for theft, and a member of the family is marked for extortion*

When the manservant from the Hall of Beauties took the invitation to South Brocade Alley, he saw only a young shop assistant behind the counter of the Auspicious Luzon Lottery Store. When he asked for Bamboo Hu, the shop assistant said, "He's not in. He's at a party in Generosity Alley."

"It's so difficult to get hold of guests today! No one's in," the manservant said with a smile.

The shop assistant looked at the invitation. It suddenly occurred to him to earn a tip behind Constant Blessing's back, so he said, "Leave the invitation here. I'll deliver it for you; how about that?"

The manservant gladly entrusted him with the task, thanked him, and left. After that, the shop assistant told the cook to keep an eye on the store while he went to Green Phoenix's in Generosity Alley. He headed straight upstairs, peeped in, and saw there was considerable confusion as everybody was about to sit down at the table. Overcome by shyness, the shop assistant did not go in. Instead, he handed the invitation to the servant girl, Little Treasure, who submitted it to Prosperity Luo. Prosperity passed it to Bamboo Hu, who, upon reading it, replied, "No, thanks." The shop assistant returned to the store, his hopes dashed.

Soon the girls called to the party turned up one after another. Twin Pearl brought along an invitation for Benevolence Hong that was also from Lichee Zhuang, so Benevolence suggested that he should start the finger game. He took his leave when the others had broken his bank of ten cups. Prosperity Luo figured that Green Phoenix would have many things to attend to, so he thought it best if the party ended early. Those at the table did not have any great capacity for wine; they were just ordinary drinkers such as Bamboo Hu. Among them, only Mallow Yao was a rowdy drinker, and he happened to have received repeated reminders to go to another party and had to leave early. So unfortunately this splendid feast on a principal festival did not last all night, and neither was it enjoyed to the full. There was nothing to tell, no conservation to relate.

When the guests had gone, Prosperity Luo prepared to return to his residence.

"What other business do you have?" Green Phoenix asked.

"Nothing. But don't you have to pack? You'll be too busy if you leave everything till tomorrow," Prosperity said.

Green Phoenix looked away and smiled. "Goodness! I finished packing ages ago. Would I have waited until now?"

Prosperity sat down again.

"Tomorrow won't be a busy day, but you'll be needed here. Don't go," she said.

Prosperity consented and told Promotion to go home with the sedan-chair bearers. But he was disturbed and annoyed by the raucousness of the finger game and the singing in Gold Phoenix's room. By the time Gold Phoenix's party was over, Green Phoenix was called to a party. He could not help feeling a little lonely. To buck himself up, he smoked three of the opium pellets Gold Phoenix had toasted.

Green Phoenix returned around midnight and bade the menservants to keep an eye on the incense and the pillar-sized candles.[1]

::

1. [This is part of the ritual for seeking blessings from the deities when a courtesan moves to another house. *E.H.*]

The menservants had asked Mama Zhao and Little Treasure to a card game to help them pass the night. There was continuous noise downstairs, and before Prosperity knew it, he had been talking to Green Phoenix until dawn. He quickly undressed, went to bed, and fell soundly asleep. As there was something on his mind, he did not oversleep. They got up together near noon and had lunch.

Early that morning, somebody had delivered a package to the room. Green Phoenix told Mama Zhao to give it to Second Sister for safekeeping, saying she would need it the next day. She also asked Second Sister to come upstairs. Green Phoenix fetched the document box Prosperity had left with her, asked him for the key, and opened it in front of both of them. The box contained nothing but an assortment of official and personal papers. When Green Phoenix told Prosperity to show Second Sister the documents, Second Sister declined with a smile. "That's all right. Someone like you would never slip up. I don't need to look."

"But you do, Mother. These are his things, and I'm taking them with me, so when you have checked them, I'll ask him to take a look as well. That way, if anything goes missing later on, it won't concern you, Mother, right?"

Second Sister had to watch as Prosperity checked the contents of the box and locked it up again. Green Phoenix then told Mama Zhao to put it together with the package they had received earlier and to ask the bookkeeper to come up with the account book of clothes and jewelry.

This was a novel term to Prosperity, so he looked on with interest. It turned out that the first half of the account book listed items of jewelry while the second half listed items of clothing with annotations about the state of their repairs and alterations written in clear, small characters. He was much impressed by such thoroughness.

With Little Treasure's help, Mama Zhao took three cases of jewelry out of the wardrobe. Green Phoenix opened one of them and put all the items on the table. She asked the bookkeeper to read out the list from the top. As each item came up, Green Phoenix handed Second Sister a piece of jewelry to check. Second Sister then handed it to Mama Zhao, who put it back in the case. When it was all done, Second Sister was asked to lock the cases. Altogether, there was one case of gold, one of pearls, and one of green and white jade. Every item in the three cases was intact, and nothing was missing.

Mama Zhao called two menservants upstairs to take out ten red lacquered trunks from behind the bed and the mezzanine room. Green Phoenix opened one of them, took out all the clothes, and put them on the divan. She then asked the bookkeeper to read out the list of clothes from the top. As each item came up, Green Phoenix took a garment and handed it to Second Sister to check, who then passed it to Mama Zhao to put back into the trunk. When it was all done, Second Sister was asked to lock the trunk. Altogether, there were two trunks of heavy furs, two of medium furs, two of light furs, two of padded garments, one of lined garments, and one of unlined or silk garments. Every item in the ten trunks was intact, and nothing was missing.

Green Phoenix then asked the bookkeeper to turn to the last two pages of the account book and read out all the subsidiary items. These were the *huali* and purple cedar furniture, clocks and silver water pipes, and so on. Item by item, Green Phoenix pointed them out in the room. Second Sister just grinned and nodded, not really paying attention.

Green Phoenix went on to say, "Then there're the clothes I wear at home and all sorts of playthings that are not listed; they're in the communal trunk. Please check them when you have time, Mother."

Second Sister smiled and said satirically, "You must be tired! Have a smoke from the water pipe and sit down for a while."

Green Phoenix did feel tired out, so she sat down face-to-face with Second Sister. Pearl Phoenix hurried over to fill the water pipe for her. Gold Phoenix, who had been chatting with Prosperity, fell silent. Everybody looked at one another; no one spoke. The bookkeeper, perceiving that his presence was no longer required, took the account book with him and led the menservants downstairs. Mama Zhao and Little Treasure also went out of the room.

Green Phoenix now addressed Second Sister in a calm and controlled manner, "All these clothes and jewelry of mine, well, they may not be much, but they weren't exactly easy to come by, either. Today I'm handing them over to you, Mother, and you really should have a little more sense. If you let your lovers cheat you out of them again, you're going to fall on hard times! All your old lovers are con men and gangsters; there's not a single reliable one among them. I've seen with my own eyes how much they have cheated you out of. Fortunately, I held firmly on to my things on your behalf, so they haven't been taken by the con men. If these had been in your possession, nothing would've remained. I've been doing grown-up work for four or five years now and have earned these things for you, Mother, so today I can say that I've done right by you. My business here is finished, but your lack of judgment worries me a bit, Mother. Once I'm gone, who is there to put you right? If you listen to your lovers, in four or five years' time they'll have cheated you of your money and your possessions, and you'll end up with nothing but hardship. If you fell on hard times because of your lovers, you'd surely be too embarrassed to ask anyone to look after you, right? You'd be too ashamed to ask for help."

This little speech left Second Sister wishing she had somewhere to hide. She bowed her head and fidgeted with a bunch of keys in her hand. Prosperity smiled ever so slightly.

"Mother," Green Phoenix carried on, "Please don't be angry with me for speaking like this; I'm doing it for your good. Though I'm buying back my freedom, the only kin I have is you, Mother. Wherever I go, I'll be the girl from Second Sister's place. If you do well, I'll feel honored, too; if you don't do well, we'll all be humiliated. You're good in many ways, Mother; you're a keen businesswoman and a wise manager of the household. Your only weakness is letting your lovers take advantage of you. I'm saying all this because it's all been too much to put up with and in the future I won't be in the position to say anything. You *must* have a sense of proportion, Mother, for you're over fifty now. If you behave in the same way as before, you'll make yourself a laughingstock to the youngsters. Even I would feel ashamed for you."

Hearing this, Second Sister didn't know where to put herself. Her face gradually turned a bright scarlet. Green Phoenix did not have the heart to continue, so she changed the subject. "I suggest you buy another girl with the thousand dollars. With the clothes and jewelry ready at hand, the business she'll do should be enough to pay the expenses. In a couple of years, Gold Phoenix will put up her hair and carry on the business. It's perfect timing. Pearl Phoenix is a useless girl; if anybody wants her, you might as well let her go to a good place. Gold Phoenix, on the other hand, can't be faulted. She'll definitely be one of the leading fashionable courtesans. Even if she doesn't make it to the top, she'll at least be like me. If you do as I say, Mother, it'll be your good fortune."

Prosperity nodded repeatedly in agreement and cut in, "Now this is proper advice. She's quite right, you know."

"D'you mean what I said to begin with was wrong?" Green Phoenix demanded.

Second Sister responded quickly, "It was all good advice. There was nothing wrong." Having said that, she got up and paced about, murmuring to herself, "They ought to be here any minute now. I'll go and wait downstairs." She turned around to go back to her small room.

Green Phoenix pointed at her back and said to Prosperity in a low voice, "Look at her! The more you tell her off, the more thick-skinned she becomes. From now on, I'll say no more. If she wants to suffer, it's her own lookout."

"As far as madams go, she's rather miserable. She didn't even dare utter a word when you gave her such a dressing-down," Prosperity commented.

"Listen to the way you talk! Is there a good person among the Seven Sisters? If I had made the least mistake, she'd have beaten me to death," Green Phoenix said.

"I don't believe it."

"Well, if you don't, just look at Gold Flower," she replied. "Of the Seven Sisters, I've met three. Third Sister Chu is much nicer than my mother; she only gave Gold Flower a couple of beatings. If that girl had been sold to my mother, she'd have a life so terrible that she'd have wished to die, and that would've taught her a lesson."

He smiled but said nothing.

She sighed. "My mother aside, if you look at the Shanghai brothels, where d'you find a madam who's a good person? Would a good person be making her living off a brothel? There's this Mrs. Filial Guo whom you know a bit about. Now that she doesn't own a girl herself, she goes to help Third Sister beat up Gold Flower. Now doesn't that make your blood boil?"

As she was talking, there was suddenly the sound of footsteps coming up the stairs. Three men, led by Second Sister, walked ahead of the bookkeeper straight into Gold Phoenix's room. Astonished, Prosperity asked what it was about.

Green Phoenix held up a hand to silence him. She said in a whisper, "They're gangsters. My ransom papers have to be written in their presence."

Upon hearing this, Prosperity lowered the bamboo blinds.

Green Phoenix told Pearl Phoenix to go and entertain them and not to leave without orders. Gold Phoenix, however, did not return to her own room. She just sat there silently, looking dazed. When Prosperity saw the pensive expression on her face, he pulled her close to him and asked kindly, "You'll be lonely when Elder Sister is gone, won't you?"

Gold Phoenix frowned and answered with tears in her eyes, "I don't mind being lonely. I was thinking, when Elder Sister is gone, I'll be the only one left to do business. With rent and taxes, the expenses are *so* high! No matter how hard I work, there'll just be a few drinking parties and some party calls. Now if Mother gets worked up over that, it'll be death for me. What am I to do?"

Green Phoenix laughed. "Come, if you can be expected to pay for all the expenses as a virgin courtesan, Mother would be making a fortune overnight."

Prosperity also comforted her pleasantly, "Don't worry, why should Mother scold you? Pearl Phoenix is a year older than you, so if there's any scolding she'll get it first."

Gold Phoenix responded, "It's not in her nature to think about things, so she's not worried. But in my case, Mother is always saying, 'Your business ought to get better!' Elder Sister also says so. But actually this season's earnings turn out to be even a bit less than last season's!"

"Don't you worry yourself about these things. Just work hard at your business, and you'll be fine," Green Phoenix said.

Prosperity also said, "Now remember what Elder Sister tells you; then you'll be in Mother's good books, too."

Second Sister happened to come over then from Gold Phoenix's room. When she heard the word "Mother," she asked what they were talking about. Green Phoenix repeated Gold Phoenix's remarks to her.

"Good girl! So thoughtful for one so young!" Second Sister said rather offhandedly.

This embarrassed Gold Phoenix, who buried her head in Prosperity's arms to hide her face. Everybody laughed and let her be. Second Sister then fished out of her sleeve a gold watch and a gold toothpick that had been strung together and offered them to Green Phoenix with both hands. "You said you won't take anything with you, and I understand how you feel. But you've always carried these two things around, and you'll be inconvenienced without them. Take them along. They're just a token, so they don't count."

Green Phoenix neither pushed them away nor accepted them; she did not even take a proper look at them. Instead she said disdainfully, "Thank you, Mother. I've said I don't want anything, so if you insist on being so kind, Mother, you'll only make me laugh."

Her hands still stretched out, Second Sister looked deeply embarrassed. In an attempt to smooth things over, Prosperity suggested, "Why don't you give them to Gold Phoenix?"

Second Sister thought for a moment and reluctantly did so.

"I might as well tell you this, Mother," Green Phoenix said solemnly. "After I move to Prosperity Alley, if you want to look in on me, you're welcome; but if you send me anything, then you must forgive me, Mother, for I won't even tip the messenger."

Second Sister, caught in an awkward position, could not find anything to say in response, so when she saw Mama Zhao come in with an invitation, she jumped at the opening and asked, "Where's the party?"

Seeing that the invitation was written on the stationery of Peace Restaurant, Prosperity knew it was for a regular seasonal party given by his bureau. Green Phoenix ignored the invitation and sat there with great dignity and haughty reserve. Second Sister felt completely out of place and, after hanging around uneasily for a little while, made for Gold Phoenix's room.

As Prosperity got up to leave, Green Phoenix reminded him, "Be sure to come back later. We need to check if they've written the ransom papers right."

He gave his promise and walked out to the parlor. There, he saw that Gold Phoenix's room was brightly lit but dead quiet. He stood at the door, peeped in through a gap in the curtain, and saw that the bookkeeper, with his spectacles on, was writing at the table. The three gangsters and Second Sister were whispering together about something. Pearl Phoenix and Little Treasure stood in attendance on one side.

Without disturbing them, Prosperity went off to the dinner party. Once he arrived at Peace Restaurant, it was the usual merry round of finger games and party calls. Mindful of Green Phoenix's parting words, Prosperity did not indulge himself to the full. Having mingled for a while, he took the first opportunity to slip away.

On his return, he found there was a dinner party in progress in Gold Phoenix's room. Four platters and eight dishes had been ordered for the gangsters, who chewed the food greedily and smacked their lips noisily. Their laughter mingled with curses as they yelled and howled. Prosperity surmised that the ransom papers must be ready. When he saw Green Phoenix, she produced an agreement and a receipt. The writing was little better than a scrawl and barely legible, but the wording and logic were clear enough. He knew these were based on a master version handed down through generations, so there was little possibility for error.

Green Phoenix, however, was not reassured. She insisted on his explaining every sentence to her. Only after she had weighed every word did she tell Little Treasure to take the agreement to Second Sister for her to press her thumbprint and stamp her seal on it. Prosperity remembered that beneath the date there was a row of names and addresses. Besides the name of the scribe, those of three witnesses were listed: Clement Zhou, Verdure Xu, and Muddy Dragon. He asked if Muddy Dragon was a nickname.

"Actually," Green Phoenix replied, "that's Mother's lover. He's a quiet one but full of cunning. Just now he came up with some new trickery, but would I be taken in by him? That'll be the day!"

Having read through the ransom papers, Prosperity looked around uncomfortably and made as if to leave. Green Phoenix again insisted that he stay, saying, "We'll go there together tomorrow." He had to go along with her. They waited until the three gangsters had left before going to bed.

Green Phoenix was vigilant even in sleep and got up at dawn to call for Mama Zhao to get a parcel from Second Sister. It contained her complete attire. Green Phoenix sat on the edge of the bed and loosened her foot bandages to change into new ones. A drowsy Prosperity went back to sleep again. When Green Phoenix had finished her toilet, she woke him up.

The minute he set eyes on her, he looked her up and down in astonishment. She was actually dressed in the colors of mourning: off-white cotton blouse and skirt, pale brown hair yarn, plain black cloth shoes, and plain silver hair ornaments, pins, and earrings. It was an outfit for deep mourning.

She explained without waiting for his questions, "I lost my parents at eight and haven't had a chance to wear mourning since I entered this house. Now that I'm leaving, I'll make up for it with three years of mourning."

On hearing this, he praised her again and again, but Green Phoenix stopped him, saying, "Enough of that; just get going."

"Let's go then," he said.

"You go ahead. I'll come when I'm ready."[2] And she told Little Treasure to follow him downstairs to get the document box from Second Sister and put it into his sedan chair.

Prosperity went to Prosperity Alley in his sedan chair, where he saw a private ricksha was already parked at the door. When he entered the house, a newly hired servant girl knew him by sight and took him to the main room upstairs. Promotion respectfully handed him the document box and withdrew. Looking about him, Prosperity found that not only was the room fully furnished but there was also a complete array of everyday household utensils. He was full of praise for the arrangement and wanted to see the spare room as well. But the servant girl stopped him, saying there was a guest there.

Soon a string of firecrackers was set off at the front door. Promotion and Mama Zhao rushed in to report, "She's here!"

The servant girl hastened to light a pair of tall candles in the center room. Green Phoenix came gracefully up the stairs, holding some incense sticks, and knelt down to kowtow toward the direction representing her parents' spirits. Prosperity tiptoed out of the room and hid himself behind her to watch, but she sensed his presence, turned around, and beckoned to him, "You come and kowtow, too."

He gave a titter and stepped back.[3]

"If you don't kowtow, you have no business gawping. Go back into the room." She pushed him through the door and took out the ransom papers from her inner pocket, asking him to check them again.

::

2. [She does not want Vigor Qian to see her arriving at the new house in the company of Prosperity Luo. *E.H.*]

3. [If he did, he would be behaving like a son-in-law. *E.H.*]

Everything was in order. She then went behind the bed and took a document box out of a red lacquered trunk. It looked rather similar to Prosperity's document box and contained a new account book and a dozen sales slips.

She put her ransom papers in the box, locked it, and then put it away in the trunk behind the bed together with his document box. Now that things were more or less in order, she told him to stay in the room and then went over to the spare room to send Vigor Qian home.

CHAPTER 50 :: *A rascal's tactics are aimed at faultfinding, and a slight interruption brings a beating*

On the day of Green Phoenix's move, Prosperity Luo ordered two double tables for both lunch and dinner to give a good showing. At noon, after Vigor Qian had gone home, the guests began to arrive. The first to come was Elan Ge. After inspecting the three upstairs rooms, he was much impressed by the elegant and exquisite decor. He then walked out to the balcony at the rear and saw that it faced White Orchid's room in Nobility Alley. Through her window, he could see Iron Hua and White Orchid drinking together, enjoying themselves. They nodded in greeting when they saw Elan.

Iron Hua unexpectedly pushed the window open and called out, "Come over if you have time. I'd like a word with you."

Elan surmised that it was still too early for the meal to commence, so he explained to Prosperity Luo and then walked over to Nobility Alley. He saw to his surprise a group of gaudily dressed ruffians standing at the door as if waiting for something.

After Elan Ge entered the house, a mandarin's sedan chair followed at his heels and came straight into the parlor. Elan hurried upstairs. White Orchid came out of her room in welcome, invited him in, and asked him to sit down. Iron Hua knew Elan was not much of a drinker and did not bother with the etiquette of pressing wine on him. Elan asked why he had been summoned.

"Did you get Second Bai's invitation? What's it about?" Iron Hua asked.

"I've just learned about that from Cloudlet." Elan told him about Devotion Yin's demand in exchange for the pornographic pictures they had seen at Flora Zhang's.

"No wonder," Iron Hua said. "I was just saying, it may not be possible to invite people to Wenjun's place on account of Lai the Turtle, but why hire a function hall at the Old Banner? So, it's all down to Devotion's high spirits."

As he was speaking, the maid, Sister Gold, came in to get the teacups. She whispered something in White Orchid's ear. Greatly startled, White Orchid ordered her servant girl to bring a bowl of rice. Iron Hua asked what the matter was.

"Lai the Turtle is here," White Orchid replied in a low voice.

Iron Hua stuck out his tongue in mock fear. He also asked for rice to be served. As they ate, they heard something shatter in the mezzanine room at the back. It sounded like teacups had been broken. This was followed by loud curses and attempts at mediation. As voices were raised, three or four of the hooligans barged noisily into the parlor as though they were on patrol. They came straight to White Orchid's door and peered in.

Elan Ge did not feel like staying, and Iron Hua asked him to wait a minute so they could leave together. Not daring to detain them, White Orchid hastily put down her rice bowl, wiped her mouth with a dry towel, and hurried out. She saw Young Commander Lai shouting wildly that he wanted to see what kind of a favorite client was in her room. His underlings were rubbing their fists, spoiling for a fight. Sister Gold and the servant girl tried hard to explain, tugging and pulling at the hangers-on, but there was no holding them back. White Orchid had to go up and press Lai to sit down in his chair and, with a smiling face, gently apologize. Such reasonable behavior made it impossible for the Young Commander to act up, so he restrained himself with a smile. His underlings also changed their tack and blamed the maid and the servant girl for having been tactless.

Presently Elan Ge and Iron Hua left hastily, vacating the room. White Orchid did not dare see them out. "Let's go," she said to the Young Commander.

"Go where?" he pretended not to know.

"Into my room," she said.

He stretched out stiffly in the chair and bellowed, "I'm not going into that room just to fill in a gap!"

When the hooligans and hangers-on heard this, they also put on a rowdy display and refused to budge. But White Orchid held Lai by both hands and pleaded humbly and sweetly with him. At this, Lai submitted and followed her into her room. Sister Gold and the servant girl also did their best to persuade the hooligans to go in.

Young Commander Lai, with his eyes on the floor, walked in and bumped his head into a hanging lamp. It was just a tiny scrape and there was no bleeding, but he looked up and said in annoyance, "Even your rotten lamp tries to bully me!" So saying, he gave the lampshade a tap with his ivory fan, and the glass shattered.

White Orchid remained silent and unconcerned, but Lai's hangers-on continued to elaborate on his comment. One said, "The paraffin lamp doesn't recognize you, that's why you got hit. Now if you were the favorite client, that wouldn't have happened. It seems the lamp is quite clever."

"The lamp can't talk, you see," said another, "so hitting you in the head is its way of showing that it wants you out, understand?"

Still another said, "We have no business being here in the main room. Don't blame the lamp!"

Young Commander Lai paid no attention to these remarks. He merely looked over his shoulder at White Orchid and said, "Never mind the damage. I'll pay for it."

She smiled deprecatingly. "Don't be silly, we didn't hang our lamp right, so why should Your Young Excellency pay for it?"

Lai was displeased. "Are you turning me down?"

She changed her tune at once. "Why would we turn down generosity from Your Young Excellency? Just now you were saying you'd pay us back, that was why we didn't dare accept."

In a good mood again, Lai smiled. His underlings were utterly confused and switched back and forth between criticism and flattery. White Orchid just ignored them and concentrated her attention on Lai.

Lai summoned one of his runners and gave the order that the Complete Imported and Cantonese Goods Store should send over paraffin lamps of all shapes and sizes immediately. Soon the runner returned with a shop assistant. Lai ordered the man to replace all the old lamps in the room with paraffin ones. Following his orders, the shop assistant hung up a bunch of ten such lamps. Seeing that Lai's displeasure had not completely subsided, White Orchid had to let him do whatever he wanted. Lai, for his part, saw that though she was attentive, she showed neither warmth nor coldness in her attitude and wondered how she was disposed toward him.

Presently he took her by the hand, sat down side by side with her on the edge of the bed, and plied her with questions. She took special care that she answered his questions but did not volunteer any other information. When he asked who had been in the room just now, she was inclined not to tell him. Yet she feared he would use that as an excuse to make trouble, so she told him plainly it was Iron Hua.

He jumped up. "If I'd known it was him, I'd have asked to meet him."

She made no comment.

The hangers-on clamored in support. "Iron Hua is staying at the Qiao residence on First Avenue. Shall we invite him here?"

"Good idea. Invite him as well as Fourth Qiao," Lai said in delight. The invitations were written at once, and several other names were added. White Orchid let him do as he liked and neither encouraged nor tried to stop him.

Lai was in high spirits and engaged in all sorts of antics, but he noticed White Orchid was as aloof as ever and his displeasure grew. When the runner returned from his mission to report that the guests were either busy or not at home and that not one was coming, Lai flared up. He called the runner a string of names and dismissed him angrily and then said in a huff, "If they're not coming, we'll have a party ourselves."

Whereupon the call chits for courtesans were written out in a flurry. Lai called more than a dozen girls. As it was already getting dark, a double dinner table was set. Terrified that Lai might find fault with her again, White Orchid signaled Sister Gold to light all the paraffin lamps. The glare dazzled her and the heat made her feverish and sweaty, but Lai was delighted. He applauded and shouted wildly. This was echoed by his hangers-on, and the sound was thunderous. Seated at the table, she waited for the called girls to arrive so she could extricate herself. But as it turned out, Lai just left the called girls sitting around while he forced his attentions on her. It so happened that she received no party calls that night so she had no way out.

In the beginning, she poured a cup of wine for him as routine required, but he raised the cup to her lips and told her to drink it for him. When she turned away, he slammed the cup down on the table. She glanced at him sideways, picked up the cup, and said with a smile, "If you want me to drink, you should offer me a cup. Now you're giving me what I offered you. Don't you appreciate a courtesy?" She put the cup down in front of him, also with a bang.

This made Lai smile. He drained the cup and then filled it again and gave it to her. She downed it in one gulp. Everybody at the table gave a cheer. His spirits soaring, Lai wanted to match her cup for cup.

"You please go ahead, Your Young Excellency. I'm not much of a drinker," she said, frowning.

"You're still trying to fool me!" he said in astonishment. "You're well-known for your capacity. How dare you say you're not a drinker?"

"Your Young Excellency is going to be the death of me," she said with an icy smile. "With us, drinking is an acquired technique. We can down a large tumbler of wine and then make it come up again; that's how we learned to drink. At parties, when guests see me draining cup after cup, they all say I can hold my liquor. Little do they know that when I get home I have to bring it all up before I feel all right."

Lai also sneered. "I don't believe it, not unless you drink a large tumbler of wine now and then bring it up to show me."

White Orchid deliberately digressed. "Bring up? Is Your Young Excellency suggesting that I lay something on for you?"

All this while when Lai had been talking to her, she neither teased nor joked, so he was overjoyed at this remark. He stretched out his right hand to pull her into his arms, but she was too quick for him. Pretending to be upset, she screamed coyly and ran away from him. Just then she caught sight of Sister Gold signaling for her behind the bamboo curtain, so she left the room to find out what the matter was.

It turned out that Iron Hua's household slave, Loyalty, had been sent there to find out how Lai was behaving.

White Orchid gave a brief account of things and then said, "Tell your master that he's made a racket all this time and has got it in for me. Ask your master if he can do anything about it."

Before Loyalty could reply, everybody at the table was calling "Maestro," so White Orchid had to return to the room. Holding his breath and taking care to avoid detection, Loyalty lifted the door curtain and peeped in. He was immediately hit by a gust of hot air. He saw that those seated at the table were either bare-headed or bare-foot, and some were even bare-chested. It was even hotter for Lai as he was completely hemmed in by more than a dozen courtesans.

The Young Commander barked at them to make way for White Orchid and told her to come up to the table to join him in the finger game. She excused herself, saying, "I don't know how."

He banged the table and shouted fiercely, "How can anyone not know how to play the finger game?"

"But I've never learned, so I really don't know how. Since Your Young Excellency wants to play the finger game, I'll learn the game tomorrow and play with you after that," she said.

He glared at her ferociously. Fortunately, a hanger-on interceded on her behalf. "Well, with the maestros, the rule is that they sing; they don't play finger games. Let's just tell her to sing something."

Since she had no excuses for not singing, she started tuning her *pipa*.

Loyalty saw that the hangers-on were either the spendthrift sons of rich families that had gone down in the world or overseers on the warships garrisoned at Wusong. Fearful of being spotted and questioned about his presence, he withdrew and returned to the Qiao residence on First Avenue to report to his master. Iron Hua gave the matter some thought but could not come up with any good idea, so he set it aside.

The next day, a manservant bearing White Orchid's card came after lunch to invite Iron Hua to the house. After pondering for a moment, Iron Hua sent Loyalty to find out where Lai had gone to seek his pleasure. He himself then went by sedan chair to White Orchid's in Nobility Alley.

The minute White Orchid saw him, she broke down in a torrent of tears and set before him her endless grievances. Iron Hua could do nothing but comfort and console her. Worried that Lai might come again, she was anxious to consult with him, but Iron Hua heaved a sigh, at a loss what to do about it.

"I'm thinking of staying at Conical Hat Garden for a couple of days. What d'you think?" she said.

Iron Hua was dead set against the idea; he shook his head and said nothing. She asked why. He replied, "You don't understand, there're lots of problems. First of all, I can't speak to Harmony Qi about this. Lai the Turtle is a family friend of his, so it'll be awkward if he knows about this."

"Wenjun Yao is there because of Lai the Turtle. What's so awkward about it?"

His argument collapsed, Iron Hua said nothing.

"Humph! I know what you're like," said White Orchid after a long silence, "Whenever I need you to do something for me, no matter how easy it is, you never agree to it. Don't worry, I'm only telling you first; I'll speak to His Excellency myself. If Lai the Turtle learns about it, it'll have nothing to do with you."

Iron Hua applauded this. "That's fine. Later on, we're going to the Old Banner. There's your opportunity to speak if you want to."

She snorted and said nothing. They were both of a quiet disposition. Now, with a disagreement between them, they sat facing each other with nothing to say.

Presently Loyalty came back to report, "The Young Commander is taking a carriage ride. He'll be coming here on his return."

When Iron Hua heard this, he became quite unnerved. He finally opened his mouth and said to White Orchid, "Let's go."

The news about Lai had fanned White Orchid's anger. She paused for a long time before replying, "As you like."

Iron Hua told Loyalty to stay behind. If Lai showed up to make trouble, he was to go quickly to the Old Banner and report it. White Orchid left word with Sister Gold to bid Young Commander Lai welcome and just tell him the truth, that she had been called to a party at the Old Banner.

Iron Hua and White Orchid went downstairs together, and each got into a sedan chair. They had barely come out of Nobility Alley when they heard faintly the sound of wheels and hoofs turning into Pebble Road and gaining on them at lightning speed. Soon it was traveling alongside the sedan chairs. Thinking it was Lai, Iron Hua looked out through the curtain. It turned out to be Nature Shi and Second Treasure riding south in separate carriages, probably heading for the same party given by Second Bai. After the carriages had passed, the sedan chairs made their way slowly across Beaten Dog Bridge and along First Avenue in the French concession to the Old Banner.[1] Here, Iron Hua saw an array of sedan chairs and carriages parked in front of the restaurant and realized that Nature Shi must have arrived before them. Many more sedan chairs were coming in behind them.

Iron Hua and White Orchid stood to await the new arrivals, who turned out to be Elan Ge, Amity Zhu, Cloud Tao, and their girls, Snow Scent, White Fragrance, and Belle Tan. There was the usual round of mutual greetings before they went in.

Having spotted them, Second Bai came out in welcome with two Cantonese prostitutes in tow. He said, laughing uproariously, "The notes hurrying the guests have barely been dispatched, and here you all are. And Nature arrived ahead of you. It's as if you planned to turn up together."

They walked up the steps in a file to the banqueting hall. Besides Nature Shi and Second Treasure, three others had arrived early: Devotion Yin, Modesty Zhu, and Jade Tao. After everybody had exchanged greetings, Second Bai said, "That leaves only Cloudlet Chen and Harmony."

They deferred to each other before finally taking their seats, after which they examined the banqueting hall. The decoration was indeed novel and distinctive, completely different from what they were used to in the Shanghai brothels. The folding screens and window frames were either carved or inlaid, with bases of expensive wood such as *huali*, gingko, poplar, and sandalwood. The curtains and hangings were painted or embroidered on colorful Huzhou crepe, mandarin gauze, Ningpo silk, and Hangzhou weave. Pillars, beams, walls, and doors had pictures painted and carved in vibrant green and red; tables, chairs, couches, and cabinets were highly polished and gave off a luxurious glow. To complement these, there were rare flowers in pots, excellent calligraphy and paintings on the walls, valuable curios on display, and fine fruit and tea offered to guests.

::

1. [According to Chen Boxi's *Shanghai yishi daguan* (Shanghai: Shanghai shudian, 2000), p. 404, the Old Banner was on Ningbo Road, that is, north of the International Settlement. *E.H.*]

Those in the gathering then turned their attention to the Cantonese prostitutes, who took turns keeping them company. There were twenty or thirty of them, and they looked completely different from women in the Shanghai brothels. Some wore their hair in a stiff bun sticking straight out, others had a loosely braided pigtail trailing down the back; some had two round green plasters pasted to the corners of their eyes, others wore a quivering red pompon at the back of the heads. What astonished them most was that the women's cheeks were rouged scarlet, making them look as if they had been slapped round the face, and their willow waists were as stiff as if they had hurt their backs. Their sleeve cuffs flapped loose like pig's ears, and their leather slippers made a noise on the floor like tortoise shells. Their physical strength was terrifying. As Amity Zhu made a joking remark, a prostitute laughed and cursed, turned around, and gave his arm a little pinch through two layers of clothing, which sent him howling with pain. He hastened to take a look and found three finger marks on his arm already turning a purplish blue, like ripe grapes. At the sight of this, everybody gave warning to one another, and none of them dared joke or tease any more. But the prostitutes would not quiet down and still jabbered on endlessly.[2]

Fortunately, someone came in to announce "His Excellency Mr. Qi is here." The gathering rose and lined up to wait on him. Harmony Qi came in followed by a group of local prostitutes who swayed gracefully as they walked. They were River Blossom, Twin Jade, Flora Zhang, Green Fragrance, Wenjun Yao, and Aroma, the six girls called to the party. The Cantonese prostitutes, unable to join in the conversation, finally stopped bothering them.

CHAPTER 51 :: *A fugitive hides from an unwelcome guest, and a slave artiste vies with a courtesan*

By then, countless lamps and candles were lit, the banquet was set out in the middle of the hall, and the Cantonese prostitutes asked

::

2. [Canton, or Guangzhou, had a much longer history in foreign trade than Shanghai. Cantonese merchants in Shanghai were therefore generally thought of as wealthy. However, the areas around Shanghai were traditionally the nurturing ground for literary talent. This, combined with a difference in customs and aesthetic taste, meant that the Cantonese were often considered uncouth. *E.H.*]

them to come to table. In accordance with the rules, they each called a girl of the house in addition to those they had brought to the party. The resident prostitutes, who played various musical instruments, belted out the unfamiliar sounds of Cantonese songs. According to Cantonese custom, they should have taken turns to sing continuously before dinner, but Second Bai thought the noise would be too much and put a ban on that. Now they were seated for dinner, Harmony Qi also lost his patience and again stopped them before they could finish the first song. Only then was it possible for them to talk and play drinking games as usual.

Presently, Iron Hua's bond servant, Loyalty, came up to report in a whisper, "The Young Commander has gone to Third Treasure's in Tranquillity Alley. He didn't go to Nobility Alley."

Iron Hua gave a slight nod and quietly informed White Orchid to reassure her. Harmony Qi happened to notice and asked what the matter was, so Iron Hua took the opportunity to tell him about Lai the Turtle.

"In that case, come stay in our garden," Harmony offered at once. "You can keep Wenjun company, wouldn't that be nice?"

White Orchid took it up. "I was thinking of going to Your Excellency's garden, but *he* said it might be inconvenient."

Harmony turned to Iron Hua. "What's inconvenient about it? You can come as well."

Iron Hua counted the days on his fingers. "Well, she can go today, but I have something to attend to. I'll join her on the twentieth."

"That's fine," said Harmony. "Nature Shi also said he'd come on the twentieth."

Now that White Orchid's business was settled, Iron Hua recalled his own business and wanted to take his leave. Second Bai, knowing he had no taste for partying or whoring, did not press him to stay.

Iron Hua's departure left White Orchid unattended; it was awkward for her to stay on. Harmony, sensing her difficulty, said, "Here they have things on such a scale, they're definitely going to have an all-night party. I'm ready to go home and go to bed."

Second Bai knew that Qi was used to taking a nap whenever he felt like it, so he dared not press him to stay.

Harmony Qi invited White Orchid to join him and Aroma in taking leave of the others, and they left in their sedan chairs. It took an hour to reach Conical Hat Garden. The moonlight looked brighter than ever in the garden. The swaying shadows cast by flowering bushes, bamboos, and trees crisscrossed on the ground. Harmony gave the order that they should be taken to the Moon-worshiper's Chamber, which meant going round the northeastern corner of Conical Hat Lake. As they emerged from behind the artificial hills, they heard peals of laughter. They had no idea who this merry lot could be.

When they got to the courtyard wall of the Moon-worshiper's Chamber, they stepped out of their sedan chairs. Harmony walked in front, followed by Aroma and White Orchid walking hand in hand. As they entered the courtyard, they saw some dozen girls from Pear Blossom Court wrestling on the ground, kicking a shuttlecock, and playing blind man's buff. They were boisterous and quite out of control. Suddenly, they looked up and saw their master. They scrambled to their feet in fear and ran off in all directions. Only one girl remained. She stood with one hand against a cassia tree and bent down to straighten her cloth shoes, which had come off at the heel, muttering, "Why run away? A bunch of kids with no manners!"

Harmony looked at her in the moonlight and found to his surprise that it was Pendant. He went up to her smiling broadly, took her by the hand, and said, "Let's go in."

Pendant took two steps and then turned around to look at another cassia tree, where a dim figure was peeping out. "Hairpin, come here!" Pendant shouted angrily. Hairpin hurriedly came out from the shadows, and Pendant continued to scold her, "How could you join them in running away? Have you no shame?" Hairpin dared not answer back.

They all went into the Moon-worshiper's Chamber. Harmony, a little tired, leaned back on a settee and chatted with White Orchid. He asked about Lai the Turtle and said a few words to comfort her. Seeing that White Orchid felt ill at ease, he told Aroma, "You go with Maestro White Orchid to Panorama Hall. If her room lacks anything, tell them to fix it."

White Orchid was only too eager to go. She left hand in hand with Aroma.

Harmony called for the manservant standing on duty beyond the bamboo curtain and told him to extinguish all the lights except the five paraffin lamps at the center of each room. The manservant carried out his order and withdrew. Harmony then used a twist of his lips to signal Pendant and Hairpin, indicating they should sit by the couch. He closed his eyes and drifted off and was soon snoring. Pendant quietly left her seat and picked up the teapot. It was hot to the touch, so she wrapped a handkerchief around it to keep the tea warm.

Hairpin went to lower the bamboo curtains at the windows in the back. "Shall I fetch a woolen coverlet?" she asked in a low voice. Pendant thought for a moment and then held up a hand to indicate "no."

The two of them sat facing each other in silence. With nothing at hand to kill time, Pendant just watched the reflection of the moon on Conical Hat Lake. Hairpin opened a drawer and found a box of ivory dominoes, so she started a quiet game of solitaire. Pendant looked at her severely, but she pretended not to notice. She picked up several tiles, brought them close to her mouth as if in prayer, and then blew on them for luck and started playing again. Angry at her disobedience, Pendant snatched a tile and hid it in her pocket. Hairpin anxiously brought her palms together in a gesture of entreaty and smiled ingratiatingly, but it was all in vain: Pendant ignored her and looked away. Hairpin then grinned and gesticulated, indicating that she would search Pendant to find the tile. Pendant, who was extremely ticklish, adopted a grim and angry look in the face of this ordeal.

As they were about to start wrestling, they heard the sudden tinkle of the curtain hook at the door to the center room. They went out in a hurry to find that it was Aroma and her servant girl, Greenie, coming in. Pendant pointed silently at the couch, and Aroma realized that Harmony was asleep. Fortunately, she had not wakened him. After checking that everything was in order, she turned around and spoke to Pendant in quiet entreaty, "My elder sister is asking me to go over to her place to do some sewing. Would the two of you please look after His Excellency for me? When he wakes up, just tell Greenie to call for me."

Hairpin, who was standing to one side, promised to do so. Aroma left them after she had spoken. Pendant immediately sent Greenie away, telling her there was no need for her to be in attendance. Greenie was only too glad to be free to roam about.

Pendant settled herself in her seat and sniggered derisively. Then she told Hairpin off, saying, "I've never seen a fool such as you. You'd say yes to anything, no matter what it is."

Hairpin pondered over the conversation just now and was thoroughly bewildered. "But what's wrong with what she said?"

Pendant snorted. "Is she your madam, so you have to attend to a client when she says so? What's wrong indeed!"

"Then let's go elsewhere," said Hairpin.

Pendant glared and said in annoyance, "Why should we go elsewhere? His Excellency told us to sit here. Whether we attend to him is none of *her* business."

Only then did Hairpin understand what she meant. Pendant snorted again. "She talked as if His Excellency belongs to her. Ridiculous!"

As they talked, they had quite forgotten about Harmony, who was sleeping on the couch. With their growing vehemence, their voices rose higher and higher. Harmony happened to turn over just then. The two of them covered their mouths in alarm and waited, but nothing happened. Pendant tiptoed over to the couch and saw that

Harmony was lying on his back, his slightly opened eyes looking frighteningly bright. Pendant straightened the lapel and sleeves of his gown and then withdrew on tiptoe. No longer in the mood for solitaire, Hairpin packed up the ivory dominoes and returned them to the drawer. There was a complete set of thirty-two pieces, not one missing, and she had no idea when Pendant had returned the tile she had taken. The two of them again sat facing each other in silence with nothing to do to kill time.

It was almost evening when Harmony had slept enough and stretched himself. Hearing him, the manservant standing beyond the curtain brought in warm water in a basin. After Harmony had wiped his face, Hairpin brought a mug of water for him to rinse his mouth. Then Pendant took the pot of tea she had kept ready and tasted it. It was warm and pleasant, so she filled a teacup and gave it to him. He drank some of it.

"Where's Aroma?" he looked around and asked.

Pendant pretended not to have heard.

"She said she was going over to your lady concubine's place," replied Hairpin.

Harmony told the manservant to fetch Aroma. Pendant took the teacup from him, set it down offhandedly, and sat down to one side with her face turned away. He wanted more tea and asked her for it repeatedly, but she remained motionless and answered coldly, "Aroma will come and pour it for you. I'm too clumsy to pour tea."

He laughed heartily and then stood up to get the teacup himself. Hairpin, smiling pleasantly, came up to pour the tea and handed it to him. Having finished the tea, he sat beside Pendant and tried to soothe her tenderly for a long while. But Pendant just stared in front of her, silent and expressionless.

"Now you're being silly," he changed his tone and reasoned with her seriously. "Aroma is an outsider. Even if I'm fond of her, she can't compare with you—you're family. Family are always here, but Aroma will go away in a year or six months. Why should you be jealous of her?"

When she heard this, Pendant replied loudly, "Where's your sense of proportion, Your Excellency? What do I know about jealousy?"

Harmony smiled, a little embarrassed. "Don't you know about jealousy now? Well, I'll teach you something useful: the way you behaved just now is called jealousy."

She pushed him away. "Go and drink your tea. Aroma is here."

He turned around to look, which gave her the opportunity to extricate herself and call out to Hairpin, "Aroma's here. Let's go."

Sure enough, he saw the figure of Aroma in the distance, so he thought it a good time to send them away: "Everybody to bed. It's getting late."

Hairpin assented as she followed Pendant down the steps. They found themselves face to face with Aroma.

"Hurry up, maestro," Pendant said. "His Excellency is waiting."

Aroma did not stop to reply. Pendant and Hairpin walked slowly back to their rooms along a moonlit path.

CHAPTER 52 :: *A young woman in a lonely bed dreads an empty room, and hospitality means a shared bed and chatting through the night*

Pendant and Hairpin chatted as they walked in the moonlight.

"The moon tonight is brighter than it was at the Midautumn Festival. Then there was merrymaking all night, but tonight it's all quiet," said Hairpin.

"Well, what they did doesn't count as viewing the moon, does it? Now *we* are really viewing the moon," Pendant said.

"I suggest we go to Dragon Range and sit in the Mid-sky Pavilion where we can see the whole garden. That's the best place for viewing the moon."

"D'you know where you should go if you want to do it properly? On the podium in front of Right Target Hall, there're lots of machines and instruments for looking at the moon and the stars; with these, you can even look at the sun. What's more, you can make all sorts of calculations. They say it's the same as the emperor's observatory, only smaller," said Pendant.

"Then let's go there. We don't need the instruments either. We'll look at the moon just as it is," Hairpin said.

"What if we run into a guest there? It wouldn't do."

"Come on, guests won't be going there."

"We'd better go to Panorama Hall and look in on White Orchid instead. That'd be nice, wouldn't it?"

Hairpin was all eagerness. "Let's go!"

Instead of returning to their courtyard, the two of them headed for the Bridge of Nine Twists, where they saw the green roof tiles of Panorama Hall enveloped in a light mist, glistening in the moonlight. When they got to the ground floor, it was quiet all around. The windows were all shut, and it was pitch-dark inside except for the windows on the southwest corner where White Orchid's room was. There, a faint light came through beyond the layers of gauze curtains. They looked around, unable to find a way in.

"I'm afraid she's asleep," Pendant said.

"Let's give a shout and see."

Pendant did not object, so Hairpin called out loudly, "Maestro White Orchid!"

No answer came. But there appeared on the curtain the silhouette of a woman tilting her head to listen. Hairpin called once more. The woman rolled up the curtains and opened the window to call down, "Who's there?"

Pendant recognized White Orchid's voice, so she spoke up, "It's us looking in on you. Are you going to bed now?"

On seeing them, White Orchid was overjoyed. "Come up now. I'm not going to bed yet."

"But your doors are already shut," said Hairpin.

"I'll open them. Just a minute!"

"Oh, don't bother. It's bedtime for us, too," said Pendant.

White Orchid was so anxious for them to stay that she stamped her feet and waved at them, saying, "Don't go! I'll let you in!"

Seeing how eager she was for company, Hairpin encouraged Pendant to stay a while. White Orchid's servant girl came to open the doors and light the way for them with a candle in an imported candleholder.

White Orchid came up to meet them and said, "I want to ask a favor: would you mind sleeping here tonight?"

An astounded Pendant asked, "Why?"

"Just think, there're so many rooms in Panorama Hall, and my servant girl and I are the only ones staying here. It's really creepy, and I'm too frightened to sleep. I was just going to call on you at Pear Blossom Court when you called out for me. I'd be ever so grateful if you'd keep me company for one night. I'll be all right tomorrow."

Hairpin dared not make the decision; she turned to ask Pendant.

After pondering over this, Pendant replied, "Basically, it's OK for us to sleep here, but it's best if we avoid any possible awkwardness. If you don't mind roughing it at our place, it's better for you to come with us."[1]

"It's indeed better that way. That won't be roughing it at all," White Orchid replied.

And so the servant girl blew out the oil lamp and held the candlestick up high to light the way down. She then shut and secured all

::

1. [As members of the family's theater troupe, the two girls have a lowly position and cannot stay in the guest quarters. It is only Qi's fondness for them that makes Pendant say, "It's basically OK." E.H.]

the doors. Pendant and Hairpin did not linger to admire the scenery but led White Orchid and the servant girl straight back to Pear Blossom Court. On finding the courtyard door tightly shut, they knocked repeatedly for a long time. It was quite some time before a sleepy old crone tottered out to open the door for them.

"Is there any hot water?" Hairpin asked at once.

"Hot water? You're asking for the impossible! D'you have any idea what time it is? The tea stove went out long go!" the old woman replied.

"Just shut the door and go to bed, and shut your mouth as well," Pendant said. Only then did the old woman hold her tongue.

The four of them went up to Pendant's room in the dark. Hairpin struck a match to light the candle the servant girl had brought and invited White Orchid to sit down. Pendant wanted to offer White Orchid her bed, but White Orchid would not permit it and instead suggested they share it. Pendant complied. Hairpin saw to the servant girl, settling her on the couch in the outer room. Pendant then found a copper tea kettle and burner and fetched water herself to make tea while Hairpin produced a big platter of Cantonese snacks. They put these before White Orchid, who felt uneasy for having caused them so much trouble.

The three of them sat around under the lamp, talking heart to heart. When they came to questions about family, it turned out that none of them had living parents. This increased the bond of sympathy among them.

"To be orphaned when you're little, now that's really miserable," Pendant said. "However caring your brother and sister-in-law may seem, they're always thinking how they can take advantage of you. A child doesn't know anything, not even when she's been swindled. If I had a father or mother, would I be here now?"

White Orchid responded, "Exactly. My parents had just been dead for three months when my paternal uncle sold me as a slave girl for a hundred dollars. Luckily I got wind of it and told my maternal uncle, who paid off the other uncle with his own life savings. That was when I entered the business. But I had no idea my maternal uncle was rotten as well. When my business got a bit better, he swindled five hundred dollars out of me and never showed his face again!"

Hairpin, seated beside them, listened in silence, her eyes bright with tears. White Orchid turned to look at her and ask, "How long have you been here?"

Pendant answered on her behalf, "Her case is even more disgusting. When she came here, her father came with her. At least she called him Father. Later, when I asked her, I found out that it wasn't her father at all. It was her stepmother's lover!"

White Orchid said, "The two of you are quite lucky to have ended up here, but my fate is destined to be a sad one. The trouble is I don't have a friend by my side. Whenever anything important happens, I brood about it all alone. Who can I talk to? When I'm upset about something, I just bottle it up because there's no one I can tell. It's *so* difficult to find even a maid or a servant girl who I can get on with."

"But you also have cause to feel satisfied as well; you're much better off than the two of us. Though we're together, what's the use? We haven't got the least bit of freedom, so how can we help anyone else? Besides, who knows if we'll still be together in a couple of years' time?" Pendant said.

"When it comes to the future, nobody can tell. Who knows where we'll end up? There's no other way but to live one day at a time and just see what happens."

Hairpin broke in, "Yes, you're right, for us it's living one day at a time. As for you, what's so hard about figuring out your future? Mr. Hua is extremely taken with you, and once you marry him, you can sit back and enjoy life. That's not difficult to foresee, is it?"

White Orchid burst out laughing. "You make it sound so easy. Well, if you put it that way, His Excellency is very nice too. Why don't you two marry him?"

"One moment you're speaking seriously, the next you want to make fun of us," Hairpin complained.

Pendant, however, nodded. "This is serious talk as well. When all's said and done, to be women in this world means we all have problems that we can't put into words. How would anyone else know about them? We're the only ones who do. I suppose you don't find Mr. Hua, good as he is, completely satisfactory, right?"

White Orchid put her palms together in silent applause. "You've hit the nail right on the head. A pity I'm not staying here long term. It feels good talking to you."

Hairpin commented, "Well, that's hard to say. We don't know if we'll be leaving this place, or if you'll be coming here, do we? As you said, we'll see what happens."

"If we get on well, it's not necessary for us to be together all the time. We'd feel happier even when we're not together."

On hearing this, White Orchid said excitedly, "Why don't the three of us be sworn sisters?"

Hairpin responded immediately, "Fine! Once we're sisters, we can look out for one another."

Just as Pendant was about to speak, there was a rustling sound outside, and, being timid by nature, she took a candle and pulled Hairpin along to check what it was. The moon had moved across the roof of the building; the bright stars had dimmed. Cocks were crowing in the surrounding countryside, but nothing stirred in the courtyard.

Having checked all around, they returned to the room, and the servant girl sleeping on the couch was awakened. Too tired to open her eyes, she asked, "What're you doing?" They told her. "The sound came from downstairs," she said. And, sure enough, they heard the rustling sound again. It was the girls in the troupe who slept downstairs getting up to use the chamber pots.

After calling aloud to confirm it was the girls, they returned to the room, closed the door, and said to White Orchid, "It's almost dawn. We ought to go to bed."

White Orchid agreed. Hairpin invited her to have more tea and snacks and then put the things away and tidied up before returning to her own room next door for bed. Pendant got up onto the bed and laid out two coverlets and then asked White Orchid to undress and take her place.

Having missed her usual bedtime, White Orchid could not sleep. She tossed and turned, but Pendant was quiet and motionless. Hairpin next door was snoring faintly. Then a crow skimmed over the rooftop, cawing. White Orchid lifted the bed curtains to peer out and found the white of dawn had illuminated the windows. She called Pendant's name in a low voice, but no answer came. Draping her clothes over her shoulders, she decided to sit up in bed. Actually, Pendant was not asleep; she was just resting with her eyes closed. When she heard White Orchid sitting up, she did the same, and they started chatting.

"What d'you say to our becoming sworn sisters?" White Orchid asked.

"It seems to me we can look out for each other even if we're not sworn sisters. But if we want to do it, let's do it today."

"Good, we'll do it today. But how?"

"For us, it's all a matter of how we feel, so we can do without the empty show of feasting and presents. We'll just buy a set of incense and candles, and when night time comes, the three of us will quietly kowtow several times. That'll be all."

"Fine. I think the less fuss the better."

Seeing that it was already full daylight, Pendant wound up her hair simply, got off the bed, felt for her slippers, and then went to the area behind the bed. After a while, she came out, washed her hands, blew out the oil lamp on the dressing table, and returned to bed, where she sat hugging the coverlet. She asked White Orchid in a relaxed manner, "As sworn sisters, we're like family; there's nothing that can't be said between ourselves, so I'd like to ask you about Mr. Hua. He seems quite all right to us. Why d'you find him unsatisfactory?"

White Orchid sighed before she spoke. "Even talking about it makes me feel frustrated! There isn't anything unsatisfactory about him as a person, and we get along very well in every way—except for one thing. He is a man who fails to get ninety-nine things done out of a hundred. Anything that involves him personally, he won't do. Even if you ask him to do the tiniest thing, he'll consider thoroughly every aspect from every angle and make sure there's no catch before he agrees. And if any busybody says it's no good, then that's the end of it. Now think about it, with a temperament like that, can he possibly marry me? Even if he wanted to, he'd never get round to it."

"We always thought it was so easy for maestros and misses if they wanted to marry; they could choose whoever is a good sort and marry him. Having heard what you said about Mr. Hua, it seems you have your difficulties as well."

Now it was White Orchid's turn for questioning. "I want to ask you, too: do the two of you think you'll get married?"

Pendant also sighed before she answered. "Things can't be any more difficult for us. As we're alone here, it doesn't matter if I tell you a little about it. We've been here since we were little, so naturally we have to let His Excellency have his way with us. But because of that, things are now really awkward. His Excellency is over sixty, and should anything happen to him, we'll be caught in between—neither mistress nor servant. What'll people think of us? It'll be too late to think of marrying then!"

"Hairpin was saying you might leave this place; is this what she meant?"

"She's an intelligent girl; the only problem with her is the way she talks. Though she's already fourteen, she doesn't know anything about weighing her words and speaks whatever comes into her head. Just think, how can we say things like that at this time? Fortunately, she said it in front of you. If it had been somebody else, who then told His Excellency, we'd have been in a fine fix."

Pendant yawned as she spoke, so White Orchid suggested, "Let's sleep a while longer."

"Indeed we should."

White Orchid also made a trip to the place behind the bed. She saw a ray of sunlight had come in through the window, and the old women downstairs were getting up to open the gate and sweep the courtyard. It was around seven o'clock. The two of them hastened to lie down. "When you get up, please wake me as well," White Orchid said.

"We'll have a lie-in. It doesn't matter," Pendant replied.

Exhausted both mentally and physically, they fell asleep before they knew it and did not get up until one o'clock in the afternoon. When Hairpin heard them, she came in to tell them merrily, "There was a big joke today. It was said that two courtesans in the garden had run away. A huge number of people ran around creating havoc everywhere, and that went on until I got up and explained what happened."

White Orchid could not help smiling.

Pendant told the old woman to relay the order to the household buyer to get a pair of large candles with cash payment and not to list them in the accounts. White Orchid also gave orders to her servant girl, "Make a trip home after lunch and on your way back go to the Qiao residence again and see if there's any message for me."

The servant girl left on her mission together with the old woman.

"Are we going to become sworn sisters today?" Hairpin asked anxiously. White Orchid nodded in reply.

Pendant warned her, "Would you please mind your tongue? All that talk about 'runaway courtesans'! If Aroma had heard you, she'd have started imagining things. For that matter, this business of our becoming sworn sisters must be kept from Aroma as well. If she knows about it, she's sure to want to join in. That'd be such a letdown."

Hairpin gave her promise repeatedly, saying, "I haven't told anyone about it."

White Orchid said, "Well, don't mention it before we become sisters. Once the ceremony is over, it won't matter. It's all open and aboveboard, and we're not hurting anybody by doing so."

Hairpin again promised to act as instructed. As they were talking, Aroma arrived and started interrogating the old women downstairs. On hearing her voice, Pendant called out "Maestro" from the window, and Aroma came up to greet them and deliver the host's request for White Orchid's company at lunch. White Orchid immediately took her leave from Pendant and Hairpin and followed Aroma to the Moon-worshiper's Chamber.

When Harmony Qi saw White Orchid, he said, "It didn't occur to me last night that no one else was at your place. Today I'll have Aroma keep you company, and tomorrow night Iron Hua will be here."

"Oh, please don't!" White Orchid said in a panic. "I'm quite comfortable at Pear Blossom Court. We've agreed that I should go there tonight as well."

"Then let Aroma go with you. You'll have one more companion for your conversation," Harmony said.

"I can't agree. Aren't I the same as Maestro Aroma? If you treat me as a guest, Your Excellency, I'd be too embarrassed to stay on. I'm going home!"

Upon hearing this, Aroma tugged at Harmony's sleeve. "Don't interfere if you don't know what's going on! They're such a merry crowd at Pear Blossom Court, what would I do there?"

Harmony smiled and brushed the matter aside.

Soon Jade Tao, River Blossom, Modesty Zhu, and Twin Jade all sent word to excuse themselves from lunch, while Second Bai, Wenjun Yao, and Devotion Yin arrived one after the other and joined them at the table. Second Bai and Wenjun Yao, who were suffering from hangovers, did not drink. Devotion Yin, who felt exhausted, just rubbed his eyes and stretched himself, not even bothering to eat. Knowing White Orchid could hold her liquor, Harmony Qi told Aroma to urge her to drink. White Orchid barely wetted her lips and then upended her cup and begged to be excused.

They dispersed after the meal. Devotion Yin returned to his room to rest, while Second Bai and Wenjun Yao sauntered about. White Orchid also stepped into the courtyard. Aroma noticed that she was going back to Pear Blossom Court. She smiled and was about to say something to Harmony but thought better of it and checked herself. Harmony noticed this, however, and said, "Whatever you were going to say, just go ahead."

Aroma was searching for an excuse when Greenie came in to say that the lady concubine wanted to trace some embroidery patterns. Aroma looked at Harmony, awaiting his wishes. As it was time for his afternoon nap, he said to her, "All right, go on ahead."

"Would you like me to fetch Pendant?" Aroma asked.

He gave it a moment's thought and then answered, "No, never mind."

Aroma left word with the menservants standing on duty beyond the curtain to wait on Qi attentively and then went with Greenie to the inner courtyards.

Harmony Qi had a good nap. When the clock struck four, and there was still no sign of Aroma, he took a walk to kill time. As he strolled along, he found that he had passed through the garden's inner gate, which led to the residence. He was going to look for Aroma, but now he suddenly thought of Dragon Ma, so he turned around and made for the study. There, he and Dragon Ma talked tirelessly until nightfall. He had supper there before he took his leave, ready to return to the inner courtyards.

He had just left the study when he ran into Aroma, who, all agitated, shouted the minute she saw him, "Why on earth did you come here all by yourself? I looked for you everywhere in the garden; it's worse than hide-and-seek!"

He calmed her down a bit, took her by the hand, and ambled along with her. When they got to the fork at the inner garden gate, she urged him to go to Panorama Hall. Though not enthusiastic, he obliged. They walked back into the garden and passed the lake house occupied by the Taos and Zhus without going in. When they approached the Bridge of Nine Twists, Aroma deliberately turned around and exclaimed in fake surprise, "Is that the moon?"

Harmony turned to look. He saw bright lamplight shining from the windows of Pear Blossom Court. Reflected by the whitewashed walls, it illuminated the entire courtyard, turning it a glowing red.

"I wonder what they're doing," she said.

"Playing mah-jongg, perhaps?"

"Let's go and find out."

"Oh, let's not be a nuisance. We shouldn't break up their party."

And so she reluctantly followed him to Panorama Hall, their original destination.

CHAPTER 53 :: *Flowers of different types are forcibly grafted together, and mating birds are driven asunder by a sudden alarm*

Harmony Qi took Aroma with him to Panorama Hall. It so happened that both Second Bai and Wenjun Yao were in Devotion Yin's room. There were greetings all round. Second Bai had a slim, roughly bound volume in his hand and was about to start reading. Harmony Qi saw from the label on the cover that it contained exercises in civil service examination essays written by the announcer, who had brought it to Devotion Yin to ask for his opinion and help. Harmony asked Devotion, "Has he made any progress lately?"

"Not bad. He's showing some spark," Devotion replied.

As they were talking, Wenjun Yao was also engaged in an animated conversation with Aroma. The latter could only manage to get a word in now and then. Harmony heard they were talking about mah-jongg, so he called out to Wenjun, "White Orchid is having a game now. Go over there if you feel like it."

"I'm sure they're not playing. If they are, they'd have sent for me, wouldn't they?" Wenjun replied.

"Are you a really good player then?" Harmony asked.

She just grinned.

Aroma cut in, "She plays an awfully aggressive game. Only Pendant can match her. I'm always losing."

"I wouldn't call her aggressive," Second Bai said.

Wenjun responded, "Of course I'm not aggressive. The aggressive one, sadly, played a bad hand!"

"I didn't play a bad hand the other day," Second Bai said. "I just failed to get the right tiles."

Wenjun stood up abruptly, yelling, "You didn't play badly, eh? Get the tiles out and show everybody the hand!" So saying, she turned to Devotion, "Where's your set?"

Devotion hastened to stop her. "All right, all right, there's nothing worth seeing. You're never wrong and that's that."

But would she just drop the matter? She opened the cupboard to search for the box of mah-jongg tiles.

"It's not in the cupboard. Pendant borrowed it and hasn't returned it yet," Devotion lied.

Frustrated, Wenjun turned around to face them and gesticulated histrionically as she recalled the tiles in Second Bai's hand, recounting his every move and asking them to be the judge. Harmony and Aroma laughed.

Devotion said with a frown, "Don't you have any sense of shame? You two are always fighting or quarreling, and I have the rotten luck to be staying in the room across from you and be disturbed by the racket you make."

Second Bai just laughed, but Wenjun said icily, "Aren't you bored with yourself? You're always repeating the same thing over and over. Everybody has heard it before. Haven't you got anything new to tell us?"

This left Devotion completely stumped. Second Bai rubbed his hands and laughed uproariously. When Harmony changed the subject, Wenjun let the matter rest.

After a while, the moon rose and was level with the treetops. Everyone was a little tired, so Harmony and Aroma got up and took their leave. Devotion saw them out at the door, while Second Bai and Wenjun, who were returning to their own room, saw them off at the stairs. Holding Aroma by the hand, Harmony slowly descended the stairs in Panorama Hall, crossed the Bridge of Nine Twists, and saw that Pear Blossom Court was still brilliantly lit. Now that the moonlight was shining on it, however, there was no red glow.

"Let's go and see if they're playing mah-jongg," Aroma egged him on.

"Why are you in such a hurry to find out? Just ask White Orchid tomorrow," Harmony said.

Aroma could not very well insist. They left the garden behind and returned to the inner courtyards, where they went to bed together. No more was said.

The next morning, Harmony rose at eight. Servants came in to relay the message that Mr. Hua was here. He went straight to the garden and asked Iron Hua to meet him at the Moon-worshiper's Chamber.

"I guessed right; I knew you'd be the first to arrive today," Harmony began by teasing him.

Iron Hua looked embarrassed. Harmony told the menservants to ask Maestro White Orchid to come over at once.

In a moment, Jade Tao, Modesty Zhu, Second Bai, Devotion Yin, River Blossom, Twin Jade, Wenjun Yao, Aroma Su, and White Orchid all arrived by different routes. Iron Hua greeted them, bowing.

White Orchid asked in a low voice, "Mr. Hua, were you busy yesterday? Are you quite well?"

"I'm all right," Iron Hua replied. "When everything was settled yesterday, I thought I'd look in on you, but I saw your servant girl, so instead of coming here I just gave her a dozen bottles of champagne to take back with her. Did you get them?"

"Yes, thank you. How could I ever drink a dozen bottles? I gave half of them away as gifts."

Devotion Yin pointed at them behind their backs and joked in a hushed and merry voice to Modesty Zhu, "Look, the two of them are *so* polite. It's as if they haven't seen each other for ages."

Second Bai heard him and joked back in a similarly hushed voice, "Oh, this involves real style beyond description; it's not mere politeness."

They all laughed, covering their mouths with their hands. Although Iron Hua and White Orchid were standing some distance away, they knew the joke was on them and immediately stopped their exchange. This caused Harmony Qi to say with regret, "It was just getting interesting, and your laughter killed it all!"

At this everyone laughed louder than ever. Pretending not to notice, Iron Hua tried to make conversation. "Devotion, where're your two ladies?"

"They haven't arrived yet," Devotion replied with a smile.

The words were hardly out of his mouth when in came Cloud Tao with Belle Tan and Flora Zhang and Amity Zhu with White Fragrance and Green Fragrance. The general greeting that ensued was friendly and informal. Amity Zhu took an opened letter from his sleeve and respectfully handed it to Harmony. Harmony looked at the envelope and found that it was from Whistler Tang to Amity, posted in Hangzhou. The gist of it was as follows: "Having given his consent to the marriage, Script Li has asked Crane Li and Old Merit Yu to serve as matchmakers. They'll take the small steamship on the evening of the twentieth, arriving in Shanghai after a journey of a day and a night. Everything will be settled in face-to-face consultation, but it is important that the groom's family invite one more person to serve as matchmaker," and so on.

When Harmony had finished reading, he put the letter down. "Who're you asking?"

"I've just asked Cloud," Amity replied.

"I'm all keen to be a matchmaker, yet you didn't ask me," said Harmony.

"You've done it before; this time it's my turn," Cloud said, at which everyone laughed.

Modesty, however, was stunned by this news. He drew near the table and peeped at the letter, but before he could read more than a phrase or two, his brother Amity put it away. Modesty's heart thumped wildly, yet his face revealed nothing. He paced back to where he had been sitting and glanced surreptitiously at Twin Jade. Seeing that she did not seem to notice anything wrong, he felt a bit more at ease.

Next a manservant came to report, "Mr. Ge is here." They saw Elan Ge come in with Snow Scent and Sunset Wei.

"Did you bring Sunset here?" Harmony Qi asked in surprise.

"No, we met Sunset at the garden gate," Elan Ge replied.

Realizing his own mistake, Harmony told the manservant to ask Secretary Ma to come at once.

Devotion said to Harmony, "These two are going to have a son soon. If you like matchmaking, why don't you make a match for them?"

Before anyone else could respond, Cloud said, "They don't need matchmakers. The two of them quietly lit a pair of big red candles and performed the wedding rites at her place. I was at their wedding feast." Everyone roared with laughter.

Aroma went up to Harmony Qi and took his arm. "Do you know what Maestro White Orchid was doing last night if she wasn't playing mah-jongg?"

"I haven't asked her," Harmony said.

"Well, I did. She, too, lit a pair of big red candles and performed all the rites."

Harmony was very much amazed. White Orchid then related in detail how she and the other two girls had become sworn sisters.

"It's nice to be sworn sisters, but why just the three of you?" Harmony said. "Why not everybody all together? I'll sponsor the union. Last night doesn't count. Today, when all the maestros and misses have arrived, you'll all kowtow once more and be sisters, all right?"

White Orchid was silent, while Aroma put a fingertip between her teeth to stop herself laughing. None of the others noticed anything.

Harmony told Greenie to summon Pendant and Hairpin.

Second Bai said to Harmony, "Now, this is right up your alley. You're so enthusiastic about this that you don't even want to match-make any more."

"If this is right up my alley, I've got work for you, too. Write me a preface in parallel prose on the theme of sworn sisters. At the end of that, we'll list the names of the members of the union, each with a short biography giving details of age, appearance, where she comes from, and whether her parents are alive or dead. You will each be responsible for the biography of your lady love, and I'll do the ones for Aroma, Pendant, and Hairpin. The title will be *A Collection of Flowers on the Sea*. What d'you think?"

Everyone was ready to follow his instructions. Harmony told the announcer to get writing materials ready, while Second Bai deliberated on a draft of the essay. Nature Shi happened to come in just then with Second Treasure, and Dragon Ma, Pendant, and Hairpin also arrived in the Moon-worshiper's Chamber. Everyone eagerly told them about the idea of sworn sisters and the biographies. Both Nature Shi and Dragon Ma responded, "I'm at your service."

The men took up their writing brushes and dashed the biographies off in no time. It took less than an hour for the biographies as well as Second Bai's preface in parallel prose to be completed. Harmony Qi asked Devotion Yin to take a look at the whole collection before giving it to the announcer to make a fair copy. After having done so, Devotion commented, "It turns out to be quite interesting. Second Bai's preface is just what we would expect—full of learned allusions that show depth and wide knowledge, and it's beautifully written. The biographies are well worth reading, too. Pendant, Hairpin, and the two Fragrances have joint biographies. Second Treasure's and Flora's biographies complement each other. River Blossom's is based on the life of Water Blossom. Aroma's does not mention her elder sisters directly, but their presence is obvious. The rest are based on their words or on events in their lives or are discursive in nature. There is infinite variety, and each one is excellent in its own way."

Everyone was delighted to hear this, Harmony Qi most of all.

By then it was noon. The menservants on duty got the tables ready for lunch. Hairpin took the opportunity to pull Pendant over to the porch surreptitiously and asked, "His Excellency is telling everybody to become sworn sisters. Shall we do it?"

"Of course we should do as His Excellency says. It matters little that we join the rest."

"But what about the three of us becoming sisters, will it mean that doesn't count?"

"Oh, you're so mixed up. Why shouldn't it count? The three of us became sworn sisters because we are fond of one another. As sisters, we're just fonder, that's all. Now His Excellency tells us to be sisters with the others, but whether we like them is up to us. His Excellency can't do anything about that, right?"

Hairpin nodded silently, her misgivings dispelled. When they heard the guests taking their seats for lunch, they went unobtrusively back into the room and stood to one side. Unexpectedly, Harmony told the two girls to join them at the table and to sit on the humble side of Aroma. Pendant and Hairpin sat with their hands tucked away and their heads bowed, feeling ill at ease in that company.

When the wine had gone three rounds and two sets of dishes had been served, Harmony Qi said to Nature Shi, "This time you brought many things to Shanghai, none of which is of use. There's just one good thing I want from you, but you won't give it to me. Now that I'm giving you your farewell dinner, if I'm still too polite to ask for it, I'll never get it. Couldn't you spare me some?"

A little startled, Nature asked, "What is it?"

Harmony laughed. "What I want is in your head. Even Second Treasure has a pair of scrolls you wrote for her, and I don't even have that. Isn't that too much of a slight?"

Catching his drift, Nature said, "I didn't know what to write because you have so many fine pieces on the walls here. If you insist that I make a fool of myself, Uncle, I will of course obey. Just give me time, and I'll present my effort for your correction."

Harmony saluted him in thanks, after which Iron Hua asked why this was a farewell dinner.

"I got a letter from home. They want me to make a trip back before the end of the month," Nature replied.

"If you want to see him off with a dinner, you can pair up with Elan Ge. You might as well make it the twenty-seventh and have it here. That'd be nice, wouldn't it?" said Harmony.

"We could do it earlier," Iron Hua said.

"Well, that's the earliest day available. Starting from tomorrow, the twenty-fourth, everybody is occupied. The twenty-fifth is Gao's and Yin's farewell dinner for him, the twenty-sixth is Tao's and Zhu's, so you and Elan will have to wait till the twenty-seventh," Harmony said.

Iron Hua called out to Elan to make the appointment, and Nature saluted them in thanks.

Just then, the announcer submitted a meticulous copy of *A Collection of Flowers on the Sea* for Harmony Qi's perusal. Harmony told the menservants to relay orders for a table with incense to be set up in Right Target Hall and then had the announcer pass the copy of *A Collection* around the tables. Elan Ge saw that the handwriting was modeled on the famous clerical script of the Taoist classic *Flying Spirit* by the famous Song dynasty calligrapher Wang Xizhi. It was so elegant and appealing, he could not help eyeing the announcer.

"Don't you underestimate him," Second Bai said with a teasing smile. "His title is 'Fine Son of an Announcer; Brilliant Student of a Genius.'"

Devotion cut in, "If you like being the butt of sarcasm, you're welcome. Just leave me out of it."

The announcer chuckled beside them. Elan did not understand what it was all about.

"His father is the ceremonial announcer," Devotion explained. "And he often writes poems and essays for me to correct. Because of that, Second Bai played a trick on him. He gave him a line to match: 'Fine son of an announcer.' He couldn't match it, so Second Bai said, 'Let me do it for you: "Brilliant student of a genius."' Isn't it a perfect match?"

Elan recited it once over and said, "Very well matched."

The announcer had just taken the copy of *A Collection* to the other tables. Devotion now whispered in Elan's ear, "He may be young, but he's wicked! His father asked him, 'Why didn't you match the line Mr. Gao gave you?' He said, 'I did, but because Mr. Yin was there, I couldn't say it.' When asked what his match was, he said, 'Unworldly crony of a minister.'"

Elan laughed uproariously. "It might as well be 'whoring crony.' Let it all hang out!"

Both Second Bai and Devotion laughed over this for quite a while.

When the last four courses had been served, the menservants came to replace the wine cups with large wine tumblers, but everybody stopped them. In anticipation of hearty drinking that night, they did not want to indulge themselves fully just yet, and Harmony did not press them. They had rice and then left the table.

Now Harmony Qi formally invited the sisters to perform the rites and their clients to supervise the union. With a smile, the men proceeded to carry out his order, each leading his girl to Right Target Hall. They saw that the bamboo curtains in front of the hall had been rolled up. In the hall, two candles were burning bright and incense smoke was rising up. A large scarlet carpet was spread on the floor. The men spread out on both sides to oversee the ceremony. The announcer stood on the humble side and chanted out the names, and the sisters ranged themselves according to age in two rows, making the formation of wild geese in flight. They faced inward and kowtowed four times, after which they turned to kowtow four times to each other. After the ceremony, they addressed one another according to age. At twenty-three, Sunset was the oldest and was thus Eldest Sister. At twelve, River Blossom was the youngest and thus Fourteenth Sister. As it was hard to remember the order for the rest, everybody just muddled through with either the addition of Elder Sister or Younger Sister to their names.

Harmony Qi was in ecstasy. He entreated the sisters to remain cordial from then on and not to forget today's union. The sisters smiled and gave their promise and then followed the men down the steps of Right Target Hall. There happened to be a little sorrel grazing under the podium with its saddle and bridle on. To show off her skill, Wenjun Yao took the reins, mounted, and started cantering back and forth along the archery path. Everybody scattered at her approach.

After watching Wenjun, Pendant turned around and could not find Harmony Qi, so she went looking for him. She caught sight of him heading west on his own, taking a walk, so she quietly gave Hairpin a tug. They left the others behind to follow him.

Harmony did not sense their presence. He kept on his track toward the Moon-worshiper's Chamber. When he reached the slope, he suddenly caught sight of someone ducking stealthily into the bamboo grove. He thought it was Modesty Zhu going after crickets, so he also tiptoed forward, thinking he'd give him a fright. It was only when he drew near that he realized it was the announcer; the latter was gesturing, as if pleading with someone.[1] Harmony stood still and loudly cleared his throat. Filled with fear, the announcer turned an ashen gray. He immediately stood in attendance, his hands pressed flat against his body and not a sound came out of him.

"Who else is here?" Harmony asked.

"There isn't anybody," he stuttered.

Behind them, Hairpin pointed, saying, "There, over there!" Taken unaware by her presence, Harmony also got a fright. Pendant hastened to signal her with her eyes, warning her to keep quiet. But Harmony questioned Hairpin, "What were you saying?"

Hairpin had no choice but to point once more. When Harmony turned around, he saw there was indeed a figure in the shadows, threading through the bush and trees to make her escape.

Harmony dismissed the announcer angrily. He then walked up

::

1. [The announcer is obviously having an affair with a courtesan's servant girl. *E.H.*]

the steps with Pendant and Hairpin. These led up the slope at the back of Moon-worshiper's Chamber. Cassia trees had been planted all over the hill, their interlocking branches growing luxuriantly. A three-roomed little house built like a boat nestled in the green shade, bearing the signboard "Fragrant Slumber." He walked into the inner cabin, sat down on the couch, and questioned Hairpin, "Who did you see?"

She did not answer, just looked toward Pendant, so he turned to ask Pendant.

"We didn't see very clearly, to tell the truth," Pendant replied.

He sighed. "When I ask you a question, is there anything that you can't tell me?"

"It wasn't anybody from our garden. Just let them be," Pendant replied.

After a brief moment of reflection, Harmony put aside the matter and asked instead, "When I left, everybody was watching the horse ride. When did you two start following me?"

"Didn't you notice, Your Excellency? We were following you all along," Hairpin said.

"You were too busy looking in front of you to know that we were behind you," Pendant said.

"Perhaps you should have looked behind you as well. Maybe somebody else was following you," he said.

"There couldn't have been anybody else," said Hairpin.

"Unless it was Aroma," Pendant said.

Upon hearing this, Hairpin actually went outside to check. Harmony immediately stood up and took Pendant's hand, saying with a smile, "Let's go to the Moon-worshiper's Chamber." But before he could make a move, Hairpin announced loudly, "Fifth Young Mr. Zhu is here."

Greatly surprised, Harmony looked out and saw that the handsome Modesty Zhu was indeed approaching them on his own. Harmony invited him to sit down on the couch. For a long while, Modesty remained silent.

"I heard you caught an invincible warrior the day before yesterday; is it true?" Harmony asked, just to make conversation.

Modesty answered vaguely but gave no more details.

There was another long pause. Then Modesty blushed a little and stole a glance at those around him, as though he could not make up his mind whether to speak or not. Puzzled, Harmony tipped Pendant a wink and told her to order tea. At this, Pendant withdrew, taking Hairpin with her. Harmony was left alone with Modesty in the House of Fragrant Slumber.

Seeing that they were alone in the House of Fragrant Slumber, Modesty Zhu spoke hesitantly to Harmony Qi, "Elder Brother tells me to go home tomorrow. I wonder what it's about."

"Your brother got you engaged. Didn't you know about it?" Harmony said, smiling pleasantly.

"That's always the trouble with Elder Brother," Modesty said with a frown, his head bowed low.

Harmony was astonished to hear this. "What's wrong with getting you engaged?"

"There's nothing wrong, but why the hurry? Could you please put in a word with Elder Brother to cancel this engagement?"

Harmony had a good idea what was on Modesty's mind from the way he looked but decided to probe him further, "What d'you mean?" He repeated the question several times, but no answer came. Modesty just could not get the words out.

Harmony then spoke to him seriously, "You shouldn't say that to your brother. At your age, it's time to get engaged, and since you've lost your parents, naturally your brother makes the decision for you. Nothing can be better than getting engaged to Script Li's daughter; there's no warmer friendship than his. But instead of being grateful to your brother, you're telling him to cancel the engagement! Not only would he be angry, but just think for yourself: the matchmakers have all arrived, and the betrothal gifts have been prepared; is it possible for your brother to turn them down now?"

Modesty said not a word.

"Though you're engaged, it's important to make sure that everybody's willing," Harmony said. "If there's anything not to your liking, just say so, and we'll talk it over. The way I look at it, the most important thing for you is to get engaged. The earlier the engagement, the earlier the wedding; then you can take Twin Jade home at the same time. Wouldn't that be nice?"

Hearing this, Modesty swallowed hard, hesitated a while, and again mumbled, "Now that you mention Twin Jade, in the beginning it was Elder Brother who first called her to parties for me, and it was also Elder Brother who told me to have a dinner party at her place. Right after that, Twin Jade asked me if I wanted to marry her. She said she came from a respectable family and ended up in a brothel just this year, that she had only spent one season as a virgin courtesan. She wanted me to promise to marry her, and she said she would not take on another patron. Well, I did give her my word."

"If you want to take Twin Jade as your concubine, that's easy enough, but you won't be able to make her your wife. Look at Jade Tao, he wanted to marry Water Blossom after his first wife died, and he never succeeded. In your case, it'd be a first marriage, so it's hopeless."[1]

Modesty again bowed his head and frowned. After a while, he said, "That's the rub. Twin Jade is awfully stubborn by nature. Ever since she got here, she's been talking about buying back her freedom. She told me that if I take another wife, she will drink raw opium and kill herself."

Harmony could not suppress his chuckle. "Don't you worry. Courtesans all talk like that. You don't have to take it seriously."

Modesty looked chastened, but inwardly he was deeply agitated, so he said helplessly, "At first, I didn't believe it, either, but Twin Jade is not like the others. From the look of it, she isn't bluffing. Now if anything happens, it won't be funny."

Harmony waved his hand to show he disagreed, "What can happen?" he asked. "I guarantee the show will go on, all right? Don't you worry."

Modesty saw that they were talking at cross-purposes, so he knew it was no use saying anything else. Just then, the manservant from the tea kitchen brought tea, and Harmony politely urged him to drink. Having taken a sip, Modesty got up to take his leave. Harmony walked him to the door and offered this advice: "I suggest you tell Twin Jade at once that your elder brother wants you to be engaged. If she has anything to say, just put all the blame on your brother."

Modesty acknowledged this absently.

When they ambled out of the House of Fragrant Slumber, Pendant and Hairpin were waiting for them at the door and followed them down the slope of the hill, where they went their separate ways. Harmony Qi headed west with Pendant and Hairpin to the Moon-worshiper's Chamber, while Modesty Zhu walked eastward by himself. He thought, "Harmony is well-known for being the leader of the love cult, yet even he wouldn't help bring a happy ending to this romance. What's to be done? If Twin Jade learns about this, there's no telling how far she'll go." He pondered long and hard but could see no way out. When he reached the archery path, he found that all those who had been watching the horse ride had dispersed. Only two menservants remained in Right Target Hall to make sure that the

::

1. [Despite Qi's earlier claim that he could have brought a happy ending to Jade Tao and Water Blossom by adopting the latter as his daughter, here he shows his true feelings about the proper position for a courtesan. *E.H.*]

incense and candles did not start a fire. Modesty retraced his steps and ran straight into Aroma. "Where's Our Excellency gone off to; did you see him, Fifth Young Master?" she asked cheerfully.

"He's at the Moon-worshiper's Chamber."

"But I didn't see him there," she said.

"Well, he has just gone there."

On hearing this, she turned to go at once. He called to stop her, asking, "Have you seen Twin Jade?"

She pointed and said something that he did not catch, but he followed the direction she indicated to continue his search in the lake house. As he entered the courtyard, he caught a whiff of opium scent and knew Amity must be smoking in his bedroom. Instead of disturbing him, he returned to his own room, where, sure enough, he found Twin Jade. A large number of porcelain bowls littered the table, and she was feeding the crickets with powdered lotus seeds. When she saw Modesty, she happily conferred with him on how to take the crickets home the next day.

Modesty was listless. Twin Jade thought he was unhappy about their temporary separation and comforted him with loving words. He tried to tell her about his betrothal several times but each time stopped for lack of courage. It also occurred to him that it would be unseemly if she made a scene there, so he decided to leave it until they were home. He tried his best to converse and joke as usual.

When evening came, lamps were lit and the feasting began. The hall was filled with musicians to entertain them. Harmony was in high spirits, pressing wine on everybody and asking them to join in the drinking games. After the merrymaking, he produced *A Collection of Flowers on the Sea* and wanted a eulogy for each of the sisters appended to the biography. Everybody applauded the idea, so Modesty Zhu, too, had to do his part somehow. He managed to get through the night.

The next afternoon, carriages and sedan chairs awaited the guests. Apart from Dragon Ma, Second Bai Gao, Devotion Yin, and Wen-jun Yao, only Iron Hua and White Orchid had been persuaded to stay on. The rest, including Nature Shi, Elan Ge, Cloud Tao, Jade Tao, Amity Zhu, Modesty Zhu, Second Treasure, Snow Scent, Belle Tan, River Blossom, White Fragrance, Twin Jade, Sunset, Flora Zhang, and Green Fragrance, all took their leave to go home.

Harmony said to Jade Tao, "You're just going for Water Blossom's 'spirit return day.'[2] Come back as soon as it's over."

::

2. [It is believed that the spirit of the dead revisits her old home on the twenty-first day after her death. That day marks the end of the rituals of mourning. *E.H.*]

"I think I'll go home tomorrow," Jade said. "I'll definitely come again on the twenty-fifth."

Since Jade was going home, Harmony could not very well insist. He turned to Modesty Zhu instead. "You can come right away tomorrow, can't you?"

Afraid he would reveal the matter of the betrothal, Modesty evaded the question.

The group left Conical Hat Garden and went their different ways. Modesty's and Twin Jade's carriage made straight for Sunshine Alley, where Twin Jade bade him in no uncertain terms, "Come as soon as you can."

Modesty gave his promise repeatedly and watched as Pearlie helped Twin Jade into the alley, supporting her by the elbow, before he returned to Middle Peace Alley. He saw that his brother, Amity, was already home and was attending to various matters in the parlor. At loose ends, Modesty went to the study, where he sat brooding, thinking that Twin Jade absolutely must not be told. "I'll keep it from her for now and talk it over in due time," he thought.

When it was almost four o'clock in the afternoon, the doorman came in to announce, "Mr. Tang is here." Etiquette demanded that Modesty go out and greet him. Dispensing with the usual greetings, Whistler Tang told Amity urgently, "Pragmatic Li came with us. He and the others are still in the boat."

Amity immediately dispatched three invitations and three mandarin's sedan chairs to the pier to fetch Old Merit Yu, Pragmatic Li, and Crane Li. Then he sent a servant to West Civic Peace Alley to ask Mr. Tao to come at once. Unexpectedly Cloud Tao was not at Belle's place, and neither did they know his whereabouts.

Amity had become quite agitated by the time Cloud presented himself without being summoned. Seeing Whistler Tang, he said by way of greeting, "It's been a while."

Amity could hardly wait to ask him, "Where did you go? We couldn't even find you."

"I was in East Prosperity Alley," Cloud said with a smile.

"What were you doing there?" Amity asked.

Cloud smiled and then frowned, "It's Jade again. We've just wound up Water Blossom's affairs and up pops River Blossom. It's quite an awkward business."

"Whatever's the matter?" asked Amity.

Cloud sighed before he spoke. "When Water Blossom was still alive, she had said something about having Jade marry her younger sister. So now Fair Sister Li has handed River Blossom over to Jade and said he should take her as concubine when she's a bit older."

"Well, that's not a bad thing," Amity said.

"Except Jade would have none of it. He said, 'I've ruined one life already; I'm not going to ruin another. If River Blossom comes to me, she'll be my adopted daughter, and I'll marry her off.'"

"Well, that's not a bad thing, either," said Amity.

"But Fair Sister insisted on giving her to Jade as his concubine! She said poor Water Blossom never got to marry Jade, so now River Blossom is to be her surrogate. If River Blossom is lucky enough to have a son by him, Water Blossom would be considered the source of such a blessing, and there'd be someone who'd remember her."

Having heard all this, Amity nodded in sympathy. Whistler Tang cut in, "Every one of them makes sense. It really is an awkward business."

"I've thought of a way out, though, so it's all right," Cloud said.

As he spoke, Longevity came running in with two red calling cards to announce the arrival of guests. Amity and Modesty Zhu hurriedly put on their hats and formal robes before they went forth to welcome Old Merit and Crane Li. The two men alighted from their sedan chairs and walked into the parlor, saluting their hosts, and then seated themselves on the divan, where they were served tea.

"Why isn't your esteemed uncle coming?" Amity inquired.

"Uncle is not feeling very well. He's here to see a doctor. He appreciates your kind invitation, regretting that he can only enjoy your hospitality in spirit, and told me to convey his thanks."

Amity turned to exchange a few pleasantries with Old Merit and then invited them all into a reception room by the parlor where they could remove their hats and formal robes. Cloud Tao and Whistler Tang were asked to join them there. Everybody made small talk, but Modesty Zhu said nothing.

Soon Old Merit got to their chief business. He told them of Script Li's wishes and conferred with them over the betrothal and wedding ceremonies. Modesty was glad to take this opportunity to excuse himself.[3] Longevity, thinking he would get into Modesty's good books, snatched a free moment and went to the study to congratulate him, going down on one knee. Disgusted with the man's interfering nature, Modesty glared at him angrily. Longevity withdrew in embarrassment.

That evening, Longevity came to ask Modesty to attend the banquet, so Modesty had to return to the reception room and keep the dinner guests company. By then, the arrangements for his marriage

::

3. [The bride and groom are not supposed to have any say and would be considered extremely immodest if they did not absent themselves during such discussions. *E.H.*]

had been settled, and nothing was said about it at the table. When dinner was over, Old Merit, Crane Li and Cloud Tao thanked their hosts and took their leave. Amity and Modesty saw them to their sedan chairs. Though Whistler Tang stayed behind, he was such a close friend that there was no need to entertain him, so Modesty withdrew again to the study. Nothing more needs to be said.

On the twenty-second, Amity was busy finding out which were the most auspicious dates for the betrothal and the wedding, which he had to submit to the bride's family for approval. Modesty, though at leisure, dared not leave the house. His opportunity finally came at dusk, when someone invited Amity to a sing-song house party. Modesty then slipped off for a rendezvous with Twin Jade in Sunshine Alley.

When he arrived, Benevolence Hong happened to be in Twin Pearl's room, so Modesty went over to tell him about the betrothal and bid him to keep it from Twin Jade. Benevolence understood his situation and relayed the message to Twin Pearl at once. Twin Pearl then told Orchid Zhou, who ordered the entire household to keep the news under a tight lid.

Everyone obeyed her, with the exception of Twin Jewel, who, gratified by this turn of events, began to make fun of Twin Jade through hints and innuendoes. Twin Pearl happened to catch her at it and called her into the room to admonish her, "How dare you still wag your tongue like that! Have you forgotten the incident of the silver water pipe? If Twin Jade picks a quarrel, no good will come to you."

Twin Jewel dared not answer back. She went silently downstairs.

The next day, Orchid Zhou left a bunch of keys in Twin Jewel's room when she went there to get some clothes from the trunks. She happened to see Pearlie and told her to look for them. When Pearlie had found the keys and turned to go, Twin Jewel grabbed her and asked in a whisper, "Aren't you going to Fifth Young Mr. Zhu's to congratulate him?"

"Don't talk nonsense," Pearlie answered offhandedly.

"Fifth Young Mr. Zhu is getting married, haven't you heard?"

Knowing Twin Jewel had a loose tongue, Pearlie had no intention of being drawn into an argument. She said loudly, "Let go of me this minute, or I'm going to call Mother!"

But Twin Jewel would not let go. Just then, they heard Worth calling out in the parlor, "Pearlie, somebody to see you."

Pearlie asked, "Who is it?" and took the opportunity to extricate herself. She found out that it was her old colleague, Goldie the servant girl. Momentarily taken aback, she asked, "Has anything happened?"

"No, I just thought I'd look in on you," Goldie replied.

Pearlie rushed off to hand over the keys to Orchid Zhou and then came out, took Goldie by the hand, and walked with her to a corner of the alley, where they stood by the whitewashed wall for a heart-to-heart.

"Things are getting impossible. Even the couple of old clients are keeping away, not to mention Mr. Wang. There aren't any new clients, either. At the end of last season, my share of tips came to just four dollars. We're worried to death, but she's still taking carriage rides and going to the theater and seems quite happy," said Goldie.

"Little Willow is doing very well, so why should she be glum? The way I look at it, you should just quit."

"I will. They're renting a little hideaway and want me to go with them at a dollar a month. I'm certainly not going."

"I heard Mr. Hong say that they need a servant girl at Mr. Wang's house. D'you want to give it a try?" Pearlie said.

"Fine. Will you speak for me?"

"If you like, I'll ask Mr. Hong about it later. I'm busy tomorrow, so I'll go with you on the twenty-sixth, at two in the afternoon."

The appointment made, Goldie took her leave, and Pearlie returned to the house. On the morning of the twenty-fifth, a call chit came from Conical Hat Garden, so Pearlie accompanied Twin Jade to the party. The next day, Pearlie came home with the message: "The young maestro won't be back until the twenty-eighth." Orchid Zhou made no comment. Not long after lunch, Goldie showed up to go with Pearlie to the Wang residence on Fifth Avenue.

When the two of them arrived at the door, a young man charged out as if the devil were after him and dashed off with his head down. It was Lotuson Wang's nephew. They had no idea what it was about. The two of them pushed the door open and went in. It was all quiet inside, with no one around. They had gone as far as the parlor when Talisman came out from the back of the house. On seeing them, he held up a hand to indicate that they should not come in, so they stood still. Pearlie asked in a low voice, "Is Mr. Wang in?"

Talisman nodded.

"Has anything happened?"

Talisman approached her and was about to whisper into her ear when the sound of whacking came from upstairs. Then all hell broke loose, and they heard shouting and loud crying. The two women could tell it was Constance's voice, but they did not hear Lotuson Wang. Next came the sound of running feet—bound and natural. They ran into the center room, and then another bout of whacking followed. Constance was shouting incessantly, "Help! Help!"

Pearlie could stand it no longer. "Go and intercede," she urged Talisman.

He hung back, not daring to go. Then came a thump that shook the ceiling, sending the dust flying down. They knew it was Constance falling on the floor. Lotuson Wang never uttered the slightest sound; he beat her in complete silence. Constance rolled and writhed all over the floor. Pearlie wanted to intercede but felt she was in no position to do so, so she did not dare go, either. As there was no one else present, Lotuson Wang could beat her to his heart's content. Gradually, Constance's voice became hoarse, and she no longer had the strength to roll around or call for help. Only then did they hear Lotuson Wang stop. He heaved a long sigh and then withdrew into the inner room.

Pearlie surmised that it was best not to disturb him, so she whispered good-bye to Talisman. Goldie, still transfixed, only came to her senses when she saw Pearlie leaving. As they slipped out the door hand in hand, they again heard Constance howling a couple of times; it was a really chilling sound.

Goldie could not help lamenting, "I wonder what brought this about?"

"What do we care! Let's go and have a cup of tea."

This cheered Goldie up no end. They went out of the alley, turned a corner, and made their leisurely way to Splendid Assembly Teahouse on Fourth Avenue, where they went upstairs. It was the peak hour, so tea drinkers were coming and going in droves. They chose a table that overlooked the street and ordered one pouring cup to share. They drank slowly and chatted.

"We all thought Mr. Wang was such a nice person, but now he's beating his concubine! Isn't it strange?" Pearlie smiled and said.

"It would've worked out well if our maestro had married Mr. Wang when he was in love with her. If that had happened, would he have dared beat her?" Goldie responded.

"But Little Rouge is not cut out to be a respectable woman, is she? There'd have been even more of a hullabaloo," said Pearlie.

Goldie sighed. "It's all our maestro's fault. One can't blame Mr. Wang for marrying Constance. To think that she was a top courtesan in Shanghai, and now she's come to this!"

"Well, this isn't the end of the road for her yet," Pearlie said with a sneer.

As she spoke, the waiter came to pour more hot water into their cup. He showed them a ten-cent coin in his hand and pointed to a table further back, saying, "Your tea is paid for. They've paid."

The two women craned their necks to look. There were four people seated at that table, all unknown to Goldie. Pearlie thought they looked familiar; she seemed to have seen them a couple of times in Conical Hat Garden, but the only one she recognized was the young man, Second Treasure's brother, Simplicity Zhao. Since Simplicity was dressed in a formal, wide-cut robe, looking uncommonly distinguished, Pearlie refrained from greeting him. She just nodded in acknowledgment and smiled.

A moment later, a smiling Simplicity came over to their table. Pearlie invited him to sit down and handed him a water pipe. After an appraising glance at Goldie, he made conversation with Pearlie. "Your maestro is at Rustic Retreat. How come you're back here?"

"I'm going there now."

Simplicity turned to ask Goldie, "Who do you work for?"

Goldie replied that it was Little Rouge.

"She's looking for a job right now," Pearlie cut in. "If you know anybody who wants a servant girl, please give her a recommendation."

Simplicity was all ears. "Flora Zhang of West Civic Peace Alley mentioned that she wanted another servant girl. When she comes back, I'll ask her about it."

"Fine. Thank you," Goldie said.

After asking for her name, Simplicity made an appointment to give her an answer on the twenty-ninth. "You might as well wait a couple days," Pearlie said to Goldie. "If it falls through at Flora Zhang's, then you can go to Mr. Wang's."

Goldie was full of gratitude. Simplicity took a few puffs on the water pipe and then returned to his own table.

Soon it was getting dark. Pearlie and Goldie went to say good-bye to Simplicity before they left. As Simplicity and his friends were also going, they walked down the stairs of Splendid Assembly Teahouse together and went their separate ways.

CHAPTER 55 :: *Second Treasure is plagued by doubts despite her lover's promise of marriage, and Verdure Xu is embarrassed for sharing a whore's bed with his friends*

Simplicity Zhao returned home to Tripod Alley, where he told his mother that Second Treasure said they should give a farewell feast for Third Young Master Shi and also prepare a dinner for him to take on the road. The food had to be exquisite and plentiful. Having made his report, Simplicity went in search of the servant girl, Clever. Taking advantage of Second Treasure's absence, they flirted outrageously, engaging in mock fights and uttering playful curses. Seeing that recently Simplicity had been smartly dressed and flush with money and looked quite the rich young gentleman, Clever gave her all to play up to him. This put an end to his affair with Second Wang. He had even dropped his friends of former days; Little Wang being the only one he was close to now. They promised to be sworn brothers, and through Little Wang he got to know Loyalty Hua and Felicity Xia. The four of them often went out together.

On the twenty-eighth of the eighth month, Simplicity knew Little Wang would be in Nature Shi's entourage, so he asked Loyalty Hua and Felicity Xia to a dinner in Wang's honor. It would also serve as a farewell feast. The sound of horse bells did not approach their door until sunset. When it did, a flustered Mrs. Zhao and Simplicity went out in welcome. They saw that Third Young Master Shi and Second Treasure had alighted from their sedan chairs in the parlor and were coming in. Simplicity stood to one side. Nature Shi smiled slightly at Mrs. Zhao and then went up the stairs in slow measured steps.

Second Treasure greeted her mother and then pulled her into the little room at the back, closed the door, and quietly instructed her, "You mustn't act this way, Mother. You're his mother-in-law now! He hadn't even invited you to come out, and yet you dashed out there of your own accord; isn't it embarrassing?"

Mrs. Zhao just grinned and kept nodding her head.

Before leaving her, Second Treasure gave her further instructions. "I'm going up now. Later, if he asks to see you, I'll tell Tiger to wait on you. When you see him, just greet him as 'Third Master' and that's that. Don't say anything else. If you say the wrong things, you'll make him laugh at you."

Mrs. Zhao was all obedience. Second Treasure left the room, and at the staircase she ran into Simplicity helping Little Wang carry bundles of clothes and miscellaneous things.

"Just leave them to it. You're fawning in all the wrong ways!" she said in a low growl.

Simplicity hurriedly handed the things over to Tiger to take upstairs. Second Treasure also went up to get changed into more comfortable clothes, after which she went to keep Nature Shi company. She sat opposite him, talking and laughing, and no mention was made of Mrs. Zhao.

Presently the banquet was served in the study across from Second Treasure's room, and Tiger came to invite them over. As Second Treasure had intimate things to say to Shi, she did not invite a single guest for company.

"Ask your mother and brother to eat with us," said Third Young Master.

"They're not up to it. Here, I'll keep you company." She asked him to take the seat of honor and poured three cups of wine for him and a small cup for herself before she sat down by his side.

When he had drained the three cups, she said unhurriedly, "You're going home tomorrow. I want to ask you something: what you've been saying all along, can it be done? You may be happy talking about it now, but what if when you get home, your family won't allow it? Isn't it going to be awkward for you? You might as well speak plainly; I won't mind."

Third Young Master stood up, looking very perturbed. "Don't you trust me?"

Second Treasure gently pressed him back into his chair and said with a smile, "I do trust you. But I have become a courtesan because my brother is a good-for-nothing and got us into dire straits. I've frequently thought to myself: how could there be a happy ending for me? You want to marry me as your wife; that's something I never even dreamed of. But you already have a wife at home, so how can you take another wife as if she doesn't exist? Don't let's get carried away and then see it all come to nothing."

"Don't worry," he consoled her. "If I myself wanted to take three wives, then maybe it couldn't be done. Now, it's my adopted mothers' idea for me to take two more wives,[1] so who's to object? I might as well tell you: my adopted mothers had their eyes on a match quite a while ago, but I didn't take it seriously, so no matchmaker has been sent. Now, once I get home I'll ask a matchmaker to see to that match, and when it's settled I'll come back to fetch you for a joint wedding ceremony. It'll just take a month; I'm sure to be back in the tenth month, don't you worry."

Second Treasure was overjoyed when she heard this. She sought further reassurance by saying, "Then you *must* come back in the tenth month. When you're gone, I'll keep to myself, stay in the house, and refuse all clients, and I won't feel at ease until you come back, so please don't put it off on any account. If your lady at home won't let you take me as a wife, I'll be willing to marry you as your concubine."

As she said this, Second Treasure burst out crying; tears streamed down her face. Looking into his eyes, she clung to his shoulders and said, "I've made up my mind to be yours for life. However many wives and concubines you take, don't you ever cast me off. If you do,

::

1. [In an extended family where only one brother had male progeny, it was a common practice for his son to carry on the lines of his brothers as well, particularly if his brothers had died. Nature Shi is obviously the only male child of a man with two childless brothers; his "adopted mothers" are his aunts. *E.H.*]

I . . ." Choking, she could not finish what she had to say and instead started crying again. Unnerved by this, Third Young Master folded her into his embrace. He wiped her tears gently with his own handkerchief as he tried to console her. "Don't talk nonsense. What you should do now is be happy, shop for all the small items you'll need, and get things ready. If you cry again, it'll just be silly!"

She took the opportunity to snuggle into his arms. Holding back her tears, she said plaintively, "You don't know my predicament. People in my home village have been bad-mouthing me. Now you say you're going to make me your wife, but these people won't believe it; they're laughing at me. If this falls through, the shame will be so great, I'll have nowhere to hide."

"How can it fall through? Not unless I drop dead," he replied.

She sat up immediately and covered his mouth with her hand. "Don't say that! Now I won't talk to you anymore."

With a smile, he brushed the matter aside.

She poured a cup of warm wine and handed it to him. Having drained it, he diverted her attention by asking her about sights in her home village. She understood his intention and cast off her melancholy to joke with him.

"We have a temple of the warrior god in our village, and in the ninth month, opera performances are held there,"[2] she said. "Countless people come to see the show, so much so that the tree branches are hanging with people. I've just seen it once, with Flora Zhang. We built our own viewing podium and then climbed onto the wall. With the sun beating down, it was hot as hell, but everybody said, 'Wonderful show!' It was so unlike how things are at Panorama Garden, where it's nice and quiet and you're all by yourself in a box. Now, if you ask me, I'm not interested in that!"

The Third Young Master nodded in agreement.

She offered him two more cups of wine. "I'll tell you a joke. Next door to the temple lived Blind Man Wang; he was said to be awfully good at telling fortunes. The year before last, my mother called him to the house to study the birth dates of the three of us. When he saw mine, he said I'd be a lady of the highest official rank and that but for a small flaw I'd get to be empress. We thought it was all nonsense, but it seems he came pretty close, right?"

::

2. [One of the most valiant generals in the Three Kingdoms Period (221–265), Guan Yu was deified in later generations and worshiped as an icon of loyalty and justice. Interestingly, both the police and gangsters adopted him as their guardian god. Operas performed on temple grounds (to entertain the gods) were a major entertainment for Chinese villagers. E.H.]

Third Young Master smiled and nodded in agreement.

The two of them drank sparingly as they poured out their feelings to each other, and dinner was over only when they had fully enjoyed themselves. Third Young Master walked over to the bedroom and called out, "Little Wang."

Second Treasure, who came in behind him, interceded, "With me here, what d'you want them for?"

"Is Little Wang here?" he asked.

"My brother has invited him to a restaurant for a farewell dinner. What d'you want him for?" she said.

"Nothing, except to tell him to go back and pack and to come early tomorrow."

"We'll tell him later."

He did not say anything. After a long rest, they retired for the night.

The next day, Second Treasure rose extremely early. She performed her toilet in the center room and dispensed with all makeup and jewelry. She then changed into clothes of subdued colors. When Third Young Master got up, she asked him, "Do I look like a respectable woman?"

"That looks nice and neat," he replied.

"From today on, I'll always look like this."

She had breakfast with him, after which he told Tiger to ask Mrs. Zhao to come upstairs. He took a money order from his purse and handed it to her, saying, "I have to make a trip home and will be back in a month. I'll see to the gifts for the bride when I get home. Here's one thousand dollars for you to buy whatever small items she'll need. The trousseau can wait until I come back."

Mrs. Zhao dared not accept the money. She looked at Second Treasure.

Second Treasure snatched the money order and asked, "What's this for? If you were paying the season's bills here, then all I could say would be 'thank you.' But you said you're coming back to marry me, so why are you giving us money? Though we're poor, we can still afford to buy whatever small items that'll be needed. You don't have to worry about that."

When he heard her put it like this, he bowed his head thoughtfully. Mrs. Zhao chimed in, "Third Master is *so* mindful of etiquette! We're family now, so we can be more relaxed."

Second Treasure immediately signaled her with a glance to stop her talking. Mrs. Zhao took her leave and went downstairs.

He had no choice but to put away the money order. He then called out to Little Wang to have the sedan chair ready. Second Treasure also took a sedan chair to see him off. They first went to his residence to dispatch his luggage. When lunch was over, a stream of people came to say farewell to him. This kept him busy until four o'clock, when he finally got ready to board the boat.

Second Treasure went aboard with him and saw that her brother, Simplicity Zhao, was looking after the luggage in the cabin for Little Wang.

"Has the dinner for his journey been delivered yet?" she asked in a low voice.

"Yes, it's here," he reported.

She knew there wasn't anything else for her to do and thought she'd go home. Firmly holding Third Young Master's hands, she bade him, "Write to me when you get home. Though I'm physically still in Shanghai, my heart is going home with you. Don't you go and tarry anywhere else." He gave his promise. Then she continued, "When are you coming back in the tenth month? Write to me again once you've settled on a date. Best if you can make it early. Your early arrival will make my whole family breathe easier."

He again gave his promise. She was going to say more when the boatman, ready to set sail, hurried them, so she had to let go of his hands and climb ashore. They looked at each other with tears in their eyes as the boat pulled away, with Nature Shi standing at the bow and Second Treasure sitting in her sedan chair. Not until the mast was lost to sight did Simplicity Zhao order the sedan-chair bearers to go home.

Second Treasure was a proud and willful woman. Ever since Nature Shi had talked about the idea of marrying three wives, she had set her mind on marrying him. Afraid that he would look down on her, she had tried hard to put up a facade of respectability. She had refused to let him settle his bills at her house, on the basis, "since you regard me as a wife, I won't regard myself as a prostitute." Immediately after the Midautumn Festival, she had her name slip removed from the door and refused all clients but Nature Shi. When he left, saying that he'd come and fetch her in the tenth month, she had checked that she still had four hundred Mexican dollars at home, which was plenty to live on, so she felt completely at ease.

When they returned home from seeing Shi off, Simplicity Zhao went to Flora Zhang's to recommend the servant girl Goldie, while Second Treasure went to confer with her mother. "He said the trousseau can wait until he comes back, but I think the bride's family should pay for it. If we let him do it, I'm afraid his servants would talk and we'd feel humiliated," she said.

"Well, in that case, you won't be able to have the best, for we only have four hundred dollars," Mrs. Zhao said.

"Humph! You're always like this, Mother! How can you have a

trousseau for four hundred dollars? What I'm thinking is: we'll borrow the money to get things ready and then pay it back when he brings the bride price."

"Well, that's all right, too," Mrs. Zhao replied.

Second Treasure turned to Tiger. "D'you know where we can borrow some money?"

"You can't really borrow very much," said Tiger. "It'd be better to get things on credit. We know people in all the silk shops, import shops, and furniture stores, so we can just pay up at the end of year."

Delighted, Second Treasure sent Tiger out every day to get all the necessary articles for a trousseau from the various stores on credit. She herself was kept busy evaluating and selecting the things brought back to her and was only interested in the most fashionable items of the highest quality.

With nothing to occupy him, Simplicity Zhao became deeply entangled with Clever. The two were like a pair of lovebirds, inseparable. Knowing that he would become Third Young Master's legitimate brother-in-law, Clever tried harder than ever to please him. Simplicity made a secret vow to marry her. And once married, she would be a lady, sister-in-law to Shi. Second Treasure was too preoccupied to pay attention to them, and the others naturally did not bother.

One day, a manservant from the Qi residence suddenly turned up to deliver a letter from Third Young Master. Simplicity read it and then related the contents in detail to Second Treasure. Shi spoke first of his safe arrival and of having asked a matchmaker to propose to the other family. Then he said that autumn was a most enchanting time and if Second Treasure was bored at home, she could go and amuse herself in Conical Hat Garden. Having received this letter, Second Treasure speeded up the purchase of her trousseau, thinking that once Third Young Master returned, she would have her perfect marriage.

Not having seen Qi's steward, Xia, for some time, Simplicity asked the manservant about him and was told that he was drinking tea at Splendid Assembly Teahouse just then, so Simplicity went to look for him right away. Sure enough, he found Felicity Xia and Loyalty Hua at tea at Splendid Assembly.

As soon as Loyalty saw Simplicity, he asked, "You haven't been out and about all this time; what's happened?"

Felicity Xia jumped in with an answer, "He's got a little game going at home, understand?"

"What game?" Loyalty asked in surprise.

"It's not clear to me, either. You'll have to ask Little Wang," said Felicity Xia.

Simplicity just smiled awkwardly and sat down. The waiter brought him a lidded teacup and asked, "Would you like to order tea?" Simplicity waved his hand to indicate there was no need.

"Let's go then," Loyalty suggested.

"Fine, let's look for some fun," said Felicity Xia.

The three of them came out of the Splendid Assembly and turned into Treasured Merit Street, where they spent some time observing the courtesans in their carriages. Then they ambled into the Virtue Tavern, where they ordered three bottles of warmed Peking wine and three small dishes of food. After supper, Felicity invited the others to smoke opium. He led them to Third Pan's in Security Alley and knocked on the door. The maid answered from inside but did not come to the door for a long time. Felicity Xia knocked again.

"Coming! Coming!" the maid said repeatedly. She came out very slowly and opened the door.

When they went in, they could hear the scuffling of feet in the bedroom; it sounded like two people pulling and tugging at each other. Felicity Xia knew there was another client and stopped at the door of the room.

The maid closed the front door and said, "Please go in."

Felicity Xia lifted the curtain and ushered the other two into the room. They heard the other guest going out via the back door and then the thumping of his footsteps as he went up the stairs. The room was dark, lit only by an oil lamp on the dressing table. Third Pan closed the back door and came up smiling to greet "Master Xia." The maid hurriedly lit a foreign lamp and the opium lamp and then went to get more teacups.

Felicity Xia asked Third Pan in a whisper who the guest was who had gone upstairs.

"It wasn't a guest; it was the friend of a guest," she replied.

"That's a guest all the same, right?" Felicity Xia said. He pointed at Loyalty Hua and Simplicity Zhao and asked, "Don't you consider them your guests?"

"Enough of your nonsense. Now have a smoke," she said.

Felicity Xia lay down on the couch. Just when the pipe was ready, they suddenly heard someone knocking at the door.

"Who is it?" the maid called out loudly in the parlor.

"It's me," a man answered.

The maid let him in. Instead of coming into the room, the man went straight upstairs. Knowing that he must be from the same clique as the guest upstairs, they did not pay him any attention.

Felicity Xia's opium habit was slight, so after two pellets he invited Simplicity Zhao to smoke while he took a water pipe and moved over to the humble side of the couch. Loyalty Hua and Third Pan sat side by side by the window chatting. Suddenly, they heard somebody knocking at the door again.

"Aiyo!" Felicity Xia exclaimed, "your business is certainly booming!" So saying, he put down the water pipe and stood up to peep out the window.

Third Pan came up to stop him. "What's there to see? Go and sit down!"

Felicity Xia heard the maid open the door and go out to talk for some length to the man, whose voice sounded familiar. Felicity Xia pushed Third Pan aside and rushed out to see who it was, but the man had made off to avoid him. Felicity Xia ran out into the alley and by the light of the glass oil lamp hanging over the door recognized the man as Verdure Xu. He called out his name.

Verdure Xu had no choice but to turn around. He called out, asking quite unnecessarily, "Is that you, Felicity?" When Felicity replied in the positive, Xu saluted him repeatedly, saying, all smiles, "I never expected to see you." He followed Felicity Xia into the room and greeted Loyalty Hua and Simplicity Zhao.

Simplicity recognized Verdure Xu as the man who had brutally beaten him up, wounding him in the head and face. He was scared stiff by this unexpected meeting. Verdure also recognized Simplicity but pretended he didn't.

After a round of mutual introductions, everyone settled in their seats. Felicity Xia asked Verdure Xu, "Why did you run away when you saw me?"

Verdure blustered, "I didn't know it was you. I just came to ask whether Yang from Hongkou was here; when I learned he wasn't, I turned to leave. How would I have known you were here?"

"Humph!" was Felicity's only response.

Verdure looked at Third Pan and grinned. "I haven't seen you for a long time, Third Miss. Looks like you've gained weight. Is it because our friend Felicity has been giving you something nice to eat?"

Third Pan glanced at him from the corner of her eyes. "Because you haven't seen me for a long time, you miss my scolding and are craving it, right?"

"Exactly. Bull's-eye," Verdure Xu said, clapping his hands. He then turned to Loyalty Hua and Simplicity Zhao, gesticulating and laughing as he spoke, "The last time when Felicity was in Shanghai, Third Miss was the only one he visited, so our gang all came here to look for him several times a day; it was as if this were the Splendid Assembly Teahouse. We all got cruelly cursed by Third Miss. Now Felicity doesn't come anymore, so none of our gang comes here either."

Loyalty Hua and Simplicity Zhao made no comment. Verdure Xu

turned to ask Third Pan, "Why did our friend Felicity stop coming here? Did you offend him?"

Before she could reply, Felicity Xia shouted at him, "Cut the cackle. I have official business with you."

CHAPTER 56 :: *Third Pan, the underground prostitute, plots a theft, and Yao, the daytime patron, stays the night*

As Felicity Xia mentioned that he had official business, Third Pan left the room and went upstairs to entertain her other guests. Verdure Xu solemnly asked what business it was.

"What kind of police work are you people supposed to be doing? Did you ever go and investigate our Rustic Retreat?" Felicity Xia.

"Has anything happened there?" Verdure Xu asked, aghast.

"I have no idea," Felicity said with an icy smile. "But this morning, His Excellency told us that a gambling den in Rustic Retreat draws a big crowd and goes on day and night, and a single game of dice has a stake of thirty to forty thousand. He said things are getting completely out of hand. I've been told to ask you if you know about that."

Verdure laughed. "Hasn't there always been a gambling den in Rustic Retreat? I thought a bandit was holed up there! You gave me a real fright. I'll go there tomorrow and tell them to stop gambling, all right?"

"Don't you take it lightly. If anything went wrong in the future, it wouldn't reflect well on anybody."

Verdure moved his chair closer. "Felicity, my friend, I've never taken a single dollar from the gambling den in Rustic Retreat. You know very well who's running it. Lots of their customers are officials, some from our yamen as well, so how dare we say anything when we go there? Now that His Excellency wants to bring them in, nothing's easier; I'll gather my team right away and go and arrest the lot of them, how about that?"

Felicity pondered. "If they stop gambling, His Excellency is not actually set on punishing them. Go and pass the word around first. If that doesn't put an end to it, naturally you should arrest them."

Verdure slapped his thigh. "That's what I meant. Several of their customers are actually His Excellency's friends. We're not in the same position as the police in the foreign concessions; things are very tricky for us."

Felicity was clearly displeased by what he said. "The only gambler among His Excellency's friends is Eldest Master Li, and that has nothing to do with us. Who in our house has been gambling? Let's hear it."

Verdure tried to excuse himself at once, "I didn't say it was anybody in the house. If that had been the case, wouldn't I have told you?"

Only then did Felicity drop the matter.

Verdure Xu turned to Loyalty Hua and Simplicity Zhao and said jovially, "Our friend Felicity is a man who has what it takes! There're over a hundred people in the Qi residence working under him, and nothing has ever gone wrong."

Loyalty Hua made some noise to show polite agreement, while Simplicity Zhao rose from the opium couch and asked Verdure Xu to take his place. Xu deferred to Loyalty Hua. Just as they were pulling and tugging to make each other take precedence, the back room door suddenly creaked open, and somebody tiptoed in, making straight for the couch. They saw it was Longevity Zhang and asked in surprise, "When did you get here?"

Without a word, Longevity bowed low and grinned, turning his eyes into mere slits. Loyalty Hua asked him to lie down and smoke.

"Who is it upstairs?" Felicity Xia asked in a low voice. Longevity responded similarly, saying it was Second Kuang.

"Well, then he should come and sit here with us for a while," Felicity said.

Longevity immediately held up a hand to stop him. "This is like an underground whorehouse for him. Don't let's disturb him."

"Humph! People are behaving very strangely lately. I wonder why!" Felicity pointed at Verdure Xu. "Just now he came to talk to the maid, and when I called out for him, he tried to run away. Isn't that strange?"

Verdure Xu grinned at Longevity Zhang. "Our friend Felicity has been rebuking me all this time, as if I looked down on him. I put it to you, is that possible?"

Longevity Zhang smiled but said nothing.

Felicity Xia said, "A brothel is a place where *everybody* comes to have fun. If Second Kuang thought I'd be jealous, he's got it all wrong."

"He's not hiding from you, though; he's afraid that if his employer learned about this, he'd get a lecture," Longevity replied.

"There's something else I'd like to tell him," Felicity said. "He should give his employer a word of advice: don't go to the gambling den in Rustic Retreat anymore."

Longevity promised to relay the message. After smoking a pipe of opium, he thanked the four of them and took his leave to return upstairs, where he found Second Kuang and Third Pan rolling around in a heap on the couch. On seeing Longevity, Third Pan sat up unhurriedly and said to Second Kuang, "I'm going downstairs, but you're not allowed to leave. I have something to say to you." She turned to Longevity and said, "Sit for a while, don't go." After that, she went downstairs.

Longevity took the opportunity to have a quiet word with Second Kuang. Half an hour later, they heard the confused noise of the four men downstairs taking their leave. Third Pan ritually tried to detain them, and then the maid saw them out. The door was closed.

"Come on down," Third Pan called out.

Second Kuang invited Longevity to come with him to the down-stairs room, but the latter had to leave because he still had duties to perform. Second Kuang thought he'd go with him, but would Third Pan let him go?

"Have another pipe of opium, do," she urged Longevity Zhang as she pulled Second Kuang by the hand and made him sit down in the rattan chair by the bed and then settled herself in his lap for a lengthy heart-to-heart. Longevity could only wait. She talked for a long time, but he did not know what it was about. He saw Second Kuang nodding repeatedly in agreement but making no reply. When she finally finished, she walked away, but Second Kuang was still preoccupied with what she had said, looking lost.

"Are you coming?" Longevity Zhang called out, which alerted Second Kuang. At the door, Third Pan whispered into his ear, and he again nodded in acknowledgment. Finally, he walked out of Security Alley with Longevity Zhang.

"What did she say?" Longevity asked.

"It was a lot of tripe! She said once she's paid her debts, she's going to get married."

"Why don't you marry her then?"

"Where do I get all that money?"

Presently they separated; Second Kuang went to Grace Yang's in Generosity Alley while Longevity went to Green Phoenix's in Prosperity Alley. From the distance, he saw seven or eight courtesans' sedan chairs at Green Phoenix's door. He guessed that the party was still going on. As he went in, he met Talisman.

"Are all the girls here?" Longevity asked.

"The party is about to end," Talisman said.

"Who did Mr. Wang call?"

"He called two of them: Little Rouge and Twin Jade."

"Is Mr. Hong still here?"

"Yes, he is."

Longevity Zhang thought that Golden must have accompanied

Twin Pearl to the party. He took the opportunity to slip upstairs and peep in at the edge of the door curtain. A loud and energetic finger game was in progress, and the fumes of heated wine hovered over the table. Prosperity Luo and Mallow Yao joined forces to form a bank of unlimited penalty, calling themselves "the bottomless pit," which naturally aroused the indignation of the others. Lotuson Wang, Benevolence Hong, Amity Zhu, Elan Ge, Whistler Tang, and Cloudlet Chen formed a united front and took turns to do battle. No one allowed their lovers, maids, or servant girls to drink in his stead. Everyone was loud and aggressive, each trying to best the next man. It was an even merrier crowd than usual.

Seeing that Twin Pearl's maid, Golden, was standing idly to one side, Longevity Zhang took a small whistle from his pocket and blew it softly. Nobody at the table noticed, but Golden heard it and slipped out of the room. She made a secret appointment with him to meet the day after the next. Overjoyed, he went back to stand by downstairs while Golden returned to the room. Those at the table, engrossed in the finger game and drinking, paid them not the slightest attention.

This rowdy dinner party did not break up till midnight, when all the guests were more or less drunk. As the girls called to the party were eager to please, not one left before the men.

About to leave, Mallow Yao saluted Lotuson Wang and the others, saying, "Please honor me with your company tomorrow. You gentlemen are all invited to keep him company." He turned around to point to the girl he had called to the party, "At her place, Auspicious Cloud Alley."

Everyone assented and asked, "Is your lady love called Cassia Ma? None of us has met her yet."

"I've only just started seeing her. Originally a friend of mine called her to parties, and then he recommended her to me, so I thought I'd give it a go," replied Mallow Yao.

"She's very nice," they all said. After that, everyone took his leave, and they trooped downstairs one after another. With the maids and servant girls supporting them in front or covering them from behind, no one was in danger of falling down drunk. Having seen them off, Prosperity returned to the room. Green Phoenix took a glance at him and saw that he was not too drunk, so she sat down to keep him company.

"Why is everybody giving dinner parties in honor of Mr. Wang?" she asked.

"He's been given a posting in Jiangxi. As his old friends, we naturally have to ask him to a farewell dinner," Prosperity replied.

Taken by surprise, Green Phoenix let out a sigh. "Oh, dear! Now

Little Rouge will really have a tough time. If Mr. Wang stays, she can try to please him, and he might renew their relationship, which will be a good thing for her. Now that he's leaving, she's in for it!"

"Just now it looked as though Mr. Wang was showing some fondness again for Little Rouge. I wonder why," said Prosperity.

"It's no use now however fond he is. Little Rouge got it all messed up right from the start. If she had married Mr. Wang, everything would've been all right now. She could either go with him or, if she wanted, go out to work again."

"Little Rouge was intent on having a good time, and she got hooked up with an actor. Would she have been willing to get married?"

Green Phoenix sighed again. "Plenty of courtesans have relationships with actors, but she's the only one who suffers for it." Having commented on this, the two of them got ready to go to bed.

The next day was Sunday. In the afternoon, Prosperity wanted to visit Luna Park and ordered Promotion to call two carriages. Just then, Second Sister happened to drop in. When she came into the room, she greeted them as "Mr. Luo" and "Eldest Maestro." Green Phoenix still called her Mother and invited her to sit down. After the usual pleasantries had been exchanged, Green Phoenix asked how her business was doing.

Second Sister frowned and shook her head. "Don't even mention it! With you there, business was always quite brisk, but now things are impossible. Even Gold Phoenix seems to be getting fewer party calls. I wanted to buy a girl but was afraid she'd turn out no good, like that Gold Flower. It won't do for me to muddle along like this. That's why I've come to talk it over with you to see if there's any way out."

"That's up to you, Mother. I'm in no position to say anything. Buying a girl is terribly difficult, it's true, and even if she's good, there's no guarantee as far as business is concerned, is there? I myself don't have much business either," Green Phoenix replied.

Second Sister, deep in thought, said nothing. Green Phoenix just ignored her. A moment later, Promotion came in to report, "The carriages are here." Second Sister had to take her leave and walk home, a forlorn figure. Prosperity Luo, attended by Promotion, and Green Phoenix, attended by Mama Zhao, each took a carriage. When they reached Luna Park, they ordered tea in the main parlor.

Prosperity made a comment about Second Sister. "Your mother is hopeless. She'd be better off with you keeping an eye on her."

"Why should I do that? I told her to buy a girl, didn't I? But she scrimped on the money and wouldn't listen to me. Now that her business has declined, she turns around and asks me if there's any way out. Should I just give her some more money?"

This made Prosperity laugh.

Green Phoenix turned to the subject of Little Rouge again. "Little Rouge is what I call a hopeless case. When Mr. Wang went with Constance, it was the best thing for him that could have happened. Now, you didn't tell Mr. Wang directly what you knew, but you pushed him to a revelation; that was really shrewd."

As she was speaking, Little Rouge strolled by alone, so Green Phoenix said no more. Prosperity saw that Little Rouge had the sallow complexion of an opium addict and was visibly thinner than he had noticed at the party. Little Rouge also saw them but pretended not to notice and cut across to the foreign-style building. A while later, the male lead of the Panorama Theater, Little Willow, came along. He had on brand-new clothes of summer silk and lined gauze that showed his trim figure to great advantage. On his feet were thick-soled Peking shoes that made a clicking noise as he walked. A thick shiny braid trailed down his back. He came straight into the main parlor and deliberately circled round Prosperity Luo's table, scrutinizing Green Phoenix. Now, Green Phoenix was dressed all in white and wore very little jewelry,[1] but the pair of black gold bracelets on her wrists had been bought at the Japanese Jewelry Exhibition and was worth a thousand dollars. Having heard about it some time ago, Little Willow thought he'd take the opportunity to look at such a rare item.

Green Phoenix, however, misunderstood his intention. She stood up abruptly, flapping her sleeves in irritation against the table, and said to Prosperity, "Let's go." Prosperity naturally acquiesced. They visited the various parts of the park before boarding their carriages at the garden gate and driving back to Prosperity Alley. When they entered the house, they saw Jade Wenjun seated alone at the window of the side chamber, bending over the table, totally absorbed in a book. Prosperity Luo approached the window to peek in, standing on his toes. The book was *A Thousand Classical Poems,* and Jade Wenjun's eyes were only two inches from the page. She was oblivious to the fact that somebody was looking at her through the window. Green Phoenix quietly tugged at Prosperity's robe, forbidding him to tarry. Bit-

::

1. [True to her word, Green Phoenix is still wearing white, the color of deep mourning, in honor of her dead parents. Such an outfit is of course also very effective in showing off her elegance. In portraying her thus, the author, Han Banqing, obviously has in mind an episode from chapter 20 of *The Story of the Stone,* when Green Phoenix's namesake Wang Xifeng dresses in white mourning to visit her rival and also manages to appear stunningly beautiful. *E.H.]*

ing back his chuckle, he went upstairs, and as soon as they were in her room, he asked in a low voice, "Jade Wenjun is quite well known, isn't she? How come she behaves like this?"

Instead of replying, Green Phoenix merely pulled down the corners of her mouth to show contempt. Mama Zhao, who was standing to one side, said in a low merry voice, "It's funny, isn't it, Mr. Luo? We run into her sometimes and talk to her, and it's such a tickle! She says Shanghai is like an empty place, with not one creditable courtesan in the foreign settlements. Fortunately, she's here now to set an example of a good show." She chuckled, and Prosperity laughed long and hard.

Mama Zhao continued, "We asked her, 'Have you managed to put on a good show yet?' She replied that she had indeed, but unfortunately there weren't any creditable clients in Shanghai. If there were, they'd all patronize her and no one else."

This made Prosperity laugh uproariously. Green Phoenix hastened to signal that this would be audible downstairs, and Mama Zhao stopped talking.

At nightfall, Promotion submitted an invitation slip to Prosperity. Seeing that it was from Mallow Yao, he set out at once. When he walked past Jade Wenjun's door, he heard the sound of poetry chanting. Who in Shanghai would patronize a courtesan like that? he wondered. Promotion helped him into the sedan chair, and he was taken straight to Cassia Ma's in Auspicious Cloud Alley, where he was met by Mallow Yao. When all the others had arrived, they took their seats at the table, giving each other precedence.

Mallow Yao, as host, naturally exerted maximum pressure on everyone to indulge his capacity for wine and merrymaking. Lotuson Wang drank so much that he felt sick and bent over the table. "What's the matter?" Little Rouge asked. He just held up his hand and suddenly gagged and threw up all over the floor. Amity Zhu, realizing he, too, had had too much to drink, left the table and lay down on the opium couch, where White Fragrance prepared a pipe of opium for him. Before he had taken a couple of puffs, he dozed off.

Elan Ge, who at the beginning made excuses to avoid drinking too much, ended up clamoring for more when he got drunk. Snow Scent barely said a word to stop him, and he was already up in arms. They almost got into a slanging match.

Seeing Elan in such high spirits, Prosperity yelled repeatedly, "Great fun! Wonderful! Let's play the finger game." He played Elan for ten large cups. Elan lost three times and barely managed to get the wine down. Prosperity, who prided himself on his ability to hold his liquor, had already drunk quite a lot, so after these seven cups he could not stay upright. The only ones who remained clear-headed were Benevolence Hong, Whistler Tang, and Cloudlet Chen, all of whom took evasive measures whenever wine was set before them. Seeing their four friends in such a drunken state, they pleaded with the host to put away the wine and end the party, after which they escorted their friends to their sedan chairs before going their separate ways.

Mallow Yao, a good drinker, did not feel the effect of the wine until he stood up to see his guests out, when all at once he felt dizzy and wobbly on his feet. But for Cassia's supporting him from behind, he would have fallen down. When all the guests had gone, Cassia and her maid helped him over to the bed to lie down and then took off his outer garments and put a blanket over him. Oblivious to all this, Mallow Yao fell soundly asleep. The next morning, he woke up to find that he was not in his own bed and that someone else was lying beside him. Only then did he realize he had spent the night at Cassia's.

Mallow Yao's wife kept a tight rein on him. He had to report home every night by ten, and the least delay invited immediate sanction. If he had official business that prevented him from going home, he had to send someone to inform her, and she would check that it was all genuine before she let it pass. Formerly, when he was seeing Sunset Wei, though they were quite fond of each other, they had never spent an entire night together. Ever since her humiliation by Sunset, Mrs. Yao had made a scene several times, adamant that he should not see Sunset again. Mallow Yao thus had no choice but to effect the break.

To cater to business connections, however, he could not avoid entertaining some prominent people in the brothels, as Mrs. Yao well knew. It happened that one of their maids, named Ma, was a distant relative of Cassia Ma's and often sang Cassia's praises in front of Mrs. Yao, with the result that Mrs. Yao actually encouraged Mallow to patronize Cassia. Even his daily homing hour became slightly more flexible: he was allowed to stay out till midnight.

Now Mallow had spent a night at Cassia's quite unintentionally, because he was drunk. This was his first time and the best thing that had ever happened to him. But he could only think of his wife and the doubly fierce scene awaiting him. If he told her a lie, and then the sedan-chair bearers exposed him, things would be even worse. He kept worrying about this and could see no way out.

Cassia, thoroughly exhausted, was still asleep. Though he could not sleep, he was loath to get up. He lay there with his eyes open until noon, when the menservants suddenly called out in the parlor, "Miss Cassia called to a party."

The maid, who was in the next room, asked, "Who's the client?"

"The name's Yao," the manservant replied.

At the very word "Yao," Mallow's heart jumped into his mouth. He sat up in bed and cocked his ears to listen.

The maid responded. "Among our clients only Second Young Master is named Yao; there's nobody else besides him."

The menservants chuckled. Their voices dropped, and there was a lot of twittering that Mallow could not make out.

Mallow shook Cassia to wake her and then hurriedly dressed, got out of bed, and called the maid into the room to question her. The maid had a call chit in her hand, which she submitted to Mallow, grinning, "Mrs. Yao is said to be in Sky in a Wine Pot and is calling our miss there. It was none other than your sedan-chair bearer who delivered the ticket, Second Young Master."

As if hit by a lightning bolt, Mallow stared, dazed and speechless. Cassia, however, seemed very sure of herself. A smile slowly spread across her face as she said, "Coming," and told the sedan-chair bearers to get ready. She then sent the maid to fetch warm water so she could immediately wash and do her hair.

Having composed himself a little, Mallow conferred with Cassia, saying, "I suggest you don't go. I'll go instead. It doesn't matter for me; she can do whatever she likes. She can't chop off my head, can she?"

Cassia was momentarily puzzled. "But she called *me*, so why can't I go?"

Mallow frowned. "If you go and she makes a scene in a Western restaurant, how would it look?"

She broke out laughing. "You just put your mind at ease and sit here! If she wants to make a scene, she can do it anywhere, why go to a Western restaurant? D'you think your missus has gone mad?"

Mallow dared not say anymore. He looked on helplessly as Cassia finished her toilet, got changed, and went out to get into the sedan chair. He bade the maid to tell the sedan-chair bearers to report back to him if anything untoward should happen. The maid assented and set off behind the sedan chair.

CHAPTER 57 :: *Honeyed words pacify a jealous wife, and persistent questions reveal a story of adultery*

Cassia Ma's sedan chair headed straight for Sky in a Wine Pot and stopped at the door of the restaurant. Cassia, leaning a hand on her maid's shoulder, walked in and went upstairs. The waiter led the way to the number one function room where a smiling Mrs. Yao stood up to welcome her. Cassia stepped up to her with the greeting "Second Mistress"; after that, she also greeted the maid, Ma. Mrs. Yao took Cassia by the hand and sat down with her on a foreign-style leather sofa.

"I was inviting you to a Western meal, but the bookkeeping office here got mixed up and sent a call chit instead," Mrs. Yao said. "What would you like to eat? Just place your order."

Cassia made excuses. "I've already had lunch, Second Mistress. Please order for yourself."

But Mrs. Yao insisted and made a few choices for her. The waiter wrote it all down and sent the order downstairs.

After pressing her to drink tea, Mrs. Yao just made small talk; the subject of Mallow did not come up. As Cassia had decided on what to say beforehand, she took the initiative to recount how Second Young Master gave a dinner party the night before, how the guests took turns at the finger game, how everybody got very drunk, how Second Young Master was overcome by sleepiness and unable to leave, how she and the maid carried him to the bed, how he blamed himself that morning when his head had cleared, and how he had no recollection of events of the night before. She told Mrs. Yao all the details without the least fudging.

Mrs. Yao had heard that Cassia was an honest person, completely different from other courtesans. What she was saying now bore this out, so Mrs. Yao was very pleased. Just then, the waiter brought them their noodle soup. Mrs. Yao insisted that Cassia should sit with her at the table. As Cassia humbly and repeatedly declined, Mrs. Yao glanced at her maid, Ma, instructing her to persuade Cassia. In the end, Cassia had to comply. After the noodle soup came fish.

"So, is Second Young Master up now?" Mrs. Yao asked as she ate.

"Yes, just before I left. When I was setting out to answer your call, Second Mistress, Second Young Master became very agitated, afraid that you would give him a talking-to. But I said to him, 'Don't worry, Second Mistress is one who goes by the rules. What she fears is that you'll waste your money and ruin your health into the bargain. If you see to it that you keep within decent limits, why would she want to lecture you?'"

Mrs. Yao heaved a sigh. "I find it exasperating just talking about him. Instead of blaming himself for lacking a sense of proportion, he makes it sound as if I nag him constantly. Once he goes out, regardless of where he is or who he meets, he starts complaining about me. He says I'm fierce, that I keep a tight rein on him and won't let him go out. I expect that's what he told you, right?"

"Well, not really. Second Young Master may be a little lacking in sense, but in his heart of hearts, he knows what's right. If Second Mistress lectures him now and then, it's always for his own good. Sometimes, I also offer him a word of advice. I said, 'Second Mistress can't be compared to women in sing-song houses. When you come to our house, you're just a client. Whether a client is sensible or not doesn't concern us, so naturally we don't lecture you. You and Second Mistress are family; her welfare is linked to yours. It's not that she wants to control you or forbid you to go out; she only wishes you well, that's all. If I got married and my husband went beyond the limit, I'd lecture him, too.' "

"From now on, I'm not going to lecture him anymore. He can do whatever he wants. He doesn't listen to me anyway; he just takes the side of those in the brothels. I got a real mouthful from that Sunset, and he, that coward, went to appease the damn woman, said I'd offended her! Where does that put me? Lecturing him indeed!" As she talked, Mrs. Yao started huffing and puffing, and the blue veins showed on her swelling face.

Cassia dared say no more. Presently the five courses of a Western meal had all been served. Cassia merely tasted each course and then asked the maid, Ma, to eat it. After they had wiped their mouths with a hot towel, they left the table to sit around.

Cassia said with deliberation, "Perhaps I shouldn't say this, but Second Young Master does tend to go overboard and needs you, Second Mistress, to keep him under control. If he had his way, he'd have a go at all the courtesans in the foreign settlements. He's at least a bit better with you keeping on eye on him, right, Second Mistress?"

Although Mrs. Yao made no reply, she permitted herself a slight smile. A few minutes later, she took Cassia by the hand and went out to the balcony, where they leaned on the railing together. She asked Cassia how old she was, whether her parents were alive, and whether she had ever been betrothed. Cassia told her she was nineteen, her parents died leaving debts that forced her into the business, and she'd be forever grateful to anyone who'd save her from this pit of sin. Mrs. Yao sighed copiously over her fate.

Cassia then asked Mrs. Yao, "Would you like to hear a song? I'll sing a couple for you, Second Mistress."

Mrs. Yao stopped her, saying, "Never mind, I'm leaving." Then they turned around and returned to their seats. The maid was told to go and settle the bill.

Mrs. Yao sighed again. "I quarreled with him several times, and that has given me a bad name. No one knows how unjust it is! Now that Second Young Master is seeing you, my heart's quite at ease. If I'm jealous, why don't I quarrel with him anymore?"

Cassia smiled. "You see, Sunset is a top-class courtesan, a real maestro. They're a cunning lot. People like us, on the other hand, are down to earth, with just a few clients. Once we get someone like Second Young Master, all we hope for is that his business prospers, his health is good, and he'll go on patronizing us."

"There's something I'd like to say to you," said Mrs. Yao. "Since Second Young Master is at your place, I'm placing him in your care. When he goes to the foreign settlements, don't let him call another courtesan. If he insists on doing so, tell the maid to send me a message."

Cassia repeatedly gave her promise. Still holding her by the hand, Mrs. Yao went downstairs in slow graceful steps, and they came out of the restaurant together. Cassia waited until the maid, Ma, had left with Mrs. Yao's sedan chair before going home in her own. She found Mallow Yao lying on the couch smoking opium.

"You're certainly taking it easy!" Cassia said mockingly. "Second Mistress is going to give you a beating. You'd better watch out."

Since Mallow's spies had already made their report, he was totally unconcerned and just sat there grinning. Having changed out of her party clothes, Cassia recounted in detail what Mrs. Yao had said and how she'd behaved. Mallow was so jubilant, he scratched his ears and his cheeks, not knowing what to do with himself. But Cassia gave him these instruction: "Later today, after you've been to the party, go home early. When Second Mistress asks about me, you should always say I'm nothing much, no comparison with Sunset Wei."

Before she could finish, he shouted, "How can I mention Sunset Wei? That'll really mean a beating for me!"

"Then just say second-class houses are uninteresting. If she asks you whether you'll continue to come here, tell her just now you don't have any courtesan that suits you, so you'll just continue for a while. A couple of remarks in this vein will make Second Mistress very pleased."

Mallow could not say "yes" fast enough. They conferred a little longer before he left in his sedan chair for the bureau to attend to some official business. At nightfall, when the work was done, he went straight to the party. This evening, it was Elan Ge's farewell feast for Lotuson Wang, held at Snow Scent's in East Co-prosperity Alley. The company remained the same. Mallow had set his mind on going home early, so he left before dinner was over. The others, having drunk too much several nights in a row, were no longer in the mood for wine. They just sat for a while after dinner and then dispersed.

As the party had ended early, Lotuson Wang walked with Benevolence Hong to Twin Jade's in Sunshine Alley for tea and sweetmeats, and they sat together in Twin Jade's room. Twin Pearl came over to greet them with this opening remark: "You look much better today. The way you drank last night was pretty scary!"

Pearlie, who was toasting opium and rolling it into a pellet for Lotuson, said, "You should drink less, Mr. Wang. Smoking opium after you've had a lot of wine doesn't make you feel so good, right?"

Lotuson smiled and nodded in agreement. Pearlie placed the pellet in the pipe. When he started smoking, Lotuson sucked in the leftover opium gunk in the pipe. Scrambling up in a panic, he spat into the spittoon by the divan. Pearlie immediately took the pipe and cleaned it with a metal borer. Twin Jade, seated at a distance, signaled Clever Baby with her eyes, and Clever Baby took a large covered glass jar from a dressing table drawer. It contained crabapple preserves, which she offered to Mr. Wang and Mr. Hong. Something stirred in Lotuson's memory, and he sighed.

Having cleared out the pipe, Pearlie held it over the opium lamp for Lotuson to smoke, asking, "Is it true that at Maestro Little Rouge's, there's just her mother waiting on her at parties?"

Lotuson nodded.

"Not even a servant girl then, after Goldie left?"

Lotuson nodded again.

"It's said she'll be moving to a hideaway, is that true?"

"I don't know," Lotuson said.

Pearlie had only filled the pipe for him twice when he had had enough. He sat up cross-legged, indicating he wanted the water pipe. Clever Baby fetched it. As he smoked, two teardrops ran down his face. Pearlie could not very well inquire into the matter. Twin Pearl and Twin Jade looked at each other in silence. It was so quiet in the room, all they heard were the crickets chirping.

Benevolence knew what was on Lotuson's mind and realized there was no way to console him, so he just made small talk with Twin Pearl. They caught sight of the door curtain being slightly lifted and a head poking in. It seemed to have been a child.

"Who is it?" Twin Pearl shouted harshly. No answer came. "Come in," she shouted again.

Only then did the boy sidle up to her awkwardly. As she'd thought, it was Golden's son, Eldest. He jabbered and gabbed, telling her goodness knows what. "Humph!" was Twin Pearl's response. Eldest dithered about and withdrew. Then the sound of slippers came running up the stairs and into the room. Seeing it was Golden, an angry Twin Pearl just ignored her. Golden slipped out to the parlor to confer with Eldest, shame written all over her face. Benevolence laughed in spite of himself.

Lotuson lay down again to smoke another couple of opium pellets and then told Pearlie to order Talisman to get the sedan chair ready. Benevolence, Twin Pearl, and Twin Jade saw him off at the top of the stairs. After Lotuson had left, Benevolence went into Twin Pearl's room. Having finished tidying up, Pearlie came over to ask Benevolence why Mr. Wang was in such a bad mood.

Benevolence sighed. "You can't blame him really."

"Now that Mr. Wang has an official posting, he should be happy. What's there for him to be angry about?" Pearlie said.

"Mr. Wang had been fond of Little Rouge all along. He only married Constance because Little Rouge let him down. Who'd have known that Constance would let him down as well? Now because of that, he's been seeing Little Rouge again. But though he's seeing her, he's still angry at heart."

"How did Constance let him down?" Pearlie asked.

"Well, she did, and there's no point in talking about it."

Now Pearlie told him about her visit to Lotuson Wang's residence the other day and how she had overheard the beating of Constance.

"That was a near thing!" Benevolence said. "Mr. Wang gave her a beating and wanted to cast her out. Then Constance took raw opium. In the end, it took several of us old friends of his to persuade them to make up. The nephew was driven out of the house, and that's supposed to be the end of it."[1]

Pearlie sighed. "Constance is such a letdown! Little Rouge will be overjoyed when she hears about it. She'll choke with laughter!"

They were talking away merrily when menservants shouted downstairs. "The Younger Maestro is called to a party." Pearlie went back to the room across the way to accompany Twin Jade to the party.

Benevolence turned to Twin Pearl. "It's a pity Mr. Wang is leaving. Otherwise he could take up with Twin Jade. That'd have been nice."

"Now that you mention Twin Jade, I'm reminded of something. My mother wants to ask you a favor, but I forgot to tell you," Twin Pearl said.

"What is it?" Benevolence asked urgently.

"Twin Jade has refused to have any guests stay overnight since she came back from Rustic Retreat. Mother and I have spoken to her several times. She said Fifth Young Master is going to marry her, that it's all been settled. We can't very well tell her the truth. Could you please go and ask Fifth Young Master what he wants? If he wants

::

1. [From the scene in chapter 54, it's clear that Constance and Lotuson's nephew had an affair. E.H.]

her, he should take her home; if not, he should tell her, so she can start working again, right?"

"I'd never have thought Twin Jade had it in her to hatch such ambitious schemes," Benevolence said.

"With the two of them, it's all castles in the air. Even if Fifth Young Master is not betrothed, could he ever marry Twin Jade as his wife?" said Twin Pearl.

Before Benevolence could answer, Twin Jewel, who had not seen him for some time and decided to snatch this opportunity to come over, stepped into the room. She said right away, "Oh, a wife! Where is she? Let's have a look."

Twin Pearl, disgusted with her loose tongue, glared at her, which made her shut up and withdraw to sit on one side. Golden followed her into the room and whispered in her ear, and Twin Jewel whispered back. Golden swore softly, turned around, sat down, took out a set of ivory dominoes, and started fiddling with it. Benevolence asked Twin Jewel how things had been with her lately.

Soon Twin Jade returned from the party, and on hearing her Twin Jewel made herself scarce. Twin Jade came over and chatted for a while. When the clock struck midnight, Clever Baby brought them congee. Golden put aside the dominoes to wait on Benevolence, Twin Pearl, and Twin Jade. When they had finished eating, Clever Baby put away the bowls and chopsticks and Golden returned to her dominoes. Benevolence saw Eldest hiding in the darkness of the doorway and called out, "What're you doing?"

Eldest tiptoed away, only to return again to hover by the door. Twin Pearl was so disgusted that she just let him be.

Presently they heard the menservants remove the lamp over the front door and shut up for the night. Twin Jade took her leave to go to bed, and Clever Baby brought them another basin of warm water. Only then did Golden put away her ivory dominoes to wait on Twin Pearl as she washed her face and removed her jewelry. The paraffin lamp was blown out, the lamp on the dressing table lighted, the multicolored embroidered quilt on the bed removed, leaving just a light coverlet, and the bed was made. Clever Baby having left, Golden returned to where she had been sitting, her head bowed. Eldest edged into the room and cuddled up against her. Benevolence thought, "Let's see how this will turn out."

As Golden dawdled, Worth came in with a kettle to freshen the tea. He then turned around and stared at Golden, saying coldly, "Going home?"

Golden pouted without replying, took Eldest by the hand, and went ahead. Worth followed close behind. Once they got to the foot of the stairs, there was bedlam: the noise of cursing and beating from Worth, weeping and yelling from Golden, howling and hopping from Eldest was intermingled with Pearlie's and Clever Baby's attempts to make peace, the menservants' effort to pull them apart, and the sound of Orchid Zhou berating them all. The din was relentless.

Benevolence did not want to miss any of it, but as he peered down from the top of the stairs, he could see nothing. All he heard was Worth swearing as he beat Golden, demanding, "Where on First Avenue did you go? Tell me, where on First Avenue did you go?" He repeated this one question over and over again. Golden neither confessed nor begged for mercy; she just cried and yelled for all she was worth. In a turmoil of confused activity, Pearlie, Clever Baby, and the menservants pulled and tugged but failed utterly to separate them or block his assault. In the end, it was Orchid Zhou who, driven to a show of ferocity, stopped him with a desperate shout, "You're killing her!" As she shouted, Worth's hands slackened enough for the others to pull Golden away. Pearlie and Clever Baby immediately pushed her into Orchid Zhou's room.

Still in a rage, Worth seized Eldest instead and questioned him, "What did you go with your mother to First Avenue for? A fine son you are, you swine!" A blow hit Eldest with every curse, making him howl and hop all the more, his squeaking reminiscent of the squealing of a pig being butchered. The menservants tried to snatch the child away, but Worth, who had grabbed hold of Eldest's little pigtail, would sooner die than let go.

At this point, Twin Pearl had had enough. With her hair all unkempt, she rushed onto the landing and called out, "Worth, you're having a fine time lashing out like that, aren't you? He's a child, what does he know?"

Seeing that Twin Pearl had spoken, the menservants rushed up and pried loose Worth's hands. They carried Eldest into Orchid Zhou's room as well. Since there was nothing he could do, Worth made for the front door and strode off.

As Benevolence and Twin Pearl turned around to go to bed, they saw Twin Jade standing at her door, her hair uncombed, trying to find out if Golden was badly hurt.

"Worth just wanted to humiliate her. If he hurt her badly, she couldn't work, right?" Benevolence said with a smile.

Thereupon they all went to bed. Golden and Eldest slept in Orchid Zhou's that night.

The next morning, Benevolence got up before Twin Pearl. Golden happened to be in the room, sweeping the floor. Her eyes were still tearful, and a deep frown showed her gloom. Benevolence wanted to say something to comfort her but found it hard to do so. After breakfast, he had to be on his way and did not want to disturb Twin

Pearl, so he told Golden, "I'm off to Middle Peace Alley. Mention it to Third Maestro when she's up." Golden promised to do that.

Leaving Twin Pearl's house, Benevolence only had to walk down a couple of streets to reach the Zhu residence. At the sight of him, Longevity Zhang thought something terrible had happened. He asked in a panic, "What's the matter, Mr. Hong?"[2]

Slightly taken aback, Benevolence answered, "Why, nothing. I'm just looking in on your Fifth Young Master."

Reassured, Longevity led him straight into the inner study, where he met with Modesty Zhu. They sat down according to etiquette and began a conversation. Benevolence gradually came to the subject of Twin Jade. He praised her determination in refusing to receive any other overnight clients and suggested that perhaps Modesty should take her home. It would surely make for a nice romantic anecdote. But if Modesty were unwilling to do that, Orchid Zhou hoped he would explain this to Twin Jade face-to-face so she would not waste other opportunities just sitting around waiting for him.

Modesty merely made noises acknowledging his request, and when Benevolence insisted that he give a firm answer, he prevaricated by saying he would do it another day. There was nothing Benevolence could do but take his leave and report back to Orchid Zhou.

Having seen Benevolence out, Modesty returned to the study. He thought if he wanted to take Twin Jade as concubine, Harmony Qi was still the best person to consult. But Twin Jade had set her mind on becoming his wife and might be unwilling to be demoted to concubine. It'd perhaps be best to keep it from her until after their wedding ceremony. That way, she would have no choice but to accept a fait accompli.

In the afternoon, having found out that his elder brother, Amity, had gone out, Modesty took a sedan chair and headed for Conical Hat Garden. The menservants there, who knew him well by then, led his sedan chair directly into the garden and on to Panorama Hall. When he got off, they reported to him that His Excellency was taking his afternoon nap and invited him to sit for a while in the secretaries' room. Modesty nodded in agreement, so a manservant on duty led the way upstairs. He was greeted by the sound of ivory tiles clicking on a table, so he knew they were playing mah-jongg. As he hesitated, the manservant had already lifted the bamboo door curtain and asked him to enter.

::

2. [Obviously, Longevity has already got news that his lover had been given a beating the previous night and was worried that something worse could have happened. *E.H.*]

As Modesty Zhu entered the center room of Panorama Hall, he saw that the four mah-jongg players were Crane Li, Second Bai Gao, Devotion Yin, and Aroma Su. They all stood up to greet him. Aroma said promptly, "I've lost a lot of money for His Excellency. Why don't you take over for a while, Fifth Young Master?"

Modesty made an excuse, saying, "I don't know how."

"That doesn't matter. Aroma will help you," Second Bai Gao said.

"Don't you believe him. Who was it who played mah-jongg with Twin Jade at the Phoenix Pavilion if it wasn't him?" Devotion Yin cut in.

Modesty was thus obliged to join in and take a seat. They had just played four games when Harmony Qi, having had his siesta, came in at a sedate pace. Seeing him, Modesty immediately stood up to give him his place at the table.

"You carry on," Harmony Qi said. But Modesty adamantly refused, so Harmony told Aroma to take over again while he chatted with Modesty. With all these people present, Modesty could not mention what was on his mind. He kept procrastinating until Harmony Qi decided to return to the game. He told Modesty, "You stay here tonight. Later, you can send for Twin Jade and spend a couple of days here. Don't go home till after we've had the viewing of the chrysanthemums."[1] Modesty stuttered his acceptance of the invitation.

It was getting dark when the mah-jongg game was over. They left Panorama Hall and strolled southward. Harmony Qi pointed across the water and said, "Well, it turns out that the chrysanthemum hill is completed and only the viewing shed is yet to be finished."

Crane Li and Modesty Zhu looked into the distance, but all they saw were three or four workmen squatting on the rooftops of some

::

1. [One of the major seasonal events, the viewing of chrysanthemums in autumn involved major planning and preparation. Numerous potted plants were used to create hill-shaped formations called "chrysanthemum hills," and to afford a better view of the flowers, raised structures were put up for the viewers.

Viewing chrysanthemums was also a major event in the calendar of second-class brothels. The "chrysanthemum hills" in the brothels were just small-scale formations and figurines placed on a table. Wealthy patrons who normally did not frequent second-class houses would host banquets there for the viewing. It was therefore an opportunity for the second-class brothels to attract new clients. *E.H.*]

building in the southwest corner of the garden; there was no sign of any chrysanthemum hill. They looked left and right and caught sight of a section of vermilion railings in the midst of sprouting bamboos.

"We're right behind the chrysanthemum hill, so we can't see it from here," Second Bai explained.

"Don't worry about that! It won't be ready for another day," Devotion Yin said.

As they were talking, they had reached the fishing bank, where there was a magnificent building with three rooms. The signboard hanging over the door declared it to be the Crisp Air Abode. The spirited calligraphy made the words look as if they were in flight. The sunset glow turned the sky into a myriad colors and illuminated all the rooms in the building. They walked around outside to admire the scene before they entered the house together. The menservants had already set the table for a banquet. When the girls called to the party—Grace Yang, Twin Jade, Wenjun Yao, and Flora Zhang—had all arrived, Harmony Qi invited his guests to come to the table.

Grace Yang took an invitation out of her sleeve and unobtrusively passed it to Crane Li, who read it, tucked it into his sash-purse and began fidgeting. Preoccupied with leaving, what interest did the wine hold for him? Modesty Zhu, who was also preoccupied, was not in the mood for drinking, either. Things were therefore rather quiet at the table.

After all the dishes had been served, Crane Li made an excuse and rose to take his leave. Harmony Qi smiled cynically and said, "Don't you try to deceive me! I know what important business you have. Your timing is perfect."

Crane Li was too abashed to say anything else. Soon the banquet was over, and the guests left the table to sit around. Only then did Crane Li and Grace Yang thank the host and take their leave. They got into their sedan chairs in front of Crisp Air Abode, and when they reached the garden gatehouse, they parted company. Grace Yang headed back to Generosity Alley while Crane Li turned north and after a couple of yards stopped by a gate. Second Kuang pushed open a side door, and somebody came out with a lamp to greet them, saying, "Eldest Young Mr. Li, you're a bit late today, aren't you?"

Crane Li saw that it was Verdure Xu. He nodded at him and then followed him into the house. When they reached the inner door, where there was a brass lamp set in the wall, Verdure Xu stopped there and let Crane Li and his servant go in by themselves. They passed through a maze of brightly lit corridors to the main hall. There, some sixty or seventy people were crowded together in the middle of the room. Peddlers of snacks and fruit threaded among them, but everyone was quiet. The only sound came from the dealer, who occasionally called out "blue dragon" or "white tiger." This was the "cash only" table.

Crane Li stood on tiptoe and saw that the banker was Muddy Dragon. He walked away from the crowd toward the back of the main hall. Seeing him, the doorkeeper hastily let him and his servant through. It was the way to the parlor, and the attendants came running out to welcome them. One man took Second Kuang somewhere else to entertain him while another asked Crane Li into the parlor. At one end of the room was a tall counter, and behind it stood Clement Zhou, the bookkeeper. This was where chips were bought. Crane Li produced a money order for two thousand dollars and handed it over.

"Best of luck! Best of luck!" Zhou said repeatedly as he issued Crane Li with the chips.

Crane Li smiled in acknowledgment. Then he was ushered upstairs. There, three rooms were opened up to make one airy space that was as brightly lit as day. At the center of the room was a large table with a fitted cover of baize cloth. Some dozen people were seated around it. All was quiet.

Third Shu, the banker, was on a winning streak, which, naturally, made Crane Li envious. When Third Shu stepped down, Fourth Qiao succeeded him. Crane Li looked around and then asked, "Why isn't Lai the Turtle here?"

"He's gone home," Third Shu replied. "We were just saying that with the Turtle gone, there's one less person who'll be banker."

Crane Li said, "That's a pity."

Fourth Qiao displayed his dice, and the game commenced. Crane Li took a pencil and a piece of foreign paper to draw a chart of the numbers that had come out and then placed his bets accordingly, but he failed to get a winning string, so he stopped betting and went to the opium divan to smoke. A while later, Fourth Qiao lost heavily to Willow Yang and Eminence Lü, who had bet on the same numbers several times in a row. Qiao had no choice but to pick up his dice and leave.

The thought that no one but Lai the Turtle would place a big bet made Crane Li rise swiftly from the opium divan. Confident and emboldened, he sat down at the head of the table, fetched his dice out of his pocket, and shook the bowl as banker. He started off winning more than he paid out and managed a profit of about two thousand. Suddenly, several punters won on the same number, and his takings were not enough to pay the bets. Full of regret, he thought about stopping right there, but he wanted to break even. Unfortunately, his luck had turned, and he threw two losing combinations in succession. All the punters won while he had lost as much as five or six thousand.

In his hurry to recoup his loss, he threw caution to the wind, with disastrous consequences. Fourth Qiao led the way by placing a thousand on ascending numbers. Third Shu followed suit with a thousand plus another five hundred on a line sequence. Then others followed with three to four hundred or seven to eight hundred, all betting on ascending numbers. Crane Li, unaware of the danger, thought gleefully: how can they be sure the numbers will be ascending? As he lifted the lid, all eyes were on the bowl. There neatly sat the four dice: 1, 2, 4, 6. Crane Li just stared in anger, too upset even to speak. The others worked out for him that he needed to pay out some sixteen thousand. The money order he had brought along, together with a dozen or so gold ingots, only amounted to a little over ten thousand. He was frantic, not knowing what to do.

"What's the worry?" Fourth Qiao said with a smile. "Borrow some money for now to pay the bets. You can pay it back tomorrow."

Thus reminded, Crane Li asked Willow Yang and Eminence Lü to be his guarantors for a loan of five thousand from Third Shu. He wrote out an IOU then and there specifying the loan was to be repaid in three days. That enabled him to settle all the winning bets, after which he went back to lie down on the opium divan. But the more he thought about his loss, the angrier he felt. Before dawn broke, he called for Second Kuang to light the lamp and walked out along the original route, got into his sedan chair, and headed back to the Long Peace Inn on Pebble Road. Once there, he hammered on the door until it was opened and went into his room to sleep without even enquiring about his uncle Pragmatic Li. Not until the next day after lunch did he ask Second Kuang, "Where's Fourth Master?"

"Where else but Great Prosperity Alley?" Second Kuang answered, smiling.

It occurred to Crane Li that a few days before he had bought a thousand baskets of Niu Village cooking oil together with Pragmatic, who held the sales receipts that could serve as a guarantee in lieu of cash to tide him over the emergency. He told Second Kuang to keep watch while he walked over to Perfection Chu's in Great Prosperity Alley. There, he saw an empty sedan chair at the door, and three sedan-chair bearers standing in the courtyard. He was a little puzzled and apprehensive.

Third Sister Chu recognized Crane Li and came out from the parlor to welcome him, calling out, "Do come in, Eldest Young Master. Fourth Master is here."

Crane Li went in and asked, "Is that Fourth Master's sedan chair?"

"No, it's the doctor Fourth Master sent for, called Hill Dou. He's upstairs. Please come and sit upstairs, Eldest Young Master."

Crane Li went upstairs. Pragmatic Li, who was stretched out on the opium divan, sat up to greet him. Perfection greeted him bashfully. Dr. Hill Dou, however, just sat with his head bowed, writing out his prescription, and did not even acknowledge Crane Li's presence.

Crane Li sat down casually. He saw that Pragmatic still had several scars from eruptions on his cheeks and temples. A stack of bamboo paper stood ready in the opium tray to be used for wiping away the pus. Perfection Chu, though her face was still flushed and her eyes had dark circles around them, was not the least bit scarred.

In a minute, Hill Dou finished his prescription and took his leave. Only then did Crane Li ask Pragmatic for the receipts.

"What do you want them for?" Pragmatic asked, astonished.

"Yesterday, Old Zhai mentioned that the cotton crop this year is interesting. I want to buy some," Crane Li answered with a lie.

At this, Pragmatic smiled derisively. He was about to question him when he heard Third Sister Chu coming slowly up the stairs. She came into the room with a tray heaped full of snacks. She first took a lidded cup of tea from the tray and brought it to Crane Li and then placed four plates on the table. The plates held sweet buns, savory buns, steamed cakes, and watermelon seeds. She then put two pairs of chopsticks on the table.

Pragmatic asked, "Why did you buy all this without telling us?"

Grinning, Third Sister Chu made no reply; instead, she pushed Perfection Chu forward. Perfection Chu took an unwilling step toward Crane Li and said, "Please have some tea, Eldest Young Master."

Her voice being a bit faint, Crane Li did not take notice, so Third Sister Chu went up to him, saying, "Do have some, Eldest Young Master." As she spoke, she took a pair of ivory chopsticks and picked up one of each of the snacks for Crane Li. Before he could stop her, she had put every variety, including melon seeds, on his plate.

"Just eat whatever you like," Pragmatic said to him with a smile.

To show appreciation for her hospitality, Crane Li broke off a piece of a cake and washed it down with a sip of tea. Third Sister Chu, who was standing by his side, suddenly thought of cigarettes. She hurriedly took a packet from a drawer, drew one out, and offered it together with a lighted spill to Crane Li, saying, "Eldest Young Master, please have a smoke."

Crane Li, with a teacup in his hand and cake in his mouth, couldn't take the cigarette or smoke it; he started to laugh. Embarrassed, Perfection Chu tugged at the hem of Third Sister's jacket, which finally made her step back.

Now Pragmatic handed the prescription to Third Sister Chu. She asked, "Did the doctor say anything?"

"All he said was now that I'm improving, I should be careful," Pragmatic replied.

"Buddha be thanked! Now you're getting well. When you came down with it, we were worried to death." Then she turned to say to Crane Li, "Eldest Young Master, Fourth Master got into the habit of smoking a little opium. Now, in the country, it's not like in Shanghai; the small opium dens there are all filthy places. I suppose Fourth Master got contaminated by the poisonous air there without being aware of it. When Fourth Master had just arrived, it looked so horrible; it was all over his face. We wondered, 'Where on earth did Fourth Master catch it from?' And Fourth Master neglected himself so; even he had no idea where he got it from. Perfection and I, the two of us, attended him day and night, not getting any sleep. Fortunately, with this doctor, he got better after several doses of medicine. Otherwise, Perfection and I could have caught it from Fourth Master. Now, if we both broke out with those eruptions, that would've been the death of us! Don't you think so, Eldest Young Master?"

Crane Li marveled at the fact that she had the audacity to say something like that. He eyed Perfection Chu appraisingly.

Third Sister Chu continued, "D'you know, Eldest Young Master, there're people who don't know the truth, and they spread wicked rumors about us; it's maddening! They say Fourth Master caught the disease at our place. Now, there're just the two of us here, Perfection and me, both neat and clean. We don't have eruptions, do we? If Perfection has them, is Fourth Master blind, can't he see?" So saying, she pulled Perfection toward Crane Li and pointed to her face, "Do look, Eldest Young Master, does our Perfection have anything on her face like Fourth Master's?" Then she showed him Perfection's arms, turning them this way and that. "Look, not a trace!" Perfection was so embarrassed, she wrenched herself free and stood to one side.

Crane Li did not say a word. He thought to himself: this Third Sister Chu is truly an old fox. If Pragmatic fell for this, he would be in great trouble.

A little annoyed, Pragmatic told Third Sister off. "What d'you care about rumors? I never said this of you; that's all that counts."

She responded with a smile. "Of course you didn't, Fourth Master. If you had blamed us, then we'd . . ." She stopped in midsentence and went downstairs, smiling all the way.

Only then did Pragmatic turn to Crane Li. "As for you, stop playing your tricks. If you gamble your own money away, it's none of my business. But if I let you take the receipts from my hands and you lose them in gambling, what am I to say when I get home?"

Crane Li, though silent, was much displeased.

"The receipts are in the small leather suitcase at the inn. If you want them, go get them yourself. I can't very well hand them over to you," Pragmatic continued.

After the briefest moment of pondering Crane Li got up to go.

"D'you want the key?" Pragmatic asked.

Crane Li was in too much of a huff to ask for it. Downstairs, Third Sister Chu tried to detain him. "Eldest Young Master, do stay a little longer." He ignored her, too, and walked out of Great Prosperity Alley to make his way back to Long Peace Inn. He thought: Pragmatic didn't want to be held responsible, and yet he told me to get the receipts myself. Does that mean he'll accuse me of stealing? Such a mean and stingy man! No wonder Third Sister tricks and manipulates him! I don't want anything to do with him now, but what about my debt to Third Shu? After thinking hard about it, he decided that all he could do was to take the deeds of the two houses he owned and ask Whistler Tang to use them as collateral for borrowing ten thousand dollars. He took the sedan chair to the Zhu residence in Middle Peace Alley in search of Whistler. The latter promised to help and told him to get an answer that evening at Grace Yang's. Crane Li was to go there early and wait for Whistler.

Having seen Crane Li out, Whistler calculated that they did not have enough cash at Amity Zhu's, so he needed to confer with Prosperity Luo. He went to Green Phoenix's in Prosperity Alley right away, where he found Luo in her room. He was invited in and greetings were exchanged. Second Sister happened to be there and also greeted him, saying, "Mr. Tang."

Whistler nodded in acknowledgment. "Haven't seen you for a long time. How's business?".

"Oh, business is impossible. It's fallen off very badly."

Green Phoenix snorted and cut in, "You just aren't interested in doing business. What's so impossible about it?"

As Whistler Tang had no idea what she meant, he brushed the remark aside and took the deeds out of his sleeve to show Prosperity Luo, explaining to him Crane Li's request for a loan. Prosperity knew Whistler was a reliable man, so he agreed immediately and left with him to get a money order at a Chinese bank.

Now that Prosperity Luo and Whistler Tang had gone and they were alone in the room, Second Sister said to Green Phoenix, "I looked over a respectable woman the other day. She's not bad, so I thought I'd just buy her. The only thing is, she's new and doesn't know how to do business. Just for the year-end season, we'll be three to four hundred dollars short. I'm so worried!"

Green Phoenix bent her head and said nothing.

"Could you think of a way out for me?" Second Sister asked. "Should I get a partner? Or maybe rent out the upstairs rooms?"

Green Phoenix still kept her head down and looked as if she were thinking. Her expression made Second Sister hopeful, so she continued to plead her case rather shamelessly, "I'm much obliged to you! All the things you told me, I'll do as you said. If business gets a bit better, I'll never forget you. I'd be much obliged if you could think of something for me."

Green Phoenix finally spoke. "The trouble with you is greed. I can't think of anything now, but even if I can show you the way to make three or four hundred dollars, you'll just complain that it's too little."

Second Sister could not protest fast enough. "That's not true! I'll be delighted to make whatever I can. I'd never dare complain it's too little!"

Green Phoenix resumed her silent contemplation for close to half an hour, during which time Second Sister wisely waited on one side, keeping very quiet. Then Green Phoenix opened her eyes and looked at her appraisingly before signaling for her to come close. As Green Phoenix whispered into her ear, Second Sister listened intently, bending low. Green Phoenix talked for close to half an hour, and Second Sister picked up many useful tips.

Just when their discussion came to an end, Prosperity Luo came back. He handed Green Phoenix the collateral documents, telling her to put them in a safe place. Second Sister, who followed Green Phoenix to the area behind the bed to hold up the lid of the trunk for her, asked in astonishment, "How come there're two of Mr. Luo's document boxes?"

"Well, one of these is mine. It holds my ransom papers," Green Phoenix replied.

Prosperity heard her lock everything up securely, and then Second Sister took her leave. "Humph! I guessed right, didn't I? She wanted to borrow money from me."

"Again?" Prosperity asked, surprised.

"D'you think *she'd* ever learn to be sensible? It's not even been two months, but the thousand dollars are all gone."

He didn't pay this much attention. It was in one ear and out the other for him.

Two days later, Second Sister again came to plead with Green Phoenix, but the latter was determined not to part with even one cent. For five days running, Second Sister kept pestering Green

Phoenix, who just ignored her. This angered Second Sister, and she turned nasty. It was all too much for Prosperity, so he tried to make peace between them. But he had not expected Second Sister to ask for as much as five hundred dollars. When he tried to persuade her to settle for less, she went on and on about how good to Green Phoenix she had been. "Now that she's good at business, she's forgotten what she owes me. I definitely won't have that. Ransomed or not, she's still my daughter. Can she run away to a foreign country?"

Finding it impossible to talk to her, Prosperity repeated her remarks to Green Phoenix.

"I have the ransom papers, so why should I be afraid of her? She's welcome to try whatever tricks she likes," Green Phoenix responded with a smile.

CHAPTER 59 :: *Second Sister employs an old ruse to filch important documents, and Jade Wenjun begs for a poem to boost her fame*

One afternoon, Second Sister went to Green Phoenix's, ready to make a scene. Green Phoenix's reaction was to tell a manservant to summon two carriages and then to go with Prosperity Luo for a ride to Luna Park, leaving Second Sister to her own devices. By the time they had their tea in Luna Park, Green Phoenix was still laughing scornfully. "I've got the ransom papers, let's see what tricks she can come up with."

"You should have told your servant girl to keep her company," Prosperity said.

Green Phoenix jerked her neck to look away. "Just let her be. Why should anyone keep her company?"

"This won't do!" he said.

"Why? Are you afraid she'll steal my furniture?"

"She wouldn't want any furniture, but she knows the ransom papers are in the trunk. Wouldn't she steal them?"

Reminded of this danger, Green Phoenix stared straight in front of her and let out a cry, "Aiyo! I'm in for it!"

Mama Zhao, who was standing by her side, was also momentarily stunned. She said, "Oh dear me! Let's go home at once."

Prosperity told Green Phoenix to go first, but she said, "Naturally you're coming with us. If the papers have been stolen, at least we'll be able to consult you about what to do."

And so the three of them rushed home in their original carriages.

As soon as she entered the house, Green Phoenix asked, "Is Mother upstairs?"

"She just went home a minute ago," the menservants replied.

Green Phoenix rushed up the stairs and into her room. She saw that the furnishings and ornaments were all there. Then she went behind the bed and opened the trunk. It gave her such a start that she stamped her feet, shouting, "Now I'm done for!"

Prosperity ran up after her and saw the hinges of the trunk lying on the floor. When he lifted the lid, he saw just one document box inside. In desperation, Green Phoenix stamped her feet, weeping and cursing, vowing she'd fight Second Sister to the death. Prosperity and Mama Zhao tried to persuade her to sit down and talk it over.

"What's there to talk about? She wants my life. If I die, what good will it do her?" Green Phoenix said.

"You should put my document box somewhere safe; then we'll talk about it." Prosperity said.

When Green Phoenix took the document box from the trunk, she suddenly cried out in astonishment, "Why, this is *my* document box!" Then the truth dawned on her. "She took the wrong box! She's got Mr. Luo's document box!" So saying, she burst into hearty laughter.

Prosperity panicked when he heard this. "Where is my document box then?"

She held up the box in her hands to show him, saying in great merriment, "She took the wrong box! She took yours. Mine is still here."

His face turned an ashen gray. He slapped his thigh and exclaimed, "Now that's really bad."

"Your document box will be all right. It's of no use to her. Would she dare to sell it? She wouldn't know where to go even if she did."

He sat there in a daze thinking about this. Green Phoenix called Mama Zhao over and gave her these instructions: "Go and tell Mother that she's got Mr. Luo's document box. Ask her why she has taken it. Tell her Mr. Luo needs it and is waiting for it. She's to bring it back."

Mama Zhao went to carry out her orders. Prosperity remained uneasy and nervous, but Green Phoenix was sure that Second Sister had absolutely no reason to hold on to the box.

A little later, Mama Zhao returned. Before she spoke, she clapped her hands merrily and had a good laugh. Then she reported, "It's really funny! They didn't even realize they'd taken the wrong box; they were still rejoicing over it. When I said it was Mr. Luo's box, they were stunned, couldn't get a word out. I just laughed and laughed! They told me to bring the box back with me, but I said 'None of my business!' and walked out of there."

Prosperity stamped his foot in frustration, "Goodness! Why didn't you bring it back?"

"Since they took it, let them bring it back themselves," Mama Zhao replied.

"It's all right. They'll come and return it later," Green Phoenix said.

Like an ant on a hot stove, Prosperity could find no rest whether he sat or stood. He was consumed by anxiety. Seeing how worried he was, Green Phoenix wanted to send Mama Zhao to speed up the matter, but Prosperity stopped her. Instead he summoned Promotion and told him to demand the document box from Second Sister. He further instructed him, "Don't mention anything else, just say I need the document box for some business and you're to bring it back quickly."

Having got his instructions, Promotion went straight to Second Sister's in Generosity Alley. When Second Sister saw him, she was all smiles as she invited him into the little room at the back. Promotion delivered his master's message and demanded that the document box be handed over instantly.

"The document box is here, but I have something to say to Mr. Luo. Don't be in such a hurry; do sit down," Second Sister said.

Promotion had no choice but to sit down. Second Sister called out for somebody to make a cup of tea and then said to him very calmly, "You came at just the right moment. I've got lots of things to say, and I hope you'll convey them to Mr. Luo. When Green Phoenix was here working for me, we did booming business, so much so we were run off our feet. But our expenses were great, so there never was much money left. After Green Phoenix bought back her freedom, things went downhill. There's no business at all, but the expenses remain the same. The thousand dollars she paid for her ransom was gone before I knew it, and I didn't know what to do. I asked Green Phoenix for a loan of a few hundred dollars, but she flatly refused. I went to see her several times, and each time she said she didn't have it. Now when Green Phoenix was a child, I was the one who combed her hair and bound her feet, who groomed her all the way, treating her like my own daughter. And she turns out to be so ungrateful! This was the first time I asked for a loan, and she didn't have any scruples about turning me down. The anger nearly killed me! Now I'm done with talking to her. I had intended to take her ransom papers so I could get her back to work for me, and if she wanted to buy her freedom again, I wouldn't have settled for less than ten thousand. As it happened, I took the wrong box; instead of the ransom papers, I now have Mr. Luo's box! Mr. Luo has always been a good friend to us, always giving us business and sometimes lending me ten or twenty dollars. I'm not ungrateful like Green

Phoenix; I'm always mindful of Mr. Luo's kindness. So as soon as I learned it was Mr. Luo's box, I wanted to send it over at once. But then I thought, Green Phoenix and Mr. Luo are as if one, and Mr. Luo's box is no different from hers. I'm disgusted with Green Phoenix, so I'm borrowing the box from Mr. Luo as security and asking Green Phoenix to ransom it for ten thousand dollars. When she delivers the money, I'll return the box to Mr. Luo. You just go back and tell Mr. Luo he has nothing to worry about."

On hearing this little speech, Promotion stuck out his tongue in awe, not daring to make any comment. He returned to Prosperity Alley and reported everything in detail. Before Promotion was through, Green Phoenix jumped up and shouted, "How dare she talk like that! The woman was farting through her mouth!"

Prosperity also trembled with anger. He lay paralyzed on the divan, unable to say a word.

After looking dazed for a moment, Green Phoenix abruptly stood up and headed for the stairs, saying, "I'll go."

Prosperity grabbed her. "What are you going to do?"

"I'll ask her if it's my life that she wants."

He stepped up to block her way, "Hold on a minute. If you go, there'll be nothing but angry words. I'd better go myself. Let's see if she has the audacity to say the same thing to me. Even if we give in to her, it'll only be a loan of a few hundred dollars."

Green Phoenix gritted her teeth. "You're infuriating! How can you even think about paying her off?"

He called for Promotion to get his sedan chair ready and went on his way. Little Treasure welcomed him and invited him into the room formerly occupied by Green Phoenix. Gold Phoenix and Pearl Phoenix greeted him as "Brother-in-law" and said, "You haven't been here for a long time."

"Where's your mother?"

"She's coming," Little Treasure replied.

Indeed Second Sister was at that moment entering the room. Smiling sweetly, she walked up to Prosperity and knelt down to kowtow to him, apologizing all the way, "Don't be angry, Mr. Luo, I'm kowtowing to you for all that I've done. Your document box will just be kept here for a couple of days; it's as safe as keeping it at Green Phoenix's. You have always been a good friend to me, Mr. Luo, would I dare damage the valuable things in the box and bring you trouble? You might as well keep out of it, Mr. Luo, for Green Phoenix will have to ransom it, never fear. When she gets desperate and comes to see me, then we will talk. Would someone like Green Phoenix cough up ten thousand dollars unless she's desperate?"

All this nonsense infuriated Prosperity. Yet he controlled himself and asked, "Enough of this silly talk. How much d'you want to borrow from her? Let's hear it and see."

"This is no silly talk, Mr. Luo," she said, smiling. "At first, I only wanted a loan of a few hundred dollars, but now it's different. Green Phoenix is ungrateful, so in the future if I'm short of money again, she won't be lending me any, and I won't want the embarrassment of going to her again. Now that your document box happens to be here, it's a heaven-sent opportunity for me to get a tidy sum out of her once and for all. Ten thousand is not too much! The collateral papers Mr. Tang brought the other day, don't they come to ten thousand, too?"

"So you're trying to extort money from me. It's got nothing to do with Green Phoenix," he said.

She defended herself immediately. "That's not true, Mr. Luo! How would Green Phoenix have ten thousand dollars? Naturally she'd have to borrow it from you. Your party bills at the house come to a thousand per season. If you take it out of the bills, it'll be cleared within three years. Right, Mr. Luo?"

Unable to respond to that, Prosperity snorted and walked away. She saw him out, apologizing repeatedly, "I owe you many apologies, Mr. Luo. It's all because we have no business and our money has run out. After all, when you're facing starvation, would you be afraid of any unpleasantness? If Green Phoenix remains stubborn, I might just set the lot of it on fire. If that happens, how is she going to face you, Mr. Luo?"

He pretended not to hear her and departed in his sedan chair. When Green Phoenix came up to ask how it went, he just groaned and sighed and shook his head. Only when she pressed him did he give her a brief account. Green Phoenix went through the roof. She seized a pair of scissors and was determined to kill herself in front of Second Sister. At a loss what to do, Prosperity did not stop her. But as she rushed downstairs, she ran into Mama Zhao, who wrested the scissors from her and, half by persuasion and half by force, managed to carry her upstairs.

Still struggling, Green Phoenix said, "I'm going to die anyway. Why are you all ganging up to help them? Why don't you let me go?"

Mama Zhao pressed her down firmly into a chair and spoke to her gently, "Eldest Maestro, it's no use even if you kill yourself. If you died, they'd be faced with punishment by death, in which case they might indeed burn the document box in revenge, and Mr. Luo's loss would be in the tens of thousands."

Upon hearing this, Prosperity also chimed in to stop Green Phoenix, who was so angry that she skipped supper and went straight to bed. Prosperity's fury kept him awake all night. Rising early in the morning, he went to consult Whistler Tang at the Zhu residence in Middle Peace Alley.

"Green Phoenix bought back her freedom for just a thousand dollars," Whistler said, "and now they're asking for a loan of ten thousand; it's a clear case of extortion. But you can't really bring in the police because, first, you have committed the offense of consorting with prostitutes and, second, you may not find the stolen objects on their premises as evidence. Besides, you have to be wary of the possibility that they'd burn the evidence in order to deny everything. Your document box contains official as well as private papers. To obtain duplicates for all of them involves not just tremendous expense but may also cause thorny problems."

On reflection, Prosperity realized he had no way out, so he asked Whistler to act as middleman in the negotiation, which Whistler promised to do. Prosperity then went to the bureau to attend to his work. It was not until dusk, when official business was over, that he returned to Green Phoenix's by sedan chair. As he entered the house, he saw Jade Wenjun seated at leisure in the parlor. She greeted him cordially, so he stopped and nodded in acknowledgment with a smile.

"Did you see the papers today, Mr. Luo?" she asked.

Greatly alarmed, Prosperity turned pale and asked urgently, "What's in the papers?"

"It says a guest's friend—now what's his name? It's a real tongue twister . . ." She tried hard to remember the name.

"Never mind the name. What about him?"

"Oh, nothing. He wrote two poems dedicated to me. They're said to be in the newspapers."

"I don't understand poetry," he said with a chuckle and went upstairs without looking back.

Rather put out of countenance, Jade Wenjun turned around to say to a manservant, "Just now I was telling you Shanghai is full of uncultured men. Well, it looks like Mr. Luo's not too cultured, either. He's a client of this house, and he doesn't even understand poetry; what a fine state of affairs!"

"Here comes your cultured man," the manservant responded. Looking up to find that it was Thatch Fang, Jade Wenjun complained to him, "All this sarcasm! Isn't it maddening?"

Thatch Fang walked into the study on the right and then replied, "That's a minor point. But why talk to these people at all? Doesn't the smell of vulgarity sicken you?"

She repented, saying, "Of course! Thank you for reminding me."

Thatch Fang sat down and took out a newspaper. "Here're the poems the Romantic Lyricist dedicated to you. Have you seen them yet?"

"No, not yet. Do show me."

Thatch Fang spread out the newspaper and pointed the poems out to her.

"What's he saying? Please tell me," she said.

Thatch Fang put on his glasses, recited the poems, and then explained them. She was overjoyed.

"You should address two poems to him in reply," he said. "I'll correct them for you. For a title, you can use 'In Answer to the Romantic Lyricist, Using His Original Rhyme.' Wouldn't that be nice?"

"That'd be in the form of the eight-line regulated verse. I don't know how to do the parallelism for the four lines in the middle. Why don't you write them for me?"

"Now that'd take a lot of work. Tomorrow is the meeting day of our Poetry Club On-the-Sea, how would I find the time for it?"

"Please, just write something, anything."

He looked sternly at her. "Mind what you say! Poetry is a serious and important matter. How can one write just anything?"

She apologized hastily for her mistake, after which he continued, "But since I'm writing for you, I do have to go a bit easy. If it shows too much craftsmanship, it won't look like a poem by you, and no one would believe you wrote it, right?"

She thoroughly agreed. And so he closed his eyes and wagged his head, humming under his breath. After a while, he abruptly lifted a finger, poked at the marble tabletop several times, and drew some lines on it. He then said with a frown, "The rhyme he used is very difficult. It can't be done offhand. I'll go home and write a couple of fine lines for you."

"Do stay for supper," she said.

"Another day," he replied. She bade him to keep the matter secret, as they said farewell.

Thatch Fang strolled out of Prosperity Alley, mumbling to himself all the way, still engrossed in constructing a poem. Suddenly, a maid rushed out of a side alley and grabbed him by the arm, saying, "Where're you going, Mr. Fang?"

Taken by surprise, Thatch Fang did not know how to react. He gazed at the woman, squinting, and dimly recognized her as Laurel Zhao's maid, the one she called Grandma. So he also greeted her as Grandma just to be polite.

"Why don't you come to our place? Let's go," said Grandma.

"I don't have time now. I'll come tomorrow."

"Nonsense! Our young lady misses you terribly. We invited you several times, but you never came." Brooking no protests, she dragged him into Laurel Zhao's in Generosity Alley. Laurel welcomed him into her room and asked, "Have we offended you in any way, Mr. Fang? You never even came once."

Thatch Fang smiled and sat down. Grandma attempted to make conversation, "Except for a party call to Sky in a Wine Pot last season, you haven't seen us at all. It's been over two months now; aren't you embarrassed?"

"He's bewitched by Jade Wenjun," Laurel chimed in. "How would he think of coming here?"

Thatch Fang shouted at once to stop her, "Don't talk nonsense. Jade Wenjun is my girl pupil. It's all very proper and polite, so don't you try to smear her. It's absurd!"

"Humph!" was Laurel's only response.

Grandma spoke to him in a low voice as she prepared a water pipe for him. "There's no deceiving you, Mr. Fang, as to our miss's business. Last season, with you looking after us, we managed to get by, but now even you don't come anymore. We haven't even had a party for several days now. While Grace Yang downstairs has mah-jongg and drinking parties, a real lively crowd, we're all quiet and deserted up here. Isn't it humiliating?"

Thatch Fang cut in, "Mah-jongg parties and drinking parties are so vulgar. Remember I got Laurel's name into the newspapers a while ago? Everyone in all the eighteen provinces of China has seen it, and they all know there is a Laurel Zhao in Shanghai. D'you think mah-jongg parties and drinking parties can compare with that?"

Following his track, Grandma continued her efforts. "Would you look after us a bit just like before, Mr. Fang? You could carry on seeing Jade Wenjun, but please also come here now and then, OK? Throw a couple of drinking parties and mah-jongg parties. We'll try our best to please you."

"Mah-jongg parties and drinking parties are *so* commonplace! Wait a couple of days, and I'll write another couple of poems for her."

"Mr. Fang, parties may be commonplace to you, but they're good for us. You take all the trouble to write something, but it's no use to her. Even if you don't want mah-jongg and drinking parties, give her a party call when you go to a dinner; that would be good, too."

He laughed derisively and said, "Oh, such vulgarity!"

Seeing that Thatch Fang was too dumb to see her point, Grandma turned to Laurel and said something in street slang. Laurel just nodded. This was of course beyond Thatch Fang. When Grandma had filled the water pipe, Laurel asked him to place his order for supper. He begged off strenuously but to no avail, so he told them instead not to order from a restaurant but to get some smoked and salted meat. Grandma relayed the order to the menservants, and when the food came, she took it upstairs along with the homemade dishes and rice.

CHAPTER 60 :: *An old man gets an opium addict for a wife, and the keeper-turned-thief performs a vanishing act*

After Thatch Fang and Laurel Zhao had had supper, Grandma cleared the things away and went downstairs. Thatch waited a little while before he took his leave. Laurel, having tried in vain to make him stay, saw him to the staircase landing and called out loudly, "Grandma, Mr. Fang is leaving." Upon hearing this, Grandma caught up with him. "Mr. Fang, hold on a minute. I'd like a word if I may."

Thatch asked, "What is it?"

She whispered into his ear, "I suggest you stop going to Jade Wenjun's, Mr. Fang. Our place is just the same. I'll be your matchmaker; how about that?"

This abrupt proposal both startled and gladdened him. His heart thumped wildly, and his body turned quite numb with excitement. Thinking he was still hesitant, she again whispered, "Mr. Fang, you're a guest of long standing; it doesn't matter. We'll count it as a party call, and on top of that, there's just the servants' tips. It won't come to much, don't worry."

He grinned silently, which showed her he was willing, so she dragged him back upstairs.

Laurel asked on purpose, "Why were you in such a hurry to leave? Eager to see Jade Wenjun, right?"

Grandma answered before he could, "He sure was, but he's not allowed to go now."

"Jade Wenjun is calling for you; beware! If you go there tomorrow, you'll get a beating," Laurel said teasingly.

"Stuff and nonsense!" Thatch Fang said repeatedly.

Having played her role, Grandma went off. Laurel prepared a pipe of opium and offered it to Thatch, but he shook his head, saying, "I don't." She then smoked it herself. Seeing this, he asked, "How much of a habit is it for you?"

"I just do it for fun. A pellet or two can't be called a habit," she replied.

"All addicts get the habit from smoking it for fun. It's best not to touch it."

"Don't worry. How can I work if I'm addicted?" she replied.

He went on to ask about her situation, and she asked him about his work. It happened that one of them had no surviving family, and the other had neither wife, nor concubine, nor children. This lonely old couple thus developed a certain empathy for each other.

"My father was a brothel owner," Laurel told him. "When I was a virgin courtesan, I didn't lack for clothes, jewelry, and furniture; they were all my mother's things. But we were swindled by a client who left unpaid bills worth a thousand dollars. As a result, the house closed down and my parents died. After that, I rented these rooms and have ended up in debt for three hundred dollars."

"Shanghai is full of such heartless swindlers, so it's hard for all you working girls. Now, with people like us, who have been in the city for decades, we give the occasional party call or come for a tea party. While it's not lucrative business, we always honor our bills, so all the sing-song houses say we're respectable people and treat us very cordially."

"I don't have any vain hopes anymore. This is not an easy line of work, and I certainly won't get the best kind of business. I'm willing to make a home with any guest who'll pay my debts for me."

"Settling down is of course the best thing, but do be careful. If you should get swindled again, you'd suffer for the rest of your life," he said.

"It's different now. When I was young and ignorant, I liked handsome young men who talked big. That's why I got swindled. Now I'm going to choose a client who is honest and straightforward, so how can I go wrong?"

"You can't, except where do you find a client like that?"

As they talked, Thatch Fang yawned twice. Laurel knew he liked an early night, so when it struck ten, she called for Grandma to bring congee and get ready for them to go to bed.

Unexpectedly, Thatch Fang caught a cold in the night. He woke up feeling dizzy, with a blocked nose and a sore throat. Laurel suggested that he should stay in bed and rest there for a few days, so he asked for a writing brush and inkstone and wrote a note requesting sick leave from the poetry club. As a result, several of his friends in the club came to inquire after him. They were amazed to see Laurel waiting on him attentively and with great intimacy and considered it a lucky encounter for Fang.

Laurel sent for the fashionable doctor Hill Dou, who prescribed herbs that encouraged perspiration. She then brewed and administered the medicine with her own hands. For three days, she did not leave Thatch Fang for a moment. In the daytime, she gave no thought to food or drink, and at night she slept fully clothed in a bed in the outer room. How could he but feel grateful to her?

On the fourth day, when his fever had gone, Grandma seized the opportunity to encourage him to marry Laurel. Thatch Fang reflected that a bachelor life in an inn was really not a suitable long-term arrangement. Since Laurel did not mind his poverty and his age, surely he shouldn't miss this chance for a good marriage? He was well disposed toward the idea. By the time he had fully recovered, he took his leave from them with thanks and went straight to the Longevity Bookstore in Bowling Alley to tell Old Bao about it. Old Bao was all for the idea. Overjoyed, Thatch Fang asked him to act as matchmaker and to go with him to Generosity Alley to discuss the matter in person.

As soon as Old Bao came through the door, the courtesans, maids, and servant girls in the two side chambers shouted in unison, "Hey! Old Bao is here!"

Crane Li happened to be in Grace Yang's room. When he heard the shouting, he peeped out the window. Seeing Old Bao, he was about to call out in greeting, but the sight of Thatch Fang stopped him. Instead, he told Thrive to go upstairs and ask Mr. Bao to come and have a word.

In about the time it took to have two or three meals, Old Bao finally came downstairs. Crane Li welcomed him and invited him to sit down.

"What's it you want to talk about?" Old Bao asked.

"I asked Third Shu to come for a drinking party, but he declined. You've come just in time," Crane Li said.

"What d'you take me for?" Old Bao demanded loudly. "Someone to fill up an empty seat at dinner tables?"

Crane Li hastened to put on a smiling face to persuade him to stay, but Old Bao put on a show of walking out. Grace Yang took him by the arm and asked in a low voice, "Is Laurel getting married?"

Old Bao nodded. "I'm the matchmaker. She gets three hundred dollars to settle her debts and two hundred for expenses."

"Laurel Zhao actually has a client who'd marry her?" asked Crane Li.

"Don't you belittle her. At one time, she, too, was a popular courtesan," Grace Yang said.

As she was speaking, the man sent out to invite guests came to report back. "The other two gentlemen can't be reached. At Sunset's, they said, 'The Second Young Mr. Yao hasn't been for a long time now.' At Twin Pearl's, they said, 'Since Mr. Wang went to Jiangxi, Mr. Hong doesn't come often.'"

Crane Li said, "Now if on top of all this Old Bao is leaving, too, I'm aggrieved."

"Old Bao was just joking. He's not leaving," Grace Yang said.

Not long afterward, the four guests that were coming—Amity Zhu, Cloud Tao, Whistler Tang, and Cloudlet Chen—arrived one after the other. Crane Li then gave the order for the table to be set and hot towels brought in. They took their seats and chatted as they drank.

"Has your esteemed uncle gone home? I never even saw him once," Amity Zhu asked.

"He's still here. Old Merit went back by himself," Crane Li replied.

"There're too few of us today. Why not ask your esteemed uncle to join us?" Cloud Tao suggested.

"He'd never agree to come to a sing-song house party! Last time, it was only because Script Li grabbed hold of him that he had to call several girls to the party," said Crane Li.

"Your esteemed uncle is a truly capable man," said Old Bao. "In Shanghai, he counts as an old playboy, too, but he never spent much money. He actually managed to make some to take home!"

"It seems to me if one wants to have a good time, it's better to spend some money. Look at my uncle now; can you say he's enjoying himself?" Crane Li responded.

"Have you had good fortune this time round?" said Cloudlet Chen.

"I've actually lost a bit more than last time. I owed Third Shu five thousand dollars that I only managed to pay up a couple of days ago. And I owe Prosperity Luo as much as ten thousand. I'll pay him back when the oil is sold."

"D'you have any idea of the danger your deeds were in?" asked Whistler Tang, who then recounted in detail how Second Sister Huang had stolen the document box and held it for ransom. He also told them that in the end he acted as middleman in the negotiations, and Prosperity Luo had had to pay five thousand dollars to redeem the document box. Everybody at the table shook his head and made faces, saying, "So, Second Sister turns out to be a serious blackmailer."

Grace Yang laughed as she said, "All the madams in Shanghai are blackmailers. Old Bao would know, right?"

Old Bao stood up to object to being dragged in. Afraid that he would play rough, she ran out to the parlor. Old Bao, in hot pursuit, got to the door when it so happened that the girls called to the party were arriving, and Jewel Lu lifted the curtain and walked into the room. Old Bao bumped his head against hers, evoking uproarious laughter.

Old Bao massaged his forehead and returned to his seat. A smiling Crane Li made peace by calling Grace Yang back into the room and making her drink a cup of wine as punishment, but she considered it unfair. Collective judgment then sentenced Jewel Lu to a penalty cup as well, and that settled the matter. Old Bao then suggested that the finger game should commence. He set up a bank, and everybody took turns to play and drink to their hearts' content. The party did not break up until eleven o'clock.

After Crane Li had seen his guests out, he wanted to fetch something and asked for Second Kuang. The maid, Thrive, reported, "He's not here. He dropped in briefly during the party and then left."

"When he comes, tell him there's something I want him to do," Crane Li said to Thrive. Then he sent the sedan-chair bearers away, saying, "When you see Second Kuang, tell him to come here." The sedan-chair bearers took their orders and left.

The next morning, as soon as he got up, Crane Li asked, "Where's Second Kuang?"

"The sedan-chair bearers are here, but Master Kuang isn't," Thrive said.

Astounded, Crane Li shouted at the sedan-chair bearers, "Go and get him at the inn."

Not long afterward, the sedan-chair bearers reported back, "The waiters at the inn said Master Kuang didn't go back last night."

Crane Li thought that it was just because Second Kuang was loath to leave some streetwalker's lair. As he did not want to wait any longer, he decided to return to the Long Peace Inn on Pebble Road in his sedan chair. There, he entered his room and opened the trunk to get what he wanted. He was shocked to find that the trunk, which had been packed full, was now completely empty. Dumbfounded, he was at a loss what to do. When he opened the other trunks, he found they had all been cleared out. In desperation, he shouted, "Waiter!" The waiter, also panic-stricken, asked the bookkeeper to come up. The bookkeeper took a look and frowned. "Our inn is completely aboveboard. How would a thief get in here?"

Crane Li, who knew it had to have been Second Kuang, stamped his feet in bitter regret. After saying a few words of consolation, the bookkeeper went off to report to the police. Meanwhile, Crane Li ordered the sedan-chair bearers to go quickly to Perfection Chu's to fetch Pragmatic Li.

Pragmatic rushed back as soon as he received the message to check his own things. He found they were all untouched. Only eight leather trunks, two covered baskets, and a pillow box belonging to

Crane Li had been ransacked and all the valuables stolen. What was more, pawn tickets were found in a drawer, presumably left there by Second Kuang so that his master could redeem the things he had pawned. This made Crane Li feel a little better.

In the midst of the bustle and confusion, a foreign policeman and two detectives arrived. They had come to examine the scene of the crime. Finding the roof, door, and windows all intact and seeing no sign of intrusion, they decided that it was an inside job. When Crane Li revealed that Second Kuang had not showed up all night, the detectives asked in detail about Kuang's age, facial characteristics, and accent. Then they left.

The waiter now told them, "Last week, we saw Master Kuang go out a few times carrying a large bundle on his back. We couldn't very well ask him about that, could we? Who'd have known he had stolen things to pawn them?"

Pragmatic Li said rather gleefully, "He's quite an interesting character though. You're a big spender who can take the loss in your stride, so he targeted you. Otherwise, why didn't he take my things?"

Crane Li, though angered by this remark, had no choice but to ignore it. He thought that as a stranger in town he had better not act rashly. On reflection, he decided that Harmony Qi was the only person he could consult, so he promptly set off for Conical Hat Garden in his sedan chair. As he was well known to the menservants at the garden gate, they led his sedan chair through the front gate and all the way to the second garden gate.

Crane Li saw that the main entrance was now padlocked; only a narrow side entrance was left open. As he puzzled over this, a manservant saluted him with one knee on the ground and reported, "His Excellency got a telegram and went home. Mr. Gao is the only one who's here. Please make yourself at home in Panorama Hall, Mr. Li."

It occurred to Crane Li that it would be a good idea to consult Second Bai, so he followed the manservant into the garden at a leisurely pace, heading for Panorama Hall.

"Aren't you lonely staying here all by yourself?" Crane Li asked.

"That matters little, but it's a real pity about the chrysanthemum hill. Mr. Dragon Ma spent quite a lot of thought on it, and now it just sits there, neglected," Second Bai replied.

"Then you should invite us over," Crane Li suggested.

"All right, I'll have a party tomorrow then."

"Sorry, I can't make it tomorrow. We'll see in a couple of days."

"What's keeping you so busy?"

Crane Li recounted briefly how Second Kuang had run away with his valuables. Second Bai was shocked. Crane Li then asked him, "Should I report it to the magistrate?"[1]

"That's just a formality. It's hard to imagine that the thief will be caught and the stolen goods returned."

"In that case, how about not reporting it?"

"I'm afraid that won't do either. What if he gets into further bad trouble elsewhere and people demand that as his employer you deliver him to court? That's something you can do without."

"You're so right," Crane Li said repeatedly and then stood up to take his leave.

"There's no need for such a terrible hurry, is there?" Second Bao said.

"I'll go and wind this up and then come back to see you, how about that?"

"I'll be waiting," Second Bai said with a smile. He walked with Li all the way to the inner garden gate where Li saluted him and left in his sedan chair.

Second Bai was just turning to go when a young man rushed up to him and saluted him with one knee on the ground. Second Bai did not recognize him, so he asked for his name. It turned out to be Second Treasure's brother, Simplicity Zhao, who was trying to find out if there had been any letters from Third Young Master Shi.

"None," Second Bai replied.

Simplicity could not very well pursue this, so he drew back and stood respectfully to one side as Second Bai went back into the garden and ambled westward toward the chrysanthemum hill, which was erected in front of the Parrot Tower. The tower was a two-story building with five very spacious rooms on each floor laid out like an inverted "V." As there was space in front of the tower, the chrysanthemum hill was also constructed in the shape of the inverted "V," parallel to the building. The hill was as tall as the eaves on the tower, and the many pathways within led in all directions. A sightseer walking along the path would feel as though he were in a maze, "lost his way among the flowers," as the poet says.

Second Bai, however, knew the place well. He took a shortcut from the south side, along a stone path and across a bamboo bridge, and soon had left the chrysanthemum hill behind.

::

1. The Chinese police and judiciary and those in the foreign concessions are completely separate. As Li is not a resident in the foreign settlements and Kuang may well have left Shanghai, the question of reporting to the Chinese authorities is an urgent one because employers may be held accountable for their servants' misdeeds. E.H.]

Having viewed the chrysanthemums, Second Bai returned to his room. The next day, as he had nothing to do, he looked through the notes sent by various people asking for his calligraphy or painting and wielded his brush to fulfill many of these obligations. The day after that was spent in a similar manner. Feeling a little tired after lunch, he thought that a walk in the garden would keep sleepiness at bay, so he put his brush down and descended the stairs at a leisurely pace. It was a fine day, with wisps of cloud drifting by and the sun shining brightly high in the sky—a sight that cleared the head and gladdened the eyes. As he strolled through the front porch of Panorama Hall, he saw a handyman carrying a five-foot broom of shredded bamboo, ready to sweep the fallen leaves in the courtyard. At this sight, Second Bai recalled that at the break of dawn he had heard the sound of gusty wind and heavy showers; these leaves must have fallen during the storm. His thoughts turned to the chrysanthemum hill: could it have withstood such a trampling? It'd be a shame if the flowers had been crushed and the hill were unworthy of further viewing, for Crane Li had been looking forward to admiring it. Could anything be done about it? As he pondered this, he headed northeastward, thinking he would first check on the state of the lotus pond since that should be a good indication for the rest. As he stepped onto the Bridge of Nine Twists and looked down the stream, he saw that the black door of Pear Blossom Court was tightly locked, but against its whitewashed wall lotus flowers were blooming quite vibrantly.

Somewhat reassured, Second Bai walked on to Moon-worshiper's Chamber to check on the cassia blossoms. These had fallen thickly, carpeting the ground and cushioning his feet as he walked. His cloth shoes were soon covered in flower buds.

He went into the courtyard. Here, all the windows were shut, and the soft bamboo curtains on the porches were rolled up high; the place looked long deserted. Where the menservants on duty had gone, he did not know. Shading his eyes with one hand, he looked through a window. The room was undecorated, with all the furniture stacked up.

As he turned to go, he heard seven or eight crows taking flight and then circling overhead, cawing. That meant someone was coming. He went around Moon-worshiper's Chamber and made for the slope on the east side. There, he saw several handymen and the menservants gathered under a tall tree. They had put a ladder against it, intending to tear down a crow's nest in the tree, but the ladder was too short, and the nest remained out of reach. Everyone had an opinion about what should be done, but no one could actually work it out.

Second Bai looked up at the nest. It was just the size of a watermelon, as yet unfinished, and was lodged firmly on a forked branch. He ordered a manservant to fetch a bow and arrows from Right Target Hall. After estimating the distance, he took a couple of steps back, bent the bow, took aim, and shot. The men only heard a whistle in the air; they did not even see the arrow. The nest, however, was now hanging off the branch and swaying perilously. Before they could cheer, another shot whistled through the air, and the nest fell to the ground. The men broke into joyful applause while a manservant picked up the nest with the two arrows in it and brought it forward to show Second Bai.

He acknowledged this with a nod and a smile and then walked away aimlessly via the southeast bank of the lake and past Phoenix Pavilion. He was seen by the menservants on duty there, who rushed out to invite him in. He held up a hand to stop them and turned toward Parrot Tower. As he threaded his way into the chrysanthemum hill, he heard the sound of talk and laughter in the small pantry, where the menservants were probably playing mah-jongg. He decided not to disturb them. The chrysanthemum hill, he discovered, was protected by the mat shed and therefore undamaged. Still, it seemed to have lost some of its radiance, and in time the structure would collapse and the flowers wilt. He thought he should send out the invitations early so the chrysanthemums would have a party in their honor.

With this thought, Second Bai returned hastily to Panorama Hall, where he penned seven invitations, worded as follows: "Awaiting the pleasure of your company at the chrysanthemum feast tomorrow at noon." He handed them to the menservants for dispatching. Not long afterward, he heard a piping voice downstairs, talking and laughing away; it was evidently Wenjun Yao. He thought the menservants had got mixed up and had called her before time. When she came upstairs, he asked at once, "What're you doing here?"

"Lai the Turtle is back in Shanghai!" she replied.

He now realized the reason she had come, so he said with a smile, "I'm giving a party tomorrow, and here you are already."

They walked into his room hand in hand as they talked. Active by nature, she immediately removed her outer robe and went out alone to see the various sights in the garden. When she returned, she said to Second Bai, "Things have fallen off badly since His Excellency's departure. Even the chrysanthemums look downcast."

Second Bai applauded, saying, "Wonderful. There speaks the poet in you." That evening, the two of them just whiled away their time in his room.

The next day was the fifteenth of the tenth month. Elan Ge and Snow Scent were the first to arrive. Sitting in Second Bai's room, they waited for Wenjun Yao to finish her toilet and accompany them to Parrot Tower. Elan Ge brought the message that both the Tao and the Zhu brothers were busy and sent their apologies. Second Bai asked what was keeping them busy, but Elan had no idea.

Next came Iron Hua with White Orchid. The usual greetings over, they all sat down. Second Bai said, "Maestro White Orchid had better stay here for a couple days. I heard Lai the Turtle is here."

"Didn't he go home a long time ago? How come he's here again?" Elan Ge asked.

Iron Hua said, "According to Fourth Qiao, Lai the Turtle has returned to punish several swindlers. It seems that the last time Lai went gambling with Crane Li and Fourth Qiao, they got swindled by a gangster who worked with a group. The three of them lost well over a hundred thousand in total. Luckily for them, a couple of the small-time crooks who did not get their cut let the secret out. Lai the Turtle is determined to get even with the gang."

Second Bai and Elan Ge both said, "Gambling in Shanghai is getting out of hand. It's time someone gets punished."

"Well, it won't be easy. I saw his wanted list. It's headed by a mandarin of the second grade with followers numbering over a hundred, including policemen at the yamen as well as courtesans; they're all in it," Iron Hua said.

"Who are the courtesans?" White Orchid, Snow Scent, and Wenjun Yao asked in unison.

"I only remember one name: Grace Yang," said Iron Hua.

Everybody looked at each other, astounded. Before they could find out more, the menservants announced the arrival of none other than Crane Li and Grace Yang. Everybody made them welcome, and the subject was dropped.

"Did you report the theft to the Chinese magistrate?" Second Bai asked.

"Yes, I did," Crane Li replied.

Grace Yang stared at him angrily, "So it was you who took it to the magistrate, was it?"

"It's got nothing to do with you," Crane Li said, smiling.

"Of course it's got nothing to do with me! You can report all you like!" Grace Yang retorted.

"You've got it all mixed up. I'm talking about Second Kuang," Crane Li said. Grace Yang fell silent.

As noon approached, Second Bai told the menservants to get the feast ready. Since the guests were few, two square tables were put together, and the four guests and their girls sat on three sides so they could all look on the flowers as they drank.

Eventually the talk got round to the subject of Lai the Turtle again. Grace Yang laughed sarcastically and then said, "Yesterday, Lai the Turtle came over to our place to say he would arrest Clement Zhou. The man is a well-known gangster in these foreign settlements, and all the sing-song houses know him. Last time Eldest Young Master played mah-jongg with him, I knew he would have some tricks up his sleeve. But would those of us who make our living in the sing-song houses dare offend a gangster? Even if we saw them at their tricks, we could only keep quiet. Now Lai the Turtle turns around and accuses us of conspiring with Clement Zhou! How can that be?" As she spoke, her face was suffused with anger, and her eyes were filled with tears.

Crane Li both laughed and sighed with exasperation, while Iron Hua and Elan Ge tried to comfort her: "Would anyone believe anything Lai the Turtle says? Let him talk away. What does it matter?"

Second Bai wanted to change the subject. He saw the announcer standing in attendance and recalled that he had told him to write a poem on chrysanthemums as part of his lessons, so he asked the announcer whether he had finished the poem.

"Well, I have, but I don't know if I got it right," the announcer replied.

"Go and fetch it. We'll have a look," Second Bai said.

The announcer assented but remained standing there, which surprised Second Bai.

"Second Treasure of Tripod Alley has sent a man over to see you, Mr. Gao," the announcer reported.

As he spoke, a young man emerged from behind him and performed a salute with one knee on the ground. Second Bai recognized that it was Simplicity Zhao, the same man he had run into at the garden gate the other day. He asked the purpose of his visit and found that it was to enquire about letters from Nature Shi. "There's none," Second Bai said, "perhaps you should try elsewhere, ask around."

Simplicity Zhao could not very well pursue this further, so he followed the announcer out to the porch. The announcer went off to his own quarters to fetch the poem he had written and submitted it to Second Bai. The poem was entitled "Back in the Company of the Chrysanthemums: A Sixteen-Line, Five-Character Verse."

Second Bai merely laughed heartily after he had read it and then passed it on to Crane Li, Elan Ge, and Iron Hua without any comment. When they had passed it around, he asked with a smile.

"May I ask what you think of this poem?"

The others looked at one another. Crane Li was the first to speak. "It seems to me there isn't much to it."

Elan Ge nodded in agreement: "True, but there's nothing wrong with it either."

"I've been sitting here thinking all this while to see if I can come up with a couple of good lines on the subject, and I failed. That shows this poem definitely has its merits," said Iron Hua.

Still smiling, Second Bai turned to the announcer and told him to fetch an inkstone and writing brush so that the three gentlemen could each write out their comments. Crane Li praised the poem's rhythmic felicity and efficient use of rhyme; Elan Ge singled out the poem's structure as its greatest strength; while Iron Hua commended the unflinching focus on the subject matter.

"Second Bai should write a commentary, too. Let's see what *he* thinks," Crane Li said.

Second Bai chuckled and dashed his comment off in a single stroke: "A poem penned with tears and blood, its apparent ease camouflages supreme effort."

"This is a comment that says no comment is possible," they all said with a smile.

"Well, it seems you did all right," Second Bai said to the announcer.

Well pleased with himself, the announcer left with the poem and the inkstone and brush to reread the commentaries on his own. On the porch, however, he was grabbed by Simplicity Zhao, who pleaded with him, "Could you please ask for me once again? It's been said that Third Young Master has come to Shanghai; is it true?"

The announcer went back to relay the question. Second Bai said, "He got it wrong. The one who has come back is Young Master Lai, not Shi."

Simplicity Zhao heard this outside the window and realized that he had made a mistake. He waited until the announcer came out so he could take his leave. The announcer walked him out part of the way.

Deeply depressed, Simplicity Zhao returned home to Tripod Alley to report to his mother that there had been no letters from Nature Shi. He also recounted that his alleged return was a mistake. Second Treasure happened to be sitting with their mother. She was so angry at the news that she just stared, unable to speak.

Mrs. Zhao heaved a heavy sigh and then said, "I'm afraid Third Young Master is not coming! It's all over for us!"

"I wouldn't be so sure. Third Young Master isn't that kind of man," said Simplicity.

Mrs. Zhao sighed again. "Well, you can't tell. It would have been all right had she gone home with him. But now she's left hanging in the air. How's it all going to end?"

Second Treasure tossed her head and snapped, "Mother, stop talking nonsense!" This was enough to make Mrs. Zhao shut up and lower her head. Simplicity, at a loss what to do, slipped out of the room.

The maid, Tiger, who had heard everything outside the door, felt she had to come in and offer some advice. She said, "Second Miss, you're too young to appreciate the problems of the brothel business. You shouldn't listen to the things clients tell you. You never told us what Third Young Master said to you, so we know nothing about it. Now there's been no letter from him for more than a month. It seems things aren't quite right, wouldn't you think so? If Third Young Master doesn't come, you'll have to work things out yourself. The bills you've run up at the jewelry stores, silk shops, and import stores come to three or four thousand dollars; how are you going to pay them? I'm not trying to interfere, but it's best if you're prepared. Otherwise you'll just lose face when the time comes."

Second Treasure flushed crimson but dared not respond. Suddenly, they heard Tailor Zhang calling out that he needed colored threads to be bought for immediate use. Tiger simply ignored this and sauntered out of the room. Mrs. Zhao had no choice but to tell the servant girl, Clever, to buy them, but Clever did not understand what colors were needed and kept pestering Tailor Zhang. When Simplicity saw this, he said, "I'll go get them."

This scene further annoyed Second Treasure. Unable to find relief for her rage, she went listlessly back to her room and lay down on the bed; she thought the matter over and over but still had no idea what to do.

At nightfall, Tailor Zhang delivered a newly made ensemble consisting of a dark blue satin cape lined with ermine and a scarlet crepe skirt. He asked Second Treasure to examine it, but she did not even get up. She just said, "Leave it there."

Tailor Zhang did as he was told and then asked, "There's another ensemble with fox fur lining. Shall I start on it?"

"Of course you should. Why ask?"

"Then the lace trimming, the satin trimming, and the lining border should all be purchased tomorrow," he said.

She grunted assent faintly.

After Tailor Zhang was gone, it was all quiet upstairs. When it was past nine o'clock, Clever and Tiger brought dinner for Second Treasure.

"I don't want it," she said.

Clever, in her naïveté, tried to pull Second Treasure up. Annoyed, the latter barked at her to keep off. Clever could only sit down with Tiger to eat with her. After they had finished, they removed the dishes. Tiger brought a hot towel for her own use and did not ask Second Treasure if she wanted to wash her face. Clever, however, made a pot of tea for Second Treasure.

Tiger opened the trunk to put away the new clothes. Holding the candlestick for her, Clever said admiringly, "This ermine is so fine! Did it cost a lot?"

Tiger sneered. "Humph! It takes real good fortune to wear clothes like this. Without the good fortune, even if you have money, you don't get to wear them."[1]

Second Treasure, lying on the bed, pretended not to hear. She was fuming inside, but Clever and Tiger paid her no attention. Later in the evening, they each went to bed, but Second Treasure did not close her eyes all night.

CHAPTER 62 :: *Simplicity Zhao's affair with the servant girl is exposed, and Twin Jade overhears gossip about "wives"*

Second Treasure thought hard all night. At daybreak, she got up and tiptoed downstairs, her hair still uncombed, and went into her mother's room. Mrs. Zhao was asleep in bed, snoring loudly. There was a small bed off to one side for Simplicity Zhao, but it was empty. Second Treasure woke Mrs. Zhao and asked, "Where's Brother?"

"No idea."

Second Treasure, though, had a pretty good idea. She went back upstairs and walked into the mezzanine room, where she lifted the servant girl Clever's bed curtains. Sure enough, Simplicity and Clever were lying together, sound asleep. Second Treasure's fury exploded. She shook and slapped them mercilessly, waking them both. Simplicity got off the bed, naked except for the underpants he somehow managed to put on; he ran out of the room. Clever was so embarrassed, she hid under the quilt and stayed there, not daring to show her face.

Second Treasure scolded and cursed for a long while before she

::

1. [The clothes were bridal ensembles for an official's wife. Ordinary women were not entitled to wear them, let alone prostitutes. *E.H.*]

went back to her mother's room. Mrs. Zhao was sitting in bed with her clothes draped over her shoulders. Second Treasure's eyes bulged and lips trembled as she sat down bolt upright on the edge of the bed.

"Who was making a row upstairs?" Mrs. Zhao asked.

Second Treasure made no reply. She thought this affair had to be hushed up and she could use it to her own end, so she consulted with Mrs. Zhao about sending Simplicity to Nanjing to seek out Third Young Master Shi and ask for a definite answer from him. As Mrs. Zhao also believed this was the right course of action, Second Treasure called out loudly, "Brother!"

A fearful Simplicity showed up and stood in trepidation to one side. Second Treasure prodded Mrs. Zhao to indicate that she should speak, which she did briefly, telling Simplicity to commence the journey that very day. Simplicity dared not object.

Second Treasure gave him repeated instructions, "When you get to Nanjing, make sure you ask Third Young Master face-to-face why he hasn't sent any letters and when he is coming to Shanghai. Don't forget."

Simplicity assented repeatedly. Only then did Second Treasure go back to her room to comb her hair. As she went up the stairs, she saw Clever, who was sweeping the floor and crying buckets of tears. Second Treasure just ignored her.

On this day, the Yangtze steamboat sailed at midnight. After supper, Simplicity rolled up his bedding and asked Mrs. Zhao for some money for traveling expenses. Mrs. Zhao instructed him to return as soon as his mission was done. The maid, Tiger, interrupted, "After all this time, we should have a clear idea by now. What's the point of going to Nanjing? I bet you won't get to see Third Young Master Shi. If he never comes here again, what's the use even if you do get to see him?"

"But she's not convinced. A trip to Nanjing will bring back a definite message, then she'll be convinced."

"If Second Miss is not convinced, then you, her mother, should make her see the light. In her heart, Second Miss still thinks Third Young Master Shi will come back; that's why she wants to ask for a message. Well, who're you going to ask? Even if you do see Third Young Master, will he tell you the truth even if he has decided not to come? Of course not! He'll say, 'It won't be long now.' If Second Miss is taken in again and keeps waiting till the end of the year, then she'll truly be in a fix," Tiger said.

"You may well be right," Mrs. Zhao replied. "But let's wait till after the trip; then we'll see."

"It's got nothing to do with me, really. I'm just worried about the three to four thousand dollars we owe the shops. If it had been a lesser young lady, I wouldn't have run up such huge bills for her at the stores, but Second Miss was really popular; in the fifth month alone, she had numerous mah-jongg and drinking parties. If she gives up Third Young Master while there's still time and concentrates on pulling in business, by the end of the year she'll be able to pay up some of the bills and borrow money to cover the rest. But if you let this drag on, it'll be too late."

Mrs. Zhao was silent, so Simplicity said, "I'll go and ask for an answer. If Third Young Master is not coming, then of course it's back to business for us."

Tiger laughed coldly and walked away. Having put his traveling money in a secure place and picked up his bedding, Simplicity took his leave and departed.

The next day, Second Treasure ordered Tiger to go to Snow Scent's in East Co-prosperity Alley to fetch Little Sister. Tiger realized the affair had been detected, so she took her orders and went. Second Treasure then told her mother what to say and to keep things simple.

Soon Tiger came back with Little Sister and took her to see Mrs. Zhao. Second Treasure smiled and invited her to sit down.

Mrs. Zhao said, "At the end of the month, our whole family will be going to Nanjing to look for Third Young Master, so Clever should go and look for another job. Her wage is a dollar a month, and we'll pay her to the end of the year."

Little Sister was stunned. After a slight pause, she said, "She can leave when the time comes. It's early yet."

It was Second Treasure who responded. "Since we have stopped working, there isn't anything for Clever to do. The earlier she leaves, the earlier she can find another job, right?"

Little Sister had no answer to that. She told Clever to go and pack up. Second Treasure told Mrs. Zhao to give three dollars to Little Sister and then ordered a manservant to carry the baggage and see them out. Little Sister led Clever away after thanking them.

After they had left, Tailor Zhang wanted to be paid for his work in advance. Second Treasure again told Mrs. Zhao to give him ten dollars. Tiger whispered to Mrs. Zhao behind Second Treasure's back, "You mustn't let Second Miss have her way in everything. She has too little sense. How much money do you have left? How can she go on having those clothes made? Clothes like that can wait till she's married. What's the hurry?"

"I've spoken to her about it. She said the work can stop when the fox fur is done," Mrs. Zhao replied.

Tiger sighed and gave up.

Unexpectedly, Little Sister brought Clever back to see Mrs. Zhao early the next morning. Pointing her finger at Clever, Little Sister said to Mrs. Zhao, "The girl's my husband's niece. Her parents entrusted her to me and told me to find her a job. It's her own fault that she did such a shameless thing. Even I'm ashamed of it. How can I face her parents? I've sent a letter to tell them to come to town. You just hand her over to them, for I'll have nothing to do with it."

"What're you talking about? I don't understand," Mrs. Zhao asked, totally lost.

"In that case, you should ask Clever. Let her tell you herself." After saying this, Little Sister walked out.

Second Treasure had just got up. When she heard their voices, she hurried downstairs. Little Sister had already left, while Clever was seated facing the wall, hiding her face and weeping. Second Treasure glared at her in rage, but there was nothing she could do to get rid of her. Mrs. Zhao was still asking what the matter was.

"There's no point in asking her!" Second Treasure said. She then told her mother what had happened two days ago.

This news got Mrs. Zhao truly worried. She cursed Simplicity repeatedly for being a good-for-nothing who had got them into trouble. Second Treasure wanted Tiger to convey a message to Little Sister that they were willing to give her some compensation money if she would take Clever back.

"Little Sister is a minor problem. Let me ask the girl first," Tiger said. She pulled Clever to one side and talked to her at length in whispers, after which she came back to report, "I thought so! The two of them have it all settled between them. They want to be married. She doesn't want money, so all you need to do is wait till her parents are here and ask for her hand."

Mrs. Zhao was overjoyed. "Then you'll be our matchmaker."

Second Treasure jumped up and shouted in anger, "It won't do. Am I to have this shameless little hussy as a sister-in-law?"

Mrs. Zhao looked at her dumbly, not daring to make any decision.

"If you ask me, it's quite acceptable for a brothel owner to marry a servant girl," Tiger said.

"I won't have it!" Second Treasure yelled.

Mrs. Zhao was forced to promise Clever's folks fifty dollars outright. Tiger was told to go and talk to Little Sister.

"Brother is by nature a low-life hooligan," Second Treasure said between clenched teeth. "Third Young Master wanted to give his head steward's daughter to him in marriage; what an honor that would be! But instead of waiting for that, he's got himself hooked up with a stinking servant girl!"

Though Mrs. Zhao was pleased to learn this, she was afraid Little Sister would not let the matter rest. When Tiger returned, she anxiously asked how it went.

Tiger shook her head. "Nothing doing. Little Sister said, 'Your daughter happens to have a pretty face and so she became a miss; Clever is somebody's daughter, too, only she doesn't have a pretty face, so she became a servant girl. The one who's a miss costs so much to deflower, so much to stay overnight with, so why should it be different for a servant girl? Your son slept with her for several months, how can fifty dollars begin to make up for it? It's just empty talk!' "

Very much shaken, Mrs. Zhao looked at Second Treasure, waiting for her decision.

"We'll wait till her parents are here and see how it goes," Second Treasure said.

Mrs. Zhao, being timid by nature, felt extremely uneasy about this. Soon, three days had passed, and before Clever's parents turned up, Simplicity returned from Nanjing. As soon as Mrs. Zhao saw him, she gave him a thorough dressing-down.

Second Treasure stamped her feet. "Mother, let him make his report first!"

Simplicity put down his bedding and said, "Third Young Master won't be coming. I found my way to the Shi residence, but none of the seven or eight menservants at the gate was known to me. At first, I said I was looking for Little Wang, and they just ignored me. I then said I was sent by His Excellency Mr. Qi to see Third Young Master, and they invited me into the gatehouse and told me Third Young Master had got betrothed right after he returned from Shanghai, that now he was in Yangzhou and Little Wang had accompanied him there. The wedding is to be held in Yangzhou on the twentieth of the eleventh month, and he'll be spending a full month there before returning to Nanjing. Doesn't that mean he's not coming?"

When Second Treasure heard this, everything turned black in front of her. Something went boom in her head, and she fell backward to the floor. Everybody panicked and rushed forward to help her up, calling her name. She was unconscious, foaming at the mouth.

It so happened that Little Sister came in at that moment with Clever's parents. Seeing the situation, they could not very well say anything. Little Sister joined in to try and revive Second Treasure. Mrs. Zhao started howling, tears streaming down her face. Simplicity and Tiger, on either side of Second Treasure, pinched her under the nose and forced hot ginger soup into her mouth. It was all chaos and commotion.

A while later, Second Treasure threw up some phlegm, and her breathing became easier. While everybody was arguing about how to carry her back to her room, Tiger just rolled up her sleeves, picked Second Treasure up round her waist, and struggled up the stairs. Everybody crowded behind them, following them into the room. Second Treasure was laid on the bed and covered with a quilt. The crowd dispersed, leaving Mrs. Zhao to sit with her.

Second Treasure gradually came to. She opened her eyes and asked, "Mother, what're you doing here?"

Mrs. Zhao, relieved to see that she had awakened clear-headed, said to her, "Second Treasure, you scared us so! What happened to you?"

This brought back to Second Treasure what Simplicity had said. She recalled all the details, every single word. Though feeling wretched, she tried to suppress her emotions for fear of upsetting her mother.

"D'you feel bad?" Mrs. Zhao asked.

"I'm all right now. Go downstairs, Mother."

"No, I'm not going. Clever's parents are there."

Second Treasure frowned as she thought the matter over. Then she sighed and said, "Brother will just marry Clever and that's that. Since her parents are here, you can ask Tiger to be the matchmaker."

Mrs. Zhao expressed her agreement and immediately called Tiger up to tell her to propose the match.

"Well, I'll try, but I don't know if they'll accept," Tiger said.

"Please try," Second Treasure said.

Tiger took her time going down to make her proposal, expecting to be told off. But Clever's parents were good, timorous country folk to whom putting the squeeze on someone was an alien idea. The minute Tiger proposed the match, they consented right away, without making the least difficulty, so Little Sister could not very well hinder it, either. Mrs. Zhao and Simplicity were overjoyed, but Second Treasure felt sadder than ever.

Tiger then told Mrs. Zhao, "You're relatives now. You should at least go and keep them company for a bit."

"Their son-in-law is with them. I'm not going," Mrs. Zhao replied.

Second Treasure tried to persuade her. "Mother, you should go and entertain them for a while. I'm all right here."

Mrs. Zhao still hesitated.

"If you don't go, Mother, I'm going." So saying, Second Treasure forced herself to sit up, tidied her hair a little, and tried to get off the bed.

Mrs. Zhao quickly stopped her, saying, "I'll go. You stay in bed."

Second Treasure smiled and lay down. Mrs. Zhao bade Tiger to stay with her and then went downstairs to entertain Clever's parents.

Second Treasure beckoned to Tiger to come near and sit on the bed and then consulted her about what settlements to make for the shopping bills. Now that Second Treasure had turned around, Tiger tried her best to help make a plan: they'd return goods that could be returned and sell or pawn the rest. This way, by her reckoning, their loss would be limited. The only big problem was the new clothes. Second Treasure wanted to keep the clothes and dispose of everything else, as Tiger suggested, to pay the bills. They worked out that this way she'd still be over a thousand dollars short.

Tiger said, "If we have the same amount of business as we did in the fifth month, a debt of a thousand doesn't matter. By the end of the year, we'll be able to pay it back."

"The fox cape should be ready today. Go tell Tailor Zhang he needn't come tomorrow."

"Whatever you do, you're always in too much of a hurry. Take these clothes, for example; it would've been much better if you had ordered a fox jacket instead of a cape, don't you think so?" Tiger said.

"Let's not talk about this anymore," Second Treasure said impatiently.

A little put out, Tiger went out into the center room to relay the message to Tailor Zhang, who merely acknowledged it. The other tailors lost no chance to joke about this. Naturally, Second Treasure could hear them, but this was the least of her concerns.

When evening came and supper was over, Mrs. Zhao, still worried about Second Treasure, came to see her. She told her Clever's parents had gone back to the country, and Clever would stay to work there. The wedding would take place in the New Year. Second Treasure just said "Good." Mrs. Zhao asked her this and that and consoled her solicitously before going off to bed. Second Treasure sent Tiger off to bed as well. Her door was closed but left unlocked, and she was left alone.

Lying in bed, she relived the time she had spent with Third Young Master, how she had fallen for him at first sight, how warm and loving they had been at the moment of their union, how kindly he had treated her since then, how congenial and tender they were. In daily life, his manner and behavior were always gentle and moderate, yet patrician and well-bred, without a trace of the flippancy and dissoluteness so commonly seen in the sing-song houses. Who'd have that his faithlessness was worse than the whoring playboys'? At this thought, sorrow and anger surged up her chest, so strong that she could no longer suppress it. Hers was no ordinary weeping; it rose and fell, abruptly stopped and then started again—it was sad beyond words.

She cried the whole night, but no one heard her. The next morning, when Tiger came in, she saw her sitting in bed, her eyes swollen like walnuts.

"Did you get any sleep at all?" Tiger asked, just to make conversation.

Second Treasure did not reply. Instead, she asked for a basin of warm water and then got up to wash her face. Clever came in to clean the furniture while Tiger got ready to dress Second Treasure's hair.

Second Treasure ordered Clever to summon Simplicity and then told him to write her name slip and post it at the door that very day. Simplicity assented silently. Second Treasure also told Tiger to go out that very day and invite various clients to drop in. Tiger, like Simplicity, took her order in silence.

After that, Second Treasure powdered and rouged herself and then changed into brand-new clothes before she went downstairs to see her mother. Mrs. Zhao was awake but still lying in bed, facing inward; she seemed to be groaning. Second Treasure called to her in a low voice. Mrs. Zhao turned around and, seeing her, said, "Why are you in such a hurry to get up? If you're not feeling well, stay in bed."

"I'm all right," Second Treasure took the opportunity to tell her about starting to work again.

"You should rest for a couple more days. You've only just got a little better so you really can't afford to strain yourself. If you should catch a cold on the way to a party call, what are we to do?"

"Mother, you shouldn't worry about me anymore. Now, we owe the stores three to four thousand; if I don't work, how are we to pay them? It's as though I'm held as collateral here in Shanghai!" Her voice choked, and she could not carry on.

Overcome by misery and concern, Mrs. Zhao asked in a trembling voice, "Even if you work again, how are we ever going to get three to four thousand?"

Second Treasure sighed and then told her what Tiger had said about converting the goods into cash. She went on, "You might as well leave it to me, Mother. As long as I'm here, you don't have to worry. If you're happy, I feel better, too, so don't be sad because of me."

Mrs. Zhao could only acknowledge she was right. Then Second Treasure asked, "Mother, why didn't you get up?"

"I have a headache."

Second Treasure reached under the quilt to feel her temperature, which was a little high. "Mother, you may be running a fever."

"I do feel a bit hot."

"Shall we get a doctor so you can take some medicine?"

"What for? Just keep me warm, and I'll sweat it out."

Second Treasure found another quilt and made sure that it covered her mother well and then left her so Mrs. Zhao could sleep again. Second Treasure went back upstairs to confer again with Tiger. This went on until the afternoon, when Tiger went out to attend to the shop bills and to invite their clients.

The message was soon spread all over town. Within three days, Cloudlet Chen heard about it. He was shocked because he thought Nature Shi was going to make Second Treasure his wife—a wonderful thing—and that she chose instead to remain a fallen woman because she loved the brothel scene. He was just going to inquire into the matter when he came across Benevolence Hong on Third Avenue. When Cloudlet suggested that they have a chat in a teahouse, Benevolence said, "Let's sit for a while at Twin Pearl's instead."

The two of them headed for Sunshine Alley. There happened to be clients for tea parties in both the upstairs rooms, so Worth showed them into Twin Jewel's room on the ground floor. Twin Jewel welcomed them and invited them to sit down, after which Cloudlet told Benevolence the news about Second Treasure's working again.

Benevolence clapped his hands and laughed. "You're an intelligent man, how come you were taken in? I never believed it from the very beginning. Third Young Master Shi can have the pick of womanhood, so why would he want a courtesan for his wife?"

Twin Jewel also clapped and laughed. "Why is it that all these maestros and misses want to be wives? First there was Water Blossom; *she* wanted to be a wife so badly that she died. Now there's this Second Treasure, who also doesn't get to be one. The one at our place is actually number three!"

Cloudlet, who had no idea what she was talking about, asked who was number three.

Twin Jewel signaled with her mouth. "It's Twin Jade. Isn't she Fifth Young Mr. Zhu's wife?"

"But he is engaged to be married!" Cloudlet said.

Twin Jewel just smiled and did not comment. Benevolence hurriedly held up a hand to indicate that they should drop the subject. When he looked up, however, he saw Twin Jade standing in front of him. Sudden fear wiped Twin Jewel's smile off her face; she hastily withdrew. Benevolence knew they were in for it and could not think of any small talk to divert Twin Jade's attention. The look on their faces made Cloudlet feel more puzzled than ever. They all stared at one another transfixed.

The clients who were having a tea party in the upstairs rooms were Lai the Turtle, Iron Hua, Fourth Qiao, and Seventh Qiao. Fourth Qiao had been a regular client of Twin Pearl, so he had called Twin Jade to parties several times for his brother Seventh Qiao. That was why, though the four of them had come together, they occupied two separate rooms. When Benevolence Hong and Cloudlet Chen arrived, Lai was chatting with Twin Pearl. Since Benevolence was an old client, Twin Pearl did not have to hurry downstairs to entertain him, so she just talked on with considerable animation. Twin Jade, hoping to ask Benevolence to pass on a message to Modesty Zhu, went downstairs and used the back door of Twin Jewel's room as a shortcut. That was how she heard Cloudlet Chen and Twin Jewel talking and then saw Benevolence holding up a hand in warning. Twin Jade, shocked by what she had heard, was anxious to get to the root of the matter. But on second thought, she realized Modesty Zhu's betrothal was probably to be kept under wraps and she had to be circumspect, so she walked into the room and greeted Cloudlet Chen and Benevolence Hong and then sat down to keep them company, not showing that she was in the know.

Presently Twin Pearl came in, and Twin Jade took the opportunity to go back upstairs. She waited until evening when the clients had all gone and the house closed for the night before she went to see Orchid Zhou. The latter, all kindness, told her to sit down.

Twin Jade said gently, "Since you bought me, Mother, I've dedicated myself to working for you. Except for you, I don't have any other kin, and aside from work I never think of anything else. Now that Fifth Young Mr. Zhu is engaged to be married, that's a business opportunity for you, Mother. You should invite him here and let me ask him about it, then you won't have to worry he won't give you money, Mother. Why did you keep it from me? For fear that he would give you too much money and you'd be too polite to take it?"

"I didn't keep it from you," Orchid Zhou replied. "Fifth Young Mr. Zhu said he was afraid you'd be unhappy if you heard about his engagement, so he told us not to talk about it."

"You must be joking, Mother. I have so many clients, someone even better than Fifth Young Mr. Zhu won't be too hard to find! Are you afraid no one will marry me? Why should I be unhappy?" said Twin Jade.

When she heard this, Orchid Zhou broke out into laughter. She then told Twin Jade all about Modesty Zhu's betrothal to Script Li's daughter at the end of the eighth month. Now Twin Jade recalled that during the last two months the word "wife" had always been on Twin Jewel's lips. "She was mocking me!" she thought. Anger filled her heart, and she could no longer suppress her tears. Her weeping gradually grew louder.

Orchid Zhou regretted saying the wrong thing. Twin Jade resumed, "Elder Sister and I work for you out of filial duty, Mother, and you have never said a cross word to us. What bugs me is Twin Jewel. She gets no business at all, and the money that the two of us earn for you goes to feed and clothe her. She sits there with nothing to do and spends her time thinking up ways to laugh at me and run me down!"

"She wouldn't dare, surely!" Orchid Zhou said.

Twin Jade then recounted in detail Twin Jewel's innuendoes and sarcastic remarks, adding a little embellishment. The information made Orchid Zhou so angry she shouted repeatedly for Twin Jewel who hurried in, trembling with fear. Not bothering to question her, Orchid Zhou just picked up an opium pipe and aimed it at her head. But Twin Jade reached out and caught it in her hand, saying, "Mother, don't! If you beat her now, she'll just take it out on me later, and you'll never know about it. If you're fond of Twin Jewel, just let her return to the room upstairs. As for me, you can send me to work in a second-class house. There I wouldn't be laughed at and abused, so I'd get some peace and work even harder to bring in more earnings for you, Mother."

Outraged, Orchid Zhou threw down her opium pipe and demanded, "Am I fond of Twin Jewel? The only reason she's still here is that your elder sister said that we're sometimes too busy and it's good to have Twin Jewel around to substitute at parties. Otherwise she'd have been sent away long ago. Why should I be fond of Twin Jewel?"

Twin Jade laughed ironically. "Mother, you're always saying you'll send Twin Jewel away, but she's still here, right? And you say you're not fond of her?"

Orchid Zhou became furious, "That's not a problem. I'll send her away tomorrow. Save your breath; there's no need to dwell on this."

"Don't be angry, Mother. Twin Jewel and I both belong to you. It doesn't matter whether you're fond of us or not. Even if someone has to be sent away, the matter should be discussed first. What's the hurry?"

Orchid Zhou pondered over this, her anger subsiding somewhat. Then she shouted at Twin Jewel to clear off and asked Twin Jade quietly what there was to discuss.

"Mother, I'm sure you can work it out yourself. Twin Jewel's purchase price was three hundred dollars. Even if that was money down the drain, that'd be your total loss. But if she stays here, she brings no business, and her expenditure is exactly the same as ours. If that goes on for several years, won't it be a terrible waste of money? The way I look at it, Mother, it's better to let Twin Jewel go."

Orchid Zhou nodded in agreement. Twin Jade continued, "Elder Sister's business is good, so she needs Twin Jewel to substitute at parties. My business is just so-so. When Twin Jewel's gone, I can substitute for Elder Sister at parties."

Orchid Zhou again nodded. So it was that she and Twin Jade made the decision to resell Twin Jewel to Second Sister Huang's house and Twin Pearl heard nothing about it. The next day, when Orchid Zhou told Pearlie to go to Second Sister's and talk to her, a surprised Twin Pearl asked what it was about and only then did she learn of the decision.

"Mother, at your age, you really should do some good deeds!" Twin Pearl remonstrated with her. "Second Sister Huang is not the same kind of person as you. Under her, Twin Jewel will be wretched. If you've made up your mind you don't want Twin Jewel, Mother, I suggest you talk it over. The client named Ni from the general goods store is quite close to her. We can invite him over and ask him if he wants her. If he does, then Twin Jewel will have a good place to go to, and we don't lose on the ransom price, either. Don't you think that's the right way, Mother?"

Orchid Zhou, seeing the logic of this, recalled Pearlie and sent Worth instead to Great Prospects Grocery Store in South End with Twin Jewel's card to invite the owner's son, Mr. Ni, to come. Twin Jade was resentful of the fact that this arrangement would bring Twin Jewel a good match, but as it was Twin Pearl's idea, she dared not object.

Shortly afterward, Worth returned, followed by Mr. Ni. He went into Twin Jewel's room, where Orchid Zhou greeted him and proposed the match. Ni was overjoyed and agreed at once. But then a thought struck him: aside from the ransom price of three hundred, he needed another two hundred to pay for the wedding. How could he raise so much money at once? He began to hesitate. Afraid that the matter would fall through, an extremely worried Twin Jewel went secretly to beg Twin Pearl to think of a way out. Twin Pearl took the exceptional measure of inviting all her best clients, including Benevolence Hong and Fourth Qiao, and told them about this. She then suggested that they club together to help make up the deficit. As they were all kind-hearted people, none demurred. Benevolence even told Modesty Zhu about it. He also contributed a share but kept it from Twin Jade.

Soon it was the wedding day. Mr. Ni came with a band, lanterns bearing his family name, and a bridal sedan chair—the full regalia for marrying a wife. Twin Jewel kowtowed to his ancestors alongside him, drank with him from the same wine cup, and then sat beside him on the wedding bed, where they were inspected by the wedding guests. Three days after the wedding, she came back for the bridal home visit accompanied by Ni. Both of them kowtowed to Orchid Zhou, and he addressed her as "Mother-in-law" as he knelt down. Embarrassed by this, Orchid Zhou hastily bought a set of standard gifts for the son-in-law—a pair of boots and a hat—and gave it to him. She also gave a banquet in their honor, and they did not leave until late at night.

After Twin Jewel's marriage, Twin Jade no longer had an enemy, so life was quiet and peaceful. Orchid Zhou wanted to persuade her to receive overnight guests again but had not yet spoken about it outright. Twin Jade, who was aware of this, made a plan. First she went to the kitchen and freed all the crickets she had been keeping in the hollowed centers of pears. Then she told Worth to buy very strong sorghum spirit on the excuse that she needed to clean opium stains on her clothes. Finally, she sent Pearlie to invite Fifth Young Mr. Zhu over.

Having heard that news of his betrothal had leaked out, Modesty Zhu knew a row was inevitable. Since there was no escaping it, he answered her summons apprehensively, overcome by shame and guilt. Surprisingly, a smiling Twin Jade welcomed him. She held his hand and made him sit down, looking as high-spirited as ever. Modesty, who could not make out her intention, just looked at her in silence. When evening approached, he got up to take his leave, but she drew him to one side and whispered tenderly, asking him to stay the night. He did not have the heart to say no, so he nodded and obeyed.

Soon it was time for the party calls, which came one after another. Twin Jade changed into party clothes and went out, leaving Clever Baby behind to serve Modesty a simple dinner in her room. After Twin Jade came back, a succession of clients came for tea parties; she was run off her feet. It was not until midnight that the carriages gradually left and the smoke in the room dispersed.

Twin Jade closed the front and back doors and bolted them. When she turned around, she saw Modesty taking off his shoes to get into bed.

"Let's not go to bed yet. There's something I need to do," she said with a smile.

He asked in surprise what it was. She came over to sit beside him on the edge of the bed and leaned forward to put both hands on his shoulders. Then she told him to put his right arm around her neck and press his left hand on her heart. Looking him in the face, she asked, "When we were in Conical Hat Garden in the seventh month, we also sat together like this; do you remember what we said?"

Modesty knew they had vowed then to be husband and wife and to live and die as one. He was struck dumb, unable to answer, but Twin Jade pressed him. Finally, he just said, "Yes."

"I thought you would," she said with a smile. "I've got something nice here. Do have some." She took out two teacups from a drawer. They were filled with a dark liquid.

"What is it?" he asked, startled.

"This one is for you. I'll keep you company, too." She was still smiling.

He took a sniff and detected the burning smell of sorghum spirit. "What's in the liquor?" he asked in alarm.

She put the cup to his lips and urged him with a charming smile, "Come on, drink up."

He tasted a little with the tip of his tongue and found it extraordinarily bitter. Realizing it had to be opium, he pushed it away. She had thought he probably would refuse to drink it, so she pinched his nose shut and, as he opened his mouth to breathe, forced most of it down his throat. He fell back onto the bed. As the bitter and fiery taste exploded in his mouth, he tried his best to spit it out. Finally, it spurted out like a red shower, covering the bedsheets and quilt. He propped himself up and was just going to spit some more when he saw Twin Jade pick up the other cup and gulp down its contents. He did not even have time to shout for help; he just threw himself at her, snatched the cup, and smashed it on the floor. Then she tried to grab what was left in the other cup. He managed to sweep it onto the floor, too. Only then did he shout for help.

Orchid Zhou, who was downstairs, had paid no attention when she first heard the sound of the cups breaking. When Modesty called out, however, she suspected something had gone wrong. Holding an opium lamp in her hand, she came upstairs to look around. Modesty rushed forward to unbolt the door and ushered her in. Orchid Zhou was shocked to see that his hands, mouth, and clothes were all stained by opium. Then she saw Twin Jade lying back stiffly in the leather chair panting, with opium smeared all over her face.[1]

"What happened?" she asked in a panic.

::

1. [Eileen Chang was of the opinion that Twin Jade uses fake opium (made of black pear paste) to stage this scene in order to get what she wants. E.H.]

Modesty just stuttered and stamped his feet in futile anxiety.

Fortunately, Twin Pearl, Clever Baby, and Pearlie had not yet gone to bed. One after the other, they came into the room and, seeing the situation, guessed what had happened. Twin Pearl immediately asked, "Well, did you drink any?"

Modesty just pointed urgently at Twin Jade. Twin Pearl understood and called out for a manservant to go quickly to the Hope Hospital to get an antidote.

Clever Baby fetched warm water for Modesty and Twin Jade to wash their faces and rinse their mouths. Modesty cleaned his hands and face and spat out the remaining opium. Twin Jade, furious, stood up abruptly, her eyes round with fury. She cursed him between gritted teeth. "You heartless rascal, you deserve to be chopped up into a thousand pieces! You said we'd die together, so why didn't you die just now? When I go before the king of hell, I'll come back and drag you there with me, you damned scoundrel! Let's see where you're going to hide!"

Orchid Zhou was still stunned, so Twin Pearl tried to reason with Twin Jade. "It's true Fifth Young Master is at fault; he shouldn't have got engaged. But you're young, and there're things you don't understand. You shouldn't listen to the nonsense clients tell you. Even if Fifth Young Master is not engaged, would he be able to make you his wife?"

Twin Jade shouted before Twin Pearl could finish. "Who's talking about wives? You ask him, who was it who said we'd die together?"

Modesty slapped his thigh in frustration and said in tears, "It's not my doing! Elder Brother arranged it all. I couldn't get in a single word!"

Twin Jade rushed at him and poked him hard with her finger, cursing, "You swine, you're good for nothing! Of course your elder brother arranged it! I'm asking you why won't you die?"

Modesty was so frightened, he backed hastily away from her. In the midst of all this confusion, the manservant returned with a bottle of antidote that Pearlie hurriedly poured into two glasses. Modesty suspected that he had not yet spat out all the opium, so he immediately took a sip. Enraged, Twin Jade snatched the glass and threw it right at his face, splashing the solution all over his head. Fortunately, he twisted sideways, and the glass flew by his ear, missing him. Standing at a safe distance, he pleaded with her, "Please drink some of it. Once you take the antidote, I'll do whatever you want, all right?"

"What do I want?" Twin Jade yelled. "I want you to die, that's all I want!"

Orchid Zhou and Twin Pearl said in unison, "Leave the matter of dying till later. Just drink the antidote now."

Pearlie and Clever Baby also tried everything they could think of to persuade her to take the medicine. Twin Jade snorted. "Stop all this wheedling! Just put it down, and I'll take it," she said. "Since he refuses to die, why should I die in front of him? I won't take my own life until he drops dead." So saying, she picked up the glass and sipped at it slowly. Clever Baby wrung a hot towel and proffered it. Twin Jade gave her face a quick wipe. Soon she felt her stomach churn. It was followed by a gurgling noise in her throat, and she brought up some water. Orchid Zhou and Twin Pearl supported her on either side and told her to concentrate on bringing up the opium. She kept cursing as she vomited. This lasted until daybreak, when her stomach finally settled somewhat. Everybody felt relieved, but it was too late for bed then, so an order was given to the kitchen to start the coal stove and heat up some congee for a snack.

Modesty knew that Twin Jade would not leave the matter alone, so he secretly begged Twin Pearl to think of a way out.

Twin Pearl frowned. "You know what Twin Jade's temper is like, Fifth Young Master. Would she listen to anybody? Besides, we're her own people, so it wouldn't be right for us to speak about this. Even if we do, it'll be no use. But if you ask a friend to come and persuade her, she may be willing to listen."

Thus reminded, Modesty immediately wrote a note and told a manservant to go quickly to South End to invite Mr. Hong of the Flourishing Ginseng Store there. The others helped Twin Jade into bed and dispersed; Modesty, who had not slept himself, stayed to keep watch alone. His vigil lasted until noon, when Benevolence Hong graciously answered his summons. After welcoming him, Modesty asked him into Twin Pearl's room and told him in detail what had happened the night before. He beseeched Benevolence to talk to Twin Jade.

Benevolence promised to do so and then walked over to Twin Jade's room. He found her propped up in bed, her head down, taking a nap. Benevolence drew near and called her name softly. She opened her eyes and, seeing him, got up and asked him to sit down.

"Feeling all right?" Benevolence asked casually.

Twin Jade laughed derisively before replying, "Mr. Hong, don't you act as if you haven't heard anything. I know Fifth Young Master asked you to come and talk to me. I haven't got anything else to say except I'm determined to die with him. Wherever he goes, I'll follow, and there'll be no end to it till we've died together. That's all I've got to say."

Benevolence said gently, "Twin Jade, don't be like that. Fifth Young Master has always been fond of you. The engagement was his elder brother's decision, so you shouldn't blame him for it. In this life, what does it matter if you're called wife or concubine? Let me be the matchmaker, and I'll see to it that you marry Fifth Young Master. How about that?"

With all her strength, she spat out, "Me? Marry that heartless scoundrel?" After this remark, she lay down, closed her eyes, and pretended to sleep.

Seeing no opening, Benevolence recounted the conversation to Modesty, for what it was worth. More worried than ever, Modesty groaned and sighed, not knowing what to do. Benevolence probed Twin Pearl about what Twin Jade really had in mind. To his surprise, Twin Pearl had no idea, either.

"Is there somebody behind this, telling her what to do?" Benevolence said.

"Does Twin Jade need to be instructed by anybody? As for us, we'd only be telling her to work. Would we want her to make a scene?" said Twin Pearl.

Benevolence thought about it from all angles and still found it inexplicable.

"I suspect that Twin Jade behaves like this for two reasons: one is Fifth Young Master, the other is Twin Jewel," Twin Pearl said.

Benevolence laughed and applauded. "You're right! Now we're getting to the heart of the matter."

As Modesty stood there respectfully waiting to be enlightened, Benevolence pondered over the matter again. Then he laughed and clapped his hands again, saying, "Yes! I got it!"

Modesty inquired about his theory, but Benevolence said, "You keep out of it. You said whatever Twin Jade wanted, you'd let her have her way. Was that true?"

"Yes," Modesty replied.

"I'll untie this karmic knot for you, but it will cost seven or eight thousand, maybe up to ten thousand. Are you willing to pay?" Benevolence said.

"Yes."

"Then everything will be all right."

Modesty asked what ultimately would be the solution.

"I won't tell you just now. When everything's ready, you'll see."

Faced with a puzzle he was unable to work out, Modesty could only tell Pearlie to order dishes for a simple meal with Benevolence. Benevolence beckoned Twin Pearl to sit beside him. He put a hand on her shoulder and whispered into her ear. It was a long and secretive conversation. Twin Pearl was perfectly in tune with him from the beginning, but when the conversation had finished and she had thought it over, she hesitated and said, "Well, we might try, but I'm not sure it'll work."

"I'm sure it will. It's nothing to them," Benevolence replied.

Thereupon Twin Pearl went into Twin Jade's room as negotiator. Pearlie brought in the dinner just then, so Benevolence told her to set it out in Twin Pearl's room. He and Modesty drank together, sitting opposite each other.

Presently, Twin Pearl returned to report on her mission. "There was some slight interest but also the fear that the matter would fall through and she'd be even more of a laughingstock."

"Go and tell her that if it doesn't succeed, I'll hand Fifth Young Master over to her," Benevolence said.

Twin Pearl again went to relay the message and then came back to report, "Everything is fine. She says Fifth Young Master is handed over to you for now."

Benevolence laughed and clapped his hands in delight.

CHAPTER 64 :: *Anger makes Second Treasure pawn her bracelet, and a kick in her chest causes internal injuries*

Having finished lunch in Twin Pearl's room, Benevolence took Modesty into Twin Jade's room to settle the matter face-to-face. Benevolence volunteered as guarantor so that Modesty could leave with him. Her face suffused with anger, Twin Jade glared at Modesty for a long, long time before she said, "Ten thousand dollars buys you your life; you got a bargain."

Modesty, hiding behind Benevolence, dared not say anything. To lighten the atmosphere, Benevolence talked and joked as they walked out the front door. On their way, Modesty asked how the ten thousand dollars would be spent.

"Five thousand will be her ransom price, and the rest buys her trousseau so she can get married, and that'll be the end of it." Benevolence said.

"Who'll she marry?" Modesty asked.

"That's the troublesome part, the marriage. You keep out of it. Just get the money ready, and I'll see to the rest."

Modesty wanted Benevolence to go home with him to consult with his elder brother, Amity Zhu. Benevolence reluctantly accompanied him to the Zhu residence in Middle Peace Alley, where he talked to Amity in the outer study. Modesty made himself scarce.

Benevolence took his time relating the reason for Twin Jade's suicide attempt and Modesty's intention to buy her off. He then asked Amity to make the final decision. Amity went through a gamut of feelings: shock, regret, and utter devastation. As the matter had reached this state, there was nothing he could do. He sighed and said, "If spending all this money means there'll be no entanglement afterward, I'll go along. Still, ten thousand seems a bit much."

Benevolence could only make a few noises to show agreement.

"I'm entrusting everything to you now," Amity said. "If savings can be made somewhere, please use your admirable discretion."

Somewhat shamefacedly Benevolence agreed and took his leave, so Amity walked him to the door, performed a salutation, and watched him depart. Benevolence walked out of Middle Peace Alley to look for a ricksha, but he saw none. Instead, he spotted a young man walking southward with a swaggering gait. At first, Benevolence paid no attention, but when the man drew near, he saw that it was his sister's son, Simplicity Zhao, who was now much better turned out than before, being dressed in a fairly new lambskin-lined Nanjing silk robe and jacket. Simplicity stopped and greeted him. When Benevolence acknowledged him with a nod, Simplicity reported respectfully, "Mother has been ill for quite a few days and got a little worse yesterday. She misses you often, Uncle. Would you please come over and chat with her?"

Benevolence hesitated for a long while and then heaved a sigh and walked away without looking back.

Simplicity watched his receding figure helplessly and then returned home to Tripod Alley to report back to his younger sister, Second Treasure. "The doctor will be here soon." He also recounted his encounter with Benevolence.

Second Treasure laughed derisively. "He looks down on us, but we don't think much of him, either. A store owner like him is not much different from us courtesans who run brothels."

As they conversed, the doctor arrived. After taking Mrs. Zhao's pulse, he said, "The old lady is greatly weakened in her constitution. A little Jilin ginseng should be used." He wrote the prescription and left.

To buy ginseng, Second Treasure took a small jewelry box out from beside Mrs. Zhao's pillow. But when she opened it, there were only two dollars in the box. In a panic, she asked Simplicity where the money had gone. The latter replied, "We paid the rent this morning. That's all we have left."

Afraid that her mother would be distraught if she found out about this, Second Treasure decided to remove the jewelry box. She returned to her own room to consult Tiger, intending to meet the emergency by pawning the five new suits of fur-lined clothes.

"It's all right if you pawn your own things," Tiger said, "but you haven't paid the silk shops yet, so it doesn't seem right to pawn the clothes, if you don't mind my saying so."

"The bills only amount to a thousand or so. D'you think I'll fail to repay them?" Second Treasure said.

"Second Miss, now it may seem like very little to you. But when you run out, even a dollar is hard to come by, let alone a thousand!"

Second Treasure refused to feel crushed. She took off a gold bracelet and told Simplicity to pawn it.

"If it's Jilin ginseng we need, why don't we get some from Uncle's store?" Simplicity asked.

Second Treasure spat at him before replying, "You're the limit! How dare you speak of Uncle again!"

Simplicity covered his face and hurried off. Second Treasure went downstairs to check on Mrs. Zhao and found that she was drowsy, drifting in and out of sleep. When she called out, "Mother," Mrs. Zhao stirred slightly and grunted faintly. She asked, "Would you like a sip of tea?" A long time passed, and still there was no reply. Second Treasure was deeply troubled.

At that moment, she suddenly heard Tiger call out laughingly, "Why, if it isn't the Young Master! When did you arrive in Shanghai? Do go upstairs." This was followed by the sound of boots going up the stairs.

Second Treasure left her mother's room at once. Seeing a group of men in uniform clustered in the parlor she felt certain it was Third Young Master Shi. She flew upstairs and ran straight into Tiger.

"Who's in the room?" Second Treasure asked.

When Tiger said it was Third Young Master Lai, not Shi, Second Treasure instantly lost heart. Her legs gave out, and she leaned against a pillar, panting.

"Third Young Master Lai is well known as Lai the Turtle," Tiger said in a low voice, "but he's really a good customer, unlike Shi, who's just empty show. You haven't had much business for over a month now; it's time for you to try extra hard. If you get Lai the Turtle, you'll be able to meet your expenses by year-end."

Before she had finished speaking, someone started yelling in the room: "Quick, tell the wife to come! Let me see if she really looks like a wife."

Tiger immediately urged Second Treasure to go in. Second Treasure saw two men occupying the seats of honor. One of them was Iron Hua, so the other had to be Third Young Master Lai.

Since Lai had been cheated of a considerable sum in gambling during his last visit to Shanghai, this time he decided to stick to a few respectable friends. Having heard that Twin Jade was the third of the "wives," he had asked Iron Hua to bring him here to see what Second Treasure was like.

When Second Treasure walked up to him, Lai took the opportunity to pull her toward him for a good appraisal. Then he chuckled and said, "So this is Third Shi's wife! Good! Excellent!"

Although she did not understand what he meant, she knew he was mocking her. She ignored him and turned instead to Iron Hua, "Have you heard from Young Master Shi?"

"No," Iron Hua replied.

Second Treasure complained to him briefly about how Shi had asked her to marry him and then gone back on his words and married in Yangzhou.

"Did he settle his party bills?" Iron Hua asked.

"Before he left, he was going to give us a thousand dollars, but I said to him, 'Since you'll be coming back soon, there's time enough to settle everything altogether.' We had no idea then that that would be the last we saw or heard from him."

As soon as Lai heard this, he jumped up, shouting, "Third Shi welshing on his brothel bills? That's ridiculous!"

Iron Hua said with a smile, "I suppose there must be some reason behind it. How can you believe a one-sided account?"

Second Treasure immediately avoided all mention of the subject.

Tiger eagerly assisted in the entertainment of Lai. Second Treasure was open and polite in her manners. Unfortunately, Lai had taken a fancy to her and kept staring at her until she felt annoyed. She looked down and played with her handkerchief. He reached out surreptitiously, took hold of a corner of the handkerchief, and snatched it away. The handkerchief was torn, and with it two of Second Treasure's long fingernails measuring over two inches. Shock, pain, and anger flooded over her; she would have given him a piece of her mind, but for the sake of business, she controlled herself. With her handkerchief in his hand, Lai gloated. Tiger took a pair of scissors and handed it to Second Treasure, who cut her fingernails off and put them in a pocket.

She thought she would slip away to avoid Lai when Simplicity peeped in opportunely at the door. Second Treasure walked into the center room, where Simplicity gave her the ginseng he had bought and accounted for the money from the pawnshop. She told him to go downstairs and brew the ginseng; then she counted the money and put it away in the wardrobe in her room.

Lai, faking surprise, asked, "Where does the young man come from? He's a looker!"

"He's my brother," Second Treasure replied.

"I thought he was your husband," he said.

"That's nonsense," Tiger said. She turned around and pointed at Clever. "Over there! He's *her* husband."

Clever, who was filling the water pipe for Iron Hua, was so embarrassed, she turned her face away.

Second Treasure, thoroughly disgusted, left her guests and hid herself in Mrs. Zhao's room. Iron Hua, sensing her annoyance, straightened his robe and made to leave. Lai, however, could not tear himself away. Egged on by Tiger, he called for the menservants to set the dinner table for a party. Iron Hua could not very well stop him. Lai then asked where Second Treasure had gone off to.

"She's downstairs, looking in on her mother," Tiger said. "Her mother's ill." She told him about the illness, making up the details as she went along. This went on for a long time, and still there was no sign of Second Treasure, so Tiger told Clever to go get her. Wishing to give a slight hint to the unwanted guest, Second Treasure took her time in coming. Burning with impatience, Lai rushed up to her the minute he saw her, hoping to take her in his arms. She backed off in alarm. He got into such a state that he just waved his arms around and beckoned wildly. She stood at a distance from him, refusing to go near. Anger began to take hold of Lai's heart.

"What's your mother's illness?" Iron Hua asked, pretending to be concerned.

Second Treasure picked up this lifeline at once. She put on a show of being deeply worried and talked incessantly with Iron Hua. Only then were Lai's high spirits dampened.

Soon afterward, the menservants came in to set the table for dinner. Second Treasure again took the opportunity to slip away. Instead of inviting guests, Lai just called seven or eight girls. He also called three for Iron Hua, White Orchid not among them. Once the call chits had been taken downstairs, he dragged Iron Hua to the table and sat down, not even waiting for hot towels to be brought in. The menservants hurriedly sent up the wine pot, but Second Treasure was not even there to pour the wine for them.

Seeing that nothing was as it should be, Tiger rushed down to Mrs. Zhao's room. She saw Simplicity sitting in a corner holding the candle, and Second Treasure feeding Mrs. Zhao the medicine with a teaspoon.

Tiger stamped her feet in frustration. "Second Miss! You must come! They're already seated at the table! I told you to try to please the client, and you give him the cold shoulder instead."

Second Treasure snapped at her in a low voice, "Who told you to fawn on him? He's a pest! I don't feel like seeing him."

"If you don't want someone like Third Young Master Lai for a client, why're you in the business?" Tiger demanded.

Second Treasure turned red in the face.

"You're the miss; I'm just the maid. It's of course all up to you. Once the shopping bills and the money I put up have been settled, it's none of my business."

Second Treasure realized the hold Tiger had on her; there was nothing she could say. Tiger, now in a sulk, also ignored the party and instead just sat around the kitchen. Clever was left to cope alone at the table, trying her best to make conversation and tell jokes.

Simmering with anger, Lai looked like thunder, but Iron Hua interceded, saying: "I've heard Second Treasure is a devoted daughter. Now I can see it's true. She must be attending to her mother and can't get away. This is admirable, truly admirable!" Thus placated, Lai smiled.

Having fed Mrs. Zhao the medicine, Second Treasure helped her lie down again and then returned to her own room to entertain the guests. It happened that the called girls were arriving just then.

"We didn't call Second Treasure to the party, did we? Why has Second Treasure come without being called?" Lai gave voice to his displeasure.

Second Treasure pretended she did not hear. To prevent a row, Iron Hua asked for large wine tumblers to be brought and challenged Lai to the finger game. Lai gleefully stretched out his hand to do battle. Unfortunately, he was on a losing streak and went down a dozen rounds or more. He drank three tumblers himself; the rest of the wine was taken by the courtesans and their maids. Tiger also came in and drank a cup for him.

Refusing to admit defeat, he kept on playing. Toward the end, he lost another round, and when he looked around, he saw Second Treasure was the only one who had not drunk for him. He specified that this cup was for her, and she drained it in one gulp. When he reached out to take the tumbler back, he happened to touch the back of her hand. She resented the liberty, snatched her hands away, and tucked them in her sleeves.

This reminded him of her previous behavior. He put the cup down, grabbed hold of her collar, and ordered her loudly to come close. She fought against him as if her life depended on it and struggled free. His anger surged, his boot flew up, and he kicked her in the chest, sending her tumbling to the floor. Tiger and Clever rushed to the rescue, but it was too late.

Unable to scramble up right away, Second Treasure started crying and cursing. This made Lai still angrier, and he carried on kicking wildly at her. With nowhere to hide, she rolled all over the floor, crying and cursing all the while. Tiger held Lai around his waist and kept shouting for him to relent. Clever, who blocked him with her body, was kicked to the floor as well. Fortunately, Iron Hua was there to plead for them, and Lai finally stopped.

When Tiger and Clever helped her up, Second Treasure's hair was in disarray and her makeup completely smeared. She looked like a demon. Her sense of grievance made her reckless. She jumped straight off the ground and, crying and cursing, was determined to kill herself by hitting her head against the wall. Would Lai have stood for such a scene? His temper flared, and he barked, "Come!"

His four sedan-chair bearers and four menservants immediately appeared at the door, standing at attention. Lai swung his arm and barked, "Smash!" The eight men instantly tucked up the hems of their robes and, swinging their arms and brandishing their fists, started to smash everything in sight. Furniture, drapery—nothing escaped save the paraffin lamps.

Knowing Lai was beyond persuasion, Iron Hua slipped away and left in his sedan chair. The called girls also escaped in a swarm. Tiger and Clever, shielding Second Treasure, fought their way out of the crowd. Stumbling and half carried out of the room, Second Treasure was so deeply shocked that her tears dried up.

Lai liked nothing better than smashing rooms and was extremely thorough about it. If any item remained intact, his servants would be thrashed for it, no excuses allowed. It was hard to imagine what karmic debt Second Treasure owed from her last life to run into such a fiend. Everything in her room, regardless of size or value, was laid waste in the blink of an eye.

Simplicity Zhao the timid brothel keeper was nowhere to be found. As for the menservants, who among them would come forward to beg for mercy? Mrs. Zhao heard the noise faintly and kept asking, "What's going on?"

Second Treasure ran tottering into the study across the way and lay down on the opium divan. Clever followed close behind and stayed with her. Tiger, seeing how badly things had gone, just walked into the mezzanine room in a daze to think things over. Lai was left to do as he pleased until he saw fit to stop and lead his ferocious pack away. Only then did the menservants go and find Simplicity so they could check how things were.

The room was covered in debris; they could not even set foot in it. Even the bed and the wardrobe had been knocked over and left with gaping holes. Only the two paraffin lamps hanging from the ceiling were left to burn brightly.

Simplicity, not knowing what to do, looked around in vain for Second Treasure. Then he heard Clever call out across the way, "In here." He rushed over to find the study was pitch-dark. When a manservant brought a wall lamp in, he saw Second Treasure lying stiffly on the divan.

"Where have you been injured?" Simplicity asked in a panic.

"Second Miss is all right. What about the room?" Clever said.

In reply, Simplicity could only shake his head mutely. Second Treasure abruptly stood up. Supporting herself on Clever's shoulders, she dragged herself slowly and painfully to her room. When she took in the state of the room, her heart contracted in pain, and she howled in misery. This finally brought Tiger out of the mezzanine room. Second Treasure was persuaded by everybody to control her tears. They helped her back to the opium divan and discussed the matter together. Simplicity wanted to take it to the magistrate.

"Taking Lai the Turtle to court?" Tiger said. "You can forget about the county and the district courts, and even the foreigners are scared of him, so where can you take the case?"

"Just from the way he talked, one could tell he wasn't a decent sort. It was your fault for sucking up to him!" said Second Treasure.

Tiger held up her hand dismissively and countered in a harsh voice, "Lai the Turtle came here uninvited; I wasn't the matchmaker. You were the one who offended him, and now you got hurt, you blame it on me! Fine, we'll have this adjudicated tomorrow in a teahouse, and if I lose, I'll pay the damages." Having said that, she turned around abruptly and went off to bed.

This further added to Second Treasure's anger and misery. She told Simplicity to supervise the menservants in cleaning up the room and then managed to make it painfully down the stairs, supported by Clever. The minute she saw Mrs. Zhao, her tears flowed.

"Mother . . ." She did not know what to say.

Mrs. Zhao, unaware of what had happened, told her to go. "You go upstairs and keep the guests company; I'm quite well now."

This made it doubly difficult for Second Treasure to tell her the truth. Instead, she told Clever to warm the reboiled medicine and give it to Mrs. Zhao in bed.

"I'll be all right here. You should go," Mrs. Zhao again hurried her.

Second Treasure bade her to take care and lowered the bed curtains. Clever was told to stay behind to keep watch while Second Treasure made her way slowly upstairs. As her room was covered in dust and debris, she returned to the study. Then Simplicity came in, carrying a drawer in both hands. It contained odd bits of jewelry and a small bundle of silver dollars.

"The money and pawn tickets were scattered on the floor. I don't know if anything is missing," he said.

Second Treasure could not bear to look it over, so she pushed it aside. After Simplicity had gone, it was all quiet. She tried to think things over but could see no way out. She wept silently for a long time. There was a dull ache in her chest and her legs were sore, so she went over to the opium divan and lay down.

Suddenly, there was clamoring and banging at the front door. "Oh, no! Lai the Turtle is back," Simplicity rushed in to report.

Second Treasure felt no fear; she stood up straight and stepped out. Seven or eight menservants who had swarmed up the stairs bent down on one knee to salute her, smiling ingratiatingly. "Third Young Master Shi is now the county prefect of Yangzhou. He asks Second Miss to go there at once."

Her joy was beyond description. She rushed back into her room and called for Clever to dress her hair. Her mother came in wearing the phoenix headdress and serpent-patterned jacket of an official's wife. She called Second Treasure's name fondly and then beamed. "Didn't I tell you? Nothing could go wrong with a man like Third Young Master! He's sending for us now, isn't he?"

"Mother, when we get there, don't mention what's happened before."

Mrs. Zhao kept nodding.

Clever was calling for "Second Miss" from downstairs. "Miss Flora has come to congratulate you," she said.

"Who told her the news? It beat the telegram," Second Treasure asked, surprised.

Before she could go out in welcome, Flora Zhang was already standing before her. Second Treasure smiled and asked her to sit down.

"You're all dressed. Are you going out for a carriage ride?" Flora asked abruptly.

"No, Third Young Master Shi is asking us to go to him," Second Treasure replied.

"That's nonsense! Third Young Master Shi died a long time ago. Didn't you know that?"

Second Treasure thought for a moment, and it seemed to her that Third Young Master Shi was indeed dead. She was just going to question the menservants when they turned into monsters and jumped at her. The fright made her shout with all her might. She woke up covered in a cold sweat, her heart palpitating.

AFTERWORD

*Eva Hung*

*The Sing-song Girls of Shanghai,* a novel of manners and romance written in late-nineteenth-century China, captures the golden age of
Shanghai's high-class brothels. While the novel's main setting is
the expensive sing-song houses in the International Settlement and
its chief protagonists are the courtesans and their clients, the networks of relationships it portrays give the reader a richly textured
picture of Shanghai's Chinese society. Featuring some 120 characters, it is a huge and finely woven tapestry depicting a world that
was at once alluring and dangerous, narrated by someone familiar
with its workings.

Aside from the interest its subject matter may generate, *The Sing-
song Girls of Shanghai* also stands as a landmark of literary innovation.
First, it is an unsentimental and realistic account whose narrative
method and structure differ significantly from traditional *zhanghui,*
or episodic, fiction and that ends with a distinctly modern touch.
Second, the dialogue of the whole novel is written in the Wu dialect,[1]
the main language used in the brothels, making it the most substantial literary work in nonstandard Chinese and a major experiment
in evoking authentic voices in fiction. In terms of familiarity, on
the other hand, the author clearly states that he derived his narrative
technique from the Qing dynasty novel *Ruilin waishi* (*The Scholars*). He
also borrowed from another masterpiece of Qing dynasty fiction,
*Honglou meng* (*The Story of the Stone*), both in characterization and setting, and from Tang dynasty stories about courtesans and their often
faithless lovers. Exemplifying the evolution of Chinese fiction, these
properties obviously make for an interesting work.

Despite its attraction for a small number of aficionados, however,
*The Sing-song Girls of Shanghai* never achieved great popularity. The fact

that the dialogue is not easily accessible has been seen as a major obstacle, but an even more important barrier must have been the rapid decline of the brothel world in the twentieth century, when the glamorous and alluring soon became outdated and seedy. The sing-song house, with its special rules and rituals, was a familiar scene to the author Han Bangqing and his contemporary readers, but to twentieth-century readers used to an ever-quickening pace of life, it is part of an alien and distant past. Though readers of the novel in translation are shielded from the problem of dialect, they are at least as unfamiliar with the novel's world. I hope that my essay "The World of the Shanghai Courtesans" will bridge some of the knowledge gaps.

*About This Translation*

One the most famous aficionados of *The Sing-song Girls of Shanghai* was the Chinese writer Eileen Chang (1920–1995). Her belief that it deserved a wider audience made her begin work on a Mandarin version as well as an English translation some three decades ago. Though her standard Mandarin version of the novel has been available to readers for over two decades (Taipei: Crown, 1981), except for two chapters, her English translation was never published.[2] After Chang's death, her literary executors, Stephen and Mae Soong, donated her manuscripts to the University of Southern California. Discovered among the various papers in this collection were different versions of *The Sing-song Girls of Shanghai* in translation. Inspection revealed that these were rough drafts in which personal and place names showed no consistency, romanization followed no particular system, and occasionally a paragraph or a page was missing. The biggest problems, however, were those of language, cadence, and style. Chang seemed to have opted for an almost word-for-word approach, with the translation often following Chinese—rather than English—syntax. The translation of wordplay, idioms, and literary clichés also proved to be a major hurdle.

When Columbia University Press first approached me in 2001 about making Chang's draft publishable, I was more than a little reluctant. What finally persuaded me to undertake this task was my role as a translation historian. Collaborative translation has been a significant part of China's cultural tradition for some two thousand years, starting with sutra translations in the mid-second century. Since one of the duties I envisaged for myself as editor of *Renditions* was that of advocating teamwork, it seemed that I should put into practice what I preached. Thus began twenty-two months of extensive revision. In terms of translation approach, use of language and prose rhythm, as well as choice of names for the characters, roughly 60 percent of this published text represents my work rather than Chang's. Her assessment of the strengths and weaknesses of this novel cannot be faulted, however, so the structural changes made in this translation—in the form of deletion and minor rewriting—are mostly based on choices made by Eileen Chang.

The major deletions center on occasions when some of the brothel clients flaunt their literary talent.[3] The most important reason for the decision to omit these is that refined poetic composition was not Han Bangqing's strong suit, and so the pieces attributed to the "talented young men" in the novel fall far short of the standards of those with true talent.[4] Other than such literary scenes, the only major deletions occurs at the beginning and the end of the novel, as explained in Eileen Chang's preface.

Chang's approach to the translation of personal names is one that may arouse objection: she decided against transliteration in favor of semantic translation of all personal names. While this approach makes perfect sense in the case of the prostitutes—whose names were given to them by their owners when they entered the profession and were chosen to convey various aspects of feminine allure—it may be more problematic in relation to other characters. The primary objection is that such names may cause each character to be perceived as a representative of a certain human trait, suggesting a kind of allegory similar to *The Pilgrim's Progress*. The obvious and simple solution is to adopt a bifurcated approach (as David Hawkes did in *The Story of the Stone*), with semantic translation for names of prostitutes and straightforward romanization for other characters. After careful consideration, however, I decided that Chang's decision was backed by sound reason.[5] Chinese personal names in general carry a much more obvious semantic and cultural load than English ones: to put it in the simplest way, they reflect the background, good wishes, and ambitions of the parents or name givers. In the case of fiction, they are of course one of the easiest means of characterization. Indeed, the majority of names in this novel serve more than the simple purpose of identification; they also tell us something about the background or personality of the characters concerned. Unlike what occurs in *The Pilgrim's Progress*, however, names are not used uniformly in this novel. Cases such as Simplicity Zhou and Juvenity Zhang are direct and obvious: they are young and unsophisticated men whose personalities and lack of experience are central to their roles in the novel. In cases such as Prosperity Luo and Dragon Ma,[6] their names mainly indicate their circumstances in life, while those of Devotion Yin and Second Bai Gao are indicative of certain personality traits.

Then there are the somewhat ironic cases, notably Constance (who despite her apparent good nature is not constant) and Benevolence (who is good to his friends but fails to look out for his kin). Finally, some names characterize through literary reference: Green Phoenix bears more than a passing resemblance to another "phoenix"—Wang Xifeng in *Honglou meng*—and Water Blossom reminds us of Lin Daiyu, who is represented by the water lily in the same novel. As long as readers bear in mind that this is a *Chinese* novel, where the webs of relationships—cultural, semantic, and social—are different from English ones, the translation of personal names should be a bonus rather than a distraction. After all, besides the reasons stated above, translated names—unlike many romanized according to *pinyin*—are pronounceable and easier to remember.

In translating place and street names I have relied primarily on late-nineteenth- and early-twentieth-century English maps of Shanghai. Names of small lanes and alleyways—the sites of the brothels—are not recorded in the English maps I consulted, however. With reference to these, my decision was again to translate rather than transliterate, for the same reasons as those pertaining to personal names.

It is the practice of most academic translations to provide footnotes on all sorts of minor details in the text. Readers will find that, with very few exceptions, in this translation footnotes are only given where they make a direct contribution to the understanding of characterization and plot. The reason is simple: *The Sing-song Girls of Shanghai* is a novel, so this translation is meant to function first and foremost as a novel. The advantage of providing peripheral information has to be weighed against the aesthetic disruption footnotes entail. Scholars with a good appreciation of translation discourse know that footnotes are a cumbersome means of conveying factual information and are not conducive to literary appreciation. A far better way of giving essential information on social and cultural background is to do so comprehensively in a separate text—an approach similar to providing a new visitor with a city guide and a street map for orientation. I would therefore urge readers of this novel to read the essay "The World of the Shanghai Courtesans" to get their social and cultural bearings. The street map of old Shanghai is provided for the same reason. Readers who have visited the city—or who care to check a contemporary map—will find that they can easily follow the characters through its streets and alleyways.

Like most episodic fiction written by men educated in the old style, this novel contains occasional passing references to older works. In terms of frequency, however, mention of popular opera ranks the highest. Since most such references are just an indirect reflection on the popular culture of the day, footnotes are only provided in cases where the information contributes to an overall understanding of events and characters. There are, of course, various sourcebooks on Beijing opera and Kun opera that detail their storylines and sources, and the interested reader may want to consult these. With reference to literary allusions, annotation is only used when the primary meaning would be obscure if the source of the allusion were not revealed. Where the allusion serves only a secondary or peripheral function in terms of message communication, the preferred approach here is manipulation of style and register rather than annotation. After all, allusions are used at all levels of discourse in all literary cultures without distinctive markers (such as footnotes) tagged to them. Imagine the tears of boredom that would drown us all if every time someone said "lend me your ears," we had to endure an aside stating: "*Julius Caesar*, act 3, scene 2, line 79" or the unnecessary complication that would ensue if every "good-bye" were followed by the tag "a corrupt form of 'God be with you.'"

*Acknowledgments*

After twenty-two months of revision, my impression of *The Sing-song Girls of Shanghai* changed substantially. With the realization that this is a novel meant for repeated reading, what began as a duty eventually became something of a pleasure. This transformation would not have been possible without the following people: Professor Joseph Lau of Lingnan University and Professor David Wang of Columbia University, who cornered me into accepting the project; Professor Yuan Jin of Shanghai University, who first showed me traces of old Shanghai in 1997 and who later obtained for me various sourcebooks on the late Qing and early Republican eras; Mrs. Mae Soong, who assured me that my extensive rewriting of Chang's draft would be a favor rather than a sacrilege; my research assistants, Kaman Chan, Audrey Heijns, and Maggie Leung who undertook the hefty task of proofreading three revisions of the translation; and my secretary, Alena Chow, who helped me with word processing and compiling the "Cast of Major Characters." The person to whom I owe the greatest debt is my husband, David Pollard, who is my most reliable source of information on matters related to realia as well as language and whose appreciation of this novel contributed significantly to my own reevaluation of it.

*Editions of Haishang hua Used*

*Haishang hua liezhuan.* 1926. Reprint, Taipei: Tianyi chubanshe, 1974.

*Haishang hua.* Ed. Wang Yuanfang. Shanghai: Yadong tushuguan, 1935.
*Haishang hua.* Ed. Eileen Chang. Taipei: Crown, 1983.
*Haishang hua.* Ed. Jiang Hanchun. Taipei: Sanmin chubanshe, 1998.

## Notes

1. Eileen Chang noted that the only exception is one line spoken by Lai the Turtle, probably to show that Lai is a northerner.

2. Chapters 1 and 2 of her translation were published in *Renditions,* nos. 17 and 18 (1982). It seems that Chang did look for a publisher for the full novel. The manuscript, however, never reached the stage where it was publishable.

3. As a result of such deletion, the titles of chapters 10 and 33 have been rewritten.

4. Liu Fu, who was vehement in his condemnation of the introduction of the Rustic Retreat group of characters into this novel, was of the same opinion. See Liu Fu, "Du *Haishang hua liezhuan*" (On reading *Haishang hua liezhuan*), in *Haishang hua,* ed. Wang Yuanfang (Shanghai: Yadong tushuguan, 1935), pp. 21–24.

5. Many of the personal and place names that Chang used proved problematic and have been replaced.

6. Dragon Ma's personal name in Chinese—Longchi, or dragon pond—suggests that he is a man of great talent (dragon) trapped in a small space (pond), that is, someone with unfulfilled ambition.

## THE WORLD OF THE SHANGHAI COURTESANS
*Eva Hung*

*Foreign Concessions and the International Settlement*

The transformation of Shanghai from a settlement with a small walled city to a major metropolis began in 1842 with the Treaty of Nanjing that resulted from the Opium War. Shanghai, as one of the five designated treaty ports, was declared open to foreign trade on November 14, 1843. A stretch of rural land bordering the Huangpu River was assigned for the use of several hundred foreign traders, and Western-style houses as well as godowns began to appear.[1]

The earliest boundaries that marked the areas designated for foreign settlement were the Huangpu River in the east, the Yangjing-bang Creek in the south, and present-day Beijing Road in the north; the western boundary was never defined. This land, which remained nominally Chinese, was leased in perpetuity to the foreign powers. It was divided into three settlements: the French concession occupied the area between the Chinese walled city and Yangjing-bang Creek;[2] the British concession stretched from Yangjingbang to Suzhou Creek, while the United States took up the land along the Huangpu River to the northeast of Suzhou Creek. In 1863 the Americans and the British decided to join forces, turning the areas they occupied into the International Settlement. Since there was no fixed boundary on the western side of the assigned land, there were repeated—and some very successful—attempts to extend the settlements into the Chinese countryside. Each of the foreign concessions had its own administrative setup, police force, and volunteer fire service, while the walled city and the small areas of land bordering the concessions remained under Chinese administration.[3] Residents came under the jurisdiction of their respective zones, and a mixed court was established to deal with cases that involved both

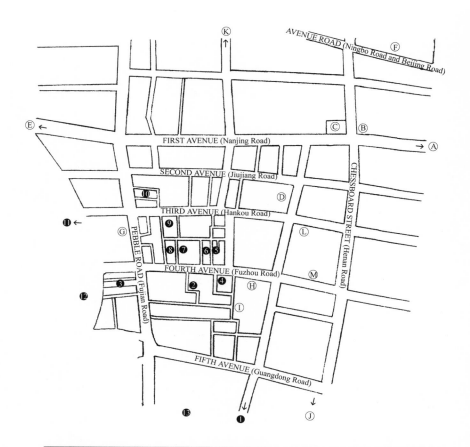

**LOCATION MAP OF THE BROTHEL AREA AND ENVIRONS IN THE INTERNATIONAL SETTLEMENT**

❶ To Beaten Dog Bridge
❷ Generosity Alley
❸ Nobility Alley
❹ Civic Peace Alley
❺ East Co-prosperity Alley
❻ West Co-prosperity Alley
❼ East Floral Alley
❽ West Floral Alley
❾ Co-security Alley
❿ Sunshine Alley
⓫ Tripod Alley
⓬ Tranquility Alley
⓭ West Chessboard Street

Ⓐ The Bund
Ⓑ Hope Brothers
Ⓒ Bowling Alley
Ⓓ Fire Bell Tower
Ⓔ To Bubbling Well Road (Nanjing Rd. W.)
Ⓕ Chinese traditional banks
Ⓖ Tailors
Ⓗ Jewelry shops
Ⓘ Silk shops
Ⓙ To French Concession and Chinese walled city
Ⓚ Suzhou Creek
Ⓛ Central Fire Station
Ⓜ Central Police Station

Chinese and foreign interests. Despite the administrative independence of the different zones, the currencies in common use were the same: the gold-based Spanish Carolus dollar, the Mexican dollar, and the Chinese tael of silver.

In the settlements' early days, Chinese residents were originally prohibited, but this soon changed. The majority of the employees of foreign firms were Chinese, and Chinese merchants who dealt in silk, tea, opium, and other goods were constantly coming and going. However, what changed the nature of the settlements and the composition of their populations was the refugees, including many wealthy households who rushed there to escape from the peasant uprisings against the Qing government. The first wave of refugees came when the Small Sword Society, which revolted in 1831, occupied the Chinese walled city between 1834 and 1845. By the end of that rebellion, the Chinese population in the settlements had exploded to fifty thousand. An even greater impact came with the Taiping Rebellion (1850–1864), which permanently changed the topography and nature of the foreign concessions. These settlements' development into a thriving city was linked intrinsically to their huge and ever-increasing Chinese population, which by 1862 had reached half a million. The refugee migrants found in this city not just protection from rebels but also new business opportunities. In 1870 Shanghai became the fifth largest port in the world.

By this time, Chinese people could move quite freely among the various administrative zones in normal circumstances. The major restrictions were related to the walled city, which still upheld the Chinese curfew rule and closed its gates at night; it was also off limits to horse carriages. In such a small area overseen by different administrations, the rules for residents and businessmen were considerably more complex and cumbersome than in other places. For example, all the transport vehicles for hire, such as sedan chairs and rickshas, had to obtain licenses for all three zones.[4] It was a situation the locals found they could deal with, however. With time, such Western practices as participating in town councils and obtaining insurance coverage became the norm for well-to-do Chinese.

### Brothels in the International Settlement

Since *The Sing-song Girls of Shanghai* was written before China's defeat in the Sino-Japanese War of 1895, the Shanghai in this novel predates the city's industrialization.[5] Areas under all three administrations were dominated by commerce and entrepôt trade. The action takes place almost exclusively in the International Settlement as that was where the high-class brothels, or sing-song houses, congregated. During the Taiping Rebellion, high-class brothels were set up in the new lanes, such as Nobility Alley in the International Settlement, with Fourth Avenue (present-day Fuzhou Road) serving as the core area for sing-song houses. Later, the first-class houses moved westward with the expansion of the foreign concessions, while the second-class ones remained around Chessboard Street (present-day Henan Road). Though the French concession was also home to a large number of prostitutes, they belonged mostly to the lower rungs of the ladder, probably because for a long time law and order in the French settlement was less than ideal.

The prosperity of the foreign concessions and the growth of the Chinese population were of course major reasons for sing-song houses to have been established in the International Settlement, but another important reason was that the area was outside Chinese jurisdiction. In the Qing dynasty, officials were strictly forbidden by law to have liaisons with prostitutes. Since this rule did not apply to the foreign concessions, it created a major opportunity for prostitutes to entertain officials of all grades, as well as their associates. That was why, despite their Chinese clientele, all the high-class prostitutes in Shanghai operated in the International Settlement. This situation also brought flourishing business to trades that benefited from the custom of courtesans and their clients, notably tailors, jewelry stores, embroidery shops, fabric shops, restaurants, and food stalls. These were set up in clusters around the core brothel areas. In addition to Chinese prostitutes originating in the areas around Shanghai, there were also establishments serviced by women from other regions and nations (including Japanese, European, and American women). Prominent among the regional groups were two from Guangdong province: the Tanka girls, who lived and worked on boats, and the Cantonese girls, who worked in Cantonese brothels. The only non-Shanghai group that features in this novel is the Cantonese one, represented by their best-known brothel, the Old Banner. The short episode on Cantonese courtesans is of considerable interest as it demonstrates the differences in aesthetic taste and fashion, as well as customs, among different regional groups.

Prostitution establishments, like opium shops, were perfectly legal in the foreign concessions, and there were intermittent attempts to tabulate the number of prostitutes working there. One of the earliest, based on statistics compiled by health officials in 1871, stated that there were 1,632 prostitutes in the International Settlement and 2,600 in the French concession. These figures, however, do not differentiate between origin and categories, and neither do they include the majority of unlicensed streetwalkers.[6] The main concern of the administrations was to prevent prostitution activities from invading the streets; what went on within the brothels was not considered a major source of nuisance.

Brothels were subject to license fees and taxes and monitored under various police regulations. For the sing-song houses, the fees varied depending on the quality of the house and the number of girls working there. The demarcations among different grades of brothels were reflected in the fee structure; the license fees for mature courtesans offering a full range of service were also considerably higher than those for virgin apprentices. Landlords also charged a higher rent for brothels than for other shops and households.

Since sexual and entertainment services were sought by all classes of people, the prostitutes in Shanghai fell into many categories, which catered to different clienteles. They all have a role to play in this novel. Streetwalkers, or "game birds," were unlicensed and roamed the teahouses and alleys for custom. They always claimed to be respectable women forced by circumstances to take on the occasional client and often used a small *shikumen* house as a business base.[7] The lowest category establishments were the knocking shops, where sexual services were provided without any complex preliminaries, and it was not unusual for girls to be summoned to the shop only when clients arrived. A slightly higher category was the "flowered opium den," so called because the women who waited on the smokers in the opium house also offered sexual service. They congregated in the French concession and were mostly set up in *shikumen* houses. The high-class brothels, or sing-song houses, were divided into two categories: first-class, or *changsan* (meaning "all three"), and second-class, or *yao'er* (meaning "one two").[8] The somewhat strange reference to numbers originated with the fees charged: at the first-class houses, the charge for a dinner party or a party call was a flat rate of three dollars, hence "all three"; at the second-class houses, a tea party cost one dollar, and a party call or dinner party two dollars, hence "one two."[9] These names remained long after the charges had gone up with the passing of time. Sing-song houses were marked by a lamp hanging above the front door as well as the names of the courtesans written on red paper posted at the door. Some second-class establishments had a name for the house, such as "Hall of Spring" or "Hall of Beauties," but the first-class houses were always referred to by the names of their leading courtesans.

While the lower class establishments offered only sexual service and basic amenities such as tea, opium, and tobacco, the sing-song houses served functions other than that of providing sex, food, drink, and drugs. Entertaining in brothels or in the company of courtesans was part of the daily routine for officials and businessmen alike. This is evidenced by the fact that in the late Qing and early Republican eras, tabloid papers specializing in reports on the brothel scene also provided new and prospective clients of sing-song houses with basic information on brothel rules and etiquette to help them fit in. Thus the sing-song house was an important meeting place for friends and business associates, a place where social networks were extended, business discussed, and advice sought and given among friends and colleagues. This was particularly true of the first-class houses whose courtesans were expected to act as a social lubricant and to be discreet.

*The Courtesans*

Like the establishments they worked for, the higher-classed prostitutes were divided into different grades. The top-class courtesans claimed their lineage from the female minstrels who became popular in Shanghai shortly after the Taiping Rebellion. It is said that the original female minstrels performed storytelling in songs and did not openly sell their sexual favors. They were addressed as *xiansheng*, a form of respectful address that normally applied to men. This title remained in use even after prostitution became their main business. It was then adopted by first-class courtesans who were also trained in singing and music, often from a young age. (In this translation, the term "maestro" is used to call attention to this unusual application of address and the sense of respect it originally conveyed.) Traces of the facade of respectability remained: clients and courtesans were not permitted to talk directly about establishing a sexual relationship; a third party always acted as matchmaker (this could be a friend, another courtesan, the maid, or the madam). In many cases, even the simple matter of summoning a first-class courtesan to a dinner party in a restaurant also involved some sort of introduction by a person she knew.

At the period depicted in this novel, female minstrels no longer existed, and the word "maestro" referred only to courtesans who worked in first-class houses. The second-class girls, less accomplished and often less good-looking, were addressed as "Miss" (a title also used for other prostitutes, including streetwalkers). In the second-class establishments, there were some girls who only entertained at home and did not answer party calls,[10] but it seems that they were a small minority. In this novel, the contrast between the behavior of Jewel (a young courtesan in a second-class house) and her first-class peers such as Green Phoenix and Lute clearly demonstrates the perceived differences between the two categories of girls:

second-class courtesans were more blatantly sex-oriented and far less refined in their attempts to ensnare new clients. Thus there was no intended irony when a client praised a courtesan by saying that she was like a respectable woman.

Leading courtesans in Shanghai were minor celebrities and trend-setters in fashion. Readers will notice that while descriptions of the looks of various girls are few and far between, detailed descriptions of their clothes and ornaments can be found in almost every chapter of this novel. This was a period when a well-endowed figure was frowned on, so the women wore tight undershirts to flatten their chests. On top of that, they wore several layers of clothes made variously of silk, brocade, crepe, or fur. There were clear distinctions among clothes worn in the house, for daytime trips, and for dinner parties, with the last being the most ornate. As the practice of footbinding was still at its height, almost the first thing a brothel owner did when she acquired a young apprentice was to bind her feet tightly in order to create the desired form of the "three-inch lotus," hence the repeated references in the novel to "bound-feet shoes." Besides exquisite clothes and shoes, a leading courtesan was always adorned with expensive jewelry, mostly gifts from her many clients.[11] Instead of individual items, they often asked for sets of jewelry comprising rings, earrings, hairpins, and headbands made of gold, pearls, or green jade.[12]

The relationship between courtesans was an interesting and tricky one. While those who belonged to the same house were placed on a hierarchical order according to seniority and popularity, courtesans of comparable status from different establishments were guided by much more complex considerations. On the one hand, they were all potential business rivals; on the other, they were well known to each other as they met regularly at parties hosted by their clients. Where the relationship was cold and distant, they avoided addressing each other directly; where the relationship was friendly, courtesans adopted the Manchu term "A ge," used as both a title and a form of address for princes of the royal house, to circumvent the questions of age and hierarchical seniority. This is because the title "A ge," unlike the normal words for "brother" or "sister" in Chinese, does not indicate the relative age of the addressed and addressee, a highly sensitive issue for courtesans. In this translation, the unusualness of this form of address is preserved through the term "my peer," which stresses the obliteration of age and rank considerations and also remotely hints at the term's palace origin.

Since sexual service was only part of a courtesan's trade, all those who entered the profession as apprentices were trained in singing and playing musical instruments. Those who joined the profession as adults, however, had no such training and had to rely on their natural charms to please their clients. (In chapter 20 of this novel, there is a short account of the investment an average owner made to ensure that a courtesan acquired the necessary skills as an entertainer in addition to being physically attractive.) Despite the various skills the high-class courtesans had to learn, the majority was illiterate. Thus even the most intelligent courtesan in this novel (Green Phoenix) relies on a client to read for her the most important document in her life, and even a courtesan with literary pretensions (Jade Wenjun) must depend on someone else to read her the poems dedicated to her. As Christian Henriot points out, the literary courtesan was just a myth.[13]

Given the large number of prostitutes in Shanghai, the question of their origin naturally arises. It is not easy to determine the native places of individual courtesans, as the majority claimed to have come from Suzhou, where a dialect was spoken that was considered most pleasing to the ear. Given this common perception, girls from these areas would have attracted more attention from abductors and traffickers. It was certainly a fact that the Suzhou dialect dominated the sing-song houses, as courtesans from other regions also used it to sustain the claim that they were from Suzhou.

Whatever their geographical origin, one factor that featured prominently in the supply of prostitutes was poverty: the sale of female children was a frequent occurrence among desperately poor families, and in years of flood and famine little girls were sold openly on the streets; most of them ended up as servant girls or prostitutes. While some girls were sold by their relatives, others were kidnapped by gangs that specialized in human trafficking. Other factors, however, including family background and personal choice, also led girls into prostitution. The courtesans in sing-song houses were mostly daughters of courtesans and brothel owners who were introduced to the trade from childhood (such as Twin Pearl, Water Blossom, and Aroma), girls sold to brothel owners (such as Green Phoenix, Twin Jade, and River Blossom), or women who voluntarily joined the profession (such as Second Jewel and Flora Zhang). Women in the last group normally started business as free agents who rented rooms in a brothel, but when they ran into debt,[14] they would end up in situations little different from girls who had been sold.

For both the young apprentice and the sing-song house, the transition from virgin courtesan to one who offered sexual service was an important occasion. The event was treated like a mock wedding, with large red candles lit in the courtesan's room. Hence the sing-song house term for the deflowering of a virgin courtesan was "lighting red candles." The client, who had to pay a substantial amount of money for the privilege, was chosen by the madam with a view to establishing a relatively long term relationship. It was also well known, however, that such occasions were often used to swindle clients. One of the usual ways of doing this was to line up two or more inexperienced clients for defloration and try to pass the courtesan off as a virgin several times over. Another common practice was for the courtesan to arrange for her favorite client to enjoy her services as soon as the defloration night was over so that he would not have to pay the hefty fee.[15]

While a popular courtesan normally had two or three regular clients and was not supposed to show that she favored any one above the others,[16] it was only human nature for her to have preferences, so it is not surprising that courtesans also had romantic attachments. Besides favoring certain clients, they were also known to have relationships with actors, something that was decidedly discouraged and could ruin their careers. In this novel, even the most businesslike of courtesans—Green Phoenix—plays tricks on the house in order to benefit her favorite client,[17] while the willful Little Rouge comes to ruin because of her liaison with an actor.

With looks and youth being vital factors in determining a courtesan's popularity, the length of a courtesan's career was limited. Normally, there were two exit paths for those who were reasonably good in the business: marrying or setting up their own sing-song house. Since courtesans were used to comfortable surroundings, and the men they met were mostly their clients, marriage for the majority meant becoming a client's concubine. Though such an arrangement could be for life, there were many cases of courtesans leaving their husbands to return to the trade. Some no doubt made that decision because they could not get along with their husbands' families; others just missed the relative freedom they had compared with the restrictions placed on a married woman in a large household. As long as their husbands consented to their leaving, they could return to the trade, although some did so without such consent.

Those who wanted to set up their own establishments had to find the necessary funding to buy their own freedom, purchase young apprentice girls, rent a house and all the furnishings, and hire the required staff. Without the generous financial help of their regular clients, at least in the initial stages, such an enterprise was quite impossible.

As for courtesans who were unlucky in business or who became heavily indebted through drug habits and other indulgences, the ending could be extremely miserable. As they lost their looks and popularity, they went down the rungs of the prostitution ladder until they ended up destitute in the streets.

### The Owner and the Coterie

The majority of owners of sing-song houses were madams with long experience in the business. Most of them started life either as courtesans or as maids, and as they grew older they bought young girls and set up their own establishments. The family atmosphere of the sing-song houses centered around the madam who was "Mother" to all the girls who worked for her, whether they were her real daughters or just girls she had purchased. One way the madam had of showing ownership was brand-naming: a newly bought girl was given a new name that tied her to the madam and the brothel: the madam's family name, followed by a personal name that included a word that appeared in the names of the other girls in the house, the same way that real sisters in normal families were named.

Since many courtesans were sold to the sing-song houses as little orphaned girls, the feelings they had for the madam and the house could be somewhat complex, particularly if the madam was not overly exploitive or abusive. The madam, on her part, always stressed the fact that she treated girls sold to her the same as her own daughters. This was of course seldom true, but the fact that young purchased girls represented a long-term investment that might produce very handsome returns over a decade or more did give their owners an incentive to maintain a good relationship with them. Moreover, owners were responsible for members of their houses. If a girl was pushed too hard, she might take the drastic step of ending her life. Should this happen, the madam not only lost out financially but could find herself faced with an investigation and legal consequences.

Maids played a crucial part in the life of a sing-song house. They were familiar with all the daily routines and etiquette and accompanied the courtesans on all party calls as well as helping them entertain at home. The working relationship between courtesan and maid is perhaps best symbolized by this practice: the maid carried the courtesan's personal silver water pipe and nutmeg box—items essential to entertaining guests at home and at parties—hence, wherever the courtesan went, the maid followed. A maid was usually the best person to smooth over lovers' tiffs and was often required to intercede during negotiations or quarrels by either suppressing an impetuous courtesan or speaking up for one who failed to stand her ground.[18] Though some maids were employees, others had money invested in the establishments or courtesans they worked for. Thus the hierarchical relationship between courtesan and maid could be even more complex than that between madam and courtesan. As a shareholder in the courtesan's business, the maid, despite her apparently inferior position, could put considerable pressure on the courtesan. This could be one of the reasons that maids had a bad reputation. In addition to being deemed vulgar and ugly, they were also said to be rampantly promiscuous—this despite the fact that most maids were married women.

Besides madams, courtesans, and maids, the sing-song houses had to employ a substantial staff including servant girls, menservants, and sedan-chair bearers. The great majority of servant girls and menservants originated from the countryside and regions around Shanghai. Since job hunting was done almost entirely through personal references and family connections, positions of servant girls and menservants were often filled by the relatives of people who were already working in the brothels. Though the positions were lowly and the pay was low, because of their constant contact with clients these employees received tips on a regular basis. In addition to tipping at the end of each season, clients who spent the night at the brothel were also expected to tip all the servants.

While some sources say that servant girls openly offered sexual services to brothel clients, such a possibility is only hinted at in this novel. Han Bangqing seemed to be of the opinion that no refined client would lower himself to accepting the services of a servant girl (the unrefined, however, were quite another matter).[19] In terms of prospects, a servant girl could aspire to becoming a maid after she had learned the necessary grooming skills and knowledge of the trade.

Menservants in the brothels were called by a special term: *xiangbang*, or helpers. They were responsible for keeping an eye on the front door, announcing the arrival of clients, bringing hot water for tea, serving hot towels, setting tables for dinner, running errands, delivering invitations and call chits, and so on. Menservants were often looked down upon as lacking both brains (if literate, they could be bookkeepers) and physical strength (required for sedan-chair bearers). In the tabloid papers specializing on gossip about brothels, they were frequently accused of indulging in illicit relationships with servant girls and courtesans.

Sedan-chair bearers or ricksha pullers were essential to a sing-song house as courtesans were not supposed to go anywhere on foot. Virgin courtesans were sometimes carried on the backs of menservants to answer party calls, but by far the most frequently used means of transport was the sedan chair. Other employees in the brothel included a cook (homemade food was one element that contributed to the mock-family atmosphere of sing-song houses) and a book-keeper responsible for accounts and records. They, however, had little direct contact with the clients.

### Life in a Sing-song House

The Chinese year followed the lunar calendar, with each year starting in late January or early February. In the brothels, the fiscal year was divided into three seasons, each marked by a major Chinese festival: Dragon Boat Festival in the fifth month (usually early June), Midautumn Festival in the eighth month (usually mid- to late September), and Chinese New Year. At the end of each season, a ceremony was held to honor the money gods by burning paper ingots and incense as offerings. This was also the time for the brothel to audit its books, the maids and servants to be paid, and clients to settle their accumulated bills. On the day of the ritual, a regular client of a courtesan was duty-bound to give a sumptuous dinner party in her room. Since failure to attract such parties was not just a serious loss of face for the girl but might well bring on the wrath of the brothel owner, these could be trying times for the less popular courtesans. (In this novel, there is an example of how a second-class girl relies on her better-connected sister to arrange for a dinner party on such an occasion.) For courtesans who were in demand, however, these were extremely busy times. In addition to parties hosted by their regular clients, they also had to attend those given by their clients' friends.

Besides the festivals marking the end of the three seasons, second-class houses had another special day in the year: the Chrysanthemum Festival in autumn. This was the only occasion when they could attract wealthy clients (normally too snobbish to visit a second-class house) to give parties on their premises. Pots and bowls of chrysanthemums were piled in a hill formation in the central courtyards where banquets were served.[20] Though chrysanthemum viewing was part of the literati tradition in China, the origin of this practice in second-class brothels is unknown.

Another familiar ritual in brothel life was the recitation of Buddhist and Taoist texts, called "treasure scrolls." This was done on special occasions, such as the birthday of a leading courtesan, and also to ward off evil and cure diseases.

The day in a brothel started late for everyone except the servant girls, who had to do the washing and cleaning before others were on the move. Courtesans normally did not get up till noon, when the maids would comb their hair and help them dress for the day. Until clients began to arrive, they would smoke, sew, play solitaire domino games, or just take naps to while away the time. The working day for a popular courtesan began soon after late breakfast, with clients coming for tea parties or taking them out on trips. At the arrival of a client for a daytime tea party (called "adding teacups"), the courtesan and her coterie were immediately mobilized. Tea was prepared by a servant girl with hot water brought in by a manservant. The courtesan then offered melon seeds and sweetmeats to the client while the maid readied the courtesan's water pipe for the client's use.[21] Smoking—whether tobacco or opium—was one of the core entertainments for brothel clients. Those who were interested in opium were invited to lie down on the opium divan and smoke opium pellets that the courtesan would roast for him.[22] In the case of regular clients who had a long-term relationship with the courtesan, the maid or young virgin courtesans in the house would take over this duty.

Toward evening, courtesans had to prepare for dinner parties held in their own rooms and answer banquet calls from clients attending parties elsewhere. For the latter, call chits made of red paper were delivered by hand, with the courtesan's name and the location of the party clearly written. Since a courtesan was supposed to entertain but not to eat at dinner parties, she had to have a simple meal before she started her evening rounds. At parties, first-class courtesans would entertain their clients with song and music as well as conversation; some courtesans were even trained to perform excerpts from operas. In most cases, however, the consumption of alcohol remained the core entertainment, and various kinds of drinking games were played. By far the most popular was the extremely noisy finger game that features prominently in this novel: Two opponents would each stick out as many fingers of one hand as they liked, at the same time shouting out what they guessed to be the total number of fingers in a formulaic way. The person who guessed correctly was the winner, and the loser had to drink a penalty cup of wine. While courtesans were not supposed to eat at parties, they and their maids were expected to drink at least some of the penalty wine on behalf of their clients. While literary games also featured in parties among the educated elite, they could not rival the finger game in popularity.

A sought-after courtesan could find herself answering three to four party calls a night in addition to hosting a dinner party in her own room. It was therefore normal for her to retire to bed (sometimes with a client) only in the small hours of the morning. The sedan-chair bearers naturally had to take her to all the parties. As the maids were responsible for attending to the courtesans and their clients and the servants girls for cleaning up, they had to wait till the courtesans retired before they could go to bed.

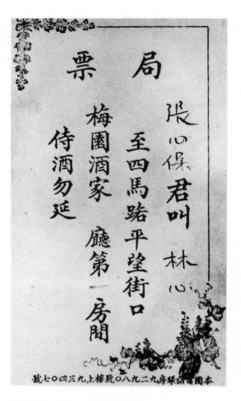

局
票

張心俁君叫林心

至四馬路平望街口

梅園酒家　廳第一房間

侍酒勿延

甍七〇四三九上楼批〇八九二九房联点聚園本

Call chit for a courtesan called Lin Xin
issued from the Meiyuan Restaurant on
Fourth Avenue.

The better sing-song houses were quite spacious, with rooms spread over several stories. Rooms on the upper floors were considered the best and therefore reserved for the use of courtesans, while rooms on the ground floor and mezzanine were used by maids, servants, and the madam. The kitchen and other service areas were at the back of the house.[23] Most of the second-class houses were three stories high and partitioned into a far larger number of rooms than were first-class houses because they normally had a larger number of girls.

Regulations required that a lantern be hung outside the entrance of a brothel as a mark of identification. Since the high-class brothels congregated in a dozen lanes in the western part of Fourth Avenue, this actually created a rather festive atmosphere at night. Doors within the sing-song houses were normally left open throughout the day. To provide some privacy, curtains were hung over the room doors. Depending on the weather, the curtains were made variously of thin cotton or quilted material. At the arrival of a client, menservants would loudly announce it at the front door or in the courtyard, and the client would always head straight for the room of his regular courtesan. A maid or servant girl would accompany him and lift the door curtain for him to enter.

Each courtesan had her own room in which all the daily activities and entertainment, including dinner parties, were held. The standard furnishing for a courtesan's room included a bed with embroidered curtains, an opium couch, a dressing table, side tables, a dining table (on which a large round tabletop could be placed to create extra seating for parties), a considerable number of chairs, paintings and calligraphy scrolls on the walls, and elaborate lamps or chandeliers. The bed, instead of occupying a corner or one end of the room, served as a partition: the space behind the bed was curtained off as the lavatory area. Trunks for storing clothes and other essentials were also placed here. A back door, used only by members of the house, including the madam, led to the passageway outside. The high-class houses also had an upstairs parlor where larger-scaled banquets or mah-jongg parties were held. Additionally, there had to be a spare room for the popular courtesan who might well have to entertain more than one overnight client.

*Etiquette and Manners*

One interesting rule about sing-song houses was that once a man patronized a certain girl, her house had the right to send someone to his home or place of business and invite him to visit again. Even if such attempts proved inconvenient to the client, it was not considered harassment. After settling his bills for the season, however, the client would be free to take his patronage elsewhere.

People hosting dinner parties, whether in a sing-song house or a restaurant, were expected to have written invitations delivered by hand to their guests not once but twice. The first was an invitation card listing the day and venue for the party; the second, a note to "hurry the guest," was sent after the host had arrived at the venue. It was normal practice for guests to set off only after they had received the second note.

When friends met in a sing-song house, the normal rules of manners and etiquette applied. Everyone had to stand up as soon as another guest entered the room. There were three different gestures of greeting. The first, referred to as an "informal salute" (or simply "salute") in this novel, involved forming a fist with one hand, wrapping the other hand over it, and then slightly moving the joined hands back and forth a couple of times. It is the normal gesture for saying "hello" and "good-bye" as well as "thank you" and was the commonest used among friends. The second gesture involved bowing while performing the "salute." In cases when someone wanted to acknowledge deep gratitude, the joined hands were raised above the head, and the person bowed as he brought his hands down. In this translation, the term "formal salute" is used to describe this form of greeting. The third gesture of greeting was derived from Manchu practice and used only by some inferiors to greet their employers or elders on very formal occasions. The person performing it knelt on one knee, with head bowed and one hand touching the ground. Finally, there was the kowtow, which was performed as part of certain rites and on special occasions.

After greetings had been exchanged, everyone could sit down again. For casual conversation, there was no seating order, but for dinner a strict etiquette was normally observed. A courtesan called to a party had to sit slightly behind her client rather than shoulder to shoulder with him. The seat of honor faced the door, and the right-hand side was considered the honored side. Seating order was determined by such usual considerations as status, age, and generation. One rule was given precedence over other considerations, however: a first-time acquaintance was always honored above others and would occupy the seat of honor even if he were younger than the rest. The same rules applied to walking in and out of a house or a room.

When in the presence of seniors and figures of authority, it was a sign of respect to approach them with one's body turned slightly away instead of facing them directly. Similarly, when withdrawing it was rude to turn one's back to them, hence the expression "walking sideways" in this novel. This was of course not required among peers and friends.

Readers will notice that "smile" is one of the most heavily recurrent words in this novel. Since it was considered bad manners for women to laugh out loud, a smile was a much more proper expression. Showing one's teeth in laughter was decidedly bad manners. That was why women covered their mouths with their hands, a handkerchief, or their sleeves when they laughed; even men often did the same.

### The End of an Era

A study of historical sources, be they biographical, journalistic, or anecdotal, clearly shows that the world of the Shanghai courtesans had a certain allure for its patrons as well as chroniclers. In a society where men and women occupied distinct spheres and marriage had little to do with personal feelings, for educated men the courtesan was both an embodiment of romantic possibilities and a channel for sexual gratification. For clients of the high-class brothels, sex was not necessarily their top priority. The etiquette of the sing-song houses demanded that the client go through a gradual, well-charted process before he could establish an intimate relationship with the courtesan of his choice. This, in some ways, was like a courtship process and carried with it a sense of excitement, longing, and uncertainty that was in itself as enticing as the final gratification of desire. As social norms changed, however, the nonsexual aspects of the courtesan's service became less and less relevant.

Among the patrons of the sing-song houses, the weakening of the leisurely scholar class (the main support for the romantic myths associated with the courtesan) and the rise of those associated with a trade economy (including merchants and administrators) were a reflection of the changing times. The continuing expansion of the prostitution trade, both in numbers and modes of service, also quickened the demise of the nonsexual aspects of the courtesan's work. The result was a leveling off of the prostitution field, what Henriot sums up as the sexualization and commercialization of the high end of the trade.[24] Meanwhile, a revolution in social attitudes and practices in relation to women was brewing. This was to result gradually in the breakdown of many of the former boundaries between men and women. High on the agenda of the New Culture Movement that swept through China in the second and third decades of the twentieth century was autonomy in love and marriage.

This completely changed the emotional landscape and expectations of the average educated young man, thus eliminating the courtesan's role as a romantic figure. Within the first quarter of the twentieth century, the world of the Shanghai courtesan as described in this novel was to become little more than a faded dream.

*Notes*

1. At this time, the local Chinese population, living in the walled city and its vicinity, was around twenty-five hundred.

2. This small creek, which gave its name to the pidgin English spoken in Shanghai, was filled in in 1914 and became the Avenue Edouard VII (present-day Yan'an E. Road).

3. The Chinese walled city, measuring approximately three-and-a-half miles in circumference, was administered by a magistrate.

4. Sedan chairs, rickshas (introduced from Japan in 1874), and horse-drawn carriages were the only means of transport in Shanghai until 1902, when motorcars and trams were introduced.

5. The unequal treaty resulting from the Sino-Japanese War in 1895 allowed the Japanese to build factories and mills in Shanghai. As a result, other treaty powers also followed suit, and the cityscape of Shanghai changed considerably.

6. Statistics immediately after the First World War showed that Shanghai was the city with the largest number of legal prostitutes on a pro rata basis. The second was Beijing and the third Tokyo. According to a map showing the distribution of various categories of prostitutes in 1860 in Christian Henriot, *Belles de Shanghai. Prostitution and Sexuality in Shanghai: A Social History, 1849–1949*, trans. Noel Castelino (Cambridge: Cambridge University Press, 2001), p. 208, most flowered opium dens were in the French Concession, while common prostitutes worked in the Chinese walled city as well as the International Settlement and sing-song houses and Cantonese brothels were located in the International Settlement.

7. *Shikumen* is a form of terrace house developed during and after the Taiping Rebellion as a result of an influx of well-to-do refugees from the countryside. It is an architectural form local to Shanghai, and a small number can still be seen there. These houses have extremely strong stone portals and a thick wooden front door that lead onto a small courtyard—a reflection of the concern for security in the early days. The house itself is of Chinese design and layout, with the kitchen and service area in the back. These houses, compact in design, suited the purposes of unlicensed prostitutes.

8. For more details about the categories of brothels and courtesans, their modes of operation, and changes that occurred in Republican China, see Gail Hershatter, *Dangerous Pleasures: Prostitution and Modernity in Twentieth-Century Shanghai* (Berkeley: University of California Press, 1997).

9. Unlike the second-class houses, the first-class ones did not charge cus-

tomers for dropping in for tea. This was done on the understanding that clients who did so would give regular dinner parties at the house.

10. In this novel, Constance, Lotuson Wang's new flame, is thought to have belonged to this category, though her rival Little Rouge claims that she was originally a streetwalker. Incidentally, while it was not unusual for streetwalkers to set up as first-class courtesans with the backing of a wealthy client, the chances of a second-class girl being promoted to a first-class house were said to be slim.

11. If the girl was sold to the house, all the gifts she received in fact belonged to the brothel though she was the one who actually wore them.

12. It was the fashion to wear what looked like a thin headband studded with jewels just above the forehead.

13. Henriot, *Belles de Shanghai*, p. 30.

14. The reader will notice that many of the courtesans in this novel are in debt, a fairly accurate reflection of the real situation. The reasons for courtesans going into debt were various. Some became addicted to opium, while others gave money to their lovers (it was very fashionable for courtesans to take up with actors). Many prostitutes, however, were cheated by clients who just disappeared after running up huge bills.

15. This must have been a well-known practice, as there was a technical term for it: "waiting by the city gate." This saying probably originated with the curfew laws. The Chinese walled city closed its gates after curfew, during which time the gates were only opened when government officials needed to go through. Commoners who wanted to pass during the night therefore waited by a gate and rushed through when it was opened for an official.

16. It was also considered bad form for her regular clients to show feelings of jealousy.

17. See, for example, chapter 22, in which Green Phoenix goes to bed with Vigor Qian in his home so that he will only be billed for a party call.

18. Goldie, who works for Little Rouge, is perhaps the best example of an effective maid in this novel.

19. Thus we have the episode in chapter 23 when Clever complains about brothel clients "horsing around" with servant girls.

20. Normally, dinner parties were held in the courtesans' rooms.

21. Tobacco was smoked through small water pipes, made of silver in the sing-song houses and of a yellowish copper alloy in other establishments. The body of the pipe, containing the water compartment and the tobacco bowl, could fit into the palm of the hand.

22. Opium divans were wide enough for two people. Normally, the client lay on one side and the courtesan on the other. Besides an opium lamp used for roasting the raw paste into pellets, other equipment for opium smoking included a pick, an opium pipe, and a box for roasted pellets.

23. Given this arrangement, it was very upsetting for a courtesan to be moved to a downstairs room, as is illustrated in the case of Twin Jewel in this novel.

24. Henriot, *Belles de Shanghai*, p. 354.

## Selected References

Chen Boxi. *Shanghai yishi daguan* (Panorama of Shanghai anecdotes). Shanghai: Shanghai shudian, 2000.

Cusack, Dymphna. *Chinese Women Speak.* Sydney: Halstead, 1958.

Dong, Stella. *Shanghai: Gateway to the Celestial Empire.* Hong Kong: FormAsia, 2003.

Henriot, Christian. *Belles de Shanghai. Prostitution and Sexuality in Shanghai: A Social History, 1849–1949.* Trans. Noel Castelino. Cambridge: Cambridge University Press, 2001.

Hershatter, Gail. *Dangerous Pleasures: Prostitution and Modernity in Twentieth Century Shanghai.* Berkeley: University of California Press, 1997.

Hu Shi. *"Haishang hua liezhuan xu."* (Preface to *Haishang hua liezhuan*), in *Haishang hua,* ed. Wang Yuanfang, pp. 1–36. Shanghai: Yadong tushuguan, 1935.

Huang Jun. *Hua sui rensheng an zhiyi* (Memories of the hut of flowers and figurines). Shanghai: Shanghai shudian, 1998.

Liu Fu. "Du *Haishang hua liezhuan*' (On reading *Haishang hua liezhuan*), in *Haishang hua,* ed. Wang Yuanfang, pp. 1–34. Shanghai: Yadong tushuguan, 1935.

Pott, F. L. Hawks. *A Short History of Shanghai, Being an Account of the Growth and Development of the International Settlement.* Shanghai: Kelly and Walsh, 1928.

Sargent, Harriet. *Shanghai: Collision Point of Cultures, 1918–1939.* New York: Crown, 1990.

Tang, Zhenchang. *Xiandai Shanghai fanhua lu* (Records of the prosperity of modern Shanghai). Taipei: Commercial, 1993.

Wang Zhongxian. *Shanghai suyu tushuo* (Illustrated book of Shanghai slang). Illus. Xi Xiaoxia. Shanghai: Shanghai shudian, 1999.

Zhang Wei et al. *Lao Shanghai ditu* (Maps of old Shanghai). Shanghai: Shanghai huabao chubanshe, 2001.

WEATHERHEAD BOOKS ON ASIA
Columbia University

*Literature*
David Der-wei Wang, Editor

Ye Zhaoyan, *Nanjing 1937: A Love Story*, translated by
Michael Berry

Makoto Oda, *The Breaking Jewel*,
translated by Donald Keene

Han Shaogong, *A Dictionary of Maqiao*, translated by
Julia Lovell

Takahashi Takako, *Lonely Woman*,
translated by Maryellen Toman Mori

Chen Ran, *A Private Life*,
translated by John Howard-Gibbon

Eileen Chang, *Written on Water*,
translated by Andrew F. Jones

Amy D. Dooling, editor, *Writing Women in Modern China:
The Revolutionary Years, 1936–1976*


*History, Society, and Culture*
Carol Gluck, Editor

Michael K. Bourdaghs, *The Dawn That Never Comes: Sihimazaki
Toson and Japanese Nationalism*

Takeuchi Yoshimi, *What Is Modernity? Writings of Takeuchi
Yoshimi*, translated by Richard Calichman

Richard Calichman, editor, *Contemporary Japanese Thought*